About the Author

Michael Dunn has been writing for many years, but has only recently decided to do something about publishing. He currently resides in Newcastle, New South Wales, with his two cats; who do their best to drive him insane.

The Fortress Saga
Book One

THE DRUMS OF WAR

Michael Dunn

All characters, events, organisations and places etc in this book are fictitious. Any resemblance to actual people, events, organisations and places is purely coincidental.

First published 2013

ISBN: 1490388389
ISBN-13: 978-1490388380

Cover art by Laura Wickham

Visit www.fortresssaga.com

TO;

Laura,

You there. Book that cover!

And to;

Shane,

For always turning up at the right time.

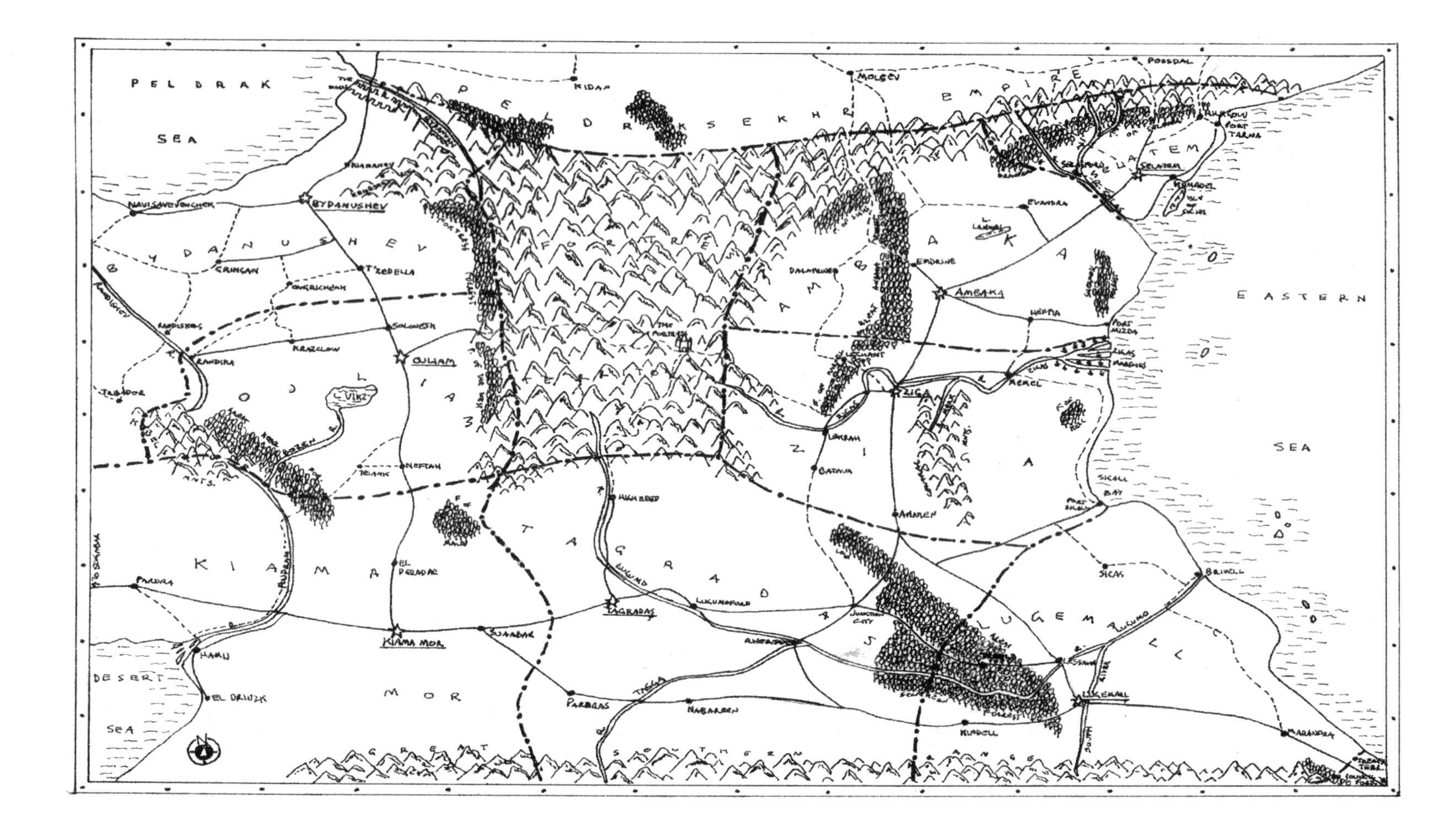

PELDRAK SEA
PELDRAK SEKHR EMPIRE
KIDAP
MOLSEV
POSSDAL
FORT TARNA
SELATEM
EVANDRA
EASTERN SEA
NAVISAVEVONCHEK
BYDANUSHEV
BYDANUSHEV
CRINGAN
T'ZEDELLA
SOLONESH
KRAZCLOW
RANDIKA
TABADOR
OJLIAM
OJLIAM
VIKZ
NEFTAH
THE FORTRESS
AMBAKA
EPDRINE
DALATRUND
HEPPIA
PORT MIZDA
MEMEL
ZIGA
LAKRAH
BATAVA
AMMEN
SKALL BAY
SICAS
BRIVELL
HIGH REED
TAGRADAS
LUKUMOFORD
JUNCTION CITY
AMSARAN
LESSAMI
LUKEHALL
LUGEMALL
KIDDELL
NABARREN
PARBRAS
SUAABAR
KIAMA MOR
EL PERADAR
PARDRA
HAMU
EL DRIJUK
DESERT
SEA
KIAMA MOR
GREAT SOUTHERN RANGE
MARANDRA

Prologue

Being a generalised account of the colonisation of the Mervabda System in the twenty-seventh century. Extracted from the **History of the Galactic Alliance of Light - Second Period. Volume VIII.**

The Mervabda System had first been discovered and noted in the twenty-second century by the Reconnoitre Probe Project. The system contained a total of eleven planets, two of which fell within the ranges of habitation. The physicality of the system was unremarkable. A standard G type star, and the expected variations in planetary types. There was only one rather small asteroid belt, and only a few minor cometary trails. Geologically the various planets would be able to provide large quantities of base metals and materials, but nothing in the order of natural transuranics that might have made any colony attractive as a major energy production centre. The outer habitable planet was noted as having a higher concentration of crystalline structures within the planetary crust than would otherwise have been expected. There were no foreseeable problems with this fact, and may have eventually spawned industries to mine them for decorative and religious markets on other worlds.

For many years after its discovery, no need was seen for any colony in that area of the galaxy. However when the Hamazdian Coalition seceded from the Alliance in the twenty-sixth century, over the Gordanka Prime Affair as it later became known (See separate entry for details), the need was soon realised.

The system now lay only a few light years from the new border.

The system, which up until this time had been of little interest to any one, suddenly became of strategic importance. If it were somehow colonised by the Hamazdians it would represent a potential threat to the Alliance of great proportions. The actual decision to colonise the system was a unanimous one of the Congress of Sentients. This was a unique situation for something, which in any normal circumstance would have been merely a bureaucratic decision, out of the hands of the legislative branch of government. The fact that the Congress made a decision on the colonisation of a planet helps us to understand the importance that was placed on this issue.

The fact that two planets in the system were habitable was also an opportunity too good to pass up. It allowed the various functions of the individual colonies to be spread out and therefore have less impact upon each other. It also gave rise to the possibility of higher populations in the future, making their long-term viability more certain.

'Project Trident' was the name given to the colonisation plan. This was because there were three main aims to the project. One- the establishment of another rural and cultural colony in a non crowded sector of space; two- the establishment of a military outpost and base close to the new Hamazdian border, with which to provide a first line defence; and three- to provide new areas for both biological and high energy experiments which could not be conducted in densely populated areas due to both planetary and spatial environmental considerations. These experiments would be accomplished through the establishment of a major annex of the Galactic University Technical School.

Some concerns were raised in various quarters over the inclusion of military functions in the colonies, however the functions of this section of the colony, which was to be located on Mervabda II, were generally limited to vessel and communications monitoring and threat force tracking and analysis. Some facilities would be available for maintenance, resupply and repair, but there would be no independent shipbuilding or weapons manufacturing. The need for a new "military" base in this area was too great to be either overlooked or ignored. While the concerns, mainly about exacerbating the situation with the Hamazdias, were genuine and quite rightly raised, the needs for the defence of the Alliance were simply too great. The "limited" breadth of functionality of the facility was a concession towards those concerns.

The project was accepted and commissioned by the Congress of Sentients and administered by the Galactic Light Military Council (GLMC). Plans were made and huge sums devoted to finding hardy, intelligent and stable people to form the main body of colonists. Several months were spent manufacturing the needed supplies, and preparing several colonisation ships for the journey. The ships required minor refits in order to accommodate as much of the materials and personnel as possible, as time was of the essence. The colonisation effort was to be conducted in one voyage if possible. The four ships, *Gasbeake*, *Selatamas*, *George Rydner*, and *Trustee*, were all given extra storage bays as well as modified systems to handle the increased loads.

In charge of the overall expedition, at least for the transit stage was Leonard Ojam, the famed retired member of the Council of Sentients from Sirius. Having sat on both the Council Military Oversight Committee, as well as the Colonial Administrations Board meant he had a great deal of experience in the areas of concern for the establishment of the new colonies. It also meant that the new colonial governments would be taken more seriously with someone such as he involved. His track record in defending individual and planetary rights, as well as his first hand knowledge of the operation of the Cabinet made him the perfect and popular choice.

A colonial constitution was drawn up, as well as a set of general laws and operating protocols, which would form the basis of the new colony's legal and political system. In accordance with the Alliance Constitution, every colony had the right to a level of self-governance. The Mervabda Colonial Constitution provided for strong personal safeguards, freedoms and liberties by using the Alliance First Law, that "All sentients are born equal in ability, right and independence and shall not be hindered from the pursuit of personal perfection" as the primary guiding principal of the colonies.

The two colonies were intended to operate as both independent and unified entities. Their representation to the Alliance government would be by a single member, however each colony would be allowed a great deal of freedom to administer its normal operations and to guide its own future, and could if necessary, make separate representations to the Alliance authorities.

During the planning stages the Alliance Military decided to use this opportunity to test several new technologies. The vessels that would be used to transport both people and materials to the colonies would use the new Hyperspace Wave-Guide system. This new navigation system was intended to provide safer transport and prevent vessel losses in hyperspace. This of course prompted further modifications to the four ships used.

The second major technology to be implemented was the Hyper-dimension Gateway, using similar technology and theory to normal Hyperdrives. A network of interconnected gates would be built on each planet to allow a full range of testing and applications to be examined on a planetary scale.

Late in the planning stage, the Alliance Psychical and Telepathical Administration requested that a new training school be built on one of the colonies. The next nearest school, on Gabria, was strained with the number of students it was teaching from the surrounding sectors and it was felt that a relief campus would be a good inclusion, allowing both of the new colonies and indeed other colonies, bases and member worlds in the immediate surrounding sectors to go here instead of to Gabria. The possibilities of this school being located near a military facility, and also a potential area of activity was not lost on the GLMC who quite quickly approved the inclusion. Over the last two decades or so the number of graduates from the APTA to military careers had fallen and the military was keen to try and correct this. It was felt that direct exposure to some of the military possibilities might help recruit more trainees.

The GLMC approved these decisions and so in the year 2609 the colony fleet left for the Mervabda system, three months away.

The fleet arrived on time and initial surveys were conducted and landing sites chosen. On Mervabda IV (the furthest habitable planet) a massive communication array was constructed on a mountaintop. This was intended to provide easier communication with the rest of the Alliance. It also housed an H.S. Wave-guide transmitter. This would be one of the furthest beacons in the new network, and would allow more heavily trafficked systems closer to the Alliance core to be quickly added to the network.

Full and proper surveys of the planets were conducted from orbit and careful examinations of both plant and animal life were undertaken before any of the colonists were allowed to settle. While there were no exceedingly dangerous animals on either world, it was felt that proper examination of migratory patterns and food sources would be beneficial. Allowing the new colony sites to be situated in areas of least impact.

Once the colonies had been established and completed their initial start-up programs, the inevitable protests from the Hamazdia began. They claimed the colonies were within their territorial boundaries, which was clearly incorrect. The Congress of Sentients met with delegates from the Hamazdian Representative Chamber at the colonies to discuss a peaceful solution to the problem.

From these meetings came the Hamazdian colonisation of Salador Cova. The Cova system had for many years been considered strategic given it's location in neutral space, and certain mineral deposits in the system that might be useful for both energy production and weapons manufacturing. The Alliance had for some years been seeking a way to colonise the system without breaking the Treaty of Arden V, which proclaimed the whole area as neutral territory.

The Alliance realised that by giving the system to the Hamazdia, colonies from which the Allaince could obtain these resources through trade, could be established without any cost to the GAL. The Hamazdia knew of the Allaince's great interest in the system, and hopefully would see it as a prize worth taking. Which they did.

For the time the situation had been defused. The process of the Hamazdian colonisation of Salador Cova took several years and there were signs that Hamazdian attitudes towards the Alliance were changing. The possibility of future interaction with the Coalition was welcomed strongly in the Alliance.

However in the year 2694, seventeen years after its colonisation by the Hamazdia, Salador Cova was all but destroyed by one of the rarest natural events in the galaxy. The Salador Cova System contains fifteen planets and a total of one hundred and forty eight satellites. Once every two hundred and fifty thousand, nine hundred and forty years (by best calculations) all these bodies line up in a single file stretching out from the systems primary. A beautiful, yet disturbing sight. The resulting gravitational stresses produced (thought for several centuries to be mere hysterical myth) resulted in massive tectonic forces that almost tore apart the surface of the bodies. Salador Cova was destroyed.

A massive rescue effort was launched by the Alliance, who were the first to receive the garbled distress call from the ravaged colony. Hamazdia was quickly contacted and a rescue fleet of their own also travelled to the system. More than 90 per cent of the population had been killed in the massive seismic events, which had completely reshaped the surface and landmasses. The systems primary had also become somewhat unstable; a testament to the forces at work, though it did settle after several years.

Despite the possibility of a better relationship, due to the mutual rescue effort, the Hamazdians' naturally suspicious nature won out. The Hamazdian Coalition charged that the Alliance Congress had purposely let them colonise a doomed planet. The Congress stated this was not the case and allowed the Coalition to remove all traces of their colony from Salador Cova and choose another planet in the sector.

The Hamazdians refused this offer and demanded the immediate removal of all colonies in the Mervabda System. The Congress tried once again to find a diplomatic solution to the crisis, but after many meetings and much heated discourse, this effort failed.

By mid 2701 the Hamazdian fleet entered the sector and began to attack shipping before making their way toward the Mervabda System. The Alliance was notified by the Mervabda II colony and warships were sent to assist.

The war that followed did not in fact destroy the Mervabda colonies, as many had believed it would. It did not last very long, mainly due to errors made by the Hamazdians, probably because they expected a quick conflict; the area of contention being so far from the Alliance core. The Alliance vessels were able to draw the attacking ships away and chase them back to Coalition territory. This rather humiliating defeat was not forgotten by the Hamazdians and prompted them to desire vengeance against the Alliance for the perceived loss of honour.

For several years after the conclusion of the Coalition War, as it was then called, GLM vessels were regularly stationed in the sectors systems and patrolled the surrounding space. Improvements to the military facilities were proposed and accepted. If completed this would have seen a major improvement in the facilities at the colonies including shipbuilding docks and long-range defence platforms and possibly the construction of a starbase. The population would have been increased dramatically, and this may have had impacts of the original purposes of the colony, not to mention large changes to supply routes and communications.

Economic conditions during the 2710's, warranted a more gradual implementation of the plans than had been originally envisioned and as such the plans were only ever partially completed. Historians argue over precisely what role this fact plays in the second conflict and it's outcomes. Though all agree it did play a part.

The Second Coalition war began in 2724, less than two years after the Alliance had reduced its military presence in the system due to a perceived reduction in the threat to the system posed by the Coalition. This perception was a result of misinformation and indeed misinterpretation of legitimate information. The improved military capabilities for the colonies were still being enacted, though now at their somewhat slower pace. This misinformation was later learned to part of the Hamazdian plan for a renewed conflict. This time however the Hamazdians intended to take the Mervabda system, not destroy it. They attacked several other systems and bases as a distraction, then descended on Mervabda before any one was ready.

The defensive campaign that was mounted rather sluggishly at first, due to a perception in the Alliance that this war would proceed much the same as the one previously, only achieved minimal success, liberating some minor systems and wasting more lives and resources than was acceptable. The conflict also saw the first tactical deployment the the Hamazdian "Harness" weapons (see entry for technical details). These powerful subspace weapons caused the loss of at least thirty-five Alliance starships, including the sixteen destroyed in what became known as the Mervabda Miscalculation. Eventually, after a stalemate was reached, the Congress decided that it was time to end the war.

Conferences were held and after several months of negotiation a cease fire and later a proper conclusion to the conflict was reached. The Hamazdians refused to even consider the idea of them giving up the territory they had gained. Attempts were made to convince the Hamazdians to allow the Alliance to remove the colony. Predictably the Hamazdians refused to consider this idea as well. As such the Alliance was forced to relinquish some of its citizens. Something that had never happened before. There was much moral angst in the Alliance over this fact, but there was not much more that could be done about it, if peace was to be achieved.

Guarantees were sought from the Hamazdia, that the citizens of Mervabda would be given all the rights and privileges of both Alliance and Coalition citizens. Whilst the Hamazdians officially agreed, other agreements have prohibited investigation.

Many in the Alliance believe the people of Mervabda are treated as second-class citizens, slaves or are even dead, as some kind of retribution for the perceived embarrassment of the Hamazdians.

However there is currently no way to substantiate this belief.

Chapter 1

He was torn from his slumber.

The storm continued to rage outside. By the soft firelight from across the room he could see he was bathed in sweat. That dream again!

Climbing unsteadily from his bed, the young man went to the table, unstoppered the decanter and poured some wine. He drank quickly, his eyes closed. The spiced wine warmed him as it slid down his throat and started a cosy, almost toasty reaction in his stomach. Silently padding to the window on bare feet he gazed into the tempest. A flash of lightning revealed his nakedness to the world. Lucky this was a high room. He would have been rather embarrassed otherwise.

It was a dream that was worrying him. Why was he having it? It scared him. He was somewhere, a building of some sort. Huge it was; dark and gloomy. He was running from something. Something that chilled him to the bone. Even now after he had awakened. He would be running, turning down twisting corridors; in and out of strange rooms. He'd continue until he came to a room with a gold throne at the far end. He would run to it, looking for a way out. There never was one. Then that noise. An inhuman screaming, that made every part of his being shudder in absolute terror. Then the black came. The far end of the room started to disappear into blackness. It gradually came closer. He would cry out for help from any one. His father, mother, the guards, Mac. But it was no use. It got him.

He closed his eyes.

Why? What did it mean?

He replaced the glass on the tray and looked back at the bed. Mac lay there asleep. How anybody could sleep with him having a dream like that was beyond him. He could see the rumpled patch of sweat on his pillow next to Mac. The bedclothes on his own side of the bed also rumpled and twisted. How could he sleep through that?

He watched Mac.

'I did choose well', he thought. 'Of all the people you could have got, you chose the right one.'

Mac lay in the bed with one arm over his head. His chest moved up and down rhythmically to his breathing. His soft snoring floating around the room.

He hated this dream.

He shouldn't think about it. Tomorrow would be an important day. The Ambassador from Selatem was coming to meet with the King. His daughter was coming with them. It had been years since he had seen her.

Absently he reached for the lump of crystal at his chest. This amulet gave him inner strength when things got tough.

He slowly walked back to the huge bed. 'Yes Dorm, you did make the right choice.' Mac looked so beautiful lying there. Dorm slipped into bed and ran his arms around Mac.

Mac wrapped his own around Dorm and moaned 'Dorm' softly. Dorm kissed him lightly on the forehead, and closed his eyes.

He held Mac tightly, hoping that would protect him from the dream. He really hoped it would. He didn't want to look tired or distraught in front of their international guests.

He had a certain reputation to maintain.

After all, he was the Prince.

~* * * * *~

Drat this storm.

Drat, Drat, Drat it. Stupid weather. She wouldn't be able to see the sunrise. She hadn't seen one in years.

'Well there's nothing else for it now' she thought. 'I'll just have to go back to bed and sleep all morning.' She would only need an hour or so to prepare for the conference. It's not like she was actually part of it. She was just here for show. But that was alright. She like to show.

But what ever she did, she was not wearing the pink dress! That was final. That pink dress made her look like she was a little girl. She was definitely *not* a little girl. She wasn't wearing the pink dress, no matter what her father said. 'Very becoming' indeed. What a load of...

She did love her father, despite the fact he was a stuffy old fashioned so and so. Sometimes she wished her mother were still alive to soften him. That was something she'd never been able to master. Whilst she was definitely her mothers' daughter, she had never been able to control her father the way so many times her mother had.

Which was a shame because it might have been fun.

She was looking forward to seeing the Prince again, and the King. They were both nice people. So was Dorm's other half. She didn't know him as well as she should have, but that was something she was determined to work on during her stay here. There were relationships she needed to develop.

Right now though she'd have to pick something to wear, maybe something blue, so that she could literally just slip into it before her father came and made her put on that wretched pink dress.

SHE WASN'T WEARING THE PINK DRESS!!

There, that felt better.

~* * * * *~

She peered into the darkness.

Her quarry was there. She could tell that much.

The bastard wasn't going to get away this time. Silently she unsheathed her dagger, then held it close to her chest.

A movement. Only tiny. But she saw it. It had to be him. He was the only one it could be. She took aim very carefully. When she flung the dagger, it didn't make a sound. He wouldn't even know it was coming.

It struck home. She heard a muffled cry of pain. As she moved from the shadows towards him, she removed her gloves triumphantly, with a hint of satisfaction.

"So, how does it feel?" she asked him haughtily. "How does it feel to know it's all over, you scum?"

His answer was only a groan of pain.

"Don't think that you suffering from a dagger wound is going to make me help you. You'll have suffered much more by the time I'm finished with you."

She unlatched the bonds from her belt and prepared to tie him.

"Zacravia, it is my great pleasure to place you under arrest for attempted murder of a member of the Royal Family of Ambaka. You have the right to remain silent. Anything you say at this time may be used in a court of law as evidence against you. From here you will be taken to a place to be held until a trial for your crimes can be organised."

Pulling him out of the shadows into the dim light, the situation changed.

What!

"Wait a minute, you're not him." She stared into the face of a stranger.

Suddenly a massive weight landed on her shoulders. Her knees buckled and she fell to the ground collapsing on top of the man she had arrested. A person rolled off her as she tried to right herself.

"Not today I'm afraid Senior Constable," Zacravia sneered. "I'm not your prize tonight." And he ran back into the shadows.

"Zacravia!" she called after him, springing to her feet. "You bastard. I'll get you." But he was gone.

~* * * * *~

"Good evening sir," the officer saluted.

"Commander," he returned the salute. "I thought you had retired for the evening?"

"I was going to but decided to catch up on some work," the Commander indicated the sea of parchment before him.

"It doesn't go away when you become a flag officer," he replied.

"Don't tell me that sir, I'll get depressed."

He laughed. "Well good night Commander. And good luck."

"Thank you Admiral, Good night."

He walked back up on deck and slowly paced around. Looking out over the city, lights twinkled back at him, and the rain continued to fall. Pulling his cloak tighter about himself, he slowly worked his way towards the forecastle, pausing briefly to admire the figurehead beneath the bowsprit. Water dribbled off her breasts. 'Poor mermaid' he thought.

He headed back towards the gangway. He would make his inspection of the *Avenger* another time. Right now he needed sleep. And that meant he had to walk to the far end of the quay to the *Conqueror*. He almost slipped off the plank as he made his way hastily down. How embarrassing, he thought. Luckily the two sentries didn't appear to notice.

"Good night gentlemen," he said as he passed them. They returned the sentiment as he strode along the quay past the *Devastator* and the *Sacrificer*. At last he arrived at the gangway that led to the *Conqueror* and his nice warm bed. Quickly making his way to the rear cabin with its large, aft facing windows, he barely acknowledged the sentries on duty. Once inside, he drew the curtains and doused most of the candles. He glanced at the drawing of his six daughters and smiled, remembering their faces. He removed his uniform coat and hung it on a peg. Removing his shirt, he shifted his amulet.

He lay down and sighed heavily. What a day.

Hopefully tomorrow would be better.

~* * * * *~

"Who's stolen my purslane?"

They all looked at her blankly.

"Someone's got it, because it's not here where I left it."

"Well I haven't got it."

"Nor me."

"And don't even think about me."

"Well who has it then?"

They all looked at each other accusingly. The door opened.

"Was it you?" she pounced, not even knowing who it was.

"Was what me?" he asked angrily.

"Who stole my purslane?" she told him.

"Was that the purslane that was sitting just here?" he said resting his hand on the desk.

"Yes it was. You stole it didn't you. Give it back."

"I didn't steal it at all, the window was open and it was blowing all over the room. So I picked it up and put it in here." He said giving her a small bag, inside which were the small round leaves.

"Well the next time you do something like that, leave me a note or tell someone."

"Sorry," he said sitting down.

"Never mind," she said closing her eyes in frustration. "I have patients to attend to." She picked up her things and left the room.

"Students," she muttered to herself as she strode down the corridor. She descended to the next level and walked quickly to the ward. There were only a few wards in the collage. Most people had to be content with the few hospitals in the city. Or their own beds.

Her quiet footsteps slipped into the near silent ward and moved slowly past the beds, watching each patient sleep peacefully. Most of these people only had minor ailments. But a few, such as the woman she was going to see this evening, had serious conditions.

She sat down beside the bed and watched the elderly matriarch sleep. Her breath rasped in and out as she slept. Slowly she opened her eyes and looked at her. A small smile touched her lips.

"Here drink this," the young woman said tipping a small cup to the elder one's lips.

She drank. "Thank you my dear," she said sincerely.

"You're welcome. And call me Bianeska."

"Thank you Bianeska," the elderly patient replied as she closed her eyes.

'What for,' she thought. 'I can't cure you.'

~ * * * * * * ~

'Perfect'

The mason stood and moved to the colossal plinth. He placed the stone in its slot and pushed it in firmly, he smothered the top of the stone with some cement. Quickly he went to tidy up the faces on the next stone.

He was annoyed that he was doing repairs, he had the talent to make statues in their own right. One day he'd do it. One day.

The Phirinos had begun additions to the great temple of Karoks four months ago. Several small statues and the processional way had been completed but the additions to the actual temple itself were somewhat far from complete. Of course then his majesty had wanted to repair the statues of his father who had ruled before him. "The glory of the Polsain Dynasty will shine for ever," he had said. Or at least until the next Phirinos decided to add something or change something.

They seemed to do that a lot.

When he finished this evening, he would work some more on his project. His pride and joy. An edifice of the god Hep. It would be magnificent. Nearly two hundred feet high. Coated in pure white alabaster to catch the sun. Inlaid with gold, bronze and lapis lazuli where appropriate.

If only he could get a sponsorship to begin construction. But so far he'd only been laughed at. But he'd show them all. He could feel that there was a change coming. An opportunity. He just had to be ready, and recognise it when it came.

He placed the next stone and cemented the top. Tomorrow they would be placing the new limestone cover stones over the plinth. Then they could move onto the next statue, and the next, and the next.

The foreman came over a few moments later and announced the end of the day. There would be a brief meal then the dedications to various deities, including the Phirinos. Then at dusk they would all troop off home.

Then he could work on his statue.

Soon they wouldn't laugh.

~ * * * * * * ~

"Goats, sir."

"What?"

"Goat's Your Grace."

"Goats?"

"Yes sir."

"Goats," stupid animals. "I don't believe it."

"Neither did we sir, but that's the way the figures came out."

"Goats are the main economic support of this jarldom?" he still didn't believe it. "We must do something about that. I want you and your.. little.. group.. of people to think of some ways to promote the ah… economic growth of other industries. I won't have this jarldom falling flat on its face the next time there's a livestock disease."

"Very well, Your Grace. We'll work on that and I'll report next week."

"Very good Mishon. That will be all."

"Good day, Your Grace." He bowed and left.

'Now for breakfast' he thought lifting the covers of the dishes. Smells and steam rose to his nostrils as his breakfast hit the atmosphere. He began to eat with great appreciation.

This was his favourite time of the day. First thing in the morning with the fire on. It was autumn out side. Whilst it hadn't snowed last night, the remnants of yesterdays brief fall, the first of the season, still clung to the corners and the wind had been ice cold for days.

He had to tour the shipyard today and finish his report for the royal court. He hated tax time. It was annoying, pedantic and stressful. After that he had some meetings before he could get some time to himself.

This was stupid. He was a warrior, not a politician. He should be out there chopping limbs from enemies of the king, not fussing over income rates or currency conversion tables, or whatever else. Blood and guts. That's what he'd always been trained for. But the world had changed. And he'd had to change with it.

What a depressing thought that was. A little violence now and then never did any harm. Well, except the ones upon whom the violence was being done. But as long as they deserved it, everything was all right.

He finished his breakfast, wiped his mouth and combed his hair and beard. Then he left to meet the day.

~ * * * * * * ~

"Oh Artur could you get him."

"Alright." He slid out of bed and crossed the room to the crib. He lifted the crying baby out and held him close. He walked quietly out to the kitchen. It was cold now; the fire had burned low. He soothed the distraught baby who slowly began to relax. His crying subsided.

"That's it Galam, shhhh."

He kissed the child's forehead lightly. "My son," he whispered.

Galam was only a few weeks old and already he felt he was missing too much of his son's life. But they had to live and there were trees to fell. He knew though that it would only be a few years until he could start to take Galam with him during the day to work. It would go fast. It already had. Sometimes it seemed like those few weeks of his sons' life had been just a day or two.

Galam began to fondle with the chain of Artur's amulet. He instinctively put it into his mouth. He'd noticed that almost anything Galam touched went into his mouth. Everything except the food they gave him. And seeing as most of it was liquid, their mop had been used a lot lately.

Once Galam had begun to nod off again, he moved quietly into the bedroom. Artur slowly placed the baby back in his crib and covered him. He watched his sleeping child for a moment.

Artur wished sometimes that he could experience the peace and innocence that his son was now enjoying. Moving to the bed and getting in, he covered up against the cold and hugged his wife.

"Hello," he said to her.

"Hello," she replied sleepily, snuggling against him.

'North field tomorrow,' he thought as he drifted off to sleep.

~ * * * * * * ~

"Accounts Receivable. Accounts Receivable." She moved some parchments aside. "I know I had that here somewhere, now where is it?"

It was so late, and she needed sleep. Especially since she had been chosen to present this information to the King tomorrow morning.

The storm raged outside. She took a brief drink from her glass then kept searching.

"Oh there you are," she said crawling on the floor to pick it up. "Now where's that figure?"

She skimmed the list until she found the one that she wanted. "Now you go in … there," she said as she transposed it. 'Now I have to figure out you.' Quickly pulling out her counter she began to flick the beads to the right in quick succession. Adding in the second figure, she found her answer. She scrawled it in then sat back to admire the page in full. 'Most professional' she thought with pride. 'Now I can finally go home.'

She tidied up the desk, replacing her quills and inkpots, before placing the final reports in their special folder featuring the crest of the Royal Accountancy.

Dousing the candles she quickly finished her drink. Then putting on her cloak and hood, she left the room and then the building, the two guards at the main door bidding her a good night, even though it was early morning by now. It was raining heavily as she hurried down the street. She did her best to avoid getting too wet, and even found a little fun jumping to avoid puddles.

It was lucky she didn't live far from the Accountancy. She saw only one person as she made her way home, a night watchman. He smiled at her as they passed.

Reaching the house where she lived she found it was dark and she slipped inside quietly. Taking off her wet cloak as she entered her rooms.

Now to get some sleep, she thought. She wasn't even going to follow her normal retiring routine. She simply removed her dress and climbed into bed.

'Tomorrow,' she thought as she drifted off to sleep.

~ * * * * * * ~

Idly, the captain listened to the creak of the wood, and the wash of the water against the hull. She always had liked this time of night when she could relax. Everything was still and she could stand at the tiller and watch the world slowly glide by. This evening was cool and a breeze blew gently, carrying the scent of rain coming from the south.

Tomorrow would be another hectic day on the river. The town of Memel was in her opinion the most fussy and pedantic town in all of Ziga. If they managed to unload in time, she would be able to reload the barge and then set sail before she had to put up with them for too long.

That was the plan anyway.

Gormall came up onto the aft deck. He sidled silently up behind her and slipped his arms around her hugging her close. The warmth of his body and his affection, were an effective defence against the slight chill in the air. "Lovely night isn't it," He said.

"Yes it is," she replied.

"Looking forward to tomorrow?"

"You've got to be joking?"

He laughed. "Now, now. They're not that bad."

"Yeah right."

"Well the seasons almost over. We can move onto other parts of the river then," he reminded her.

"Gormall dear, you always know how to brighten my day," she said turning to him and patting his cheek. She tugged on his beard.

"Ow!" he said. "That is attached remember."

"Sorry," she apologised, with a mischievous grin.

"Well I'm off to bed," he announced. "I'll see you in the morning."

"Good night," she said.

She gazed out over the prow, then up to the jewelled canopy of night above her. 'Enjoy the beauty now' she thought to herself. 'Because tomorrow you'll be breaking backs unloading this barge.'

They drifted off into the night.

~ * * * * * * ~

She could feel it. It was there.

All she had to do was pinpoint its exact location. She was getting closer.

The blazing gold disc of the sun beat down overhead. The sand was hot on her sandalled feet. The light breeze whipped at the edges of her hair and clothes.

Cresting the next dune, she turned rapidly. There it was. It was stronger in this direction. She followed it. The others watched her from a distance. Her every move could be important, so they paid close attention.

That was one good thing about being a dowser. She held everybody's attention. Of course, being as stunningly beautiful as she was helped as well.

She was surprised there wasn't an oasis around somewhere, the way the energy was surging. It was usually a good indication. But not this time. Oh well. The world was full of surprises.

Tumbling sand, she started down the flank of the dune. She heard the others follow her. It was definitely getting stronger. Suddenly it overwhelmed her. Gripping her temples for a moment, she steadied herself.

"Here," she called behind her. "Dig here. Now."

They did so.

She sat back and rested as the men began to dig through the sand to the precious water below. Meanwhile, others had begun to set up the tents for the camp that night.

After performing the brief ceremony of thanks for the water, she then retired to her tent. Right now, she wanted to be left alone.

~ * * * * * * ~

The sun slowly set.

The sky was ablaze as it sank behind the horizon. It was quite beautiful, she thought as she played absently with the end of one of her long blonde tassels.

Some rather heavy footsteps approached from behind her. Spinning around she saw it was a watchman.

"Oh Sergeant Makor," she recognised him. "It's you."

"I'm sorry Miss Tissievilla," he replied. "I didn't mean to startle you."

"That's alright."

"You should be gettin' inside now."

"I know. I just wanted to watch the sun set. It's very beautiful."

"Yes Miss," he replied blandly.

"I've always wondered," she mused absently. "Why the sun rises and sets in basically the same position each day."

"I'm sorry?!" the Sergeant replied somewhat bemused.

"Well it must get rather dull after a while, doing the same thing everyday."

The Sergeant shook his head in disbelief. "The sun isn't alive Miss. It's just… the sun!"

"Yes but still," she paused in thought for a moment. "Oh well. I guess that it's happy to do it. Otherwise it wouldn't I guess. I suppose I should go inside. Thank you Sergeant and goodnight." She flittered off down the battlements towards the door.

"Oh my god!" Makor said out loud. "That woman is the dumbest… Agghh."

He slowly walked toward the same door hoping to put some distance between them. That way he wouldn't have to put up with her insane conversation.

He went back into the palace as the sun continued to set.

~ * * * * * * ~

She sketched the finishing touches on the design.

It would only take an hour or so to make. A bit longer to cool, of course.

She admired the design. Simple, functional, yet with a certain artistic flare. Master Jolin will find it "fun". He always seemed to find weird ways to describe her work. It was never good or promising or even dramatic. It was always fun, unanticipated or swish.

What did swish mean?

This design would not be started on for a few days yet. They still had several items to finish off before they could start some free work. It had been a heavy season. They would only have a month or so before all the work began again.

She put down the charcoal stick and looked over her work. Enough for today, she thought. It was evening and she had some work to do before her evening meal and retiring for the night.

Standing, she crossed the room, opened the door and brought in some wood from the pile next to the door. Placing them next to the hearth, she checked over the room for the things she needed to do.

Quickly she shifted her amulet then paced purposefully across the room. She began tidying up small messes and misplaced items. Her rooms needed to be clean tomorrow. A group of deans from the Collage of Arts were visiting tomorrow. She had to make a good impression, if she wanted to get in. And she did.

The deans would examine everything about her. Starting with her habitat. With a little luck she would be successful. She squeezed her amulet in thought, then proceeded to clean like she'd never cleaned before.

~ * * * * * * ~

"I think that looks about right," she said. "Now you can go on to the great cabin, get Labin to help you."

"Yes ma'am," he said and scampered off.

She glanced about the room at the many draughtsmen and women pouring over their tables. The designs were coming along nicely. They should be completed early next month. Three long years. It had taken that long to get to this point. But, it would be worth it. These two ships would be worth it.

She watched them studiously working on their rigging arrangements, their capstan alignments, and their deck layouts. Everyone in this hall had worked hard on this project. She was grateful to them all. Without them, her dream would never have gotten this far.

The 'Warqueen' and the 'Royal Rikaway' would be the greatest warships afloat, and the world would have her to thank for it.

She took a sip of water and continued reading the letter from the king. The design needed to be completed soon. Too much money had been pumped into this project already.

So? What had that to do with anything?

~ * * * * * * ~

The rogue watched intently.

The watched crept up to the target. His hand reached out ever so slowly, at times appearing not to move. It lightly touched the kerchief protruding slightly from the pocket.

He held his breath.

The hand gently began to pull the kerchief. The pocket tugged ever so slightly.

"STOP!"

Everyone froze.

"You were perfect up until then!" he cried angrily. The child looked at him in fear. "There was no noise as you approached the target, you gained access to the target without being noticed. But!" He drew in a deep breath. "You removed it too forcefully. You're not reeling in a fish."

"I'm sorry," the child began.

"Sorry won't do you any good in front of a magistrate, will it?" He paced the room his hand holding his forehead.

"Gallim I want you to show him again, and all the younger ones. You children will be the finest thieves in all of T'Zedella, in all of Bydanushev, or the Alliance. That is a promise, but you need to work harder. Now back too it."

He moved to the table and poured some vodka into a goblet. He downed it quickly, shook slightly, turned and stared out across the room, as Gallim took over the instruction. He hated this deal he had had to make. But to not make it would have been a worse outcome. Far, far worse. He just hoped it would be enough to smooth things over. Best to just get on with the job he had to do and return home as soon as he could. He hoped that they were doing well without him. Gallim would make a fine master for this den when he left. If only the den could live up to him.

Well they were getting better, slowly.

He poured another drink.

~ * * * * * * ~

He'd always hated Pardra.

It was such a depressing city.

Its walls seemed only half finished. It's minarets haphazard and its streets small and chaotic. It was also perhaps the dustiest place in the world. At least out in the desert the wind could carry the dirt and grit away. But here in Pardra, there was no such luck.

He moved quickly down the crowded streets, heading towards the more seamier parts of town. Which is to say the smaller streets. All of Pardra was pretty seamy.

His appointment would only be brief, but it was necessary. He had to sell the herd he had or he would have to take them on to Rindiya or Kiama Mor. And the prices there were not as good.

He entered the doorway and saw the fat merchant. He sat down next to him.

"You're late," said the merchant, shovelling grapes into his mouth.

"It's busy out there."

"What have you got for me this month?"

"Twenty"

"Twenty," the merchant looked at him. "Is that all?"

"They are from Rimlanns' herd," he replied slyly.

"How did you get some from Rimlann?!"

"That's for me to know. How much?"

"Going rates forty crowns. But these are Rimlanns', so we'll say fifty."

"Fifty, you must be joking. They're worth at least seventy."

"SEVENTY!" the merchant screamed, grapes spewing across the table.

"They are Rimlanns'"

"I'll give you fifty-five."

"Sixty-five."

"Sixty."

"Done," they shook hands. Somewhat reluctantly, but with a big grin so as not to let on. "Well Golann let's go sign some contracts."

~ * * * * * * ~

They pounded on the door again.

She simply stared at it.

"Well are you going to answer it?" Gossan asked.

"Just tell him to go away," Lianka said.

She wiped her face with her hand, smearing flour all over her cheek. She then straightened her apron, fluffed her hair and strode to the door. She stared at it a moment as it was pounded on again. Then grasping the heavy iron handle she tugged it open.

"Yes, can I help you?" she enquired sweetly.

"Good Morning Miss," the soldier replied. "I'm sorry to disturb you. But I bring a request from His Royal Highness Prince Varain."

"I see," she said as monotone as she could achieve. " And what does he want today?"

"Miss, he requests your presence at a public gathering to be held next week at the royal palace for the ambassador from Bydanushev. He wishes you to accompany him."

"This is getting tiresome," she said half to herself. "Captain, would you be so good as to tell His Highness that I will be unable to do so.

"I understand Miss," the Captain said in a sympathetic tone. The poor man had done this many times over the past several months. He was as sick of it as she was. "But he will want a reason."

"Yes he will won't he," she mused. "Tell him I'm rearranging my socks," she said after a moment.

The Captain thought for a moment. "As you wish Miss. I'm sorry to have disturbed you. Good day." He saluted, strode to his horse, mounted then he and his men rode away.

"Socks?" Gossan asked.

"I think it's great," Lianka said supportively.

"It will work," Kanilma said. "For today."

~ * * * * * * ~

"I do not agree," one announced.

"Neither do I," said another.

No surprises there. For either of them.

"May I ask why?"

"To allow ordinary women to view and participate in these proceedings is to invite danger. Think of the repercussions."

"Yes. Firstly it is very unfair to subject them to such complicated matters as politics. Their minds cannot understand. It would be cruel of us to try and force them to."

"And secondly," spoke another. "If some of the more ambitious ones get it into their heads to actually run for a seat in the Great Council, it would spell disaster for us all."

He sat silently for a moment. "Well I have heard all the arguments, both for and against, and I will pass them on to his Excellency. He of course will have the final decision."

"Your recommendation will carry much weight, Chief Archon. Which will you recommend to him?"

"Neither. I do not have an opinion. However I would remind you of the wise words of the ancient philosopher Moloss, who said 'that is the desire of the gods for mankind to grow. To develop and to enlighten.' Does that not also include those of the female?"

"Moloss was speaking of men. Not of women"

"The Archon is right."

"Perhaps. Perhaps not. But should we not move on to other matters. Archon," he turned to the councilman who kept the agenda. "What is next?"

The Archon began to explain. Arapofia wasn't listening. He was too busy thinking of philosophical and religious arguments for and against the notion of women in the Great Council. Many arguments had been made throughout history. Other cultures had concluded that women should be allowed into politics. And it was true that they had been accepted into almost every other profession. But there was still concern of those times. Those times each month, when women were hijacked by their bodies. If only there was a way to help them overcome it. They didn't deserve that punishment. He felt the gods had been too harsh on that matter.

But then who was he to argue with a god.

~ * * * * * * ~

"Daddy."

"Yes darling?"

"Mother says it's time for breakfast."

"Okay, tell her I'll be there in a few minutes," he told her.

"Yes daddy." She started to return to the house.

"Be careful walking back," he cautioned her. "And stay away from Povel. He's not very happy today."

"I will," she promised then tottled off towards the house in the distance.

Poljazak finished milking the cow and then sent her back into the field. Several more cows blinked at him, their lack of intelligence shone brightly from their eyes, their jaws moving constantly, chewing their cud. "Sorry girls, you'll have to wait till after my breakfast."

One of them lowed as if in response.

"Is that right?"

Stopping briefly to check that Povel was all right, Poljazak headed towards the house. The old bull had come down with something. He wasn't sure what yet.

When he arrived at the house he slipped off his muddied boots and washed his hands and arms in a bucket on the large verandah. As he dried his hands on the piece of towel he looked out over the misty valley. Grey clouds were moving in over the distant tree topped hills and a cool breeze blew through the valley.

He went inside and greeted his wife with a kiss then said hello to his son and daughter, then sat down and began to eat.

"How's Povel?" his wife asked.

"He seems okay," he told her. "But I still might go into the village and ask Morras to come take a look at him."

"Probably better if you do. We can't afford to loose him now."

"Not this close to the breeding season, no."

"What's wrong with Povel, father," his son asked.

"I'm not sure yet."

"Is Povel going to die?" his daughter asked.

He and his wife exchanged a glance. She was starting to get to that age where she was asking certain questions. They still weren't quite sure how they wanted to handle them. "Do you really think that old grouch is ever going to die? He wouldn't give us the satisfaction."

She giggled.

Unfortunately he could well do. That's what had him worried.

~ * * * * * * ~

"Glory be to Asen," he chanted.

"Glory be to Asen," she repeated.

"Glory be to Asen," the chorus intoned.

He returned to the alter to prey silently. All heads in the chamber bowed in silent benediction.

But her thoughts were not of her God.

The old fool thought he was immune to the ways of the world. Everyone knew that the only reason he was still the high priest was because the Phirinos feared civil war if he was replaced. If the Phirinos had his way, Avek wouldn't be high priest.

But he was old anyway. And accidents can happen to older people. Especially those that thought no harm could come to them. She just had to figure out how. That was the problem. She had no idea.

Once she became high priest, she would make sure she was liked and respected. Not at all like the dottering old fool who now had begun to pour libation oil into the ceremonial platter.

She stood slowly ready to begin the next phase of the ritual. The many pieces of jewellery clinking softly as she rose. She also felt the amulet around her neck shift. If only she was allowed to wear it outside her garments. Her mother had believed it was part of an ancient crystal throne. The one the first Phirinos had been given by the gods, millennia ago. Who knew? But its very sight would inspire fear in the old man.

He looked at her with a look of anger. Her mind had wandered. She smiled sweetly and stood next to him.

Soon, she thought. Soon and it will be me standing there.

~ * * * * * * ~

He sat down wearily on the seat.

He sighed with effort and relaxed a little.

"You look tired," she said.

"I am. I'm not as young as I used to be," he replied.

"Neither of us is," she agreed. "Perhaps you should see the physician again."

"Oh I'm alright," he assured her. "Those physicians just poke and prod me so they can get their hands on our hard earned money. You worry too much my wife."

"Do I?" she asked him seriously.

He glanced at her sideways, then looked out across the plains. The farmhands were out tilling the fields, and the sun was rising behind the heavy clouds.

"Perhaps you should consider taking it a little easier from now on," she said. "Like you said, you're not as young as you used to be."

"That might be nice," he agreed quietly. "I could do with an extra hour or twos sleep each night."

"Well then that settled." She took his hand and squeezed it gently. He smiled and looked at her. She smiled back. "Would you like a cup of tea to calm you?"

"That would be nice," he said and patted her hand.

Moving into the kitchen, the woman poured several small spoons of tea leaves into the iron kettle. She took the simmering water off of the fire and pored it into the pot. She then arranged this and several large mugs on a large wooden tray and carried them back out to the veranda.

He still sat in the chair. His eyes were closed. She put down the tray and looked at him. He didn't seen to be breathing. A shiver ran through her.

"Marcava?" she said. She reached out and shook him gently.

He woke with a start. "Oh Endilla," he said. "I'm sorry. I must have dozed off."

"For a moment I thought..." she left it hanging.

"No. When I do, I will be doing it with you here. I want the last thing I see to be the face of the woman I love," he told her.

"It's been a good fifty years, hasn't it?" she asked.

"They couldn't have been better," he smiled.

She poured the tea. They sat together and drank in silence.

~ * * * * * * ~

The prey was wary.

It knew it was being stalked. But it didn't know from where or by what. It was clever prey. Good. That was more of a challenge.

He eased his foot forward, carefully setting it down on the soft grass. The prey kept grazing, looking around warily.

Slowly he raised the blowpipe to his lips. He inserted the dart into the other end. He steadied himself. He inhaled and exhaled through his nose several times to calm himself.

Slowly he then drew in his final breath, filling his lungs. Then he let it out.

There was a faint rushing sound and the dart rocketed out of the tube. A second later, the prey jerked. A hit.

He waited for a moment. The prey walked around not sure of where the attack had come from. Then the potion started to take effect. Its head nodded and its eyes closed. It lay down on the ground and drifted off to sleep.

He walked out from behind the scrubby trees and sat next to it. It was only small but it would be food. He quickly gave the traditional prayer for a successful hunt then swiftly killed the animal. He skinned it and then lit a small fire to cook the meat.

As he ate he reflected on his journey. He had seen many strange things in his dreams. His father and mother. His brothers and sisters. The tribal elders, the medicine men, the shaman, but they had not yet spoken to him. Neither had any of his guides or the animals he had encountered on his journey so far.

He would just keep walking.

It would come eventually.

Chapter 2

The day was clear and bright. Clouds filled the sky and all was still wet from the downpour last night. But the city had taken on a cleaner appearance. Most of the dust and dirt had been washed off the buildings. It seemed that the city and Mother Nature had conspired to allow Lugemall City to present its best face during its conference.

The people of the city had been preparing long for these three days. The conference was not that important in terms of its outcomes. It was essentially a chance for the monarchs and diplomats to get together and re-affirm their friendship. In other words, lots of drinking, eating and other strange behaviour.

Banners flew from all the main civic buildings; and from the flagpoles in front of the palace, now flew the flags of the participating countries.

All morning guests and dignitaries had been driven into the palace by coach, from inns and embassies within the city and from country estates on the outskirts of the capital. The city was abuzz. Preparations had been under way for several weeks. Townsfolk bustled from shop to shop. Not that they had anything to do with the conference, but they seemed to sense the heightened anticipation, emanating from the palace. Yet the palace was in a state, publicly at least, that all was calm, orderly and stately. But behind the façade pandemonium reigned.

No matter how much careful planning had been done before, no matter how much had already been completed, human beings had an amazing habit of creating confusion and disruption on a grand scale.

And this occasion was no different.

Tables were still to be set, decorations still to be hung, carpets still to be laid and guest beds still to be made. There was much carting and hauling and much dashing and darting going on in the halls of the palace. Chambermaids ran frantically trying to get it all done, while deliverymen were being instructed to move "faster, faster. As though your life depended on it!"

In the expansive kitchens on the lower floor of the palace, it was chaos. Cooks nervously, but frantically poured over bubbling pots, spit jacks turned meat like it was a lathe; bakers kneaded dough as if they were rowing a boat. Dishwashers scrubbed till they nearly took off the glazing. And above all the noise, yelled instructions glided across the room. Howls of frustration at some problem or other echoed from the walls. Conversations were impossible, over the noise. Luckily there was too much work to be done.

Mac watched the scene before him as Toloc, Chief head Steward of His Majesties Household yelled over the din in the kitchen, for the Head Chef Kolon. The two men had worked at the palace for years, probably decades, and were the best of friends. Not that you would know it by the way they spoke to each other at the moment.

Toloc was fairly tall, and this attribute would have normally stood him in good stead in a crowded room like the kitchen was at this time. But not today. There were too many baskets and sacks and goodness knew what else being carried around the room that it was next to impossible to pick out one man. Kolon was the complete opposite of Toloc. Short, rotund and rosy cheeked, more so in the heat of *this* kitchen. The two men could not have been more physically opposite, but they ran the Kings kitchen with patience, intelligence and exquisite taste. Mac personally liked the men, but for different reasons. Toloc because he was always helpful, and had never judged Mac when he had first arrived at the Palace. He just added one more name to the list of people he looked after. And Kolon because he was how a cook was supposed to look. He may have been fat, but he didn't care. He was good at his job and he knew it. Damn good as it happened.

Kolon of course couldn't hear Toloc because of all the noise.

Despite the pandemonium Mac actually felt comfortable here. It reminded him that real people still existed. That the common man was still thriving.

Finally after several more abusive and rather uncharacteristic screams across the kitchen, Toloc noticed Mac in the corner near the door.

"Ah, Mac. A normal person in this room at last."

"I see what you mean."

"If I have to yell once more above this racket I'll go hoarse. Then the King will have me beheaded." He sighed heavily. "What can I do for you?"

"I was going to take some tea up to His Highness," Mac replied.

"Ah yes of course," he turned and reefed a tea tray out of the hands of one of the serving girls who was just passing by heading towards the reception. "Here you are sir. I hope His Highness approves. You, get another."

Mac stifled a grin as the serving girl scuttled off pulling a face.

Mac made his way upstairs to their apartments. Several times people held doors open for him and everyone greeted him with a certain nervousness. At first he wasn't sure why. No one normally spoke to him like that. Was there something he didn't know? He decided it was the conference. He hoped it was the conference.

He entered the room and set the tea tray down on the table and began to prepare a cup of tea. He heard a struggled gasp and looked around the corner to see the prince struggling to clasp the collar on his tight and expensive doublet.

Mac looked at him for a moment. Dorm continued to struggle with the clasp. It was always rather funny to watch someone trying to do something they couldn't and probably shouldn't do in the manner that he was. He had a tendency to pursue things in this manner. But that was Dorm for you. He sighed to himself for thinking such 'negative' thoughts about his partner.

Dorm was definitely the perfect man for him. Well he thought so anyway. Dorm was tall, but not overly so. He had a defined body, while not being grossly muscled like some of the palace guards, and he actually had a brain. Dorms best features, in Mac's opinion were his eyes. A perfect shade of blue. A blue he could get lost in. They set of his features perfectly. A strong chin, without being all pointy, and dark hair that Mac just loved to play with. Especially when Dorm didn't want him too.

But then of course there was the person inside. Dorms' personality and intelligence were what really made him perfect. He rarely yelled. He always had a kind word for people, and took the time to get to know them. He knew the names of just about everyone in the Palace and always knew their stories and what was happening in their lives. He was patient when he needed to be, firm when it was called for, and took his responsibilities as future monarch seriously. Everyone knew he was rather intelligent. He could sometimes recall facts everyone else in the room had forgotten. He knew both Lugemall's and the Alliance's history well, and was familiar with all the laws and practices of the country. But despite being so knowledgeable, he was modest about it. He hated blowing his own horn, and sometimes even tried to hold back some of his knowledge so that he wouldn't appear too superior.

In short he cared what people thought about him. He wanted people to like him.

But above all that he was kind, and generous and caring. Everything any one could want in their partner. And Mac was so utterly grateful to have found it. He still remembered their first meeting and how they had come to be together. And what Dorm's actions that day meant to him. Whenever he had doubts about their relationship, he only had to recall that day and they vanished. Mac knew that Dorm loved him.

And oh how he loved him.

Mac himself could never quite understand what Dorm saw in him. He was a commoner for a start. But Dorm had never cared. In fact he often claimed it was one of the reasons he loved him so much. Mac personally felt his hair was the colour of dried horse manure, but Dorm always said it was rugged and shone in the right kind of light. He was shorter than Dorm, and felt that green, nearly hazel were completely the wrong colour eyes for him. He had improved his physique during his time at the Palace, that was true, but he still felt his knees were too knobbly, and don't even start on his nose. Dorm said his nose was one of his best features. Mac always accused him of being drunk when he said that. Only far too often he wasn't. Mac would often catch Dorm just staring at him, while he was working. Mac had taken on some of the minor things that Dorm didn't have time to do, and they often worked together in Dorm's study. Mac knew he blushed when he caught Dorm doing that. Dorm always just smiled that sweet smile of his, that spoke volumes.

Theirs was a relationship that they both treasured beyond, riches, or station. And the best thing about it was that they were happy. Really that was all anyone could ask for in life, wasn't it?

"Wait," Mac said crossing quickly over to him, after tearing himself away from his reverie. "Let me or you'll wreck it. Breathe in."

Dorm sucked in a huge breath and held it while Mac calmly clasped the collar. "Thank you," he said as he let out his held breath noisily.

"You're welcome," Mac replied laying his hands on Dorms' shoulders and kissing him. "Good morning by the way."

"Yes that too," Dorm said striding to the tea tray. He quickly finished making the tea then raised it to his lips.

"You know..." Mac began.

Dorm held up his hand for silence whilst he took a sip. A look of relaxed ecstasy, oozed slowly across his face. "Now, what were you saying?"

"You won't have time to finish it."

"I'm the Prince. Let them wait."

"And what will your father say?" Mac reminded him.

Dorm made a face.

The banquet room was crowded with people all milling around in preparation for the opening ceremony of the conference. It was normally a rather gloomy place, as it didn't get used much. Normally the grey stone walls and buttresses made it a rather uninviting room, but currently it was bright and airy. Many candles and sconces had been lit, and flowers and bunting and flags placed here and there to liven up the colour. It had turned out quite well in the end, and Dorm had starting thinking of all the things that could be done with the room, now that he had seen it this way. The large tables chocked full of platters of food, and an army of goblets filled with a deep red wine certainly helped make it a more inviting place as well.

Over the light din of the hundreds of conversations, a small string orchestra plucked and plicked their way through a repertoire of airs, on a variety of lutes, violins, violas, cellos and harps. The clink of crystal glasses mixed with the tinkle of expensive, and rather heavy jewellery and the rustle of even more expensive gowns.

The conversations revolving around the room covered a huge range of topics; from political decisions, court gossip, social reform policies, court gossip, rural production quotas, court gossip, military recruitment levels, court gossip, public construction efforts, court gossip, scientific development, and of course court gossip.

The official reception line weaved its way from the large oak entry doors towards the centre of the room. The official representatives of the attending nations, greeted the entering peerage of Lugemall, the various attending diplomats, bureaucrats, officials, attendants, assistants, military escorts and other un-notables.

His Royal Highness Prince Dormal of Lugemall, heir to the throne, Prince Lord of all the Marches, Knight Commander of His Majesty's armies and Crown Prince of the Realm, stood in the long line beside his father, His Royal Majesty King Mac Lavin III of Lugemall, Field Marshal of the Armies of Lugemall, Patron of the Royal University, Keeper of the Peace, High Marshal of Justice, Leader of the Marches, Sovereign of the People, greeting the entering nobodies.

Dorm's father was shorter than his son, and looked older than he was. Despite this and his sometimes appearance of the onset of dotage, he commanded the respect of everyone and indeed any one who knew him. He had a close cropped beard of steely grey and a mane of flowing white hair. The fact that his hair had turned white so early in his life was a source of unending amusement to the King who continually teased his son that his hair would go white "not five minutes after I'm dead, you'll see."

At the moment he was wearing the simplified version of his royal robes. The full Lugemallan royal robes were a huge cumbersome arrangement that were only ever brought out at coronations. You simply couldn't move in the damn things! The king wore his rich silk edged blue doublet and hose and his normal half high boots, though for once Dorm noted they were polished. He wore his ceremonial dagger at his waist, meant to be for self protection, and his heavy knee length cloak with the furry edges. As a child Dorm had liked playing with the fur on the cloak, and often wandered around his parents rooms wearing it, trailing along behind him. He wore the Day crown on his head, which was not the formal crown; again something far too heavy to wear on a regular basis, as well as his various rings and the large necklace of office. As if anyone couldn't tell he was the King, what with the crown and all, the ancient Kings had been given a fancy necklace with gold and jewels. Each panel representing one of the ancient clans of the Kingdom.

Dorm noted that his father was again all in blue. He seemed to have a penchant for blue. He was *always* wearing it. Now Dorm didn't have anything against blue. He quite liked blue, and wore it often himself. But even a blue linen shirt under his doublet? That was a little excessive wasn't it?

King Mac Lavin was considered by many to be the epitome of Lugemallan kings. Intelligent, just, compassionate, firm, confident, and forward thinking. He often told his son that his father, had taught him from a young age, what it meant to be a king of Lugemall. The responsibility, the privilege it was. The honour the position bestowed on the bearer of that title. But also the enormous responsibility that went with it. "'Being a king", he always said. "Is not about a fancy chair, fine clothes and food, and being waited on hand and foot. It's about making peoples lives easier and better. And if at the end you cant point to at least one thing you've done that has achieved that... then I'm afraid you've failed." And he had tried to instil this philosophy in Dorm.

Beside Dorm stood his best friend, Her grace the Lady Tellsandra, daughter of Lord Kardranos, Niece to her Imperial Majesty Queen Olda Victasia III of Selatem.

Telly was, well beautiful, to put it mildly. She too was tall and always carried herself with an air of confidence and grace. Today her wealth of dark, almost black hair cascaded down her back, several strands of pearls being woven into it. They matched well with her pale and flawless skin. Her grey eyes seemed to be everywhere as she greeted the incoming guests. But her sweetly voiced platitudes to the entering guests were not fooling Dorm for a minute. He knew her too well to think that she was really as sickly sweet as all that. In fact that was one of the reasons he liked her so much.

Close behind Dorm stood Mac. As a technical member of the lower class, he was not permitted to stand in the line, though many of the guests knew him and greeted him all the same.

Tellsandra let fly a huge sigh. Luckily there was a break in the line at the time, so no-one noticed. "I hate standing here for hours on end, smiling and bowing and shaking hands. It makes me feel like a twerp."

"Twerp???" Dorm asked quietly.

"Yes Twerp," Tellsandra replied. "Haven't you ever heard that word before?"

"No"

"Dear me Dorm," she replied exacerbated. "Where have you been for the last ten years?"

"I could tell you," Mac said quietly from behind them. Dorms' face turned a brilliant shade of red.

"Oh Mac really!" Tellsandra said superiorly. "You mustn't be so rude. It's frightfully unbecoming." She grinned at him "You'll have to tell me later."

Mac chuckled, and grabbed Dorms' hands as Dorm, his face cascading to a brighter shade of crimson, glared at Tellsandra who merely turned back to face the newly arrived guests.

The procession of various people continued for a little while longer. Finally it finished and the last of the new arrivals joined the throng and began to seek out people they knew, wanted to impress or gloat to and left the line alone.

Lord Kardranos moved over next to his daughter. His greying hair was a serious clash to his small, dark black moustache. He was shorter than his daughter, but moved with a cat like walk that made it seem like he was about to pounce at any second. He was a man who was known to have been a formidable warrior in his younger days. His expertise with the sword was common knowledge. As was his intelligence, wit and charm. He had apparently given all his children some instruction in swordplay as well, hoping it would give them more opportunities in life. He now seemed to work directly for the Seltamese queen on various endeavours, that no one really fully understood. "Tellsandra my dear," he said taking her arm and kissing her on the cheek. "I thought you were wearing pink today?"

"No I wasn't," she told him through clenched teeth. "Ah you remember Prince Dormal don't you Father?"

"Well of course I do my dear. I may be old but I'm not senile. How are you my boy? You've certainly grown since the last time I saw you."

"Yes Your Eminence," Dorm replied. "It seems to be going around."

"Witty as ever I see. And how are you Mac Ravin?"

"Quite well sir, thank you for asking," Mac replied.

"Dormal I wanted to ask. How's your father?" his voice lowered somewhat at this.

Dorm had been hoping he wouldn't. His fathers health had been of some concern for a little while now. He had been afflicted with an illness the year before. Everyone had just thought it was a cold at first, but then it had gotten worse, and hadn't gone away. He hadn't been able to perform his regal duties for several weeks, and Dorm had effectively had to take over. While his condition had improved considerably over the last few months, it was clear that he was still ill. Everyone was hoping he would get better, but secretly fearing he wouldn't.

"He tires easily," Dorm replied. "But he is still determined to be the king."

"Well we are all concerned about him. Her Majesty instructs me to pass on her best wishes to both you and your father."

"Be sure to thank her for me."

"I will." He looked across the room, noticing someone. "Would you excuse me. There's someone's bubble I need to go and burst."

"Of course."

"Daughter dear," he said kissing her again. "Your Highness" He bowed to both Dorm and Mac, before scuttling off with a barely controlled sense of anticipation in his stride.

"Well I don't know about either of you young boys, but I'm thirsty," Tellsandra said. "Shall we?"

Dorm took her arm in his and with Mac they moved quickly towards the groaning drinks table. After obtaining their refreshments they moved up to the dais where King Mac Lavin now sat in his throne talking with the King of Tagradas, Corm Sanell.

The two old men were chuckling and grinning like schoolboys when Dorm approached them. The two monarchs were old, old friends. They were distantly related, and because of their similar ages had in some ways grown up together. When their parents had visited each other during their childhoods it had been natural that the two of them would end up together and become friends.

Corm Sanell was slightly taller than Dorm's father and his hair still had much of its colour, but it was rapidly starting to go a dark grey. He had a wicked sense of humour and could easily find the funny side in any situation. He was though a very good monarch, cut from much the same cloth as Mac Lavin. When the situation called for it he could be serious, even verging on single minded. Dorm had only seen that once or twice, and it worried him a little.

"Oh Dormal," Corm Sanell said as he approached. "Your father's still as perverted as he was when he was your age."

"Don't tell him that," Mac Lavin said. "It's not true my son. In fact, I'm actually worse."

Corm Sanell laughed loudly again. "Sit down boy," he told Dorm. "Oh and the lovely Tellsandra, and the ever present Mac Ravin. Sit both of you. There is much naughtiness to discuss."

Huge grins abounded.

As Corm Sanell began to tell one of his tall stories to Tellsandra and Mac, Dorm leaned closer to his father.

"Are you going to be alright to make the speech Father?" he asked quietly.

"Don't worry about me my boy," he said warmly. "I'll be alright." He smiled at his son.

A while later a herald came and told the king that the last of the guests had been admitted and that the opening ceremony could begin whenever he was ready. Mac Lavin rose slowly aided by Dorm. The crowd was brought to a quiet and they turned to face the dais.

"My assembled guests," Mac Lavin began in a shaky, but strong voice. "I, as host, would like to welcome you all to the humble capital of my Kingdom, for the seventy-fifth East Alliance Conference on Economic and Agricultural Mutual Assistance and Co-operation. May all of us be blessed, during these coming days, with wisdom, respect, and above all patience. For what we decide here and how we act will be an example to the generations to come. With faith in each other and in the Fortress, I hereby declare this conference open."

The crowd applauded politely then took a sip as a toast to the success of the conference.

Dorm helped his father back to his throne as the crowd returned to their activities and the music resumed. "Thank you Dorm," he said as he sat. "Now take Mac and go get something to eat. You're starting to look thin."

"Father!"

Mac Lavin laughed. "Go on my son. I'll be alright."

"As you wish Father." Dorm stood, turned, took Mac's hand and said, "Come my darling. His Majesty has ordered us to eat."

"Well I guess we can't refuse then," Mac said standing.

"Would you care to join us My Lady?" Dorm asked Tellsandra.

"Why of course Your Highness," she replied with all the pomp she could muster. "I would be honoured."

The three friends proceeded to the table.

After another hour or so the opening ceremony concluded. All the assembled guests departed, painfully slowly. Those not participating in the conference circuited the room farewelling all those people they deemed important enough and bade them well, arranged lunch meetings and got in a final gloat or two. They were then escorted to a fleet of waiting coaches to take them home, as those principal participants in the conference moved to the Great Conference Hall in the North Wing of the palace.

There in the comfortably and heavily blue draped and upholstered room, more introductions took place, this time introducing all the attendees to each other and making sure they knew each other.

Next came several long-winded, flowery worded and hypnotic speeches by several of the main participants, outlining their aims at this conference and personally thanking King Mac Lavin for his hospitality and kindness.

Dorm sat through all this into the early night, only because he had to. Mac and Tellsandra had gone off after the reception to the gardens and were probably now enjoying a sumptuous meal; while he sat here listening to the economics minister of Ambaka briefly outline how well his nation had done fiscally last year.

Several times both he and his father began to nod off. Luckily Mac Lavins' long time aide, and friend from childhood, Ellin kept a careful eye on both of them and gave them a discreet nudge to wake them.

Finally the last speech finished and then the session ended and they were all allowed to go. It was obvious by the heavy sighs of relief from all those in the room that it was a welcome development. Servants were then called to escort all the dignitaries back to their rooms. Corm Sanell lingered for several moments to talk with Mac Lavin to organise a visit. The two ageing monarchs were almost like brothers thought not related to each other anywhere near that closely. After their brief discussion about the choice of liquid accompaniment, Corm Sanell then began towards his quarters with his aide and Finance Adviser in tow.

Dorm walked slowly with his father and Ellin back to the royal apartments.

"Father I wish you would let me do more for you," Dorm said as they neared their destination.

"Oh, trying to usurp my crown are you son?" Mac Lavin joked.

"You know what I mean Father."

"I know Dorm. But I'm alright for the moment. A good nights rest and three square meals a day will see me through."

"I'm just worried about you, that's all."

"I know you are my boy," said the King gently. "I know everyone is. And I appreciate it. But I'm fine. Really." He looked at his sons' face for a moment. "You know there were many who said you'd never make it to be king. If only they could see you now."

Dorm blushed.

The King chuckled at his son's discomfort. They entered the rooms and Mac Lavin sat in a heavily upholstered chair. "Where are you off to now?" he asked.

"To my rooms. Then to get some dinner and see what Mac and Telly have gotten up to."

"No good I should imagine, if I know those two," the king laughed.

"You should get some rest Father."

"Stop fussing over me son. You aren't my mother."

Dorm looked at Ellin. "Can't you talk some sense into him?"

"Don't look at me Your Highness. I'm just his oldest friend. What could I possibly know about him?" Ellin said sarcastically.

"Well good night Father. And if you hear raucous laughter during the night, it's just us. Try not to worry to much about it." Dorm kissed his fathers cheek then left.

"My dear. These young people today Ellin," Mac Lavin sighed, watching where his son had left. "Not like us when we were that age eh?"

"No of course not Your Majesty," Ellin replied without the least hint of sarcasm in his voice. "We would never have stayed up till the wee small hours of the morning drinking ale, and singing and making all manner of loud noises keeping the whole palace up, would we?"

Mac Lavin turned and glared at his friend. "Be quiet. I have a reputation to maintain."

Chapter 3

They laughed.

"I've never heard it told quite like that."

"You should have seen Fathers' face," Dorm said.

"I can imagine," Tellsandra said. They laughed again.

The rain continued to fall. They had retired to Dorm and Macs' apartments and had stayed up talking and reminiscing. It wasn't often that any of them got the chance to do this. The responsibilities of station usually robbed them of the simple pleasures in life. That and the fact that they lived in different countries separated by hundreds of miles.

"Mac," Dorm said reaching across and shaking his partner. "Wake up so you can go to bed."

"Huh what?" Mac said waking up suddenly. "What's going on?" he said innocently.

"You're falling asleep," Tellsandra told him.

"I am not," he said defensively.

"What rot, you were too," Dorm told him. "Why don't you get into bed now. That way I won't have to try and carry you there."

"Oh alright," he said, wearily rising to his feet. "Good night everyone." He ambled towards the huge canopied bed, stopping briefly to kick off his shoes and strip off his doublet. He crawled into the bed and promptly returned to his slumber.

"Would you like a top up?" Dorm asked her pointing to her glass of fruit juice.

"Just a little bit," she replied handing him the glass. He quickly poured her some more and topped up his own glass of wine, before settling back down. A crack of thunder crashed into the room.

"I always liked storms for some reason," Tellsandra said mysteriously, looking towards the rain streaked windows.

"Me too," Dorm mused. "Something primeval, powerful and primitive about them."

"That was nice alliteration," Tellsandra complemented him.

"Yes I thought so too."

"We should do this more often," Tellsandra said. "We have so much fun, the three of us."

"I know," Dorm said sadly, "But you live so far away, and there's never any one around here willing to stay up till the wee small hours with us."

"Well maybe you'll just have to find someone to join in the fun," Tellsandra told him.

"Either that or you could move here."

"From Selatem?!" she said. "That would take a year just to think about."

"Probably but we'd have lots of fun."

"Now don't talk like that. You'll make me actually consider it."

"That's the idea," Dorm said and laughed.

"Oh Dorm... You always were a good and true friend," Tellsandra told him. "I'm glad I knew you."

"And Mac?" Dorm asked.

"Mac is thoughtful, intelligent, sensitive, resourceful, loyal, courageous, funny, probably a million other things I can't think of, and he's one hell of a good looking boy."

"Believe me," Dorm said. "He's no boy. He's a man."

Tellsandra blushed slightly. "Thank you for that insight."

Dorm laughed.

"I guess it's too late to go trudging back to my apartments now," Tellsandra mused.

"Well you'll just have to curl up here. I'm sure we can spare a blanket or a sheet or something for you. And we have more pillows than I know what to do with."

"Why thank you Your Highness," Tellsandra said curtsying.

"My pleasure My lady," he said bowing.

Dorm fetched a sheet and blanket off their bed and laid them out with two pillows on the largest settee in the room. She looked at him as he stood back up.

"I'm glad I came here today," she said to him. "Despite the difficulties we had some years ago. I am very proud to have you as my friend Dorm."

He blushed at her for a moment. "And I you Telly," he said, slipping into the familiar name she only let people close to her use.

She hugged him close and he responded in kind.

She stood back from him and patted him on the cheek. She then began to remove her cumbersome dress before snuggling down under the blanket.

"Good night old friend," she said.

"Good night," Dorm said as he made his way to the bed taking off his own doublet and throwing it onto the bed covers. He got into the huge sleeping chamber and snuggled up next to Mac, who instinctively snuggled back. Very soon he was asleep.

The storm continued to rage outside.

Dorm slowly closed the door to the bathroom and sleepily began to make his way back towards his nice warm bed. Sleep. What a wonderful idea man had come up with there. He passed the table strewn with cups and plates from supper and shuddered at the thought of how much he'd eaten... and drunk.

He looked back across the pitch-black chambers towards his bed. Suddenly he crashed into something soft, warm and fragrant. He almost yelled in terror until he heard her voice.

"Who are you?" she asked.

"Dorm," he replied.

"You scared me half to death."

"Well I'm not far behind."

"What are you doing up at this time?"

"I could ask you the same thing."

"I'm going to freshen up and powder my nose," she said in mock arrogance.

"You too," he giggled.

A flash of lightning lit up the room, washing all colour away so everything looked grey. They glanced at each other and grinned. Suddenly Tellsandras' hand shot to her chest. She held it there as if waiting for something.

"What is it?" Dorm asked concerned.

"I thought for a moment..." she began. "Where did you get that amulet?" she asked pointing at Dorms' chest.

"This?" he said lifting it up to look more closely at it. "It's a family heirloom. Father gave it to me on my sixteenth birthday. Why?"

Tellsandra reached inside her bodice and pulled out an almost identical amulet. "That's why," she replied.

"How did you..." Dorm began.

"It was my mothers'. Father gave it to me shortly after she died. He said it was an heirloom of her family, and that she had apparently intended to give it to me on my sixteenth birthday."

"This is too weird."

"Don't tell me Mac has one as well?"

"Not that I know of," Dorm rubbed his cheek in thought. "Something tells me we'd better have a word with our fathers in the morning."

"What a brilliant idea."

"Father we need to talk," Dorm said.

"Yes we do," Tellsandra echoed, glaring at her father.

The room in the west atrium was rather crowded. The meeting had something to do with defence spending and co-operation. Dorm couldn't remember the details. Seated around the large oak table were Mac Lavin with Ellin beside him. Tellsandra's father, Lord Karranos, as a representative of the Queen of Selatem was present as well. Selatem had probably the largest and best navy in the Alliance. Sitting with him was Fleet Admiral Travanos, also from Selatem. The Admiral was a man of large bearing with a neat grey beard. His barrel chest and tall stature gave him immediate authority in just about anything he wished to speak on.

Corm Sanell sat with his aide next to Dorm's father. Several others, mostly bureaucrats sat in various chairs at the table and around the room.

"What about Dorm?" Mac Lavin asked a little nervously.

"It's about this," he replied removing his amulet from under his doublet. "I need to know everything there is to know about this amulet."

"Well there's not much to tell really," the monarch said. "It's a family heirloom, passed from father to son on their sixteenth birthday. I have no idea why. It's just a piece of crystal. Why do you ask?"

Tellsandra removed her own, almost identical amulet and held it up for the group to see.

"That's a clever trick," said Ellin.

"You wouldn't be able to shed some light on this at all would you?" Tellsandra said looking at her father.

"I know about as much as His Majesty, I'm afraid. It was your mothers. She was given it by her mother when she turned sixteen. Unfortunately she died before you were."

"Yes I know all that Father," she said with a tinge of sorrow in her voice. "But what is it?"

"This may seem strange," Admiral Travanos said, "But..." he reached beneath his uniform and revealed an identical amulet.

"Now this is getting weird," Mac said.

"Three identical amulets," Ellin said astonished.

"Admiral you wouldn't by any chance have been given it by your father on your sixteenth birthday?" Mac Lavin enquired.

"As repetitive as it sounds. Yes," he replied a little bemused.

"Three of them," Lord Karranos said in an astonished voice.

"Make that four," said a young woman sitting in a chair against the wall. She pulled another from her bodice.

"I think I need a drink," Corm Sanell said reaching for the decanter.

"Come her child," Mac Lavin said gently.

"Yes Your Majesty," she curtsied and walked to the group.

"What's your name?"

"Rhynavell. I work at the Royal Accountancy." She seemed nervous. Understandably, since she was probably only meant to be here to present some financial report. She was an attractive young woman, with a full figure. She was of a similar height to Mac, and had a wealth of auburn hair, which at the moment was tied back. She wore a rather nondescript but formal looking dress, probably something resembling a uniform.

"Let me guess," Dorm said. "Your mother gave you that amulet when you turned sixteen?"

She nodded.

"How *did* you guess that Dorm my love?" Mac said sarcastically.

"Well it would seem we have a little mystery on our hands," Ellin said

"So how do we figure out what it means?" Kardranos asked.

"Well as our old tutor always used to say ''To the library'" Mac Lavin said pointing into the air.

The library of the palace was situated on the top three levels of the great west tower. Beneath it were records office and several scribing rooms as well as several rooms that were normally filled with bureaucrats. These were frequented by many of the kings' scribes and assistants and by the various government bureaucrats from all the different government offices in the city. It even had a special entrance portico where they could enter without having to go through the main ceremonial entrance.

The lower level of the library kept important legal documents, court decisions, the full registrar of laws and several other important constitutional tomes and their various sub-volumes, commentaries and annotations.

The second level contained hundreds of various historical texts of the kingdom, as well as extensive plans of all major buildings throughout the country.

The third and highest level, which was rarely visited, contained more historical records, as well as many fantastical and somewhat heretical accounts of magical happenings and prophecies and other such nonsense.

The great search for the answers to the crystal amulet mystery began on the second level. Dorm, Mac, Mac Lavin, Corm Sanel, Ellin,

Tellsandra, her father Lord Kardranos, Fleet Admiral Travanos, Rhynavell and Corm Sanels' aide, Thovin marched into the great vaulted chamber to the stunned look of the few scribes and librarians that were there.

They all began examining documents, scrolls, books and the like, while the poor librarians struggled to continue their work without interrupting this sudden barrage of royalty as they scrounged through the collected works.

It soon became apparent that there was a serious flaw in their plan. When one researches something, one usually has some knowledge of the topic and is therefore able to formulate specific questions one intends to answer. This research was different. The question was not specific.

"Tell me more about these amulets," does not help in identifying what volumes to look in. Should one examine the catalogue of all the royal jewels? Should one scour the works of the great jewellery makers? Perhaps an examination of the whole history of the kingdom is in order. No one knew. So at first the group blindly flipped and read through tomes and scrolls that might in some way have the ability to give them some inspiration as to where to look.

After an hour or so of pottering around the room looking at various things, a messenger entered to inform Mac Lavin that the participants in the next session of the conference had arrived at the conference room. Mac Lavin and Corm Sanel looked at each other then apologised profusely and hurried from the room like naughty school children, followed by their aides.

The remainder of the group stayed behind and continued to rummage aimlessly through the many volumes. Fleet Admiral Travanos continued to mutter to himself as he tried to remember anything about the amulets that might be useful.

After several hours of fruitless search they sat around the table in the centre of the room, deflated and feeling rather useless. After about half an hour of dejected sighs, Rhynavell suggested, "Perhaps I should look through my mothers things. She died only last year and I've not had chance to go through all her things. There might be some clue in there."

"She's as clever as she is beautiful," Mac said.

"Hey!" Dorm said looking at him.

"Oh don't worry Dorm. I still think you're beautiful too," Mac told him, patting his cheek.

"Father?" Telly asked then. "Do we still have Mothers' things?"

"Well most of it," Kardranos replied. "It's stored at home. There was very little I didn't keep."

"We should look through that."

"You're not suggesting we go all the way back to Selatem?" he asked.

"No."

"Well that's good."

"I'm suggesting you do. I'm staying here."

"What!" he rose in his seat.

"Moving right along," Dorm said quickly.

Travanos spoke. "I think we should let Miss Rhynavell search her mothers' things before we continue. There really isn't much point to rifling through this library until we have more information."

"I agree," said Mac.

"Well then that's settled," Dorm concluded. "Rhynavell will search her mother's things and see if she can find anything that may help us."

"She did have a lot of things. It might take me some time," Rhynavell said quietly.

"Then I volunteer to help you," Telly said.

They all looked at her.

"And so do all of you," she concluded.

The next day it showered. Clouds scudded across the sky and a cool wind rose and fell.

The conference continued at the palace, but was confined to minor dignitaries natting out problems in contracts and proposals before their final submission to the decision makers.

Overnight Dorm, Mac, Telly and Travanos had assisted Rhynavell to delve through all her mothers stored belongings. There weren't many papers, mainly clothes, linen and personal items, however they did find her diary. A meticulously kept journal of each days events. It started from when her mother was about fifteen years old.

Before long they found the entry of her sixteenth birthday. Her mother recorded what her own mother, Rhynavells' grandmother, had said to her. She wrote that her mother had told her how the amulet was passed from mother to daughter on the commencement of her sixteenth year. Her mother had said that the amulet was very old, and that when her mother had received it from Rhynavells' Great-grandmother, she had hinted that it may have something to do with the Fortress, but she hadn't understood what and so had disregarded it.

This seemed to be a breakthrough. A possible connection with the Fortress. The question was, what sort of a connection? And so with a slight reluctance the group had returned to the palace library in order to do more research.

They had entered early and asked the librarians and scribes to bring them any documents dealing with the Fortress.

And so the librarians complied.

That was the first mistake.

As the group sat around the large central table, the staff of the library proceeded to place tome and volume, scroll and parchment upon the table. All of it in some way dealing with the Fortress.

The majority of it was the now ancient and well known rules imposed upon the Alliance countries by the Fortress when the Alliance was first chartered millennia ago.

These documents most likely had nothing to do with the amulet unless their secret purpose had been to assist economic co-operation. They considered the possibility they may have been some sort of symbol worn by the ancient kings, to indicate that they were part of the alliance. However there was no mention of this.

They seemed once again to be lost.

"I think my eyes are beginning to go funny," Mac said.

"What do you mean funny?" Telly asked him.

"Well I'm not sure. My head hurts too much"

Dorm patted him on the shoulder. "So what do we do now?"

"If this is all we're going to find, I think give up," Rhynavell said.

"I agree," Telly said laying her head on the table.

Dorm looked across to the head librarian. "Are you sure that this is all?" he asked.

"Well Your Highness, he said. "We have exhausted all works on both levels of the library."

"Both levels?" Dorm said. " What about the top level?"

"Your Highness really," the librarian protested. "Those are all the *other* works. We never go up there. We don't even consider that to be part of the library."

"I know," Dorm said. "But at this point I'm willing to entertain anything."

The head librarian sighed heavily, took a large key from his pocket and headed over to his desk. He unlocked the lowest draw and withdrew a dusty, leather bound tome. He struggled with it over to the desk and dropped it with great effort, and a large boom, in front of Dorm. A cloud of dust rose into the air giving everyone cause to cough.

The librarian bowed slightly then tottered back to his desk.

As the others moved around to see, Dorm opened the hard blue leather cover.

The first page was blank.

The second page contained nothing except a small mark, a date and the name of a city. Presumably where it was scribed.

The next page contained the title.

'Royal Library of Lugemall. Palatial Annex. Primary Catalogue 3. Works dealing with religious, prophetical and occult subjects, as well as quasi-mystical volumes from all kingdoms in the Fortress Alliance. Annoted, indexed and cross referenced. See sub indexes for further information and reading.'

"Well it's a start," said Mac hopefully.

The next page contained some information on those who compiled the catalogue. Also listed was information on how to contact them for further information. A dubious prospect, as the last of them had died over a thousand years ago.

Next came the main index. It listed in alphabetical order, just about every subject to do with the topic areas covered by the contents of the library. This gave page numbers within the catalogue. Finding the appropriate page gave information on the various works dealing with that topic, a brief synopsis, and how to find them in the library.

"So what topics do we want to look up?" Dorm asked.

"Amulets?" Telly suggested.

"Seems as good a place as any," Travanos agreed.

"Ok then," Dorm said.

Under amulets there were five main groups. Regal Amulets, Vice Regal Amulets, Family or Positional Amulets, Mystical Amulets and Others.

They were fairly certain they were not Regal or Vice-Regal of any sort. So they moved on to Family or Positional amulets. It listed several hundred amulets that belonged to the ancient great houses of the various kingdoms as well as amulets held by various ancient magicians and wizards of the long forgotten kings, as symbols of their positions and authority, at the dawn of time. They skimmed through the description of them, but none seemed to be the amulets in question.

Mystical amulets did give some clues. It listed all the amulets mentioned in various ancient sagas that supposedly held great magical powers. Many of the amulets mentioned were supposedly capable of incredible things. Splitting mountain ranges and such.

Finally they came to Others. This was for all the amulets that didn't quite fit into any of the other categories or could be put into more than one. About halfway down the list was an entry. "Keystone Prophecies, Crystal amulets", with several pages listed.

Turning to these pages, Dorm read the brief description.

"Crystal pieces fashioned into near identical amulets passed down family lines for safekeeping. See also: Keystone prophecy."

"That sounds more like what we want," Telly said.

"Good. I was beginning to feel unlucky," Travanos replied.

"Well shall we go upstairs to investigate?" Rhynavell asked

They all looked at each other. "Let's eat first," Mac said.

There was no argument.

The meal was brief, somewhat frugal, considering it was the palace, and silent. They all seemed to want to get through the meal as quickly as possible, though all realised they needed it. They ate and drank in silence staring at each other with sparkles in their eyes. They all felt on the verge of finding that vital clue that would unlock the secrets of the mystery.

Dorm felt this was a little strange. He already felt comfortable with these people. Mac, and Tellsandra of course. He had known them for years. But Travanos and Rhynavell he didn't know at all. And yet, somehow it felt right to have them here. Almost as if they had been friends for years as well.

After they finished eating, and the servants had cleared away their dishes, they all sat finishing their wines, or in Tells' case, tea. Still nothing was said. All seemed to savour the excitement and anticipation. Finally Dorm drained his goblet and spoke.

"Well my friends, this is it."

"It looks like it doesn't it," Travanos said. "The answer."

"It's a little nerve racking," Rhynavell said.

"A little!" Mac looked at her. "I can't speak for you my dear, but I'm a nervous wreck!"

"Well the sooner we get upstairs the sooner we will have our answer," Telly said.

"Exactly," Dorm agreed. "Well then, if everyone has finished, and there are no objections..." he left it hanging as he looked around the table.

They all shook their heads to indicate no.

"Then lets go," he said.

They climbed the stairs to the top level. It was dark and rather easy to tell that it wasn't frequented. The head librarian led the way with a large bunch of keys in one hand and a lamp in the other. At the top of the stairs they stopped on a landing, the large oak doors barring their way. Mac lit a wall sconce with a taper and shed some light on the subject.

The librarian looked once again at Dorm, sighed at the Princes' nodded urging to proceed, then unlocked the door. "If you need anything Your Highness, I'll be downstairs."

"Thank you Mavin," Dorm said as he descended.

"Well this is it," Mac said quietly.

"Then let's get on with it," Telly told him.

Dorm gently pushed the doors inward. They creaked slightly as they moved.

The library's third level was very dark. Thick drapes hung on the few windows, and no lamps were lit. In the dim light, shelves could be seen, filled with books scrolls and the like.

In the centre of the room sat a large table and five chairs.

They entered slowly, their footsteps echoing slightly. They all paused for a moment, as if unsure of how to proceed. Telly then crossed the room to the windows and began to draw the drapes as Mac lit various candles and braziers around the room.

The late afternoon sun streamed in through the windows. Everyone winced slightly at the sudden inrush of light.

Travanos moved to the table with the catalogue, lowering it onto the table as Rhynavell dusted off the chairs.

All came together at the table once more to decide how to proceed.

"Well let's just start with that Keystone thingy. That sounded promising," Mac said.

"I agree," Telly said.

"Okay," Dorm said opening the great tome and finding the appropriate pages. "Here's all the listings of the various works. Let's all look for some."

All the works in the library were stored numerically. Each shelf section contained a range of numbers. This meant that the various documents were spread all over the room, on various shelves. A lot of walking backwards and forwards, and climbing on the small stepladders provided was done before the first few documents had been collected.

They all began to read the documents they had collected. Most simply contained tantalisingly cryptic allusions to the amulets. All of them were suitably vague and not very helpful. Almost all of them mentioned the amulets and their great importance, but most never went far beyond that. One or two mentioned this keystone, but none of them said anything about it in any detail. They got the impression that whoever was meant to read these things was also meant to know what it was. One crackling parchment had a rather ominous line that read "Beware the fire from above when the Keystone amulets have been found, for it brings death." Everyone paused at that one and contemplated what it could mean. All in all most of their time was spent chasing up fleeting glimpses. But then Travanos found something.

"I think I have something," he said quietly, as they all turned and looked at him. "The Keystone Prophecy."

"That was mentioned in the catalogue tome," Dorm said.

"Looks like we've found it," Telly agreed.

"Let's find out then," Mac said.

Travanos grinned as he looked at the page, cleared his throat and began to read.

"It shall be that, centuries from now, the Alliance of the Fortress shall have both prosperity and strength. And shall have proven it's worth in both combat and peace. It shall have endured and proven it's value to all. In this time the enemies of the Alliance and of the Fortress shall band together to destroy it.

"They shall plan long and hard to overthrow us and that which we have caused to be. They shall seek, not just to conquer, but also to destroy. And to destroy that which is most sacred to us. And most necessary for all that we seek to achieve.

"Those who now hold the pieces of the lobe of the Great Keystone, that was broken in that past moment of fear, shall discover each other. The revelation shall cause them great angst, but they shall be stronger than they think. Shall those who first discover their meaning journey all across the Kingdoms of the Alliance and beyond and gather to them all those who now hold those pieces, as now fashioned into amulets.

"These Questers shall be diverse. They shall be disparate. They will have their confrontations and turmoil. But these shall come to nought in the end. For they are the Questers. And their nature as such such shall bind them to each other in ways most profound and most personal. And most special.

"They shall cause to be the beginning of the possibility of a new era for the Alliance, but that new era shall not be able to begin until the outcome of this prophecy has been reached.

"Shall they finally journey to the Fortress itself. And there shall they be instructed and told of their fate. And of the true meaning of the amulets and what it is that they signify, not only for these noble Questers but for all the Alliance. Shall they then journey forth to confront these enemies who seek to destroy all that we have built. And pass where we have not seen before and cannot know. And in this journey shall they discover the true danger that we face, and that I cannot see.

"Though I cannot say whether or not they shall be successful, the more we of the Fortress prepare ourselves, shall we better be able to prepare them, and then shall they, those chosen to take on this task by fate, be prepared to confront and then defeat that which seeks to destroy us.

"At the start of their quest shall they number five. By the end shall they number twenty five. Be prepared for ultimate sacrifice. It will come. That cannot be avoided. And in fact may be of help in the final confrontation, even though the pain of it tears at the heart.

"Shall we all prepare ourselves for this great time. For this great challenge to come. Let us all pray that our strength shall become their strength. That our wisdom shall become their wisdom. For then, may we have a chance of victory."

Chapter 4

They had decided to go north.

After much discussion through the night it had been finally settled. They would head north towards Ambaka. It seemed logical, given the evidence, that there would be two people from each kingdom. And since the two from Lugemall and Selatem were already present, Ambaka seemed fairly sensible. They could then head to Ziga, then on to Tagradas.

Further searching in the records in the library had revealed only a few more clues about this 'prophecy' and this 'quest'. There had been some vague statements about this 'Great Keystone'. It was obviously of great importance to whoever had written the prophecy down, though they were still a little uncertain as to what exactly it was. Though they guessed it was at the Fortress itself. There was a mention in one crumbling scroll that dated from the time of the Second Peldraksekhr Invasion that mentioned ever so briefly a man by the name of Fanim, apparently in connection with it, but not what he had done to merit being mentioned, nor why.

There was mention of the 'enemy's great plan', and how it would cause concern and disruption. But not who this enemy was, nor any details about the plan with which to recognise it. This was starting to become hard.

The very idea of a quest itself was rather insane. Once they had realised that that was what was being asked of them, they had a brief moment where they thought this had all been some sort of practical joke. Quests were constructs for literature, not events in reality. Sure there had been times where certain individuals had had to go off into the world to gather people or supplies for certain reasons, but they were all sensible things like allies in a war, food during a famine. Not mystical objects. It made a nice story but not reality.

And yet here they were.

The reality began to dawn on them that this was in fact real. Dorm didn't want to say anything but for some reason that he couldn't put into words, he *knew* that this was real. There was just a rightness about it. Even though the idea itself was ludicrous.

The idea of this journey stretched before them. Dorm of course had been to all the countries of the Alliance on various official trips, but never all of them one after the other, all in one big long trip. The very thought of it was exhausting.

Another thought that worried them was this idea of going to the Fortress itself. The very idea was difficult to understand. Travel to the Fortress was forbidden without prior permission; which was rarely given. If your presence was required there, they would let you know. Not the other way around. Transgressions were punishable in rather horrible ways. Many who had tried had never been seen before, and those few that were, more often than not came back bereft of their senses. Spending the rest of their lives locked in small rooms surrounded by very soft furnishings. And some few of those would spend most of their time sobbing uncontrollably. Or screaming endlessly.

Their decision to leave quietly was rather quickly made. Corm Sanel was informed and he promised to do his best to identify those who held the amulets in his kingdom. He promised to be discreet. There were doubts.

King Mac Lavin was a little reluctant to let his son go traipsing off around the world. Though he realised it was probably necessary.

The two of them had discussed the situation at great length.

To both of them, the very thought of going off on some ‘quest’ was a little laughable. Mac Lavin had decreed that quests were something made up to entertain during long winters, or to give hope to the downtrodden or oppressed. They weren't real. And probably never had been. Yet here it seemed that it was. Well it at least seemed that something was going on. Something beyond their immediate understanding. Otherwise coincidence was in reality very commonplace.

Preparation for their departure had been taking place all day. The five travellers, or questers as they reluctantly allowed themselves to be called, had been scouring the supplies of the various royal storerooms, for all the various odds and ends needed for an extremely long camping trip. They had to be careful, as there were still a lot of foreign guests in the palace, as well as all the palace staff. No one particularly wanted information of what they were doing to get out. If it was something important, that might spell trouble, if it wasn't then they'd all look pretty silly. And they'd just as soon avoid that if possible.

They had not planned to leave until shortly after all the conference members had left, which was tomorrow. That way news of their sudden, mysterious departure would not be carried from one end of the Alliance to the other, before they got out the city gates. The last thing they needed was fussy do-gooding monarchs throwing banquets in their honour everywhere they went.

So this day would also be spent wrapping up the conference, and biding all the delegates farewell and safe journey. The sneakiness would come after.

Dorm had protested when Mac had told him he was coming with them. It wasn't that Dorm didn't want Mac to come. Far from it. He just didn't want him to come. Dorm knew he wouldn't win the argument, but it was expected, so he played along. It turned out to be a good argument. Mac was one of the best. In truth it was one of the things Dorm like about him. Mac's final argument was perfect

"I'll only follow you as soon as your back is turned anyway. And I'll probably have a battalion of your fathers troops with me when I do. How will that look eh?"

Tellys' father also did not want her to go along. Or if she was going to insist, then he was going to accompany her. Tellys' face was quite emotive while her father told her this. She then asked Dorm, Mac, Rhynavell, Travanos and Mac Lavin to leave. None of them heard what was said, and they did try. But when he left the room, Lord Kardranos had been brought round to her way of thinking.

They suspected not entirely of his own accord.

Rhynavell was given an indefinite, Royally signed, leave of absence from the Royal Accountancy, which duly impressed her co-workers.

Admiral Travanos wrote a flowery three-page letter to both the Chief officer of the Royal Selatem Navy and their Queen Olda Victasia III, telling them of a family crisis that he couldn't avoid. And that he apologised for such short notice but he wouldn't be returning to work for some time. He also wrote a separate three-page letter to his wife.

And so all the members of the group had organised to be free to participate in the quest.

The official closing ceremony of the conference proceeded smoothly. All the customary speeches and obligatory thank yous were spoken, then began the wining and dinning. Hours of conversation and dancing and more conversation and eating and drinking, and more dancing, followed by more conversation, this time with hoarse voices, which was all about as interesting as doing ones taxes.

Those members of the special group of 'questers', for the most part, sat quietly. Participating in the frivolities only if it was necessary. Though no one seemed to notice, they were resting themselves for their departure tomorrow.

The banquet wound up late at night and the guests were ushered off to bed quickly, so as to be asleep very soon. This had been arranged by Mac Lavin, who not only was eager to get rid of everyone so he could go to bed too, but because he wanted to give Dorm and his friends more chance to rest and prepare. The guests were all leaving during the morning. The last group scheduled to leave were the Selatemese officials, who would be leaving aboard their flotilla of warships.

The group woke fairly early and while Dorm was required to help his father bid goodbye to all the conference guests, the others quietly prepared. This involved preparing horses and packs, which Mac oversaw. He knew what needed to be arranged and what sort of horses would be needed. Dorm as Prince had access to several horses, and Mac had a few as well. The others would be able to chose from quite a selection of some of the best mounts in the kingdom.

The day remained cool and cloudy, though it didn't rain. As the guests left one by one, Dorm felt the anticipation grow. He knew he was about to step into the unknown. He had no idea what to expect. He had read many great adventure stories as a child. His mother had read him the great saga of Trogan, all seven volumes of it. It had captivated him. He had wanted to step into the pages and help Trogan battle the Legans, to walk with him into the great crystal city of Mess'ahn and luncheon with its all-powerful queen, Elsi'a.

But of course that was just a story and he had only been a boy. Now he was a man, a man with intelligence and who knew the difference between reality and fantasy. At least he thought he had.

But here he was about to participate in something that, at least at this stage, seemed to be almost a fantasy. He just hoped that at some stage someone would explain it to him.

The Selatemese diplomats left for the quays and Dorm and his father returned to the palace. A brief lunch and the group met once again to finalise how they would proceed.

Within an hour their horses had been prepared and they had been packed with their supplies. And so it was time to leave. The hard part.

As Tellsandra quietly said goodbye to her father who had not travelled with the rest of his country's' diplomats, Rhynavell and Travanos spoke quietly. Mac stood nearby checking the horses packs and quietly watching Dorm and his father.

"Remember to dress warmly," Mac Lavin said.

"Father," Dorm began. "I'm not a child any more."

"I know, but I'm your father. I'm supposed to be a fuss pot."

"Well you're getting to be too much of one lately."

Mac Lavin looked at his son for a moment. A curious expression crossed his face. "So much like your mother," he said quietly.

"Father..." Dorm began emotionally.

"Oh it's alright," Mac Lavin said. "I'm not upset. It's just that you remind me so much of her sometimes. And I know that you miss her too. So do I. And I know she would have been proud of you."

"And of you too father."

"Well perhaps..." Mac Lavin embraced his son. " Look after Mac for me, will you. He's become somewhat indispensable around the palace. We can't afford to lose him."

"Of course I will," Dorm said. He noticed Ellin standing near the doors. 'Look after him' he mouthed to him.

Ellin nodded and mouthed back 'I will Your Highness. Don't worry.'

Dorm smiled. He stood back and looked at his father. "Do what Ellin tells you to, father."

"Ellin!" Mac Lavin said. " He's getting to be a grouch in his old age."

"I heard that," Ellin said from the door.

Mac Lavin gritted his teeth and winced. "You did that on purpose," he accused his son.

"Well someone has to keep you on your toes." Dorm moved over to the horses to check his saddle. Mac moved next to the monarch.

"Look after him for me will you Mac," the king told him quietly.

"Of course sire. You know I will."

"Mac I think we know each other well enough now for you to call me Mac Lavin. It is my name," he paused. "You could always call me father. You are practically my son-in-law."

"I'm not sure I could do that, Your Majesty."

"You're a rascal Mac," The king grinned and pushed Mac's shoulder. "Go on get ready."

As the group mounted up, the two fathers stood next to each other watching. Kardranos watched his daughter with a calm but concerned look on his face. It was clear he was thinking the same things as Mac Lavin. The king smiled at the group.

"Your Majesty," Dorm said. "We are ready to proceed on our journey, with your permission."

"Good luck and good speed to you. Bring us back something from your trip."

"I'll do my best sire," Dorm smiled.

"Then begin your journey, Your Highness."

"Thank you Your Majesty," He bowed in his saddle. "My friends, are we ready?"

"Well I'm not sitting here for my health," Telly said sarcastically.

"I believe all is in order Highness," Travanos told him.

"I'm as ready as I'll ever be," Rhynavel replied.

"Lead on Dorm," Mac said as Dorm looked at him.

Dorm turned to the king. "Then lets ride!" They turned their horses and rode off into the city with the midday sun breaking through the clouds.

The journey through the streets of Lugemall City was erratic at best, though all things considered they made good time. They proceeded down Grand Avenue past the Basilica, and then the two massive government bureaucracy offices on either side, linked high above the street by a special two story high corridor bridge that allowed the various bureaucrats passage between the two.

They continued down the cities widest street passing smaller ones off to left and right, passing various buildings as they went. The Avenue was crowded, though it didn't teem as yet. It was only just after the lunch time break and as such people tended to try and take time to get back to work.

As they passed the Temple and the Shrine opposite, they turned into Capital Street and continued slowly out of the city. There were as usual not many people here. Both buildings were ancient and had some arcane history that no one really understood any more. They had become meeting places where people could exchange ideas. Some very good ideas had even come out of them from time to time.

"Perhaps we should have taken a side street," Telly said.

"Then we'd have taken even longer," Rhynavell said. "Everyone always takes the side streets to get back to work after the lunch break. At this time of day we'd never get through."

"She's right," Dorm agreed. "We'll be much quicker on the main streets."

They continued along, passing business offices and opulent mansions as well as various public buildings. Market stalls dotted the street as merchants sold food and all manner of other wares, though many of them were business related. Ink, quills, parchment and the like.

After another quarter of an hour they passed the Stockade, a now decorative and largely symbolic series of ancient fortifications that had been superseded several centuries ago by newer walls, though the city had in sections spilled outside of these too. The several guards on duty at the gatehouse in the Stockade didn't seem to recognise Dorm, who was perhaps a little hurt by this.

After the Stockade came more houses and shops. Squares filled with fountains, statues and markets. As they proceeded further from the city centre the buildings became smaller, less grandiose, though none were exactly shabby. Those buildings dominated the quayside areas.

Eventually they reached the main gate. The heavily fortified structure was also well guarded. The group passed through without incident and travelled through one of the clusters of shops and houses that had spilled outside the city's walls. Several new buildings were under construction so obviously the trend was continuing. Some attempt had been made to fortify this section as well, several small wooden palisades with small platforms adjacent had been built. Though none were connected fully.

Finally they left this and entered the open country. Dorm looked back at his home, sighed and turned back to the road ahead.

The main road north from Lugemall City was a well-maintained and well-travelled highway. Merchants, goods caravans and private citizens plied the road all day. Occasionally a small number of troops from the Lugemallan army marched past heading back towards the capital. Still no one recognised them.

As they proceeded north they had planned to stay at inns as they came to the various villages and towns that dotted the countryside. Dorm had travelled this region extensively during his many years of public service and hoped not to be delayed by overjoyed citizens pampering the prince of the realm.

The problem with this journey was that they were not exactly sure where it was that they had to go. In all of the countries' population it was probable that only two people had the amulets. Two from millions would be a needle in a haystack to say the least. They had decided that it would be best if they headed to each capital city and decide from there. They just had to hope fate would lend a hand.

The sun continued to shine intermittently through the clouds and the cool wind continued to blow, but it didn't rain. The green countryside of central Lugemall passed by them slowly as they flowed along with the northward traffic.

"How far are we expecting to travel today?" Telly asked after an hour or so of their trip.

"Not all that far," Dorm told her. "It was after midday when we left. I'd expect we should stop about sunset. That should put us somewhere just this side of Kessahh."

"I have no idea where Kessahh is Dorm," She told him. "So I'll just trust you alright?"

"Okay," he said smiling at her.

"Do we think we are in a hurry?" Travanos enquired. "Or do we think we have plenty of time?"

"That's a good question," Mac said.

"I have no idea," Dorm admitted. "The problem with this 'quest' is that we have very little to go on. All we can gather is that there will be twenty more people coming. Most likely two from each nation. Though I'm not sure which ones."

"Well we know Selatem and Lugemall," Rhynavell said.

"True and the prophecy hintimated that all the other Alliance countries would be involved," Telly agreed. "That would give us another twelve. That's... seventeen."

"That leaves..." Mac began to subtract.

"Eight," Rhynavell told him.

"Thanks," he said. "I was never very good with numbers."

"You're welcome," she replied smiling. "I'm an accountant remember."

"What about Szugabar?" Telly asked.

"Maybe," Dorm admitted. "They are associate members of the alliance. It makes a certain sense."

"Then that leaves six," Rhynavell counted them off.

"Perhaps Rikaway," Travanos suggested, referring to the country to the south of Lugemall. There had been a long history of trade and negotiation between Lugemall and Rikaway. The depth of that contact had fluctuated over the centuries, but had usually been cordial. "It's not impossible that something from the Fortress could have gotten to the south. There were mentions of the southern allies during the first Peldraksekhr invasion. We just thought it was Tagradas, Lugemall and Kiama Mor; but perhaps...” he left it hanging.

“Good point,” Dorm conceded.

“And during that time we still had contact with ancient Plezjdark,” Telly reminded them. “They were very good friends of the Alliance then. Perhaps some went there?”

“Well if they did,” Dorm began. “Then they’re probably lost to us. No-one has been able to contact the Plezjdark for centuries.”

The great nation of Plezjdark had become somewhat of a mystery over the last few centuries. Telly's description of the relationship was accurate. They had been very good friends with the Plejzdans. But then for apparently no reason they had cut off contact. Several attempts were made at the time to try to find out what had happened, but the Plejzdan navy had turned them back each time. Over the centuries their name had become a byword, for unsolvable mystery. Many in the Alliance were eager to see the contact renewed.

“That would account for all but two,” Mac said. “Do you suppose they could be from Peldraksekhr?”

“I’m not sure. That wouldn’t make much sense,” Dorm said. “The creation of the amulets from the ‘focusing lobe’, whatever that is, seems to have been done to stop the Peldraksekhr from doing something. I'm guessing that they are the 'great enemy' it speaks of. I can't think of any one else that fits that bill. It wouldn’t make much sense to give them amulets.”

“Then perhaps there are two countries with three people,” Rhynavell suggested.

“Or another country in the world we don’t know about,” Travanos said.

“Who knows. Maybe the tribes to the south of the Alliance have them,” Mac said light heartedly.

The tribes were a virtual unknown. They knew they existed and that was about all. Well strongly suspected that they existed might be a more accurate description. Explorers had often come back with tales of seeing dark skinned strangers in the lands to the south, but had never made contact with them. Every attempt to breach the mountains and find a way through, had met with failure. The nomads of Kiama Mor as well as the occasional Rikan merchant or noble would mention strangers from those wilds, but nothing ever certain. And nothing that could lead to any way of confirming their existence, let alone contacting them.

"Don't wish that upon us," Dorm said. "It'll be hard enough finding the ones in civilised countries, let alone trying to find amulets held by two members of nomadic tribes. We'll have enough trouble with that sort of thing in Kiama Mor."

"Wherever they are," Telly said confidently. "We'll find them."

"Well I'm glad you have faith in us," Dorm said. "Because I have a feeling we may be in for a long adventure."

"Well I could use a holiday," Rhynavell said. "Do you have any idea how annoying the national accounts can be?"

"I can imagine," Dorm said. "Got any advice for my father and I?"

"Spend less," she said. "I prefer smaller numbers." They laughed heartily.

"I'll pass on the message," Dorm promised.

"Well I hope we don't take too long," Travanos said. He sat very rigidly in his saddle. It was obvious he was not a frequent rider. "I don't want to lose my sea legs."

"Hopefully we'll have you back aboard a ship before too long."

"We'll the sooner we ride quicker the sooner that will be," Telly pointed out.

"Then lead on mighty leader!" Mac said to Dorm pointing in the direction they were heading.

They all looked at him with curious expressions.

"Stop it," he said defensively. "I'm having fun."

They picked up the pace a little and continued the journey northwards as the afternoon wore on. As time went by, the number of travellers thinned and the temperature dropped. It looked like it was going to rain again overnight. They passed several small villages but decided to continue on into the dusk, until they came to Kessahh, which was the first major town north of the capital.

The group approached the town as the sun began to set. Kessahh was a stately, thinly walled affair that was known for its hospitality and its yearly cheese festival.

Making their way through the streets, as the few, wary townspeople finished their days business and hurried home, they arrived at a large inn near the centre of the town.

The inn was a large three-story building with a slate roof, equipped with stables and surrounded by a decorative wall. Several tall trees shaded the now gloomy courtyard and a small grassed garden lay opposite the stables.

The stable hands took their horses and placed them in stalls as the group entered the main door and stopped at the front desk. Dorm rang the small bell on the unattended counter as they all waited patiently.

"Your Highness," Rhynavell began quietly. "May I handle this?"

"Well I suppose," Dorm replied a little confused. "Though I'm not sure why."

"Trust me," She assured him. "I know these sort of people."

Dorm indicated for her to proceed and stepped aside as she approached the desk.

A thin, balding man entered from a door behind the counter and stood in front of Rhynavell. "Can I help you?"

"Ah yes," Rhynavell began confidently as she opened her purse. Her Royal Accountancy crest and badge was clearly viable hanging from the top. "My companions and I require rooms for the evening."

The innkeeper glanced surreptitiously at her identification, hanging seemingly forgotten from her purse, and reacted hastily. "Of course. How many rooms in total?"

"I think three should suffice."

"Very well. I shall give you the top floor. There are four bedrooms and a communal sitting and dinning room as well as bathing facilities. Would you like an evening meal?"

"Ah... Yes thank you, that would be lovely."

"Excellent." He jotted down several notes in a large red leather book. "We shall endeavour to please." He picked up a small bell from behind the counter and rang it three times. Two young boys in smartly pressed clothes appeared as if from nowhere. "Assist these people to the top floor," he instructed.

The two boys grabbed several of the groups packs each and headed to the large staircase off to the side of the counter. The group passed the second floor observing the lengthy corridors off to both left and right.

Arriving at the top floor, the two bellboys placed their bags neatly in the common room, and disappeared as quickly as they came.

"So what was all that about?" Dorm asked curiously.

"Inn keepers are business men," Rhynavell explained. "I'm an accountant. He doesn't want to give me any excuse to go through his books."

"But I'm the Prince. We could have gotten everything anyway."

"Yes but you would just be treated as a prince. I will have us treated like gods. This innkeeper will go out of his way to please us. Just to keep his money safe."

"I'm glad we brought her along," Telly said putting her arm around Rhynavells' shoulder and grinning from ear to ear. Rhynavell followed suit.

"Why does this picture scare me?" Travanos said looking at the two grinning women.

"I'm not sure," Mac said. "But I'm scared too."

The next morning they rose, dressed and ate and prepared to get under way. Rhynavell settled the account with the overly-happy innkeeper, and obtained a slight discount from him as well.

They left quickly and headed north through the centre of town, making their way through markets and doing their best to avoid being stopped by all the merchants and their fabulous, well priced merchandise, that is rare beyond your wildest dreams!

Finally they left the town and returned to the open countryside. Farms, mainly dairy and goat farms dominated this region of Lugemall, hence the local cheese festival. It was pleasant country and the weather remained fair as they continued northward on the main highway.

They stayed in a variety of inns both large and small over the next few days, but as yet had not had to sleep out under the stars, which was what Dorm was secretly hoping to do and Tellsandra was desperately hoping to avoid. They crossed the River Lugomo and passed through

Lessahn which was the second largest city in the country. This city did teem rather as there was a lot of activity because of the yearly stock sales that were now under way.

They managed to find some rooms in an inn, though not as fancy as the one in Kessah and did their best to appear to be farmers. None of them was terribly convincing and so they just decided to try to be as uninteresting as possible.

They left Lessahn slightly earlier than originally planned in the morning and continued on their way north.

They managed another week of staying in small towns and villages, before they finally had to camp. They didn't do too badly, though Telly did complain a bit. Though Dorm suspected more because they had expected her to, more than anything else. They crossed the border into Tagradas and continued northward towards Ziga. Whilst they were on the road Tellsandra had taken to wearing her amulet on the outside of her clothes. Eventually it transpired that they all did it. It became almost like a mark of identity.

As they approached the Tagradas/Ziga border at about mid-morning, a group of three cloaked men carrying bows came walking towards them from Ziga. Their cloaks were all a dark blacky blue colour and had hoods, which they wore up even though it was rather sunny. Tellsandra and Rhynavell were chatting on about something womanly that Dorm wasn't really paying attention to. He was just thinking to himself. He wasn't even paying much attention to what Mac and Travanos were saying.

Suddenly the three men stopped and stared at them. Dorm noticed them first. "Good morning," he nodded politely. At that the three of them pushed back their hoods and inclined their heads as if in great respect. All were youngish and had neatly trimmed beards. As they passed them the others noticed as well and gave them similar greetings, as they rode by.

"How curious," Travanos said looking back at the three men who still stood with their heads bowed.

"Who were they?" Rhynavell asked.

"I'm not sure but I think they might be Rangers, from the Fortress," Dorm said also looking back. "I've only ever seen them once or twice, with messages for my Father. And I've never seen them with weapons before?"

"Aren't they the ones who look for people suffering from magic?" Telly said.

"Yes, perhaps they think we might have it?" They all looked at each other for a moment.

"Well perhaps we should go and explain things to them?" Travanos said. "If they are indeed from the Fortress then they may be able to help us."

"Good idea," Mac said turning in his saddle. "Hey! Where'd they go?"

They all looked. Despite the fact that it was still rather sunny, and that the land was fairly flat in this area, the three cloaked men were nowhere to be seen.

"Okay, now I'm a little scared," Telly admitted and pushed her horse a little faster. It wasn't long before they were all keeping pace with her.

After crossing the border, at which none of the border guards could remember the three cloaked and hooded men, they continued up the highway towards the waiting landscape of Ziga. The large highway which they followed lead eventually to the Zigan capital itself. They continued to think about how they were supposed to find these people they were looking for, and each night they would discuss different options once they reached Ziga itself.

They all fairly quickly agreed that going to the King and asking him was out of the question, as was going to any of the government offices as it would quickly reach the King that Prince Dormal was in town, and 'he simply must have dinner with us' would inevitably follow.

The Zigan countryside was 'picturesque' as Telly described it. Fields bordered with low white stone walls and hedges, crops waving gently before the wind. Cows, sheep and other farm animals grazing peacefully in their paddocks. There were not too many travellers on the road at this time. Mainly just the odd caravan. The merchants were always friendly and willing to share information about what was ahead.

They continued to stay in inns, mainly in villages and small towns, getting ever closer to Ziga. On the third night inside Ziga they stopped at a small village called Ik Lafahn. It was rather small consisting of only about twenty or so small stone cottages, a small inn, a large livery and blacksmiths, and a general merchant, which by the time they arrived, Tellsandra insisting she could make out a village just over the next rise, no she meant the next rise, was well and truly closed. They entered the inn and were shown to their rooms before returning to the cheery common room to take a small evening meal. The people of the village were friendly in a closed sort of way.

The cook brought them the meal himself then returned to bring them something to drink. As they ate the few villagers in the room, sat quietly and conversed about their days events. A much different conversation than what they were used to hearing.

Just after the cook had delivered their drinks and started back across the room, a young man, not much older than Dorm entered the inn and was greeted firstly by the cook then by the villagers. They all greeted him and several shook his hand warmly. He sat and was brought a mug of ale which he began to drink.

He was fairly nondescript, being of average height and wearing simple peasant clothes, though with a heavy looking hooded coat of dark green wool on now given the time of evening. He had sandy brown hair and seemed to have fairly well developed muscles on his upper body. It was clear he was some sort of labourer, not uncommon for a village like this.

He had a plain but kind face, one that spoke of a simple life and a simple philosophy, but also of someone who cared. Someone who gave a thought about his fellow villagers, who tried to do the right thing by them, and worried about them when times were tough.

"So how's that wee little son of yours doing?" One of the older men in the room asked.

"He's doing well," the man replied, pushing back the hood on his coat. "And Lassahna's doing well too thanks for asking." He grinned at them.

They laughed heartily.

"So are you moving onto the Western ridge near Falloms' farm tomorrow?" One of them asked.

"Yes starting at the southern end first thing," he said taking a swig from the tankard that was offered to him. "Why you want to lend a hand?"

"Well you know I'd like to Artur," the older man replied. "But you know all about..."

"My back!" they all sang in unison, then laughed again.

The cook brought out a pot of tea for Tellsandra, and the man named Artur noticed them for the first time. He smiled at them and watched for a moment. He seemed to notice something then. Something that made him look closely. His face changed to a curious expression. Confusion and worry played across his face at the same time as curiosity. He watched them for a moment, to the point that Rhynavell started to get worried.

"He keeps staring at us," she whispered. "Perhaps he recognises us?"

"How could he recognise us?" Telly asked her, also in a whisper. "None of us has really ever been here except for maybe Dorm."

They all looked at him. "Only a few times, and I've never stayed here before. I don't even recall passing through this village. Perhaps he just thinks we look weird."

"Whatever could give him that impression," Travanos said sarcastically.

Just then the man stood up and crossed to the counter while the rest of the villages kept talking. He refilled his mug with ale, then moved slowly over the their table. He sat down at a spare seat next to Tellsandra.

"Hello, welcome to Ik Lafahn. My name is Artur."

"Yes we heard," Dorm said politely.

"Ahh, I'm not really sure how to ask this," he began. "But I couldn't help noticing your amulets."

"Oh this old thing," Tellsandra said lifting hers up and looking at it. "It's just a little something we have in common."

Artur paused for a moment. "It's just that... well." He reached inside his tunic and pulled out an amulet. The group exchanged glances. "Well I guess you can see what."

"Well, that wasn't as hard as I thought it would be," Mac said suddenly.

"What wasn't?" Artur asked.

"Perhaps this isn't the best place to discuss this," Travanos said pointing surreptitiously at the curious glances they were receiving from the other patrons.

"Yes, you're probably right," Dorm said. "We are staying here overnight. We had planned to be moving again at first light but it seems our plans have changed."

"Well perhaps we can discuss this at your home," Tellsandra said giving Artur that look that made most men weak at the knees. "I'd love to see this baby of yours."

"Well I guess that wouldn't be so bad," Artur mused. "Provided we don't talk for too long. My wife isn't expecting visitors."

They made ready to leave for the moment giving the cook a small extra fee simply because they were feeling lucky.

The air was crisp and cool, and the stars twinkled merrily in the velvet sky, as they walked through the quiet village. Crickets chirped in the distance and other animals could be heard moving around.

"So what is this all about?" Artur asked. "How do you people have copies of my amulet?"

"When your father gave it too you on your sixteenth birthday, did he tell you it was a one of a kind?" Travanos asked.

"How did..?" Artur stopped walking and looked at them for a moment. "How did you know that my father gave it to me on my sixteenth birthday?"

"That's what were here to try and explain," Dorm said patting him on the shoulder.

If possible, Artur looked even more confused.

Chapter 5

The firelight now flickered brightly, as Artur sat back down in the chair.

They had made their way to Arturs' small cottage where his wife, Lessahna, was preparing their meal. She was a little worried and slightly angry at Artur for bringing home all these guests without telling her, especially since she had no food to give them. When Dorm assured her that they required no food, she relaxed a bit but was still understandably upset.

Lassahna was slightly shorter than Artur and had long auburn hair. It was redder than Rhynavells, but the two women did look rather similar. She wore a simple grey woollen dress, with a plain linen apron over the front. She kept a very neat house and it was plain to see that while the couple didn't have much they took pride in what they did have.

They had allowed Artur the time to eat and check on his infant son, who both women in the group instantly went all clucky with, before he finally sat down next to them for a moment while they waited for their tea to brew. After stoking up the fire a bit he now sat down again. A little nervous to say the least.

"So what is this all about?" he said quietly.

"Well that's an interesting story," Mac began. "We don't exactly know yet."

"I'm sorry?" Artur said.

"Well let's see if we can't explain it a little better," Telly began.

"We all have these amulets. We all were given them by either our mother or father on our sixteenth birthday. We all know that it has been passed down through our families for many years. We also did not know that there were any others like it."

"It was only after we discovered that we all had them that we started to find out some answers," Rhynavell explained.

"What answers?" Artur said curiously.

"Well it seems that these amulets aren't so unique after all," Travanos told him.

"In fact it appears that there are about twenty five of them." Dorm explained.

"Twenty five?" Artur was a little shocked. He'd obviously been under the impression, like they all had been not too long ago, that his amulet was special, or at least unique. Now it seemed that he was denied even this.

"Well what do they mean?" Lassahna asked.

"Well we're not entirely sure about that," Dorm admitted.

"We do know it has something to do with a prophecy," Telly told him. "And perhaps the Fortress as well."

"The Fortress!" Artur said in awe, tinged with fear. He cast a brief look off in the general direction of the Fortress Territory before he looked at Lassahna. She too held his gaze.

They were probably going to have to get used to that reaction, Dorm realised. The Fortress was just about the most mysterious thing known to any one in the Alliance. It gave the Alliance not just it's name but was responsible for the structure and operation of the Alliance itself. Yet no one knew very much about it. Everyone knew that people afflicted with magic went there, but that was about all. It communicated with the various kingdoms on occasion, but usually it was silent. Travel there was not permitted except with prior permission, which apart from the odd extraordinarily rare occasion, was never given. To try to go there without permission was to invite the wrath of the Fortress. And everyone knew the legends, of how in ancient times, before the Alliance had been formed, the old kings of that time had lost whole armies to the Fortress, without them losing a single person.

"Though we aren't entirely sure what," Rhynavell said quickly.

"If indeed anything." She was trying to sound reassuring. She was almost convincing.

"All we really know," Dorm began. "Is that there are about twenty five of these amulets, and that we need to find all the people who have them. Something is going to happen. And the people who have the amulets are going to have to do something when it occurs. We don't know what, but it would seem to be important."

Artur stared into the fire for a few moments, lost in thought. His face was hard to read. This was obviously a lot of information to digest all at once. He sighed heavily. "You want me to go with you don't you."

"That would seem to be indicated, yes," Travanos said quietly.

"What?!" Lassahna exclaimed standing to her feet. "You can't expect my husband to go running off around the country with people he's only just met. We have a son. How do we know you're not some sort of confidence artists, or shamsters"?

"A good question," Mac said looking at Dorm. "You want to go first or shall I?"

"I suppose I should," He replied. "I have the highest rank." Dorm stood for a moment then sighed obviously not wanting to reveal their identities. "I guess some introductions are in order." He glanced at Tellsandra who nodded. "Permit me to introduce us. My name is Prince Dormal, heir to the throne of Lugemall, son of King Mac Lavin. This rather fine young man here is my partner, Mac Ravin."

Mac grinned and waved.

Dorm went on. "These two young ladies are Rhynavell departmental chief of the scribing section of the Lugemall Royal Accountancy, and her ladyship Tellsandra, daughter of Lord Kardranos, Earl of Bravia. And this fine gentleman is Fleet Admiral Travanos of the Royal Selatem Navy, Viscount de Salvin."

Artur and Lessahna stood motionless for a moment. They both stared directly at Dorm. Their eyes wide. For a moment Lessahna looked as if she was about to topple over, before she regained her footing enough to slowly lower herself back into her chair. Artur who had stood to calm his wife during her brief tirade, remained standing. He seemed unable to move. For a moment he too seemed like he was about to fall, but he remained upright. His brain was obviously going through thoughts at a mile a minute. Either that or it had stopped working altogether. It was clear that this simple village couple was now rather confused and worried about the group of people they had invited into their home. Their rather simple home.

"Artur," Dorm said moving a little closer to him. "Are you alright?"

Artur opened his mouth but no noise came out.

"It's all right we are still rather ordinary people," Telly said reassuringly.

"Ummmmm..."

"Oh dear," Travanos said. "Perhaps that wasn't such a good idea."

Slowly Artur sat back down. Dorm sat too watching him. "Are you alright now?" he asked quietly.

"I think so," he said then looked at him wide eyed. "Your Highness." He then bowed his head.

"Oh I think we can dispense with the court manners for the moment."

Artur looked at his wife. "I don't think I have much of a choice dear," he said quietly.

"No," she whispered. "Seems that way."

The next morning, Dormal wrote a letter to the local baron of the area, claiming that Artur was on a permanent assignment for the Lugemall government and that it would be greatly appreciated, and a mark of continued friendship between the two countries, if all of Lassahnas' and Galems' needs for the foreseeable future were taken care of.

The group returned to their inn late in the night after explaining as much as they could to Artur and Lessahna about the prophecy and their discovery of it. As such they rose later than expected, but the fact that they had already found their first companion was a good sign. They packed quickly and headed back to Arturs' house to pick him up.

The good bye was emotional.

There was lots of hugging and kissing, and lots of looking away on the part of those on horses. No one denied them this. It was hard enough to leave ones home, but to do so when you've only just recently had a child arrive... well no one wished that pain upon Artur and Lessahna. Finally Artur was on his mount and they rode slowly northward out of Ik Lafahn.

Ziga remained pleasant country to travel through. As they headed north, they attempted to explain to Artur as best they could everything that they knew about the amulets and the prophecy they had discovered. Much of it was still not quite believable to them so getting Artur to believe it as well was hard.

The towns along the main highway grew steadily larger as they progressed towards the capital. Like all the nations in the Fortress Alliance it shared its name with the country it now governed, the nations having grown from primitive city states many millennia ago. Dorm had been to Ziga a few times in his life on state visits, but had not gotten the chance to see a great deal of the city. Though this was the least of their troubles. The main problem they faced was how to proceed. The luck in finding Artur was not expected to repeat itself, and the way forward was impossible to see.

Since these amulets had obviously been intended to be kept secret until this time, there was not likely to be any record of them anywhere, the only people who would likely know about it, were the wearer and the wearers immediate family. Tellsandra however cleverly pointed out that the likelihood was that the wearer they were looking for in Ziga was probably a woman.

"What makes you say that?" Mac asked.

"Well we've gotten people from two countries already," she explained. "Both countries have a woman with an amulet, Ryhnavell and I, and both have man. Dorm and Travanos. Mac of course is just here to look pretty..."

"Hey!"

"Since we now have Artur," she went on. "It stands to reason that the next person from Ziga will be a woman."

"Hmmm," Dorm thought about it. "That does make sense I guess. And it helps in our search. If we have a better idea of who we're looking for and we can eliminate half the population."

"So we're looking for a woman..." Travanos said. "In Ziga."

"Yes," Dorm said confidently.

"Artur, you wouldn't know by chance the approximate population of Ziga would you?" Travanos went on.

"Ah I think its about two and a half million. Maybe a little more," he answered.

"So removing the men from the list will leave us with about one a quarter million," Travanos concluded.

"Oh," Rhynavell said shortly.

"I couldn't have said it better myself," Mac looked at her.

"What are you saying?" Telly asked looking at the admiral.

"I'm saying we might want to consider buying a house here, milady. This is going to take a while."

"Well perhaps we'll just have to hope that fate steps in again," Dorm said. "It helped us find Artur, maybe it will help us find this woman."

"That's a pretty big maybe, love," Mac said looking at him.

"I know," Dorm replied. "But right now it's about all we've got."

They finally entered the city of Ziga a week and a half after finding Artur. In that time they had seen a lot of the country, and indeed a lot of woman. None of them had seemed to have an amulet, at least no one jumped out them demanding to know why they had stolen her jewellery.

Ziga, much like Lugemall city was a large bustling place filled with people. Its buildings varied from the simple almost rustic to the obsessively ornate. There were, the group noticed, a great many squares filled with bubbling fountains and statuary at various intervals along all the main streets. It gave the impression that they were trying to build you up to something. The something was of course the royal palace. While the palace Dormal shared with his father was certainly ornate in many ways, it also had a great deal of functionality to it. The palace of King Wilista II seemed to try to outdo itself in ostentatiousness the higher it got.

The palace was large to say the least, with extensive grounds stretching for several hundred yards in all directions. Large trees and ponds dotted the landscape, and while they didn't go in, several large sections of the wall surrounding the palace contained elaborate metal grillwork, with just enough room between the bars to let you gawk in envy at the wealth on display.

They passed the palace and headed to another high-class inn not far away. They stabled their mounts and obtained rooms. After organising themselves and arranging a meal, they all sat around waiting for someone to come up with a brilliant idea as to how to proceed. These ideas of course were not forthcoming and so it was finally decided to momentarily take their minds off their troubles and visit the markets.

The nearest market to their inn was located in a large square, dominated by a fountain, which slashed water all over a scantily clad lady holding a trumpet. The majority of the stalls sold foodstuffs of varying sorts, though there were quite a number of stalls selling other items. As they perused the stalls pretending to be looking, but really just trying to waste time, they all began to get the growing feeling of anticipation. Perhaps fate was going to lend a hand. It certainly had with Artur. Why not again?

Tellsandra came to a jewellery stall and examined the items hoping to find something that looked familiar. When the merchant finished with his customer he turned to her.

"Can I help you find something in particular miss?" he said.

"No, thank you," she said smiling. "I'm just searching."

"Searching for what?" the merchant enquired sensing the potential for money.

"Oh, I'll know it when I see it." She continued to examine items.

As they stood there, the merchant noticed Arturs' amulet which had slipped outside his tunic. "Ah sir," he said pointing. "Could I take a closer look at that amulet of yours?"

Artur looked at the others. As the newest member of the group he was a little unsure of how to act around them, and tended to defer to their judgement. In this instance it was clear he wasn't sure whether he should let the merchant see the amulet. Dorm nodded slightly to him to indicate that it was alright. "Ah I suppose," he said stepping closer.

The merchant held it in his fingertips turning it this way and that. Watching the light catch on its angled surface. "What kind of crystal is that? I don't think I'm familiar with it."

Looking at the others for guidance he said, “I’m not sure to be honest.”

“Well its beautiful,” merchant said rather quietly, a touch of awe in his voice. “Where did you come by it?”

“Its a family heirloom.”

Dormal stepped forward at this point. “Tell me friend merchant,” he began. “You say you’ve never seen the like of this amulet before?”

“No never.”

“Well this amulet is part of a set of amulets that were stolen from this man’s family. I am helping them re-obtain them. Outside of the family they have little actual value apart from their great beauty. If by any chance you happen to come across any more like it, say someone tries to sell you one, it would be greatly appreciated if you could let us know.”

“Indeed?”

“Yes it could be quiet profitable for any one who helped my employer regain his property.” Dormal leaned forward conspiratorially, jangling his purse slightly.

“I think I get your meaning sir,” the merchant said slyly. “Where might you be staying?”

They left feeling rather happy with themselves. If nothing else it was a start.

With assurances from the jewellery merchant, whose name was apparently Xaband, that he would inform all his contacts and fellow merchants about the ‘missing’ amulets, they felt that they had set up a small network of eyes to do their looking for them. Though in all probability it wouldn’t amount to much, since the owners of the amulets weren’t likely to be selling them for any reason except for total destitution. Still they all felt it was a step in the right direction, and since they had no real idea of what they were doing, any steps in anything remotely approaching the right direction were more than welcome.

They visited a few more minor markets in the hopes of finding something out, but with no luck, so they returned to their inn to contemplate their next move.

The sun had just set and the shadows were growing long, when a porter knocked on their door to inform them they had a visitor. Dorm and Telly went downstairs to see who it was, to find the jewellery merchant Xaband waiting impatiently in the foyer.

"Friends," he said as they came down the stairs.

"That was quick," Telly said.

"Well it's not much at this stage I'm afraid," he admitted.

"At this stage anything's better than nothing," Dorm said. "What is it?"

"Well as I said it's not much I know," he began. "But I told several people I know about the merchandise. I described it as best I could. From the description I gave, one of them said he might have seen a woman wearing something similar recently. Though he doesn't actually know her."

"Well its better than a slap in the face with a wet fish," Dorm said. "Go on."

"My friend said she worked near the docks along the river side. I can tell you where exactly tomorrow. If you come by my stall."

"Of course friend," Dorm said shaking his hand. "We'll see you in the morning."

Xaband left and Dorm and Telly headed back up to their rooms to inform the others.

"If this woman is as easy to find as it seems, then we might be moving on tomorrow," Telly said.

"Do you really think it could be that easy?" Dorm asked glancing at her.

"Well no I suppose not," she admitted. "Still it's a break. We might be able to find her soon. That's something at least."

"True. We could use some help."

They walked for a moment. "Better than a slap in the face with a wet fish?" Telly asked.

Dorm looked at her. "It's one of those silly things Mac says sometimes. I guess he's starting to rub off on me."

"Indeed?" Telly said raising an eyebrow.

The next day they rose and headed back to the large market in the square, and saw the merchant. He left his stall in the hands of his assistant and guided them through the city towards the docks. Ziga was a riverside city, so there wasn't the usual stench of an ocean port, though they certainly knew they were approaching them by a change in the atmosphere. The buildings changed, more merchant shops, and trading houses as well as large warehouses began to dominate the area as they proceeded.

After almost an hour they arrived at their destination, a large open warehouse right near the water. They caught glimpses of the river and the many large flat barges that plied its waters. Xaband went to find his friend who had seen the woman in question. They milled around trying not to look out of place, while around them bustled the industrial life of Ziga. Horses and carts, laden with goods, the shouts of dockworkers, the towers of goods stacked in the warehouses awaiting transport, the clink of money changing hands.

Dorm had been in several areas like this in his years, but not as the crown prince. His father had always told him it was important to listen to the needs of the people. Not necessarily what they were saying with their mouth, but more what they were meaning. As such he had many times travelled incognito around various parts of Lugemall City and the surrounding towns. He had learnt a great deal about the aspirations and expectations of the people he would one day rule. There had of course been concerns about his safety, and he understood why, but he was good with a sword, and he knew where most of the intelligence safehouses were in the city.

It had been in one such locale, not too different from the one he was in now, where he had first met Mac. Though the situation was rather different. Still it was similar enough that he noticed Mac was a little uncomfortable. Dorm moved closer to him.

"Are you alright?" he asked quietly.

Mac looked at him. His eyes were slightly distant. As if he was trying not to remember things. "I'll be alright," he said, giving Dorm a weak smile, and squeezing his hand.

They waited still.

Eventually Xaband returned and said that his friend had told him that the woman he had seen with the amulet worked further along the quay. They followed him as he weaved his way between scurrying workers, horses, carts, barrows and large piles of goods and equipment. For a man of his stature and girth he moved very rapidly and with a great deal of dexterity. They had to stop for a few minutes, as a large herd of sheep was unloaded from a nearby barge.

As they waited, they noticed a young boy struggling to lift a heavy bolt of cloth. The boy tried to lift it, and then tried to stand it on its end. He considered rolling it but quickly realised it would unravel. Mac walked over to him.

"Here," He said kneeling down and helping him. "Let me help you. You see the secret is to lean back slightly as you lift, and to bend your knees." He helped the boy struggle upright with the bolt, that was obviously too large for him to carry. The boy waddled rather awkwardly over to a cart filled with other bolts of cloth of varying hues and dumped it on top.

The boy turned and smiled at Mac. "Thanks"

"You're welcome," Mac said ruffling his hair. He turned and walked back to the others. He stopped next to Dorm and his hand quickly sliding into Dorms. He looked Dorm square in the eyes. His own were a little haunted and slightly glistening. "Sorry," he said quietly.

Finally the herd of sheep had moved on and they progressed.

They continued down the quay for a little longer. Telly moved in next to Dorm and managed to throw him and enquiring look. Dorm shook his head slightly to indicate 'not here' and she seemed to understand.

They arrived at their destination and waited for their merchant friend to find someone in authority. He found the person he was after and told them who they were looking for. The warehouse manager said he didn't know the woman but would recognise her if he saw her again. Apparently she had been there offloading her barge earlier that morning but had since left.

Leaving their details the group left, not really wanting to hang around the noisy, dirty quays all day. So still not knowing who this woman was, or in fact if she really existed, they returned to their inn to wait.

After a few hours and dinner, they sat around in the small

common room taking and discussing the day's events. Dorm went to one side and sat near the window, thinking. The others continued their animated conversation near the hearth. After a while Telly came over and sat down next to him. For a moment she was still. Simply looking out the window.

"Do you want to talk about it?" she asked finally.

"I'm not sure there's anything really to talk about," he said quietly.

"Well obviously something upset Mac today," she said. "What was it?"

Dorm thought for a moment. "Memories," he whispered finally.

"Memories?" Telly looked back at the others. "Of what?"

"Of the past."

"Something around that dock reminded Mac of his early life?"

"All of it did. I'm surprised he managed to keep it together that long."

"Was it really that bad?" she was a little shocked.

"Oh Telly," Dorm began getting a tear in his eye. "Some of the things that happened to him... and I only know some of it."

"What?"

"He wasn't the most able bodied child. And in the poorer districts of any nation, children work. It's always happened, probably always will. But most of the jobs they make children do, he wasn't suited for. Oh he tried, but he could never quite keep up."

Telly reached out her hand to Dorms. He took it and held it tightly.

"He went from one job to the next. Getting beatings and all sorts. Eventually when he was about fifteen, he took a job in a tavern in one of the worst parts of Lugemall City. Repairs, serving, cooking, that sort of thing. But after a few years the owner of the tavern forced him to become one of the 'help'." He emphasised 'help', and looked sternly at Telly.

"Oh?" She began, then it dawned on her. "Oh. That's horrible."

"There are plenty of people in the world who do it, but they all choose to, no matter what reason they have. Mac was threatened that not only would he lose the only job he'd ever been good at, but that his family would be threatened as well. Mac loves his family. So he did it. And for nearly two years he was made to do that. All his income was kept by the tavern owner. He became a virtual slave..." His eyes glazed briefly with tears, before he blinked them away.

Telly was rather shocked by all this. This was not the sort of thing she'd expected. Mac had always been so confident. To learn this was difficult to understand.

"And that was where I found him," Dorm continued quietly. "Some sickening old merchant. Mac had finally had enough. When I tried to help him, they got a little angry. But I got him out of there. Oh Telly the things he's told me."

Telly was a little lost. She didn't know what to say, or what to do.

"I fell in love with him the second I clapped eyes on him. I wasn't going to sit there and let it happen. So I took him away from it. And for some crazy reason, he stayed with me."

"Because he loves you Dorm," Telly said putting her arm around Dorm's shoulder. "Just like I do."

At that point Mac turned around to look at them. He caught the look on Dorms face and that of Tellsandra. His grin slowly drained from his face and was replaced by a look of infinite sadness and regret, tinged by loneliness and sorrow. He stood and left the room.

That night. Dorm lay in bed next to Mac. He stared at the dark beamed ceiling, listening to the wind blow outside and to Mac's rhythmic breathing. He knew Mac didn't like to talk about his past. It had taken Dorm months to coax it out of him. He moved his hand slowly across the bed until he found Macs hand resting on the covers. He touched it lightly. Mac didn't respond at first then he grasped Dorms hand tightly.

"I'm sorry," Dorm whispered.

"I know," Mac said with tears on his voice.

Dorm turned in the bed and drew Mac closer to him. "I love you," he whispered into Macs' ear.

"I know," was the only response.

Next day they returned once again to the quayside in search of their mystery woman. They again met their merchant friend and went to the warehouse. The manager of the warehouse told them that her barge was due to return to unload later that day. But that he could not give them and exact time due to the volume of cargo he was unloading and the number of barges in the city. As a result they were forced to wait all morning for this barge to arrive.

They did their best to stay away from the hustle and bustle of the warehouse and out of everyone's way, though this was not always easy. It seemed that confusion was the order of the day. Cargo was unloaded from the barges at the quayside. A large open shed ran along the quayside and was used to store and sort the offloaded goods. It had to be identified, inventoried and assigned. This last part was the difficulty. From what they observed, there was only so much storage room, and far too many goods coming in. As such several people were desperately running around trying to find extra room for it all. Obviously with little or no luck.

They waited patiently as barge after barge was unloaded with at least some efficiency. However as the morning wore on their patience began to wear a little thin. Several attempts to ask the foreman when this barge was expected met with screams of "GO AWAY! Can't you see I'm busy"? By the time midday rolled around, still with no barge, Rhynavell was ready to give up and go back to Lugemall, Artur was starting to consider felling the supports for the shed, Travanos was complaining that this was no way to run a nautical enterprise, and Telly was considering taking up swordplay lessons, so that she could "teach these people some manners". Dorm and Mac simply sat quietly next to each other. Mac grasping Dorms hand tightly.

They got some food and drink from a passing food merchant who seemed to have found a rather lucrative niche market in supplying lunches to all the dock workers. And sat for another hour or so. Then the warehouse supervisor came over and told them that the barge they were waiting for was in the queue now and would begin unloading in about another hour and a half.

Relief mixed with utter frustration, was the only way to describe that hour and a half. It seemed to drag on forever. Rhynavell was the one who noted thoughtfully, that "When you want something to happen it takes forever, but when you don't want something, it's there, ready for you in a jiffy all gift wrapped and everything".

Eventually they interrupted the foreman long enough to find out which barge it was. Their merchant friend returned and told them that he had found out that the woman was actually the captain of the barge. The barge was berthed and tied up, and a small herd of dockworkers went aboard to begin unloading the goods. They watched this ant like army for several minutes before deciding that they would try to find her. They made their way to the broad gangways that rose up onto the barge, where a tall man wearing heavy clothes, despite the warm sunshine, and with a dark beard, was marking off various items being removed from the barge on a long list he was carrying.

"Excuse me sir," Dorm began. "We're looking for who's in charge here."

"That would be me," he said without looking at him. "What can I do for you?"

"Umm we were told that it was a woman?"

"What?" the man turned and looked at him.

Telly stepped forward. "Were looking for a woman, we were told she was the captain of this barge."

The man looked at them for a moment. Obviously suspicious. "What do you need to see her for?"

"Well it's a bit of a private matter. We think she may be able to help us with something."

"And that would be...?"

"As we said it's a private matter," Travanos said in a rather final way.

"Well I'm afraid you just missed her. She had to go to an exchange house to do the paperwork. She wont be back for about an hour."

"What?" Rhynavell said between gritted teeth.

"Oh dear," Artur said in one of his rare speeches.

"You're welcome to wait," the bearded man said turning back to the unloading.

"Wait!" Rhynavell said.

"Oh dear," Artur repeated.

"Perhaps we should go and sit back where we were. At least we were sort of comfortable there." Travnos said taking Rhynavell by the hand and leading her back towards their previous waiting spot.

An hour later they returned to the quayside and the bearded man, who was still standing in exactly the same spot, still marking off things on his list, with an incredibly bored look on his face. The workers continued to unload the barge and it seemed that there was no way that all these goods could fit inside the barge. They asked the man where the woman they were seeking was.

"She hasn't returned yet," he said before yelling at some of the workers, to be more careful.

"I thought you said it would be about an hour?" Dorm said.

"I did, but obviously she's taking longer or has stopped somewhere along her way back. She does have a life you know."

"This is ridiculous," Rhynavell exclaimed throwing her hands in the air.

"Ok I think we're a little tired of waiting," Travanos said. "Where will you be berthed overnight?

"Right here," The main indicated. "We have some cargo to pick up for our return trip but it won't be loaded till the morning."

"Good. Then we'll come back then," Telly said. "There's no way in the Fortress I'm standing on this rotten quayside any more." She linked arms with the scowling Rhynavell and they stalked off.

"Well I guess we'll see you tomorrow," Dorm said. "Coming gentlemen?"

Chapter 6

That night a gentle rain fell on the city of Ziga.

Dorm, Mac and Telly sat with Rhynavell for a while listening to the rain as it beat down on the slated roof above them. They talked softly of the days events and their feelings about this quest. Mac remained very quiet. And his silence made the rest of them a little uncomfortable. Only Dorm really understood what was going through Mac's mind and even he didn't have the full story.

He cast long, knowing looks at Tellsandra often throughout the hours that they sat talking. Rhynavell noticed them and was curious but was sensible enough to realise that now was not the time to be asking about it. Telly gave her a knowing look that seemed to say "Ask me later and I'll try to explain".

Eventually they all went off to bed. Dorm lay awake for some time, thinking. Wishing he could make Mac feel better. But he knew there was little he could do. So he simply held Mac in his arms hoping that that would at least do something for him. Dorm also knew that the only way to make Mac feel better, at least in the short term was to get out of Ziga, or at least stay away from the docks. But for now that wasn't possible.

They rose with the sun and once again trudged their way back to the quayside where the barge was berthed. They waited patiently until they saw some movement aboard and then they saw the tall bearded man from the previous day. He recognised them and invited them aboard. He told them that the captain would be with them in a few minutes.

They waited again. The air was crisp and fresh despite the quayside locale, and the city was not quite as noisy yet, so it wasn't too unpleasant a time.

The man returned and with him came a woman. To say she was beautiful was an understatement. She gave Telly a run for her money. The woman was average height with a full figure, and a virtual waterfall of dark hair. Her eyes sparkled in the morning light, and she wore a somewhat flimsy but still thick arrangement that indicated she had not long risen from bed. Around her neck hung the amulet that was the cause of all their consternation. They all shot each other looks as if to say. "Well finally". She carried a mug in her hand, and smiled warmly at the man, in such a way as to subtly indicate that there was more than just captain and first mate between them.

The two of them stopped and looked at their group for a moment. "I understand you've been asking about me?" she said in a rather sensual voice for first thing in the morning.

"Yes Captain," Dorm said stepping forward. "And we see we definitely have the right person."

"I don't understand," she said confusedly.

"No I'm not surprised," Telly said.

"Perhaps we can go somewhere and talk?" Dorm suggested.

"About what?" she insisted.

"Well that sort of thing," Travanos began. "Is best not discussed in front of everyone. Perhaps your great cabin, or whatever passes for it on this barge, will serve?"

The two of them watched them for a moment. "Very well," she said. "You've intrigued me. This way. Be warned of course, that if this turns out to be some sort of con, you might find that here on this barge we don't take kindly to that sort of thing." She turned and walked back inside. They followed and the tall bearded man took up the rear.

They entered the small cabin which was dominated by several largish windows looking out over the back of the barge. A large table cluttered with the wreckage of the previous nights meal sat in the centre surrounded by several large wooden chairs. They all sat and waited while the two of them made a pot of tea and poured several mugs.

"So you want to tell me who you people are?" She asked.

"Well the last time we did that, our friend here nearly died of shock," Dorm said patting Artur on the shoulder.

"Well alright perhaps I can get the ball rolling." The captain said, taking one of the seats and throwing her leg, rather unladylike over the arm. "In case you missed it, my name is Lianna, captain of the *Longreach*, and this is Gormall, my first mate." She paused. "Amongst other things." She shot him a wicked looked smile.

Dormal looked at the others.

"Well darling," Telly said. "You did such a great job last time."

"She has a point," Travanos agreed.

"You won't get any argument from me," Artur said.

"Not you too," Dorm said wearily. He sighed and began the introductions. They took it rather well considering. And neither of them was standing up so that was good. They then went on to explain their purpose here. The amulets. The prophecy. There was of course the obligatory amulet showing, and since Lianna already had hers out, it was much easier to compare them all.

"This is a little scary," Lianna admitted.

"You're telling me," Gormall said quietly.

"Well to cut a long story short," Dorm explained further. "We need you to come with us."

Lianna looked at him for a moment. Then she began to laugh. "I can't go off with you," she looked around the group. "I have a barge to run. Besides I don't know any of you."

"Well I'm afraid this takes precedence. Considering the Fortress is involved, who knows what may be at stake here."

"And who's going to look after my barge while I'm gone?"

"Well Gormall certainly seems capable."

She looked at him. He simply shrugged his shoulders.

"I need some time to think," Lianna said quietly.

"Of course," Travanos said. "But don't take too long. We don't know what kind of a timetable we're supposed to be keeping, so we're endeavouring to be fairly speedy in our journeying."

"Well we may be able to give you a ride down the river to a place closer to the border with Ambaka," Gormall said.

Lianna turned and glared at him. "Stop that! You're encouraging them."

"I kind of thought that was the idea?"

They returned to their inn to await Liannas' decision. Though they were beginning to suspect that perhaps someone or something else was manipulating things. So far things had gone quite well. Which given the nature of what they were trying to do was a little scary. It should have logically been almost impossible to find these people, yet so far they were having a great deal of success.

They contemplated this while they packed away their things, which they hadn't really unpacked so it only gave them something to do for a short while, and waited to see if Lianna would come back with her decision fairly readily. When they hadn't heard from her by late afternoon they began to think that her decision might not be the best.

They had no idea what to do if she said no to their proposal. It wasn't like they had any authority to force her to accompany them. Dorm may be a Prince, but he was from another country.

The sun began to set and they thought about settling in for the night. Then a porter came to tell them someone was here to see them. A sense of excitement filled the air, as the possibility of success grew.

It was Lianna, accompanied by Gormall. She stood still for a moment.

"All right," she said. "I'll go with you."

"Glad we could convince you," Dorm said.

"Well we can leave Ziga then," Rhynavell said.

"Well I'm sure that will brighten our days," Travanos said turning and heading back up the stairs with Ryhnavell.

Artur stood for a moment. "I've never been outside Ziga before. I've only ever been here to the capital once." He looked at them. "But I guess we've all got to do something daring once in our lives."

"Well if that offer of the ride on the barge up the river is still open..." Dorm said.

"Down," Lianna said absently. "Down the river not up."

"What's the difference?" Mac asked.

"Of course the offer is still there," Gormall said cutting off her reply and smiling. "Get your things together and we can be off tonight."

"Very well then," Telly said. "Give us just a few minutes and we'll be along."

They left quickly after settling their account at the inn and arrived at the quayside about half an hour later. It was getting rather dark now and city employees were lighting street lamps as they made their way. The barge was also lit by several large lamps and the few windows and open hatches glowed warmly with golden light. They led their horses into a section of the hold normally used to carry cattle and then retired to several very cramped but comfortable cabins in the after sections of the barge.

Soon after the barge cast off and after being poled towards the centre of the river was picked up by the current and began to drift lazily down stream. Picking up a little speed as it did. They found on a brief tour conducted by Gormall, that the barge was simply but well appointed, with all the facilities they could need.

For a while Dorm lay squeezed into the small bed with Mac, but was unable to sleep. He decided to go topside and try to relax a bit. After climbing over Mac, who he noted had managed to drift off to sleep, and following the narrow corridors; sorry, companionways, he corrected himself; and climbing the rather steep but short ladder he reached the deck. He found Lianna standing amidships looking up at the sky. Dorm stopped near her and followed her gaze to the stars above them.

"It's beautiful," he said.

"That it is," she replied.

"I wish I had the ability to see it every night."

She turned and looked at him. "Are you really the Prince of Lugemall?"

"Yes."

She sighed heavily. "I've done it this time."

"What's that?"

"My mother always said I'd come to a bad end. I should have listened to her."

"Its not bad yet," Dorm said looking back at the stars. "And with your help our chances may just have increased a little."

"You really think this is something to do with the Fortress?"

"I don't know. But maybe."

She was silent for a moment. "Well all that being that. I think I've had a rather hard day so I think I'll go get some sleep. Good night"

"Goodnight." He watched her go, before looking back at the sky and returning to his own thoughts.

None of them was really used to sailing, except of course Travanos. Dorm had once or twice. The Lugemall royal family did have an official yacht, but it was hardly ever used. And Telly had openly said she hated the sea. Travanos seemed to delight in their situation, finding joy in examining the barge in every detail and offering his advice at every opportunity. The others however were not so entertained. While no one was actually sick, there was a certain uneasiness.

The barge proceeded leisurely downstream as the day wore on. The river was quite wide and every so often another barge would pass them heading up the river. The occasional village dotted the landscape and most seemed to have at least a few small piers sticking out into the flow of the river. The sun shone and all was pleasant.

Dorm noticed that Mac brightened considerably and was gradually returning to his normal self. Artur was also a little louder, joining in more with the conversations. They had noticed that he seemed a little taken aback by the people he was in company with. Though now it seemed that he had loosened up a little since Lianna had had a similar reaction upon discovering who they were.

They had decided that their quest should now move on to Ambaka. Proceeding on the assumption that there were only two people from each nation, meant they could skip onwards. Though once again, when they arrived inside Ambaka, they would have no idea of what to do then.

The river they followed came to within about a hundred miles of the border. As such, once they disembarked and returned to their horses, it would only be a few days to the border.

Of course no one knew precisely what to do then. Though there seemed to be a general agreement among the group that they should proceed to the capital at Ambaka and see if their luck would hold.

It took nearly three days to reach the wide bend in the river that was close to the border. The wisdom in transporting goods via the river and then by road into Ambaka had not been lost on someone in the past as a large trading town was situated there. It was called Memel and Dorm noticed a distinct aroma of garlic that seemed to hang everywhere. Lianna informed him when he mentioned this that garlic was a major commodity in the area. Given the late hour at which they arrived at this town they decided to wait until morning before proceeding. Their last night on the barge was spent mainly going over their general plans and how they would go about trying to find these next two amulets.

Gormall also announced that he had decided to accompany them. It was obvious that his reason had nothing to do with seeking adventure, but rather his feelings for Lianna. It took some doing but they eventually persuaded him that he was best to stay, given that they had no idea what they were getting into. Dorm told him that they would have to pass back this way when they left Ambaka, and that they would see him then. Liannas' argument was a little more concrete. She practically ordered him to stay and run their business so that she would have something to come back to, stating that he was the only one she trusted enough not to bankrupt her or cheat her out of her money.

He did grumble a bit but eventually he capitulated. Overnight they slept once again in their cramped little cabins, after taking a meal. It was the first time that Dorm noticed the sound of the water. The barge was docked now. It wasn't moving with the current. The simple, measured beat of the tiny waves slapping against the barges' wooden hull, was somehow relaxing. He and Mac both woke the next morning feeling rather refreshed.

The departure was a little drawn out. Lianna and Gormall needed time to say goodbye, which nobody denied them, though after the tenth minute long kiss it was beginning to get a bit much.

They unloaded their horses and proceeded through the small town, which consisted of a large number of warehouses and merchants offices, and headed northward into the open country. The weather remained clear and bright as they continued. They noticed that Lianna was not the best horseman. While she was certainly trying hard, she didn't seem to be able to quite get the knack. On several occasions they had to stop and help her, though these pauses usually gave way to raucous laughter before too long and so it improved their mood immensely.

They continued for two days passing villages and farms. Just before midday on their second day since leaving the barge, they again encountered a group of darkly robed travellers.

As before in Tagradas, there were three of them. Though this time one of them was clearly a woman. These three also wore their hoods up, again despite the sun. They stopped and stepped to one side pushing back their hoods, and inclining their heads forward. All three were young and looked hard travelled yet at the same time they looked as if they had just come back from a month's holiday. All three seemed to "glow", was the only way Dorm could think to describe it. Curious, he stopped his horse next to them.

"Good morning," he said.

"Good morning," said one of the two men.

"This may sound like a bit of a strange question," Dorm began. "But am I correct in thinking that you people are Rangers?"

"You are correct Quester," the woman replied.

"Quester?" Telly asked.

"We recognise who you are," said the other man.

"Well I'm glad someone does," Artur piped up.

"Any advice you can give us?" Dorm asked.

"Unfortunately that is not permitted, Quester," said the first man again.

"Great we're still lost," Mac said.

"Not lost, Quester-to-be," said the woman. "You just can't quite see the path yet. But that will come to you in time. Have faith."

"Ummmm right," Mac said.

"But we have much work to do," said the other man. "We must be on our way. May all the luck we have be yours." Again the three of them bowed their heads to the group, before pulling their heads back up and resuming their walk southward.

They tried several times to arouse their attention but the three of them continued on their way without showing any signs that they even heard them.

"Ok," said Rhynavell. "These people are weird."

"Their from the Fortress," Travanos said. "I'm guessing that explains it."

"Ah where did they go?" Lianna said noticing that they had vanished.

"That's twice they've done that," Mac noted.

"They've done that before?" Lianna asked.

"Oh yes," Dorm said matter-of –factly.

"Did any one else notice that they called Dorm a Quester, but Mac they called Quester–to-be?" Telly commented.

They all looked at Mac. "What?" he said.

"Nothing Mac," Rhynavell said. "We're just wondering what's so special about you, that's all."

"I could give you a few ideas," Dorm said. Mac blushed.

They crossed into Ambaka later the next day. The countryside remained much the same, the rolling hills dotted with small clumps of trees and occasionally criss-crossed by small meandering streams. The odd small village could be seen, most set back from the main highway. The weather again started to turn, promising rain in a few days. Though it remained more than clear enough for their purposes at the moment.

As they travelled north, they made it a point to try and pass through as many villages as possible. Allowing the villagers to clearly see their amulets around their necks. If any one in the village owned one it was likely to have been seen by at least some of their neighbours. It might arouse suspicion that perhaps their friend had been robbed. They didn't mind the possibility of being chased for a little bit, as long as it led to them eventually being able to locate their next quester.

Their conversation with the group of Rangers was still fresh in their mind. The Rangers had definitely implied that the Fortress had something to do with this quest of theirs. That opened up all sorts of strange possibilities. They had also implied that there was much more going on than what there appeared to be. They seemed to suggest that there were even some "rules" governing what was going on. Things certain people were allowed and not allowed to do. Dorm was almost tempted to go to one of their chapterhouses and start asking questions. Though he had no idea where they were in Ambaka, and he also got the feeling that he could talk till he was blue in the face and they wouldn't answer him.

On their fourth night in Ambaka they stopped at a small village named Leff and stayed in a rather small but homely inn. After stabling their horses and stowing their packs in their small rooms, they made their way to the common room and ordered a meal. The meal was simple but very filling and didn't taste too bad considering. There were various local characters scattered around the rooms benches, at various stages of drunkenness. Whilst always trying to keep to themselves as much as possible, they always tried to keep an 'ear to the ground' as Artur described it. Keeping abreast of local events and conditions might help them in their journey ahead. This night, most the conversations in the room consisted mainly of just the local goings on that were inevitably lost on their group. However one person in the room, who was obviously a local merchant of some description, had recently returned from a nearby large town named Heffia.

"Kicking up quite a fuss over there in Heffia," he mentioned to one of his compatriots when asked about his recent trip.

"Oh really?" replied the other man. "What about?"

"Oh all the usual stuff," replied the merchant. "But also there's some royally appointed police person going around all over the town looking for someone. She's having a right go of things she is." He took a large gulp from his tankard, leaving foam in his beard. "Bending peoples noses all out of shape with her attitudes and her questions. But none of them locals can do much about it, what with her being appointed by the King himself."

"What's she looking for?" asked the other man.

"Not what, who," he explained. "Apparently from what I heard this here man she's after is wanted for all sorts. Theft, embezzlement, fraud, maybe even murder."

"Murder!" Whispered the older man shocked. "Do you think so?"

"Oh I don't what rightly know. All I knows is what I heard in Heffia" He waggled his finger in the air for a moment. "But they're circulating his likeness everywhere they can. Shouldn't be too surprised if they don't turn up here eventually."

"It wouldn't do no wanted criminal good to come here," said the older man. "No wheres around here for no one to hide from all us locals." He almost turned in their direction.

"Well be that as it may, this royal police woman is certainly on a crusade she is. You can see it in her eyes. Flashing that big sword of hers around, and that big badge they all carry and that great dangly medallion of hers."

That caught their attention.

"Oh well if she was to turn up here, she wouldn't end up staying long cause she'd find nothin'."

Later that evening they all gathered in the room Dorm and Mac shared to discuss their discovery.

"A great dangly medallion?" Telly was saying. "Sounds like it could be worth a look."

"Yes but if this woman is as single minded as the merchant implied we should tread carefully," Travanos cautioned.

"If she's a royally appointed officer, we may end up having to see the King to get her to come along," Rhynavell pointed out.

"Lets hope not," Dorm said. "I've never really liked King Hevandra. I don't think he and my father get on. And it seems to have rubbed off on me."

"You'll just have to use your charm my sweet," Mac said sarcastically.

Dorm made a face.

"Let's just hope this criminal she's searching for doesn't show up, she might get distracted if he does."

"You know Artur, "Telly said. "I think that's the longest sentence I think I've heard you say."

Artur blushed fiercely before Telly put her arm around his shoulders.

"Then I guess that means we're going on to Heffia tomorrow," Lianna concluded.

"It does a bit doesn't it." Dorm agreed. "any one else get the feeling that we're being led around a little here?"

They all cast nervous looks at each other.

"Hmmm. That's what I thought."

Heffia it turned out was a large town situated on the main highway that ran east-west from the city of Port Mizda to the capital, Ambaka. So their 'side' trip there was not a waste at all. Heffia was, like most towns, large, sprawling, unplanned and with a unique set of odours.

The towns buildings seemed to be predominately brown, though many of the civic buildings near the centre were a light greyish white, obviously meant to imitate marble. One however, the Ducal Palace was a bright sandstone yellow.

As they headed through the town looking for a suitably inconspicuous inn at which to stay, they caught snatches of conversation about this 'wanted criminal'. It seemed that the merchant back in Leff had not been exaggerating. They saw posted drawings off the wanted man, looking rather evil and intimidating at various offices and at almost every corner.

Eventually they found an inn and got rooms. They decided to go out and try to pick up the trail of this policewoman to see her 'great dangly medallion'. They went to several markets in the area of their inn, and listened to the conversations for a while before picking up that she seemed to be staying in the Ducal Palace itself, by order of the King. This presented its own problem. If they went there, there was a good possibility that the Duke, Tollina might recognise Dorm or Mac or Tellsandra or even Travanos. It was decided that Rhynavell and Artur would go and ask to speak with her. If they could at least get her alone then they might have a chance of getting at least an idea of what the medallion was. They had to come up with a credible sounding sighting though, and that was the problem.

They entered another square filled with a market, and began to move around the various stalls. At one Dorm, Mac and Telly paused to view a selection of local vegetables, possibly to purchase, when a shortish man of around fifty stood next to them.

"You look like an intelligent young lady, my dear," he began.

"Why thank you," Telly replied. "It's obvious your eyes work then."

"Yes indeed, they do," he said. "I wonder if I might propose something?"

"And you would be??" She asked.

"Forgive me, my named is Druvand, merchant and purveyor of fine items, at your service." He swept his hat off his head and bowed low to her. His foppish blond hair flopped over his face as he stood back up, causing him to brush it aside. It was hard to tell what sort of physique he had in the clothes he was wearing, but Dorm suspected that he was more powerfully built than being a simple merchant would suggest. He had a small goatee beard that for some reason didn't look right. Dorm wasn't sure why.

"And why do you want to propose something to us?"

"I'm staying at the same inn as you" he began. "And I couldn't help but overhear one of your conversations this morning. Am I correct in thinking that you are heading in the general direction of the capital?"

"Yes we are," Dorm told him. "And that is of concern to you why exactly?"

"I see you are a cautious man sir," Druvand said grinning. "And I can see why with so lovely a wife as this."

Dorm was about to say something but Telly beat him to it. "No they're the couple I'm the bodyguard. What is it you want?"

"Oh how silly of me. I do apologise," he said bowing again. "Let me explain. You see as I said I am a merchant. I deal primarily in fine silks, jewellery and fine spices. Many people know this. I've worked this region for almost a decade now. Unfortunately with this fame comes a certain amount of risk. You see, even in these peaceful times, brigands and the like scour our highways and roads, preying on the unwary traveller."

"I'm sure they do," Telly said.

"Yes well you see, I seem to be in a bit of bother, my normal group that I travel with have decided that now is a good time to go get hired by someone else."

"And you want to travel with us so you don't get robbed," Dorm said.

"I knew you were an intelligent man."

They looked at each other for a brief moment. “I guess that would be acceptable.” Dorm told him. "If it’s only as far as Ambaka.”

“Oh yes. I will be there for several weeks,” Druvand grinned again.

“Very well then, friend.” Dorm shook his hand.

Later that evening back at the inn, Dorm briefly introduced their new travelling companion to everyone before he retired for the evening. Rhyn and Artur then gave them a report on their days activities. They had tried to get in to see the policewoman at the Ducal Palace, but apparently she had gone off to another nearby town to investigate another lead. She wasn’t expected to return to Heffia for several days.

“Should we stay or should we continue?” Dorm asked.

“Oh could we stay,” Lianna said wearily. “My bottom would really like that.”

They laughed. “Since we don’t know what sort of time table we’re running to I think it would be best if we pressed on,” Travanos said “Bottoms not with-standing.”

“He’s probably right,” Artur said.

“I agree,” Mac conceded.

“Alright, but in deference to the bottoms, we shall leave a little later than normal.”

The next morning they headed out of Heffia along the highway to the capital. Druvand the merchant seemed to get along well with everyone, though both Telly and Artur thought that he looked vaguely familiar, though they couldn’t figure out why.

Once they were out of view of the town, they all relaxed a little, and began to talk more freely, though they were still rather guarded since they now had a guest. After an hour or so, the sun had climbed higher in the sky and the day turned warm. Not hot, but warm enough that metal chains around ones neck, no matter how small, will cause one to sweat. As a consequence, everyone began to take out their amulets. It also meant people could see it, including Druvand.

“I say,” he said when he noticed Liannas’. “I don’t mean to be rude, but why are you all wearing the same amulet?”

Everyone looked at each other, not knowing how to respond.

“It’s a sign of our mutual connection,” Travanos said slowly.

“I see, what connection is that if I may be so bold?”

“It’s a sign that we all come from the same people.” Mac said quickly.

“Fascinating,” Druvand said. “Who are these people? Where do they come from?”

“It’s an ancient tribe near the mountains of southern Tagradas.” Dorm said casting a worried sideways glance at Telly.

“Amazing. My family originally comes from Tagradas. They moved to Ambaka several centuries ago. I guess that would explain it.”

“Explain what?” Rhynavell asked him.

“This,” he said reaching into his embroidered black jerkin and pulling out his own.

“Oh,” was all she could say.

“This is wonderful. I must be distantly related to you.”

“Ummm yes, you could say that,” Mac said looking at the others.

“Any one else get the feeling this is all scripted?” Artur commented.

Druvand sat grinning and holding up his amulet as they rode. "Perhaps we should stop soon for lunch and explain a few things?” Telly said.

“What a good idea,” Dorm agreed.

“Is something the matter?” Druvand asked.

“No, nothing,” Travanos said. “Just a few issues that need clarifying, and perhaps some plans that need changing.”

“Oh I see,” Druvand said, his face dropping.

Chapter 7

Things were definitely getting better.

They were all certainly getting the hang of it. Druvand had taken it all rather well. He had seemed a little worried at first, his eyes kept darting around the group nervously. Not a scared nervousness, more of a "Damn my plans will have to change" nervousness.

His story was essentially the same as everyone else's. His father had given him the amulet on his sixteenth birthday. He hadn't known much about it, so he hadn't been able to tell Druvand very much, except that it was a family heirloom that had been passed down through the family's generations, since time immemorial.

They had camped that night in a grove of trees set back from the highway, and had told him everything they had found out about the amulets, and their apparent mission, as well as its connection with the Fortress.

Everything seemed to have gone down well with him. He seemed to accept that his business would have to be put on hold, once they returned to the capital. He almost seemed eager to start the adventure.

Now they were on the road again, heading east through the sunshine and pleasant, rolling countryside. It was going to take at least a week to reach Ambaka, and everyone was eager to get there and start their search. They frequently travelled at a trot or a canter and occasionally a gallop, and the miles went by rather quickly.

Another three days out from Heffia they were approaching a large village, Sevann. It was typical of villages in this part of Ambaka, large barns and warehouses. Small homely houses with thatched roofs, several large windmills, a few animals roaming freely in the streets. As it was just before midday they weren't planning on stopping. They rode quietly through the villages' main square as other travellers passed them by and the locals all nodded politely. They passed out of the village and headed again into the open country. Cresting a small rise they saw several farms scattered about on either side of the highway. Not too far ahead they saw a group of people on horses heading in their direction. They seemed to be in a hurry and so, the group began to drift over to one side of the road to let them pass.

Instead the group, which consisted of two men and a woman, wearing all very official looking clothes and deep blue cloaks, came to a halt directly in front of them.

"Halt," said the woman. "I'm sorry to stop you, but I must ask you a few questions."

"By all means," said Dorm curiously.

"I am Harmia, Chief Investigator of His Majesty King Hevandra IV. Have you heard that there is wanted man in these parts?"

Dorm took note of her appearance. Her blonde hair was cut rather shorter than he would have expected for a woman of her years. Her face was round, and presently dominated by a set expression that seemed to say 'don't bother trying to play games with me'. It was hard to tell how tall someone was when they were sitting on a horse, but it was clear that she was well muscled and knew her way around weapons.

"Yes we heard something about that," Telly replied.

"What is he wanted for?" Lianna asked.

"He attempted to kill the Princess Royal," she told them.

"An assassination," Travanos said. "Most dastardly."

Harmia reached into one of her saddlebags, and pulled out a picture. "Have any of you seen this man?" She said holding it up. It was the picture they had seen back in Heffia.

"No, none of us have," Dorm said. "We all passed through Heffia not too long ago so we saw all the pictures there."

"I see," Harmia replied. "That is where I'm stationed at the moment. I've been following leads through out this area." She paused for a moment thinking, or more Dorm thought, studying their faces. "Well if you see any one, or hear of anything suspicious, then alert the authorities immediately, they will let me know."

"What's his name?" Rhynavell asked. "In case we hear it."

"His name is Zacravia. He has been wanted for many years on many different charges, but never murder before. I have been chasing this man for several years now."

She paused for a moment again. Looking at each of them in turn. Then she seemed to notice their amulets all of a sudden. She opened her mouth to say something, but then stopped. She had lifted her hand, which now hung in mid air. A tingle of anticipation ran through the air around them. Dorm chanced a glance at Telly, who slyly smiled at him.

"You have one don't you?" he ventured.

"One what?!" She said sternly, snapping her mouth shut and glaring at him.

"One of these," he said lifting his amulet.

"What if I have?"

"Then we need to talk."

The two men behind her looked at each other. One of them leaned forward. "Ma'am.." he began.

"Quiet!" she snapped cutting him off. "About what?"

"Oh, many things," Mac said.

She glanced around the group once again. She paused. Peering intently. "You in the back there," she said pointing.

"Me," Artur said, a panicked look on his face.

"No behind you," she said.

Druvand glanced around from behind Artur. "Me ma'am?" He said. His voice was a little more nasally than normal.

"Yes come here. Now!"

He moved forward a little way. She stared at him her eyes boring into her face. She paused. Her brain ticking over furiously. Then quite suddenly, recognition crossed her face. "Clever," she whispered almost to herself. "Seize Him!!" she roared then, drawing her sword. The two men behind her did likewise and rushed forward to grab him. Druvand reached behind him and produced a pair of daggers.

Dorm pulled his own sword, as did Mac and Travanos. Liannas' hands sprouted daggers, and suddenly Artur, had an axe. No one had noticed it before.

"All right!" Dorm said. "That's enough. What's the meaning of this?"

"Out of my way peasant!" Harmia said between clenched teeth. "That man is Zacravia. I WILL have him!"

"This man is a merchant named Druvand."

"No he's not!" She replied. "Look at him. Use your eyes man. Now out of my way."

Everything was happening so fast. Dorm tried to recollect the details of the drawings of the wanted man that they had seen, and to study Druvand's face. Harmia's horse danced beneath her as it sensed the urgency and the anger in her. Before he had a chance to realise what she was about to do, she pushed her horse forward, her sword raised. Dorm moved in front of her, and brought his sword up against hers with a clang.

"What is the meaning of this!" She said viciously. "Interfering with a police matter. You shall all hang for this."

"This man is under our protection," Dorm said. "You will not harm him."

"Who are you to tell me this?"

"I'm His Royal Highness, Prince Dormal of Lugemall, and I somewhat outrank you, my dear. Now put away your sword, and let us talk to you!"

"You lie!" she spat.

"No actually he doesn't," Telly said then.

"He is wanted for crimes against the Kingdom of Ambaka!"

"Yes and he shall pay for them, just not today. Now calm down and let me explain!" Dorm urged her.

Infuriation crossed her face, as she struggled to comprehend everything that had happened. Her loyalties to her job, her King, and to her own vengeance, fought against Dorms request. If he really was a prince, even a foreign one, he had the right to grant protection and even asylum to any one he deemed fit. Even if that person was a wanted criminal somewhere else. She struggled against her feeling for what seemed an eternity before finally dropping her sword. The vitriol was clearly etched on her face as she did so.

"You have ten minutes. And if I'm not satisfied he comes with me, and you can complain all you want, Prince or no." She glared at Dorm with a look of hate. "Men. Don't take you eyes off of him."

"Yes ma'am," they both said and moved towards him.

"Everyone else, stay here. Make sure things don't get out of hand," Dorm said.

"We shall Highness," Travanos said reassuringly. He turned back and looked at the three men.

Dorm, Mac and Telly rode with Harmia a short distance away.

"You have an amulet like these, correct?" Dorm asked.

"Yes. What of it?"

"You'll notice that we all have one too. Except my friend here. Druvand... or Zacravia, if indeed it is him, has one too."

"And what exactly is that supposed to mean?" she said crossing her arms.

"Dear, he's trying to tell you that since we all have them and since you have one too, it means you're one of us." Telly said.

"What do you mean?"

"Well this is going to sound a little crazy, but we are all on a quest."

"A Quest?!" She laughed. "That's ridiculous."

"Yes that's what we thought a little while ago," Mac said looking at the other two.

"This quest we are on has something to do with the Fortress. Now we don't know precisely what it is that we have to do, but I'll be damned if I'm going to let you ruin our chances of completing it." Dorm was enjoying this tirade. "It means that you have to come with us. If nothing else, that means you can keep an eye on your prisoner. But it means you cannot kill him, nor can you have him thrown in a dungeon somewhere. We all have an important part to play in this quest. If any one of us dies, or is taken away from the group, we all lose. Maybe the whole world loses. I don't know." He paused and moved a step or two closer to her. "Do you want to be the one to find out?" he asked quietly.

"What makes you think I'm going to believe this ridiculous story?" she spat back at him.

"Use your eyes you stupid woman," Telly said angrily. "We all have the same amulet. Surely the fact that when your mother gave it to you when you turned sixteen and told you it was a unique family heirloom, a one of its kind, and now you are confronted by seven more identical pieces should tell you that something is going on here!"

She looked at them for a minute with eyes like steel. Her face set. It was clear that Telly's words had struck a chord with her. It's was hard to ignore the fact that here were seven more amulets the same as her formerly "unique" one. She struggled with the idea for a while as she obviously wanted her prey but felt the need to find out what all this 'quest' talk was about.

Finally she said, "I will accede to your request. For the time being. And I will journey with you. But I swear. If he does anything wrong, even a little. I'm not be responsible for my actions."

She turned and walked back to the group. Dorm gave the others a look that said it all. 'We'd better watch this closely'.

Harmia was talking quietly with the two policemen she had been travelling with, there were rather stunned looks on their faces as she explained what was happening. Dorm moved over next to Druvand, if that's who he really was.

"Is she telling the truth?" he asked shortly.

He looked back at him for a moment. "I'm afraid she is," He doffed his felt hat at Dorm. "Zacravia at your service, Your Highness."

"Why? Why did you lie to us?" Mac asked.

"Now there's a stupid question if you don't mind my saying so. The first thing you would have done if I'd have told you, would be to hand me in. Strange Fortress amulet or no."

"That's not true," Rhynavell said. "We can't do this without everybody."

"I'm sorry my dear, but I've learnt not to trust people over the years. I tend to live longer that way."

"Did you really try to kill the Crown Princess?" Telly asked.

Harmia came back at that point. "Of course he did," she said angrily. "He was found in the palace grounds with three poisoned daggers. We'd known he was trying to for several days but we hadn't been able to catch him."

Zacravia stared at her for a moment. “You really have no idea, do you Senior Constable,” he said quietly, almost to himself.

“Right we’d better make a move,” Dorm said in a businesslike tone.

Everyone began to rearrange themselves for travel. Dorm pulled Travanos and Lianna aside and asked them to ride close to Zacravia so as to keep him safe. Safe at least from Harmia. Both of them were a little unhappy about it, but they also realised it might be necessary.

“Senior Constable,” Dorm began. “Ride with us, we should share our information. You can tell us your story and we can tell you what we know about our situation.”

She looked at him for a moment before inclining her head in agreement.

“Lets move out,” Dorm said and the group began to move. As they did, Harmia sidled in briefly next to Zacravia. Just long enough to lean in close to his ear and whisper, “When this is over, I tell you, I will kill you.” She spurred her horse forward to join the others. Zacravia smiled to himself.

That night they decided to stay at an inn in the village they arrived at, at dusk. It was a normal village affair, small but sturdy and homely. It had just enough room for them all.

"After today’s events I think I need a drink," Dorm said wearily. "Any one want to join me?"

"I will," Mac said his hand slipping into Dorms.

"Why not," Travanos said. "All this riding is making me forget I'm a sailor. I think I need something to remind me."

"I suppose one won't hurt," Artur said with a smile.

Lianna opened the door. "Well are you all coming?"

They all made their way down to the common room, ordered ales and some food, and drank while they waited. The ale was a dark local brew that was rather good.

"Won't you have something to drink Ma'am?" Rhynavell said to Telly.

"Yes my tea is coming and how many times do I have to tell you to call me Telly?" She replied.

"Sorry I'm still trying to get used to that." She said sheepishly. "But I meant something a little stronger than tea."

"No thank you, I never touch the stuff."

"Oh whys that?" Lianna asked.

Telly paused for a moment glancing at Dorm and Travanos. "Well you see," she began. "My mother was killed when I was much younger. Right in front of me. We were out in the capital and this coach came out of nowhere and hit her. It turned out that the driver was drunk. So drunk in fact he couldn't give the police his name for two days. His driving was so erratic he eventually ended up snapping an axle. That's what stopped him."

Everyone was quiet.

"I vowed I would never touch the stuff. And I can be rather annoying to drunk people."

Mac took her hand and held it. They'd all heard the story before. They knew how much it hurt Telly to remember that day.

"I'm sorry," Rhynavell said quietly. "I didn't mean to bring up bad memories."

"No it's all right dear," Telly said patting her hand. "It's been quite a few years now. It doesn't hurt nearly as much any more."

Their plans were to head to the capital so that Harmia could make some sort of excuse to her superiors, hopefully without letting the cat out of the bag. They had decided to head towards Tagradas, though the trip would most likely take several weeks. Lianna had kindly offered to try and get a lift at least part of the way on her barge. After consulting the map, Dorm decided to take her up on the offer, since it was likely to take at least a week off the trip. The lack of a timetable for this adventure was still worrying those who'd started in Lugemall, though they tried not to pass it on to the others. They were back to simply following their noses and hoping for the best.

The city of Ambaka was much the same as most of the major cities in the world. A walled, lofty, imposing affair, studded with towers and spires, and fluttering flags. As was normal for a capital, the streets of the city teemed with people. Merchants bustled with workers, artisans, and officials, as everyone went about their duties. Several large open squares were distributed around the city, and each one faced one of the important civic buildings. Harmia led them to the imposing yellow facade of the Ministry of Justice and Internal Security. They dismounted out the front and paused while Harmia tried to think of an excuse. She still wasn't happy about this situation and Dorm was worried that she wasn't thinking very hard. In the end however she suddenly set her shoulders and strode towards the stairs. Mac went to grab her, but Travanos grabbed his shoulder and spoke quietly to him saying, "It will look rather suspicious, my young friend, for you to go after her."

And so they waited. They expected her to take a bit of time, depending on where abouts in the building she had to go. But half an hour came and went, and they were starting to get suspicious. Quietly Dorm and Travanos agreed that everyone should get ready to run at the first side of trouble. Not long after that, Harmia emerged from the building and walked slowly down the steps and over to them.

"Well?" Dorm asked.

She paused. "It is arranged."

"What is?" Mac said.

"I have not told them the truth. I have said that a close friend of mine is gravely ill and I wish to be with her. I feel like a traitor to my country."

"Well if it is any consolation," Travanos said. "You are doing the right thing."

She didn't seem reassured.

They stayed that night in a small inn near the western walls of the city. Harmia was still very angry and said little except when directly asked. However her eyes were very much alive. Constantly watching everyone, especially Zacravia. Her hatred of him was obviously deep. Dorm was beginning to get a little worried as to how deep.

They left fairly early the next morning and rode west out of the city. Dorm was glad to have avoided the King. He didn't want to have to see him and protest his never-ending friendship with a fellow monarch, especially when he couldn't stand to look at the man. He just had one of those personalities that Dorm couldn't stand to be around for very long.

The countryside on this side of the capital grew slowly more hilly.

Gently rolling country that undulated slowly, gradually rising in height to the foothills of the Fortress Mountains. Dorm looked at them. Even at this distance they cast an imposing view. Huge mountains, perhaps the tallest in the world, reared up towards the heavens. Most of the higher ones were perpetually covered in snow for most of their height. From this place it wasn't fully apparent, as the mountains appeared hazy in the distance. The Fortress Mountains had always invited fear and suspicion amongst the populations of the Fortress Alliance. No one entered the Fortress Territory as it was grandiosely called. It was forbidden for all except the chosen few. Dorm began to get the sneaking suspicion that one day, in the not too distant future he may be forced to walk those paths. Even here in the peaceful sunny countryside of Ambaka, that prospect filled him with a cold dread.

They rode a little harder than they had been as there were less towns and villages on this side of the capital and they were spaced further apart. No one really wanted to camp yet, though they had tents with them to do so when the need arose. Lianna had sent word with one of the many couriers in Ambaka for her barge to meet them at a particular point on the river in about a fortnight's time. They just hoped that Gormall got the message with enough time to get there.

As they rode Harmia slowly softened. If only a little. She seemed to be a very driven young woman, someone who had sacrificed a lot of fun and happiness to get as good as she clearly was. She constantly watched Zacravia as they rode. He didn't seem to mind and just rode on admiring the countryside. He seemed quite ready to talk, though everyone seemed a little less comfortable, knowing that he was a criminal.

Two days after leaving Ambaka, the group rounded a long southward bending curve in the road. In the distance they caught sight of three figures walking towards them.

"Are they who I think they are?" Mac asked.

"Looks like it," Dorm replied.

"I'm not sure I'm in the mood for riddles this morning," Travanos said.

"I don't think we'll have much of a choice," Dorm told him.

"Perhaps if we went into a gallop?" Rhynavell suggested.

"I doubt it," Lianna said, "They've seen us already."

"Well, let's get it over with then," Telly said with a sigh.

The three Rangers approached with their steady gait. They stopped a short distance in front of them and bowed. They pushed back their heads and smiled.

"Yes, yes we know," Mac said. "All the luck in the world, peace be with us, riddles, riddles."

"Quester-to-be thy tone suggests that you have lost faith."

"No it's not that," he told her. "It's just this is the third time we've come across you people, and we're just as confused as the first time."

"He has a point," Rhynavell said. "I got the impression you people were supposed to help us."

"And we shall," said one of the others. "It is just not the right time yet. If we were to try and help you now, we could very well disrupt the prophecy."

"Well we couldn't have that now could we," Telly said quietly.

"We understand thy frustration Questers," said the third. "But thou art where you should be. You have done what you should have done. There is no need to hurry. You have done well."

"Finally some encouragement," Artur said under his breath.

For a moment they were silent and seemed to be contemplating something, though by the look on their faces, Dorm got the impression there was a lot more happening.

"Set aside thy anger and hatred, Quester," said the woman Ranger. She took a step forward and looked directly at Harmia. "There is much that thou dost not know. You must embrace that which you have longed to destroy. It is necessary."

"What do you mean?" Harmia said slowly.

"Indeed," replied the Ranger.

"I'd have thought that part was obvious," Zacravia said.

"And you, Quester," she said turning to him. "You must also put aside that which has kept thee in fear all this time. Now is the time for truth."

"I think I understand," he said a little hesitantly.

"You shall find strength and confidence from this," she said.

She took a step back to the others. They all bowed again and moved to the side of the road. They pulled their hoods back up and began their steady rhythmic walk again, continuing the way they had been going.

"Does any one get the feeling that we should camp somewhere tonight?" Dorm said. "I don't think the conversations we'll be wanting to have would be right for villagers to overhear."

As dusk approached they moved quickly off the road and headed to a shallow valley not too far away. The "valley", if it could be called such, as it was more just a dip in the land with a small stream running along the floor, was well wooded and would provide them with effective cover from prying eyes. Cows could be heard lowing in the distance and it was obvious that they were not too far from civilisation should anything occur. They camped quickly and set up a fire and proceeded to cook the evening meal. Everyone of course had different tastes but after a few brief arguments about the best way to cook eggs, the meal was served.

After eating and washing the utensils in the stream they sat down to begin the conversation.

"So it would seem that we are on time," Dorm began.

"So it would seem," Travanos concurred. "Though this lack of a timetable, or at the very least some indication of when approximately we should be at certain places is still troubling."

"I agree," Lianna said. "It makes things very difficult to plan. And we can't make sure we don't get behind our schedule, if we don't know what it is."

"Maybe if we tried getting the next group of these Rangers to give us something of an indication of just where we're supposed to be at certain times. Nothing too specific, just like the season. That'd be something."

"I get the feeling these Rangers aren't going to be very forthcoming," Mac said.

"What if we asked some of them to ride with us?" Artur said suddenly.

"The man's a genius," Telly said grinning at him from ear to ear. "If they say no then we haven't lost anything, and if they say yes then their presence might give us some insight as to what's going on."

"Hmm I'm not sure if I like the idea of those syntaxicly challenged people hanging around us all the time." Mac said.

"You're just nervous because they always talk about you, Mac," Dorm said.

"Yeah well how would you like it?"

"The day people stop gossiping about me Mac, is the day I die."

"Point taken."

"I just have a strong feeling that they will say no," Rhynavell said. "I mean they didn't seem like they were ready to significantly help us this morning."

"True but its going to be at least several days before we see them again. Things can change in an instant." Dorm thought for a moment. "If nothing else we can always say we're scared and need their reassurance."

"It wouldn't be that far from the truth," Mac said.

“You two seemed very important in the eyes of the Rangers," Telly said looking at Harmia and Zacravia. "What was all that gibberish about hatred and confidence and the rest?"

"Ahh now there’s the thing," Zacravia said. "I'm surprised none of you got it. And here I was thinking you were all clever people."

"I think I understand," Travanos said. "Harmia needs to stop loathing Zacravia, and despising the ground he walks on and the air he breathes."

"I see now why you're an Admiral."

"Fleet Admiral actually."

"My apologies," Zacravia said inclining his head towards the navy man. “But seriously he is right. My dear you need to learn to let go. It's obvious that this situation we find ourselves in is much, much bigger than our petty squabbles."

She turned on him with fire in her eyes. "Petty... petty. You tried to murder the Princess Royal. And that’s just one of your crimes. The full list of your crimes goes back decades and is longer than my whole body, let alone my arm."

He sighed. "That old story. I hate to disappoint you my dear, but reports of my criminal master mindedness are greatly over exaggerated."

"What do you mean Zacravia," Dorm asked him.

"Well that has to do with the second thing the Ranger said this morning. She said to me that I also had to let go of something. That I would find strength and courage from telling the truth." He paused. He looked a little deflated, perhaps a little sad. "The truth is... I am a nothing. I'm no great thief. I'm not a very good embezzler. I hate having to try and remember all the lies I have to tell. I'm not a very good businessman when it comes to selling stolen merchandise. I have no abilities as a forger. I am a nothing. A small time petty operator. I have the criminal abilities of a local magistrate. Nothing more."

"But your name is legend in the criminal world." Harmia accused him.

"Yes even I've heard of Zacravia," Lianna said.

"Well tell me my dear, would you be scared or awed or want to do business with someone who was widely known as being a nothing? I may not be very good at what I do, but I am at least clever enough to realise that in this world image and the perceptions of other people carries a lot of weight. If people think I'm a clever infamous criminal mastermind, people are more willing to let my mistakes slip past. They tend to look for the fault in themselves, not in me. I find I live longer that way."

"You should still hang for trying to kill the Princess."

"Senior Constable. You have no doubt studied extensively the long list of my exploits over the past thirty or so years. Tell me my dear; is there anything in there, even remotely that suggests I'd be capable of murder? I am many things, I admit. I am a liar, a thief, a cheat, a swindler, completely untrustworthy, treacherous, and the worst cook in the Kingdom of Ambaka *but...* I am no murderer."

"What are you trying to say?" Mac asked.

"I'm saying my young friend, that I have had many chances in my time to delve into murder. Many times when I've been caught and the simplest and safest option for me would have been to commit a murder. But I never have. I can't do it. The thought of taking a life that didn't deserve it terrifies me."

"Are you trying to deny that you were on the palace grounds to kill the Princess?" Harmia said angrily.

"No not at all," Zacravia said matter-of-factly. "That's precisely what I was there for. But tell me Senior Constable. How many murderers that you know, who are intent on killing their target and getting away with it, take rests on marble benches in palace grounds next to brightly lit, frequently patrolled paths?" He looked at her intently. "Any ideas? I'd hazard to guess none. You know as well as I do that that is where I was discovered. Sitting quietly. The only reason I escaped later on was because I realised that I would hang for something I hadn't done, and didn't want to do."

"Then why did you go there?"

"Ask yourself one simple question Harmia," he said leaning towards her. "What would killing the Princess Royal get me? Hmmm? She's no threat to my interests. She's not my rival. She didn't cheat me out of anything. She didn't steal from me. What possible reason did I have to kill her?" He let that stew in her mind for a moment or two. Everyone else was thinking hard trying to see where this was going. "She might however be one of those things to someone else. Ever think of that? You see my dear Harmia, I was hired. Hired to kill the princess."

Everyone was shocked by this. Political intrigue was not new or out of the ordinary. But it occurred so infrequently that it was hard to believe when one heard it.

"So the real question you need to ask yourself," he continued quietly. "Is who hired me to kill her? Answer that question, and you'll find the real criminal in this affair."

The directness of the question was indisputable. If someone had hired Zacravia to kill the Princess Royal then that person was the real criminal. It would obviously be something political that sparked it. But what. Princess Allandra was only fifteen years old. She was expected to take the throne after her brother had it once King Hevandra died. Her brother Prince Morice was a very ill young man. And despite his iron determination to take the throne and rule for several years, it was known that Princess Allandra would have to take over as the Prince was unable to father any children due to his illness. Everyone knew the circumstances as to how King Hevandra had come to the throne. It had been common knowledge in the Alliance for years. The untimely death of his brother the previous king, and father to the Prince and Princess. There had been a lot of speculation as to how King Afrem III had died. No one had thought that the children could be targets, at least not openly. Obviously someone was trying to end the family dynasty, but why. Dorm filed this information away carefully. Himself being an heir meant that this information might come in handy one day when he became king.

Everyone was thinking their own thoughts now. There wasn't much left to be said. Everyone was intrigued yet at the same time a little worried. What if the police found them again? What if the people who had hired Zacravia came looking for him? Since there wasn't anything they could do to answer these questions, or deal with the issues they prepared for sleep as they all agreed it would be good to get an early start.

Since they had always previously stayed in local inns camping was a new organisational exercise in itself. Some people knew where they'd be sleeping. Dorm and Mac for example and Telly and Rhynavell always got on well together. But since Harmia was still reluctant to let Zacravia out of her sight despite his revelations meant that Arturs invitation to share a tent now included Harmia bedding down with them. A very cramped night was had by all.

Chapter 8

The weather began turning the next day as they rode.

The cloud cover began to increase and the breeze picked up. There was a definite chill in the air. It wasn't quite time to get out the cloaks but the fact that everyone knew that winter was on its way certainly made them think about it.

Mid-morning the day after they crested a small rise and looked out over the large plains below, stretching off into the distance and rising slowly as it headed west. And the trees! This was the start of the Great Ambakan Forest. A huge expanse of trees that seemed to go on forever. Dorm knew that there were several Royal hunting estates here as well as several small villages. But they weren't expecting to meet too many people. The main industries of the area were, obviously logging, as well as hunting and fur trading from the various small woodland creatures that inhabited the region. Everyone was awed by the size of the forest for a few moments, all except Artur who seemed to be almost in a state of ecstasy over the thought of all that wood he could cut.

"Are you all right Artur?" Rhynavell asked him after she noticed the curious look on his face.

"Oh yes," he said almost dreamily, his fingers twitching near his axe handle. "I'm fine. Just fine."

"I think he's in love," Dorm said laughing.

They rode on.

Entering the forest was almost like entering a new world. Fir trees and birch seemed to dominate though occasionally they saw oak and spruce. The road was still quite wide, however the sudden appearance of great numbers of trees on either side of it, made the world seem to suddenly shrink. It closed in on them. It was cooler in the forest. The breeze didn't reach them as much but all the air sitting under the trees was shaded and so seemed cooler.

It was also much quieter under the trees. There were still birds chirping and so forth, but there seemed to be an almost expectant hush over everything. Like the world was holding its breath, waiting for something.

They rode on quite quickly as it was agreed the area was a little unsettling. Harmia informed them that there was a fairly sizable village about a days ride into the forest.

Everyone agreed that they should try to camp as little as possible in this wood. So they proceeded with a certain amount of haste. They stopped only briefly for a meal before heading off again.

It was getting dark when they arrived at the village. The village was set in a large cleared area and consisted of a fair number of small houses all whitewashed with thatched roofs. They found the inn and got rooms. They noticed that many of the villagers stopped and stared at them. No doubt it was strange and maybe a little intimidating for a large group of travellers to arrive right before dark.

The night was a good change from camping for the last two nights though the hooting of several owls on their nightly hunt, kept Dorm awake for several hours. Mac, he noticed fell asleep almost instantly. The man would probably sleep through the roof of the palace falling on his head sometimes, Dorm thought.

They headed out fairly early the next morning after confirming that the next village along the main road was probably too far to reach in one day, since there were several hills they had to climb.

The going was still good thanks to the well maintained road, and they felt like they were making good time. But as dusk descended upon them they realised the innkeeper back in Tahlona had been right. They weren't going to make it to the next village.

They moved back off the road and set up their tents fairly close to each other and kept their fire to a minimum, as much to hide their location as to not set fire to the forest. There was something in the air. The wind had picked up and the trees all creaked and shuddered. It looked like it might rain but the near full moon, shed its blue light over everything, and kept popping out from behind the clouds. They all retired fairly early.

It was several hours later that Dorm awoke. The wind had picked up. And he could tell from the canvas that it had rained a little while he'd been asleep.

Just then he heard voices. He strained for a moment to listen. He couldn't hear what they were saying but it was definitely Harmia and Zacravia arguing about something. Poor Artur mustn't be getting much sleep. He didn't know how the quiet Zigan had managed to put up with them for as long as he had.

Dorm was about to roll back over when a persons' shadow passed by the tent. At first he didn't think anything of it but then it stopped and came towards his tent. It was definitely a male figure, but he couldn't think who would want to talk to him in the middle of the night.

The tent flap slowly undid and peeled back. The moon went behind a cloud again and it got dark. A head looked inside the tent, Dorm couldn't make out any features and he doubted the person could see him since it was so dark. Just then the moon re-emerged from behind the cloud and gave Dorm enough light to see by.

His midnight caller was unrecognisable.

Reacting instantly, Dorm threw himself at the man and tackled him to the ground. The struggle woke everyone up and people emerged from their tents. Quickly realising what was going on, they frantically grabbed weapons.

The man was not alone.

As Dorm did his best to fight him, while trying not to freeze in the frigid air, several other men came into the clearing and grabbed him. Travanos and Mac pointed swords at them. Artur hefted his axe menacingly. Telly unsheathed her short sword that Mac always joked was a very girly weapon, and wouldn't see any real use. It appeared he had been quite wrong.

Both Harmia and Zacravia stood side by side brandishing pairs of daggers that seemed to appear from no where. There was no hint of animosity towards each other in their faces, in fact there was almost an unspoken camaraderie between them. Both had affixed the same determined expression. Both were serious enough to know that this situation took precedence.

Even Rhynavell held onto a large frying pan, since she didn't have a weapon of her own.

"You appear to be out numbered gentlemen." Dorm said.

"Yes," Travanos said. "Why don't you be good boys and give up."

At that, several more people emerged from the woods.

"You were saying?" said one of the men holding Dorm.

Dorm locked eyes with Mac. It was time to revert to training. They usually spent several hours, three times a week practising with various weapons. Swords and daggers mainly, though they also practised with both longbows and crossbows. The palace had several training rooms as well as its own archery range and even a horse training circuit. Dorms' father also had a collection of several foreign weapons, including sabres from Kiama Mor and ancient battle-axes from Plezjdark.

They had both gotten quite good. And enjoyed practising. It also meant that they had begun to be able to communicate certain things without talking. Not full conversations obviously, but intents. Feelings. When they were sparring with each other this had the habit of being a drawback. The opponent could anticipate certain moves the other was making, by these signals that were usually given unconsciously. But this situation was different. When facing an enemy who hadn't had the benefit of sparring with you you could communicate to your allies without them knowing. This was one of those moments. Dorm only needed to look at Mac, catch his eye and hold it long enough to convey his intent. Mac would do the rest.

Mac gave him the slightest smile. He understood.

Without warning Mac spun and slashed at the man standing behind him. Travanos had obviously sensed that something was coming and quickly took on the man that Dorm had tackled. Zacravia quickly pinned one of the men holding Dorm in the shoulder with one of his daggers, while the other decided to see what the man had had for dinner.

Dorm grabbed his other captors arms and flipped him over, probably reefing his shoulder out of joint. Harmia had dispatched another man while Rynavell and Artur took on yet another together. Telly parried with a much larger man, who thought he'd gotten the luck of the draw, confronting a woman with a small sword. Little did he know...

Dorm retrieved a sword and quickly took on another of their assailants, soon after hearing a gong like sound, as Rhynavell sent her attacker off to sleep.

Dorm then caught glimpse of Mac out of the corner of his eye chasing after the man. Telly on his other side was grinning from ear to ear at the man who thought this fight was a mere formality. He thrust his sword at her. She danced effortlessly out of its way. This was one of her strengths. She was quick and light on her feet. He thrust at her again, but she was again ready for him. Slapping his sword blade aside before striking home. He groaned and staggered back. Looking at her in pain. He tried for a slash, and again Telly danced out of its way before cutting him across the shoulder.

This seemed only to infuriate him and he tried for a lunge. Which Telly countered with a lunge of her own. Straight through his stomach.

Dorm parried quickly scoring minor hits on the man's hand, and receiving a small cut on his exposed chest.

'Alright' he thought. 'I'm too cold for this'. He thrust quickly taking the man off guard. He looked down at the sword now protruding from his lower chest. He looked back at Dorm, who simply shrugged. "Sorry," he said as the man slid off and fell to the ground.

Dorm looked around. There were now three dead bodies and three dying ones as well as two men lying in comatose heaps thanks to Artur and Rhynavell. Lianna had quite cleverly dispatched her attacker by neatly slitting him up the middle. His insides didn't much like becoming outsides and he died rather quickly.

Telly was still grinning. Travanos was complaining quietly to no one in particular about such uncivilised behaviour. Lianna was softly humming to herself while she cleaned her blade. Harmia and Zacravia seemed to have come to some sort of compromise and so were now comparing daggers. Zacravia admiring the workmanship on the police issue daggers she carried. Artur was inspecting Rhynavell's weapon of choice and assuring her he could fix the large dent in the middle. Only Mac remained unaccounted for.

"Where's Mac?" Dorm asked worriedly.

"I think he went off in that direction," Travanos said indicating.

"Mac!" Dorm called out.

There was no response.

"Mac!" He called again, quickly joined in by the others.

"What!" he said suddenly appearing out of the gloom. "Gawd you people would wake the dead with that noise. And we've killed them once already."

"Mac, I was worried," Dorm said hugging him and kissing him on the forehead.

"I'm fine. I just had to chase him. He seemed intent on trying to get away. That didn't seem fair somehow. Oh you've been hurt Dorm," he said noticing the cut.

"It's nothing love," Dorm said touching it.

"Look stop poking it and let me fix it. Telly would you get the medicine pack."

They fixed up any minor injuries and broke camp very quickly. Dorm tried questioning the surviving attackers but they seemed to be on the way out, and so weren't much help. They rounded up the horses that had tried to run away from the fight and headed back to the road. It was clear they wouldn't get much sleep tonight.

The wind got wilder and rain started to come down in splats, stinging their faces and making them cold all over.

They knew they had to go somewhere, that they could protect themselves from both the weather and possible attack. It was likely that their attackers were just bandits but they couldn't be sure.

After several miles they saw a smaller road branching off from the main one. Set a little back among the trees stood a large barn or warehouse. They checked to see that there wasn't any one on the road and they quickly headed for it.

The warehouse appeared to be used to store cut wood, presumably before it was taken into the nearest village. But at the moment it was empty and mainly dry. They moved inside quickly and closed the door. The wind began to howl and they heard the rain failing heavier on the high wooden roof. They got out their blankets and huddled together. Everyone was a little scared to sleep, but they did fall asleep eventually.

The attack had left them rattled to be certain. It wasn't everyday that you were waylaid. It also drove home just how dangerous this "questing" business could be. All the tales of old spoke of such things, but as with everything else to do with the topic everyone had all but dismissed the danger. They all knew the world quite well. The thought of being attacked in the middle of the night had never really entered their minds.

The next day they all rode warily. The slightest noise caused a nervous apprehension in them all. They rode close together and rode quickly. They reached the next village just before midday and decided to stay for a few hours.

They asked around about the next village and were told of a small hamlet about six or seven hours further along the road. After replenishing their supplies they set out at a fairly quick pace, hoping to reach the hamlet before nightfall.

The shadows were long when they did, but it wasn't quite dark yet. Everyone was relieved to not be spending another night under the stars. Though they knew that eventually they would have to again.

They slept that night in one of the local farmers barns and while there wasn't a great deal of room, what with them, their horses, the farmers' four horses and several cows as well, but it was safer than sleeping out. The farmer and his wife and their son told them that there had been several reports of bandits and other assorted brigands stalking the roads in the forest more than usual lately. The local police had had some success, but the attacks still continued.

The next day they came to the junction in the highway they had been following and the road that would take them south to the vicinity of the border and then onto the river bend where they were hoping to meet up with Lianna's barge again. The new road they followed was smaller than the previous one, but was still well maintained. Several hours after turning onto it they passed a maintenance station. Several soldiers and police were stationed there as well as a work crew who repaired any damage to the road. They stopped long enough to water the horses and find out about the conditions ahead. The soldiers and police had arrested several brigands two days previously, but they didn't think they'd gotten the whole gang. They informed them of their encounter and the sergeant of the post took details and thanked them for their assistance.

That night they were forced to camp again. Everyone was a little wary, and as such they pitched their tents even closer. The openings practically all touching. Nothing happened and they all got a decent enough nights sleep, considering the fear they all experienced.

Unfortunately travelling south meant they had to travel almost entirely inside the forest itself. There would only be small parts of the road that briefly wandered outside of it. The next day they passed through the town of Sembol, which was the major centre in this part of the country. The town was awash with rumours of bandits and such. The group kept to itself not wanting to add to any of the hysteria.

Several days later they crossed the border. It was a fairly uneventful crossing, the guards at the post seemed very uninterested in checking their belongings, and Dorm made a mental note to see what the border guards were like in Lugemall.

They continued on through the autumn weather, which remained fine but cool. The nights got increasingly colder, but there wasn't any sign of more rain or Fortress forbid snow.

It took another two days to reach the spot where they turned off the main highway again and followed a smaller road back deeper into the forest. Here it was called the Forest of Marvell, but was really just the same sea of trees marching ever southward. Here though the trees were spaced out a bit more and the undergrowth was not as dense. It only took two days of good riding to get through it and emerge into the plains on the other side. The day after they finally arrived at the spot on the river where Lianna had arranged for Gormall to meet them. It was a large sweeping bend in the River Zigas, with large marshy banks. Tall reeds waved in the breeze as they rode down to the water. The barge was tied up to a tree and there seemed to be no one about.

They stopped and waited expecting someone to come out.

"Well what are you bloody waiting for?" Lianna yelled.

Suddenly Gormalls' face appeared out of a hatchway. He beamed.

"I was expecting you hours ago," he called back.

"We took our time," Lianna replied. "I wanted to make sure you'd have enough time. I know how you like to dawdle."

They all climbed on board and with some effort got the horses on as well. The barge cast off and they began to move upstream. There was of course the obligatory reunion. Everyone was glad to see a familiar face. The introductions went well, and Gormall seemed to just accept that these were the people that Lianna had fallen in with now.

The journey along the river was relaxing. There wasn't much chance of being attacked there. Everyone got back their humour and was able to get a decent nights sleep. Gormall was obviously worried when he heard about the attack and almost tried to get Lianna to reconsider, but she looked at him sternly and he obviously thought better of it.

The Zigas River meandered its way southward and they all just relaxed and enjoyed the trip. They again passed all the small villages that were spaced out at various points along the rivers course. Gormall told them they would take about three days to reach the port of Batava at Lekrah. The city of Batava, probably the second largest after Ziga itself, was not actually situated on the river, but since its importance had grown so much, a special purpose built river port town had been established to give Batava and its region access to the important waterway, and the commercial opportunities it represented. Lekrah was also the 'end of the line' as far as barge sailing was concerned. While the river was certainly navigable upstream for some miles yet, and smaller barges connected the various towns and villages there, it soon grew too small and was frequented by rapids as the river climbed higher into the mountains.

They had decided to disembark at Lekrah and travel overland to Batava and thence on to Tagradas.

The river wound closer to the mountains at this point. While they were still many miles away, Dorm could see them much more clearly. They were huge to be sure. And they still held that sense of foreboding.

On the second day of their journey down the river, everyone was on deck enjoying the cool sunshine about mid-morning, when Rhynavell noticed something that made them all a little wary.

"Umm everyone," she called out. "I hate to ruin everyone's

morning but it seems our friends have returned."

They all looked, and sure enough, on the road that ran beside the river was the familiar figure of three rangers. Their swaying gait unmistakable.

"You don't suppose they're following us do you?" Lianna asked.

As if in response to her question the three rangers stopped, turned to face them as they flowed past and bowed to the barge. The barges' crew looked perplexed at this strange incident. The questers were more annoyed at this disruption to their happy mood.

The barge continued downstream and eventually the three rangers disappeared from view.

Later that day they passed under the large bridge that carried the main road between Ziga and Batava. Several caravans were traversing its span as they silently passed beneath. Dorm had heard about such large bridges but he'd never really seen them. Most of the river bridges in Lugemall were either small stone country lane affairs, or were built low to the ground. This bridge however was very high. Probably so that it could allow barges to pass safely underneath.

The vegetation continued to change slowly as they headed further south. Willows dipped their elongated leaves into the waters edge in imitation almost of the Rangers. Dorm wasn't quite used to all this supplication before him, especially from trees.

That day ended with Lianna and Gormall getting into a screaming match with the masters of several other barges and a Rivermaster at the town of Sabronne. The town seemed to be mainly industrial and commercial, at least what they could see of it. The argument seemed to stem from the fact that there was a main river crossing here. An east west highway crossed the river by punt at this point and it was always quite busy. Apparently these punts had right of way. A fact that was not expressed to the *Longreach* until they were almost in the flow of the punts. Apparently in all the other towns along the river barges had the right of way. Hence the screaming.

Finally though they arrived at Lekrah the day after. It was large though not nearly as large as any of the major places they'd been to. It also seemed to be dominated by warehouses and merchants shops. There were several public facilities as well as a fair number of inns, and other entertainment venues. The houses were small but seemed sturdy. The streets were cobble stoned and they clattered their way through the streets once they'd finally gotten away from the waterfront. They decided to stay at an inn for the evening and start on toward Batava first thing in the morning. Gormall decided to stay with them for the evening instead of being on the *Longreach*.

Gormall and Lianna described Batava to them so that they could have some idea of what they were walking into. Everyone went to sleep fairly early so as to get a proper nights sleep, as they were hoping to cover the distance between the two towns as quickly as possible.

The weather was fine but cool as they travelled south to Batava. As the day wore on caravans began to head northward towards Lekrah with a certain regularity. They missed most of the southward heading ones since they had left earlier. About half way, they stopped at a large open air market, complete with inns and various merchant shops, and ate a brief meal. They continued on their way south, stopping briefly mid-afternoon to help a caravanner who had lost a wheel on one of his wagons.

They passed large farms and mills, as well as olive presses and vineyards. It was very pleasant countryside, and Dorm was almost tempted by it. Herds of cows and goats could be seen grazing on various hills, and as they got closer to Batava increasing numbers of sheep flocks. Finally as dusk began to settle, they crested a hill and looked down into the wide low valley and beheld the town of Batava.

It certainly was a large city, and several large buildings could be seen clearly. The number of caravans on the road at this time was diminishing but there was still enough traffic that they would make it to town before the gates were closed.

It was dark by the time they arrived and quite late. They looked quickly for an inn that had enough room for them and booked in for the night, before retiring.

In the morning they took time out to replenish their supplies and have a brief respite in civilisation. It was obvious that Batava was still primarily an industrial city, by the number of mills, and presses, and smiths, and other mercantile activities that were contained within the city walls.

Harmia always kept Zacravia within sight, but it was clear that she had relaxed somewhat towards him, since she didn't hover over his shoulder like a vulture waiting for his demise. Everyone else did relax a bit as well, and Batava was a welcome change from the road. A little after midday they all met at an inn looking out over the main square and considered their next move.

"How long will it take to reach Tagradas from here?" Rhynavell asked.

"Well it's about another few days or so to the border," Dorm explained. "Then to reach the capital will probably take about a week and a half. Maybe two."

"And once we're there?" Lianna asked.

"Well King Corm Sanell might have some information for us. He promised to try and see if he could find out who in his kingdom might have them."

"Won't we just get bogged down if we go to the palace," Zacravia said. "I thought we were trying to avoid such things."

"We are," Dorm said. "But Corm Sanell and my father are childhood friends. He's almost like an uncle to me. He won't hold us up. When we want to go, he'll let us. He might even provide us with an escort."

"Oh what joy," Telly said sarcastically.

"What if the King hasn't found them?" Artur asked.

"Well then I guess we do the work," Mac said.

"Great we get to scour the countryside, checking every woman's' bodice and every mans' neckline and try not to get ourselves arrested," Lianna joked.

"Well we do have a police constable with us. I'm sure she'd know a trick or two to get us out of some troubles," Telly said.

Harmia looked at her as if she was serious.

Dorm listened to his friends talking about Tagradas and their adventures so far together. It was curious how he now considered them all friends. Even Zacravia and Harmia to a certain extent. He hadn't expected that kind of speed. He looked out over the square at the bustling of the city. The Ducal palace stood proud in the centre flags fluttering from its short, round towers. Then he noticed something else.

Something disturbing.

"Oh no," he said.

"What is it Dorm?" Mac asked worriedly.

"I think I may have been spotted. Look." He nodded in the direction of the palace. From across the square a small troop of soldiers, well more glorified guards came marching towards them. In front of them was a rather fussy looking man in black velvet and frilly lace, with a bald head. Dorm tried to hide, hoping they'd go away.

They didn't.

The guards stopped and stood to attention. Everyone near by stopped what they were doing and stared.

"His Grace the Duke of Batava sends greetings and compliments to his Royal Highness Prince Dormal of Lugemal and requests the company of His Highness and companions to be his honoured guests at a banquet this evening," the man announced. He thrust out an official looking parchment tied with a red silk ribbon.

"I'm sorry, me!" Dorm said pointing at himself.

"Yes Your Highness," the man replied.

"Oh I'm sorry you confused me there for a moment when you started talking about princes. My name is Mord" Dorm remembered the name as a real person at the palace in Lugemall. "I'm a messenger. Can I deliver a message for you?"

The man raised an eyebrow.

"Your Highness, I understand your reluctance, but It is just a dinner. I am under orders to bring you safely to the Dukes house."

"Dorm," Telly whispered in his ear. "It would seem that our cover is already blown."

"Indeed," Dorm sighed dejectedly realising the fact for himself. To try and get out of it would have been to invite more notice than what they already had. "Your name is...?" he said to the herald."

"Trabet. Chief Steward."

"Mister Trabet." Dorm continued. "We're only too happy to go to dinner with the Duke, but we would like to keep this as quite as possible."

"Of course, Your Highness," Trabet continued uninterested. "The Duke is entertaining several important guests at the moment and he insists that you attend as well"

"Well who are we to argue with a Duke feeding us all." Dorm replied dejectedly.

They were escorted to the Ducal palace and given appropriate changes of clothes. It was a little daunting, especially for Artur, Lianna and Zacravia, who were not used to attending official functions at all. Harmia tried to insist on going back to their inn for her uniform, but was eventually forced into a father flattering blue dress.

"My dear Senior Constable," Zacravia said admiringly. "You look wonderful. I can almost forget you're a police officer."

"Shut up," was her response.

"Right, let's get this over with as soon as possible." Dorm said. "Etiquette isn't going to let us out of here before midnight, but we can insist on returning to our inn for the night. I doubt the Duke will refuse a Prince that. Hopefully if we're clever enough in the morning, that by the time they come to get us to drag us back here for more insanity we can be out of the city and halfway to the next town."

"Perhaps one of us should fain illness later on?" Travanos suggested.

"No they'll just send for the Dukes personal physician," Mac replied.

Several pages came back to escort them to see the Duke before the banquet was to begin that evening. Apparently the Duke had visited Lugemall several times, and was eager to talk to Dorm, something that Dorm was not looking forward to. They wound their way through the palace past various ornately decorated rooms, and offices. Finally they were led into a large chamber near the centre of the palace draped heavily in crimson and lit brightly by a large glass dome in the ceiling.

His Grace, Jekass, Duke of Batava, was a tall man with greying hair and a rather silly looking twirly moustache. He wore expensive clothes made from a rather ugly looking greenish velvet. His short jacket was embroidered with small sequins and jewels and other superfluous nonsense.

"My dear Prince Dormal," he began extending his arms wide. "It is a great honour to have you here in my palace. Welcome." He grasped Dorms shoulders and shook them heartily in what was obviously meant to be a sign of affection.

"Your Grace," Dorm replied forcing a smile on his face. "It is an honour to visit you."

"I'm so glad you could join us," the Duke went on. "It's not everyday we get to entertain foreign royalty. And who are all these other guests."

"May I present my partner Mac Ravin, Her Ladyship Tellsandra daughter of Baron Kardranos of Selatem, Fleet Admiral Travanos of Her Majesty's' Selatem Navy, Rhynavell of the Lugemall Royal Accountancy, Lianna Captain of the *Longreach*, Senior Constable Harmia of the Royal Ambaka Police, Zacravia... a Merchant friend of ours and Artur." Dorm paused for a moment. "My bodyguard," he concluded.

The Duke seemed pleased, his face beaming. "Welcome all. I'm delighted to meet you. I would introduce you to my wife, but she hasn't come down yet. Perhaps a little later. I believe you've already met my Chief Steward, Over here is Captain Killda head of the Town Guard, here is..." the introductions went on, and on, and on. Eventually every important civic and business leader of Batava had been introduced to the group. Eventually the end of the line was reached, and for a moment the Duke looked upset.

"There were several other important guests I wanted you to meet in particular, but they seem to not be here at the moment. No matter you shall meet them later."

The mingling began then. Wine was handed out and conversation began. Most of the group of questers tried to stick together. Dorm and Mac obviously couldn't avoid being talked to. Nor could Telly. Rhynavell it seemed was also rather popular, and several boat builders cornered Travanos.

After some time, another group of people entered the room. One of whom was the Dukes wife, Duchess Vessana, a tall, large lady, with an equally large bust, draped in pearls and gold, with a high warbly voice that seemed to be everywhere in the room at the same time. Several ladies in waiting and their daughter accompanied her. Also entering with her were two curious gentlemen, who wore what almost appeared to be expensively trimmed and decorated bed sheets.

"Your Highness, this is the man I wanted you to meet especially. Your Highness Prince Dormal of Lugemall, may I introduce Ambassador Lassius, honoured servant of his Imperial Majesty Junistia III, Emperor of Peldraksekhr."

"Your Highness," the Ambassador said in a heavily accented voice. "It is an honour to meet you." He bowed slightly to Dorm. He smiled his perfectly white teeth at odds with his olive skin. He smiled sweetly at him, and Dorm smiled back. However Dorm did not trust this ambassador. The Peldraksekhr were mortal enemies of the Alliance. They had sworn to obliterate the Alliance for centuries, and for them to suddenly start exchanging ambassadors this way was very out of character.

"Likewise Ambassador," Dorm replied warily.

Chapter 9

The evening was long and boring to be sure. Dorm was not particularly interested in anything any one had to say. He was however very worried by the appearance of the ambassador from Peldraksekhr.

The Empire had never liked the Alliance. And numerous wars and border disputes had emphasised that dislike over the centuries. But perhaps nothing quite so cataclysmic as the Second Invasion.

The Empire had started off being all nice and open, and allowing trade. But then after a while they had started to change. Suspicion was whipped up about the Alliances' motives. They eventually restricted trade so much and recalled their emissaries that the Alliance realised that something had to be in the planning. It was almost too late. The Second Peldraksekhr Invasion had resulted in the complete capturing of Bydanuushev and most of Ojliam. Attacks along the eastern coast had caused much damage in Selatem, Ambaka and Ziga as well.

The Empire had finally been defeated in the Battle of Ojliam, where the Alliance's army had ground the Empires legions into the ground. Almost at the expense of themselves. The war had devastated the Alliance and all but wiped out a generation. A third smaller Invasion several centuries later had also been repelled, but at great cost.

The Empire quite openly claimed that it had been wrong in its invasion plans but they always stopped short of apologising for invading in the first place. Quite a few emperors since then had openly said that it was one of the main goals of the Empire to one-day crush from existence the Fortress Alliance. Junistia III while not being quite so antagonistic about it, had never done anything to show he disagreed with that opinion.

Ambassador Lassius stated that he had been sent in order to assess what potential there was for commercial contacts between the Empire and the Alliance. This despite numerous attempts since the wars to restart trade from both sides, that always ended in nought, due mainly to the Pepdraksekhr refusing to allow Alliance merchants to travel within the Empire. It didn't fit. It was certainly possible that the Peldraksekhr had changed their mind, but Dorm was unable to shake the feeling that there was some ulterior motive.

Lassius talked diplomatically and often about opening dialogues and establishing contacts. He continued to emphasise that it would be as good for his people as it would for the Alliance, and might help bring the two societies together.

The very fact that the Peldraksekhr had an ambassador, something they had never bothered with for centuries, was a revelation in itself. He didn't appear to be armed, other than a small ceremonial dagger, which looked more like a letter opener. He spoke often of money and business and seemed to try to avoid matters of a tactical or military nature.

"And what is your opinion on whether the Empire should pay some form of compensation to the people of northern Bydanushev, for the slaughter of the villages there a decade ago?" Dorm asked provocatively.

"I try not to get myself involved in such tragic matters, Your Highness," he replied.

"Then you agree that the Peldraksekhr are to blame for that atrocity?"

"I never try to attribute blame either sir." His smile was beginning to irritate Dorm.

"So you don't feel any sense of guilt at all over what happened?"

The Duke intervened at that point. "Perhaps Your Highness would care to have something to drink." He said rapidly filling Dorms goblet with wine. The Ambassador had since been whisked away by some of the other guests and was now chatting to them as if nothing had happened.

"Please Your Highness," the Duke began to whine. "I'm trying to make a good impression here. The business opportunities here are enormous."

"Your Grace, did it ever occur to you to stop and think, why? Why all of a sudden after centuries of hatred and war, they suddenly want to do business?"

"Well I was a little curious at the beginning, but Lassius explained that the richest merchants in the Peldraksekhr Empire are starting to pressure the Emperor to open up trade with us. And the Emperor fears the kind of wealth they can throw around."

"Plausible I suppose," Dorm mused. "But something doesn't add up here. How long has Lassius been here in Batava?"

"A little over a week."

"Have you heard of an other major commercial towns being visited by Peldraksekhr 'ambassadors'?"

"Well not personally. But Lassius has told me that there are several others exploring the possibilities in several kingdoms of the Alliance."

"Is that so," Dorm was having thoughts. Not all of them good.

"Would you excuse me for a moment Your Grace." Dorm wound his way back towards Travanos.

"What are you thinking?" Mac asked quietly on the way.

"I'm not sure," Dorm admitted. "But I don't like the feeling I'm getting."

"I thought you were going to punch him out before?"

"Who Lassius or the Duke?"

"Take your pick."

Travanos had heard a few little comments from various people about the Peldraksekhran ambassador. Mostly from merchants. They were all a little wary, but all sensed the possibility of enormous wealth and so were willing to look past it. Several of them had noted to the Admiral that he seemed very interested in roads and rivers, and the like. How goods got to different places. What were the fastest routes to take. That didn't make much sense to any of them. Dorm filed it away.

The night continued. More food and wine was brought in, and the Duke and Duchess continued to glide around the room chatting incessantly. Dorm tried to keep an eye on Lassius. Several times he noticed the man quickly snatch a glance at him. His look was unreadable. Dorm strolled out onto the large balcony overlooking the garden. He needed some air. This night had not been what he'd expected. He would have to let his father know what was going on. If he didn't already.

He felt a hand on his shoulder. "Are you okay?"

"I'll be alright love," Dorm sighed. "I just needed some air."

"Yes it is getting a little stuffy in there isn't it." Mac kissed him and put his arms around his shoulders. "You're very tense Dorm. This ambassador really has you worried doesn't he?"

"I can't shake the feeling there's more to this than a simple commercial exchange. Much more."

"You think it might have something to do with us?"

"I don't see how." Dorm actually hadn't considered that possibility. "It just doesn't make sense that after hundreds if not thousands of years of hatred and violence, they suddenly want to be friends. They have tried that with us before remember. And look where that got us."

"Two countries invaded and probably millions dead."

"Exactly. So why would they think we would trust them all of a sudden?"

"Well it is late. Perhaps we should start thinking about going back to the inn?"

"I always said you were a smart boy."

"Oh so that's why you love me is it? Just for my brain?"

"And a few other things as well." Dorm smiled wickedly.

Mac kissed him deeply. His hands begin to explore.

"Get a room you two," Telly said making them both jump.

"Actually we were just discussing that." Dorm said. "Perhaps we all should."

"Well I'm sure Rhynavell will thank you. I think if she has to say 'transaction' one more time, she'll faint. And poor Artur is having a wonderful time trying to avoid talking to any one."

They went back inside and gathered their group. Once they were all together, Dorm quietly told the Duke that they were leaving. Jekass wanted to announce that his honoured guests were leaving, but Dorm was able to talk him out of it. They quietly told some people that they were going to the Dukes office to further discuss something.

As they moved through the corridors towards the main doors, the Duke was interrupted several times by guests wishing to talk with him. It became apparent as the interruptions grew more frequent that it was going to take longer to get back to the inn. Waiting patiently for the Duke to finish talking with some unimportant nobody, Dorm noticed Ambassador Lassius' aid moving quietly along the hall. He then turned quickly down a side passage.

The Duke turned back having finished his conversation. "Sorry about that everyone, shall we continue?"

"Tell me Your Grace, what's down that corridor?" Dorm asked.

"Ah some of the guest quarters. A few offices, and storerooms, and the main records office, why?"

"What is kept in the main records office?"

"Well, records my dear boy," he began laughing. He was clearly somewhat intoxicated.

"I think he means specifically," Telly said impatiently.

"Well let me see now," he said scratching his chin. "There's records on the tax regimes. Plans for some of the civic buildings here in Batava. Government contracts. Maps. Plans of the sewer system. A few legal notices. Some local history texts. All that sort of thing. Nothing terribly exciting I can assure you. I hardly ever go in there myself."

"Let's have a look shall we," Dorm said moving towards the hallway.

"Well yes I'd be delighted to show you, You Highness," the Duke said following him. "But I thought you wanted to leave?"

"Well we couldn't rightly leave without visiting your records office now could we?" He turned back and gave them all a serious expression.

"I think he's gone mad," Rhynavell whispered to Lianna.

"Why exactly do we want to see the records office?" Zacravia asked.

"I'm feeling lucky," was Dorms' reply. He strode off down the corridor with the Duke and eventually the rest of his companions trailing after him.

The records office was well lit, but unattended. Several large bookshelves stood around the edges. A large table surrounded by chairs sat on a deep red carpet in the centre of the room. Heavy drapes hung from several long slender windows that looked out over the courtyard.

"Hmmm what's something interesting to read in here I wonder?" Dorm said louder than he needed to.

"Well I don't know," Duke Jekass said looking sternly at the floor for a moment. "What do you feel like reading?"

"Oh I don't know I'm sure something will spark my curiosity." He strode to the centre of the room and stood next to the table. The others filed in.

"What is going on Dorm?" Mac asked curiously.

"Yes do let us in on your little secret?" Telly said sarcastically.

Dorm caught a glimpse of a shadow in the corner.

"Maybe something over here." He disappeared behind one of the bookcases. When he emerged he was dragging the ambassadors aid behind him. "What about this?"

"What are you doing in here?" Jekass demanded.

"Nothing Your Grace. I needed to be alone for a moment."

"Alone my foot," Zacravia said.

"Perhaps you would care to explain why you're reading this?" Dorm said taking the large piece of parchment from the man and giving it to Jekass.

"This is a map of all the recent changes we've made to all the local roads after the landslides late last year."

"And what would you want with them hmmm?" Dorm asked

"Nothing. I just was looking."

"He also marked in where some of the barge stops are."

"Why would you want to know that?" Lianna asked.

"A very good question." Travanos said moving a step closer. "Why would any 'ambassadorial aide' need to know any of this? And why would he want to steal a map? Which is clearly what you intended to do."

The door opened.

It was Lassius.

"Your Grace is something amiss?"

"Ah Lassius. Perhaps you can explain this," Jekass said quite seriously.

"Yes. Lets hear it," Telly said.

"Explain what my friends?"

"Why your man is trying to steal maps from the Duke? Maps showing all the important transport information of this area."

"I'm shocked, Your Grace. I cannot fathom why. I assure you he shall be severely punished." Lassius stalked forward and grabbed his attaché by the arm. He shot a look of utter contempt at Dorm. "This isn't over Prince," he said under his breath. He quickly pivoted and dragged his cowering man towards the door.

"Perhaps an interrogation by your police would be in order, Your Grace," Harmia suggested. She had obviously picked up that there was something not quite right about this situation.

"A capital suggestion my dear," the Duke said heartily. "We'll soon get to the bottom of this." He thrust his head out the door and called for guards.

It wasn't long before several guards and Captain Killda came into the room, obviously worried something terrible had happened. The Duke quickly filled them in on the situation and ordered that he be interrogated.

The guards and Captain Killda took him away quickly.

"Well Your Grace," Dorm said. "I think our work here is done."

"Thank you, Your Highness. We'll soon have it sorted out."

Dorm caught a last glimpse of Lassius watching them, his face fuming, as they left the room.

They headed back to the main doors, and were only interrupted once. They got into several coaches and were taken swiftly back to their inn, all feeling quite pleased with themselves.

It rained a little that night. It took Dorm some time to drift off to sleep. He lay awake thinking about this encounter with Lassius. Obviously Lassius, if not the Peldraksekhr government was up to something. The question was what?

It was possible that the man had been paid by some merchant to try and steal information so that they could try and earn more money by planning travel routes and ways in and out of places. But it was a little far fetched. There were other more disturbing possibilities that entered Dorms' mind, but he tried not to dwell on them too much.

They rose early the next morning and left just as the sun was beginning to peek above the rooftops. They made their way quickly to the south gate. Merchants were moving about at this time, as were members of the town watch. But most other people were still asleep. Once out of the city they pushed their horses into a gallop for about half an hour in order to put a fair bit of distance between them and Batava.

"Well that was an interesting experience," Telly said. "Remind me never to visit Batava again."

"It was a little odd," Lianna admitted. "Even for the people of Batava. Most of the time they seem obsessed with money, but consorting with the Peldraksekhr? That's a new one."

"Do you think Duke Jekass will investigate it properly?" Rhynavell asked.

"Probably at first," Dorm replied. "But I'm sure that somewhere along the way someone's purse strings will start to loosen and the investigation might start to dry up."

"A rather normal sort of end in my experience," Zacravia admitted.

Harmia looked at him angrily. "Are you questioning my integrity?" Her eyes flashed venomously.

"Not at all my dear. You are probably one of the very few that doesn't work on."

"I think that's meant as a compliment," Mac said leaning towards her.

"You don't think that Peldraksekhr ambassador was after us do you, Your Highness," Artur asked a little nervously.

"No I can't see how they'd know anything about us," Dorm said to him. "And how many times do I have to tell you to call me Dorm?"

"I'm sorry Your... Sir," Artur began, blushing. "Dorm."

"That's better."

"So what is the plan now Dorm," Travanos asked.

"I'm not sure. I think we should just continue onto Tagradas and see."

"Sounds like a plan," Rhynavell said.

"Not a very well thought out one," Telly whispered loudly in a hoarse voice.

"I heard that," Dorm said.

Telly smiled sweetly at him.

The weather continued its gradual march towards winter as they continued along the highway. The days grew milder and the nights colder. Rain showers became more frequent and after a few days small frosts began to silver the countryside of a morning. Also at dusk they began to notice mist hovering in the air over the local watercourses.

They crossed the border into Tagradas, and continued on their generally southward tack. Farmland continued to dominate the area, but every now and again a village or small town showed some evidence of industry.

After several more days they sighted the Forest of Losh. The sea of trees stretched into the distance, eventually becoming part of the Great Southern Forest and reaching all the way into Lugemall. It took about another week to travel around its periphery, and reach the large town of Junction City.

Junction City was rather appropriately named because it had grown up around the junction of two main highways. One heading into Lugemall, the other into Ziga. These roads were ancient and so had had millennia to develop huge volumes of yearly trade. As a consequence, some clever local landowner had decided to open a hostel and blacksmith where the two roads met. This then required him to build an inn, and a livery, several small granaries and so forth. Eventually other people decided to get in on the act, and after several hundred years a fierce competition had arisen. And so Junction City was born. The city was a major commercial centre, and Dorm was hoping to get some information about the condition of the world here. He was hoping he might hear word of any other Peldraksekhr 'ambassadors' that were roaming about the countryside. He was hoping that Lassius' claim that several others were operating was wrong. But he feared it was probably true.

They stayed for two days in Junction City sampling good urban living once again. However they didn't find out much information. It seemed that the most exciting thing that had stayed in people's minds recently was the record price for cattle.

Feeling a little dejected and deflated they left Junction City heading for the capital at Tagradas. They expected to take just over a week to travel, though if the weather turned they might take longer. Dorm was sincerely hoping the Corm Sanel would let them enter and exit the city with as little or no pomp and ceremony as possible. Usually Dorm had a way with 'Uncle Sanel' as he had called him when he was a boy. The fact that Dorms' father and the King of Tagradas were such close friends, almost brothers, lent the western monarch to regard Dorm almost like a son of his own. Dorm had never really gotten to know Sanel's real son Prince Gormik, as Gormik was several years older than Dorm and so had always been in lessons, when Dorm was around.

He was hoping the Sanel had had luck with finding the next two questers, something everyone else agreed with.

The weather did turn after two days. A light drizzly rain that took a few hours to actually wet you, but very shortly after that had soaked you through to the bone. Everyone huddled inside their cloaks as they rode, blinking water out of their eyes, and feeling rather cold and morbid.

They stopped at every sensible opportunity and tried to dry out a bit for the next leg of their trip. Needless to say it didn't really work very well as they still wanted to maintain a good pace. It was a rather unpleasant time for everyone.

After three days of the rain and doing their best to stop in towns and villages, of which the only sizable one was the town of Lugumoford, where they were rather overcharged, according to Rhynavell, they crested a rise and looked down into the valley of the River Lugumo. Its sluggish grey waters, constantly rippling in the drizzle, did nothing to brighten their moods. The highway ran down and then along the bank for at least another days travel. Though at the rate they were travelling Telly suggested that it might take a week.

It didn't. It only took them a day and a half. Then the road turned to the river and ended abruptly at a ferry stop. The large ferry barges sat on opposite banks of the leaden grey water. Several small buildings clustered around the ferries on both sides. Dorm, Travanos and Rhynavell entered what looked like the main building and asked when the next crossing would be.

"Another four hours," they were told. "If the rain clears a little."

"If?" Dorm said a little angrily.

"Yes its dangerous to take people across in this kind of weather. One false move and you could slip over the edge, and the currents a lot stronger than it looks."

"And if the rain doesn't let up?" Travanos said to deflect the argument as much as to know the answer.

"Then we'll give it another go four hours after that. If not then, then we'll try tomorrow."

"Tomorrow isn't good for us," Dorm said.

"I'm afraid that's the best I can do," the ferry master concluded. "You're welcome to use the stable to keep out of the rain yourselves."

"Thank you Ferrymaster." Rhynavell said. "That's very kind of you." She led Dorm from the building and back to the others, who stood shivering next to their horses.

"Well?" Mac asked.

"We get to use the stable," Dorm told him sarcastically, with just a hint of malice.

"How long till the ferry departs?" Harmia asked.

"If the weather improves, four hours," Travanos siad.

"And if it doesn't?" Artur asked a little nervously.

"Then we'll probably end up waiting till tomorrow." Dorm concluded.

"Well the ferry master has given us permission to use the stables for now." Rhynavell said. "Why don't we get out of the rain and see what happens."

"See I keep telling you us women think better than you men," Telly said.

They moved into the stable and tried to dry themselves. There wasn't a huge amount of room in the stable, but they managed to squeeze inside and remain comfortable after a fashion.

The rain didn't let up and in fact several times got heavier, over the next four hours. Their stay was restful, but not very cheery. At about the appointed time the Ferry master came to his door and looked about for a moment. He went back inside and came out wearing a long wet weather cloak. He strode over to the rivers edge and looked about. Dorm and Travanos watched him closely trying to ascertain if he was going to cross. He went onto the ferry barge and disappeared into the mist. He came back several minutes later and walked slowly towards the stable.

"All right," he said as he entered the doorway. "The currents slackened off a bit so we're going to give it a try. But you have to try and stay as close to the centre of the ferry as possible."

"We understand," Dorm told him.

They all put their now damp cloaks back on and headed out into the rain.

The precipitation had definitely slackened but was still annoying. They led the horses onto the barge while the ferry master and two of his assistants grappled to erect a canvas awning over the centre of the barge in order to give their passengers some relief from the inclement weather.

The other side of the river was almost completely obscured by the drizzle. Dorm could just make out the buildings, nothing more than dark blocky shapes.

The ferry master signalled for his crew to start taking them over while he held onto a tiller at the rear. Two men began turning a windlass at the front of the barge. It looked like hard work, especially since the deck was very slippery. The barge moved slowly out of the small "dock", which was really nothing more than a wooden landing jutting out into a small enclosure dug into the side of the river. As it entered the river proper the current began to tug at it. They could feel the barge shivering as the fast flowing water eagerly pushed against the starboard side trying to snatch it away. The ferry continued to crawl across. Eventually Dorm, Travanos, Mac and Artur assisted the two crewmen in turning the windlass and their speed increased.

Just over half way the current picked up again. A peal of thunder, some distance off, momentarily distracted one of the two crewmen. He suddenly lost his footing and slipped. He grabbed at the windlass but missed. The barge was on a slight lean to port, and so the man slipped towards the edge. He managed to grab onto one of the ropes strung along the side of the barge, and began to haul himself up.

At that moment another surge of water hit the barge. Everyone had to grab on. Artur didn't make it. He was flung over the edge. The ferryman managed to grab Artur's cloak as he sailed past him. Artur hit the water and began splashing about. It was obvious he couldn't swim. Travanos and Mac grabbed onto the ferryman to prevent him from falling too. Dorm lay down on the deck and tried to reach out to Artur.

Artur however was having enough trouble simply trying to stay afloat. The water surged around him. Foam splashing over his face periodically.

"Dorm!" he heard someone call out. Suddenly a coil of rope landed on his head. He grabbed it and flung it out to Artur. Once he realised what it was, Artur eagerly grabbed it. Dorm began to haul it in. It was hard to pull Artur against the current, and even more so since Dorm had to remain lying in order to prevent himself from ending up in the river. He then felt a tug on the rope behind him. Zacravia and Lianna and grabbed the end and begun to haul as well.

It didn't take long to get Artur on board after that. And the others had managed to haul the ferryman back up as well. Everyone lay gasping for breath. Artur was shivering in the cold. Telly threw one of the spare blankets about his shoulders and took him under the awning.

By now the barge had turned almost lengthways with the river. It took a considerable effort to bring the barge back in line and haul it to the other side. But eventually the barge bumped gently into its little dock on the other side of the river. They all disembarked quickly and got inside. They sat Artur in front of the fire in the Ferry masters office and all tried to get dry and warm. After a few more hours it became apparent that the rain wasn't going to let up before night fall, so they asked to stay in the warehouse on this side for the night. The ferry master agreed and gave them a meal before retiring.

That night they all tried to keep warm though the rain continued to fall. A wind picked up as well.

They might have lost Artur today. Dorm wasn't sure what damage that might do to this quest of theirs. But the prophecy they had read seemed to indicate it would be catastrophic. He hated to contemplate what would have happened if they had. More than that though, Artur was a friend. He realised that now. If he had been lost then he would have lost someone important.

By the morning most of the rain had blown away, though the sky was still grey and occasional drizzles still blanketed the landscape in grey mist periodically. They left quietly fairly early on, and struggled onward through the wind and the rain. It was another two days before they crested the low rise that gave them their first view of Travanos. The city was large, dark, and from this distance foreboding. Though Dorm knew it wasn't such in real life. They entered the city about mid-morning and just before midday they arrived at the palace gates. Dorm wrote a note to Corm Sanel and gave it to one of the head guards, with instructions that it should only be given to the king. About twenty minutes later the Guard returned and admitted them. They stabled their horses in one of the largest stables Dorm had ever seen.

They were then escorted into the palace proper and told that they were to be given presentable clothes. Dorm refused saying he wasn't here to be gawked at, he was here on business. The chief steward complained a bit, but a bit of eyelash flashing from Telly soon made him give up.

His Majesty, King Corm Sanel of Tagradas, Lord of the Plains, monarch of the High Glen and various other assorted meaningless titles, was seated on his throne, before several official looking persons he was giving court to. Dorm and his companions entered and waited quietly at the back of the chamber while the herald went and told the King they were there. After a brief whisper in the monarchs ear, he waved his hands at his guests.

"I'm afraid we'll have to postpone this till later, Your Honour. I have urgent business to attend to."

"But Your Majesty, I have waited..."

"I said LATER!" Sanel said leaning forward. "Begone little man!"

The guest puffed out his chest in defiance, but smartly turned and strode from the room, his assistants following him.

Dorm and the others moved forward. Sanel got off his throne and descended the dais. He clasped hands with the Prince.

"My boy," he began grinning from ear to ear. "It is wonderful to see you again. I was beginning to think you weren't coming to visit me."

"Sorry Your Majesty, we had a few minor delays."

"Oh I can see that. You all look like you've been in a pickle jar. Come now we'll retire to some more comfortable quarters, and then you can introduce me to all your new friends."

"At least we know no one will faint this time," Telly observed.

Chapter 10

"Oh this is heavenly," Telly said.

Sanell had led them into a small study just off the throne room. It was primarily furnished in various shades of yellow and cream, but was quite homely and inviting. The room also contained a large hearth, which was crackling away pleasantly. The air was delectably warm and smelt of comfort too. Everyone crowded as close to the fire as they could, and began to dry off. Sanell had servants bring refreshments, of breads, cheese and wine. Remarkably he also ordered a pot of tea, "just in case someone doesn't want wine" he said knowingly.

After warming and drying, everyone sat and relaxed around the room. Including Artur who Dorm would have expected to be rather nervous in such surroundings. Sanell wanted to know who everyone was so after the introductions, with some glossing over of Zacravia's occupation, Sanell was up to date and quite pleased to meet everyone.

They told him about their activities so far on their trip, and how they had seemed to be almost led to where the various members of this quest were. Sanell then went and produced some documents, and began to tell them what he had found out about their location in his own kingdom.

"At first I didn't want to make it too public. I just did some private research in our library here in the palace," he explained. "Needless to say there wasn't much there, just a few curious references here and there that didn't lead me anywhere. I'll give you copies of it all, though I don't think it will be of much use. Eventually I decided to go 'public'. I had to make up a story though. Eventually we came up with the idea of telling everyone they were a lost part of the Crown Jewels, which everyone was sure to believe, since there aren't much of them in the first place. Everyone thinks they are lost. Anyway," he said waving a hand about. "We offered a reward for knowing their location. We got a lot of fakes in of course, but eventually we found them. We've kept them secret from each other, and from the public, but I'm glad to say that they are both here in the palace."

"You let them stay here?" Telly asked. "That was very kind Majesty. And saves us a lot of trouble."

"Well not exactly my dear." Sanell said. "You see one of them worked here, and the others' father does. So it didn't really take that long to find them."

"They both were already here?" Dorm asked incredulously.

"Essentially yes."

"Umm I think we've been had again," Rhynavell said.

"Clearly," Travanos said looking at the group.

"Yes it does seem a little convenient, doesn't it?" Sanell said.

"Hmmm well no use fretting about it now," Dorm said. "We can meet these people tomorrow and then move out."

"Oh Dorm, do you all have to leave so soon?" Sanell said, almost as if his friends were leaving in the middle of a party.

"I'm afraid so Uncle," Dorm said smiling. "Since we don't know what kind of a timetable we are actually on, we don't want to take too long getting there. It's always better to arrive early."

"True enough I suppose," Sanell said accepting the argument. "Oh I almost forgot." He stood up and moved toward the door. "Several letters arrived the other day for some of you." He opened a door that led into another part of the palace, and spoke quietly with a servant. The servant disappeared quickly and returned after about a quarter of an hour with several sealed articles.

"Now lets see," Sanell said leafing through them. "One for Dorm, one for Mac. One, no sorry two, for Travanos. One for Tellsandra, one for Rhynavell, another one for Dorm. And one for Artur. There you are my friend. Well I've arranged quarters for you all. I'm sure you will all like to be alone to read them and to freshen up. I'll have someone come to call on you for dinner this evening. And don't worry its nothing fancy." He smiled and quietly left the room as a servant entered and began to show them the way.

The servant led them to a wing of the palace specially built for guests. The rooms Dorm and Mac were shown to were reminiscent of their rooms back in Lugemall, the predominant colour being a soft grey. Expensive looking blue drapes hung from the windows and the door onto the balcony overlooking the courtyard. The bed was also decked out in blue. Several paintings and tapestries added splashes of colour, as did the small fire on the hearth.

After the servant had left Dorm settled down to read his letters. The first one was from his father, the second was from Ellin, Ellins' letter could wait. Dorm already had an idea of what it would say. He opened the letter from his father.

Dormal,

I'm not sure exactly where you will be when you read this, but I am sending it to Corm in the hopes that you haven't reached there yet. I trust that everything is going well. I hope you are looking after Mac, and he you. To be honest I'm still a little perplexed by all this quest business. It sounds so ludicrous.

My son, I only wish I had the strength to go with you. I don't like the thought of you traipsing around the world. I admit that I have grown used to you being near. You have so much of your mother in you and with you near I don't miss her quite so much.

But I know that you must do this. I know that, in spite of how much I want it not to be true. I only hope that this journey of yours comes to a conclusion soon and that you can return.

It is only to you Dorm, my son that I can admit that I am getting old. Now don't fuss, like I know you will when you read that. It's true. Oh I'm not ready for the pyre just yet. But I know that you will be king before too many years have passed. And I know that you will be an even better king than many say I am. I know this. I only hope that you know it too.

I know I should tell you this to your face, and I have tried many times, but this seems easier somehow.

I shall write more letters in the hopes that they reach you.

Good luck my son,

Father.

Dorm folded the letter back over. He closed his eyes for a moment. Then brushed away the single tear that poised in the corner of his eye. He opened his eyes.

"What did he say?" Mac asked.

"Something I never thought he'd actually say."

"Are you alright?"

"I think so."

Mac crossed to him and held him.

Later a servant came and told them dinner would be soon, so they washed, dressed and headed down to the dinning hall. They spoke briefly with the others about their letters. Lianna told them that she had received a late letter from Gormall. Their letters had been from all the expected people and everyone was glad to have received them.

Dinner was held in one of the large formal banquet rooms, the large table sat in the centre of the room with enough open space around it so that it actually felt very lonely sitting at the table. Corm Sanell sat at the head of the table and the others took places down the table. Several guests entered and took places further down after Sanel performed the introductions. The meal was fine and very hearty and filling, especially after eating so little for the last few weeks.

Two guests were obviously the two amulet bearers. At first Dorm couldn't tell which ones they were. He was sure that Corm Sanell had tried to indicate which ones they were, but he hadn't noticed.

One of the guests was Sanells' Chief Chamberlain. A confidant who knew more about the intricacies of the running of the palace than any one in the world. His name was Navagahn. He was tall in his mid fifties with a dramatically receding hairline, and wore tight fitting dark clothes that invoked a feeling of strength in those who saw him. Clearly this was a man, who despite having what could be termed a bureaucratic job, was not someone to be trifled with. With him was his daughter, Tissievilla. She was very attractive and had a full figure, and very full lips. A veritable fountain of golden hair flowed unceasingly down over her right shoulder. She wore a large flowing dress of pale blue which was adorned in various places with lace and a few jewels. Her ample bust seemed almost to levitate off her chest. Throughout the night she seem to give Dorm several unsettling looks, which made him distinctly uncomfortable. He made it a point to grab Macs' hand whenever he wasn't using it.

The other interesting guest was someone who looked like he felt decidedly out of place at this table of such important people. Sergeant Cal Makor, one of the group leaders of the Palace guard. He was a shortish man in his mid forties with dun coloured hair, that he seemed to have made an effort to try and look presentable, but was obviously not in the mood to cooperate. Years of wearing a helmet day in, day out would probably do that to any ones hair. It was clear that he would have preferred to be anywhere else but in this room. He almost seemed to be saying with his face "what the heck am I doing here?" It was clear that he didn't feel like he should be. He was only a sergeant. Surely the captain of the guard was more suited to such important guests. Dorm began to have suspicions.

The dinner seemed to drag on for a while, though the meal was deliciously filling, and a very welcome change to their meals while on the road. Later spiced warm wines were served as well as liqueurs from Kiama Mor that Sanel had recently taken a fancy to. Telly of course was brought out a steaming pot of one of the most expensive teas in the world. She seemed almost hesitant to drink it, and when she finally did, the look of sheer joy on her face was enough to make everyone laugh.

While they were sitting and talking Dorm reached into his clothes and pulled out his amulet. He flashed it briefly to Sanel, who nodded slightly before proceeding.

"Well I'm sure some of you are wondering why you're here," He began.

"Yes Majesty," Navagahn said. "I was curious."

"Well Navagahn it seems that we have an issue that can be helped in some small way to its solution. Do you notice the amulet that his Highness is wearing?"

"Yes it's..." Navagahn began. Then he seemed to notice it. "Why that's uncanny," he said. "My daughter has one very similar. Show them dear."

She reached into her bodice and after what seemed almost a struggle, produced the amulet. "It is the same, isn't it?" she said.

"Ah Majesty," the sergeant said quietly. He too pulled out an amulet from beneath his clothes. "I admit I was a little curious as to why I was here."

"Well Sergeant, now you know." Sanel said. "Dorm perhaps you had best take things from here."

"Of course Uncle." Dorm then nodded to the others and everyone took out their amulets. Navagahn and Makor both had very wide eyes, and somewhat confused expressions on their faces. This wasn't the after dinner entertainment they had been expecting.

"Blimey," said the sergeant under his breath.

Tissievilla looked for a moment. "Are they all the same?" she asked.

"Yes they are, and that's where it gets interesting."

"Interesting?" Navagahn enquired.

"Yes it's about the only thing we have to go on," Dorm admitted.

"Go on?" Sergeant Makor asked.

"Yes these amulets are the only distinguishing feature," Telly said. "Aside from that, the people who carry them could be absolutely any one. As I'm sure you can appreciate that means its like looking for a needle in a haystack."

"So you're searching the whole world for the people with these amulets, is that it?" Navagahn said somewhat daunted.

"As you can see it's a rather large job," Travanos said.

"To what end?" Navagahn asked. "I mean what do these amulets mean?"

"We're not precisely sure. We don't even know why this is happening, or exactly what it all means. But from what we have been able to learn, it indicates that the people with these amulets are a part of our quest."

"I'm sorry, did you say quest?"

"Yes he did," Mac said a little defensively.

"That ridiculous," Sergeant Makor said. "Quests are only things in stories."

"That's what we thought till this all started," Rhynavell admitted to him.

"Look all I can say is that this is real," Dorm continued. "As I said we don't know much about what's going on, or what it all means. In fact we're not entirely sure what it is that we're supposed to do. It's possible it has something to do with The Fortress. Though what precisely that might be, your guess is as good as any one else's."

"All we do know is that the two of you have a part to play in... whatever it is," Mac told them.

"Your Highness if I may," Zacravia began. Dorm indicated for him to continue. "Your Excellency, Sergeant. I can tell by the looks on your faces that you're a little sceptical. That is excellent. And very healthy. I admit that I myself was very sceptical when they first told me. I was thinking that I'd fallen in with a group of crackpots. The thought of going off on this "quest" especially when later an enemy of mine joined the group, I was about ready to leave. But since then I have seen the actions of these people, and of things that have happened to us. I'm not sure I believe in this quest/prophecy nonsense, but there is definitely something going on. And whatever it is, you're both a part of it."

"We won't be leaving the palace immediately, so there will be time for you to both make arrangements. But both of you will have to come with us."

"Now see here just a moment." Navagahn rose to his feet. "I am not letting my daughter go off with you. Prince or not. I will not leave my daughter to whatever it is you have planned for her."

"My lord Chamberlain, we don't have any choice in the matter."

"This is serious Navagahn," Sanel told him. "This is real and it's happening. Tissievilla is involved whether you like it or not. And I think that in such a large group, she would be quite safe."

That seemed to placate Navagahn at least a little. Though it was obvious that Sanel would have to convince him in private. He clearly wasn't interested in listening to Dorm at the moment. Sergeant Makor on the other hand, while still a little confused and daunted, seemed to have accepted the situation as truthful. Though it was obviously still somewhat incomprehensible. He was talking quietly with Rhynavell and Artur about the amulets and comparing his to theirs.

They left the dinner shortly after and all retired to their rooms. It was clear that if they pushed too hard this night, Navagahn in particular would put his foot down and not give an inch. They couldn't afford that to happen. Tissievilla had to go with them and if they backed him into a corner it wouldn't be good for them. After the servants had left they quickly got together in a small common room nearby to discuss what had happened.

"I hope His Majesty can convince Navagahn to let Tissievilla accompany us," Travanos said.

"If there's any one who can, it's him," Dorm told him.

"Does any one else get the feeling she's a little…." Rhynavell started. "Dense."

"Oh stop being so polite Rhynavell," Telly said sarcastically.

"I don't think Sergeant Makor will be too much of a problem," Dorm said. "He seems resigned to the fact he'll be going."

"Yes he seemed to accept it quite easily considering," Zacravia agreed.

"He handled it much better than I did," Artur said quietly. Telly grabbed him about the shoulders and hugged him close in a rough embrace.

"At least I will have another law enforcement officer handy to keep an eye on you," Harmia said, giving Zacravia a sideways glance.

"Really my dear, that's getting old."

"Well let's just see how we go tomorrow," Dorm began, preventing an argument. "I'm sure Corm will work his magic, we just need to be a little patient."

"And right now the best place to be patient is bed," Lianna said heading towards the door.

Everyone went back to their rooms and prepared for bed. Dorm and Mac were just about ready to blow out the lights when there was a light rap at the door. Dorm threw on a robe and opened it. It was Corm Sanel.

"Uncle, come in," he said opening the door wide to admit the monarch.

"I'm sorry to disturb you boys so late, but I needed to have a quick chat."

"That's alright, Your Majesty," Mac said walking over to them.

"What's wrong Uncle?"

"I've had a bit more a chat with Navagahn after dinner," the king said scratching at his beard. "I get the distinct feeling he's not going to co-operate."

"Yes we all got that feeling too."

"Oh I'll try to talk to him about it tomorrow, and convince him, but I get the feeling he's not going to budge."

"Sounds like a stubborn man," Mac said.

"Yes, and that's one of the things that makes him such a good chamberlain. Unfortunately it means that he gets a little obstinate when it comes to things like this. I can understand his point of view a little. He lost his wife, Tissievillas' mother only a few months ago. He's still in mourning essentially. I think he's afraid of losing his daughter too."

"Well I can certainly understand that," Dorm said sympathetically. "But I think the future of the world takes precedence."

Sanel looked at him incredulously. "You think it might have something to do with the future of the world??"

"I have no idea," Dorm said with a wicked grin. "But it sounds good doesn't it."

"Oooh Dorm you sneaky boy," Sanel said pointing at him and grinning from ear to ear. "You're getting to be more like your father every day."

"Doesn't bode well does it."

That night Dorm was haunted by the dream. He hadn't endured it for some time. He woke with a start, breathing heavily. Mac sat up next to him.

"You quite finished there?" he asked.

"What?" Dorm asked looking at him.

"Whatever that dream was it must have been bad. The way you were thrashing about like that."

"Sorry. I didn't hit you did I?"

"It's just a nose don't worry," he said wincing slightly.

"Sorry love. I haven't had the dream for a long time. I thought it must have passed."

"What you've had this dream before? Tell me."

Dorm briefly explained the sequence of events to him, and tried to describe the emotions of it. He realised that this episode of it was much more intense than ever before.

"Sounds nasty," Mac said when he'd finished.

"It feels it too."

"Come on lie down and try and get some rest. I'll snuggle in close. At least that way you won't whack me one."

The next morning was cloudy and dark but dry. They ate a large breakfast and met briefly in the small common room from the night before. Dorm told them all about Corm's promise to try to convince Navagahn, but also of his expectation of failure.

Dorm, Mac, Artur and Zacravia went for a stroll around the palace with Sergeant Makor as they got to know him. He was quite a likeable fellow, though occasionally Dorm felt he was holding his tongue in order not to get himself into trouble. He got the impression that Makor was used to speaking his mind, and wasn't too fussed on pomp and ceremony. Also it seemed that he had a dislike of some of the more "aristocratic" tendencies of his social superiors.

Again his story of the amulet was the same as everyone else's. His father, who he said had died several years ago, had handed him the amulet on his sixteenth birthday. He however was actually the second son in his family. His elder brother had been killed in battle during the rebellion of a minor lord against Corm Sanel many years ago. His father had known nothing about it, save its value to the family and all the same things as everyone else's father or mother.

Sergeant Makor did seem to be well liked, or at least respected by the men of the palace guard. He stopped to chat with a few of them, enquiring after family members or asking about personal things, that these people obviously had felt able to confide in him at some stage. Dorm liked this aspect of their new companion. It was far easier to integrate a new person in if they were likeable and easy to talk to and trust in the first place.

They could see much of the city of Tagradas from these lofty heights, the palace being built on a slight rise. Off in the distance he could make out hills and far off to the north the dark imposing shape of the Fortress Mountains. As he stared at them, again there was that dark sense of foreboding and doom, but also a curious sensation of an urgent need to get there.

"What is it?" Mac said quietly, standing close next to him and following his gaze.

"I don't know," Dorm said in a whisper. "It's those mountains. Every time I look at them…"

"Well they are the Fortress Mountains," Mac said.

"It's more than that. It's like an insane fear of them, yet a need, almost a compulsion to go there."

"Weird. Though I think that sums up just about everything to do with this little adventure."

"True enough." Dorm tore his vision away from those peaks and returned to the group.

Corm Sanel met them later on in one of his studies. He invited the group in and gave them all seats and drinks. Sanel sat behind his large desk, cradling a small brown cat, which purred enthusiastically as the monarchs' absent minded stroking.

"Well as you suspected Dorm, Navagahn hasn't budged in his determination not to allow his daughter to go with you. I even tried that one about the 'future of the world'. I don't think he believed me."

"Well thank you for trying again Uncle," Dorm said to him.

"I'm just sorry it didn't work." The king sighed heavily. "So what will you do now?"

"A good question," Rhynavell said dejectedly.

"We could just go on without her and hope for the best," Mac suggested.

"I'm not sure we should risk that," Telly said.

"We could try talking to the Rangers?" Travanos suggested. Everyone stared at him for a moment. "Well I mean we have encountered them several times and they have seemed to know more about what's going on than we do. Perhaps it's time they did something for us for a change."

"That's possible," Dorm thought.

"The Rangers," Sanel said in a disgusted voice. "I'm not sure you should associate with them any more than you have to. Who knows what you might end up contracting. The way they move around magic people like that."

"Aren't they notoriously hard to contact anyway?" Artur asked.

"Yes. They tend to keep to themselves, and not admit visitors."

"Couldn't Your Majesty just order him to let her go?" Lianna suggested.

"I could yes. There's just one minor problem with that. He has to witness it, to be able to prove it has come from my hand."

"Oh. That is a slight drawback I guess."

"We seem to be fast running out of options," Zacravia said glumly.

Everyone thought for a moment.

"There is one other possibility," Dorm began slowly.

"And that is?" Travanos asked warily.

"We could just leave… and take her with us."

"You mean kidnap her?" Telly asked incredulously.

"Well I was thinking more along the lines of us explaining it to her first and getting her to agree to come with us, and we just leave without telling her father."

"Would that work?"

"Well it'd give us some time to get out of the way before he finds out. At least we'd have a head start."

"I suppose I can make sure he has work to do that day to keep him busy as long as possible," Sanel suggested.

"It would take a few days to set up, which means we can allay any suspicions he might have," Mac said.

"I'm not sure I like this conversation," Harmia said.

"Don't worry," Dorm said to her sympathetically. "None of the rest of us are particularly fond of it either. But we don't seem to have much choice."

"So how exactly do we go about this?" Lianna asked.

The plotting began.

The plan they came up with was deceptively simple.

They first had to convince Tissievilla to accompany them. Since Sergeant Makor was already convinced this was a little easier, and also gave them a better way of executing a later part of the plan without raising the suspicions of her father.

For the next few days Corm Sanel would do as little paper work as possible. He purposely rearranged his schedule so that his days were filled with meetings and councils, and he postponed all the other work he had to do till later.

Next they quietly prepared all their belongings for their departure. Packing away unneeded items, and putting them back with the horses. They would usually take some small unobtrusive, and easily re-packable item away with them, so it didn't look like they were leaving. But over the few days the amount of things in their rooms diminished.

They continued to attend dinner with the king every night and attend the other functions he organised. This gave the appearance that nothing was happening at the moment, other than biding their time and resting.

They also continued to try and work on Navagahn. To no avail of course, but the illusion was important. He still steadfastly refused to allow his daughter to go off with strangers on some foolish adventure.

The stage was set for their little escapade.

The afternoon was drawing to a close. Navagahn was with Corm Sanel in his study going over some sort of budgetary thing, which would take hours. Tissievilla had now accepted their explanation that she had to come and that possibly the fate of the world rested on it. She had wanted to immediately rush and tell her father that she "simply had to go", but they convinced her that there wasn't enough time, and that they would make sure the king informed him. She had packed some of her things and was trying to organise some of her multitude of dresses and other finery into some sort of order to take with her, when Telly and

Rhynavell came to collect her.

"We don't have time for this," Telly said frustrated.

"But I can't leave without enough clothes," Tissievilla explained. "That would never do."

"Look there isn't time or the room to take it all," Rhynavell said. "Or are you expecting one horse to carry all this and you as well?"

"One horse?" She looked almost shocked. "Aren't we going in a carriage?"

The girls looked at each other. "No." they said in unison. They then took charge of the packing quickly stuffing a few dresses, cloaks and scarves as well as other items, into the bags. They had her ready to go in less than twenty minutes.

Rhynavell checked the corridor before they left and headed towards the stables. Meanwhile everyone else had gotten their horses ready and organised a horse for Tissievilla.

Elsewhere in the Palace, Dorm and Mac waited with Sergeant Makor near the study where Corm Sanel and Navagahn were working. Makor was nervous about his part, small though it was, in the escape plan. But he was willing to do it. He walked and quietly knocked on the door. A voice inside called out and he opened it.

"Your Majesty could I borrow you for a moment. I need you to sight something for me."

"Of course Sergeant," Sanels voice drifted out to them. Mumbling was heard for a moment and Sanel stepped out into the corridor, shutting the door behind him. He slinked down the corridor to where Dorm and Mac were waiting. "I guess you're leaving now?"

"Yes Uncle," Dorm confirmed.

"Well my boy," the monarch said taking him by the hand and shaking it warmly. "Good luck to all of you. I hope to see you on your way back."

"We'll try Uncle, but no guarantees."

"Of course. Look after yourself too Mac. And him," he pointed at Dorm.

"I will. You can be sure of that."

"And Sergeant," he said turning to Makor. "Make the country proud. And good luck."

"I shall try to Your Majesty."

"Well I'd best get back before he comes looking for me. Good luck"

He trotted back to the door and opened it looking back at them as he did and saying "Thank you Sergeant. Keep me apprised." He stepped inside and closed the door behind. They quickly left and headed to the stables where the others waited.

"How did it go?" Travanos asked.

"So far so good" Dorm replied. "We just need the others."

Lianna helped Sergeant Makor to his horse and got him ready.

After a minute or two Telly, Rhynavell and Tissievilla came out into the gardens and hurried across to the stables.

"Are we ready?" Dorm asked when they approached.

"I hope so," Telly said. "But let's not hang around to find out."

They helped Tissievilla onto her horse and secured her packs. After just a few minutes they were ready and rode quietly out of the stables and through the main gate, back into the sprawl of the city.

Chapter 11

They left Tagradas behind fairly quickly.

They intended to put as much distance as possible between themselves and the city as quickly as they could. Corm Sanel had promised to keep Navagahn busy for the rest of the day and he wasn't likely to notice Tissievillas' absence until evening. So there probably wasn't any chance of him coming after them until the following day. But they agreed it was best to get away as far as possible. Just in case.

The weather remained adequate for travelling. Large grey clouds interspersed with bits of blue sky. The breeze was nice and refreshing, and they made good time along the highway. The region was dotted with towns and villages, as well as farms and other industries. As they travelled they got to know Tissievilla a little better. Their original belief that she was a little "dense" was not exactly accurate. She wasn't slow. She was just not very fast. Telly described it as a natural by product of blonde hair. Travanos was a little offended by this since his wife had blonde hair and didn't seem to be similarly afflicted.

She seemed to now understand their mission better. Though she still seemed a little vague on some of the more complex parts, like what a quest was and so forth. But she did have a positive attitude to the whole affair, which was more than most of the others had at this point.

She did seem a little saddened by having to lie to her father. Since her mother had died, she and her father had grown much closer. It had obviously become a relationship they hadn't previously enjoyed;

presumably because Navagahns' work always kept him busy. Since her mothers death, Navagahn had spent much more time with his daughter, and she had come to rely on his presence. Dorm felt a little guilty when he realised this. He now began to understand another facet of Navagahns' refusal to let Tissievilla go with them. He too didn't want to lose this tenuous relationship with his daughter. Dorm was almost tempted to turn back. But the possible consequences were a little more frightening.

They continued on until dusk, when they found an inn and stopped for the night. They hadn't travelled too far from Tagradas, but far enough that they felt a little more comfortable. They planned to get up early and continue at a faster pace.

Dorm said goodnight to Telly after one of their long conversations about the group. He had come to rely on her as a sounding board. Almost as much as Mac. It was good to get a female perspective on things. And Telly did have opinions.

Dorm got into bed and tried to relax.

"How do you think it's going so far?" Mac asked him.

"Well enough I suppose," he replied.

"And how well is Tissievilla going to fit in?"

"That's a more difficult question," Dorm sighed. "She's certainly polite. She seems eager to help. Though I get the feeling people are going to get frustrated with her after a while. Rhynavell particularly."

"Why Rhynavell?" Mac asked curiously.

"They're the same age. From similar backgrounds. I think Rhynavell sees Tissievilla as an affront to everything she's worked hard for all her life. Tissie's not exactly the sharpest knife in the block."

"Dorm, love. The word is dumb." Mac said in that way of his. "She makes dung look smart."

Dorm laughed in spite of himself. "That's a little harsh I think Mac."

"Not by much."

"I think she'll be alright in the end. We just have to be a little patient."

"Well I just wish she'd stop looking at you that way." Mac said with a tint to his voice.

"What way?"

"Please tell me it's not contagious," Mac said jokingly. "She sees you as an opportunity. A good prospect. She wants to be me."

"Well she's not being you."

"Are you sure?"

"You're right maybe it is contagious."

"Just every time she looks at you that way, part of me wants to just claw her eyes out." Mac made a clawing motion with his hand.

Dorm laughed again. "Don't worry. It won't come to that. She's not going to be able to take me away from you. I like you just fine. I don't see any reason to change."

"That's not very reassuring."

The next morning they woke and left early. Tissievilla was obviously not used to getting up this early and so complained a bit and had to be made to get ready. Dorm was a little worried by this. He was a prince, not a babysitter. No one had the time to "look after" her in that way. He hoped she would begin to learn their routine.

They continued to ride westward along the highway. The weather improved slightly as the day wore on. A little after midday they heard what appeared to be thunder, rumbling in the distance. This was strange since the cloud cover had decreased steadily all day, and it didn't look like rain. Since they weren't too far from the next village they picked up the pace a little hoping to reach shelter if they were wrong. The village came into sight in the distance, but the rumbling grew louder. They realised is was a large number of horses galloping along the road. They moved over to one side of the road to allow these riders to pass.

The large group of soldiers game galloping over the rise behind them. Navagahn was in the lead. He shouted something to the lead soldiers and they bore down on the group. The soldiers quickly surrounded them. Navagahn walked his horse forward towards Dorms'.

"Your Highness," He said politely, but with a hint of steel in his voice. "I'm afraid I will have to place you and your party under arrest for kidnapping."

"That's ridiculous," Dorm replied.

"I assure you it is not!" he retorted.

"Father…" Tissievilla began.

"Silence child. I shall take you home, and these wretches shall hang!" It was obvious he was overstating things a bit. Dorm couldn't be hanged without Lugemall declaring war on Tagradas, and Sanel would never let that happen.

"You seem to be a little upset M'lord," Dorm said to him calmly.

"Upset!" He almost jumped out of his saddle. "You kidnap my daughter and you think I'm just upset?"

"Father please," Tissievilla tried again. "I went with them willingly."

"What?!" He looked at her incredulously. "You fool girl, what did you think you were doing?"

"The fate of the world might depend on it," She said dramatically. Dorm almost groaned.

"That's just nonsense they told you to get them to go with you."

"No it's not," Dorm said finally. "It may indeed be the truth. We know these amulets have something to do with the Fortress. And everything we've read seems to indicate something more important than anything else in the world right now."

"Do you really think sir, that all of us would leave our homes and families to go off on some fool errand?" Travanos asked him thoughtfully. "I assure you sir, this is very real."

"Don't try to convince me of your lies."

"They're not lies," Lianna said roughly. "It's the truth. I didn't believe it at first either, but now I know it is." Her confession was a little heartening to Dorm.

"Rubbish!" Navagahn said again with distaste.

"Not rubbish." Said a voice from behind him. "Truth."

Everyone turned and saw three Rangers standing behind the horses. They still wore their hoods up. As everyone spied them they bowed low in greeting.

"Not more of these guys," Mac whispered to Dorm and Telly.

"His Highness speaks the truth," the leader Ranger said. "You will listen to him Lord Navagahn, or you shall be responsible to the fate of the world. Whatever that may be."

"Superstition and mumbo-jumbo." Navagahn protested. Though

some of the fire had gone out of his voice. Dorm had noticed they seemed to have that effect of most people.

"No, truth." The leader said again. "The world needs your daughter."

"And these questers, need your daughter," said the female in the group. "And they shall take her with them or the world shall fail."

"I don't understand?" Navagahn said to her.

"All have their part to play. All have their own skill, and quality to bring to this event. All must participate."

"You don't have to understand Navagahn. You just have to trust." Telly said.

"Father I want to go with them. Maybe I can do some good."

"M'lord. I know you love your daughter." Dorm said to him. "I know that since your wife died the pain has been easier to bear with her around. But we all have to face the pain sometime. You need to grieve properly. On your own. We will bring her back. Of that you have my word."

It was clear he was beginning to come round.

After some more pleading from Tissievilla and continued arguments from the questers, as well as the statuesque presence of the Rangers, he eventually relented. There was a long goodbye. Dorm let that go. It was obviously necessary. He felt a little guilty at sneaking his daughter out of the city and let them have this moment. Eventually Navagahn turned his horse and began to lead his now confused soldiers back the way they had come,

Once they had moved off into the distance, Dorm turned to the Rangers. "Well it's about bloody time you people did something constructive!" he said angrily. Everyone looked at him. It was unlike Dorm to swear in such a manner.

"It was necessary, Your Highness," said their leader.

"Think of all the trouble you could have saved us if you'd just come out and done this in the first place."

"It was necessary," said the other man. "We did not mean to cause you trouble, but it was necessary."

"Necessary indeed," Travanos said.

"Well maybe you could pay a little more attention and help us out a little more often." Dorm said with a little less anger in his voice. "We are doing this for you remember, and we are operating in the dark here."

"You have done well so far, Your Highness," the woman Ranger said politely. "We cannot fault you. In the end the reasons shall become clear."

"I don't want clear reasons, I want clear instructions."

"We cannot give you that, lest we taint the outcome."

"Taint the outcome?" Mac asked.

"Yes Mac Ravin." Said the leader again. "If we did that we may cause to happen the very thing we seek to avoid."

"Well we couldn't possibly have that now could we," Zacravia said sarcastically.

"We are glad to see you agree, friend Zacravia."

"Umm nooo…" he replied.

"Rangers shall be where and when you need them most. Have no fear friends." With that they turned and began their slow swaying walk. Everyone watched them go for a few seconds. Still very confused by the whole affair.

As everyone began to move off, they again did their disappearing act.

They continued to travel westward through the rolling countryside of Tagradas. It would be at least two weeks before they reached the border with Kiama Mor, and they hoped that this time would help integrate Tissie, as she preferred to be called, into the group. She was certainly friendly, asking many questions about everyone and their background. Which made some people, Zacravia in particular, a little uncomfortable. Dorm had noticed that despite his pretence at being comfortable almost proud of his criminal background, he had begun to subtly change. He now tried hard to avoid mentioning his nefarious adventures and tried to accentuate his nice points. Dorm found this interesting. Almost all evidence of the animosity between him and Harmia had also disappeared, though she still always rode near him. She was now very polite to him, one could almost say friendly. Laughing at his jokes occasionally and even having conversations with him that lasted several minutes.

Dorm reflected on this group. Lianna and Travanos got on very well, obviously a connection with the sea, and could spend hours in conversation about meaningless nautical things that Dorm couldn't understand. Artur had seemingly taken to Sergeant Makor in the last few days, probably because Makor was also a "normal" person as Telly called them. Artur had always been quiet, and despite attempts by all of them to bring him out of his shell a little he had always remained somewhat on the outside. Dorm hoped that with Makor now in the group, this might begin to change.

Rhynavell seemed to get on with everyone. It was impossible not to like the girl. She had a good sense of humour and could always make you laugh. Dorm noticed her occasional looks at Mac when she thought no one was looking. He knew what they meant. He had seen it enough in many people. He knew nothing would happen. Mac was too faithful for that. Almost to a fault. He knew she too would never do anything. She was too good for that.

Dorm thought about this disparate group of people that fate had decided to call upon. Given the diverse backgrounds of the questers so far, he began to wonder what sort of others they might be joined by.

"A penny for your thoughts," Telly said moving her horse in beside his.

"Oh sorry," he apologised. "Didn't mean to wander off. Was just thinking about all these people."

"They are a unique bunch aren't they."

"That they are."

"We all seem to be getting on well enough though."

"I know. That's one of the things I was thinking about. How individual we all were at the beginning, and now… well we're almost like a family. It's weird."

"I know. Makes you wonder what it's going to be like once we have everybody," Telly speculated.

"Yes I know. A little frightening to say the least."

"Oh I'm sure you'll win them all over with your indelible charm," she said sarcastically.

"Now you're just being mean."

"No I think you're quite a good leader."

"Well… thanks." He said. Dorm had never been very good at taking compliments. "It's nice to be appreciated."

You're welcome," she smiled.

The next day they entered a small town called T'Kell. It was a typical small farming town, with several inns, and industries dotted about it. The people were friendly though wary of strangers, though being on the main highway they were somewhat used to new faces. They took rooms in one of the larger inns, and settled in for the night. Dorm expected to leave in the morning and reach the border by the day after.

Everyone gathered in the small common room adjacent to their rooms, to have a group meeting before retiring. It was good to have these meetings, everyone then had the chance to ask any questions they had and hopefully get an answer.

"So any more clues as to whether we're on time or not?" Lianna asked.

"Afraid not," Dorm told her. "We seem to be as lost as ever."

"Good to see some things never change," Mac said quietly.

"What's Kiama Mor like," Artur asked. "I don't really know anything about it."

"It's mainly desert," Telly said. "Though we wont come to that part of the country for some days yet."

"I've never seen a desert," Artur said."

"Depressing sort of place really," Travanos said. "Sand followed by more sand. That's about it."

"Well that's a bit of a generalisation," Hamria said.

"Sure that isn't an admiralisation?" Mac said jokingly. Everyone groaned.

"Well hopefully we wont have to go into the desert to find the people we're looking for." Dorm said. "That could get messy if we do."

"We'd have to buy camels," Lianna said. "I've heard they're expensive."

"Not to mention temperamental," Zacravia said. "And smelly."

"When were you in Kiama Mor?" Harmia asked him a little more forcefully than was necessary.

"Many years ago. Before your time my dear," he replied cryptically.

There was a knock at the door.

"Come in," Dorm said curiously. The innkeeper entered.

"Good evening everyone. Sorry to disturb you. Just wanted to let you all know that you wont have that second washroom I'm afraid. There's a group of diplomats staying with us, who have taken all the other rooms, and they needed that extra washroom. I am sorry for the inconvenience."

"Where are these diplomats from?" Rhynavell asked curiously.

"Well they're from Peldraksakhr. Can you believe it? I wouldn't normally let such people into my inn, what with their always trying to conquer us, but they are paying double…" he grinned.

"That's very interesting," Dorm said.

"Did they say why they were here?" Harmia asked.

"Something to do with trade is all I know I'm afraid."

"Who's their leader?" Travanos asked with a glance to Dorm and Telly.

"Now let me see I think he said his name was Domiticus."

Well thank you for letting us know." Rhynavell said quickly.

"No trouble at all. Good night to you all." He turned and quietly left the room.

"So the Peldraksekhr are operating here in Tagradas as well. That's very interesting." Travanos said.

"Indeed it is," Dorm said musing.

"Well if this Domiticus is up to the same tricks as Lassius, we could have some fun," Telly suggested.

"Its possible," Dorm mused. "I guess it would be our duty to the Alliance."

"Precisely," Zacravia said patriotically. Everyone looked at him. "Well we don't know that that isn't some minor part of the quest…" he suggested defensively.

"He does have a point," Telly said.

"I know. That's what worries me."

"Perhaps we should delay our departure long enough to find out a bit more about this Domiticus," Makor said. "It sounds suspicious to me… and I have no idea what you're all talkin' about."

"Well I guess that settles it," Mac said.

"Does kind of doesn't it."

It turned out that Domiticus was a rather tall man with a receding hairline. His bearing and manner indicated a military history though he had obviously lived a good life since leaving that as he was now beginning to get a "bit rotund" as Rhynavell politely described it.

Domiticus was meeting with several local merchants in the inns main common room. It was still fairly early in the morning and it seemed that he was eager to complete his discussions with them so he could attend another meeting. Dorm was interested in who this other meeting might be with, and what it might be about.

Domiticus liked to talk about all the wonderful opportunities for trade that could occur between the Empire and the Alliance, if only the leaders of both sides could put the past behind them. He liked to say how the Emperor had made some overtures of peace over the last few years, but that they had been greeted with scepticism. He conceded that he realised it couldn't happen overnight, but said he longed for the day when trade caravans could travel freely between their two powers.

After his meeting with the merchants, he stood and walked from the room, his servants following. Dorm and the others waited quietly in the common room for him to return. When he did he had changed into a flowing white toga trimmed in purple and gold. His servants and attendants had also dressed themselves up, but it was clear who was in charge, and who should be the centre of attention.

Domiticus and his entourage left and headed into the town. They followed him at a discreet distance not wanting to appear to be following him. T'Kell was not a big town by any means, but it was large enough that there was a fair amount of bustle going on in the street. Domiticus made his presence known by walking calmly straight down the centre of the street as he headed towards the main highway. Once there he paused for a few minutes at a market to talk to another merchant then headed to the towns' courthouse, which also served as the local administrative building. It was obvious he was going to see T'Kell's mayor.

He walked up the steps at the front of the building and entered. It was obvious that he was expected. Dorm began to hatch a plan.

A little later when they had prepared, Dorm and the others entered the courthouse. Several guards and attendants at the head of the building tried to stop them, but after the briefest of explanations he was allowed to pass. Dorm requested an immediate meeting with the towns' mayor, a man named Yabis. They were escorted to a waiting area and given some refreshments.

"Your Highness," Harmia asked quietly. "What are we doing?"

"Yes Dorm, do tell," Telly said. "We're all agog."

"Just play along everyone," he said cryptically. "Remember that I need it to sound natural, and try not to look surprised at anything I say."

"Well we'll do our best," Travanos told him sceptically.

Yabis arrived momentarily. He wore a dark blue doublet and hose belted with an ornate looking leather affair with a large silver buckle. He wore a small golden band on his head, obviously a symbol of his office.

"Your Highness," he said bowing to Dorm. "You do my town great honour by stopping here, Welcome sir."

"It is a pleasure to take hospitality in such a nice town Mayor Yabis." Dorm began with the flattery. "I am however here on important business for the Alliance. That's why I needed to speak to you in private."

"Of course Your Highness," Yabis relied almost in awe. "Please sit and tell me how T'Kell can be of service to the Fortress Alliance this day."

"You'll note that my companions are from many different professions, and from several countries in the Alliance. Over the last several months, evidence has been uncovered of a conspiracy within the Alliance."

That raised a few eyebrows.

"A conspiracy?" Yabis was shocked. "What is it's aim?"

"Nothing short of destroying the Alliance. This conspiracy has appeared in several Alliance kingdoms, including here in Tagradas. I have come from the capital, after meeting with King Corm Sanel. He has sent along with we this man." Dorm indicated Makor. "This is Sergeant Cal Makor. He is one of the kings most trusted advisors."

Makor tried not to look amused.

"An honour to have you here Sergeant," Yabis said nodding to him.

"Thank you, Mayor," Makor said, then after a look from Dorm… "His Majesty has instructed me to assist his Highness in gettin' information of this conspiracy to every town we can. And uncovering any evidence of it we can."

"You see Mayor," Dorm continued. "We have discovered that there are Alliance citizens, many of them merchants, who are in league with agents from the Peldraksekhr Empire. These agents are posing as merchants."

"Merchants you say," Yabis replied quietly.

"Yes. Merchants." Telly reiterated. She nodded gravely as she said it. Driving the point home.

"It seems these 'merchants' are gathering information about our countries armies. As well as our roads and highways. They are looking at ways that the Empire might invade us."

"We've also uncovered evidence that they have been embezzling money from various governments," Rhynavell piped up. "I work for the Royal Accountancy in Lugemall, and they have made off with millions."

"We fear this money is being used to build up their military, at the expense of our own," Travanos said grimly.

"And we have some evidence that they have been making contact with the criminal elements in our society." Zacravia contributed. "They appear to be planning major crimes, to keep our people off guard."

"All of this has been going on?" Yabis asked incredulously. "I've not heard anything."

"Of course you haven't," Harmia told him. "If it was made public, then those involved would know we were onto them, and then would disappear. We would never catch them."

"So that is why we are here Mayor Yabis," Dorm told him. "If you are approached by any Peldraksekhr 'merchants', or indeed by their agents. Or if your townspeople start talking about such things. Then it's quite possible that the conspirators are including T'Kell as part of their plans."

"What should I do," Yabis pleaded.

"Don't let them know you're on to them. Just find an excuse not to see them. Don't let them make any deals with your people. And certainly don't invite them to any functions."

"Functions? Why ever not?"

"One agent was caught trying to steal maps of a region near the Zigan border while at a function," Artur added in a frighteningly convincing voice.

"Now I'm afraid we mustn't linger here too much longer Mayor," Dorm said. "There are many more towns we need to see. But spread this news to all the villages near here. Tell them of this, and make sure they keep a look out."

"By the Fortress, this is terrible," Yabis moaned.

"Don't worry Mayor," Dorm said looking directly at him. "With your help, we can and will stop them."

"That went well I thought," Dorm told them all after they had left.

"I never knew you were such an actor love," Mac told him admiringly.

"I'm full of surprises."

"Do you think it will make much of a difference?" Rhynavell asked.

"Probably not," Dorm admitted, "But at least it's a dent in their plans."

"I'd love to be a fly on the wall of Domiticus' rooms when he gets back," Zacravia chuckled.

"It would be an interesting conversation," Lianna agreed.

"Sergeant, I'd like to thank you as well," Dorm said. "Your performance was perfect."

"I'll admit I was a little shocked at being introduced as one of the Kings most trusted advisors. I usually only see him once a week, and even then its from a distance."

"Well it made a difference," Dorm shook his hand.

"And where did you learn to speak so grimly like that Artur?" Telly asked.

"I don't know," he admitted. "It just seemed the right thing to say at the time."

"Well it worked." Dorm said.

They took their time heading back to the inn. After a little while Domiticus and his people came stalking up the street heading back towards the inn. The man didn't look happy. In fact he looked murderously angry.

"Well someone's in a bad mood," Lianna said as he passed them.

"Good," Travanos said. "The more he's in a bad mood, the better I feel."

They left T'Kell the next morning feeling somewhat better about things. It was a small victory to be sure, but it was just possible that this clandestine news might spread a little beyond just the surrounding towns and villages. And even if it didn't, then that was one small area of Tagradas that would be that much harder for them to use against the Alliance.

The weather remained overcast but fine for the next few days as they headed westward. It was clear by watching the countryside passing by, that they were beginning to enter the area that would eventually lead to the deserts of Kiama Mor. Telly called it savannah. She said she had learnt all about them when she was younger, since her father and mother had insisted she get a well-rounded education. While the land was still very fertile and got adequate rains, there were fewer types of crops that would grow and the number of trees would reduce. She said that eventually this would give way to grasslands and then onto the desert.

They continued to pass small villages and towns but heard nothing of any further Peldraksehkran agents. Over the days they learnt more about Tissievilla. Normally she was rather quiet. And sometimes Dorm had to think to remember the last thing she said anythng. At other times she would talk, seemingly without taking a breath about whatever topic had taken her fancy. It was clear from his looks that Sergeant Makor was somewhat used to this, as he would just refocus his eyes on something a long way away, but the others weren't. Harmia controlled it well, And Lianna appeared to be holding on ok. Artur simply stared at her when she got going, obviously wondering if she was going to run out of air and topple from her saddle. Travanos was somewhat used to it since his sister had had a habit, of "going on a bit from time to time". Telly simply gritted her teeth in an almost pleasant smile and rode on. Mac scowled beneath his brows as she talked and Dorm couldn't help but laugh to himself at the expression on his partners face.

Rhynavell however was getting increasingly annoyed by her. It seemed she wasn't used to this level of chatterboxery. While the time Tissie was quiet Rhyn seemed ok; normal even, when Tissie got going Rhyns' expression changed. Dorm sidled up to Telly and spoke to her quietly.

"When you get a chance," he began. "Probably when we stop this evening. Take Rhyn off for a chat. I'm not sure she's handling Tissievilla well, and I think it would be better coming from another woman."

"And what exactly do you want me to say to her Dormal dear?"

"I don't know. Whatever you think might help her bear all this. At least until we can get Tissie to have a normal conversation."

"I'm not sure she knows what that is."

"Yes it is a bit much at times isn't it."

"Just a bit."

They stopped that evening on the outskirts of a small village. They pitched their tents a little back from the road and settled in for the evening. It wasn't as comfortable as an inn, but this villages' inn wasn't big enough for all of them anyway. Telly took Rhyn off after a while to their chat. Tissie was busily chatting to Lianna about what they were planning to have for dinner. The two women were gone for sometime, but returned not long after darkness fell. They all sat around the fire chatting before retiring. Everyone participated in the jovial conversation, everyone saying anything they felt they could, in order to prevent Tissie from beginning one of her sessions.

The moon was out when they retired and after a little while the sounds of sleeping drifted across the camp.

Dorm began to dream. It was the same dream. But it felt different. It looked the same as far as he could tell. Everything was normal, as far as the dream went at least. But it didn't feel right. He was running through the palace, searching, still searching. He rounded a corner. There was a person standing there. That was a difference. There had never been a person in this dream before. It was a man. Silhouetted in the dark. The light behind him was bright. Piercing. Dorm had to shield his eyes to see properly. The person stepped forward. It was Mac.

"Mac?" Dorm asked in confusion. "I've been looking for you. What are you doing here?"

"Do not pursue!" It wasn't Mac's voice.

"What?"

"DO NOT PURSUE!!"

There was silence.

Suddenly he shot bolt upright in bed.

"What is it?" Mac said waking up beside him.

"The dream again." Dorm replied breathlessly. "But it was different. It wasn't the same. There was a person in it."

"I thought you said you were in the palace in that dream?"

"I am, but there's never been any one in it before."

"Who was it? Did you recognise them?"

"Yes." He paused. "It was you."

"Me?"

"Well it was you, but it wasn't you."

Mac raised an eyebrow.

"It was your face and body but it wasn't your voice. He said 'Do not pursue'."

" 'Do not pursue' what?" Mac enquired.

"I don't know." Dorm admitted. "I don't like this dream any more than the last one."

"I think maybe you need to have that looked at, love." Mac said sympathetically. "I'm beginning to get worried by all this dream business. Why don't we try to get these Rangers to answer some questions about it next time we see them?"

"Better yet, why don't we go to their chapter house in the next town we come to with one?"

"Good idea." Mac agreed holding him.

"It has to mean something. I hope they have some answers."

Chapter 12

The road through Tagradas to the border was well travelled.

Merchants and traders, as well as a good number of farmers and ordinary travellers either passed them or travelled along with them. It felt a little better to not be quite so alone on the road. It had always felt a little vulnerable to be heading along as a group with no one else around. If someone decided to attack them it would be a lot easier with no one around. And what would happen to the prophecy then?

Rhynavell was feeling a little better. Apparently whatever Telly had said to her worked. At least for the time being. Everyone also did their best to keep conversations moving along, so that Tissievilla wouldn't be able to start one of her "sentences" as Artur politely called them.

Dorm was eager to reach a large town in order to go to a chapterhouse of the Rangers. Most of the small villages wouldn't have one. He had consulted his map and the nearest large town was Lanak Cal, just before the border. It would take several days to reach it, but the going would be fairly easy.

Dorm was however worried that the Rangers wouldn't tell him anything. They certainly hadn't been very forthcoming so far. He knew they had their own agenda, but the Fortress only knew what that was. And perhaps in this instance, that wasn't just a saying. He just hoped that they might see reason and at least answer some of his questions.

These dreams had been plaguing his sleep for some time now. It had always been the same until now. He had no idea what that meant, or how it related to this quest. But he had the strong suspicion that it did relate, somehow.

On the afternoon of the fourth day out from T'Kell a large caravan came along side them. The merchant at its head, was a large, cheery faced man, wearing a green doublet that really didn't suit him. He wore several large gold rings, which he seemed to have no qualms about showing off.

"I say friend," he said to Dorm as his wagon pulled along side the Prince's horse. "Do you happen to know if the bridge over the stream ahead is open?"

"No friend, I'm sorry I don't," Dorm told him. "We're not from this area, we're only travelling through."

"Oh no matter," He said relaxing back in his seat and running his bejewelled hand over his grey balding head. "It's a nice enough day, I don't mind waiting if it isn't. Say," he said suddenly sitting up again. "Would you and your group be interested in any wares? I have many different commodities, that could relax a weary traveller."

"I'm sure you do friend, but I think we're alright for supplies just now."

"Ah well, no harm in trying is there?"

"None at all friend," Dorm smiled in spite of himself.

"So where are you heading to?" he asked conversationally.

"Kiama Mor eventually," Dorm partially lied.

"Ah, you have business there?"

"Yes, mostly family business."

"Oh I see. My commiserations my friend." He chuckled conspiratorially. "I'm sure we've all had those trips before."

"Yes, families can be that way sometimes."

"They can indeed," he laughed heartily. "My wife says the same thing about mine."

"Where are you heading to?"

"Dalag Hath, just south of Kiama Mor. I have some goods to pick up there to take back to Tagradas."

"Sounds like a long trip."

"It can get tedious sometimes. This lot tend to go to sleep in their seats for most of the trip." He gave his workers a brief look. They all seemed to be exactly as he described them.

"Seems advantageous if we travelled together for a while. It would certainly give us all someone new to talk to."

"Capital idea, my friend," he said leaning over and grabbing Dorms' proffered hand roughly and shaking it furiously. "I am Damak, trader in these parts and caravan master."

"Dormal," the prince replied. "These are my companions."

"Greetings to you all good friends," Damak waved to them all enthusiastically.

Damak and his caravan were good company, if a little quiet at first. Once all the introductions had been taken care of, everyone seemed to relax a little. Damak was definitely a talker, not anywhere as bad as Tissievilla but he was most assuredly blessed with the gift of the gab. Something that wouldn't have been completely unwelcome to a merchant.

After a while of chatting Telly sidled her horse up next to Dorms'.

"So what's the real story here?" she asked.

"What do you mean?"

"Are we travelling with this caravan all the way to Kiama Mor?"

"It seems advantageous. We get more protection. We might also find out some interesting information."

"Alright then," she said quietly. "I just want you to know that I do feel a little funny about the whole thing."

"In what way?"

"I'm not sure," she admitted. "Nothing I can put my finger on. Perhaps I'm just being paranoid. But I do find it interesting that none of them seems to have noticed our amulets…" She let the thought sink in.

She was right. None of them had seemed to have noticed. Normally peoples' eyes were drawn to them. Many commented. It had led them to several members of their group. But none of the members of this caravan had mentioned them, or asked about them.

That night they camped rather than head on to the nearest hostel, which was still some miles away. As was their custom, they met quietly before retiring to discuss the day. Everyone wanted to know why they were travelling with the caravan, as Telly had. All seemed to accept the answer, though obviously each had thoughts on the matter. Everyone had also noticed the lack of attention to the amulets. No one had known quite what to make of the fact.

They retired and slept well. In the morning they all woke early and prepared for another days riding. Dorm went to the stream near their camp to wash. The water was rather cold still this early in the morning but was refreshing nonetheless. He dried his face and chest as he looked out across the fields thinking of the day. He turned to pick up his tunic.

Tissievilla was standing there.

"Your Highness," She said.

"Good morning, Tissievilla," Dorm began warily.

"Did you sleep well?" she enquired.

"Yes, very well thank you." Dorm went to grab his tunic, but she got to it first.

"Do you think we will make it to, what was that town called again?"

"Lanak Cal?"

"Yes that was it. Do you think we'll make it there today?"

"Either today or early tomorrow," Dorm was a little worried now. The look in her eyes said it all.

"Good. I should like to sleep in a proper bed again. It's much more comfortable in a bed, don't you think?"

"I prefer my bed in Lugemall," he said quickly.

"I'm sure it's a very big bed in your apartments."

"Big enough."

Help! How in the Fortress was he supposed to get rid of her.

To make matters worse at that moment Mac and Telly came over the rise and headed towards the stream. They were laughing about something. Mac looked up. His face took on that murderous look of jealousy he got when he thought of Tissievilla. Telly grabbed his arm and tried to hold him back as he tried to storm down to the stream.

"Oh look," Dorm said suddenly, snatching the tunic from her. "Others need to use the stream too. I should go speak with Damak."

He walked quickly up the bank to the others. He threw his arms around Mac and kissed him quickly on the cheek.

"You came at just the right time, thank you," he said.

"I'm going to kill her," Mac said.

"No you're not." Dorm said sternly. "Just leave things be. I escaped. That's all that matters."

"I'll take care of him," Telly said.

"Keep him out of trouble." Mac was almost growling as Tissie passed them on her was back to the camp. She smiled sweetly at Dorm as she passed. They watched her walk away.

"Look at me," Dorm said. Mac turned to face him. "Don't do anything stupid okay? I mean it."

Mac looked at him for a moment. "I'm sorry," he said quietly.

"I know you are sweetheart."

The travel was a little tense that day. Mac stayed close to Dorm. Perhaps a little closer than usual. Lianna described it as 'protecting his investment'. The others noticed, but didn't really ask. Dorm wasn't sure if they didn't want to know or if they were just being polite.

Damak and his people seemed to notice that something was different, but didn't seem to quite know what. Dorm continued to chat to him as if nothing was the matter, and the merchant returned his pleasant banter. Still no notice seemed to be taken of the amulets.

They made good progress that day. Approaching the outskirts of Lanak Cal by late afternoon. The shadows were starting to lengthen and the sunlight turned a bright orange. They arrived within the town as dusk fell, and found a large enough inn and took their rooms.

Dorm decided to wait till the next day to find the chapterhouse. It probably wouldn't be the best thing to go wandering around in the middle of the night, in an unfamiliar environment.

The Prince explained this at their evening meeting, which was more tense than usual. Mac scowled through most of it, while Tissievilla seemed pleasantly unaware of what had transpired. No one said anything or brought the topic up for discussion. Which was just well. Dorm wasn't sure things would remain civil for long.

Privately he worried about this development. Not because he thought Tissie was nice. He had no intention or desire to leave Mac, but he wondered what this might mean for the prophecy? If Mac ended up hating Tissie would that mean he might not look out for her as much, if she ever got into trouble? Would she not do the same for Mac, if he was ever in danger? Would it lead to the group taking sides? He hated to think what that might do to the outcome of this adventure. The prophecy hadn't said anything about internal conflict. But then it had said that the readers should pray for them. Several times, he recalled.

Sleep came late that night. Macs' breathing was heavy, even a little forced. It was obvious he wasn't happy. Dorm moved closer to him, his chin resting on Macs' shoulder.

"Are you okay?" he asked quietly.

"I'm tired Dorm," he replied testily, burrowing deeper into the pillow.

"Hey," Dorm sat up on one elbow and turned Mac over by his shoulder. "Don't shut me out. I know you're upset, but this isn't good for us."

"Upset?" He was angry now. "Upset is what I get when you're late for dinner."

"You know me Mac. I'm not interested in her. I love you. Only you. You know she's a little… dense, when it comes to these sorts of things. She'll just have to have it explained to her. Just not yet. Not until we've lost our escort. We'll have it sorted out soon."

Mac just looked at him for a moment. "I'm sorry. I just don't know what to do. You know why I feel this way."

"I know love," Dorm said taking him in his arms. "I'm sorry too." He kissed him. "I want you to come with me tomorrow to the chapterhouse."

"Who else are you going to take?"

"Telly. Probably Travanos. I was thinking maybe Lianna as well. I'd take everyone, but I'm not sure how that would look."

"Probably not a bad idea though. Strength in numbers and all that. We might have better luck getting answers out of them."

"I'm not sure I'd bet money on that though."

"No neither would I." He smiled.

"There it is." Dorm said happily.

"There's what?"

"That smile."

They made up.

In the end it was decided that everyone would go. At least that way no one would have to repeat anything and accidentally forget something.

It turned out that the chapterhouse was in one of the less fashionable districts of the town. It took them a while to make their way through the narrowing, busy streets, but they finally arrived at the large barred gate in the whitewashed wall. Inside the wall was a small garden, a stone path leading to the rather ornate looking front door. Several steps led to a paved area surrounded by several columns. The group gathered in front of the door. They had been given some strange looks as they entered by people on the street. Obviously the chapterhouse didn't get too many visitors.

A chain hung on one side of the door. Dorm pulled it. The faint ringing of a bell could be heard.

After a few moments the doors opened and a Ranger appeared. He bowed before them.

"Greetings Questers," he said slowly. "We have been expecting you."

"Of course you have," Dorm said cynically as they all entered.

The foyer was large and echoey. Polished stone gave the appearance of a much more important building than the neighbourhood would suggest. There was however very little in the way of decoration. A small table with a vase of flowers on it and high above them hung the Fortress flag. Other than this there was nothing. A staircase ascended to the next level and below the flag a walkway led to a door through which another garden could be seen. This was the way the Ranger lead them. They passed several more doors before they entered the garden, which was contained in a large courtyard. Several airy balconies surrounded the open space. A fountain played quietly in the centre of the idyllic retreat, and both birds and bees buzzed about the flowers and bushes.

The Ranger led them past all of this and into the range on the other side. He led them upstairs, and finally to a large comfortably attired room, with large windows that let a cool breeze flow evenly through.

"Please wait here," he said bowing again. He then left.

"Well this is interesting," Zacravia said sitting down in one of the upholstered chairs.

"Well it's comfortable at least," Lianna said also sitting.

One by one everyone else sat down. The chairs were indeed quite comfortable.

"Is any one else as nervous about being here as I am?" Sergeant Makor said quietly, as if he was afraid of being overheard.

"I'll admit a slight trepidation," Travanos said shifting in his seat.

"It's the magic sufferers I expect," Dorm said. "We've all heard the stories all our lives. We probably can't help but feel that way. I expect it's quite safe for us though. They wouldn't have let us in otherwise."

"True enough," Telly agreed.

Steps were heard to approach then. Two Rangers, one male, the other female, entered the room. They both bowed to the group and then pushed back their hoods.

"Questers," said the man. "Let us welcome you to our chapterhouse."

"We thank you," Dorm began.

"We are glad that you have finally arrived," said the woman.

"We had no idea what our timetable was supposed to be," Telly told them.

"We understand," said the man. "I am called Sonvey, Master of this chapterhouse. This is Leness. She is our head Teacher."

"We know that you have many questions, and while we cannot answer them all, we shall give you what help we can."

"Well that's something I suppose," Rhynavell said quietly.

The two of them moved slowly and sat upon a divan, facing the group. They sat very erectly. Their benevolent smiles seemed almost chiselled on. There was very little movement in their faces. Their eyes however seemed to dance. They seemed to look everywhere at once.

"You have done well to come this far so quickly," Sonvey began.

"You have stayed true to your path," Leness intoned. "You are to be commended."

"Well that's a relief," Zacravia said quietly.

"Perhaps you could tell us what sort of timetable we are on here?" Dorm asked. "None of us much likes this running around in the dark, not knowing if we are doing what we are supposed to."

"Rest assured Quester," Leness smiled at him. "You shall always be on your correct path as long as you stay true to the path."

"Oh well that's extremely helpful," Dorm sighed.

"I think what His Highness means is," Travanos began. "We have always had the feeling that we need to have gathered all the other 'questers' by a certain time. It is a little difficult to know whether or not we are moving quickly enough to complete that task in time. At the moment we just seem to be stumbling through all this."

"We understand," Sonvey assured them.

"But you are moving at the speed you should be moving at." Leness finished the thought.

"Do not be worried by the conflicts within your group," Sonvey told them. "Over time you shall come to see them for what they are."

"And what exactly is that," Telly asked.

"Tests," Leness said turning towards her. "Tests of your character, your commitment to the journey, to the prophecy and to each other."

"Well I was never that good a student," Makor said.

"I don't think they're that kind of tests Sergeant," Lianna said turning back to him and smiling.

"Yeah I guess," He said. "But I still don't understand why we should have to go through that. I mean we're here aren't we?"

"True enough Quester," Sonvey said nodding slightly. "But there is much trial ahead of you. It will be necessary for you all to know that you can trust each other implicitly."

"That you will defend each other without regard for yourselves. That you will defend the prophecy and its outcome at any cost."

"Because one of us isn't going to make it," Dorm finished quietly.

Sonvey and Leness paused. They half turned towards each other.

"Correct Quester." Sonvey confirmed. "But in order for that to have meaning you must all respect it. You must learn to use it. For this loss will give you power to go on when all seems lost."

"Loss of a loved one, can be the most devastating thing, but it can be a source of great power as well. Power enough to change the world."

There was silence for a few moments as everyone took that in. They all thought what it would be like to lose one of them. They had all grown so close over their time together. It seemed impossible to consider their group without one of them. The thought that one of them might not survive gave everyone a sense of loss. But also a sense of determination. Both to try to prevent it, but also to not let it be in vain, should it still happen.

"I wanted to ask…" Dorm began.

"Your dreams, yes we know," Sonvey said. "They frighten you. They confuse you. Do not despair. They happen for a reason. You do not need to worry on them now. But they shall be useful to you in the future."

"It, like everything else will be necessary for the final outcome," Leness told him quietly.

There was a knock at the door. The doors swung open and several Rangers entered. They escorted a young woman, wearing a nondescript dress. She looked weary and somewhat bedraggled. She had a slightly wild look in her eyes, and she shook all over. Her hands spasmed every so often, as if she couldn't control them. The group walked towards the two senior Rangers and stopped before them as they stood.

The apparent leader of the group bowed towards Sonvey and Leness. "Master, Teacher, Apologies for the intrusion. But this young woman is a foundling."

"It is alright Debedd." Sonvey stood and walked towards the young woman. He looked at her critically for a moment. Then smiled. "Welcome child. Do not fear. We are here to help you."

He placed his fingers on her temples and closed his eyes. Everyone in their group watched transfixed as this went on. He lowered his hands after a few moments. The young woman seemed less crazed than before. As if somehow Sonvey had taken away some of whatever affliction she suffered.

"You are a most fortunate foundling," He said to her. "To be brought to us in the presence of such people as these." He turned towards their group.

"Who is she?" Dorm asked.

"She is a foundling," Leness said matter-of-factly. "She has been found and brought to us."

"I don't understand," Harmia said. "Why has she been brought here?"

"She is one of the touched. She has been brought here so we can help her."

"Touched?" Rhynavell said alarmed. "You mean she has magic?"

"Yes. That is why she is here. So we can help her."

"She has magic and you just let her into the same room as us?" Mac yelled.

Sonvey smiled at them knowingly and laughed. "My friends. Nobel Questers. You are in no danger. You cannot be affected by her magic. Magic is not a danger to you or any one else."

"But the Rangers…" Lianna began.

"Seek out those with magic yes," Leness explained. "But it is not for the reasons you think. Centuries ago, before the Rangers, people who had magic were persecuted. Attacked, murdered. All because they had abilities that others did not understand. The Fortress had need of these people. But too often they were killed before the Fortress could find them. And so the Rangers were created to find those people. The stories of what magic was, was then created, in order to try to stop the attacks. To hopefully keep the people who had magic safe, long enough for us to find them.

"Once they come here, we can teach then how to use their abilities and to develop them." Sonvey continued. "That is the main purpose of the Rangers. To seek out and find those people who have magic. To teach them, to keep them safe."

"So you're saying that it's all a big lie?" Artur asked.

"Not a lie Quester," Leness told him. "A necessary half truth."

"So a white-lie," Lianna accused.

Sonvey turned to the group of Rangers. "Please Debedd, take her to the Welcoming hall, and have her assigned a cell. She will need to rest."

"Yes Master," He bowed again. The remaining Rangers also bowed then led the girl from the room, via the other doors.

"I'm really not sure that I'm comfortable with all this," Dorm said to the two Rangers.

"There is much that you do not know nor understand about the Fortress and its' workings yet, Quester," Sonvey told him seriously.

"And I suppose you aren't going to tell us?"

"It is not our place to do so," Leness told him. "Gladly we would that it were. But there are some things that even we are not privy to."

"We have told you all we can Questers. You must return to your journey. We wish you every fortune. Remain true to yourselves and to each other."

The two Rangers bowed low to the group then walked quietly from the room following the previous group.

They stood alone in the room for a few moments, before they all made towards the door.

The journey back to the inn was quiet. Everyone seemed a little shocked by the developments. The fact that someone wouldn't survive this adventure had always been a possibility. It had said as much in the prophecy itself. But to have it articulated so clearly. And in such a matter-of-fact way was a little unsettling.

And the foundling? To have a magic sufferer right there in front of them. Sonvey and Leness had told them the "truth" about magic. Dorm wasn't quite sure if he believed it. He wanted to. But all his life he had heard the stories about magic and those that suffered from it. Could what they said really be true?

Dorm watched the faces of his companions as they moved through the town. Everyone had a far off look in their eyes. Wondering if it was going to be them who was lost. Wondering if they would realise it was about to happen, when the time came. If they would get the chance to say goodbye?

He also noticed a difference between certain members of the group. Those who lead dangerous lives, or lives with potential danger, Harmia Zacravia, Makor; all seemed to have a sense of inevitability about them. As if they were saying 'well it had to happen sometime.' Others like Artur and Rhynavell seemed to almost be asking what they had done to deserve this possibility.

Dorm wished he had an answer for them. But there wasn't one. At least not now.

They ate their meal in near silence; each lost in their own thoughts. The traders with whom they had been travelling thankfully sat at other tables and didn't bother them. Though they did cast a few looks their way.

Everyone retired early that night. The day had been tiring to say the least.

Dorm lay in bed unable to sleep. He cradled his head in his hands and stared up at the ceiling, thinking over what Sonvey and Leness had said.

"What are you thinking?" Mac asked him without turning around.

"About who it might be and how it might happen." Dorm said quietly. "And how it might affect our goal."

"I know. It's a little frightening."

"I don't think I want to lose any one. We've become almost like a family."

"If it's any consolation, it doesn't make me feel any better that it won't be me," Mac said turning over to look at him.

"How do you figure that one?"

"I'm not a Quester. I don't have an amulet remember. I'm just along for the ride."

"I hadn't thought of it like that. In a way that's good. It means I have one less thing to worry about."

"Glad I could be of service," Mac said moving in close to him and putting his arms around his waist.

Dorm held him and kissed him on the forehead. "I don't like the possibility of losing someone. Though for all we know it could be me."

"No." Mac said seriously. "It won't be you."

"What makes you say that? It could easily be me."

"I know it won't be you. You're the one who keeps us all together. If you were to go, we'd fall apart. And then the prophecy would fail. And that can't happen."

"I admire your confidence, love."

"I won't let it be you."

The journey on from Lanak Cal was quiet and a little uncomfortable. The questers tried to make everything appear normal to

Damak and his caravan; chatting politely and such, but there was still a certain tenseness in the air, that couldn't be hidden.

The weather remained clear but cool as they headed west. The landscape continuing to slowly change as they progressed. It wouldn't be long until they crossed into Kiama Mor now.

Dorm was worried what might happen there. Who the next members of their group would be. How easy would it be to convince them to join the quest.

He realised how easily he thought of it now as a quest. Initially he hadn't even wanted to mention the word, for it sounded so ridiculous. Now it seemed almost natural.

Almost.

~* * * * *~

They entered the chamber.

Flowing robes of many colours. Borders of fine intricate stitching. Heavy necklaces and large ornate head wear. The entourage flowed quietly into the room. Some sat, others stood ceremonially.

He and his companions bowed deeply, showing their respect. "You honour us again, Great Majesty, by seeing us again so quickly."

"My Viziers have reviewed your proposal, Ambassador," the Emperor began immediately. His heavily accented voice cracked in the air as he spoke. He commanded your attention without having to do anything else.

"Thank you Majesty."

"They have spoken highly of your proposal."

"I thank them also Majesty."

"I do have some questions…" he paused. His eyes glittered in the torchlight. Those eyes held great power. He was a little nervous of them. Though he would never let that show to his men. Let alone to the Emperor.

"What do you plan to do with them? How do we know you will not try to use them against us?"

"Honestly Majesty I do not believe we would be able to use them against you. Your people would find out long before we were in a position to do so. And I think your experience in battle with them, would best us."

"You speak honestly. I appreciate that."

"I'm sure we would be willing to sign an addition to our agreement to prohibit us from such action."

He lent back in his chair and looked at him coldly. There was silence for a minute. Only the sound of the torches crackling, and the faint whisper of the wind outside broke the silence.

"Then I believe we have an agreement."

Chapter 13

The crossing of the border into Kiama Mor went quite smoothly, considering the size of their group. The Tagran border guards checked their packs quickly and efficiently, before ushering them through. The border post itself was typical of those throughout the Alliance. Two sets of small neat buildings separated by a short distance, Each set of buildings had a stable and warehouse, as well as accommodation, for both the guards who worked there and travellers. Dorm knew all about the intricacies of these border posts. He had read many a report from their counterparts in Lugemall.

The guards on the Kiaman side wore rather different uniforms than most other countries in the Alliance. Their helmets were conical and wound tightly around their base with mail and cloth, which also hung down their necks, protecting them from the sun. Their surcoats were a dark blue, and studded with small pieces of metal. Their faces carried a look of seriousness, and ferocity. Yet they all remained quite calm, and their movements were slow and deliberate, almost methodical.

Dorm was careful not to reveal their identities. He had heard of the need to provide hospitality in Kiaman culture. The desire to please guests. He could do with a little pampering, but he had no intention of getting stuck for a week with every khan and margrave all the way to the capital. They'd never get there at that rate.

Everyone noticed the change in the weather. It was definitely hotter here, despite the cool breeze that blew. There were fewer trees, and the sun seemed to be everywhere. It wasn't quite a desert yet; Dorm knew that was still to come. But there was a definite change.

It would take a few days to reach the first major town, where they could re-supply, and seek some information. There were a few villages and hostels along the main highway before then, where they could stop for the night. No one fancied sleeping rough in this environment.

Damak and his people continued to be good companions. Dorm had grown to kind of like this jovial man with his numerous chins. He wasn't too pushy for information, and never really pried into their personal business. In other circumstances Dorm might have been happy to have him along. Their group was certainly better protected with them around, and inns and hostels were always much happier to see such a large group.

But Dorm knew that it would come to an end eventually, and it would go back to being just the questers. Dorm was feeling somewhat ambivalent about that day. He would be glad to be free of their companions, and having to watch what he said, but he would also miss them a little. They had proven useful.

Thoughts of who the next two questers might turn out to be filled his mind. There didn't seem to be any particular pattern to it. There was royalty, military officers, traders, police officers, criminals, labourers, soldiers and accountants. No one occupation or level of society was exclusively represented or indeed excluded. The possibilities of who the next two might be were almost endless. For all they knew it could be the Sultan himself.

Presumably though there would be one man and one woman. That had seemed to be the only constant. It made a certain sense. It kept thing balanced.

Dorm had only met a few Kiamans, as they didn't seem to be the travelling type. He had visited the country once, when he was in his early teens. Some important conference that his father had attended. He really only remembered having a bevy of young women waiting on him, and wishing he could cool down. It had been summer though, and he imagined that winter was much milder. The young women though, had seemed unphased by the heat. Their flowing robes of many colours seemed to keep them cool. Their eyes had shone like a jewels; that was another thing he remembered distinctly. It had seemed that a few of them had been interested in him. He hadn't done anything of course. Not just because he hadn't wanted to make a diplomatic incident. Ah youth. The time when all the horrible realities of ones life began to reveal themselves.

He remembered that the Kiamans he had met had always seemed polite and friendly, and eager to please. He had heard tales of their skills in battle. The occasional family feuds that would result in battles on the desert sands were legendary. Their skills with the bow and their curved swords, made them welcome additions to any Alliance army.

Everyone had loosened his or her clothes off a little to reduce the heat. The wind still blew gently, and that helped. Water would be their main concern as they headed deeper into the country, both for themselves, and their mounts. Dorm knew of the Kiaman skill at finding water in the desert. He didn't know the details; that was apparently some sort of secret ability kept within families. But however they did it, he knew he would be grateful. Many centuries ago wells and small stores had been built all throughout the arid region, to supply travellers with the precious commodity. Nowadays they were vital to the maintenance of the country's' trade networks. As well as the survival of the semi nomadic families that still roamed the sands.

The group travelled on in relative silence. A few quiet conversations being had here and there. There wasn't a great deal to talk about though. They were simply moving to the next place they would stay. They didn't expect to find their next companions out here. There were only occasional Kiaman travellers, mostly traders or herdsmen. They wore their amulets out again, in case one of their targets did happen to pass by, though the chances of that so soon after their entering the country were fairly slim. Most of the travellers on the road were from other Alliance countries. He recognised a few Zigans, and Ambakans, Several Tagradians and even a few Lugemallans. He tried to hide his face a little from them, in case they recognised him. It wasn't very likely. Lugemall was a big place, though he had attended innumerable functions and ceremonies during the last ten years or so, and his official portrait hung in more than a few places.

Trade seemed to be booming in Kiama Mor at the moment. This was generally a good thing, though Dorm worried a little that this might attract the attentions of more Peldraksekhr agents. That would not have been good. The trouble in Tagradas had been difficult enough to deal with. He wondered how it could be dealt with in Kiama Mor. One thing on their side was that the Kiamans were much more suspicious of outsiders, even other Alliance nations on occasion. In some ways this was not a good thing. In others; this situation included, it presented the possibility that it would make things harder for the Peldraksekhr. Which was not something Dorm was opposed to.

As the evening approached they neared a large hostel beside the highway. It was a sprawling, walled affair. Its walls were all made of mud brick, and had an ancient appearance, as if the buildings had been standing since the beginning of time, and would continue to do so until its end. Several trees provided shade in the paved courtyard area. A few other guests were enjoying the coolness of the breeze on the various wide verandas. They watched quietly as their horses were stabled, and then entered the main building.

They were escorted to their rooms, which were in one of the larger wings, in the west of the compound. They were provided with water and small fruits to cool them down. Everyone relaxed in the cool, dim rooms While Dorm went for a brief walk around. He felt the need to be alone for a brief moment. The lights were being lit as the sun continued to set. People were starting to make their way inside for the evening meal. Crickets began to chirp somewhere.

He found a place where he could climb up beside the wall. It was probably originally a defensive platform, where archers and pike men could have fought from. Now it was just a lookout post. Good for keeping an eye on the desert and detecting the giant sandstorms that occasionally swept across the dunes.

He sat pensively for a while, staring out across the now quite arid landscape watching the shadows lengthen. In the distance a range of high rocky hills dominated the view, though now they were beginning to become shadowed. It was quite different here. More 'dramatic', his father would have said. He heard a step on the wood behind him. Mac.

“You okay?” he asked quietly.

"Yes I'm okay," Dorm replied. "Just thinking."

"Its very different out there to what I'm used to." Mac said looking out across the scenery. "I've never been to a desert before. It's kind of beautiful, in a bleak sort of way."

"Yes it is," Dorm agreed. "It will change a lot more though before we reach the capital."

"Yes, Telly was telling me earlier today."

There was silence for a few moments.

"They're serving dinner in the common room. Everyone else was heading that way when I came to find you."

"Probably best I eat something I guess. I'm not all that hungry though."

"You've been thinking too much again by the sounds of it."

"I do that a lot. Even more so lately."

"I've noticed," Mac said putting his arms around Dorms shoulders. "Come on. You might not be, but I am hungry."

The weather remained good as they continued westward. Their travelling companions continued to accompany them, with their usual charm. As they proceeded along the highway small towns and villages would spring up every so often, some on the highway, some just off to the sides. The people all seemed cautious yet polite.

They arrived at the city of Suaabar around midday on their third day in Kiama Mor. It was a large, low walled affair, with many low, sprawling buildings. Again most of them were mud brick, and ancient. There seemed to be a great many markets in the city, all filled with large open aired tents of various hues. They bustled not only with merchants and traders but with locals, travellers and camels. Dorm had never seen a camel before, and his first sight of one was not particularly endearing. He had heard about their apparent grumpiness, and wasn't really interested in having to fight his mount all the way through the country. The doe eyed stares that the animals gave them as they passed seemed to reinforce his dislike of them.

They stayed in another large sprawling inn complex on the southern side of the city. Since they had a few hours they decided to go on another one of their reconnaissance walks to the local market square.

They broke up into smaller groups in order to appear less conspicuous. The weather was warm, and the breeze that occasionally blew through the city, while welcome, was hardly enough to make them comfortable.

Dorm, Mac and Telly walked slowly through the market, examining the various goods that were on display, and keeping an eye out to all the various peoples that were about. There were merchants from just about every country in the Alliance. Dorm even noticed a few Szugabar, distinctive in their linen headdresses.

"Can I help you with anything Miss," said one merchant to Telly as she examined some leather goods displayed at the stall they were passing.

"Oh no, not really," she said. "I was just admiring the workmanship."

"They are only three half crowns a piece."

"Three!" She said incredulously.

"I'm afraid it is the season Miss," the merchant apologised. "The clans come to town around this time of year, and they usually have a high need of all leather goods. They have the money to buy most of them before we can even get set up properly."

"Well, alright, but three?"

"It will be the same all over Miss."

"Lucky we aren't in the market then," Mac said quietly to her.

"Indeed," she said, She turned back to the merchant. "Thank you noble merchant. May you have success this day." She flashed him one of her killer smiles.

Once they had all gathered back at the inn, they all reported similar stories, that the merchants were all talking about the clans. No real information about possible undiscovered questers, but also nothing that might suggest any Peldraksekhr anywhere in town.

Damak claimed that he had some business to do in town and wouldn't be ready to leave till the day after next. They all decided that it would be best to wait and ride out with their extra large group, and that the rest would do them good. Dorm hoped it might also allow them to see more of the transient local population and therefore have more opportunity to identify any potential questers.

Kiama Mor was a much warmer and humid place than any of

them were used to, and Dorm slept fitfully that night. The thin sheets provided seemed to just make him hotter as he lay in the narrow double bed next to Mac. Several times he awoke and had to drink the cool water from the pitcher on the dresser. It didn't really cool him down a great deal, but he did feel better. The air outside did cool down considerably, and at some point during the night the heat finally left the buildings and they were able to sleep more soundly.

Their full day in Suaabar was spent much the same as the afternoon before. There were a great many market places and merchant houses in the city, and they tried to at least pass most of them. There were a great many sights to be seen. Jugglers entertained crowds, and once there was even a dance troupe; the women dressed in flowing robes and gyrating wildly to the beat of the music.

Dorm, Mac and Telly had decided to stop for a meal at a small shop next to the central market place. They sat at a table near the street watching a group performing a play. Music played in the background there was a great deal of noise from all the haggling.

" Not a very productive day," Telly said fanning herself in the heat.

"Well we can't expect miracles," Dorm relied philosophically. "We are only in one city. There is the whole rest of the country."

"Still if this prophecy wants us to find these people you'd think it would at least help a little."

"What would you like it to tell you?"

"Peoples address would be nice," she said unenthusiastically.

"Something seems to have helped in the past." Mac laid his chin on his arms. "We have had a lot of luck in finding people. Artur and both Cal and Tissie."

"I've been trying to see if I could find the Rangers chapterhouse here, but I'm not sure where to look." Dorm admitted glumly.

"Not that they would probably be much help," Mac said equally pessimistically. "Back in Lanak Cal they seemed fairly confident that we were doing just fine, bumbling along the way we are."

"Yes well they aren't *on* this quest are they," Telly said in an irritated voice.

Dorm sat waiting for their food to arrive and looked around the square. The large palace, if it could be called that, of the local margrave stood on the far side. Several onion shaped domes surmounted it, and Dorm began wondering how such things were built. He let his mind and his eyes wander over the square and the faces they milled around.

It was a moment before he realised that he had spotted Damak, as he walked briskly across the square.

Damak headed straight for the palace and went quickly up the broad steps to the entrance colonnade. He spoke briefly with one of the guards, before heading inside. Curious. Why would a merchant need to go into the palace. There couldn't be a great deal that the margrave would want to talk to him about.

"Damak just went into the palace," he informed them.

"Why would he go in there?" Telly asked leaning forward.

"I have no idea," Dorm admitted. "I can't really think of a reason."

"What do you think it means?" Mac said warily.

"I don't know. But I'm not sure it's good. I suppose it could be something innocent."

"Perhaps we should ask him?" Telly said with a slight menace in her voice.

"Perhaps," Dorm mused. As they watched Damak came out of the palace. He was carrying a roll of parchment, which seemed to have an official looking wax seal on it. Damak read from the scroll, his face serious. A slight smile played across his face.

He rolled up the parchment and walked quickly off.

"Come on," Dorm said quickly standing and putting some coins on the table. "I want to see where he goes."

Where he went was just back to their inn.

That didn't make much sense. If he were up to no good why would he go there? This only seemed to add to the puzzle.

"Should we tell the others do you think?" Mac asked as they stood outside the inn.

Dorm thought for a moment. "No I think we should keep this between the three of us. At least for the moment. No sense in worrying everyone needlessly, when we really don't know what's going on."

"Perhaps we should confront him about it? It's not like we were spying on him or anything," Telly suggested defensively.

"Perhaps," Dorm contemplated the situation carefully. "I think though that we should watch him. Perhaps he'll mention it, and it will turn out to be something innocent."

Of course there was no mention of it.

They headed out fairly early in the morning, but Damak seemed his normal jovial self. He didn't mention anything about his trip to the palace, nor did he say anything about plans having changed, or indeed anything that might indicate that things were going to change. He seemed to be acting as if everything were completely normal. Dorm, Mac and Telly exchanged the occasional wary glances at each other, as they tried to figure out what might be going on. No one else seemed to notice any changes, and indeed some of Damaks' companions even seemed to be opening up more to them.

They headed westward and the terrain grew even more arid. The few trees that still grew thinned out even more, and the landscape became more rocky and sandy. The highway was still well defined and maintained and every so often there were stopping stations where horses could be watered and shelter sought. Small towns and villages continued to appear, but they too grew fewer in number the further west they went.

They continued their slow journey along the highway for another few days. The scenery by then had changed dramatically. Sand now seemed to dominate the landscape. The mountains that were still visible on the horizon appeared to be just huge piles of rock, and the whole landscape seemed to shimmer slightly in the hot air. While the temperature had certainly risen, Dorm got the feeling that it could go a lot higher. He was glad that they were heading into winter and not summer. The weather should remain mainly fine, the nights would be very cold, but hopefully the days wouldn't get too hot.

They passed a large ruined fortress just before midday on their third day of travel from Suaabar. It wasn't much really. Just a few scattered crumbling walls, and the remains of a large keep. The vacant window and door spaces gaped at them like mouths and eyes, scrutinising their passage.

Two days later they crested a low rise in the landscape and saw in the distance the great city of Kiama Mor. It's many domes and minarets easily distinguishable from this distance. It would still take several hours to reach it, and the traffic on the highway would increase, since several other satellite towns and villages all featured roads leading into the capital.

When they finally approached the city gates, they were checked by the guardsmen and ushered in under the great yellow stone lintel. It was inscribed with complicated patterns and bore words in the ancient Kiaman language. While this language had since been superseded by the standard language of the Alliance, it was still taught at the university and certain other institutions.

The city beyond was a chaotic affair. Much like most capitals. People thronged about on their business and horses, camels and carts seemed to be everywhere. There were clearly people from all over the Alliance, but there also seemed to be a great number of the nomads, distinctive in their heavy looking flowing robes.

They wound their way through the streets to an inn in a quiet area of the city not too far from the Lugemall embassy. Dorm had planned to briefly visit the embassy in order to send a letter home to his father. He hoped however that he wouldn't be recognised.

The day was very warm and rather late by the time they had settled so it was decided to leave their investigations until the following day, when they could make an early start.

Kiama Mor was a very different city to any other in the Alliance. While there were many things that were similar, a palace, barracks, embassies and the like, they all had a difference. Most of the important buildings were large but seemed to have little or no windows as was normal in most other places. While the exteriors were elaborately decorated with relief carvings, frescoes of even mosaics, there seemed to be little in the way of a view.

Dorm later remembered this was because most buildings contained a large open central courtyard that usually contained gardens. It meant that the heat from the sun was reduced, and had less effect on the rooms inside. Every so often a breeze would billow out the bright canvas awnings that covered some of them.

The streets were broad and palm trees waved lazily in the air above them. Birds circled around and twittered loudly when they landed. There was a certain amount of dust that seemed to always float about the air. The streets were for the most part unpaved, and so a lot of dust was kicked up during a day of normal civic activity.

Dorm managed to get his letter sent off at the embassy without being recognised. At one stage he had to be extremely careful, when the Ambassador himself, one Baron Lan Camir, passed by. Camir was a career diplomat, and Dorm had had various meetings with him over the years. He knew that the letter itself wouldn't attract attention, since it was addressed to a secret name that was known only to his father and his inner circle of advisers. The name on it was fairly ordinary, but was in fact an anagram of his fathers name.

They visited various markets and public places in the hopes of seeing any one with an amulet. Artur, Lianna and Cal Makor also reported that they had visited the outskirts of the great Open Market; the massive area just outside the walls where all the nomadic clans would gather. They had decided it was too big to properly search on their own, and several of the larger clans had yet to arrive.

All in all the day was fairly uneventful.

That evening they gathered in the common room of the wing of the inn they were staying in and discussed the day. They compared their findings and where they had been. No one had seen any one with an amulet. Dorm, Telly and Mac had still been worrying about Damak and his side trip. There had still been no mention of it, and Dorm was at a loss as what to do about it.

"Perhaps you should consider going to the Sultan?" Travanos said. "He at least might be able to start something to find out for us."

"I'd like to avoid that if possible," Dorm told him. "Ojliamz Kanuza is a man who prides himself on his hospitality and generosity to others. If we go to the palace to seek his help we'll probably end up being stuck here for a month."

"But we would probably end up finding the next questers," Rhynavell pointed out positively.

"Yes and then there would have to be a celebration of that, so we'd end up stuck here for another week on top," Dorm replied pessimistically. "I think for just now we continue as we are."

"What about the Rangers?" Artur asked. "We might be able to enlist their help."

"Oh I think we can avoid that," Mac said sarcastically. "I'm not sure I want to sit through any of their riddles just now."

"I might be able to make some discreet enquiries if you'd like," Zacravia volunteered. "It may not be what we're used to but it might give us something. If these amulets have been seen they may be on somebody's list."

"You know criminals in Kiama Mor?" Harmia asked him seriously.

"Only a few," he admitted. "And most of those are originally from other countries."

"It might be worth it to follow all these leads," Telly said. "Cast our net as wide as we possibly can."

"Why couldn't we go to the police?" Tissievilla said suddenly.

Tissie hadn't said much during their journey through Kiama Mor. The heat had seemed to affect her the most. She had remained mostly quiet during the days, and seemed to drink a lot more. Rhynavell had once described her as 'wilting like a week old petunia'.

"Why would we do that?" Lianna asked her.

"Well perhaps we could say that we had had an amulet stolen from us or something. If the local police, or whatever they have here, are looking for us as well, perhaps we might find it."

They all paused for a moment.

No one was quite sure of what to make of a rather intelligent suggestion coming from Tissievilla.

"Well I'm not sure saying that it was stolen would be the way to go, but it's worth looking into," Dorm reluctantly said.

"What about saying that they are a long lost relative or something," Makor suggested.

"That would sound better," Telly agreed. "They wouldn't get arrested then."

"Yes, getting someone arrested probably isn't the best way to introduce ourselves."

"That sounds like a good idea," Dorm decided. "Well done, Tissie."

She beamed at him.

Inwardly he shuddered.

They chatted for a while longer in the room, thinking about retiring. There was a polite rapping at the door.

"Come in," Dorm said curiously.

The door was opened and Damak entered. "Good evening all," he said. "Dormal since we are now in Kiama Mor, there is something I should tell you before we part ways tomorrow."

"Oh and what is that?"

"Well that would be that we are not entirely what we appear to be Your Highness,"

Everyone started at that. They had all been very careful not to say anything in front of Damak or his people that might give them away. Even Tissievilla had managed it. Obviously either something had slipped by unnoticed or...

Damak gave a short laugh, his face beaming. "I'm sorry to have startled you all, but the ruse was necessary, I'm afraid. His Majesty, King Corm Sanel didn't want you to be interrupted in your search. He felt that if you believed we were simple merchants that you could concentrate on your job at hand."

"Exactly who are you?" Travanos asked, quickly standing.

"My name is indeed Damak, Fleet Admiral. I am a member of His Majesty's Intelligence Service. After we received reports of some of the goings on of Peldraksekhr agents in western Tagradas, the King thought it prudent for you to have an escort at least part of the way. He didn't want a repeat of what happened in Batava. And the possibility that they might want to get back at you couldn't be excluded."

"Uncle Corm, you sly old fox," Dorm said grinning. "He sent you along to protect us?"

"Indeed Highness. The men who are accompanying me are a small elite squad in the army. A kind of personal guard for His Majesty in fact. He felt that it was only appropriate that he do something to keep you safe."

“I wouldn’t be surprised if my father had something to do with that,” Dorm said looking at Mac.

“I’m afraid I can’t speak to that Your Highness. All I can say is that His Majesty was concerned for your safety on this part of your journey. He would have preferred if we could have accompanied you further, but he didn’t want things to look suspicious.”

“Well we don’t want any Peldraksekhr to start getting ideas,” Lianna said.

“Precisely Ma’am,” He replied.

“So when we saw you go into the palace at Suaabar…?” Telly began.

“Oh you saw me? I must be slipping. I think perhaps I should return to the academy for a refresher course.” He said seriously, “I was receiving some instructions from His Majesty. I assure you it was nothing nefarious. I apologise if I had you worried.”

“We were a little concerned,” Mac admitted.

“Well I am very glad to have been able to allay you fears.” Damak turned to Dorm. “Your Highness, It has been my great pleasure to serve.” He bowed then shook Dorms hand.

“We thank you for your assistance Damak.” He told him genuinely.

The news that Damak and his entourage were actually soldiers made them all feel both gladdened and concerned. The fact that they had had protection for this section of their journey made them feel a sense of security, that if anything had gone wrong, they’d have been alright. The other side of that however was the knowledge that the next stage of their journey wouldn’t be as secure. Of course if they managed to find the two next questers then their group would be larger again, and therefore better protected.

Their discussions led them to the decision to indeed contact the local authorities and enlist their aid. It was also decided that a proper exploration of the Open Market should be made. The Gathering gave them the unique opportunity to seek for the questers amongst many of the clans, which would have been otherwise near impossible to locate and examine. Though the sheer number of people that were there made the task rather daunting.

Dorm returned the next day to the embassy and sent another letter, this time to Corm Sanel, thanking him for his assistance, but requesting that future bouts of such assistance should be made notice of before hand.

Their continued wanderings through the city were long and rather boring for the most part. There were so many people that they would never get to see, and the fact that the amulets could be held by just about any one didn't help narrow the search any.

The first day after Damak had left produced nothing other than sore feet, and some frustration. The central constabulary office had taken the information and said it would do it's best, but that in a city this size might make things difficult. And of course that didn't include any other cities.

The second day dawned somewhat cooler than the previous; a few clouds ran before a stiff breeze. Winter would definitely be rather mild here in Kiama Mor. Their vagrant wanderings continued again without much success. Dorm was beginning to feel despondent by midday when they stopped for a meal.

He, Mac and Telly plonked themselves down at some more outside tables at a bustling taproom facing a broad street. The commerce of the city continued loudly around them as they were served. They ordered a simple but nourishing broth and drinks, and relaxed while waiting. None of them felt much like talking. They knew that this random wandering was a long shot to find the next questers at best.

"You're a fool Ambra," said a loud voice from another table.

"You're the fool Pavahn if you can't see the value of it," said another heated voice.

Dorm looked across to the other table. Two men sat over the remains of a meal. They both wore the flowing robes typical of Kiamans, though one also wore a large leather belt and a small jerkin, also in leather.

"There is no way that you would get that much for them. The market is groaning with herd animals of every kind. Prices are lower everywhere."

"But these are quality animals," said the younger of the two men, who wore the leather. "Or does quality not matter these days. I thought you prided yourself on the quality of your merchandise?"

"I do!" The fat man said sternly sitting up quickly. "I care not for you insinuation Ambra."

"And I care not for being cheated, Pavahn," Ambra said angrily. "I was assured that my animals would be welcomed here and that you were interested. If that isn't the case, then I can only conclude that someone somewhere is lying."

"You go too far," Pavahn grimly leant forward. "If you persist in this talk, I will have no choice but to censure you."

"And if you persist in trying to cheat me I will have no choice but to tell everyone I can what you've been doing."

Pavahn paused for a moment thinking hard. Beads of sweat began to appear on his forehead. Dorm knew that reputation was a very important thing in Kiama Mor. That a person's reputation both opened and closed doors for him. The one called Pavahn stared hatefully at Ambra for a few moments, obviously calculating what kind of damage anything Ambra said could have on his business.

"Very well," he said his voice dripping with vitriol. He quickly reached inside his robe to some hidden pocket and pulled out a small sheaf of parchments. He quickly flicked through them and pulled one out, slapping it down on the table in from on Ambra, who had to quickly lean back to avoid being struck in the face. "Fill this out and bring it to my warehouse in the morning with the goods." He lent in close. "But after this we will have no more dealings." He straightened and stormed off.

At first it hadn't occurred to Dorm. He had been caught up in the moment. The anger of Pavahn had gotten the better of him. He was worried that something 'rough' as his father sometimes said might have developed. But then it registered in his mind. When Ambra had quickly lent back to avoid Pavahns' fist, his robe had parted slightly. He was wearing a heavy chain around his neck. One very similar to a certain piece of jewellery.

He threw a look at the others, whose faces informed him that they had noticed it as well.

"It couldn't be, could it?" Telly asked incredulously.

"We'll kick ourselves if it is, and we don't follow it up," Mac cautioned them.

"Alright then," Dorm said turning back.

Ambra was just rising from his seat and putting his money down on the table. As he moved the chain he was wearing swung out from his clothes. The sunlight catching on the fashioned crystal at its end.

"Well that settles that," Telly concluded.

They got quickly to their feet, also putting coins on the table.

Dorm closed the gap between their tables before Ambra had gone more than a few steps. "Excuse me friend," Dorm began. "Ambra is it?"

"Yes," Ambra replied cautiously. "Do I know you?"

"Ah no, but I'm wondering if I might be able to talk to you. It's rather important."

"Can it wait? I have some important business to attend to."

"Not really, no," Mac piped up.

"It won't take too long and it is extremely important," Telly said in that way of hers that made people stop whatever they were doing and look at her.

"What is it about," Ambra asked irritably.

"Oh, a lot of things," Dorm replied cryptically. "Things that may change your life forever."

Chapter 14

Ambra still seemed very wary of them as they moved off. Dorm could understand that. It wasn't every day that total strangers claimed to be about to completely change your life.

Ambra had told them sternly that there was something he had to do before he could talk with them. Something to do with his business. Dorm had thought about it for a moment and then decided that it was probably better to let him take care of it. If he didn't, it would be hanging over him and distracting him. They needed Ambras' full and undivided attention for what they were about to dump in his lap.

He led them several streets over to a whitewashed stone building that seemed to be some sort of commercial office. Traders came and went from the office. Ambra explained that this was the place where various traders picked up orders for goods that needed to be taken to various places from Kiama Mor. He went inside while they waited, seated at a long wooden bench along the wall. Telly fanned herself and leaned back against the wall.

"You are planning to go back to the inn I hope?" she asked in a voice that quickly told Dorm that if he hadn't decided to do that, then he better decide to quick smart.

"Yes of course," he responded honestly. "I don't really think it would be appropriate to discuss it anywhere else."

After about a quarter of an hour Ambra returned with a large sheaf of parchment in his hand. "I will have to take care of this first thing in the morning. So I hope this conversation isn't going to go for too long."

"Oh the conversation won't" Telly said whimsically, looking out across the dusty street.

"The aftermath may be a little different though," Mac said with a grin.

"Come on then," Dorm said getting to his feet. "No time like the present to disrupt someone's life, eh?" He clapped Ambra on the shoulder and headed off, Telly and Mac following.

Ambras' expression betrayed his concern. Though perhaps concern was not a strong enough description.

They headed back to the inn, and went to their rooms. Tissie hadn't gone out that day. It had looked too hot for her. And she had prepared a nice cool meal for them so it wasn't a total waste of time. Lianna and Artur had returned not long before they arrived. They of course hadn't found anything.

Not long after they arrived Travanos and Rhynavell returned from their wanderings. They had wanted to check in. It had been decided before hand that every few hours they should return to the inn, and see if any one had gotten any leads.

Dorm offered Ambra something to drink, which he warily accepted, and they all sat down to wait.

Dorm had agreed with Mac's suggestion that they should wait until everyone returned. It wasn't long before Harmia and Zacravia returned. Zacravia had tried to make contact with certain "elements" of Kiaman society and Harmia had obviously gone with him. While she did seem to be softening up towards him, talking to him often, and occasionally even laughing at his jokes, she never let him out of her sight. It was also possible however that she was taking the opportunity to learn more about the criminal mind. If nothing it would help her in the future.

Cal returned at the same time. He had been elected to talk to the police officials and keep up to date on their progress. Essentially it meant that he went from constabulary office to constabulary office with several pieces of paper, that he would show, and then have brief, rather boring and inevitably fruitless conversations with an officer.

Everyone partook of some of Tissies offerings, which made

everyone feel better after having trudged around the city in the heat all day. Then they got down to business.

"Ambra, I told you that there was something extremely important that I had to tell you," Dorm began. He tried to go a bit slower. He had felt that he had rushed into it the other times, and that that probably hadn't helped any of them accept the idea. At least not right away. "Well I've waited will now so that all of my friends here can be here when I tell you. Since they are all involved it saves me having to update them all later."

"That sounds fair," Ambra said. He was clearly still nervous.

"It's alright dear," Telly said, patting his hand with her own. "You can relax. Nothing bad is going to happen."

He didn't noticeably calm down any.

"Several months ago, my friends and I learned that we had been chosen to participate in something. Admittedly something that we hadn't expected, and something that we are still trying to come to grips with."

"You got that right," Cal said quietly.

"I notice that you have a crystal amulet."

"This?" Ambra pulled it from his shirt. "It is a family heirloom."

"Given to you on you sixteenth birthday by your father, yes we know."

"How?" He demanded to know.

"You see that we are all carrying them too."

"Yes, I do now," he said a little worriedly. "I must have been blind not to notice before."

"Actually, it doesn't surprise me at all, the way things have been going lately," Lianna said leaning back in her chair.

"Well we all have similar stories about our own amulets. They were given to us by either our mother or father on our sixteenth birthdays'."

"I'm guessing that there's some connection then?"

"He's quick." Zacravia said honestly. "That could come in handy,"

"The connection," Dorm continued. "Is a little stranger than you might at first think. You see these amulets all come from the same place, and seem to have the same meaning."

"Place? Meaning? What are you talking about?"

"Well that's the part that's going to change your life," Telly said seriously.

"Well what do they mean then?"

"They indicate that you are a part of this group. We are journeying around the Alliance looking for people with these amulets so that they can join our group. Once we have found everybody we have a task to perform."

"What task?"

"We don't know that yet," Dorm admitted to him.

"You don't know? Where are these thing from then?"

"The Fortress."

"The Fort..." he began. He looked around the room. "How do you know this?"

"We found some information. An old prophecy in fact. It had been written by someone at The Fortress."

"A prophecy?" He laughed loudly. "What kind of a fool do you take me for?"

"I'm serious," Dorm said without blinking.

Ambra looked slowly around the room. He took in the serious expressions, the looks of concentration. "You are serious aren't you?"

"Very serious," Travanos told him.

"These amulets indicate that we are a part of something. Something important. Something that is bigger than any of us. There is some great task that we have to perform, as a group. And you are a part of that group."

"We have been getting the feeling that it is something rather earth shaking. That there may be some very unfortunate outcomes if we don't do it," Artur explained in one of his rare speeches. "At least I have."

"I think we all have Artur," Dorm admitted. "You see Ambra, someone at The Fortress thought that this prophecy, whatever it is, was important enough to create these amulets and put them out into the families of people in all the kingdoms of the Alliance, a long time ago."

"How long ago?"

"Several thousand years we think. We have people doing research for us, they may turn up more information."

"What is it that we are supposed to do?" Ambra asked them seriously. "Just wander around the world until we find these people?"

"It seems to have worked so far," Lianna said with a laugh.

"It seems that fate, the universe; heck maybe even these Gods that the Szugabar worship are helping us. All we know is that so far, we have been in the right place at the right time to find everyone. Like we did with you today."

"I don't understand any of this," Ambra said putting his head in his hands.

"It does get easier," Rhynavell said. "Sort of."

"What am I supposed to do," Ambra said his face ashen.

"For the time being…" Dorm looked at the others. "Be yourself. We don't know what our task is yet. Presumably it will be revealed to us eventually. But for right now, our task is simply to find these other people with the amulets. Once we have them all, we'll go and get more instructions."

"And where will you get them?"

"We'll probably end up having to go ask the Rangers," Harmia said. "That's a depressing thought. It will probably take us a month to figure out where we have to go the way they talk."

"Rangers," Ambra looked suddenly horrified. "You have spoken to them?"

"Yes, several times," Mac confirmed.

"Don't worry friend," Travanos tried to reassure him. "It seems that the Rangers haven't been entirely honest about magic with everyone. It isn't really a disease like we've always been led to believe. You can't catch it."

"Are you sure?"

"Well none of us has come down with it yet," He explained. "And we have been in contact with a 'sufferer'. That was some weeks ago now."

"I get the feeling that they play some part in all of this. What exactly I don't know." Lianna said.

"I got that feeling too," Zacravia said. "It was almost like they wanted us to know the truth."

"Well I suppose if we encounter anybody who seems a bit 'that way' we will be able to help them," Artur said.

Dorm looked at their guest. "Sorry Ambra," he laughed. "We were just talking shop. We've all been at this a little while now, so we sometimes just run with it. We're still all trying to work out the details ourselves."

"I get the feeling that there is a lot more going on in the world than I am aware," he said in a quiet voice.

"A lot more than any of us is aware," Travanos agreed with him.

"The short of it is," Dorm continued, "that we need you to come with us. To help us on our journey. It seems that we will all have things to do along the way that will help us. If we don't all complete our tasks during this journey, then it's possible that whatever this task is, won't be successful."

"And this task is very important?"

"Apparently so. It seems to have to do with the survival of the Alliance itself. And it may have something to do with the Peldraksekhr."

"The Peldraksekhr?"

"Yes we've encountered several of their agents along the way."

"That would be important then," Ambra agreed. "I'm guessing I don't have much choice in this matter?"

"Not really no."

"We'll probably be still here for a few days to make sure that the other amulet holder here isn't in the city. So you'll have a few days to work things out. Sort out this business you have to do and organise yourself. Are you married at all?"

He looked at Dorm quickly then averted his eyes. A strange look briefly crossed his face. "No," he said shortly.

"Well that makes things a little easier."

"Exactly who are you people anyway?" Ambra asked after a moment.

"Oh yes. I knew I had forgotten something. Sorry about that. My name is Dormal."

"Like the Prince in Lugemall?"

"Ah yes actually," Dorm fixed him with a stare.

"Oh dear," Ambra said. He suddenly fell to his knees and bowed his head. "Your Highness."

"Oh get up. I'm off duty at the moment. There isn't any need for ceremony. We're far too busy for it anyway."

Ambra slowly returned to his seat. He seemed a little wild-eyed when he looked at them

"That's better. Now for the rest of my friends."

Dorm's introductions went well. He allowed Ambra time to take each name on board before he went to the next. He seemed a little wary of the more 'important' members of the group, but seemed to relax a little more when he realised that most of them were just ordinary people like himself. He seemed to make a connection with Artur and Cal, both of them were 'working' people and so was he.

That night they stayed talking for a while. Ambra left to go back to his inn fairly early. He said he intended to go to sleep right away. Dorm didn't doubt his sincerity.

"And now we are twelve," Mac said quietly to Dorm as Ambra left the room.

"Hmmm," Dorm agreed. "Only this many more to go."

Mac looked around the room at their companions. "We're going to have to start getting bigger rooms."

The next morning Dorm, Mac and Telly, accompanied by Rhynavell rose early and went to the inn that Ambra was lodged in. They had decided it would be best to go there and make sure he hadn't decided to sneak off during the night. It turned out that he hadn't. They accompanied him as he completed the business he had arranged for that morning and then returned with him to his inn. There they discussed their journey. They explained that eventually they would leave Kiama Mor and most likely head north. Though there was the possibility of them having to journey to Szugabar.

Ambra seemed reluctant at first to want to travel, complaining that his business would not be looked after properly if he was to leave it, but eventually he seemed to realise that he didn't have any choice.

He left the rooms he had been staying in and moved into rooms at their inn. Dorm had insisted on this, ostensibly so that they could continue to tell him what he needed to know before they left. Really

Dorm just wanted to be able to keep an eye on him.

They explained to him all about the prophecy and what it had said. They briefly sketched in their adventures since leaving Lugemall City, including their run in with the Peldraksekhr agents posing as merchants.

Their stories about the Rangers seemed to shock him a little. Dorm could understand that. The Rangers had the reputation of being somewhat 'unclean' due to their association with the magically afflicted. The stories about it being an illness, despite having been told the truth, meant that the feelings were hard to shake.

To his credit Ambra seemed to take it all fairly well. He agreed to go with them, and that had always been the biggest hurdle.

That night Dorm had a dream. A different dream than his normal one. He stood in a crowded place. A market maybe. There were people bustling all around him. But they were hazy and indistinct. He could tell that they were people but that was about all. It was like being surrounded by ghosts. They flitted and spun around him with great speed, seeming to stop every so often and interact with each other. But even when they stopped he couldn't tell if they were men or women, or even if they were human.

He knew there was somewhere he had to go. But he didn't know where. He turned around looking for something that might reveal where he was, and what he should do. But alas there were only the hazy ghosts and a wavering indistinct landscape.

He woke with a start, a sick feeling in his stomach and a spinning head. He crossed warily to the night stand and poured some water from the pitcher. He drank quickly, keeping his eyes tightly shut.

There was a step behind him.

"I'm alright," he said reassuringly. "Just give me a moment."

Mac came close and held him. "I don't like this."

The following day Dorm decided that he needed the guidance of the Rangers for this. He and Mac moved through the streets till they came to the chapterhouse. It was another large affair, similar in layout to the one in Lanak Cal. They were escorted to a small but airy office that overlooked the central courtyard. They were greeted by an aged man with a short grey beard and a heavily lined, but rather gentle face. He was introduced as Master Geven.

"Noble Quester," he said rising and bowing to them as they entered. "You do this chapterhouse great honour by your visit."

"I needed some answers to some questions," Dorm began.

Geven's eyes looked distant for a moment. "Your dreams. Yes. Please sit. I can assure you that they are necessary."

"That's as maybe, but what do they mean?"

"They are…" Geven began warily. "Signposts."

"Signposts?" Mac looked at Dorm.

"Yes. They will provide meaning for you. If you take the time to listen to them properly."

"I can't understand anything about them. The one I had last night was confusing, disorienting. It made me feel ill."

Geven thought for a moment. "It is possible that something has been missed. Wait here a moment." He stood up and left the room. He returned shortly accompanied by a woman also wearing a Rangers cloak. Her cloak however was embroidered with a different symbol than the silver star that apparently denoted a Master.

She stood next to Dorm. "Your Highness, please stand," she said quietly.

He stood slowly and faced her. She reached out both her hands and placed her fingers gently on his temples. At first nothing happened, and he began to feel rather foolish standing here like this.

Suddenly as if something had given way, his mind seemed to open. That was the only way he could describe it. Sensations, feelings, thoughts, emotions, images all suddenly rushed through his mind. Sounds, smells, colours. Several faces blurred past, seeming to merge one to the other so quickly that he didn't have time to focus on any one of them.

All of a sudden the image from the dream came sharply to his mind. It seemed to pause. The image rotated slowly. The figures were still blurred and indistinct, but they now seemed motionless. He clearly saw himself in the dream. Almost as if he were looking at his dream from someone else's viewpoint.

The image from his dream slowly rotated around until it had

returned to where it had started from. At that instant a sudden rush of crazed images and sounds blurred past him and then he was standing back in the airy office.

He would have fallen if Mac hadn't caught him.

"What did you do to him?" Mac demanded.

The woman turned to Geven. She held her hand out to him, and he placed his hand against hers. They both closed their eyes for a moment. When they opened them again, they bowed to each other. "Thank you Sister." Geven said quietly.

She turned back to Dorm. "It has been the greatest honour of my service to meet you Noble Quester. I thank thee." She bowed gracefully to him then left, her feet making no noise.

Geven handed Dorm a cup of water. "Your dreams are troubling you because they have been forced upon you. You should not have had a dream this intense. Something is trying to disturb the natural flow of things."

"What things?" Mac asked angrily. "What is forcing these dreams?"

"That I may not say. But you should rest for a day or two before you continue on your way. You have time to wait before proceeding."

"Well I'm glad you think so," Dorm said wearily.

"I know that this is frustrating for you Your Highness," Geven said genuinely, leaning forward. "But if I was to reveal too much, your quest would be put in danger. And we cannot afford that."

"So are we just supposed to wait here for a few days, is that it?"

Geven thought for a moment. "There is someone who will tell you something that may lead you to more questers. *If* you are open enough to listen."

"More cryptic clues?" Dorm disgustedly remarked.

"Perhaps not so cryptic as you might think. But said in passing perhaps."

"Come on Mac, let's go."

They rose and headed towards the door.

"Your Highness!" Geven said moving over to them. He looked quickly at Mac. "I am sorry."

"Sorry about what?"

He paused. “All the things that must come to pass that will cause you pain. All of you. It is not our desire to hurt you. If we could, we would gladly, even eagerly explain all to you. But we are constrained, as are those from whom we receive our instructions. Please try to keep that in mind.”

“I know that you Rangers are genuine when you say that,” Dorm assured him. “But honestly… it doesn’t really make it any easier.”

“I know,” Geven said his face ashen. “And for that too we are sorry.”

The group decided that indeed it would be a good idea to rest for a day or two. Nobody really liked the idea of heading onwards if one of their group was unwell. Cal returned that afternoon from his daily update with the constabulary. Again they had nothing to report.

Dorm retired early that night and rose late. He felt much better. But the dream still disturbed him. He couldn’t shake the feeling that it would come back. None of the previous dreams had made him feel physically ill. They had made him feel uncomfortable. Even a little scared. But this was something new.

They continued to tell Ambra of what had happened to them on their journey and where they thought it might yet take them. They also discussed at some length what this whole journey might have been about. Of course none of them truly knew. It was all mere speculation. But it seemed to help to talk about possibilities. At least when they did find out they would have at least considered it.

Dorm continually went back over the experiences at the chapterhouse in his mind. He tried to focus on all the images he had seen in his mind. He went back over what Geven had said, trying to make sense of it all.

He knew that Geven had been honest in his apologies. It didn’t help him understand any of it, but at least he knew that if things were different Geven would explain it all to him.

The next day Dorm decided to go out into the city. Mac protested a little, but in the end relented. He, Telly and Rhyn walked to several markets to see if they could get any inspiration. The likelihood of the second quester, most likely a woman, being here in the capital itself was remote. But they couldn't ignore the possibility.

The weather continued to be warm but pleasant. The nights seemed to be growing colder, but the days were still sunny and bright. Everyone was getting a little restless. So it was clearly time to move on.

But which way.

Dorm was of two minds. He was confident that they would find more members in both Ojliam and Bydanushev. But he couldn't be sure about Szugabar. The total number of people they needed to find was twenty-five. So it was definitely possible. But the thought of a long journey directly into the desert wasn't particularly appealing.

They had stopped in a large square in the north of the city to watch some travelling entertainers performing ballads and poems. It was a pleasant distraction, but that was all. A distraction. After it had finished they realised it was getting late and that they should probably head back to the inn. They walked slowly back taking the time to observe all the passers by.

They were heading along one of the main streets of the city when it happened.

Dorm had been careful to avoid him so far, but this time there was no opportunity. Baron Lan Camir the Lugemallan ambassador that Dorm had taken great pains to hide from while in the city, came out of a building just ahead of them. He was obviously heading back to the embassy. At first Dorm didn't see him, he was busy listening to Rhyn at the time. Camir however most definitely saw him.

"Your Highness?" He called out incredulously. "What in the name of the Fortress are you doing in Kiama Mor?"

"Ah Baron Camir," Dorm replied with a measure of false interest. "Just here on family business. Nothing involving the country."

"Well I must say this is quite a surprise. I hadn't heard anything about you travelling abroad."

"My father thought it best to keep it quiet, what with it being a private matter and all."

"Oh yes of course," the ambassador agreed. "If there's anything I can do to help…"

"Oh, I think we have it under control for the moment, but thank you for the offer."

"Where exactly are you off to next, if I may enquire?"

"Well that is still a matter of some debate actually."

"If you have the time, I'm sure my wife would like to have you visit for dinner. She never gets the chance to visit the palace much these days, since I'm in various embassies for years at a time. She would appreciate the courtly company."

"That's a very generous offer Your Excellency…" Dorm began.

"Wonderful, well I can escort you there myself."

"What luck," Dorm responded with a sense of impending doom.

"You know it is most fortuitous that I saw you today," the ambassador continued as they walked.

"Oh, why is that?"

"Well in a few days my wife and I will be leaving to attend the Great Festival in Szugabar. We would have missed you."

"What a shame that would have been."

"Which festival is this Your Excellency?" Mac asked curiously.

"The yearly renewal festival My Lord," Camir explained. Many people in official circles had taken to calling Mac 'Lord' when they spoke to him. While technically Mac had no official rank, Dorm tried to encourage people to think of him as 'Lord'. Mac himself hated being called it. So Dorm delighted in using it. Often. "It is a grand occasion to be sure. Much feasting and their quaint religious ceremonies. Many of them are quite beautiful."

"Is this the same festival that lead to the invasion?" Rhyn asked.

"I'm afraid so," Camir informed her regretfully. "It's one of the reasons I'm going actually. A minor part of our continuing penance I suppose. As the nearest official Lugemallan ambassador I am required to attend. I don't mind so much. I just wish it wasn't so hot."

Everyone knew the general story of course. How millennia ago the mistaken belief that one of the Szugabarian religious ceremonies involved human sacrifice had lead to a near genocidal war, in which the Alliance was the aggressor. Once the truth had been realised, the Alliance had quickly sued for peace. Eventually it had lead to the Szugabar gaining partial membership in the Alliance. It was perhaps the sorriest chapter in the history of the Alliance.

"I've heard that the ceremonies are quite uplifting," Telly said conversationally.

"That they are My Lady," he agreed. "As I said many of them are very beautiful. It is a splendour to see." He thought for a moment. "Your Highness. This may be a bold suggestion of me. But I have an idea, if it doesn't interfere with your purpose here of course."

"Oh and what would that be?" Dorm asked him fearfully.

"Well, your fathers' government has been trying for some time now to expand trading opportunities with Szugabar. If the Crown Prince were to accompany me during my attendance, it may well go a long way to making them consider our offers."

"I'm not sure, Your Excellency." Dorm said trying to dodge the idea. "We still have things to do here."

"As I said, Your Highness, we won't be leaving for several days yet. I have some important meetings the next few days so I won't be able to interfere with your reason for being here. But it would be a great opportunity for our country."

"Well in that case how can I refuse?" Dorm felt rather deflated right then.

"Wonderful, Your Highness. I'll have to speak with the ship master in the port, but I'm certain that it won't pose too much of a problem."

"Ship master?" Telly asked.

"Oh yes. We travel by land to the port of Hamij, and then sail across the Desert Sea to Szugabar. It takes much less time than going the whole way by road."

"How long would we be there?" Mac enquired. "We still have other things to do around here and we wouldn't want to get caught by winter anywhere."

"Oh only a few days, a week at the most," Camir explained. "The whole festival goes for just over two weeks, but we only need to attend certain parts of it."

"It sounds like an interesting time."

"Oh it will be. The significance of some of their religious ceremonies are lost on me I'm afraid, but they still are interesting to watch. I'm not sure why the Fortress tolerates their religion, it seems rather strange to me, but they seem to know what they're doing."

"Perhaps there is some reason we don't know about," Mac said.

Dorm thought about it. Perhaps there was some reason, other than the purely political one resulting from the war. Maybe it also had something to do with this damned quest. Perhaps Szugabar would be the easiest country to locate the questers in, due to this religion. Dorm had noticed that the questers had been hard to find because the amulets were just 'family heirlooms'. Apparently nothing of any great significance. It was possible that in a place where a religion still functioned they might be regarded as something more important.

Perhaps this side trip to Szugabar would be a blessing in disguise.

Chapter 15

Baron Camir insisted that they all now stay at the embassy.

Of course he didn't realise how big their party actually was.

When he found out it sent the staff at the embassy into a flurry. Where exactly were they going to put twelve extra people? Not to mention their horses. To their credit though they managed it. Several people had to share, which wasn't a huge issue for them, since they'd been sharing rooms in various inns. But there seemed to be this unspoken attitude amongst the staff and indeed by the the Ambassador himself that they had somehow failed them.

They were treated as royalty, which was obviously fitting with Dorms' presence. But he didn't really like it. He was worried that this little break from their journey might disrupt the flow of things. They had seemed to have gained a momentum of late. Dorm didn't want to lose that.

They were treated to a formal dinner that evening. Various merchant barons in Kiama Mor at the time, as well as several officials from the Kiaman government attended. There was all the usual dancing and frivolities as well as the tiresome questions to Dorm about his presence here. He managed to evade most of them with cryptic answers about a personal matter, much as he had with the ambassador; some however gave clear indication that they didn't believe him, and thought that he was up to something 'official' for the king. Others clearly showed that they had no real interest in his real reason for being here, they simply wanted to try and get information out of him as to what they might expect in their future dealings with the government.

Dorm slogged his way through the evening, listening to all the tedious conversations, monotonous stories, and decidedly humourless jokes. There were occasional snatches of conversation that actually managed to pique his interest, due to his knowledge of circumstances back home, but even they had a tendency to be quickly swallowed up by the self interest of the speaker. He hated every minute of it. But he knew he had to do it. Mac of course managed to save him from some of the worst of the night, by interrupting him just at the right moments. Mac and gotten to know exactly when Dorm was sick of a particular person and had just the right level of tact to politely extract him from the nauseatingly sycophantic so and so, without giving offence. At least not too much anyway.

The night ended a little later than Dorm would have liked. He still felt a little weary from the events of the night before. But he managed to leave at just the right time to force everyone to leave before they could get too rowdy. He was the guest of honour after all.

The next few days were generally fairly quiet. The ambassador had various duties to perform so for most of the day he was busy. His wife, a woman of only minor social standing back home, who none-the-less was known for her great beauty, also seemed quite busy and it appeared that over the years her husband had been a diplomat she had decided that if she ever wanted to see him for any length of time she had best insert herself into his work. She seemed quite capable, and would often recall things that the Baron himself had forgotten. He didn’t seem to need an appointment diary either.

Most of their belongings remained packed. It had seemed rather pointless to get everything out and then just have to put it away again. The staff at the embassy included tailors and dressmakers, and they had managed to whip up suitable attire for the few days that they would be there. Dorm didn't mind getting new clothes, but he did worry about where they were going to carry them all.

Finally the day of their departure arrived and they left the embassy fairly early in the morning. The journey through the streets was uneventful as it was early enough that the city hadn’t really gotten going yet. They left the city by the west gate and headed out into the arid landscape on another well-maintained highway.

The Baron seemed to enjoy travelling. He chatted happily to Dorm as they rode along. And he seemed to smile all the time. For someone who had been raised in the lush countryside of Lugemall, he seemed to take a great joy in this arid, rugged landscape.

They stopped beside the highway for a midday meal, served by the members of his retinue, and they stopped that night in one of the hostels that were stationed along all the Alliances highways for that purpose. The manager of the hostel flew into a flustered whirlwind of activity when he found out how many people he would be having stay. That Kiaman desire to please guests was obviously making him work his hardest, but Dorm felt a little sorry for him having so many people descend on him all at once.

They were treated that night to entertainment by a troupe of travelling dancers and musicians. The dancers seemed to know exactly the right moves, and struts that were provocative to everyone, no matter what they were in to. Their costumes contained a great deal of shimmering fabrics as well as gold chains and even bells.

The next morning they left fairly early and continued on their way. The Baron explained that it would take nearly a week to reach the port at the mouth of the River Pojdram. Dorm didn't know much about this part of the world, having never travelled here before, and so the Baron explained a few things to him, about the geography.

"The Desert Sea is very large," he explained. "It's nearly the same size as Lugemall."

"That is fairly substantial," Dorm agreed.

"And of course being fed by rivers means that the water is all fresh. So we don't have to worry about salt spray getting into everything."

"None of that briny smell then?" Mac asked.

"Exactly," the Baron replied. "Which makes it a much more pleasant trip I can assure you. The Desert Sea never gets as rough as the open ocean, since there storms don't have the chance to build up."

"And Szugabar is on the far side, right?"

"Correct. They've lived there for thousands of years. They have temples that are as old as Lugemall itself. Long before we built cities.

And their mausoleums! Dear me they are magnificent. Great pointy edifices of stone they are. And there isn't a better statue maker in all the world than the Szugabar."

"Sounds like an interesting place to visit," Harmia said from behind them.

"Oh it is Senior Constable. It definitely is."

The weather remained fair as they headed west. They passed through a fairly large town, apparently called Kelb, around midday but kept going after only a brief stop. The Baron assuring them that they had plenty of time to make it to the next hostel before dark.

It turned out that the Baron was right and they spent that evening in another well appointed facility, staffed by more hospitable Kiamans.

Travelling with all these extra people made their nightly get togethers much more difficult. Since inevitably the ambassador wanted to talk to them. They did seem to get some time towards the end of the evening, since the Barons wife seemed to like getting a fairly early night.

The spoke quietly, in case they were overheard. They didn't want strange stories to get back to the Baron or his wife. It might make things awkward.

"Do you think we will find the next quester before we reach Szugabar?" Rhyn asked.

"Hopefully. If not we have to come back this way anyway, so we'll have another opportunity," Dorm told her optimistically.

"Are we sure that there are two more in Szugabar?" Zacravia said in his quiet voice.

"It make sense. We know that there is going to be twenty-five of us in the end. Two of the amulets could easily have ended up in Szugabar. It's not that far."

"That's still an odd number though," Travanos mused. "So far we have seen two from each country. It hasn't wavered from that. One man and one woman. If we are getting two people from each of these countries, it stands to reason that we would end up with an even number wouldn't it?"

"Perhaps there's going to be someone from The Fortress itself?"

Lianna suggested.

"That's an interesting possibility," Dorm agreed. "Of course it could just be referring to Mac."

"Yay, I'm special," he said waving his fists in the air happily.

The next day they continued on their way towards the port. The highway was fairly well travelled and there were frequent groups of merchants from across the Alliance passing by.

Just before midday a group of Kiaman soldiers came jingling up behind them on horseback. Their group tended off to the side of the road as the armed men began to pass them.

The Ambassador called out to their leader as he began to pass.

"Excuse me Colonel," he began taking note of his insignia. "I'm the Lugemall Ambassador to Kiama Mor. I'm wondering what is going on? Is it anything I should be concerned with?"

"Mr Ambassador," the colonel said politely inclining his head. "We are after a group of bandits that have been active in the general region of late. If you stick to the highway you should not have any trouble."

"We had been planning to take the South River Road to Hamij."

The colonel thought for a moment. "It should be safe. But if you are at all worried then you might want to continue along the main highway to Pardra then head down the South Road from there."

"Thank you Colonel, we'll consider you advice. Good hunting to you."

"Thank you. And Good journey to you Ambassador." The Colonel again bowed his head to the Baron and then rode on to retake his position amongst his men.

The patrol, which was most likely a battalion given the number of men that seemed to be passing them, moved on at their distance eating pace. Their group remained on the edge of the road until they had fully passed, before moving back into the highway and continuing on their journey. There hadn't been much chance to discuss this new information since the passing soldiers had made a lot of noise and raised a fair amount of dust.

"So which way do we think we should head?" Baron Camir asked their group.

"What's your opinion Ambassador?" Dorm asked.

"Well given the size of our group I think we should probably be safe along the South River Road. We do have a large group here. I can't imagine a group of brigands trying to attack us."

"And if we make sure we stay in hostels at night we won't have to worry about being attacked in the middle of the night," Telly advocated.

"I'm sure we can handle ourselves if something does come up," Mac said confidently.

"Are you quite sure?" Camir asked sceptically. "I don't mean to be rude, but some of your people don't really seem to be all that… shall we say… proficient in the area of combat."

"I think you'll find some of us a surprise, Ambassador," Rhyn said suggestively. "We've been through a few scrapes on our travels and managed to stay safe."

Camir looked at them all for a few moments. "Well if you're quite sure Your Highness," he still looked dubious.

"Don't worry Ambassador, it won't be on your head if anything does go wrong," Dorm assured him clapping him on the shoulder.

"I'm exceedingly pleased by that Your Highness."

It took them another two days to reach Emeresh, the small town near the River Pojdram, where the South River Road began. It too was a well-maintained and highly trafficked road stretching out across the arid landscape. Being this close to the river though there was a lot more vegetation. Mainly shrubby trees and tall grasses. Here and there at the edge of the river were pockets of reeds and taller trees. But looking inland things still remained fairly bleak looking.

The Ambassador told them how areas of this river had flood plains that allowed the locals to farm fairly extensively. The region was a productive growing region. They encountered evidence of this several hours after starting along the South River Road. A pocket of riverside farmland, tended by several industrious workers. The road swung around that area in a wide arc, which also avoided the small village of mud brick houses and workshops.

They stayed that night in a large hostel. It rained heavily for about an hour around midnight but then gradually grew warmer as the night wore on. The humidity seemed to remain about the same. Dorm began to wish that he was back in Lugemall where the humidity never got this bad.

They rose early and left rather quicker than Dorm had expected. They passed more villages and farmsteads, and the land through which the road passed began to get higher. The river passed through an area of steep gorges, and they lost sight of it for several hours at a time.

They stayed again in another hostel, which Dorm learned had been built several centuries ago by one civic minded sultan, who wanted to dramatically expand and improve trade within the kingdom, the South River Road not being part of the great highways network of the Alliance until then.

As they sat down to their evening meal they talked over the days' journey and chatted about what lay ahead. Essentially more of the same was the answer to that question. After they had eaten they enjoyed a drink or two before retiring.

It was during this quiet and relaxing time that a richly dressed Kiaman merchant entered the common room and ordered food of his own. While the quality of his clothes suggested he was fairly successful, their condition suggested he had been in a fight. He sleeves had a few small rips in them, his collar was torn on one side and he seemed to trail a pall of dust behind him, as if he had been rolling in the dirt.

They let him eat for a while before they asked him about it. It was clear that something out of the ordinary had happened to him, and it seemed quite prudent that they find out what.

"My caravan was attacked," he told them sadly in his accented voice. "I lost several good people when it happened."

"Attacked," Camir said. "By whom? Where?"

"About five leagues from here. The day before yesterday. Who they were I have no idea."

"Were you travelling east or west friend?" Dorm asked curiously.

"East. I left Hamij about a week ago with a caravan of goods from Szugabar. Mainly spices, incense, building stone that sort of thing. We were making good time. Early one morning, not long after we had left the hostel we'd stayed at the night before, they came riding out of nowhere. A lot of them. Screaming and shouting. They'd killed three of my men before we even knew what was happening. My men tried to defend themselves, but the bandits were too good." He stared into his mug for a moment.

"We saw some soldiers heading this general direction a few days ago," Travanos said. "Did you see them at all?"

"I didn't see any soldiers. If they did come this way, then they missed at least one group of bandits."

"I gather that they left eventually?" Mac said.

"Yes. They destroyed most of my wagons and the goods, and then rode off before we could get together to chase them."

"They didn't take your goods?" Lianna asked bemusedly.

"No, they destroyed them all. I will lose a lot of money because of this."

"That doesn't make much sense," Lianna mused to the others as much as to the merchant. "Isn't the point of attacking a caravan so that you can drive off the merchants and steal the goods?"

"Perhaps they didn't think they could use it? We weren't carrying food or weapons."

"But they could still have sold them surreptitiously at markets or villages. They could have made a lot of money, which would have allowed them to buy food or weapons, and with very little way for the authorities to trace it."

"That doesn't really make much sense then does it?" Dorm thought out loud.

"Whether it makes sense or not," the merchant continued. "I think I am going to give up on this area for a while. I hear the route into Ojliam is always looking for more merchants. I think I might try my luck there. Once I've had a time to rest. The world is getting too dangerous my friends." He stood and slowly walked out of the room, his face a mixture of regret and guilt.

"If these bandits are willing to attack large merchant caravans maybe they will attack us?" Artur speculated worriedly.

"Perhaps, but we'll still give them a run for their money. Merchants aren't known for their tactical strength."

Perhaps we can link up with some of the other groups here in the hostel?" Harmia suggested. If we can get our group bigger then we might not make so inviting a target if they do see us."

"That's not such a bad idea," Dorm agreed with her. "It might be the sort of thing some of the other groups might be interested, given this information. It seems to be getting dangerous in this part of Kiama Mor all of a sudden."

"I think I might be able to help persuade some of them, Your Highness," Camir said enthusiastically rising to his feet. "Let's see what they say."

Several of the smaller groups of travellers, merchants, peasants, tradesmen and the like had heard of the bandits. Most had decided to remain at the hostel until such time as they were informed by the local authorities that the area had been made safe.

Two groups however elected to travel with their company.

The first group was a young family from a nearby town who had recently bought a new business in a village further along the highway. They had gotten this far when news of the bandits had reached them. Fearing what might happen to their small group, most of whom were children and prompted them to remain. Yet the family was anxious to get to their new life and worried that if they didn't show up soon that the previous owner might sell it to someone else.

The second group were an elderly pair who had recently been visiting relatives in one of the nearby villages. They were returning home in their cart, which was pulled by an equally old horse. Their prospects of outrunning any attackers were slim.

With the expanded group, they headed out early in the morning making a good time considering the slower pace they made. The day remained clear and there was no sign of any trouble. There were few other travellers on the road as they moved along, and those that were seemed in a hurry to get anywhere. Most were also rather wary Dorm noticed, giving them as wide a berth as possible.

They stopped only briefly for a midday meal, before heading on. The old couple left them not long after, the side road to their village was rutted but the village was visible from the main road. They waited until the couple had made it to the village before moving on.

They arrived at the next hostel just after dark, having pushed themselves a bit harder during the afternoon. The evening had been a little tense but they had had no encounters. The lights of the hostel were a welcome sight and seemed to give them all a new found energy.

The next day continued much the same as the first had. They turned off about midday to head off the main road to the small town where the family was to take up residence. They had offered them food and rest at their new home, and the group had accepted. The town was not large, but was large enough that it would probably discourage most bandits.

They stayed for only about an hour before moving on again, eager to get to the next hostel before dark. Especially now that their group was back to it's original size.

Again they made the next hostel about an hour after dark. The hostel manager was at first reluctant to open the bolted gates to admit them, fearing that they were bandits. But after a few inspections, and an offer of a few extra coins, they were admitted.

The next morning they again left early, but made better time as they headed west. The wind blew stronger and whipped up the dust a lot more. They again passed small villages and farmsteads along the riverside, but again saw very few people.

They stopped only briefly around noon, in the shadow of a large outcropping of rocks beside the road. They kept a watch out, but there were no other travellers on the road. They headed off again moving quickly.

It was about two hours or so later when they passed a small group of what appeared to be tradesmen and workers heading the other direction. They passed them without incident and continued on their way. Several minutes after they had passed the group by, one of the Ambassadors' guards rode up quickly to Camir.

"Your Excellency," he said urgently. "That group we just passed…"

"What about them?" Camir enquired.

"They seem to be in a hurry all of a sudden." He pointed back the way they had come, to the rapidly disappearing group.

"This could be a problem," Camir said negatively.

"You think they might be linked to these bandits somehow?" Zacravia said nervously.

"I think it's very likely they are part of the bandits," Dorm admitted pessimistically.

"Then perhaps we should get a bit of a move on," Cal suggested as he already pushed his horse faster.

"I like the mans' thinking," Rhyn said increasing her pace to join him.

"All right lets pick up the pace a bit try and put a bit more distance between us. Perhaps if they come back and find we've moved on quite a ways they won't bother."

They all pushed their horses into a canter. They had been worried about the heat and the need to water their mounts and so hadn't pushed them that hard so far. But now the situation definitely called for it. They moved on passing well beyond the area where they had encountered the possible bandits in short order.

"Perhaps we are safe now?" Camir suggested.

"Perhaps, but lets not risk it just yet," Dorm replied. "Lets keep going until we're past this next hill, then we'll slow down for a bit and give the horses a bit of a rest. How long till the next town?"

"About another ten miles or so I think," Camir responded uncertainly. "I'm not completely familiar with this part of Kiama Mor."

"Okay then, well lets see if we can make it there fairly quickly, it might be safe enough for us."

They continued at their canter till they had passed the low hills then slowed back to a trot. They had covered a fair distance and they all felt a bit safer. It would at least cause those possible bandits an inconvenience.

They continued on towards the next village. It took about another twenty minutes or so till they crested the top of a low rise and saw it in the distance. It was a typical farming village for this part of the country, set about halfway between the road and the river. They could see fields and a few trees closer to the water.

Without any suggestion the group pushed back into a canter. It was still a few miles and they didn't want to get caught within sight of possible help. They turned off the main road and headed quickly towards the village.

Their first indication that something wasn't right was a barrow and some farm implements left beside the road. The fields all appeared normal, yet things had been left out beside the road, almost as if they had been dropped in an hurry.

They entered the outskirts of the village and realised their mistake. The houses had all been torched at some point in the recent past. Littered debris lay here and there in the streets. A wrecked wagon sat in the small central square. Thankfully there were no sign of the inhabitants.

"Now what?" Rhyn said in a pained voice.

"I'm open to suggestions?" Dorm said as everyone spun around looking for something that might offer some help.

"We could hide here?" Mac volunteered.

"It might at least give us something to help defend ourselves with," Harmia called out.

"For all we know this could be their hideout," Telly responded.

"This place looks like it has been abandoned," Travanos concluded. "I doubt very much they would use it. It might provide us with protection, but they could just as easily try to burn us out."

"Or just surround the place and wait us out," Artur suggested glumly.

"Ambra?" Dorm said turning to him. "Do you know this area at all?"

"I know it well enough. I used to come here a lot. But not in some years."

"Do you know anything that might help us?"

He looked around obviously trying to get his bearings. "If we are where I think we are, then it will take too long to get to the next hostel. But I remember some caves back a ways into the desert. If we can find them they might be able to hide us until night fall."

"Travel at night?" Camir said incredulously. "Do you have any idea how cold it gets around here at night?"

"Perhaps Ambassador," Travanos said. "But we have blankets, and at least any bandit camps will be easily avoided."

"How do you figure that?"

"We'll be able to see their camp fires long before we get anywhere near them. We can simply get back onto the main road and avoid any lights we see until we reach the hostel or a town."

"That's not a bad idea," Dorm decided. "Ambra how far away was this cave of yours?"

"If I remember correctly it was only a mile or two from the road. Though I must admit that I am not precisely sure where we are."

"Just do your best. If we have to we can distract them and lead them round in circles for a bit before we get there. Let's go!"

They turned and headed back along the side road towards the highway at a dead run, turned west again and continued on. They maintained a fast pace, Ambra carefully scouring the landscape for something familiar. After about a quarter of an hour he pointed suddenly towards the south.

"There!" He exclaimed excitedly. "I'm sure the caves are in those hills there."

Following his indication revealed a distant, low range of hills. They looked to be probably a league or two away from the road. They didn't appear to be very high but they could clearly tell that they were rocky.

"That's a fair distance Your Highness," Camir commented worriedly.

"True but we don't have much of a choice. It's still hours until dark and this land is pretty flat. We don't want to get caught out here."

"We'd best hurry whatever we do," Cal said. He looked behind them to a faint cloud of dust that seemed to be rising above the horizon. "They seem to be heading this way."

"All right lets head for it," Dorm called out as they began to quickly move off the road.

"Keep going as quickly as you can!" Zacravia called to them as he swung down from his saddle. "I'll catch up."

"I don't think so," Harmia warned him viciously. "You show your true colours at last Zacravia!" She turned her horse back around.

"You stupid woman!" Zacravia yelled at her. "Do you really think I want to risk my life with a group of bandits who destroy whole villages, out in the middle of a desert, to get away from people who mean me no harm whatsoever? Use your head Senior Constable." He pulled a small shovel that they normally used for making their fire pits, from his pack dashed back to the edge of the highway. He quickly began swirling the flat of the shovel over all the horse tracks their passage into the sand at the edge of the road had made.

He turned briefly to see that Harmia was still there. "What are you waiting for you fool? Get going. I'll be along in a minute, once this is done."

"You'd better be!" She told him gruffly. She hesitantly swung her horse around and rejoined the others. "If he doesn't come back he'd better kill himself, because if he doesn't I'll do it for him."

"Come on!" Dorm said and they pushed again out into the desert at a gallop. The horses had a harder time of it, since they were on sand and dirt, not the packed hard surface of the highway.

It was about ten minutes later as the group was climbing the side of a large low dune that Zacravia caught up with them.

"Well it isn't perfect, he admitted, but it will at least confuse the place where we left the road. With a little luck it will take them some time to figure out which way we went."

"A bit of time is better than none," Dorm thanked him. "Let's keep going."

The pushed on into the heat. The hills slowly got closer and more details began to emerge. They were not so much hills as large bumps of rock that had managed to stay above the level of the sand.

After having gone about two miles it was clear that the hills were still several miles away but were getting steadily closer. Which was just as well since the heat was beginning to affect them. They crested another small dune. As they reached the top Artur happened to glance behind them.

"Oh I think they've managed to figure out which way we went."

Back across the wide expanse they had just travelled they could see the dark brown line of the highway. A large group of figures were moving away from it at pace. A large trail of dust was being thrown up by their rapid movement. The direction the figures were moving in would take them straight to their group.

"Okay then, we don't have much choice," Dorm said. "We're

going to have to push as hard as we can. It's still at least a league to the hills. The horses wont like it but they can rest once we're safe."

They literally flew down the far side of the dune and moved out onto another flat sandy plain. They didn't slow their pace but continued on. They ate up the distance and reached the rocky surrounds of the hills where large boulders, that had obviously once fallen from the hills themselves littered the landscape.

"Which way now Ambra?" Dorm asked quickly.

"It's changed a lot. I'm trying to remember," replied studying the landscape.

"Remember quickly," Rhyn said alarmingly. Off in the distance, at the edge of that flat plain a large cloud of dust was rising.

Tissie let out a whimper. "We won't make it," she said on the verge of tears.

"Oh don't be silly," Telly snapped at her. "Of course we will." She turned and glared at Ambra. "Won't we?" She wasn't really asking.

"It's this way I think," Ambra said after a moment. "I'll know once we get closer."

They moved out quickly into the hills themselves. The hills appeared to almost be different large sections of rock thrusting up towards the sky, creating a maze of narrow pebble strewn corridors that twisted crazily back and forth. Before they entered that labyrinth Ambra briefly studied the openings of several of them before picking one and leading them inside at a trot.

It was already cooler inside the passages. The height of the rocks around them shaded them from direct sunlight. They moved deeper into the hills following Ambra.

At one point he stopped. "Wait here a moment." He moved his horse over to one wall of the passage looked behind a large boulder then disappeared behind it. He returned a moment of two later. "Not that one," he said cryptically. "Come on."

"Why not that one?" Mac asked him.

"It isn't big enough. We'd never fit all us and the horses inside."

They continued on for another few minutes. Ambra again stopped. Again he moved to a large rock next to the passage wall that seemed just the same as a dozen others he had passed without stopping. He disappeared behind this one as well for a few moments.

"This is it!" He told them quickly where he returned. "Hurry."

They didn't need much encouragement. The horses were obviously nervous about entering the dark opening but they managed to get them inside with a combination of gentle words and hard pulls on their bridles.

Behind the entrance was a twisting passageway that ran for about twenty or so yards before opening out into a cave. The cave was a rather large open space. The walls were strangely rounded and Dorm suspected that this cave had been created by water a very long time ago. There was more than enough room there for all of them plus the horses.

They calmed the horses and each other. Everyone was hushed. They all armed themselves and pushed the horses to the back of the cave.

Dorm, Mac, Harmia, Ambra and Cal made their way back towards the entrance. Travanos, Rhyn and Zacravia stood poised at the point where the passage opened out into the cave.

Once they reached the entrance Ambra paused for a moment to listen.

"I think we still have some time," He said after a moment. "Here. Help me with this." He began to pull at what Dorm had thought was simply a slab of rock that stuck out from the wall. It actually appeared to be a cleverly designed door. When it was about half closed, he paused and dashed out into the outer part of the tunnel and began furiously brushing out the various hoof marks and footsteps that were visible in the soft sand. He jumped back behind the 'door' and they resumed their pushing. The slab closed with a gentle grate or stone against stone.

"What is this place?" Harmia asked quietly.

"It used to be used by smugglers and others," Ambra explained. "Someone I used to know told me of it and brought me here once. It was some time ago though. We'll have to keep well back from here though." He pointed to a gap between the door and the wall. It wouldn't be large enough to get through, but someone might be able to look through. They looked about and took up positions that would keep them hidden from any prying eyes. They had a hurried and hushed conversation with the others before settling down to wait.

They waited in the dark for what began to seem like days. Finally however they began to hear a jingling sound. It seemed far away but Dorm suspected it was a lot closer than he would like. After a few moments footsteps could be heard and indistinct talking. There was a voice that sounded like it was giving orders. There were various hurried footfalls that appeared to be moving off in various directions. A bright light appeared through the gap into the passage. The smell of burning came strongly to their nostrils.

The light got brighter. The smell stronger and more acrid.

The torch was suddenly thrust into the gap. It didn't penetrate into their side of the passageway very far, since the gap in the door wasn't very wide. Presumably the person holding it couldn't reach very far inside.

There was a gruff bark from behind the person with the torch.

"Anything?"

"No, I don't think so. There is more of the passage beyond here but I can't see far enough into it."

"Let me see." There was a shuffling of feet and the torch wobbled slightly. "Hmm they can't have gone in there. There is not way to get through. Continue with the search."

"Yes sir." Footsteps moved off. They all remained perfectly still trying not to even breathe.

Another set of footsteps, this time slower and more measured entered the passageway. "Anything here, Hamil?" An accented voice said.

"No. Just a dead end."

"Are you sure these people aren't just ordinary travellers?"

"My men said they were not."

"Your men are fools. I should have brought more of my men with me."

"Your men are no better. At least mine are familiar with the area. They know what is what. Your Imperial spies would do well to remember that."

"You have been paid good money to disrupt this area for us. But remember who it is who is giving the orders here."

"As long as our agreement remains in effect we will follow your orders."

"Our agreement will be followed as long as you continue to do your job."

"One thing to consider Brassius. "My men outnumber yours. And our swords are very sharp." Footsteps walked away.

There was an agitated sigh, followed by another set of footsteps heading back outside.

They sat for a few moments in shocked silence.

The bandits were working for the Peldraksekhr? It was incredible. This was information that had to be gotten out. Presumably little information was getting out of the area and the Kiaman government probably thought it was just a localised situation. This clearly indicated that it wasn't, and the possibility that it could easily crop up somewhere else.

The possibilities of a connection to the activities of Lassius in Batava and Domiticus in T'Kell was not lost on Dorm. He hoped that they weren't, knowing full well the futility of that hope.

After what seemed like an hour but was probably only about a quarter of that, silence fell again over the passage entrance. They slowly rose and headed back to report what they had heard.

Chapter 16

Over the next few hours the bandits returned several times to the area. Their group waited patiently and silently in the darkness of the cave until finally they left. Silence descended over the area and a certain tension seemed to lift. Still they waited in case their enemy decided to double back after a time.

Eventually it was decided that they should at least check the immediate vicinity of the cave entrance. Dorm, Mac, Travanos and Harmia crept once again back to the slab door. They waited for several minutes to make sure that they couldn't hear anything. They checked the section of the passageway directly in front of the door before slowly opening it part way. One by one they slipped quietly past and along the twisting corridor. Near the entrance they waited again. The light outside had changed the shadows were longer and darker. It was obviously late in the afternoon now. It was clear they wouldn't be going anywhere just yet.

The area outside the cave entrance was clear. No sounds could be heard except the gentle whisper of the wind.

They headed back to their group, dusting out their footprints and closing the door behind them, and updated the others. Given that it was still a few hours until dark, they decided to get some rest so that they could move out once night had fallen.

They took turns guarding the door.

Dorm and Zacravia took the first watch. They sat in the soft sand at the door, straining their ears for any sound in the world outside. Occasionally they would hear the sound of falling stones. But there was never any other sound to indicate the presence of people.

"Why do you think this is all going on, Dormal?" Zacravia asked quietly.

"I'm not sure to be honest, my friend," he replied. "It could just be because they don't like us. Perhaps it's part of some plan of theirs."

"Plans…" he said softly. "I had plans once. They certainly didn't include getting trapped inside a cold cave in the middle of the Kiaman desert."

"What made you turn to crime?"

"Well if you can call it that." He looked distant for a moment. "I lost someone when I was a young man. For a time I lost my head. And in that crazed state I did some things that closed off what my life might have been. It was my own doing of course. But crime seemed easier than actually taking the time to rebuild my life. I don't regret it. I've made a decent enough life for myself I guess."

"But you're constantly on the run from the police?"

He laughed. "Ah but when the police are like our dear Senior Constable Harmia that is not such a bad thing to have chasing you."

"You like her?"

"Oh not in that way," he said defensively. "Oh I'll be the first to admit that she's very nice to look at. But I'm very much too old for someone like her. And besides, I'm not sure I could go there again."

"I think love can find you no matter who or what you are."

"A quaint notion Your Highness, possibly given to you by the fact that you have been fortunate enough to find someone who loves you unconditionally. You are a lucky man. Most of us don't get that."

"I think you're wrong my friend," Dorm said confidently.

"Perhaps," Zacravia mused. "But then I'm not sure I want to go through the process of finding out again. Having your heart utterly broken once is more than enough for me."

Soft footfalls sounded up the passage, and Mac emerged from the gloom. "I guess that must be my cue to go and find my replacement," Zacravia said. "Do excuse me." He stood and quietly walked off.

Mac sat down beside Dorm. "Anything?" he asked.

"Not so far. I'm pretty sure they've moved off. We should be able to leave once it gets properly dark."

Mac lent his head on Dorms shoulder. "What are we doing here Dorm?" He asked quietly. "Sitting in a cave in the middle of the desert hoping to avoid people who are trying to kill us isn't exactly how I saw this year unfolding."

"Me either love," he said taking Macs' hand in his. "But we don't seem to have much of a choice do we."

"I guess not." Mac sighed heavily. "I miss our bed. And our pillows."

Dorm laughed. "No, you miss the bathtub, that's what you miss."

"Well that too." Mac smiled. "And I miss Ellin and Sanan and Dubrika, and your father."

"I miss him too. He loves you too you know."

"I know. I'm just not used to it. Your father has been more of a parent to me than mine ever was. I'm just not sure how to respond to that."

"By being yourself." He fixed Mac with a look. He kissed him passionately.

Of course Travanos walked up right at that moment.

"Oh sorry about that dear chaps, didn't mean to break the moment. I can come back?"

"No that's okay Travanos. I think we can contain ourselves," Dorm said rising to his feet. "Keep an eye and an ear out. Hopefully we should be able to move out in a few hours."

Mac smiled sheepishly at him as he walked away.

It had been dark for about two hours when they decided to start moving. Zacravia and Harmia, being the stealthiest of them ranged out quietly around the area of the cave mouth. They came back after a few minutes to report that there was no one around.

They all lead their horses back outside. They all seemed to share a visible relief once they had reached the open air. The stars were bright, arching overhead and the moon was only a sliver.

Moving quietly and with great caution they walked the horses back through the rocky terrain of the gullies towards the awaiting dessert. They paused not far from the open sands to await what Harmia and Zacravia had seen.

"Nothing to indicate that they are anywhere around here. We didn't go too far though," Harmia told Dorm quietly.

"Not so much as a campfire. They could be waiting somewhere for us though," Zacravia added.

"Well we don't have much of a choice. We'll have to take the risk. Everyone stay together and keep quiet. The horses will be noisy enough without us adding to it. Is everyone ready?"

"Well I'll admit this isn't exactly what I had in mind when I joined the diplomatic service," the Ambassador told him quietly. "But if everyone else can do it then I'm sure I can manage."

The light humour put them all in a better frame of mind. At least it gave them a bit of confidence.

They moved out at a fast walk until they were well clear of the rocky hills. They plodded up the dune and moved out into the desert. A chill night breeze blew across the sands as they moved quickly and quietly back towards the highway.

The ride across the desert was nerve racking to say the least. Every far off noise made them think they had been caught. Several times they thought they heard hoof beats in the distance. Each time they would reign in and strain their ears to locate the direction it came from. Once they had identified a direction one or two volunteers would climb to the top of the nearest dune facing that way and see if they could determine its source. Only once did they actually see anything. A small group of riders far out in the desert apparently heading in the general direction of the hills they had just left. They fretted for a moment worrying if perhaps their tracks might get seen. But there was little they could do but press on. The other times they chalked up to nerves, echoes from the dunes, or perhaps wild animals.

They maintained an even pace hoping that the horses wouldn't get too tired. The sands seemed almost to shine in the moonlight, and the stars twinkled serenely overhead, oblivious to their emotional state. It was incredibly beautiful. Pity they had no time to stop and admire it.

It seemed to take hours. Most likely because of the nerves. Eventually though they saw the dark line of the highway stretching across the landscape. They moved a little quicker once it came into sight. Travanos pulled up just before its paved surface.

"Dormal," he said in a hoarse whisper. "Might I suggest that we stay off the actual highway for a short while longer. We know where it is now so we can follow it."

"Why not just get on the highway?" Lianna asked him.

"Once we are on those stones our horses are going to make a lot more noise, especially if we push into a gallop. And in the middle of the night the sound will carry for miles. On the sands we can make less noise and still maintain a good pace. If we see someone coming after us we can very easily get on the highway and make better time."

She thought about that for a moment. "Yes okay that makes sense I guess."

"I like the thinking Travanos," Dorm agreed with him. "Let's try it."

They passed the instructions around quickly and then turned and headed west again, following a few yards from the highway itself. It was easy to follow and their noise was definitely reduced.

Midnight came and went almost unnoticed as they swiftly rode along. They didn't stop at all during the long hours of the hight. They passed a small deserted looking village and dark, silent farmsteads along the riverward side of the road. None of them showed any signs of life, and they weren't interested in investigating.

They approached a well-lit hostel close to the riverbank, just as dawn was touching the far western horizon the lightest shade of blue. The lights of a small village shone on the other side of the river. This wouldn't be a good place for the bandits to attack. The village on the other side would too easily find out what had happened and relay that information back to the authorities.

They waited patiently outside the main gate for it to get a bit brighter before they tried to enter. Given the current circumstances in the area, Dorm wasn't going to risk his people on some nervous guardsman.

When it was light enough to see by they rang the bellpull and after some arguing and haggling were admitted. They took their rooms gratefully and all sought their beds. It had been a long, tense night, and it felt good to rest after it.

They rose late in the day, ate, and after a long consultation with each other, conversations with some of the other guests as well as the hostel staff, and a few measurings on their map, it was decided to wait until the next day before moving off. Not only would it be dark again in a few hours, meaning that if the bandits were ranging further a field they might get caught again, but also the port was only about a days travel from where they were. A full day or riding should put them out of harms way.

Everyone was a little restless going back to bed so soon, but all knew it was necessary.

They rose again early the next morning, packed and left the hostel as the sun cleared the horizon. They headed west again at a good pace and had gone a fair distance before they encountered other travellers. As the morning wore on the traffic increased, but they noted that it still seemed subdued, given that the road was the main thoroughfare between a major port and the capital.

They stopped briefly around midday in a small village and left before the villagers hopefully had a chance to get too nervous. It seemed that the current situation in this part of the country was stretching the Kiaman desire to provide hospitality.

After a few more hours they crested a small rise and saw the long gentle curve into the port of Hamij. There was a greater amount of traffic here since there seemed to be several outlying villages, farmsteads, and even large workshops. There was also a large military camp just outside the city's walls. Apparently the Sultan was at least trying to take the situation here seriously.

It took another hour or so to reach the open gates of the town. A brief conversation with the duty guards had them admitted with an escorting officer to make sure they didn't get lost. I guess rank does have its privileges sometimes, Dorm thought to himself.

Hamij bustled. That was the only way to describe it. Merchants, workers and townspeople moved quickly through the streets. Dorm also noted a larger number of soldiers than he would have ordinarily expected.

The city's buildings seemed typical of the country. Stone, mud brick, though here they were much more utilitarian. There was less decoration on the walls they passed. And what there was seemed more subtle. Some buildings seemed only to have a few parts that had been painted and nothing more. This was a working city, not something to please the visitors

The air seemed cooler here than back in the desert. No doubt as a result of the Desert Sea. Dorm had never seen the Desert Sea and it would be a sight to behold.

They were lead through various streets and squares until they came to their accommodation. Dorm had expected an inn. It was instead the local Margraves palace. Dorm groaned inwardly. Camir noticed the expression on his face.

"Don't worry Your Highness," He said as he lent closer to him. "The Margrave will be accompanying us, so we aren't going to be held up for days on end."

"At least not until we get back," Dorm replied pessimistically.

"Oh I'm sure that when we do we can pretend some urgent national mission for you. You are the Crown Prince after all. It would seem to be your duty to visit various nations for whirlwind tours."

"Whirlwind tours?" Dorm mused. "I think I like that."

"Why thank you."

The Margrave himself, Hamik by name, came to greet them. He was an elderly man of rotund figure with a large greying beard. His wife the Margravine, whose name was Lajik, wore a flimsy veil across the lower half of her face and seemed to be dripping with small embellishments of gold and jewels on her rose coloured gown.

There was a brief greeting speech that was all very flowery and probably insincere, before they were taken inside and shown to their rooms. The palace was cool and airy, with well-polished floors and wide corridors. Their rooms, on the second floor, were large and featured balconies that looked out over the central courtyard. They had whitewashed stone walls featuring tapestries and rich furniture. They also featured a small room that contained small sunken baths, which he knew the ladies would appreciate; the giggles and squeals of delight coming from the rooms down the hall confirmed his suspicions.

After a brief laugh, Mac decided to join in, stripping off his clothes and sinking in to the deep tub, sighing heavily as he relaxed in the warm water.

"Well?" he said looking at Dorm.

"Well what?" Dorm replied curiously as he unpacked some things from his bag.

"Oh you are so dense sometimes you know that." He splashed some water towards Dorm playfully. "It's quite warm in here you know."

"Most likely." Dorm watched him quizzically for a moment. "If you think I'm just going to clamber in there when any old body could come wandering in…"

"You're such a prude sometimes you know," Mac said with a smirk. "You can always lock the door."

Dorm grinned slyly. "You mean like this?" he said slowly pushing across the latch.

"Something like that," Mac replied quietly.

"I guess I could at that," Dorm replied stepping slowly into the bathing room. He stood there for a moment, as Mac swirled the steaming water around.

"You are not going to make me drag you in here are you? I'm much to travel sore for that."

"Oh I think we can work something out." Dorm reached for the ties on his tunic.

Dinner that night was sumptuous. Platters of meat, vegetables, fruits and breads washed down with various wines and sweet juices. By the end of the meal their stomachs groaned as much as the table had at the beginning.

Afterward, a group of dancers swirled their way through a frenzied repertoire to the fast paced music. Dorm noted that there were both women and men dancing. Something for everyone.

After the entertainment the Margrave spoke to them about various things, including the current 'difficulties' in the area. He admitted that he hadn't had a great deal of success against the bandits, but that now with assistance from the army he was confident of eventual victory.

He outlined their itinerary for the morning, and that he had already sent word on to the harbour master to have a larger ship standing by to carry the extra passengers. Since there wasn't enough room on the ship, their mounts would be remaining here in Hamij while they went on. They were all a little reluctant to leave them behind but there wasn't much to be done about it.

Eventually heading on towards midnight everyone began to retire. And bit by bit they all walked back to their rooms, feeling very full.

Dorm and Mac sat talking with Telly and Rhyn for a short while before they all returned to their own rooms. Everyone eyes were getting a bit heavy by now.

The evening was cool, here by the Desert Sea. A light breeze blew in through the open doors to the balcony, billowing the filmy curtains. A soft silvery light from the moon shone across everything, but drained most of the colour away. Dorm lay quietly thinking about both the days events as well as what might happen in Szugabar.

Szugabar was still a bit of a mystery to most in the Alliance. The devastating war had both caused a great wariness in the Szugabar themselves as well as making the Alliance reluctant to ask too many questions for fear of being misinterpreted. There had been at various times Szugabar ambassadors to Lugemall, and indeed a couple of times Lugemallan ambassadors to Szugabar, but the last had been several decades ago.

He knew of course about their great temples, and palaces and their massive monuments to long dead kings. But he didn't know a great deal about the people themselves. He wasn't sure how they might react to the types of questions he was likely to need to ask.

After some time he fell asleep.

He dreamt.

He felt weightless. Flying over an arid landscape. He passed out over a body of water. Not a river or lake, something larger certainly, but there didn't seem to be waves. Onwards he flew. Finally he came to a great city rising out of the sand at the edge of the water. Great spires and obelisks stabbed at the bright sky.

Domes and towers rose in the city and there seemed to be a feeling of great age. In the distance rose great stone shapes. Temples and tombs of the long forgotten. Yet somehow they seemed curiously alive. They seemed almost to shimmer. But not from heat. There was a feeling he got from them. But he had not the time to fully contemplate it before he was moved on.

His mind, for he did not seem to have a body, flew effortlessly around this great city. While he did not see any one he could tell that they were there. If he concentrated hard enough he could almost hear them.

His vision moved towards a large ornate stone building at the end of a formal avenue. Great stone pillars rose on either side of an ornate portal. Between these two pillars he moved, and on over the top of the open courtyard beyond. He wafted down into it, and felt different somehow. Like he was in someone's presence. Someone whose mind was very powerful and very quick. He floated, for that was how it felt, along a dim corridor lined with thick round columns, arriving at last to smaller dark room where a small statue stood on what could only be an alter.

That presence surrounded him again. It seemed to stare at him and examine him. For a brief moment he felt a touch against his mind. The touch of something vast, and very powerful. Something that knew very few limits, and what limits it did know were so far beyond his understanding that his mind simply shied away from the very idea of them.

"Who art thou?" he heard a voice say. It was a deep voice. There was a slight echo to it. The voice contained power, and yet somehow wisdom and compassion at the same time.

"What?" he could hear his voice in his mind, but he had no way to speak it out loud.

"Who art thou?" Said the voice again. "And why hast thou come unto me?"

"I don't understand." His field of vision swung around but there was no one that he could see.

"Ahh, I see," said the voice again after a moment. "Thou shouldst not be here young one. It is dangerous for thee to come in this manner. Given thy task."

"Task? What is going on here? Who are you?"

"Thou shalt discover this in the fullness of time. The footsteps of thy passage here to this place are as loud to me as the beat of a drum. I hear them young one. And in each step dost I know that thy fate is set, and that thy mind is ready. Even if the purpose of thy journey doth still elude thy comprehension."

"Who are you?" he whispered again.

"Thou shalt discover this in the fullness of time also, young one. E'en as thy journey seems fraught with indecision and confusion, thou hast only to look upon the face of thy true and faithful companions to know that thy journey be both righteous and just. Go in peace."

Without warning and before the thought to ask what any of that had meant had even had a chance to fully form, let alone be voiced, his vision swept back faster than anything he could imagine, out of the temple back through the city, out across the sea and to the landscape beyond. He vision disappeared in a blue haze and he awoke. Shaking slightly, staring at the ceiling.

In the morning he woke feeling like he hadn't slept at all.

Mac noticed his vagueness, and the red eyes he presented.

"Not another one?" he asked worriedly.

"Afraid so," Dorm replied rubbing his face wearily.

"Why can't they just leave you alone?" Mac comforted him. "What was it this time? Not me again I hope."

"No, not you. I'm not sure what it all was," Dorm admitted. "I was somewhere. A city of some sort. Someone was speaking to me, but what they said didn't make much sense."

"Sounds like the Rangers."

Dorm smiled. "Maybe. But the person or whatever it was… they were powerful. It was like they could have squashed me like I was a bug, and barely even noticed."

"I hope we don't have to meet them then."

"That makes two of us."

Breakfast was again sumptuous. Dorm was beginning to think that with all this eating they'd need to take two ships so that they wouldn't run the risk of sinking. Dorm was grateful for the aromatic tea that was served. He held the cup close to his face and let the steam gently waft across his closed eyes. The warmth rising from the surface of the dark liquid was soothing.

After a short bath to try and liven himself up a bit, Dorm dressed and repacked the few things he had taken out. As a group they retrieved certain things from their packs. They would be gone for at least a week and they couldn't just duck back to the inn for something if they'd forgotten it.

The Margrave had a few minor things to take care of before they left, he met with several of his town administrators and advisors. Then escorted them all to the front of the palace where a line of open coaches awaited them.

They clambered aboard and at a signal from the Margrave the coaches all moved off towards the gate to the street beyond.

Again the streets of Hamij teemed with people. The morning was quite pleasant and again a cool breeze blew in from the west. All the streets in Hamij were paved, unlike the capital. This made the port much less dusty than its national counterpart.

"I've never been on a ship before," Rhynavell was saying. "What's it going to be like?"

"Well presumably there will be significant differences to what I'm used to," Travanos replied. "At sea you have all sorts of weather and tides and currents to worry about. On an inland sea, I'm not sure how things work."

"Well at least you'll feel right at home Travanos," Telly said supportively. "The rest of us will be lost, dare I say it, at sea, in this situation."

"My dear girl," Travanos said with a tragic look on his face. "That was terrible. Besides. I'm not sure I will like it. Sailing on an ocean that doesn't smell of salt, seems unnatural to me for some reason."

"I'm sure you'll survive," Dorm said quietly.

"I hope so Dormal," the Admiral responded sincerely. "I'll never live it down if I don't"

Their carriage wound it's way through the streets of the city, passing various commercial houses and inns for the various itinerant sailors who passed through the port. After a time large warehouses and even a few silos began to dominate their view.

After what had seemed hours they arrived at an official looking building facing a large courtyard, that was surrounded by what appeared to be barracks and stores. Several soldiers moved about on their various errands.

They went inside the building and were taken to a large airy wood panelled room to wait while the final supplies were being organised. Apparently even the largest ship available in the port that day wasn't quite able to take everyone as it was and had to be slightly modified in order to provide some level of privacy to the extra passengers.

They were brought some refreshments and waited for about an hour before they were then escorted out towards the quay.

The Desert Sea stretched dark blue under a light blue sky towards the horizon. Dorm had seen the sea a few times in his travels around Lugemall as well as other countries, but this was different somehow. The mournful sigh of waves against a shoreline was missing for one, and the surface of the water wasn't broken by white caps, despite the breeze. The water rippled and sparkled in the bright light.

Their group stood transfixed for a few moments by the sight.

Their ship, called the *Star of the Sea*, was a wide beamed, high-hulled vessel, with two tall masts. The crew scurried about her at their various tasks with that typical precision of the military. Dorm was no expert on ships, but she seemed sturdy enough.

They went on board and were taken by an official looking man to various rooms below decks. The companionways were narrow, the rooms small, but it seemed that some effort had been made to make them feel bigger. The bed was well made and seemed quite comfortable. The small porthole provided a great deal of light given its small size, and there was even a mirror.

After stowing their packs, they returned to the main deck to watch their trip begin. The captain, whose name was Tamik, was overseeing the final preparations with his first mate. Travanos it seemed had already sought him out to talk shop. While Dorm wasn't sure how their captain would react to this, things seemed to be going well so far. Dorm knew that some people didn't like others coming and giving them their opinions on matters they knew all about. But Travanos seemed to be asking questions more than making suggestions. Comparing various techniques of their two different styles of sailing. Captain Tamik seemed quite happy to talk with him, and even occasionally seemed to point out things that Travanos hadn't asked about. It was obvious he was proud of his ship.

Eventually it was time to go and Captain Tamik seemed to get that invisible feeling that now it was time. He gave orders for the gangway to be removed and the hawsers slipped. Crewmen used large poles that were brought out from somewhere below and the ship was pushed away from the quayside. Several large oars slipped out, like the spindly legs of some great insect and pushed them forward slowly.

Captain Tamik ordered certain sails lowered, and when this was done, the sails flapped lazily in the breeze for a few moments, before fully catching the wind. They billowed out in such a way that you could almost feel the power of the wind pulling the ship along. Slowly they began to pick up speed and move away from the harbour. Numerous smaller boats and a few other ships gave them a wide berth as the *Star of the Sea* moved out towards the open water of the Desert Sea.

Chapter 17

Dorm wasn't sure about sea travel.

It was fine as a mode of transport, and it was good if you were used to it, but Dorm wasn't. The constant swaying feeling made him feel slightly giddy. Like he was continually walking across a slope. There was a distinct difference between this and the feelings he'd had when they had sailed on Liannas' barge the *Longreach*. There, things had been fairly gentle. The swaying was present but it was nowhere near as pronounced. Here on the *Star of the Sea* he felt constantly like he was moving in several different directions at once. To take his mind off it he took careful note of what his companions were doing.

Predictably both Travanos and Lianna buzzed about the decks inspecting things, asking questions and occasionally making comments. They didn't seem to have too much to complain about, and privately both of them even made comments of approval over certain things.

Travanos being a seaman himself seemed to have the most to say. He talked to the crew about the rigging and the sails, as well as obscure things like their shifts and sleeping berths. Dorm didn't understand most of it.

Lianna asked a lot of questions about the holds and the arrangement of stores. Presumably she was comparing how the *Longreach* was organised in comparison to the *Star*, she didn't say much when the various members of the crew answered, but Dorm could tell that she was thinking carefully on each of those responses.

Dorm noticed that several of the others seemed a little "green around the gills', was the phrase that Captain Tamik used. Telly hid it well. Rhyn tried to smile to cover it but it didn't work all that well. And Artur seemed to want to just stay in bed. He said that laying down helped.

Tissie wasn't seen for most of the voyage and once they even had to go check on her to make sure she was still aboard. Ambra seemed okay, although every time the ship shuddered at a larger wave he quickly and fiercely grabbed on to something solid.

Both Zacravia and Harmia seemed perfectly fine with things. They sat around quietly talking to members of the crew. Zacravia was trying very hard to get a dice game going with some of the crewman, but for some reason they seemed wary of him. Dorm suspected Harmia had something to do with that.

Cal spent a lot of time on deck. He said that the fresh air helped to calm his stomach, which he said felt like it was practising gymnastics. He seemed to always have a tankard in his hand too. Apparently that also helped.

Mac however had gone quiet. While it wasn't the near melancholy that he had gone through while on the docks in Ziga, he did seem a little sadder than usual. Mac had never worked on the ships themselves, but he probably had met a lot of sailors in his time. And so it probably caused his mind to wander over things he'd probably rather it didn't.

"Are you going to be okay?" Dorm asked him quietly after a few hours.

"Yes I will be," he replied. " I just need to keep my mind busy so I don't have time to dwell." He looked at Dorm and gave him a weak smile.

"If you need me, just say so," Dorm told him seriously.

"I will."

Captain Tamik set a good table. Despite the large number of crew, they seemed to eat very well. The presence of both the Margrave and the Ambassador probably meant that a few extra fancy foodstuffs had been loaded before departure, and there seemed to be plenty of wine.

The night was spent listening to Captain Tamik and his first mate telling tall sea stories, as well as one of his crew serenading the women with his songs and his tunes upon a strange Kiaman version of a lute, which had a distinctly different sound to it.

Dorm found it actually rather easy to drop off to sleep on board the ship. The sounds of the water rushing past, the creak of the wood, as well as the rhythmic gentle movement of the ship helped to calm him when he was lying down. Which was curiously at odds with how they affected him when he was standing up.

The next morning Dorm arose early. He quickly dressed and headed up onto the main deck. There was a stiff breeze blowing. It was a bright sunny morning with only a few clouds in the sky. Dorm moved over to where Captain Tamik and his first mate stood discussing something and consulting with a large piece of parchment.

"Good morning Captain," Dorm greeted them cheerfully.

"Good morning Your Highness," Tamik said briefly looking up from the parchment. "I hope you slept well,"

"Quite well thank you," he looked at the parchment. "A map I see. I hope we are still on course."

"For the most part yes," Temik replied without looking up. He was fiddling with an abacus and held a quill between his fingers.

"That doesn't sound very good."

"Oh it's normal for the Desert Sea, Your Highness," the mate informed him.

"Yes it has to do with the strong currents."

"Currents?"

"Yes, because of the rivers. All the water flows into the sea from one or two rivers, and then flows out again through the River of the Sea, off to the south." He waved his hand in indication.

"So the water moves quicker here than in the open ocean?"

"It seems to. I have no idea why, but then I've never sailed on the open ocean. You could probably ask your Admiral friend. I'm sure he could explain it."

"I'm sure he could. I'm guessing by the unperturbed look upon your face that this isn't anything to worry about?"

"Hardly," Tamik replied. "We have unaffected trips so rarely, that they are more surprising to us. We might be a few hours later arriving in Szugabar than we first thought, but not so much that you'll miss anything."

"I'm glad about that. Given the hospitality we have received so far on this voyage I'm sure a few more hours won't do us any harm."

He went below and informed the others of their adjusted time of arrival. No one seemed particularly upset by that, and Margrave Hamik even seemed to like the idea, hinting that it might let them avoid some of the more pedantic ceremonies if they were late enough.

Dorm returned to the deck after breakfast and took in the view of the waters stretching off into infinity. It was strange being out here. He had been to the coast of the Eastern Sea several times. Looking out across that ocean had not been quite the same. He had known that right behind him was land. All he had to do was to turn his head slightly to one side or the other and he would be given the perspective he needed. The ocean seemed more contained in that situation.

Here though out in the middle of it, he seemed to be adrift in an infinite nothingness. The only way he knew that they were even moving was by the wind and the slosh of the water against the ships hull. Even the wake generated by their passage seemed to fade quickly, as if it didn't want to mar the unending surface of that vast body of water. This of course was foolish. The Eastern Sea was hundreds of times larger than the Desert Sea. If anything the Desert Sea was the contained one. But out here in the middle of all that water, it didn't really seem that way.

He looked out towards the bow and noticed Ambassador Camir standing looking out ahead of them. Dorm walked over to him.

"Baron," he said quietly in acknowledgement.

"Your Highness," Camir replied. "Makes one think doesn't it?

"The sea? Yes it does."

"I've only been on a ship twice before. When I was Ambassador to Selatem some years ago. Of course on those trips we had the coast on one side of us the whole way."

"It does make one feel sort of… insignificant, doesn't it?"

"Truly," he sighed. "Your Highness, may I ask you a question?"

"Of course,"

"What is going on here?" He turned and looked directly at him. "I mean your group is a rather odd assortment of people to be sure, you all have those strange amulet things, and some of the things that have happened... I mean I've never been chased into the desert before."

"Honestly, I'm not entirely sure," Dorm admitted leaning against the railing. He had had the feeling that the Ambassador might have a bit of an idea that something other then Dorms' "family business" story was going on. "We know it has something to do with the Fortress, but that is about all."

"The Fortress? That sounds serious."

"I think it is. Given that we've encountered Peldraksekhr agents within the boundaries of the Alliance also makes me worry. And makes me think that perhaps they might suspect that something is going on."

"And what is going on?"

"If I knew that I'd be a happier man. Or at least less stressed." Dorm sighed again. "I'm sure that we'll find out eventually. Even if we don't end up liking what it is."

The day wore on much like any other day at sea. They had a small lunch around midday and then the afternoon came. It grew hotter as the hours went by, but the breeze kept things tolerable.

Around mid afternoon, Rhyn and Telly were standing near the bow gazing out to sea, when they noticed something in the water just in front of the ship. Their animated movements and the excited catch in their voices aroused Dorms' curiosity and he went to investigate.

It turned out to be a number of large silvery fish swimming just in front of the bow as they moved along. Every time they came near the surface, or breached it, the sunlight would catch their scales and flash like silver fire.

"Are those fish dolphins, that you always hear about?" Rhyn asked.

"No," Dorm replied. "I think dolphins are salt water creatures not fresh water. They might be some kind of trout or something maybe."

"Well whatever they are, I think they are magnificent," Telly said happily.

"Perhaps it's a good omen," Rhyn suggested hopefully. "We could certainly use one."

"I think we're all agreed on that point," Telly concurred.

"What do we think is really going on with all this Dorm?" Rhyn asked seriously looking up from the fish. "Why are we going to Szugabar?"

"No idea Rhyn," he admitted. He laughed briefly. "The Ambassador was asking me the same thing this morning actually."

"You mean he knows?"

"Well not everything, but he suspected that there was more going on here than what we had told him. It didn't seem sensible to keep it from him any longer. Our trip through the desert didn't really help maintain our story much."

"True enough," Telly mused. "You don't think he will present a problem at all?"

"No. Actually I think he might even be a help. He knows the people there better than we do. He might open doors we need opened. And possibly even close some we'd rather have closed."

"Well if he understands the seriousness of it all."

"I think he does."

"I hope we aren't going to have to attend too many of these festivals," Rhyn said dejectedly.

"Probably only a few, from what Camir and the Margrave have said," Dorm reassured her.

"I'm glad," she admitted. "The idea of all that religion. It just makes me a little uncomfortable."

"Me too," Telly confided. "But it might be possible that the amulets might be considered religious items, so perhaps it will be a help."

"We can hope that something good like that comes from it," Dorm agreed. "I know that having a religion makes the Szugabar a little strange, but they are our allies, and friends. I think it is a sign of maturity if we can accept the differences in our friends and colleagues, don't you?"

"You sound like Camir," Telly told him jokingly.

"Except I have a bigger badge to wave around."

"Well like they say, Your Highness," she replied sultrily. "It's not the size that counts but how you use it."

The day wore on and the ship sailed further into the never-ending expanse of water. As the sun was beginning to set a large flock of birds began to keep pace with the ship. A nearby crewman informed him that this meant that they were getting closer to land. Dorm was a little surprised by this, he hadn't even realised that they had passed halfway yet. Space and time seemed to be all jumbled up out here on the sea.

Dinner that night was again delightfully lavish for the ship. The conversation turned to Szugabar and it's people. None of their group had ever been there before and it was important to be able to get information about what to expect. The last thing any of them wanted to do was create a diplomatic incident.

They discussed generally the nature of the festival ceremonies that they would be attending, before moving on to topics of politics and such, that made both Tissie's and Arturs' eyes droop.

"Of course the thing you have to remember," Camir was saying. "Is that they see their political leaders very differently to how we do in the rest of the Alliance."

"How so exactly?" Rhyn asked.

"Well when you look at our Princely friend here," he indicated Dorm. "You see a man. An important man to be sure, but just a man. In Szugabar, the Phirinos is seen as a direct descendant of one of their Gods."

"That's ridiculous," Lianna scoffed.

"Of course it is," Camir went on. "But it is the way they see their world. It's very important to them."

"Which God is he supposed to be descended from?" Harmia enquired.

"Ah Raked, their chief God. God of the Sun and Life as well as Royalty among other things."

"Doesn't it strike them as a little odd that their divine ruler, dies every so often?" Zacravia asked.

"Oh they've thought of that. It's the same soul. But a different body. The same soul, the kingly soul is reincarnated into the new Phirinos upon the death of the old one." Camir paused for a moment staring at the wall. "Or something like that."

"Sounds complicated," Mac concluded.

"Oh it is, but they take it very seriously. Some of the Phirinos' titles reinforce that belief system. Let me see if I can remember some of them. There's Son of Light, Dispeller of Shadows, Bearer of Truth, Ahh… Divine Justice, Glory of Life. There's others but I think you get the idea. Of course the Phirinos is the King, he takes care of all the big stuff, which when you are a living God is obviously pretty big. The Grand Vizier takes care of the more mundane things."

"Mundane?" asked Telly. "Like what?"

"Oh taxation, building the roads and wharves, and forts. The mines, overseeing the garbage collection, and provision of water, that sort of thing."

"So kind of like our High Clan Chief then?" Dorm suggested.

"Quite like that yes." Camir agreed. "Only with less feasting, and rarely any quaffing."

"Our High Minister then," Travanos commented.

"How many Gods do they have in Szugabar?" asked Artur quietly.

"About ten I think it is, isn't it Captain?"

"Yes I think ten," Captain Temik said from the head of the table.

"I've never quite understood the idea of a God," Artur continued. "It seems quite… well alien to me."

"It is strange I will admit," Camir agreed. "It takes a little getting used to."

"They aren't the only ones with Gods of course," Travanos informed them. "The Peldraksekhr have several Gods."

"Apparently so too do the Rikwegians," Dorm said. "I remember reading about it in one of the reports."

"Rikwegians?" Camir asked. "Is that the right word to describe them?"

"No idea, but it sounded right at the time."

"Don't the Plejzdark also have Gods?" Lianna asked. "I'm sure I remember that from schooling."

"I think so," Camir said. "Though given how long it has been since any one has had contact with them, it's impossible to say. Things may have changed a great deal there. If indeed they are still there."

"If the old stories about the Plejzdark are anything to go by," Dorm mused. "I think it would take quite a bit to get rid of them. Which is just as well."

"Oh why is that?" Camir queried him.

"Because we may even have to end up going there."

"Do you really think so?"

"I honestly have no idea. But anything is possible in this whole quest thing."

"You must still explain this quest thing to me, Your Highness," Margrave Hamik said then. "It is still a mystery to me."

"Well Excellence, it is still a bit of a mystery to us as well. But we can't deny the fact that we are all here together."

"But a quest seems so… incredible," he went on.

"You're telling us," Ambra said.

"So what exactly can we expect when we land in Szugabar?" Rhyn asked.

"Most of the common people will probably ignore you all," Captain Temik said. "They will be respectful, but they wont fall over themselves to help you or fawn over you."

"Just as well," Dorm said. "I don't think we'll have the time."

"Yes the fawning won't start until we get to the Palace," Hamik laughed.

"And there I suppose we will be waited on hand, foot, and any other appendage you care to mention," Telly said.

"That's a fairly accurate description, My lady," the Margrave continued.

"Well I suppose if I have to endure a little abject luxury and pampering for the cause, I can be strong enough."

"I'm sure we'll all do our best to help you with it," Mac told her comfortingly.

"Does this mean we will have to meet with the Phirinos himself?" Zacravia asked a little worriedly.

"Well His Highness will. We might be able to get Lady Tellsandra and it might be possible to get the Admiral in. Maybe Constable Harmia as well. Also myself and the Margrave," Camir explained. "The rest of you I'm afraid won't rate very highly in the Phirinos' view of things."

"I hope there won't be any state dinners or anything."

"No by tradition the Phirinos and the Phirina dine alone. You may have to dine with the Princess though."

"The Princess?" Dorm asked curiously.

"Yes she's the heir. They don't have many female rulers in Szugabar, but she will be in charge when her father dies. I can't remember what her name is though."

"I'm sure we'll have opportunity to find out," Dorm sighed. "I get the feeling that Szugabar is going to keep us all busy."

"Oh very busy Your Highness."

"Great. I should probably go to bed early then tonight, and start stocking up on sleep."

Around midnight Dorm woke. He felt that there was something he needed to do, but he didn't know what. He got out of bed, being careful not to wake Mac, dressed and went out into the companionway.

He went up on deck and looked out across the dark waters. The moon was out, and bathed the scene in its cool light. Several crew members moved around the deck quietly at their various tasks. Something about night time made people move about in silence, or as near to it as they could get. He looked to the tiller and the large burly sailor who stood watch. The golden glow of lamplight touching the area around him.

Instead he walked forward. Strolling slowly past the rigging and the creaking sails. He stood at the bow looking out across the scene towards the horizon. A slight mist seemed to be hovering over the water as they sailed onward.

He stood for a few moments thinking about the evening's conversation. Szugabar sounded very different to what he was used to. He tried to recall all that he knew of them, which wasn't a great deal. There were many aspects of their society, especially their government and religion, that they kept to themselves. Probably some sort of left over concern from the war, even though that had been centuries ago.

If the next two questers where in Szugabar he hoped they would be able to find them soon. He was beginning to get the feeling that they should hurry along. They still had at least two more countries to visit, and that wasn't considering that they still had to find the other person in Kiama Mor.

He gazed out over the dark waters for a few moments listening to the sound of the water coursing past the hull before raising his face to the heavens. The stars shone brightly, and out here away from any city there seemed to be so many more of them. The great band of the heavens seemed much bigger and much deeper than he had ever seen before.

The breeze ruffled his clothes and he felt a brief chill. It was probably time to go back to bed. He did have a fairly full day tomorrow, he expected.

He turned to head back to the stairs that lead below.

Further along the railing stood a figure. At first he just presumed it was one of the crew taking a brief break in his duties,but as he watched he noticed the figure was dressed oddly. They wore a long dark cloak. It was hard to tell exactly what colour it was, given the moonlight, but he could tell it was dark. A very similar colour to a Ranger cloak, in fact.

He was about to say something, when the figure turned toward him. It was a woman. She wasn't very old. Certainly no older than Dorm himself, but she seemed to posses a face that held a great deal of wisdom. He got the feeling that there was very little she didn't know.

She stood for a moment, looking at him. Yet apparently not. She seemed almost to look through him. He stepped towards her.

"Hello?" he called quietly to her. "Who are you?"

She suddenly flinched as if she had only just realised he was there. She frantically looked around her for a moment, taking in the sight of the ship and the sea. "This is not where I am supposed to be," she said shortly. Her voice was strong, yet strangely hollow, as if she was talking down a tube of some sort.

"Who are you?" Dorm repeated.

"Quester you should not see me now," she said with a hint of fear in her voice.

"Well it's too late for that now isn't it?" he said probably a little more angrily than he intended. "Tell me who you are. You look like a Ranger."

"I am not a Ranger, but I work with them. This should not be happening."

"Well it is I'm afraid," Dorm told her. "Why are you here?"

"I am not supposed to be here. This was not where I intended to land."

"Land? You mean like a bird?"

"I do not understand. This is not meant to be."

"Where are you meant to be?"

"Yes I shall try that sir," she said suddenly.

"Huh?" Dorm stared at her realising she was talking to someone else. But there was only him here. "What does that mean?"

"It will take a few moments. And I am tired, but I shall try, if you will help me sir?" She held out her hand. After a moment her fingers closed as if she held something in her hand. Dorm got the faint impression of fingers closing over her hand, but it was so insubstantial, almost like the memory of a hand.

"What is going on here?" Dorm said confusedly.

"Quester, you sail on the Desert Sea?"

"Yes. For Szugabar."

"Once there you must proceed with caution. There are enemies abroad now. Be careful."

"Yes we've encountered some of them."

"I know. But there are more to come."

"Who are you?" Dorm asked her again after a moment.

"I may not tell you my name," she replied hesitantly. "But I am a friend."

"A lot of people have been telling me that over the past few months. I'm not sure I believe many of them either."

"Trust in us."

"Us? I don't even know who you are? Are you sure this isn't another one of my crazy dreams?"

"You dreams are necessary, they will build up your strength for what must come to pass in the future."

"Why am I even asking you really? I mean if this is a dream, and you are a part of it, you will just tell me what I want to hear, right? Maybe I should go and see Geven again. He can get that woman to do that hands thing she did to me last time."

She cocked her head to one side as if listening to something. "Of course sir, I will try."

"Huh? Who are you talking to?"

"You will discover this soon enough Highness. We are here to help you."

"Well so far you haven't really done *that* good a job. Look we really should be getting more information for this. I mean one page of writing from some "prophet" who dies thousands of years ago isn't really that informative."

"You mean… then you haven't…?" She paused and looked off to one side. "We must immediately then sir." She turned back to Dorm. "I must go now Your Highness. I wish you luck on the next stage of your journey. Be on the lookout for assistance. We shall do our best to provide it."

"And what is that supposed to mean?" Dorm asked her sternly.

But she never answered. Her image became hazy and indistinct. Dorm could actually see through her though he could still see her. After a moment she had vanished completely, and he stood alone on the deck in the chill air.

Dorm looked around feeling a little alone, but also rather embarrassed. He hoped that no one had seen him talking to this… phantom?

He didn't believe in phantoms. He didn't expect many people had conversations with them.

He walked slowly and a little unsteadily back to his bunk, being careful to avoid the spot where the woman's image had been standing. He closed the door quietly and took a drink of water. He stood for a moment trying to calm himself before he undressed and slipped back into bed. Mac instinctively moved closer to him, but Dorm simply stared at the ceiling. It wasn't every day that you had a conversation with a ghost.

But then, had it been a ghost?

She had seemed to be actually talking to him at several stages there. Answering his questions… well sort of.

She had been wearing a robe similar to the Rangers. Did that mean she was a Ranger? Or perhaps one of the people who gave them their orders, that Geven had mentioned back in Kiama Mor.

And who was this "sir" she kept talking to? And what did he have to do with this?

It was all very confusing and a little frightening. Dorm felt his head begin to ache a little in response to things it didn't want to think about.

Eventually, to the sound of the sea and Mac's breathing, he drifted off to sleep.

In the morning he awoke, feeling only marginally rested, and still very confused. The events of the night before seemed almost a dream, but when he went up on deck and saw the place where he and the woman had been standing he somehow knew that it wasn't.

He was of two minds about telling the others. He knew that they, like him would be confused and mystified by what she had said, not to mention the fact that it had happened at all. Keeping it to himself would probably make them a little angry with him, if and when they did find out.

He watched their faces as they went through their morning rituals of breakfast and conversation and the morning walk everyone seemed to instinctively take right after. They seemed blissfully unaware of the strange and momentous occurrence that had happened only a few short hours ago, right on this very deck.

He wanted to tell them, but felt that if he did it would only cause problems. More confusion wasn't something they needed right at the moment. Everyone was worried enough about everything that was going on, and that they were doing. Adding this to the mix would hardly calm everyone's nerves.

After a few hours, around mid-morning, the dark smudge along the horizon, began to grow and appear to be more than just a line. They realised that it was the coastline of Szugabar. Captain Temik scanned that coastline with his telescope looking for some landmark that he knew. When he spotted it, he took some measurements and made a quick calculation before ordering an adjustment in the ships heading to the starboard.

The crewman at the tiller swung the great wheel over and the ship slowly turned into the new course, while other crewmen made slight adjustments to the sails in order to keep the wind.

"We should be arriving at the port in Szugabar in a few hours Your Highness," Temik told him. "I'll go and tell the Margrave and the Ambassador."

"Thank you Captain," Dorm replied. He looked out ahead of the ship as the dark smudge grew bigger and details slowly emerged.

It was a rugged coastline of high rocky cliffs coloured in all sorts of golds, yellows and oranges. There were rocks and reefs along the coast but they stayed far enough away from them so that they wouldn't pose a problem. They followed the coastline northward, several ships passing off to their starboard side heading south.

There was a sense of activity as the crew prepared for the stop in port.

Dorm took that as a hint and went below to begin packing up his own belongings. They hadn't brought much with them on this side trip. It hadn't seemed appropriate. And room was at a premium. It was only a short time later when their group gathered on the quarterdeck to watch the ship dock at the large stone quay they could now see in the distance.

The harbour was a hive of activity. Large ships and small boats jostled amongst each other. Dorm noticed a large number of the small reed-made fishing boasts that were famous in Szugabar. There were also a larger number of birds in the sky he noticed.

The *Star of the Sea* inched her way towards the quay and finally after much shouting and hauling on ropes that were thrown from the sides to waiting dockworkers, the ship bumped gently against the stones and stopped. A large gangway was raised and roped on to the ship, and Captain Temik went down onto the quay with several parchments to give to the quay supervisor. After a moment of two of studying them, the supervisor apparently gave permission for the passengers to disembark, and everything was alright.

Dorm now took some time to actually look at the city itself. He couldn't see a great deal, what with all the warehouses and the walls blocking his view, but several large pillars and obelisks rose within the walls, suggesting some important buildings. Here and there a tower or rooftop peered above the walls, as if peeking at the world beyond.

The sun was bright and the temperature was definitely higher here. A few tall date palms waved slowly in the light breeze and Dorm almost felt that he was back in Kiama Mor, except that the language of the dock workers and traders was different, and the architecture was also new.

One by one they walked down onto the quay and waited, feeling a little like sore thumbs, sticking out rather nicely. Camir informed him that the Margrave was sending word of their arrival and requests for coaches to drive them to their accommodations, which were apparently a large special palace for visiting foreign dignitaries, located not far from the palace of the Phirinos.

The heat began to get a bit too much and they all had to sit for a while as they waited. Tissie pulled out a large fan and began to almost frantically wave herself with it. It wasn't long before the other women had also done likewise. The men carefully placed themselves where they too might get some of this relaxing breeze, without making it look like they were. Finally though a small fleet of carriages arrived drawn by some strange looking animals that were apparently camels. These camels were different to the ones they previously encountered in Kiama Mor. For a start they had two humps, not just one. And seemed to have much thicker fur. Their curly hair and large lips gave them a rather stupid look, but their humps were rather fascinating. Hamik began telling them how these camels could store water there and live for very long times in the desert without drinking.

These camels also wore elaborate bridles that had small bells attached to them. Some of them even seemed to be wearing veils across their mouths. Apparently this was only done to animals that had a tendency to bite people. Dorm noticed that actually quite a lot of them had them. He'd heard that camels were bad tempered, but that many?

Once everyone was boarded and their luggage packed the coaches turned away from the quayside and headed back towards the city gates, weaving their way slowly through the warehouses and workshops, not to mention the throng of dockworkers and other general workmen and merchants that seemed to be everywhere.

Finally after some time and more than a few near misses in the traffic, they finally arrived at the gates themselves and the mysterious capital of Szugabar beyond.

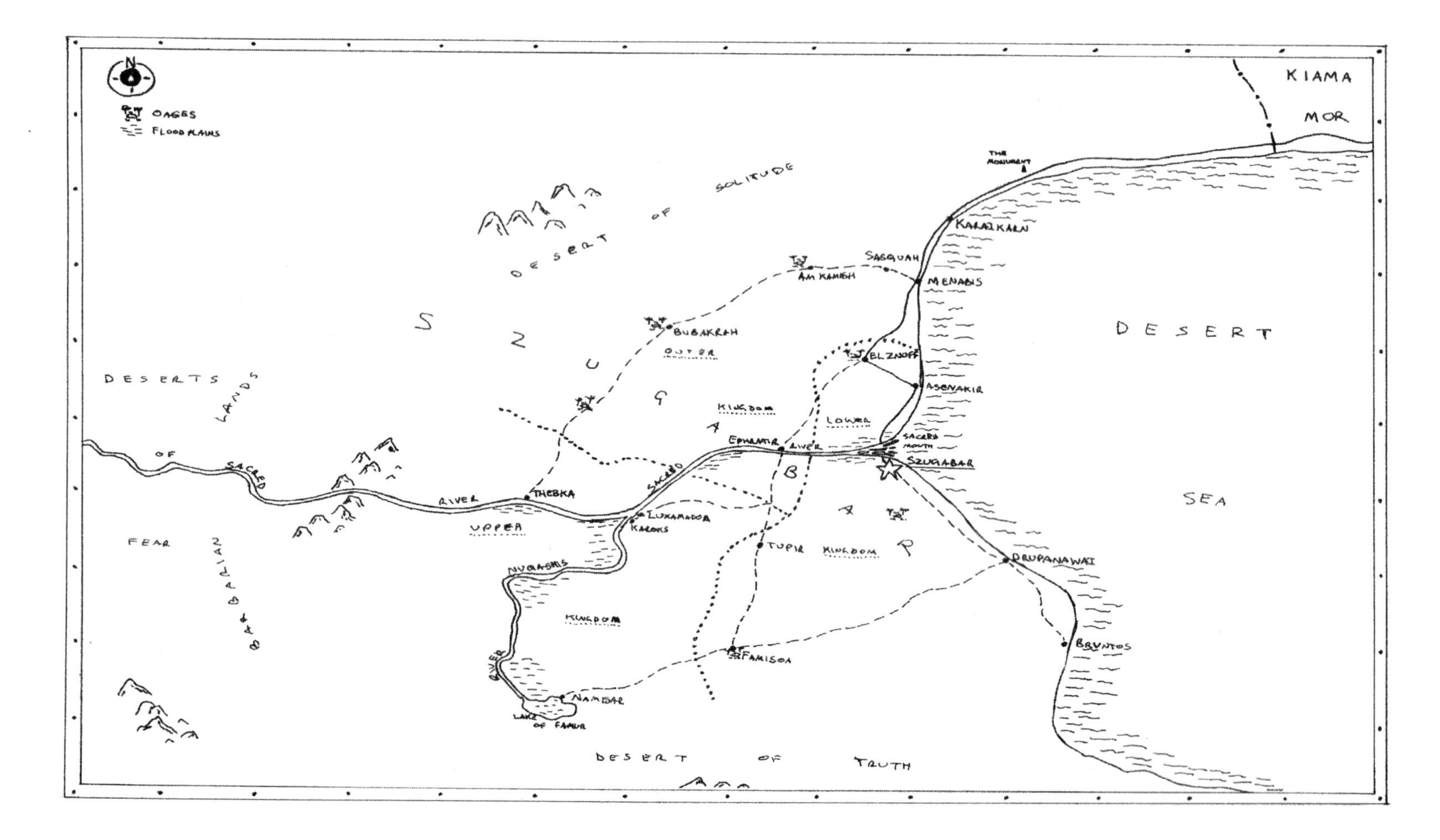

N
OASES
FLOOD PLAINS
KIAMA
MOR
THE MONUMENT
KARAIKARN
SASQUAH
AM KAMEH
MENABIS
DESERT
SEA
DESERT OF SOLITUDE
BUBAKRAH
OUTER
KINGDOM
ELZNOFF
ASENAKIR
LOWER
SACRED MOUTH
SZUGABAR
EPHRATIR
RIVER
SZUGABARP
DESERTS
LANDS
OF SACRED RIVER
THEBKA
UPPER
SACRED
LUXAMADOR
KAROKS
FEAR
BARBARIAN
NUGASMIS
KINGDOM
TUPIR
KINGDOM
DRUPANAWAI
BRUNTOS
FAMISOA
RIVER
NAMBAR
LAKE OF FAMUR
DESERT OF TRUTH

Chapter 18

Szugabar was an ancient city.

That much was obvious. It was quite possible that it was older than any city in the Alliance. The buildings seemed to proudly display their age. There was something about the vast simplicity of their construction that spoke of a different, less complicated and yet more nobler age. An age of great ideas, and even greater ideals.

Their carriages moved quickly through the city past all the teeming masses in the streets. Workmen, merchants, soldiers, craftsmen, entertainers, priests; the melting pot of Szugabaran life was there for all to see. The city seemed vast. Every street they passed seemed to stretch back for miles. They passed shops, and factories, and houses and villas, and forts, and storehouses, and temples. All made from the same yellow coloured stone.

Giant engraved pylons supported the main public buildings. Each pylon topped by one of the traditional multi-tailed flags. Tall, thin trees and even some flowers provided splashes of colour along their route. Every so often they would pass through a square at the junction of two major thoroughfares. Each square had at its centre a large stone statue or obelisk, of a God or a Phirinos of the past.

Their journey seemed almost aimless, and Dorm hoped that their drivers knew where they were supposed to be going. After about half an hour of solid travel, they passed through an ornate gatehouse in a large wall. Beyond the gatehouse the city continued, though here the buildings were much finer than those outside, being accented here and there with bright white limestone and alabaster. More trees lined the streets, and there were even occasional bunted ropes strung high above the street, to give one the impression of festivities. Dorm wasn't sure if this was because of the great festival they were here to attend or if this was just normal practice.

About a quarter of an hour after the first gate they passed through another large ornate gatehouse, into an area, which contained a series of large square, nearly identical buildings. Their driver informed them that this was the offices of the various government services, and that they were close to the centre of the city and the Phirinos' palace.

They passed through yet another gate, this time smaller, but more elaborately decorated, into a large open area that was dotted with large ornate looking houses. Apparently these were houses for the various viziers and high ranking bureaucrats, as well as the embassies of the other nations that Szugabar maintained diplomatic relations with. They turned off the main road onto a slightly smaller one, lined on the sides by low hedges and headed towards a rather much larger collection of buildings that were surrounded by yet another wall. Dorm noticed another very high and imposing looking wall off to their left. Their driver dutifully told him that that was the wall surrounding the Phirinos' palace itself.

Their accommodations were large and luxurious to say the least. Their palace, while not as big as any in the Alliance, was still large enough to get lost in and to make one feel quite at home.

Imported marble and polished granite abounded and ornately carved expensive woods surrounded the doors and windows. Sumptuous rugs, and tapestries gave the rooms and corridors a much homier feeling, and every table and desk, and even counter seemed to have bowls of flowers on them.

It took a while for them to be all shown to their rooms, and Dorm and Mac shared an apartment that was actually bigger than their rooms back in Lugemall. It looked out onto a large central courtyard, that seemed to be overflowing with trees, and flowers, and somewhere running water could be heard cascading gently over rocks.

"And what exactly are we supposed to do with all this room?"

Dorm said to no one in particular once their guide had left them.

"Enjoy it," Mac said throwing himself on the large bed and nearly disappearing into the covers.

"Sometimes I think you don't take things seriously enough," Dorm told him.

"And sometimes I think you take things too seriously," Mac replied tartly climbing back out of the bed and crossing back to him. "But I still love you none the less." He gave him a quick peck before scampering off to explore the rest of their rooms.

Dorm put his bag down on the large table. And walked slowly around the room. He went out onto the balcony through the filmy curtains and looked down into the garden. This level of luxury would take some getting used to.

At midday a servant came and informed them that a small meal had been prepared for them in one of the "informal dinning rooms", which turned out to be a large hall, with tables and chairs for more than a hundred guests. Thankfully though their retinue was allowed to eat alone, which gave them all the opportunity to compare notes on their trip through the city, and the accommodations they had been given.

While they were eating, the official Ambassador from Kiama Mor was ushered in to greet the Margrave. He apparently had been informed that they had arrived and had wanted to confer with Hamik about events back home. They went off to one corner of the hall and began an animated conversation.

Camir informed them that the festival itself would begin in two days. As honoured guests they would be invited to attend the commencement ceremony at which the Phirinos would participate in his role as the Kingdoms ultimate high priest.

Dorm was quite fascinated by the idea of a monarch also being a religious figure. It was strange and alien to him, yet at the same time held a certain interest. The idea of a monarch being a living God was itself uniquely interesting, in a strange sort of way.

As the afternoon wore on the palace grew hotter, despite all the intricate design elements intended to keep it cool. Dorm hated to think what it would have been like had these not been included. Apparently it was customary in some parts of the country to take a brief rest around mid afternoon, and so it seemed here that a silence descended over the building as everyone took a short nap.

Dorm found the nap quite relaxing. The softness of the bed, and the warmth of the air, was just the right combination to send him into a deep and restful sleep. He awoke feeling better than he had in quite a while. No dreams had plagued him, though he felt vaguely as though he had been watched.

He and Mac sat talking for a while about Szugabar and it's people. Mac always had an interest in learning such things. He hadn't had Dorms advanced education, only receiving the basic schooling that all Alliance children received. Dorm of course, being the heir to the throne, had had several tutors in various subjects for most of his formative years, and sometimes was even a little impressed himself, at the volumes of information he could actually recall. Which was doubly an achievement, as he felt that he'd slept through quite a number of his lessons.

As the day wore on, several members of their group came by to talk, and to discuss what their plans might be for the next few days. The general consensus was to play it by ear. They had no real idea of where the next two questers might be, so there was no real way to mount a search. Also the fact that they were official guests here would limit their movements somewhat.

The evening came and the sky began to grow darker. As the sun set the sky took on that blaze of orange and the light grew intense. The air began to cool noticeably not long after the sun had sunk below the line of the horizon, or in this case the walls surrounding the royal compound. The shadows lengthened and servants went around and lit the various lamps and sconces that illuminated all the corridors and rooms. Several large torches were also lit in the courtyard below their rooms.

As the night came, another servant; there seemed to be quite a few, came and informed them that their dinner would be served shortly. Again they were taken to the large hall, and allowed to eat in 'private'. The traditional Szugabaran fare was definitely something that few of them were used to, but it was delicious, and filling, and there was plenty of it.

They sat around talking for a while as the group of musicians played quietly in the background. After a while Margrave Hamik requested that they play a song he knew, and they obliged him. According to the Margrave they didn't do too bad a job of it.

Everyone went to sleep early that night, it had been a long day and they were all tired. The climate in this country seemed to induce sleep.

When he woke in the morning Dorm again had the same feeling of having been watched. Not in a malicious way, more in the nature of curiosity. He wasn't afraid of it, he just wished that whoever it was would tell him why.

They ate their breakfast and prepared themselves for yet another long quiet day. Around mid-morning however a herald arrived and soon they were all being ushered back to their carriages. They left their palace and headed back towards the main road. However when they reached it, instead of turning left toward the city, the turned right, and headed directly for the gate to the Phirinos' palace.

No one had quite expected to be taken to the Phirinos' palace quite this quickly, and certainly not without this lack of fuss being made. They had all expected some sort of formal invitation to be made. But here they were being whisked off to be taken into his presence.

After having passed through the gate, they seemed to enter a new world. Marble and limestone seemed to be almost everywhere. There were quite a few soldiers, but also a lot of servants. The palace itself was surrounded by immaculately kept lawns and trees, interspersed with beds of flowers, small pools, and statues. The building itself seemed to rear up monolithically.

It was brilliantly white, with splashes of red paint along lintels and corners. Several friezes ran around the top of the various walls. Dorm couldn't see what they depicted, but assumed given the great length of them, no one was supposed to be able to look at it all.

They disembarked in front of a short series of steps that lead to a broad landing before the main entrance to the palace. Several guards formed up around their group as an olive skinned, fussy looking man wearing a white linen outfit that resembled a cross between a tunic and a dress, came out to greet them.

"Good morning to you all," he said. "I see you have all arrived now. Excellent."

"Who are you and who are we here to meet?" Travanos asked him.

"I am Magistrate Ujan, head of His Majesties household, and you are here to see the Phirinos himself."

"The Phirinos knows we are here?" Dorm asked.

"Of course, He has requested you visit him personally," he looked across their group. "Come we haven't a lot of time for socialisation. Please follow me."

Magistrate Ujan lead them inside where it was much cooler. He walked imperiously down a wide corridor panelled in expensive looking wood. Here and there guards stood staring straight ahead, apparently oblivious to anything going on around them. Dorm had the suspicion that that wasn't really the case.

They were led into a large ornate chamber decorated with what looked like lines of tiny pictures all over large sections of the wall. A large hole in the roof admitted a great deal of light. Ujan had them wait while he went through a set of large double doors in the opposite wall, into yet another corridor.

While they waited they all curiously examined the strange pictures of the walls.

"What are these meant to be anyway," Cal said looking at one that looked vaguely like a boat.

"That is the Szugabaran Sacred writing," Margrave Hamik told them. "It can only be read by priests and the Phirinos of course.

"Any idea what this might say?" Lianna asked.

"Not really," Hamik replied. "Probably one of their great epics, or possibly prayers to keep his Majesty and his family safe. Though for all I know, it could simply be a directory of the palace. This place is rather large after all. One could easily get lost in here."

Ujan returned after a moment or two and ushered them through into the next somewhat shorter corridor. This hall also had a much lower roof. It was like they were entering some underground compound or cellar or something.

"Why is the roof here so much lower," Dorm asked.

"It is an element of our sacred architecture Your Highness," Ujan explained. "All our temples are similarly designed. The further in you go, and the closer to the centre of power you get, the smaller the areas become."

"Curious way to make buildings," Zacravia mused quietly.

They passed through yet another set of doors into a wide room. The roof was not far above their heads, and was supported by several large square columns. More of the sacred writing adorned the walls, and the only light here seemed to come from the numerous torches that hung from the columns.

Against the far wall was a single stepped dais. Upon it, sat several chairs. One was large and gilded in gold and inlaid with stones that glinted in the light. It had a high back, that seemed to culminate in some sort of disc made out of orange stone. It reminded Dorm of the sun. On the right of this chair sat another. It was smaller and not quite as decorated, but it was still quite probably more expensive than every chair in the palace at Lugemall put together. It too had a high back, not as high as the centre chair, and this ones motif at the top was different. It seemed to be a representation of water.

Also off to the right, but sitting slightly away was a smaller chair. It was intricately carved, but only had a few pieces of gold and inlaid stones. On the left of the main chair sat another carved chair, but this one was quite large, almost as large as the centre chair. At its top it carried a representation of a shield over which sat a crook and a quill.

A door at the back of the room opened and several shaven headed men entered, dressed similarly to Ujan, but without his expensive looking necklace. They moved in unison towards the dais then knelt upon the floor looking across the width of the room, seemingly looking at nothing.

A door next to the dais opened and a another shaven headed man entered. He carried with him a large ornately carved staff. He stood at the base of the dais in front of the centre chair. He faced their group and rapped his staff on the stones of the floor three times.

"Prostrate yourselves for the arrival of the great ones!" he boomed. Dorm didn't see the need for such a loud voice. They were all right here, and the room wasn't really that big to begin with.

Ujan sank to his knees and bowed his head. Hamik and Camir began doing the same. Dorm looked at the members of his group and shrugged. They all slowly sank to their knees and waited.

From the door through which the herald had entered, came a tall lean man, wearing a similar outfit to Ujan. Though his was adorned with complicated looking embroidery around the edges. He also wore a much heavier looking necklace around his collar. It was inlaid with silver and several stones. On his head he wore a complicated looking linen headress that was striped in blue and yellow. He walked to the dais as stood in front of the chair to the right. Next came a young woman. She was probably no more than twenty and breathtakingly beautiful. He hair was dark and elaborately coiled above her head. She wore again a simple gown but was dripping with gold jewellery. She wore heavy makeup around her eyes, and carried a short staff of office. She walked sedately to the smallest chair and stood before it.

Next entered a much older woman, probably in her late forties, but it was easy to tell that she was the mother of the younger woman. She too was very beautiful, with the same colour hair, and a similar looking face. Her gown was a pale blue, and she too wore expensive looking jewellery. About her neck and shoulders she wore an expensive and heavy looking collar that Dorm realised was some sort of badge of an official office.

She went and stood in front of the chair next to her daughter. She too held a staff of office, being a crook, and her eyes, elaborately made up as well, seemed to shine with a curiosity.

Next entered another man. He was of a similar age to the woman and he wore more gold and precious stones than any of the others. He wore a fancy headdress that was stripped in alternating bands of blue and yellow just like the other man's, though in the centre was a heavy looking medallion. He wore a beard that had apparently been plaited into a stiff shaft that plunged off his chin. It was bound with several ribbons, and capped in a solid gold end piece.

In his hands he carried a solid gold crook and a golden flail that still looked rather deadly despite its ornate appearance. Curiously his eyes were also lined with make up. The whole effect was strikingly beautiful, yet also somewhat frightening. Dorm knew he was in the presence of people whose power over life and death was absolute.

The group slowly sat into their chairs. The herald turned to the man in the centre seat and bowed deeply. He straightened and moved off to one side.

"Ujan," said the man in the centre. His voice carrying a great deal of power. It was a voice that was used to being heard. A voice that didn't have to strive to be heard, nor one that was ever ignored. It was the voice of power, the voice of control. "Rise and introduce our guests."

Ujan rose and bowed. "May I have the pleasure to present honoured guests from the Alliance Great One. His Royal Highness Prince Dormal of Lugemall, heir to King Mac Lavin. Your Highness, may I present his August Majesty, divine Phirinos Taslem Kanos VIII, sovereign of Szugabar."

Dorm rose slowly and then bowed deeply. "Your Majesty," he said in his best diplomatic voice. "You do me great honour by seeing me. I thank you."

"I am honoured to make you acquaintance, Your Highness."

The next few minutes were taken up with introductions, and greetings to the Phirinos, and his responses to them. He didn't seem to quite know how to respond to some of the more "common" people in their group, but he greeted them all warmly and openly, claiming them all as honoured guests. He didn't shy away from talking to lower people than himself with respect and dignity.

"And May I present to you all," The Phirinos said. "She who is my wife and my Queen. The Phirinia Tika, most gracious and august lady of Szugabar. Sacred of the Gods and mother to the country."

The Phirina inclined her head to the audience but said nothing.

"She who is my daughter and heir," the king went on. "The Princess Nefita. Favoured of the Gods, and Divine in waiting."

"Welcome friends," she said in a clear voice. She too inclined her head to their group. A curious little smile playing across her lips.

"And Grand High Vizier, Inmahop, Prime Minister of my government, and most able friend and confidant."

The man also inclined his head but said nothing. His expression almost seemed to indicate that he wasn't happy with this situation for some reason.

The Phirinos smiled at Dorm. "You give both our nation and our festival great honour by your presence here Your Highness."

"I was in the neighbourhood Your Majesty. It was no trouble. I have heard many wonderful things about your festival and I thought it was a good idea to see it first hand. I thank you for your hospitality."

"It is our pleasure. Our duty to the Gods is not complete unless we let those who seek knowledge of them receive it. While you are in Szugabar you will be honoured guests. I hope you will attend the opening ceremony?"

"I had heard about this from His Excellency, I would be very honoured to attend Your Majesty."

"All of you must attend. It will be a great day. The Great Festival is our most important time of year. To have such great and honoured friends among us during its celebrations, will please the Gods."

"We're glad we could be of service."

"It will also be good to speak to someone in such a position of authority in an Alliance Kingdom. I have thought recently that there is not enough contact between Szugabar and the other Alliance kingdoms. I have been in contemplation of addressing that. I would value your thoughts Your Highness."

"I would be most happy to give them Your Majesty," Dorm assured him genuinely. "Might I also suggest you seek the opinions of some of my other companions. They are from other Alliance Kingdoms. You could seek out the opinions of them as well."

"A most profitable suggestion Your Highness, thank you."

"I aim to please Majesty."

"I would extend an invitation to you all to dine with us this evening."

Dorm looked around at the faces of his group. "I think that would be very nice, thank you."

"Then it is settled. You will be shown to quarters while you wait. And we will discuss many things, Highness."

The rooms they were taken to were not so much bedrooms, as merely a common room, but a sumptuous common room to be sure. It was a large airy room, filled with cushions and divans and filmy, wafting curtains. A curious indoor fountain stood in the centre of the room, sending its natural music into the chamber as well as a fresh, cooling air.

After an hour or so, a servant came and escorted Dorm to the Phirinos' study.

It was a deceptively simple room. A low table, at which the king sat, seated upon a large cushion, lay at the far end of the room, before two open doors to a small balcony. Several small cupboards contained scrolls and a few books. But there was no decoration save one small wooden icon mounted on the wall above the perfectly square window between the balcony doors. The walls were plain stone. There was little in the way of colour. A breeze shifted the filmy curtains that seemed to cover every wall opening. It was a little gloomy in the room, even at this time of day, and several simple candles provided light over the desk.

"Please sit," The Phirinos said as he entered, indicating another large cushion opposite him at the desk. "You have a similar room in Lugemall?"

"Yes." Dorm admitted. "Though mine and my fathers is a little more.... Alive." He tried to make it sound inoffensive.

The king smiled. "The bareness of the room, is necessary. Ostentatiousness is something we must strive to avoid."

"Well I might agree with you there to a point. But what if there is a scroll or book you need? You don't seem to have much storage here."

"I can have it brought to me."

"Nothing personal I note too. No pictures of Her Majesty, or your daughter. My father for instance has a picture of my mother and I, which he keeps on his desk. He says it is a reminder to him of the fact that he needs to do his best every day. Because his family has to live in our country too."

"If I have the need to see my wife or my daughter I will go to them, or have them brought to me. This is a place of work. Of decision. Of contemplation. It must reflect that reality. It suits my needs."

"Of course. What was it you wanted to discuss?"

The King sighed. "My people are a proud people, Prince Dormal. We have not forgotten the war, which so nearly destroyed us. But now we understand why it happened. And we realise that there was some blame to be had on our side as well. That given the nature of the peoples of the Alliance, the war was all but inevitable given the secretive nature of our society at that time. Now of course things have changed." He paused for a moment seeming to think carefully on something. "But I believe," he went on in a quiet voice. "That the time is coming soon, when we must set aside this pain from the past, and move into the future."

"What exactly are you talking about Majesty?" Dorm asked curiously.

The Phirinos looked him directly in the eye. "Of Szugabar becoming a full member of the Alliance."

Dorm was floored. For centuries every diplomatic effort had been expended to try to convince Szugabar to fully join the Alliance. So far none had worked. And here their king was telling him that he was considering it. Dorm almost felt like running home to Lugemall right then to start the process at that end.

"Your look tells me that this would be welcome news."

"*Very* welcome Majesty. We realised very quickly that the best way to protect your people, and to prevent another war was to bring you into the Alliance. This would be a dream come true for the Alliance."

"The time is coming for change. There will of course be those in Szugabar who will not want to change. But I believe that given time and enough education on the matter, they will see the benefit."

"What has made you think this way, if I may ask?"

"The old ways are becoming less important. Some of our minor festivals are starting to be lost. We do not build the great monuments to our kings any more. Trade has started to become more important than honouring the Gods. While this saddens me, I realise the potential for improvement to my people's lives. It is something that I must pursue. Tell me, would your father allow the establishment of a permanent embassy from Szugabar?"

"I can practically guarantee it. I can probably safely say that *all* the nations of the Alliance would welcome it."

"I believe that now is the time for us to begin the process of fully integrating with the Alliance. I think that this would be a good first step."

"I would say it was an excellent first step Your Majesty."

The Phirinos paused for a moment. "I have to tell you a truth Dormal. My wife actually suggested it to me. She is much better at the subtleties of diplomacy than I."

"She sounds like a formidable woman. One of great intelligence."

"She is. The Gods have truly blessed me by giving me such a Queen. I know that such a process would take years, but I also know that there is no time like the present to grasp such an opportunity."

"Your Majesty. I think I can safely say that any move, by Szugabar to increase its participation in the Alliance, and to increase its status towards full membership would be welcomed. Szugabar has been an important friend and ally for more than two millennia. This would be the greatest present your country could ever give us."

"Then I am pleased. And I will pursue this with all the vigour I can muster."

Dorm thought for a moment. "Your Majesty, may I ask why? Why now?"

The Phirinos lent back slightly and sighed heavily. "I have had a vision."

"A vision?"

"You do not believe in visions?"

"Well," said Dorm cautiously. "Lets just say that I haven't seen any evidence to support them. We don't generally go in for that sort of thing in the Alliance."

"I see," the King said slowly. "In Szugabar visions are important. They are messages from the Gods. They must be listened to. And acted upon. My vision showed me a great battle. I know not against whom or for what reasons. But we fought alongside the rest of the Alliance, as full brothers. It was very powerful. I do not intend to ignore this message that the Gods have given me."

"Well honestly Your Majesty, I don't really care what prompts your decision. I think it can only be a wonderful thing, and I hope that you do indeed pursue it."

"I intend to Highness."

Dorm returned to their quarters feeling a little… well stunned was the only way he could describe it.

The greatest diplomatic event for the Alliance in the past millennia had just been handed to him on a platter. He knew he had to communicate this information with his father and the other kings. But doing so without arousing unwanted attention, so that details could be worked out unhindered, would be crucial.

After a brief greeting to his friends, Dorm called Ambassador Camir over.

"Something I can help you with Highness?" he asked cautiously.

"If you needed to, you could send something back to my father in Lugemall, without any one else seeing it, couldn't you?"

"Of course. Alliance diplomatic mail is protected and delivered carefully and with a great deal of care. Do you wish to send a message to your father?"

"I think I kind of have to. This is something too important to keep to myself."

"Might I be allowed to know what?"

"I've just had a very interesting conversation with the Phirinos. He seems to have had a vision."

"I see," Camir said with a hint of respect. "The Szugabar take careful note of these 'visions'. They think they help predict the future. *If* you're willing to listen to them."

"Well apparently this vision has inspired him to want to seek closer ties with the Alliance. Possibly even to the point of going … all the way."

"All the wa…" Camir stopped. The meaning of that began to dawn on him. "Oh my." He said quietly. An enthusiastic grin coming to his face. "Oh my, my my."

"Exactly," Dorm said quietly. "But just keep it to yourself for right now. We don't want news of this to leak out just yet. There are a lot of details to be worked out before we start to celebrate."

"But still. Your Highness, this could cement you and your father as the greatest monarchs in our countries history. Not to mention the prestige in Alliance history it would bring."

"Well I'm not all that interested in prestige. If the Phirinos' vision is anything to go by, there may be a lot of pain ahead. And we know that the Peldraksekhr are stirring up trouble. Let's just try and keep this from them for a little while, shall we?"

"A capital idea, I think Your Highness," Camir said winking.

Dorm composed a detailed letter to his father explaining what he had discovered. He also wrote one to Corm Sanel giving him a general description of what had occurred. As one of his fathers closest friends, and someone that Dorm respected greatly he felt he had to. He asked them to pursue this with all the urgency and strength that they could, but to make it look like nothing out of the ordinary was going on in diplomatic circles.

If the Peldraksekhr were somehow involved in all of what was going on, then the last thing they wanted was for the Empire to feel that their position was being weakened.

Dorm had to keep it hidden from even Mac. He trusted Mac with his life and much more besides, but he didn't want Mac to ever be put in a position where he might be forced to betray Lugemall, the Alliance, or Dorm and his father. He knew what that would do to him. The best way to prevent someone from revealing something, is simply not to tell them.

Dorm delivered the letter to Ambassador Camir, who quickly left the Palace to go to the Lugemallan embassy not far away. The letter to Corm Sanell would be sent on to the Tagradas embassy, with instructions that it was to be presented to him personally. Dorm had addressed it to 'Uncle Corm.' He hoped that that would be enough to arouse the Kings curiosity, and also to make sure that it was only he who read it.

Szugabars' full participation in the Alliance, would enhance both sides greatly. It was in essence, the goal that all the kings and ambassadors had been working toward ever since the end of the war. Dorm wondered at the response from the other kings.He hoped it would be as eager as Ambassador Camir's.

Dorm spent the rest of the day walking around with a suppressed grin on his face. Some curious looks from his friends, indicated that they had noticed, but none of them said anything. Camir came back during the afternoon to inform him that the letter packet had been sent off toward Lugemall. While it would take some time to get there, he felt a certain relief knowing that it was now heading towards his father.

A formal state dinner was held that night in the palace, to mark the beginning to the week of the Great Festival. As the Phirinos' honoured personal guests, Dorm and his friends were paraded around to every Nomel, Margrave and Landgrave in attendance. There was a great deal of food and wine and conversations covering every topic. Dorm's opinion was sought on most of them, and he was asked so many times if he had ever attended the Great Festival before that almost began to feel as if he had, by the details descriptions he was given.

Dancers and musicians entertained the guests during dinner. Several priests of the various gods were also in attendance. While Dorm didn't have much time to speak to them for very long, he got the impression that most of them seemed rather impressed with themselves.

There was one, an impressive looking woman with long, dark red-brown hair who was apparently a high ranking priest in one of the high temples, he couldn't remember to which God, gave him a curious look upon their introduction. She didn't saying anything out of the ordinary, but he got the impression that in another set of circumstances she would have questioned him about whatever concerned her. After their brief chat he was whisked away to another group of nobles before he could pursue it.

He caught a glimpse of her several times during the evening, but she didn't seem to be looking at him. He began to think perhaps he had imagined it.

The Phirinos gave a speech towards the end of the evening, and then the collected High Priests led them all in a prayer to the Gods to bless the Phirinos, the country and the upcoming festival.

The whole experience of the religious part of the night was a little strange. The people of the Alliance didn't go in for that sort of thing. Dorm wasn't quite sure what he was supposed to do. He tried to bow his head slightly when the priests were talking, as all the Szugabarans seemed to be doing, but he felt rather awkward. Form the expressions of his friends; he got the feeling that they did too.

They returned to their room late in the night, or was it possibly early in the morning? Everyone was too tired to worry about issues of privacy as they literally flumped down onto the various pillows and cushions and divans. The warmth of the air, and the playful melody of the water in the fountain ushered everyone off to sleep gently.

Dorm again had the "dream" where it felt as if he was being watched. This time however he could hear whispering. And the intensity of the unseen eyes scrutiny of him felt much more intense this time. It began to feel a little familiar, but he couldn't put his finger on how.

Upon waking in the morning they were again treated to a lavish breakfast and taken to rooms where they could wash and dress. During the night their packs had been brought from the other palace and they were able to change into fresh clothes.

Upon returning to their room, the Princess was in attendance. She was chatting quietly with Rhyn as the other members of their group filtered in.

"Good morning Your Highness," Dorm said to her as he approached them.

"Good morning Your Highness," she responded in her accented voice, with a low and graceful curtsy. "I trust you slept well?"

"Yes thank you."

"Lady Rhynavell has just been telling me, somewhat reluctantly of your quest."

"Her Highness was curious as to our reason for being here," Rhyn explained. "She had the impression that we weren't here just for the festival."

"Her Highness is most intuitive."

"One of the important skills in being a Phirinos," she said knowingly. "I am honoured to be alive during the time of such an important quest."

"I tried to explain that we don't like to think about the fact that we are on a quest," Rhyn told him.

"You do not see it as something noble and important?" the Princess asked.

"Important, yes," Dorm explained. "But a quest is something from literature. They make nice stories, but they don't really happen. At least, I used to think that."

"Humility and modesty as well," the Princess said quietly

watching Dorm intently. "Excellent traits in the leader of a quest. I believe you will succeed."

"We seem to have an awful lot of people being confident in us," Rhyn said to Dorm sarcastically. "Pity we aren't among them."

"We might have if we knew what we were actually doing," Dorm said.

"You mean you do not know the object of this quest?" the Princess asked incredulously.

"Well we know we have to gather all the people with these amulets," he explained pointing his out to her. "But after that, we're a little lost. We'll just have to hope that someone comes along to explain what our next step is."

The Princess thought for a moment. "You should ask the Gods for direction. There will be many times during the festival when you will have opportunity to ask the Gods directly to guide you."

"Your Gods come here to the festival?"

"Their minds do you, yes. They are with us always of course. But during the festival they hear our words more clearly. It is a powerful time to talk to them. I suggest that you ask the Gods for guidance and direction. I'm sure they will answer such as you and your friends, Your Highness."

"Well thank you for the suggestion, Your Highness."

"My father wishes you to attend the great opening ceremony today with him as his personal guests."

"I think we would be delighted. When and where does it take place?"

"It will begin at midday, outside the Temple of Raked in the South quarter of the city. You will be taken there, do not worry."

"I look forward to speaking with him on the way. He started a very interesting conversation yesterday."

"Oh you will not see him before the ceremony. My father has the most important role to play in the ceremony. And he has been in prayers all morning. About two hours before the ceremony he will go to the temple to cleanse himself. You will see him during the ceremony."

"I see. I forget that your father also has a religious role to play, as well as his political one."

The Princess looked puzzled for a moment. "He has but one role, and that is to be Phirinos of Szugabar. Whether he is performing ceremonies with the priests or meeting with the bureaucrats he is still the Phirinos, and it is all the same responsibility."

"I think this has to do with the 'divine kingship' thing that Ambassador Camir was talking about," Rhyn suggested quietly. "Probably best not to push it."

"Good idea." Dorm agreed.

"I know that in the rest of the Alliance the role of the Phirinos is not fully understood," Nefita went on. "We accept this as an unfortunate idiosyncrasy of our friends. While we might want you to understand, we know the reasons why you do not, and we accept them."

"Well, thank you for that," Dorm told her. "I'm sure that whatever it is that your father has to do tomorrow, he will do to the best of his ability."

"Of course. He is the Phirinos."

Chapter 19

The Temple of Raked was a vast sprawling complex of buildings, that dominated, or perhaps constituted the southern part of the city. Dorm had expected it be large, yes, but the word 'temple' had conjured up images of a single building. This was more like fifty, all of varying sizes, and function. And of course that was not all. There were ceremonial avenues, lined with statues. Gardens with trees, and sacred lakes. Storehouses and shrines. All were surrounded by a low wall, though the wall was broken by several different entrances.

The main temple stood opposite the main gated entrance. The gates were presently open, and they had a fine view of the ceremonial avenue leading towards it. The temple itself appeared rather plain, considering it was one of the most important buildings in the country. Dorm had rather expected something more grandiose, and decorated. This was rather plain. The ever-present pylons were decorated with what appeared to be bas-relief; it was a little hard to tell at this distance of what exactly, but Dorm guessed at pictures of Gods; presumably Raked, and there were various flags and banners. But nothing much in the way of colour. Nor were there any jewels or gold.

Most of the buildings had that same ancient feeling that seemed to be just about everywhere in Szugabar, though he did take note that there were some buildings that seemed to be in a slightly different style and looked newer. Also in one area there appeared to be actual construction under way. Camir explained that adding to various temples in the country was almost part of the job description for the Phirinos

Between the main temple and the gate in front of them was a long paved area bordered by more of those ever present date palms. The area was also lined along its edges by a long series of statues that appeared to depict lions. Camir explained that each of these "sphinxes" actually had a human head cared on it. He had the feeling they represented kings or possibly high priests.

A vast crowd had gathered in the large square before the main entrance. It almost seemed as if the whole city had turned out. Several shaded grandstands had been erected around the periphery of the square for the important guests. Priests and functionaries, came and went from the temple complex as the crowd continued to grow.

There seemed to be no real sense of order to any of it, people simply arrived talked briefly with a priest and entered the square to wander aimlessly. There was however a great cacophony rising above the mob that made it feel like an important event.

Dorm and his friends were escorted to one of the main stands. Several seats near them were separated and empty at this time. Given the decoration on them it was fairly easy to tell for whom they were intended.

Various nobles and officials were shown to seats after them. Several of them were introduced to them, but Dorm was sure he wouldn't remember most of their names.

Music was being played by a band somewhere. And several troupes of dancers and acrobats and jugglers entertained various sections of the crowd.

They sat in their seats for a while talking. Each voicing their suggestions as to what would happen in this great ceremony. Several attendants arrived and provided them with a light refreshment. After a while the seats in the various stands were full of nobles and officials, and a sense of anticipation hung over the air. The noise diminished only marginally, and the entertainers continued uninterrupted.

Dorm contemplated the various suggestions by his friends. None of them really had any great idea about what would happen, except perhaps Baron Camir, and possibly Ambra who both had witnessed it before and were much more familiar with the culture of Szugabar. They at least had had some exposure to Szugabaran customs and beliefs. It would be easier for them to understand. Since the Alliance didn't really believe in such quaint things as gods, the rest of them really had no frame of reference. They understood the basic idea of what a god was supposed to be, but Dorms' mind just couldn't quite come to terms with it. He had read in various history tomes during his youth, how it was believed that the ancient kingdoms of the Alliance had believed in such things. But that was before they had been united by the Fortress. Before the so called "enlightenment" where many of the superstitious ideas of the ancients had been abandoned. The idea was now almost laughable. Though presumably not in the polite company of any one from Szugabar.

The thought of going to a place to pray, well that was just weird. He had never understood that part of it. If these gods really were everywhere, wouldn't they hear you no matter where you were, or indeed what you were doing? Perhaps it had something to do with a shared experience. People tended to enjoy things more if they experienced it with others.

Then again, it hadn't been all that long ago that Dorm himself had thought that the idea of something like a quest was merely a 'quaint' idea. Something to be laughed at and not taken too seriously. He'd had to change his attitude about that, and some things that he had experienced and encountered so far on this journey had also started him thinking on a few others.

He decided to reserve judgement about all this religion stuff, and in particular how it pertained to Szugabar until after the ceremony. Perhaps there would be something in it that would help explain it all.

About a quarter of an hour had passed, when a commotion travelled down one of the streets to the square. There was a great flurry of movement as people jostled this way and that out of the way of the soldiers who now entered and began moving people back. They all wore ceremonial outfits, and carried impressive looking lances. After several minutes a broad avenue had been created from the side street to the centre of the square. The soldiers lined the space, holding back the crowd. A hush began to fall over the throng.

From the street came the sound of hooves. Horse drawn chariots three abreast emerged from the street and headed towards the centre of the square. Behind the chariots came a gilded carriage. It was adorned with a large orange disc upon its roof. Dorm realised that it was the same disc that adorned the Phirinos' throne back in the palace. The carriage approached the centre of the square and pulled to a halt. Several kilted footman jumped off the back and opened the double doors on the sides. They stood erect and bowed their heads.

From the carriage emerged the Phirina. She wore an elegant dress that revealed every curve of her figure. She was laden down with heavy jewellery and a large Silver crown adorned her head. It was a strange piece of head wear, as it looked vaguely like a salt shaker. But it was definitely something to get noticed in, the way it shone in the light. On the front of it was some sort of badge. It stuck out from the base of the crown and looked vaguely like a snake and a bird. Dorm got the feeling that it wasn't just there for decoration. That hat had to weight a lot, and it stuck up quite a ways from the Queens head. That badge must have helped counter balance it.

Phirina Tika stood for a moment at the foot of the carriage as beside her, the Princess emerged. She too wore a formal looking, figure hugging dress that shimmered in the sunlight. On her head she wore a small golden circlet. It seemed to have a similar badge on the front, and Camir informed it it was the symbol of the Royal house, similar to the Lugemallan coat of arms.

The two women paused as the footmen closed the doors and remounted the carriage. As it pulled away and the chariots pulled in behind it, the Phirina and the Princess began a sedate walk towards the stand. Their faces were fixed in a beneficent smile as they slowly walked forward. Several soldiers followed them close behind, but still keeping a respectful distance. A guard somewhere shouted something and like a wave all the gathered crowd knelt in reverence.

The two women approached the stairs that led to their gilded seats. They ascended them and turned to face the crowd. They paused for a moment before sitting. First the mother, then the daughter.

The crowd rose again, and the music and noise started almost as if nothing had happened. The Vizier Inmahop, whom Dorm had met briefly at the palace, approached the Phirina. He too wore formal attire.

His kilt was very long, and he had a short sword belted at his waist. He wore the same blue and yellow striped linen headdress, they had previously seen both he and the Phirinos wearing. He bowed and then spoke quietly to her. She listened intently. She nodded briefly at his conclusion and spoke a few words. He bowed again and moved off.

The Phirina glanced around at the various guest in the stand and caught Dorms eye. She inclined her head in recognition, which he returned.

"You seem to be making an impression," Mac observed quietly to him.

"As long as it leads to something productive, I don't mind so much," Dorm said.

"Meaning?" Mac left it hanging.

"Better relations," Dorm said quickly. He hadn't meant to let that slip. He didn't like keeping things from Mac, but this was too important to chance.

The crowd continued to frolic and cavort in the square as the time wore on. It was mid-morning now and the sun was already fairly high up in the sky. Despite the large awning above their heads and the light breeze in the air, it was still rather warm.

Just as it seemed that everyone in the stands was getting restless, a large number of priests began to assemble just outside the main entrance to the temple complex. They all wore lose fitting white robes, but each seemed to be decorated differently. Dorm was a little confused by it all. He asked Ambassador Camir about it.

"Each different priesthood is represented here. They each wear a symbol to represent the God they serve. They also all have different jewellery and adornments, depending upon their position within the temple," he explained.

"I don't see any symbols," Dorm admitted.

"It might be a bit hard at this distance," Camir agreed. "Let me see if I can point one out." He looked over the group of priests who seemed to be almost as restless as the crowd. "Ah there's a good one." He pointed at two priests who were standing apart, talking to each other. "The priest on the right serves here in the temple of Raked. He wears the symbol for Raked's totem. The priest on the left works for Ametsaph."

"I'm still not seeing these symbols."

"Oh of course. I keep forgetting you're new to this, forgive me." He squinted a bit at them. "Do you see that large gold shape on their left breast?"

"Yes," Dorm said after also squinting a bit.

"Well that is their priesthood symbol. Raked's looks like a falcon. That is his animal. He is the God of the Sun, Life, royalty and several other things besides. The other priest has a snake like shape. Which represents the Goddess Ametsaph, who is the Goddess of warriors and commerce."

As they watched Dorm began to make out the different animal shapes that the priests wore. As he identified a new one he asked Camir which God it represented. As such he began to recognise Salasis' lion, Heps' jackal, and Poltons' ibis. Others seemed to be represented by less priests and so he didn't get much opportunity to view them. When he had an opportunity he might take the time to look them all up.

The priests slowly assembled themselves so that they stood formally on either side of the main entrance to the temple complex. A small stone platform stood in the centre of the avenue leading towards the main temple. The priests stood, heads bowed, apparently in prayer.

The crowd slowly began to settle and quieten.

From further back towards the temple a group of people could be seen, slowly walking towards the square. They looked like more priests. They walked with a steady and timed gait that seemed rather unnecessary to Dorm. As they approached Dorm saw that there were five of them. Their group finally came to a halt at the rear of the small platform.

The priest in the middle stood for a moment then turned and bowed to the others who had escorted him. They bowed in response, and with that the man from their centre turned back and mounted the platform.

He stood for a moment. Silently before throwing back him hood and revealing the face of the Phirinos.

He stepped forward and let fall the priestly robe he was wearing. Beneath he wore a traditional Szugabaran kilt and little else. Though this kilt was adorned with gold and precious gems. He wore a golden cap, and several rather heavy looking collars from which hung more precious stones and sacred amulets. The kings arms, which were much more highly muscled than Dorm had expected, seemed to have been oiled, as his skin shone and glinted whenever he moved them. His makeup was unusually heavy and darker than Dorm remembered it.

The Phirinos bowed to the assembled crowd. They in turn bowed to him, and then knelt before he who was their ultimate priest.

"Hear me O my people," the Phirinos called loudly, his voice carrying quite well across the crowded square. "We gather here today to praise the Gods. To honour them, and to dedicate our lives and our service to them for another year."

There was a brief, though hearty murmur of agreement that rippled through the crowd.

"My people," the Phirinos went on. "Children of the sacred land of Szugabar. I am your divine King. The representative of the Gods on the Earth. It is my duty and my responsibility to lead thee in this holy duty today. I shall guide and protect thee in the journey to honour the Gods. Let us walk together that they shall know our love and respect for them, that they might bless us again."

"Bless us O Gods," the Priests intoned solemnly.

"Mighty Raked," the King said then. "God of the Sun. Giver of Life. Protector of Royalty, God of the Desert and of Time, Great Creator and Source of Rebirth, hear us!"

"See the soaring wings of Raked," sang a group of priests, all marked with the falcon shape of Raked.

"Blesséd Salasi, Goddess of Divine Right, Purity and Justice, Giver of laws, and protector of homes. Giver of the Bounties and Creator of Souls. Bless us."

"Hear the roar of Salasi," sang the priests marked with the lion.

"Learnéd Hep. God of the Arts and Literature and Learning. Teacher of Writing and mathematics. Creator of pottery and of the crafts and metals and mines."

"Hear the sacred howl of Hep," sang the jackal adorned priests.

"Silent Keda, God of the Rivers and the Sea, Keeper of the Underworld. Bringer of Storms , Master of the Sky, and Guardian of the Gates to the Underworld."

"Fear the mighty jaws of Keda," sang another group of priests. Dorm at first had a little trouble understanding what their symbol represented. Apparently it was something called a hippopotamus? Dorm didn't even know what that was.

"Fierce Ametsaph. Goddess of Warriors and Commerce. Protector of travellers, Guardian of the Ports and Roads. Patron of the Armourers."

"Hear the deadly hissing of Ametsaph," intoned the snake branded priests.

"Terrible Zebek, Bringer of Death and Destruction. Master of Chaos, Famine, disease and Crime. Master of Renewal."

"Tremble at the snapping jaws of Zebek." This group of priests wore an emblem apparently representative of a crocodile. Dorm had heard of these creatures before but had yet to see one. Though if the representation was anything to go by he was starting to reassess that idea.

"Graceful Polton. Goddess of the Moon and the Stars. Instructor of Healing. Teacher of Astonology, Divination and Medicine. Keeper of the Wind."

"Marvel at the height of Polton." These priests wore symbols representative of an Ibis bird. Dorm had seen a few around the city and understood what it meant. He did however have to lean across to Camir and ask about Astronology?

"Here in Szugabar astrology and astronomy are both a part of the same thing. You can't have one with out the other. They just simplified the name, so they didn't have to say as much."

"Powerful Nubashtes. Bringer of Earthquakes, Teacher of Mummification. Protector of the Mines. Patron of Industry. Guardian of the Mountains, the gems and the Metals."

"See the scuttling of hidden Nubashtes." These priests wore another symbol that was hard to recognise. Camir had to think for a minute to remember that it was some insect.

"Divine Asen. God of Creation. Provider of Papyrus, Teacher of Music, and Bestower of Divinity. Patron of the Gardens, the Games and the Sports. Inspirer of the Celebrations."

"See the powerful horns of Asen." This group wore a symbol that was mean to represent a bull. Dorm could *almost* see it.

"Beautiful Manateph. Goddess of Marriage and Love. Protector of Births. Guardian of Parents, Friendship and Keeper of Emotions."

"Wear proudly the gifts of Manateph." This group wore the symbol for a ram or sheep. Which when Dorm realised this helped explain what they had been on about.

"And so we have named all the sacred Gods of this land," Said the Phirinos in a clear voice. "And shall we begin again this year to honour them. To bless their names and their deeds. And to pledge to them our service for another year. Praise be unto the Gods, and Hail unto their Divine Majesty."

"All hail unto the Gods," the priest intoned in unison.

One of the priests handed the Phirinos a small bundle of what looked like sticks. The King held them aloft for a moment. Then he lent forward and placed the sticks into a shiny metal dish that sat at the forward end of the platform on which he stood. Another priest handed him a large pitcher, which the king poured some sort of libation from into the dish. The king emptied the pitcher and handed it back to the priest.

A third priest handed him several flowers, which he also held aloft for the crowd to see. These he also placed into the dish. Dorm could see them floating on the surface of the liquid from the pitcher.

A fourth priest stepped forward and handed the Phirinos a small container. Again he held this aloft, then opened it and put in his fingers. He sprinkled some of the contents across the surface of the liquid, before handing the container back to the priest.

For a moment the king paused, watching the metal dish with its various contents.

Another two priests came forward. One was carrying a small metal container that looked vaguely like a lamp, and that did indeed seem to glow, even in the daylight. The other carried a large torch. They mounted the platform and stood on either side of the Phirinos. The three of them bowed to each other.

"Behold the sacred flame of the ceremony," the king intoned.

The priest holding the lamp-like container held it aloft for them to see. Dorm now saw that it was a golden covered box that held a small flame. Presumably it was kept alight by some sort of oil. The priest opened a small glass door on its front. The light of the flame seemed to flicker for a moment before steadying again.

The other priest slowly lowered the torch she held toward that tiny flame. When the torch touched the edge of the gilt container there was a slight flash. The two priests quickly drew their objects back from each other. The flame in the box flickered again for a few moments before steadying, at which time the priest closed the small door. Meanwhile the torch held by the other priest had taken to flame. Slowly growing in intensity and brilliance.

The torch was held aloft by the priest who then, still holding it high, handed it to the Phirinos. He too held it high for a moment before slowly lowering it into the metal dish in front of him. There was a bright flash and the bowl was engulfed in a bright flame that rose quite high. After a few moments it receded down till it was a more sedate little blaze at the kings feet.

"And so we have lit the sacred fire to signal to the Gods that we are holding their great ceremony. In the name of the Gods I say this ceremony shall now commence," the Phirinos said formally. "May this light burn until the conclusion of our sacred rites."

"Praise the Mighty Gods of Szugabar," intoned the assembled priests.

"Praise the Mighty Gods of Szugabar," sang out the crowd. The Phirinos bowed in response to their voice. The priests behind him also bowed. Then there was a great deal of clapping and celebratory noise.

"Is that it? Cal Makor said.

"Yes for now," Camir told him. "There are many more individual ceremonies to come, but that is the introductory one. Why is there a problem?"

"No. I just kind of expected more," he shrugged. "Maybe some marching or something. I got the impression there was more too it that's all. Funny thing this religion. It builds i'self up to great and fun, but it seems rather boring to me. They should wave some flags or somethin'. Ooh, what about some dancing girls? That'd spice things up a bit."

The celebration of the completion of the Great Festival's opening ceremony continued for the rest of the day. There was a formal reception at the Palace for all the participants and the honoured guests. Dorm was again whisked from one person to another, and asked his opinion on just about every topic imaginable. This time however he was also properly introduced to the various priests who had taken part in the morning's rituals.

There had been three priests per God at the ceremony, and he was reintroduced to them all. Prior to the ceremony, at the reception the night before, they had just been generally introduced as the "priests conducting tomorrows rituals". Now he was actually told their names properly, and which God they represented. He knew he was likely to forget it all rather quickly, but he knew it was necessary.

The same woman was there as well. The one who had given him the strange looks across the room, at the previous reception. Her name was apparently Pianwasal. She was one of the highest ranked priests in the Great Temple of Asen, at somewhere called Asenakir. She was extremely beautiful, and wore a simplified version of the makeup that seemed to be the norm for the aristocracy here in Szugabar. She wore a long white robe that was adorned with the symbol of her order; the bull, as well as a complicated jewelled and golden broach that was fastened to her right lapel, that indicated her rank within the Asen priesthood. Her hair was a deep red-brown and her eyes carried a sense of purpose in their dark depths.

She greeted Dorm warmly, yet with an edge to her voice. Her eyes seemed to dart around him as they briefly spoke. Her gaze seemed to almost consciously avoid the amulet that he and the others wore on the outside of their clothing today.

After the priests had moved off to another part of the room, Dorm gave a signal to Mac, who rounded up their group quietly.

"What is it Dorm?" Telly asked curiously.

"I'm not entirely certain, but I think I may have found our first Szugabaran quester," he explained quietly.

"Who? Lianna said glancing around the room.

"One of the priests of Asen. Her name is Pianwasal."

"Which one is she?" Zacravia asked also looking around.

"The one with the long reddish brown hair, standing next to those two other priests near that large tapestry over there." He indicated pointing in her direction.

"Oh my, she's beautiful," Tissie said her hand instinctively going to her blonde locks.

"Yes well, that's the least of our troubles," Dorm said.

"How do you want to proceed, Dorm," Travanos asked him.

"Well we need to get her alone to talk to her, but I think I'd rather not do it alone. I think she might not respond well if it is just one of us."

"Not a bad idea," said Cal. "She looks a little… aggressive."

"That's a little strange for a priest isn't it?" Artur asked him.

"Who knows? To me priests is a little strange."

"The terrace balcony," Harmia suggested suddenly. "Everyone keeps going out there for a bit of air. We can position ourselves so that when she goes out next we can move in on her."

"Sounds like a pretty good idea," Travanos agreed.

"I hate to say it," Zacravia began. "But the Constable has made an excellent suggestion."

She looked at him sternly.

"I'm just saying," he said defensively.

"So next question," Lianna asked. "Who goes?"

"You and Telly," Mac said looking at Dorm. "With perhaps Lianna and Travanos nearby in case they need any help. Oh and Ambra as well. The fact that your country has a lot of similarities to Szugabar might be an asset. The rest of us can wait just inside the door, in case anything goes completely wrong."

"Sounds like an plan," Rhyn concluded.

They set it in motion.

They broke up and sidled around the room, having brief, uninteresting chats with a few people as they did. One by one they began to arrive in the area of the doors to the large terrace balcony, that overlooked one of the garden courtyards. It was much darker out there, the area only being lit by a few torches.

They all stood around talking quietly and watching the room. The group that would actually try and talk to this priestess stood in a close group under the crossed arms of a large statue of a traditionally garbed king of Szugabar.

After about a quarter of an hour, the priestess began to walk towards the doors. She was deep in conversation with an official of some kind. She didn't seem to notice their group as she parted company from him and went out onto the balcony. Dorm and his friends followed not far behind her.

There were only a few other people outside at the time, and they seemed intent on staying in the shadows and not interfering.

Priestess Pianwasal stood at the edge of the balcony looking up at the starry sky.

"Learnéd Priestess," Dorm said quietly.

She turned quickly. An unreadable look crossed her face when she saw who it was who had addressed her. "Yes?"

"I'm sorry to bother you. I'm Prince Dormal of Lugemall."

"Yes I know who you are. May I personally welcome you on behalf of the Priesthood of Asen."

"Thank you that's very kind. Please be sure to thank your God for me. I wanted to say well done of the ceremony today. I've never seen a religious ceremony before and for your part in making it a success I wanted to congratulate you."

"Of course," she said a little too quickly. "Thank you."

"I was wondering if I might talk with you a moment or two?"

"Ah.." she began. She seemed a little nervous. Almost as if she were trying to think of an excuse to say no. "Yes of course. What can I help you with?"

"Well I couldn't help but notice earlier when I was introduced to you, that you seemed a little taken aback. As if perhaps you had seen something you hadn't liked."

"Of course not," she said. Her eyes instinctively flicking to his amulet and back.

"It's just that it appeared to me that you seemed intrigued by this amulet I am wearing." He hefted it lightly in one hand. Then looked her squarely in the eyes. "You've seen it before haven't you?"

"No why would you think that?" She almost seemed to want to step backward though she held her position.

"Priestess, you seem nervous," Telly said. "It's actually quite alright. There's nothing wrong with having seen it."

"In fact it saves us a lot of hassle," Travanos said quietly.

"I don't understand," Pianwasal said again, her eyes darting from face to face.

"Neither did I at first," Lianna told her. "But you get used to that pretty quickly. Where have you seen it?"

Pianwasal paused for a moment. She seemed nervous for some reason. Perhaps the amulet had some negative connotation to it here in Szugabar. She slowly reached into her robes and pulled out an amulet. It glinted briefly in the torchlight.

"I see, close to home then," Dorm said.

"Please. I must not be seen wearing it. As a priest I am not permitted to wear any personal jewellery. If I am seen with it, I will be in trouble."

"That's alright, you can keep it hidden for now." Dorm looked at the others, deciding how to proceed. "I'm going to ask you a few questions about it. Please just answer them honestly. And I'm guessing quickly, if you're as concerned as you are."

"All right," she nodded quickly.

"You were given it by your mother, correct?"

"Yes."

"On your sixteenth birthday?"

"Yes"

"She couldn't tell you much about it, except that her mother had given it to her on *her* sixteenth birthday?"

"Correct."

A thought occurred to Dorm then. Something that he realised in the instant that he thought of it, that he had been noticing all along, but had never actually taken note of. He would have to ask the others about it soon.

"And sometimes, when things in your life get bad. Or stressful, or perhaps even a little scary; all you have to do is hold that crystal for a few minutes and you feel… full of energy, and that you could take on the world at anything?"

"Again yes," she said. "How did you know all this?"

"That's a long story," Mac said wearily. "One that I think can wait till later."

"Suffice to say that we have gotten your attention?" Dorm asked her seriously.

"You have indeed."

"Enough for you to hear us out on the explanation for all this?" Lianna asked her.

"I believe that would be prudent."

"Then we'll have to organise a time and place to explain all this to you properly. So that you know exactly what is going on here, and why we had to seek you out. Here and now is obviously not going to work."

"We have the day after tomorrow off from ceremonies," Mac reminded him. "Apparently there is some important ceremony that only certain high priests and the Phirinos attends."

"That is the Phirinos' renewal ritual," Pianwasal informed them. "It is most sacred. There will be a small celebration here at the palace afterward. I would say your presence would be expected."

"Would seem to be the perfect opportunity," Telly said. "We could meet her at the other palace. Seeing her here might get a little suspicious. Especially if she ends up here later on for this dinner."

"Not to mention difficult," Lianna said. "I'm not sure it would be entirely appropriate for us to receive guests in someone else's house."

"Do you think you can make that?"

"I believe so. I am fairly highly placed in my order, so I will be able to go out when I desire."

"I know this all seems a little strange Priestess," Ambra said then. "But once you have heard what you will hear, then you will understand. And it will all be made clear."

She stared at them for a moment before slowly nodding.

"Until the day after tomorrow then," Dorm said bowing to her.

Chapter 20

The following day was filled with an aggravated sense of frustration, as the hours seemed to drag by. One by painful one.

The only thing they had to attend, at the personal invitation of the Phirinos, was a special ceremony, this time inside the Temple of Raked, to honour both the Queen and the apparent relationship between Raked and Salasi; who were apparently husband and wife, or was it brother and sister. No it was father and daughter.

Maybe.

The ceremony started at a fairly respectable time, and the first hour of the ceremony actually seemed to go fairly quickly. There was music with this one so it was rather entertaining. Of course, the second hour, involved the recitation of the Hymn to Salasi. Which was rather long and repetitive. If Dorm heard the words "Blesséd be the Love of Salasi for Raked" one more time, he was likely to show them what he felt of their love.

And it wouldn't be pretty.

After that there was another hymn, this time accompanied to music, which was a bit different, and certainly easier to endure followed by a period of nearly an hour where the Phirina had to go and pray silently in a small inner chamber somewhere. The rest of them had to wait patiently in the main sanctum, tediously listening to a chant by the priests that supposedly protected the spirit of the Phirina while she prayed.

After all was done and they returned to the Palace, Dorm and his friends didn't have enough energy left for anything other than falling asleep.

The day after dawned clear and bright, and their group was up fairly early in order to witness the Phirinos leaving to go to his ceremony. It was a stately march for the king, surrounded by several of his personal staff, his Vizier and a whole company of his personal troops, not to mention the numerous priests who had come to collect him.

Again there was a recitation of some hymn or other, and a brief song, sung by a young boy, apparently some special pupil in service to the Temple, which Dorm actually found quite beautiful. The child sung it with a great deal of pride and a fair amount of gusto. He was after all performing for the Phirinos, and it probably wasn't every day that one of the people got to perform for a living God.

It took a while for the retinue to finally disappear beyond the gate. Once they had, they all quickly realised that time had now come to turn their attention to important matters. They told the various palace staff that they intended to go for a long walk into the city as a group, feigning some nonsense about not having had much time for each other in the last few days. The staff and guards didn't seem to have an issue with this and let them pass without hindrance.

They arrived at the guest palace a short time later, and left instructions with the door staff that if a priestess of Asen arrived, that she was to be brought to them immediately.

For the next few hours they all waited around nervously, biding their time until she arrived. A strange pessimism began to descend upon their group. Little was said, and the thoughts that were expressed were all positive, but they all seemed to be feeling it. Considering the possibility that in fact, she might *not* show up after all.

However about an hour before midday one of the servants arrived with the priestess in tow. There was a visible sense of relief that ran through their group as she entered the room. She was again dressed in her priestly robes, and her face bore the expression of someone who is not entirely convinced that they are doing the wisest thing.

They dismissed the servant and showed her to a seat. “I have come as asked," she said as she slowly sat down.

"We thank you for trusting us enough to do that," Telly told her.

"As we said the other night, I think it is prudent that I hear what you have to say. I make no promises, but I will admit that you have intrigued me."

"All we ask is that you keep an open mind," Dorm said to her.

"Very open," Cal said quietly on the other side of the room.

"What we have to say may sound a little unbelievable right at first," Dorm began. "But I assure you it is the truth."

"I believe that you are an honest person Your Highness," she replied genuinely. "You could not have known to ask those questions without good reason. There must be some truth to what you are about to tell me. I will of course reserve my judgement till the end."

"Of course. Well to begin…"

He briefly recounted their discovery of the amulets, all those months ago. How they had then gone on to discover the prophecy that had caused them to go off on this adventure. They told her how each new member had been gathered into their group, and each explained how, at first they too had not been sure whether to believe in any of it or not. They sketched in for her their various adventures, and their suspicions. Their meetings with Rangers and officials, and the various pieces of information they had gathered along the way.

They talked to her for quite a while until they finally arrived to Szugabar and how they had discovered her. Pianwasal seemed a little confused by the various incidents with the Rangers though.

"We have had Rangers here in Szugabar for about two thousand years, but we rarely ever see them. They seem to keep to themselves. I don't understand what they have to do with all this?"

"Well honestly we aren't entirely sure about their part in this either," Dorm admitted. "But so far they haven't done us any harm. In fact they seem to be trying to help us."

"They aren't really succeeding all that much," Cal said. "But they are trying."

"If they are trying to help you then why do they give you so little information?" the priestess asked.

"They seem to be constrained in what they can tell us for some reason," Dorm explained haltingly. "It's as if they want to tell us more, but the rules of this whole thing prevent them."

"I got the feeling that Geven was walking pretty close to the line when he spoke to us," Mac confided in Dorm.

"Yes me too," he agreed. "He seemed to be wanting to tell us more, but also not wanting to at the same time."

"As if to tell us more would put us in danger?" Rhyn suggested.

"Possibly."

"I think perhaps that's something we won't fully find out about until we reach the Fortress." Dorm told them.

"You think we will end up there, Don't you?" Harmia asked.

"I'm almost certain of it. Eventually we will have everyone with the amulets. Once we do we will need to know what to do next. There seems to be only one place we could go to get that information…" he left it hanging, the reality of it sinking in.

"So what you are saying is," Pianwasal continued. "That you want me to accompany you on this journey of yours to find all these other, what did you call them, questers?"

"Essentially yes," Telly said. "See it wasn't really all that difficult after all."

"You have an amulet," Dorm said looking directly at her. "There's no other choice. We are all connected by them in ways, I can't even begin to comprehend. We all have a part to play in this. So far, when we've had a problem or an issue to deal with we have all brought something to the table to help solve it. We all may not be able to immediately see what you will bring, but it is there and it will be something necessary and important."

"You flatter me, Your Highness," she blushed.

"No, I speak the truth."

She sat for a moment lost in thought, her fingers idly toying with the crystal in the amulet. She looked at it for a moment. Almost as if she were silently asking it for it's opinion on the matter. It's advice on what she should do.

"I have always felt that there was more to this thing than it seemed," she said quietly watching the play of light across the surface of the crystal. "That perhaps it meant much more than any one knew.

When I was a girl I used to imagine that it was some long lost indicator of royal birth. Later I used to think it meant that I was destined to be a priestess. Now I perceive it might be much, much more. Something important to the whole world."

"You begin to see why you have to come with us," Travanos said.

"I do sir," she said looking up at him. "It seems I have little choice in the matter really."

"Yes that's pretty much the conclusion we all eventually came to as well," Zacravia agreed.

"Your position in your temple seems to give you a certain freedom," Dorm suggested. "Would it be possible for you to leave?"

"For a short while yes," she said quickly. "There are numerous things I can use for an excuse."

"How long would that get you?" Mac asked.

"A few weeks at least. Possibly as long as a month."

Dorm shook his head. "I don't think that will be anywhere near long enough. We will likely be needing you for quite a few months."

"I couldn't possibly leave for that long a time," she stared at him for a moment. "There are… things I must see to personally."

"Such as?"

"Temple things," she said shortly. Dorm got the feeling there was significantly more to it than that.

"We can probably talk to the high priest of your temple," Travanos told her. "I'm sure if they understood the seriousness of the situation they might consider giving you, say… an extended leave of absence?"

"My high priest…" she began shortly. "There are things concerning him that I must attend to personally. As the second in charge of my order there is no one else who can do it."

"Well then perhaps some of those things will need to be delayed. Until you return at least."

She stared at him for a moment. "That wouldn't be possible."

"I do have the ear of the Phirinos remember," Dorm said to her shortly. He let that sink in for a moment before continuing. "He seems quite interested in cultivating a friendship with me. I'm sure if I asked him nicely enough he could make it happen."

Pianwasal stared at him for a moment a curious expression on her face, halfway between fear and anger. “You would bring the Phirinos into this?”

“If I have to.” Dorm paused for a moment, his face set. He didn’t want to have to bully her, she was meant to go with them after all, but she was being uncooperative all of a sudden. “What’s going on?”

“My High Priest is…” she briefly looked at the ceiling. “Useless to put it mildly. Since his elevation the influence of our priesthood has fallen. He seems more interested in his own comfort than in the furthering of our God’s cause.”

“Then why not simply tell someone like the Phirinos?” Mac suggested.

“Because the High Priests of all the Orders are appointed by the Phirinos,” she told him. “The Phirinos is a God on Earth. He is infallible. His decisions are final and unquestionable. To tell him that he has made a mistake… would be unthinkable.”

Dorm looked at her for a moment. There was something in her eye. The way she avoided saying her High Priest’s name. “You’re planning something aren’t you?” he asked her.

The look she gave him said it all. That same look of both fear and anger contending with each other across her face at the same time. Only this time much more intense.

“That’s it isn’t it? You have something planned to… what discredit him? No actually on second thought don’t tell me. I don’t want to get involved in your politics.”

“Then do not ask such questions, Your Highness.” She told him in no uncertain terms.

“One way or the other Pianwasal, you must come with us. If I have to ask the Phirinos to make the arrangements then I will. I’d much rather you just agreed to it and sorted out the details yourself though.”

“You do not know what you ask, Your Highness,” she almost pleaded with him.

“Actually he does,” Ambra said. “As do we all. We’ve all had to leave things behind. Artur has had to leave behind a baby son. Tissievilla; a grieving father. Lianna and I have both had to leave businesses behind. All of us have had to leave our lives behind us, because we realise that this is too important. You are no different."

Ambras' speech seemed to hit her hard. She stared at him for a moment, then slowly looked at each of the others in turn, obviously considering what they had all left behind when their group had collected them.

"I apologise," she eventually said quietly. "My calling means a great deal to me. I care about it."

"I think we can understand that," Zacravia told her leaning forward. "But we have need of you. I would probably even go so far as to say that your country needs you. And wouldn't it then be a fair enough thing to say that your God needs you too?"

"That is a very large leap sir," she told him piously.

"Perhaps, but then perhaps not," he replied. "If you want to leave in such a way as to put your High Priest on an unsure footing, and to most likely secure your place as someone known to the Phirinos, then this could be the way."

That possibility seemed to intrigue her. She sat for a moment thinking on that, a slight grin playing across her lips.

"Of course whatever it is that you have planned, will most likely have to be forgotten," Dorm told her seriously. "But then, when you return you will be in a much more powerful position. Who knows? Perhaps you'll even have the Phirinos thinking of your name for when he eventually has to choose a new High Priest."

"Of course we won't be leaving until after the Great Festival is over," Zacravia mused quietly. "She has a few days. It's quite possible that whatever she has planned could be over and done with by then."

They all looked at him.

"Sorry just thinking out loud. Any permanent solution to the problem would most likely elevate our noble priestess here to a position where she couldn't go with us. I guess my criminal nature is still very much in evidence."

Harmia's look was scathing. Dorm had noticed that over the last few weeks her attitude to him had slowly begun to change. She didn't watch him quite as closely any more, and seemed more ready to listen to what he had to say. Zacravia caught her look and smiled. "Just making sure you're still paying attention, my dear," he told her smarmily.

Dorm turned back to Pianwasal. “He has a point. We won’t be leaving Szugabar until at least the end of the festival. That’s supposing that we can find the second quester here that quickly.”

“Second quester?” she asked.

“Yes so far there have been two from each country,” Rhyn explained. “We think that is going to be the case everywhere.”

“So somewhere in your country is someone else, in this case probably a man, who also has an amulet.”

Pianawasal looked down at her own amulet for a moment. “I had thought it was unique,” she said in a small voice. “No matter,” she said then quickly raising her head and looking at them. “If I have a few days then I should use the time to prepare myself for our departure.” She seemed to think of something then. “Will it be possible to make a brief stop at my temple when we leave?”

“That all depends on where it is,” Travanos said.

“About two days easy ride north of the city. There is a small town just to the north of it. There is a dock, taking a ship would be much quicker.”

Dorm looked at the others for a moment. “We might be able to swing by when we leave Szugabar to head back to Kiama Mor. What is it that you need from there?”

“Some personal items. And possibly some things that may help us. Not knowing what we are likely to confront makes it a little difficult.”

“We noticed that too,” Artur said quietly.

“I think we can alter our plans sufficiently to accommodate you, Priestess.”

“I thank you.” She sat for a moment as if collecting her thoughts. “I think that this has been an important day for me,” She concluded.

“Possibly the most important.”

She nodded her head at that idea.

After she had left to return to her temple, they considered what had happened. Concerns were expressed about her attitude towards her High Priest and possible plans against his position. They didn’t particularly like the idea of having a wanted fugitive in their midst, something that Zacravia was a little concerned about. They assured him that he at least knew what he was doing, where as Pianwasal wouldn't, crime not being a major part of her life. Also they were concerned that if the High Priest was "taken care of" as Lianna called it, that it might fall to Pianwasal herself to take his place immediately. That could put a serious dent in their plans. Of course they still had to find the next person, but the thought of later having to try and convince her to come along all over again, when she was now in charge of an entire priesthood made them baulk.

They also certainly didn't want the wrath of the Phirinos brought down upon them, or trailing their every step across the Alliance. Taslem Kanos might not be too appreciative of his High Priests being murdered and he might want to ask them to return to explain themselves. He was after all a king, and kings often had long arms.

They ate a brief and somewhat frugal meal, considering the palatial surroundings and left to return to the Phirinos' palace around mid-afternoon. Their return was greeted with little ceremony and they retired to the great hall that seemed to be exclusively reserved for their use and relaxed for several hours. A large dinner was brought in for them not long after dark and they ate, conversing quietly.

After they had eaten they were entertained by a group of musicians and dancers who seemed to randomly roam the palace and perform. During the dancing a servant arrived and spoke quietly with Dorm, informing him that the Phirinos had returned and would like to talk with him for a while. Dorm smiled and followed the servant through the long straight halls of the palace to the other side of the building.

The Phirinos was once again seated at his low desk in his bare office. The lamplight cast a warm glow over everything, and made the room much more inviting than it seemed in the light of day. The Phirinos again sat on his cushions in a simple linen robe. He ran a hand over his shaven head as the prince entered, then beckoned him inside. Dorm sat, thanking the Phirinos for inviting him.

"I quite enjoyed our conversation the other day, Highness. I appreciate honesty and intelligence."

"I thank you for the compliment, Your Majesty. May I ask how your day went?"

"Very long and very tiring. But also very satisfying. I have given my personal pledges to all the Gods for another year, and I always feel the better for having done that."

"I will admit that I am still not entirely understanding the whole Gods and religion aspect to your country's culture. In the rest of the Alliance it is more important what a man does and thinks than what he thinks created the universe. I admit though that I find it fascinating."

"The Alliance has not had the benefit of religion. That is in some ways a sadness, and in others a blessing."

"How do you mean exactly."

"Our religion, gives our nation… cohesiveness. Purpose," he began. "We all know that we worship the same Gods, and that they care for us. Despite all our differences, we know we are together, a family if you will. It binds us in subtle yet powerful ways. It has inspired great art and architecture, great song and dance. Things that provide us a sense of belonging to this nation. Of being Szugabaran. On the other hand, there have been times where arguments about the Gods have broken out. And sometimes even wars have been started over religion." The Phirinos looked at him quite directly.

Dorm squirmed a little at the implication. "We know and readily admit our faults, Your Majesty," Dorm told him sincerely. "We know we were in the wrong. It's one of the reasons why we have pushed for Szugabar's full membership in the Alliance over the centuries. To make sure that something like that can never happen again."

The king paused for a moment, before a slow smile crept across his face. "I tease you, Your Highness. We know full well the lengths to which the Alliance has gone to, to make up for the war between us. Despite the trauma of our past, we count your peoples as among our closest and dearest friends and allies. We believe it is wrong to blame people of the present for the mistakes of the past. Especially the distant past. I assure you. There is nothing that will cause Szugabar to turn against you."

"I am glad about that," Dorm admitted laughing. "Still I admit that I know little of the complexities of all your religious beliefs. And I find it a little hard to put it all straight in my mind."

The king paused for a brief moment thinking. "That must have been it then," he said quietly.

"What must have been what?" Dorm said puzzled.

"Your meeting with Priestess Pianwasal today," he replied shortly.

Dorm was floored for a moment. He knew they had met with Pianwasal. And yet he mentioned it now as if it was the most ordinary thing in the world. Dorm was a little confused as to how he knew, and obviously the king picked up on this.

"There are those in the employ of my government whose job it is to monitor what people do. Only to make sure that no harm comes to them, and that no opportunities slip past us, I assure you."

"Spies you mean?"

"You might call them that I suppose. But they do not listen to conversations unless there is some reason to do so."

"Well I can assure Your Majesty that we have no nefarious intentions towards you or your country."

"I thought as much. So was Pianwasal indeed trying to help you with this understanding of yours?"

"Not as such, Your Majesty," Dorm said slowly. "We needed to talk to her about something important. Something vital actually."

"Might I know what exactly?"

"It has to do with the reasons for us being in your country actually."

"I thought you were here for a state visit and to witness our Great Festival?"

"Not exactly. I admit that I have been interested in seeing it, and the information you have given me about wanting closer ties with the Alliance, has certainly been worth the trip, but we actually came here on another, more urgent task," Dorm wasn't sure exactly what he should say here. He didn't want to give too much away until he had a better idea of what the Phirinos might be inclined to do.

"What is this task?" the King leant forward. "What does it involve, and why is Priestess Pianwasal important to it?"

"You have probably noticed these amulets that all the members of my group wear," he lifted it up slightly for the king to see. "We don't wear them simply for decoration. We think in fact that they come from the Fortress."

"The Fortress," the King whispered.

"These amulets appear to have originated there. We aren't entirely sure of their purpose, but we have been getting hints that it might be something vitally important to the future well-being of the Alliance. And it appears that the time for their use in that purpose may be close at hand."

"It all sounds very clandestine and exciting," the Phirinos said with an excited catch in his voice.

"Well you see, there are various people throughout the world who have these amulets. Each one of them has a part to play in whatever it is that all this is building up to. And it seems that Priestess Pianwasal has one."

The king leant back thinking for a moment, before grinning broadly. "Then I am glad that Szugabar has been helpful to you Your Highness. If there is to be a great event in our time, then I would have my people present at its conclusion."

"Majesty, it does mean taking her away from Szugabar, probably for some time."

"Oh I realise that," he replied. "But if Szugabar is to be a part of this, and if you are to succeed, then she must go. It is her duty."

"She seems a little… reluctant at this stage to be away for so long a time," Dorm tried to explain politely. "There are some… issues at her temple that she feels reluctant to abandon."

The Phirinos looked him squarely in the eyes for a moment. "You mean their High Priest?"

"Well yes, apparently there are some concerns about him."

"Then she does not have to worry alone," the king signed, closing his eyes briefly and visibly letting his shoulders fall. A look of regret passed over his face. "It is my fault. Avek comes from a powerful family. He was recommended to the post not long after I first came to the throne. I was young and still learning the ways of the world. I did not look very deeply into the man. I did not see his heart. If I had, I would not have appointed him to that position."

"Pianwasal expressed regret that he had to hold the position for life," Dorm said carefully.

"It is the way of things here. High Priests are appointed by the Phirinos for life. We supposedly are descended from the Gods and therefore infallible. We supposedly always make the right decision. But I am just a man. Nothing more. I pray to the Gods, like everyone. I feel their love upon the land. But I am no more divine than you, Your Highness."

"It is strange to hear you say it Your Majesty."

"We Phirinos' of Szugabar are not so full of our own self importance that we ignore reality. We are men, just like any other. We may have more responsibilities than many men, but we are no more noble or perfect than they. I made a mistake in appointing Avek. Nothing more. If there were some easy way to have him removed then I would have done it years ago."

"I'm humbled by your honesty, Majesty."

"It does neither of us any good for me to lie about this. I'm afraid it must rest in the hands of our Priestess friend. If she has a plan in place as you have seemed to suggest, then we must let it run its course. It will work out for the better in the end."

"You're actually advocating that she have him killed?"

"It has happened before, and I'm certain will happen again, before the end of Szugabar. As long as it isn't too messy, and that he is honoured properly after he is gone, it is all acceptable to the Gods. And to me."

Dorm was a little floored by this revelation. He hadn't expected the Phirinos to be so open about this. And the fact that he actually seemed to want Pianwasal and her co-conspirators to remove Avek the High Priest in such a way, was even more incredible. He wasn't sure what to say next. He knew he had to be careful. He didn't want to say the wrong thing, just in case this was some sort of test. But he did see an opportunity here.

"If Avek was to be needing a replacement, who would it likely end up being, in your opinion," Dorm said knowingly.

"It is customary for the Seneschal Priest to take over unless there is a more deserving candidate."

"And in this case the Seneschal Priest is…?"

"Pianwasal."

"And I'm guessing there isn't another more deserving candidate?"

"I'm afraid not."

"Well we might have a slight problem there. If she becomes the next High Priest, then she wouldn't be able to accompany us, would she?"

The Phirinos considered that for a moment. "No, most likely not. She would be required to run the Temple and the Priesthood of Asen."

"Then you see my issue?"

"I do," the king said leaning back thinking. "I believe I may have to meet with our Priestly friend. It seems that her desire to do the best for her priesthood and temple has caused us a much greater problem. It would be helpful to know the full story of her plans."

"I hope you'll try to put her at ease, Majesty. If she thinks that you are displeased she might try to do something… unfortunate."

"I see your point," the king said after a moment of consideration. "I shall be gentle in my questioning of her. We do not want her doing anything, regrettable."

"No," Dorm agreed, "That would be… bad."

He didn't want to contemplate exactly how bad.

Chapter 21

"He actually suggested that?!"

Dorm had decided to tell the others about his conversation with the Phirinos, despite some concerns. He felt it was better in the long run that they all know the position that they now found themselves in. Given the gravity of the circumstance it probably wasn't a good idea to keep those sort of secrets. He had a feeling that the Phirinos would understand his reasoning.

The situation definitely called for discretion as well as a great deal of careful treading. They didn't particularly want this information to get out, as that would only hinder their cause. Dorm didn't particularly want to be responsible for information about the Phirinos actively contemplating the assassination of a priest to make it to the streets. That opened the door to all sorts of unpleasant ideas.

It was Telly who was stating what they all were thinking. None of them could quite believe that the Phirinos had actually suggested that Pianwasal have her High Priest, Avek done away with. Given everything they now knew about Szugabaran society, the Kings admission about his divine status, or lack thereof, was also something of a revelation. Kings were not known for pointing out their faults, and this information had given them all cause to re-evaluate their opinions of the man.

"I think he wants any action done quietly and with a minimum of fuss," Dorm explained. "But yes. He did however agree that it would be better to wait a while, otherwise Pianwasal would have to take over his duties as High Priest."

"But how is she supposed to have him dealt with if she is with us?" Lianna asked. "It's not like we can double back and take care of that. What are we supposed to do, sneak into the temple one night and bang him on the head with something then sneak out again? We don't have the time."

"I expect that something would have to be arranged with her various accomplices," Dorm suggested. "If it occurred after we leave Szugabar, then the Phirinos would have to appoint an interim High Priest, until Pianwasal returns. Also it would leave her free of any suspicion of having had anything to do with it. It would probably help legitimise her when she does take it up."

No one was entirely comfortable with all this, except perhaps Zacravia, who was used to this sort of thing. Political assassinations had taken place in the Alliance before, but they were so infrequent, as to be almost unheard of. It took a great deal of anger or fear to want to commit such an act. This, of course, was slightly different in that Avek was a High Priest not a King or a councillor. But the principle was the same. They obviously would need to have a long and detailed discussion with Pianwasal about all that she was doing, before they made any decisions or plans.

They all retired not long after that. Everyone wrestling with his or her own feelings about this information. None of them liked it, that was abundantly clear, but neither could any of them see any better alternative. One that might offer a permanent solution without their being involved in murder.

Dorm tossed and turned for several hours with the issue before finally drifting off to sleep. He was plagued by dreams, normal ones this time, about him having to chase someone around to kill them. He was trying to kill them with some sort of implement in his hand that he could never quite see, and people kept distracting him, with questions and meals, and songs, and he kept having to go ask the Phirinos what it was that he was supposed to be doing.

The next day dawned clear and bright, as apparently most did here in Szugabar. This was to be perhaps the most important day of the Great

Festival. They were to go and witness the Ceremony of Sacrifice. It was the ritual that had essentially started the war between Szugabar and the Alliance so many centuries ago. He knew what an honour it would be, but there was a slightly uncomfortable feeling as well. He didn't want to upset any of the people here, and he wasn't sure how their presence would be received.

They all ate and washed before heading out to the awaiting coaches that would take them to the Temple complex of Raged once again. There were several other smaller ceremonies that they were also to witness that afternoon at the Temples of Polton, Hep and Nubashtes.

This ceremony took place within the Temple complex itself, not out in the square before the main entrance. Their carriages conveyed them through the city's streets and then down along the ceremonial avenue towards the main temple. The avenue was lined with curious statues that comprised the bodies of animals with the heads of humans. No two faces were the same. All wore the standard Szugabaran headdress, and most wore the elaborate beards that the Phirinos seemed to always have. It seemed that Camir had been right about them.

They finally arrived at a broad plaza before the main temple. They were shown to seats in another large stand that had been erected. Before them in the plaza stood a large number of strange looking wooden frames. Each was elaborately carved and festooned with flowers along the top. Dorm curiously asked one of the Szugabarans nearby about them, who simply looked at him as if he had suddenly sprouted a second head.

Various priests and officials of the Phirinos' government again also filled the stands, as did various nobles of the kingdom. Dorm was even beginning to recognise some of them he had seen them that often over the last few days.

Several large pavilions had been erected on either side of the broad paved area. Priests came and went from these as the crowd gathered. The great temple itself had seemingly not been decorated at all for the occasion, like everything else had. The great carvings of the God Raked, painted brightly, adorned the walls of the great pylons on either side of the main entrance. This close to them he was actually able to take in some of the details, and gained an appreciation of both the

Szugabaran art styles, and the scale of the work involved in creating them. A Szugabaran flag was hung over the main door, but other than that there appeared to have been nothing special done at all.

Priests came out and checked some of the frames. Tightening the garlands so they wouldn't fall off, and making sure they were standing at the correct angles. Dorm wondered exactly what they were going to do. He had read about the ceremony during his tutelage, but all the descriptions had been rather vague. They were several thousand years old though, so he could forgive them that. He did suspect however than even had those descriptions been detailed and accurate, it would not be quite like seeing the real thing in person.

The arrival of the Phirinos and the Royal party was greeted with great enthusiasm by the assembled crowd. There was much cheering and clapping as the Royal family emerged from their carriage and walked to their seats in the stand. A group of musicians somewhere played an appropriately regal composition to indicate to those who couldn't see for themselves that the God-King was now present.

The Phirinos greeted Dorm and his friends with a courteous nod in their directions. Dorm returned it and smiled hoping to show the King that he was comfortable.

The Phirinos ascended the platform upon which he was to be seated and stood for a moment before the ornate, gilded throne that was for his use. Two other golden chairs flanked it on either side, and the Phirina and the princess stood before those.

The royal party bowed deeply to the crowd, which cheered again at this. The Phirinos took a step forward and spoke, "My people. Fear not, for I, Taslem Kanos VIII, Phirinos of Szugabar, am here to protect the people and the land of our divine birth during this ceremony. Know that we are in the presence of the Gods, and their divine love protects us also."

The crowd exploded in cheering and clapping at the kings pronouncement. The Phirinos smiled and waved at the crowd as they celebrated before he sat. Dorm was a little jealous of this reception. He and his father never got this kind of welcome or response to anything they said. They might occasionally get some applause, and maybe a cheer or two, but this was something else. He began to think of a few "divine pronouncements" he could make when he got back home.

Gradually the noise of the crowd died away. Once it had, a large number of priests strode slowly to the front of the arranged stands. They bowed towards the Royal party as one. The Phirinos stood and returned the bow, as did both the Phirina and the Princess.

A tall man, wearing the robes of a priest of Raked stepped forward and pushed back his hood. His head was shaved and he wore the standard eye makeup that seemed to prevail in Szugabaran officialdom. Again he bowed. He spoke then, in a load, clear and rather deep voice.

"Divine Majesty," he began. "You have come before the most sacred House of Raked, to bear witness to the Ceremony of Sacrifice. May all assembled here today bear witness also of this ceremony, that the Gods will know truly that we have made our Sacrifices for them this day. That they may bless us and renew our land for another year."

"Blesséd be the Gods of Szugabar," the assembled priest intoned behind him.

"Blessed be the Priests who serve the Gods," replied the king in an equally loud voice.

The High Priest bowed to the Phirinos again, then stepping back he turned and bowed to the assembled priests behind him who again returned the bow.

There was an *awful* lot of bowing in Szugabar.

The priests then walked off back into their various pavilions. A few moments later they began to emerge walking with that same slow, formal march that they had witnessed previously. However this time each priest was carrying something. They appeared to be large bundles of cloth. Each was dressed and painted differently. Each priest carried their bundle to a particular frame, sometimes having to weave their way through the assembled frames to find the one they were looking for. It seemed that each bundle had a specific place that it needed to be.

Once the priest had arrived at the frame they were looking for they placed the bundles upon them and tied them to it with several short lengths of brightly coloured cord. They spoke a short prayer then bowed and stepped back slightly from it, bowing again in the direction of the Phirinos.

This went on for some time. There were quite a few frames that had to be filled and so Dorm spent a moment or two studying the bundles that had already been placed.

Each one seemed to be 'wearing' a mock version of a traditional Szugabaran costume. Short kilts. Sleeveless tunics. Headdresses. Some had what appeared to be collars made up to look similar to those worn by the nobility, and some even carried weapons. All had a face painted on them, and Dorm began to notice subtle differences in each of them. This ones eyes were large, while the one next to it had small. This one had a large nose, while this one had a normal sized one, that was positioned lower on the face. He realised that these were not just bundles of cloth in vaguely human form, but more correctly effigies. He wasn't sure who or what they were supposed to represent, but it was clear now that each one represented something different and unique.

Once all the effigies had been placed, the assembled priests intoned in unison to the crowd, "Behold, the one hundred vices of man. Assembled before you that you might recognise them and avoid them in your lives, as prescribed by the Gods."

Somewhere a gong was rung. It's low intense note resonating for some time. Each priest turned to the effigy that had placed and performed another short prayer to it. As they did the High Priest again moved to stand in front of the assembled crowd.

"People of Szugabar," he began. "We gather together in the sight and service of the Gods, to make this sacrifice this day to them. We pledge again that for another year, we will strive to avoid all that they have prescribed as wrong. That we shall seek to live a righteous life in Their divine service."

"Humbly we submit to the will of the Gods," intoned the assembly of priests.

"Divine King," the High Priest began again, addressing the Phirinos. "May we begin the sacrifice in the name of the people of Szugabar?"

"I beseech thee High Priest," the Phirinos replied. "To save the people of my kingdom, from the evils of the world."

"And so it shall be," he said turning then back to the mass of priests and effigies before him. "May the sacrifices of the evils begin!"

One priest at the end of the front row spoke then in a loud voice say, "Behold do we sacrifice Greed, that it may not hold us in its sway." The Priest raised his hand and took something from inside his robes. One by one he threw three small stones at the effigy. He paused for a moment before taking what appeared to be a ceremonial dagger and plunging it into the chest of the effigy. The priest stood back leaving the hilt of the dagger protruding from the effigy.

It was a little shocking. And slightly weird. But Dorm began to realise what the ceremony was all about.

The priestess next to the first priest spoke next, saying, "Behold do we sacrifice Ignorance, that it may not darken our minds again." She too then also threw three stones at the effigy before plunging her dagger into it.

Over the next hour or so, one by one, each priest and priestess performed this ritual with the effigy in front of them. Each sacrificed effigy represented something new. Lust, indifference, cowardice, tyranny, loneliness, contempt, bigotry, and many, many others.

With the naming of each vice, Dorm began to build up a more complete picture of the mind of Szugabar. This ceremony was their way of publicly stating their desire to strive for a better, happier society. A noble and very laudable goal to be sure, though Dorm was a little worried at the format that statement took.

Once all one hundred vices had been symbolically killed the priests then all untied their effigies and walked them to a large stone basin that stood in front of the main doors to the temple. Each threw their effigy into the basin before moving to stand on either side of it. This procession took a little while, but when it was completed, two large groups of priests stood on either side of the basin, now containing a very large pile of effigies.

Two priests came forward carrying torches. They bowed to the High Priest, then two each other.

"In the name of Sugabar, and the Phirinos, I command the bodies of our vices to be burned, so that they may not trouble us again for the coming year."

The priests slowly lowered the torches they carried, until they touched the effigies. A flame quickly took hold from each one. Rapidly the pile of "corpses" caught fire. A thin, black smoke began to rise from the fire, as the flames hungrily licked at the arms and legs of the effigies. Dorm quickly began to realise how the war came about. This ritual was a little disturbing. The idea that there was a real sacrificial ceremony conducted in this manner would easily be enough for him to want to declare war on someone. He took a deep breath and checked his anger. There was no real sacrifice he reminded himself quickly.

The priests spoke prayers quietly over the rapidly burning effigies. The whole ceremony was rather solemn but still managed to carry a certain relief, almost happiness at what had been performed. The people of Szugabar obviously took this very seriously. This was a part of their culture, their identity. They believed it was necessary for them to cast out their darker aspects in this way, as strange and unsettling as it might seem to him.

The flames eventually diminished then disappeared altogether. The smouldering ruins of the effigies were almost mournfully scooped up and placed into a large sculpted box. Once the box was full, and all the debris from the fire had been removed from the basin, several priests came forward with long poles. The poles were inserted into several loops at the top of the box, and a group of priests, eight in all, slowly lifted the poles onto their shoulders. Several more priests took up positions both in front and behind the group carrying the box and as one they all began to march off.

"Where are they taking that now?" Dorm asked Ambassador Camir who was sitting in front of him.

"Apparently there is a special garden or something that they bury it in," he explained. "I've never gotten a full answer to that. Apparently it is one of those aspects that they don't talk about too much."

The remaining priests reassembled in front of the crowd again. The High Priest who had conducted the ceremony stepped forward again. "Our ceremony is complete. Szugabar is protected for another year. The people shall not fall into the traps of the vices that haunt our path. Rejoice O ye people of Szugabar, for thy souls are safe now to travel forward on the path of life."

There was a great cheer and thunderous applause at the pronouncement.

Once the ceremony was over there was a brief refreshment. Dorm felt a little strange sipping wine and nibbling on food, having polite conversation with people after what he had just witnessed. None of the Szugabaran guests seemed in the least bit phased by all of it, so he guessed that to them at least this was all normal.

The Phirinos approached him at one stage. "Your Highness," he greeted him smiling. "You seem a little unsettled at the moment."

"I'm sorry, Your Majesty," Dorm replied. "The ceremony was not quite what I expected. And now this…" He indicated the throng around him.

"It appears normal to me," the King said looking around.

"It's just the incongruity of it all," Dorm explained. "The ceremony was very tense, very solemn. And for me a little shocking One might even go so far as to say stern. But this? This is all polite and happy, and chirpy."

The king laughed. "It is the way of things with this ceremony. The sacrifices are occasions of great power. They are extremely important. Dangerous for the priests. We know this, and honour their work, by not disturbing their activities. Once we are here however, we know that the ceremony has succeeded. And that for another year we are safe from the vices that plague us. And so we are thankful to both the priests and the Gods."

Dorm shook his head slowly. "There are many things I still do not understand about Szugabar."

The king laughed again. "As I'm sure there are things about the Alliance that we do not understand. But that is one of the goals of life. To learn and understand over time."

Mac walked up at that point. "Your Majesty," he greeted the Phirinos with a somewhat awkward bow. Mac had never really gotten to grips with that.

"Mac Ravin," the monarch responded with a nod. "It seems that there is much our Prince here does not understand about us of the desert. Perhaps you will have to teach him."

"I'll do my best, Your Majesty," Mac assured him. "Assuming I can figure it out myself," he added after a moment.

Again the king laughed. Dorm noticed that he seemed more relaxed around his guests from the Alliance. He didn't appear quite so formal. He spoke firmly when addressing any of his subjects. Even to an extent, his wife and daughter, though when he spoke to them, there was a hint of emotion in his voice. Dorm saw that he cared a great deal for his family by that factor.

After the reception, they headed to the Temple of Polton. It too was a large collection of buildings and formal gardens that covered a great deal of land. They were ushered into a large chamber near the centre of the main temple, where a large number of priests sang a long hymn to their Goddess. Afterwards a group of priests was presented to the High Priest and blessed. The Phirinos also blessed them. From the words spoken by the Priests it was clear that they were about to embark on some sort of task that would take several days. Once the ceremony had concluded and they were being taken back to their carriages, Dorm asked the Phirinos about it. His response was typically vague, though he did explain that the priests were going to pray to Polton and ask for information on the year ahead. Apparently they would also draw up astrological charts for the country, as well as the King and his family.

Dorm still didn't quite understand this astrology business, such things were not given much credence in the Alliance, but he was willing to let the Szugabar believe in it, if it made them feel better.

Next they travelled to an area of the city closer to the docks. Here another great temple stood, this time to the God Hep.

As they rounded the corner and headed down along the broad avenue towards the front of the temple, Dorm began to get the feeling that he had been here before. Of course he hadn't so it was a little hard to explain. But the feeling intensified the closer they got to the temple.

Their carriages pulled up in front of the temple, which, unlike the ones they had visited so far, was just a single building, not the sprawling complex. As he stepped down into the pavement, Dorm was taken again by that sense of familiarity. He knew he had seen this building before. But he just couldn't place it.

"Are you alright?" Mac asked him quietly, noticing that he was staring at the buildings façade.

“I just get this feeling that I’ve seen this before,” Dorm tried to explain.

They were escorted through the temple to a large courtyard at the back. Here several smaller buildings faced onto the court, and priests stood around watching a number of men sculpting at various large blocks of stone.

The men all wore loose fitting robes, and hammered and chiselled away at the stone before them. They had obviously been at it for a while, as most of the stones had begun to take shape, and piles of chips and dust lay about their bases.

The High Priest of Hep, whose name was Kamesta, came forward and greeted them all personally. He was a tall thin man, who spoke with slight lisp. But he seemed very glad to see them, and especially glad that the Phirinos and his family had attended.

“What exactly are they doing?” Rhynavell asked him, pointing at the men in the courtyard.

“They are sculpting,” Kamesta replied.

“Well yes, I can see that,” Rhynavell replied with a catch in her voice. “But for what purpose are they sculpting?”

“The final ceremony of the Great Festival, requires a likeness of each God to be present. Our sculptors here are competing to have their sculpture chosen as that likeness.”

“How is the winner chosen?” Lianna asked.

“The statue must contain the essence of the God Hep. Something that captures the aspects of our Gods essence. That is why we are so glad to have the Phirinos here. As a God on earth he is supremely qualified to chose the winner.”

There were a few raised eyebrows at that, but no one said anything.

For the next two hours the sculptors continued to fashion their artworks, chipping and scoring and later polishing and detailing. There was a brief break at one stage for the artists to take some water to drink, as it was quite warm here in the early afternoon sun.

While they worked their guests were given a brief tour of the temple itself. As they moved through the various halls, Dorm was again seized by the feeling that he had seen all this before. He even went so far as the quietly start describing some of the rooms they were about to enter, to Mac before they went inside. Mac began to realise that something was going on here, when all Dorm's descriptions turned out to be accurate.

"Beyond this door," said Kamesta when they had come to a large wooden door at the end of one of the main colonnaded halls. "Is the inner sanctum. None but myself, the Phirinos, and one or two other high-ranking priests may enter. And even then only on certain days of the year."

"It's where the statue of Hep resides," Dorm said almost distractedly.

"That's quite correct Your Highness," Kamesta said with a smile. "It is the embodiment for our God when he visits the temple."

"It sits on an alter. Plain but with a symbol carved into the front of it. The walls are white with a red band near the ceiling. The ceiling itself it painted with a depiction of Hep spinning the first man into existence. He is also shown with Polton and Raked."

"How could you know that?" Kamesta asked him incredulously. He looked at the Phirinos.

"I think perhaps there is something going on here that we do not understand Kamesta," the King said looking at Dorm.

"Do you know what's going on now?" Mac asked him.

"I have seen this before. That dream I had back in Hamij. It took me a while to place it, but this was the place I saw."

"Another dream," Telly said. "Why didn't you say something?"

"It wasn't like any of the others. This one… I… well I came here. And someone spoke to me."

"Spoke to you?" Travanos asked. "Who? What did they say?"

"I have no idea who it was that spoke. They felt… vast, and wise. That's about all I can say for certain. They asked me who I was and why I had come here. I couldn't answer them, I had no idea why I had dreamt it. Now that I've seen that this place really exists, I'm beginning to wonder who it was who was talking to me."

"This is very strange Your Highness," The Phirinos said. "It almost sounds like you have experienced a separation of soul from body."

"But why would he come here in such an occurrence?" Kamesta asked. "I don't understand. Perhaps we should have him examined by the committee of all the priesthoods?"

"I don't think we need to subject the Prince to that, Kamesta," the king decreed. "He is an honoured guest in our country after all. And I am trying to maintain good relations with the Alliance."

"This man has quite clearly been touched by the Gods, Majesty," the High Priest went on with a touch of defiance in his voice. "What he has said reveals that something special has happened to him, and this obviously has meaning. It is our obligation to investigate."

"His Highness is on important business for his kingdom," the Phirinos said quickly. "Something that also concerns Szugabar. If he has been touched by the Gods as you say, then we will just have to trust in the Prince's intellect and wisdom to discover what it is and what it means. I'm sure we will have a chance to speak of it before he leaves. Besides if the Gods are working through him, we wouldn't want to disrupt their plans would we?" He cast a look directly at the High Priest.

Kamesta didn't look convinced. He watched Dorm for a moment, obviously trying to determine how far he could push his case. After a few moments he let it drop. At least for the meantime.

As they headed back towards the courtyard at the conclusion of their tour, the Phirinos moved in next to Dorm.

"Your Highness, perhaps you could explain what is going on here to me?" he said quietly.

"I'd be happy to, Majesty. Just not here."

"Of course. I get the feeling it relates to your *real* reason for being in my country?"

"I can see why they made you king."

"They didn't really have much of a choice, but thank you for the compliment."

Arriving back in the courtyard, things had changed. All the now completed sculptures stood neatly in a row across the middle of the open space. Each stood separately on the flagstones so that one might be able to walk around them and inspect them from any angle. The sculptors stood in a row along the far wall. Several other priests stood around watching.

"Majesty," Kamesta said bowing. "Please do us the honour of showing us the choice of the Gods."

The Phirinos bowed briefly to him before walking to the first of the statues. For some time he inspected each one. Looking at them from different angles. Occasionally touching one, running his hand over certain features. It was all rather strange, and none of them had any idea what the King was actually doing.

After probably half an hour, the king had the priests move three forward from the line. These three he studied further. Pausing to look into the eyes of each, and almost seeming to listen to each one. What they might have said, Dorm had no idea.

Finally after what had seemed hours, the Phirinos finally placed his hand firmly upon the head of one of the sculptures.

"This," he pronounced with a degree of finality that couldn't be questioned. "This one captures the true spirit of your God. It shall represent Great Hep and the ceremony."

The priests all politely clapped. Two came forward bearing a scroll and stood next to Kamesta. "It is sculpture number four High Priest," said one of them.

The High Priest consulted the scroll before him. "This is the work of the sculptor Ameks. Step forward sculptor Ameks, and receive the blessing of the Gods and the Phirinos."

From the line of artisans stepped a somewhat short man, with tanned skin, probably from a lot of outdoor work. Despite his short stature he had rather powerful looking arms that seemed almost the wrong size for the rest of him. His head was shaved but with the hint of a scalp of dark hair. He wore a simple grey smock belted at the waist and typical Szugabaran sandals, that almost everyone, the Phirnios included, seemed to wear. His face seemed timid, and he wore none of the makeup that everyone in Szugabar seemed to wear, but he walked with the step of someone who had just achieved something personally important, something they had worked hard for, for quite some time.

The man came to stand before Kamesta. "Congratulations Ameks, you have done our God proud."

"Thank you Eminence," he said quietly his face beaming.

"And congratulations from me also Ameks," said the Phirinos shaking his hand. Ameks looked at him briefly before swallowing in nervousness and dropping his eyes to the ground.

"Thank you Divine One," He said bowing low. "I am honoured to have been chosen."

"Your work is truly wonderful. I may have to ask you to make some sculptures for me. I think the palace could use a little beauty. And I might have need of some work in my private chapel."

"I would be honoured to work for you personally, My Phirinos," He said looking squarely at the ground.

"Than we shall see to it."

The other priests congratulated him, as did the other competitors, whose works would be sent to the various temples of Hep throughout the country to be used at local versions of the conclusion ceremony.

As they slowly headed towards the door back into the temple, Travanos pulled in quickly beside Dorm. "Dorm," he began conspiratorially. "I don't mean to sound melodramatic, but I think perhaps you might want to just take note of the winner of the competition."

Dorm turned and looked. Ameks was standing in the middle of the courtyard, obviously deliriously happy with the outcome. He was holding something in his hand and speaking to it. Most probably sending a silent prayer to Hep, if Dorm's understanding of Szugabar was anything to go by.

Dorm was about to turn back to Travanos to ask him what he was trying to tell him, when Ameks moved his hands to give the traditional Szugabaran self-blessing. From his hand fell a large piece of greenish crystal, suspended from a chain. Dorm stopped and almost laughed at the revelation. He turned and looked at Travanos who merely smiled.

Chapter 22

Finding a way to 'meet' with Ameks had at first seemed somewhat difficult.

He wasn't the sort of person that Dorm and his companions could simply go up to and say "Hello there friend. Care for a drink with us?" The fact that the Phirinos had expressed an interest in his works and a desire for him to work for the palace, if only briefly, gave them a possible avenue, but arranging it so that it wouldn't arouse too much suspicion had them all a little stumped.

In the end the group decided that Dorm should simply go to the King and tell him what they had discovered. Given that after their visit to the Temple of Hep, he suspected that there was a lot more going on here than he had thought previously, even after Dorms partial explanation of the real reason for their being here, gave rise to the possibility that he might simply be able to arrange something.

So Dorm met with Taslem Kanos and after their usual chitchat about nothing in particular, put forward his request. The King thought on it for a moment, before readily agreeing. It seemed that he was taking this whole quest thing quite seriously.

"It is obvious that this man is one of your number," the King was saying. "And if he is then he has no other choice. He must go with you. And if that is to happen then he must be introduced to you."

"I thank you, Your Majesty," Dorm told him sincerely. "If we can get him into the palace, away from potential prying eyes, and tell him what's going on it will make things a lot easier."

"And quicker too I should think," the monarch said knowingly.

"Yes," Dorm sighed. "We still don't really know what sort of a timetable we are working to here, but I think that moving on with things is better than standing around doing nothing."

The King studied Dorm for several moments, scrutinising his features and appearance. After seemingly coming to some sort of conclusion he spoke.

"You have the feel about you of one who will change the world Dormal," he said somewhat mysteriously. "I felt it the first moment I saw you. But it is only really now that I see by how much. The world will be a different place because of you, my friend."

"I'm not really sure what to say to that, Your Majesty," Dorm told him with just a touch of embarrassment.

"Say nothing. Just listen." The king lent back for a moment studying him again. "There is much in this world that we do not understand. We of Szugabar know this. Our Gods teach us this. There is much that they keep to themselves. We merely catch glimpses of it now and again. I suspect that this quest you are on is pushing you further into that world than any one has gone before."

"You have spoken to me previously of the Fortress," he went on. "And how you believe that somehow it might be involved in this in some as yet unknown way. I believe you may be right. I have studied all that is known to Szugabar of the Fortress. And it must truly be a place of great power, but also great danger. I think before this is over, you will find out which."

"That's a little what I'm afraid of Sire," Dorm admitted. "I worry about what we might find when we get there. All the strange things that have happened to me since this began. The dreams, the mysterious encounters, the miraculous meetings of the people we have to collect. It makes me wonder."

"As I said the Gods work in mysterious ways. Ones that we can never fully fathom." The king noticed the change in Dorms face at the mention of 'Gods'. "I know you do not believe in Gods Dormal, but I suspect that somehow they are mixed up in this. Perhaps in a way that I cannot understand, but they are involved nonetheless."

"Then mayhap I will start praying to them, just to be on the safe side."

"I think that is a good idea."

The king had word sent to the Temple of Hep that the sculptor Ameks should present himself to the Palace in the morning of the next day, to meet personally with the Phirinos. It would have been interesting to have seen the reaction, not only of Ameks but of the people around him when that message was delivered.

The remainder of the day was spent quietly relaxing. It had been a very full agenda, and despite the fact that most of the time they had been sitting still, their minds were all rather worn out.

They all slept well that night. Dorm was untroubled by dreams of any sort, and he awoke feeling rather more refreshed than he had in some time. They ate breakfast in the large common room they had been given and discussed what was likely to happen that day. All knew that they were now coming to the end of their stay in Szugabar. They had managed to find both members of their group that they had come for, and now would have to head back to Kiama Mor, and hopefully find the other person from that country.

There was a certain feeling of regret at having to leave the opulent surroundings and the being waited on hand and foot and go back on the road, but at the same time a sense of anticipation that the journey would continue.

They hadn't been there long when the Princess entered the room. She spoke briefly with Dorm and Telly, informing them that her father had requested that they be present when Ameks was brought into the palace. She then went around the room and said good morning to all the members of their group, before sitting next to Tissievilla and starting a quiet but seemingly involved conversation.

"What's this?" Dorm asked curiously.

"I'm not entirely sure," Telly admitted. "They have been talking a lot lately though I've noticed."

"A problem?"

"I don't think so," she mused. "I think more in the nature of a friendship. The Princess probably doesn't have a huge number of friends she can talk to. And she is a young woman. Young women need other young women to talk to. That's something you men wouldn't understand."

"Oh really," Mac said defensively.

"It's true," Telly explained. "There are certain things that we can only discuss with other women our own age. Men are too closed. You keep things inside and don't talk about them. We're different is all."

"But why Tissie?" Mac asked. "It's not like she's good at holding a conversation. All she seems to ever want to talk about is hair and clothes."

"And sometimes we need to talk about that," Telly tried to explain. "And sometimes that's just the way to get the conversation going. And other times that's just a cover so you men don't know what we're really talking about."

"In other words lies."

"No, not lies. It is a well-known fact that when it comes to some things men just aren't cut out to talk about them. You get all squeamish and try to change the subject. So we just don't bother any more." She look at Mac, whose face seemed to indicate that he didn't really believe her. "Not convinced Mac? Well the next time I feel the need to talk about the intimate workings of the female body I'll know who to go to."

"Ahh no thanks Telly, that's alright. I wouldn't want to put you to any trouble," he said blushing slightly.

"See what I mean? You men. For all your bluster and your bravado, you really aren't much better than children when it comes to those sort of things."

"Steady on their a minute," Dorm said to her.

"Oh I still love you Dorm, never fear. It's just sometimes men can be quite silly." She slipped her arm around his.

"Thanks for the confidence boost."

"That's what I'm here for."

Ameks arrived a short time later and was taken to the Phirinos' study. Dorm hated to think how he felt. It wouldn't have been every day that a citizen of Szugabar was taken into the presence of their God-king.

After a short time the Phirinos and his rather nervous guest went for a brief walk, ostensibly for the king to be able to point out some of the ideas he had for Ameks new work. Their steps led them to the common room where their group waited. The Phirinos introduced them all, and Ameks politely responded, appearing a little unsure of what was going on. He seemed to notice their amulets but at the same time didn't seem to fully take it in. His mind was probably a little frazzled at the moment.

They all sat and talked briefly about nothing in particular before they began their inevitable conversation.

"Ameks," Dorm began. "You may have noticed that we are all wearing these amulets."

"Ah yes," he said, almost as if he had just noticed them then.

"You may be wondering how it is that we are all wearing amulets the same as the one you have," Telly said to him.

He looked at her for a moment. "How did you know?"

"We saw it, at least briefly," Travanos said. "Back at the Temple when we were leaving."

"I see," Ameks said. "I didn't steal it if that's what you're thinking."

"We know that," Dorm assured him. "Don't worry, you aren't in any trouble."

"You sure about that Dorm?" Cal said sarcastically.

"Cal, now isn't the time for jokes." Dorm sighed. "I guess I will have to explain all this first." He went on to tell Ameks about the amulets and their apparent meaning. It was a conversation they had all heard before, and it was almost beginning to become a routine. Both Ameks and the Phirinos were fascinated by it however and sat rapturously enthralled by Dorms' story. The king hadn't heard the story of how they had discovered the amulets and seemed as interested in how it had come about as any one could be.

At the conclusion of the story Dorm paused to let the full weight of it settle on the two men. The Phirinos turned to look at his subject.

"Ameks, you seem to be more important than just winning a contest."

"It does appear that way, Majesty," he said returning the look.

"You must go with these people. Szugabar must do its part to help save the world, if it should come to that."

"I'm not a warrior, Majesty. I'm just a sculptor," he protested.

"It doesn't matter what you are," Rhyn said to him earnestly. "We all come from different backgrounds. None of us is strictly speaking a warrior. None of us is exceptionally brilliant. But we all have skills that we bring to the group. And that's the important thing. We are a group. And you are a part of that."

"Our differences are what makes us good at this," Harmia told him. "They complement each other, and cancel out our deficits."

"It's the combination of all our skills that will see us through to success," Lianna said to him. "Trust me. I have no idea what fantastic ability I'm supposed to bring to this, but I'm not taking the chance that I won't be there when it's needed."

"If you don't come along we'll be missing one part of the group," Tissie piped up. "And that just isn't right."

"We know it's a lot to ask, to leave like we are asking," Mac told him. "But it is necessary."

Ameks looked over at Artur. "You left your wife and child behind?" he asked him solemnly.

"Yes I did," the woodcutter admitted. "It was probably the most difficult thing I have ever had to do. But I realised it was necessary."

"Don't you miss them?"

"Every day," Artur replied with a catch in his voice. "And there are times, where I feel like giving up and going home to them. But I know I can't do that. Not yet at least. I have a part to play in this and I have to see it though. I don't know what the consequences of all this are. I can't imagine. And I have a pretty good imagination. If it should be something bad, what kind of a husband and father would I be?"

"Then I guess I don't really have much of a choice do I?"

"That's the spirit," Zacravia said clapping him on the shoulder. "Admit that the universe has ganged up on you, and things will go much easier for you I can guarantee it."

Ameks sighed dejectedly.

They sat for a while discussing some of their adventures during their journey to Szugabar, and the various things they had discovered through conversations with Rangers and the like. During this, a servant entered and informed them that Pianwasal had arrived. The Phirinos informed them that he had taken the liberty of having her summoned, since he thought it appropriate that she be also present to welcome the newest member of their group.

She entered and bowed politely to the king, and nodded her welcome to the others. She sat and joined in the conversation almost as if she had been a part of their group since the beginning.

Ameks seemed a little withdrawn at first. He was after all surrounded by royalty, and high ranking people of various stations. While there were several people who were not high born; Dorm didn't like to think of them as common, for they were anything but, it was always difficult to relax when surrounded by people you felt were more important than you. Dorm knew that like Artur before him, Ameks would take some time to open up to them.

A meal was brought in for them and they ate continuing their conversation. Both Pianwasal and Ameks had various questions about what they all felt was going on, and what was to come. They did their best to answer their questions, though sometimes their responses were rather vague. Once it had been explained that this was not through any desire to keep them in the dark, but simply because they didn't have any real idea of what the answers were, their newest members seemed satisfied.

Taslam Kanos informed them that the final ceremony of the Great Festival would be held the day after tomorrow, and once it was concluded they would be free to leave any time they wanted. Dorm consulted with Telly, Rhyn, Travanos, and Harmia, with Mac not far away, and they decided that in order to prevent anything looking suspicious to any one who might be watching, that they would wait an extra day before leaving.

The king told them he would arrange for a ship to carry them back to Hamij. Dorm informed him that they would need to go via the Temple of Asen, so that Pianwasal could collect her belongings, and inform her "friends" of what was happening. He agreed, but then said after a moment, that he might like to accompany them there. He confided in Dorm, "I know High Priest Avek well. He will not be completely happy to have his Seneschal Priest absconding her duties."

"She isn't absconding. She's being borrowed for a time for something rather important," Dorm responded with a hint of anger.

"You and I know that, but Avek will see it as absconding," Taslem sighed. "If I am there, I may be able to temper his anger towards her. I am his King. He will control himself in my presence. I can probably also distract him for a time with private prayers only the High Priest can perform with me. That might give Pianwasal time to arrange herself." He said the last with a knowing look at Dorm.

"I have to say, Your Majesty, I'm still a little uncomfortable with this whole idea."

"As am I Dormal," he admitted. "As am I. But there is nothing to be done for it now. If something is necessary for the greater good, then it must be done, no matter how unpleasant we may find it personally. If we do find it so, then that just shows that it is important. And proves we are truly moral people."

"I'm not sure my father would see it that way. And history may say something different."

"History will say what we choose it to say. What we tell it happened. History is written by those with the will to wield the pen. Not simply by random events. This is a terrible thing to do. But there is no other choice."

"As you wish, Majesty."

The next few days were relatively quiet. There were several public ceremonies and state functions they were obliged to attend, but there were also periods where they were left to their own entertainments. They continued to meet with both Ameks and Pianwasal when they could to explain to them what they would be doing once they left Szugabar, and to bring them into their little group. Though now it was feeling somewhat less than little.

Both the new members of their company seemed to have accepted that they were required to leave behind their current lives for a time. The simple fact that they all had amulets lent itself to the idea that something important was going on. Dorm had always believed that it was just a family heirloom, made centuries ago by some ancestor as a symbol of their family. Nothing more. He knew exactly how each member of the group had felt upon the discovery that it was in fact something much more important.

The day of the final ceremony of the Great Festival finally arrived, and they took their places during the different stages of the celebration. Again it was held in the grounds of the great Temple of Raked, and again there was much solemnity. But also there was a certain amount of joy. The ceremonies were over for another year. The country had been protected and the Gods once again smiled upon the people.

After the ceremony had concluded there was a great celebration that seemed almost to encompass the whole city. As they headed back towards the palace, every square and intersection they passed thronged with joyous people, laughing and singing, and waving.

Dorm saw in their faces the joy of having completed something important and worthwhile. Something that had importance beyond his ability to fully understand. His comprehension of this 'religion' of the Szugabar changed somewhat on that ride. Before he had though of it as an important part of their culture, but not really all that intrinsic to their daily lives, if he was honest with himself. But when he saw their faces, he began to understand, at least a little, the depth of importance it held for these people. This wasn't just something they did because they had always done it. Because it gave them a few days off from their daily work every year. They did it because they knew they *had* to do it. It was a part of the functioning of their country. They could no more stop these ceremonies than they could stop planting their crops, or making cloth or bricks.

After they arrived back at the palace, there was a great banquet. A party the likes of which Dorm hadn't experienced in some time. He didn't want to think about the amount of wine he had drunk by the time he and Mac stumbled back to the rooms.

The next day was essentially spent recovering from the night before. They rose late, and ate heartily. Servants brought them soothing teas and fruits to eat, and Dorm realised with a laugh that they had had this all prepared, knowing exactly what would be required.

During the afternoon, Dorm again met with the Phirinos. They discussed their recollections of the night before, and Dorm was glad to see that he wasn't the only one who had some gaps. He also realised that once they left he would miss these chats. Taslem Kanos was a unique man. His position as a 'God on earth' would have seemed to have made him arrogant, condescending. Possibly even cruel. But the man himself wasn't. He was insightful and curious. And very intelligent. Dorm realised what the Alliance would gain if they could bring Szugabar fully into their membership. His contributions would be unique.

The King informed the Prince that he had sent word that their ships were to be readied for sailing the next day. Their baggage would be sent on ahead, and they would simply have to get themselves to the quay. The Phirinos of course would have to travel with a retinue, but he promised he would do his best to make sure it didn't delay them for too long.

That evening there was a formal banquet so that the Phirinos could say farewell to his important foreign guests. This also allowed the various nobles of Szugabar the opportunity to see that their monarch was engaging with the world and working for their nation. They of course really all just attended in order to be seen with important foreigners and therefore hopefully elevate their own status further.

The whole affair was generally rather tedious, with various long winded speeches about nothing important, whilst platters and dishes of food were constantly brought out in order to keep the guests from noticing that their plates were empty. With all the food there wasn't much chance of any one getting too far under the weather, but even so Dorm noticed that many people seemed to be going easy on the wine.

His companions sat at a large table at the head of the room, with the Royal family, the Vizier, who seemed to scowl across the room at just about everyone the whole time, and one or two other important guests such as the High Priest of Raked.

There was a lot of polite conversation between the various guests. But nothing of any great interest. That was until the Phirina spoke to Dorm.

"Your Highness," she began in her heavily accented voice. Up close Dorm now realised she was older than he had previously thought. She looked much younger from even a short distance away. Dorm wasn't sure if that was because of all the makeup she wore, or if it was just a part of the woman herself. "My husband thinks highly of you."

"Thank you, Your Majesty. I think quite highly of your husband also."

"Given the plans he has," she went on, giving him a knowing look. "I think that having a personal relationship with someone such as yourself is going to be important."

"I'd like to think that we can work on this together. And maybe even yourself?"

"That will not be possible," she said with a hint of regret. "My roles in Szugabaran government are limited and strictly defined. They are important, yes, but I must never be seen to be involving myself with things outside of those areas."

Dorm looked at her for a moment. "Your Majesty, we both know, that despite your husbands intelligence, compassion and determination to do the best for his country, that he couldn't do his job without your assistance."

She thought for a moment. "Perhaps, Perhaps not. But there are those who hold fiercely to traditional roles for people in high office. And they have powerful friends. And can sway many people. It is never wise to upset such people."

"Your husband relies on you."

"I know. As does my daughter, and select few others. My husband is a great man. He cares deeply for what happens to our country. I cannot let anything distract him from running it properly. In the future, when things are brought out into the open, it may be that you will have to negotiate with my husband and his advisors alone. I would simply ask that you consider carefully what is being asked of us, and of you. I have no doubt that it will all be done properly and openly. But I wish you to look out for us. My husband respects you. Perhaps even considers you a brother of sorts. I would like to see that continue."

"As would I, Majesty."

She smiled at him warmly then returned to her seat. Dorm was a little confused by what she had said. Of course he would try to do his best for both Szugabar and the Alliance. And he would, if he was involved, try to make sure that the Phirinos knew all that was going on.

He wasn't sure what she had been trying to ask him to do.

Mac saw his confusion. "I only heard part of it, but it didn't make much sense to me either."

"She was asking me something specific. But I'm damned if I know what."

"She probably just wants to make sure things don't go wrong for the Phirinos, or for Szugabar."

"I hope that's all it is."

The next morning they prepared to leave. They had concluded their business here in Szugabar and it would be good to be back on the road again. Dorm felt that they had probably spent too much time here, even though it had only been about a week.

There were still plenty more questers to find, and they had many more miles to travel to find them.

They saw their belongings off to the quay and their waiting ship, before thanking various members of the palace staff who had waited on them during their stay. They waited until a large number of carriages had pulled up in front of the broad steps and then climbed aboard, before heading off into the teeming streets of the city.

Ameks looked somewhat nervous about travelling in the carriage. Commoners in Szugabar it appeared didn't normally have such a luxury and so he felt almost as if he were doing something illegal. The others tried to assure him that everything was alright .

No one seemed to notice their passage. It was just another train of carriages heading through the city. Only those who stopped to pay attention to the carriages themselves, would have noticed that the passengers were not just ordinary merchants. The Phirinos sat rather nonchalantly, watching the city pass by. He wore little in the way of fancy clothes or jewellery and he wore no crown or any of his official attire. Only those who would recognise his face might have thought he was anything other than perhaps a rich merchant, or possibly some government official.

They left the city via the main gate and moved along the various quays until the came to one area that was walled off from the rest. They entered through a smaller gatehouse into a courtyard surrounded by warehouses and offices. The ringing of hammers and sawing of wood informed them that there were industrial areas not far away. They all dismounted from the carriages and were ushered though an expensive looking hallway onto a quay at which were berthed two ships. One was, unbelievably, the *Star of the Sea*, which had brought them here in the first place. Dorm, was confused at how such a thing could have been arranged, but was glad that they would again be sailing with Captain Tamik.

The other ship was quite different. Its hull was more elongated and seemed to sweep up dramatically at either end. A large red sail was attached to the single mast and a row of oars stuck out from each side. Several large canopies had been erected on the upper deck, providing large areas of shade. The ships' hull was painted in a variety of colours, over different areas, and at her bows were painted a pair of bright white eyes complete with the traditional makeup.

"The Royal Barge," The King responded to their curious looks at the vessel. "A rather melodramatic name for a ship simply reserved for the use of the Phirinos. It isn't the grandest looking ship in all of Szugabar, but she is good at what she does."

The term barge turned out to be somewhat of a sarcastic term. It implied a simple utilitarianism. This vessel was anything but. Expensive woods lined the walls of the companionways below decks and they were polished till they shone. Gold touches gave each room a certain opulence, and rich, deep carpets and airy drapes gave the staterooms vivid splashes of colour.

Taslem Kanos seemed almost to delight in showing them around the ship as they prepared to sail. It wasn't the delight of a monarch either, but rather of someone who cared about something he had helped create. He genuinely seemed proud of the beauty the vessel contained. Travanos was the only one who seemed to be unsatisfied with it. He muttered under his breath, something about warships not being meant to look like this. Apparently the royal ship used by the Queen of Selatem was officially a naval ship. He said later that he felt that the Szugabar had turned a warship into a pleasure boat.

They re-emerged back on deck after their tour, and were delighted to see Captain Tamik and his first mate present. There was a brief heartfelt reunion with the two men, and they were given instructions as to the slight deviation in their course. The conversation lasted for sometime, with Tamik expressing concerns about his ability to dock there without a proper permit, and the Phirinos assuring him that he would be given no troubles while his ship was present.

Once that was all settled they began to make their way towards the gangway so they could all take their places on board the *Star*.

“Ah Dormal,” Artur said quietly. “I hate to be a bother, but we appear to have company.” He pointed and Dorm saw the now familiar dark robed gait of a group of Rangers.

Again there were three of them. It appeared that they always travelled in groups of three. The various workmen around the quay stopped what they were doing, and watched the strange arrivals enter and head towards the ship. They lined abreast of the edge and bowed deeply. All pushing back their hoods as they rose.

“Greetings Noble Questers,” said the woman in the centre. Her dark blonde hair shone in the bright light, and her face carried a serenity Dorm had never seen before. “We would speak unto thee before thou dost depart from Szugabar.”

“Well thank you for that,” Dorm called out them. “It’s nice to know you still care.”

The woman smiled. “We understand thy frustration, Your Highness. But thy journey here has been profitable, on many fronts. You can see that I’m sure.”

Dorm thought about it for a moment. He had to agree it had been profitable, much more than he had originally expected. Not only had they gained their next two questers, but the information about Taslem Kanos’ intentions regarding the Alliance, as well as a deeper personal understanding of the culture of Szugabar, were all things he had gained throughout this little ‘side trip’.

“I see what you mean,” he told her.

Again she smiled. “Your journey here is now complete. You must continue on your way, even as you have seen yourself. But do not dally too long in the sacred place to which you journey now. There is much that still must be done. While your pause there is important, you mustn’t let it distract you.”

"And why are you telling us this?" Rhyn asked suddenly.

"We have been instructed to do so, Noble Quester," said one of the men. He was a youngish looking man with light brown hair. He looked younger than the woman, though he seemed just as wise. "We pass on that which we are told to convey."

Rhyn didn't look convinced.

"Stay safe on your journey across the sea, Questers," the woman continued. "There is still much danger in the world, and you must be careful that it does not waylay you."

"We shall offer our prayers for your safe conduct," said the other man, whose red hair seemed almost to be a fire .

Again the Rangers bowed. They then turned on their heel as one and began their slow gait again, walking back the way they had come. They watched them go for a moment taking in what they had said.

"Well that was very cryptic," said the Phirinos.

"You get used to that Your Majesty," Zacravia assured him.

"What does it mean?" he asked.

"It means that we need to be watchful," Harmia said. "At least that's what I thought."

"I think she's right," Mac agreed. "We have to make sure that we go to the Temple, but that we keep an eye out not to get trapped there for too long."

"Makes a certain amount of sense I guess," Cal concurred. "We still have another member from Kiama Mor to find."

"Not to mention Ojliam and Bydanushev," Lianna reminded them.

"Yes, yes, we have a long way to go," Dorm agreed. "But standing here wondering about it isn't going to get us there." He sighed. "Sometimes I wish the Rangers wouldn't even bother to give us information. We end up spending time just trying to understand their riddles."

"Here, here!" Zacravia shook his fist in the air to emphasise his agreement. "No more jabbering Rangers, I say."

They moved quickly then to board the *Star of the Sea* and take their berths, so that the two ships could be cast off. There was a brief delay while some other traffic left the harbour, but they were soon on their way.

Dorm settled in for another sea voyage. He listened to the shouts of orders from Captain Tamik and his senior crew, and felt the wind in his hair. The gentle rhythm of the ship began to emerge as they slowly headed up the coast.

The Phirinos' Royal Barge led the way as they headed northward. It was an impressive sight, with its large crimson sail billowing in the breeze, and its oars sweeping forward and back with military precision.

Mac came up on the deck beside Dorm and slipped his hand into his. They stood together for a while in the bright midday light as their ships headed towards their next destination.

Chapter 23

The sea was unchanged.

The two ships headed northward along the coast of Szugabar before a slight breeze. The sun shone brightly and reflected of the sheer surface of the Desert Sea, sometimes painfully, as they whiled away the time of the journey doing nothing in particular. Captain Tamik recounted his fascinating adventures in the harbour side taverns of the capital during the week and his clashes with various merchants and exporters in the hopes of getting a cargo to take back. As it turned out he didn't need to, since they now all had to be transported again. Margrave Hamik, whom they hadn't seen a great deal of during the week as he and his wife had remained in the foreign dignitaries palace while they had been in the Phirinos' house, had managed to locate the captain before he had managed to secure any return cargo and booked his ship for their return.

The *Star of the Sea* swung lazily along its passage and after an hour or two Dorm and his companions were used to its movements again. Travanos and Lianna being the obvious exceptions being used to it straight away; Travanos even trying once to climb into the rigging, before being told to leave the running of the ship to its own crew. Dorm had thought that with him being an Admiral he would have been past all of that. Preferring to leave it to the lower ranks. His response was that he started off as one of those "lower ranks" and he had never quite lost his enthusiasm for 'swinging aloft' as he called.

This part of Szugabar was generally arid. Sand dunes and rocky hills could be seen towards the horizon, while along the shoreline, sandy beaches were broken by the odd marshy area, full of reeds and mosquitoes. Occasional animals, identified by Pianwasal or Ameks as crocodiles and hippopotamus would either watch their passage or dive into the water upon their approach. Tissie was constantly worried that the crocodiles would get on board and eat her, and while the other assured her this wouldn't happen, Dorm detected a hint to their voices as they said it. They had all seen those teeth after all.

The animals of Szugabar were fascinating to all the Alliance citizens. Nothing like them existed anywhere else. Dorm had to admit that he wasn't particularly wrapped with the idea of those long, powerful reptilian jaws closing around him, or the great bulk of a hippo rushing towards him. This country was much more dangerous than it seemed at first glance.

The sounds of the creaking wood of the ship under his feet relaxed Dorm somewhat. They were finally moving again he thought to himself. While their stay in Szugabar had undoubtedly been important, and profitable, their time there had felt a little like stagnation. They had seemed so far to have things happen while moving. Here they had just had to wait around. And it hadn't felt right. Now things were moving again. They were headed back towards Kiama Mor, in a round about way. There they would have to find the other quester, before moving on the Ojliam and Bydanushev. And then…

Mac came to stand next to him. "Thinking?" he asked quietly.

Dorm watched the Phirinos' ship a short distance in front of them. It's red sail arched perfectly in the breeze. "You know me too well," he smiled.

"Well we have started to leave Szugabar," Mac spoke Dorms' thoughts aloud. "On towards the next people. Whoever they turn out to be."

"And wherever. We still have all of Kiama Mor to search yet."

Mac sighed heavily. "I'd forgotten about that. When we left Kiama Mor, it kind of felt like we had everyone. I keep forgetting that we only managed to find Ambra."

They stood in silence for a moment.

"How is everyone getting along?" Dorm asked. It was something that had played on his mind in the last few days.

"As well as can be expected given that we have two new faces. And Ambra is still fairly new as well. Pianwasals profession may cause some issues. A priest is such a strange thing." He looked back at several members of the group who were talking on the deck not far away. "I think in the end they will all be close. We're all in this together. I get the feeling that will bring us all together."

"It seems to be having an effect on you as well."

Mac looked at him questioningly.

"You haven't had anything to say about Tissie for a while," Dorm noted.

"Well she hasn't tried anything on with you lately. I haven't had any reason to."

Dorm put his arm around Macs' shoulder. "And you never will have a reason to," he assured him.

The day went by smoothly as they sailed along. Just as everyone was getting used to being on a ship again, Captain Tamik informed them that they would shortly be arriving at the temple dock where they would alight. On the horizon they could now see their destination. A slight indent in the coastline where the sandy beach had been replaced by a stone quay. Several small buildings, warehouses mostly, stood nearby and there were several figures moving about.

The ships pulled into the dock, which was only just big enough to fit them both, and gangways were raised as the crews and the dockworkers secured the lines. They disembarked quickly and headed towards the buildings. An official looking man with a large nose wearing a typical Szugabaran kilt and headscarf came forward carrying a tablet and pen.

"Stop right there please," he said in a superior voice. "Just who are you and what do you think you are doing docking here?"

Dorm was about to introduce himself, when Pianwasal stepped forward. "Dockmaster Gresik," she began. "You will stand aside, these people are official guests of our priesthood."

"Senschal Priestess," he stammered in reply bowing slightly. "I had no idea that it was you. We hadn't expected you to return from the capital for several days yet."

"There has been a change in my plans due to circumstances beyond my control. Please send word ahead to the temple that most important guests are about to arrive. I expect every effort afforded them."

"Yes My Priestess," Gresik assured her quickly bowing as he backed away.

"That was remarkably well done Pianwasal," Taslem Kanos said admiringly.

"Thank you, My Phirinos," she said with a smile. "One gets to know how to get the best out of people after a while."

"I've noticed that myself," was his slyly made reply.

She led them past the buildings to a stone archway that led to what appeared to be a formal procession way. It was lined on either side by those same human headed animal statues Dorm had seen at the great Temple of Raked in Szugabar. The procession way itself was lined with large paving stones that were quite obviously ancient. Their rather large group; given that the Phirinos couldn't apparently travel anywhere without at least a dozen armed men as escort, not to mention several servants and a scribe or two, walked calmly and evenly past the statues towards the temple. They crossed what appeared to be the main road heading back towards to capital.

"Were does this road go?" Cal asked looking around.

"Just over that ridge is the city of Asenakir," Pianwasal told him. "It is where a large number of priests and artisans live. Not to mention merchants and labourers."

"Your temple has its own town?" Rhyn asked.

"Most do. The temples are centres of worship, but when people aren't worshipping they have other things to do, and so the towns develop."

At the top of the rise, dominating the area was the temple itself.

Two tall, slender obelisks flanked the temple. Both were engraved with strange writings, which seemed to be made up of small pictures for the most part. To their untrained eyes they looked the same as those that had been in the Phirinos' palace and various other buildings they had seen. Though Dorm suspected they probably said something very different. The obelisks cast long shadows over the temple itself. Dorm began to take note of the temple as they drew closer.

It was a large stone building seemingly made of giant square blocks. The main façade was covered in the typical religious inscriptions and reliefs depicting Asen this time. The upper levels of the temple were also inscribed though there it seemed to be more writing than pictures. In the centre was a large golden plaque in the shape of the symbol of Asen. Dorm recognised the stylised bulls head that represented the God. Flags flew from the two short masts at the top of the temple. It was an imposing structure, that felt as if it had been sitting here since the beginning of the universe.

As they approached the court before the main entrance, a number of priests suddenly emerged from the cave like entrance and stood in a line across their path. Pianwasal strode in from of their group and came to a halt.

Everyone stopped. For a moment there was silence, then Pianwasal bowed.

"Who seeks entrance to the Sacred Temple of Divine Asen?" intoned one of the priests in what was obviously a ritual greeting.

"I do. I name myself Pianwasal Ab Debar. Seneschal Priest of Divine Asen. Blessed of His Name," Pianwasal replied.

"We greet you Noble Seneschal Priest of our Divine God. Welcome back to His gracious care here in His House.

"I thank you brother priest. May He spread his wisdom and love to you for protecting His House."

Again all the priests bowed. "Please inform our High Priest that I have returned. And that I bring guests, most noble and high to the House of our God."

One of the priests, a young man no more than twenty bowed deeply and walked off with a barely controlled step.

Pianwasal began to move forward and they tentatively followed. The priests fell in around them, and Dorm realised that they were fairly evenly split between men and women. Though most of them were fairly young.

They passed through the main door and the temperature

noticeably cooled as they entered the shade. The chamber was open, but rather gloomy, with an incredibly high roof. The walls were covered in paintings showing the God Asen in various postures and different actions, most of which escaped Dorm and his friends. In each of the far corners there were a block of stone stairs that led to upper levels. Various priests and other official looking people stood around in hushed conversations. Most seemed to take no notice at first, until they saw the size of the entering group. Pianwasal led them through the chamber without stopping, into the chamber beyond. This was even bigger. Its roof was lost in dark, not merely gloom. Huge rounded pillars supported the roof at regular intervals. All were engraved to look like a tree of some sort, and again the exposed walls were painted in various scenes depicting Asen.

"The Grand Hall," Pianwasal said to them loudly by way of explanation. Her voice echoed in the huge chamber.

As she walked onwards priests in the Grand Hall bowed to her and their group. It was obvious that she was recognised and respected here.

At the end of the Grand Hall stood a pair of high wooden doors. They were closed and attended by several priests. Pianwasal halted before the doors and bowed again.

"Divine Asen," she called out. "Permit me, Your Seneschal Priest to enter Your sacred temple and serve You."

The guards at the doors pushed open the doors so that they might enter.

The chamber beyond was much longer than the previous two had been. It was also much lighter than the previous ones, with small windows high on the walls and torches set at regular intervals. Several large columns held up the roof, but there seemed to be much more open space here. Rows of wooden benches were arrayed all facing towards the far end of the room. Again more pictures of Asen dominated the walls, though here they seemed to be simply carved, and left unpainted.

At the far end of the room was a dais. It took up fully a third of the floor space. Near the front of the dais was a large carved stone block, that Dorm guessed was the alter. Some distance behind it was a statue more massive than Dorm had thought possible to contain within a building. The mighty form of the God Asen stood surveying all who entered the sanctum of his temple. There was no escape from the gaze of those eyes. His face, while serene, still seemed to convey a certain hardness. As if to say, 'never try to question the will of the Gods'.

Pianwasal walked to the foot of the dais and prostrated herself on the floor. They could hear her whispering something. Dorm noticed that the Phirinos and indeed most of the other Szugabarans in his retinue, stood with their heads bowed and eyes closed. He also noticed that the members of his group also seemed to be bowing their heads slightly.

Pianwasal finished her prayer and stood. She turned towards them. "Welcome to my Temple," she said proudly.

At that moment there was some commotion from near the statue and several priests came forward. One wore a robe, that while the same cut and colour as those of the others, was obviously made of a more expensive material, and his various adornments and jewellery were heavier. His face was dominated by two things. His hawk like beak of a nose that seemed to precede him as he walked, and a pair of bushy grey eyebrows, set above two small dark eyes, that were set and hard looking.

"What is the meaning of this Pianwasal?" he said in a booming voice. "Why have you returned from the capital early, and brought strangers into the Temple of Mighty Asen?"

"High Priest Avek," Pianwasal said with almost constrained contempt. "Rejoice for our Temple is greatly honoured. We have most noble visitors. Including our Divine Phirinos."

"If the Phirinos were to be coming here," Avek began to disagree. "There would have been advance notice. The King cannot leave the capital without a large retinue and he would have sent word to us to prepare for his arrival." He spoke to Pianwasal as if she were the stupidest novice who didn't know what time of day it was. It was now clear to see at least part of the reason why she hated him so.

"This was something of a day trip, Avek," Taslem said then stepping forward. "It isn't an official visit."

"My Phirinos!" Avek said incredulously, his eyes suddenly doubling in size. "Divine Grace of Heaven." He said rushing forward and kissing the kings hand. "Please forgive me. I had no idea you would come to visit us. What great thing have we done to be afforded such honour?"

Dorm was almost sick with the sycophancy.

"I am here because of Pianwasal actually," the king went on. Aveks face fell slightly at the kings statement, and he briefly glanced at her with barely concealed contempt before regaining his composure and focusing back on the monarch. "She has a most important job to do, and it brings much honour to you and your Temple that she is involved."

Dorm was impressed. Taslem had managed to elevate Pianwasal at the same time as make it seem like it would reflect favourably on Avek himself if she was to perform it. Aveks face paused for a moment. His eyes narrowed ever so slightly as he tried to determine what this 'task' of hers might be.

"My Phirinos," he began. "I am most certain that Pianwasal has performed her duties in the capital with her usual dedication, and I'm sure that whatever job you have for her she will acquit with equal zeal."

"Oh of that I am most certain Avek," Taslem agreed smiling. "After having spoken with her over the last few days I am certain that she will be an excellent ambassador for not only the God Asen but also for Szugabar."

Avek seemed a little miffed, as Telly would have said, at the mention of Pianwasal and the Phirinos having conversations over several days. It was clear that to Avek, politics came first followed only distantly but his actual job. The High Priest fixed the Phirinos with a direct look a pleasant smile on his face.

"And what, Majesty, can my Seneschal Priest do in service to the Kingdom?" he asked pleasantly.

"She is to accompany these people on a great quest, the outcome of which holds great importance for all the free peoples of the world." Dorm thought that Taslem was laying things on a bit thick but then he had seemed to take things to a bit of a melodramatic end when they had been discussing it.

Avek simply laughed. "And who are these people exactly Majesty? Confidence men perhaps? Troubadours? What stories have they been telling?"

"You forget yourself Avek," Taslem said seriously in a quiet voice.

Aveks expression shifted slightly. "I meant no disrespect to you Majesty. Please forgive my bluntness. It is just such a preposterous idea, that Pianwasal should go off on a 'quest'? In fact that anybody should." He added the last just a little too quickly.

"We understand that, Your Eminence," Dorm agreed. "When we first started all this the idea of going on a 'quest' sounded just as ridiculous to us. But we've seen and experienced things that have changed our minds."

"But of course we only have your word for these things, Sir," Avek decreed. "I mean you people could be after anything from His Majesty."

"Only his friendship," Dorm stated unequivocally.

"I am serious Avek," Taslem said fixing his gaze squarely at the ecclesiast. "These people are esteemed guests of our nation, they are to be afforded every courtesy."

Avek didn't look convinced. After a few moments of tense silence, the Phirinos was forced to relent.

"Very well, I present to you His Royal Highness Prince Dormal of Lugemall…" the introductions went quickly. Avek began to realise that perhaps there was something going on after all. His expression slowly changed as the members of their group were announced, from one of haughty pomposity, to wary curiosity. It was clear that he wanted more information before committing to a course of action. He was in the presence of the Phirinos after all. Avek was clearly a shrewd operator, and he obviously didn't like it when Pianwasal got out from his direct observation. If she did have to go on this adventure, then he wanted to know why and what she would be doing on it.

"An esteemed group of people to be sure, Majesty," Avek said carefully. "And what does this 'quest' involve exactly?"

"We aren't entirely sure of that to be honest," Dorm told him. "But what we do know is that there are certain people that are needed and each is necessary. If any one of them is missing, then the outcome is uncertain."

"Of course you have to say that," Avek went on. "It makes you sound all concerned and heroic. Forgive me, Your Highness if I don't blithely follow your pronouncements."

There was a pause as everyone took in the High Priests flat refusal to even consider what was being said. Taslem looked at Avek for a moment. He turned then and took Dorm by the arm, leading him a short distance from the others. There were quite a few strange looks as the two moved off.

"I would have the truth of things Dormal," the monarch said quietly to him. "Is this as serious as you have said?"

"Probably more so than I have said," Dorm admitted. "I wasn't lying when I said we don't fully understand what is going on here. I'm more convinced everyday that this whole thing has something to do with the Fortress itself. And if it does... well let's just say things are likely to get a lot more complex before they get easier."

Taslem thought on this for a moment. "You have spoken truly to me during your time in my House Dormal. I appreciate that. I sense that you are an honest man. One not given to flights of fancy. Swear it is the truth and it will be so."

"I swear on the memory of my mother," Dorm said. He rarely invoked something so powerful. Despite her death more than a decade ago, his mother still loomed very large in his world. She had been the centre of his life while she had been alive. Her memory was something very powerful to him. Taslem caught the catch in his voice as he spoke. He nodded imperceptibly.

"Then it is so."

They walked back to the others. "This is a grave circumstance we find ourselves and our country in Avek. It is the responsibility of the Phirinos and his Priesthoods to ensure that the Gods are honoured and that Szugabar plays its part in the affairs of the world."

"But Majesty, the very idea that something like a quest could even occur..."

"I have heard the truth of the matter. It is as the Prince has said. We have no choice but to participate. My word is law."

"If it is the will of the Gods that a priest of Asen is to accompany this group then I for one will submit humbly to my Gods' calling for us to participate, but it is clear that Pianwasal is too important a person to participate herself. There are many priests and priestesses here and in other temples, many of whom would benefit greatly from such an experience. We shall choose one of these to accompany you."

"No you don't understand, Your Eminence," Telly replied curtly. "It has to be Pianwasal. She is the one."

"Quite out of the question, My lady," Avek said with that pleasant smiling shake of the head of someone who thinks they are in the dominant position in any argument always adopts. He clearly thought that Telly and indeed all of them, had no real understanding of who he was and what power he thought he had. "Pianwasal is vital to the smooth running, not only of this Temple, but of our Priesthood as a whole. It is clearly something that should be given to another, less irreplaceable member of our order. I assure you though, we will find someone with many varied skills that could be useful on your journey."

"I'm sorry, are you really that stupid?!" Cal exclaimed in his usual straight forward manner. "We have to have Pianwasal. Pi-an-wah-suuullllllll!" Even the Phirinos had to hide a grin at that.

Avek was somewhat aghast at having been spoken to in such a manner. "I beg your pardon sir!"

Cal threw his hands up in disgust and turned away.

"Avek," Taslem began. "There is no one else that can perform this task. She must attend to it. I have already given her permission to do so. She will go."

Avek's mouth opened and closed like a fish's for a moment before he regained his composure enough to respond. "I forbid it."

Taslem paused. All in the room knew that this was something one didn't say to the divine absolute rule of the land of Szugabar. Not if one wanted to remain healthy for very long at any rate. The monarch blinked several times before speaking quietly in an even and very calm voice. "Pardon me?"

"Majesty, this cannot be allowed to go on."

"I am the Phirinos of Szugabar. I have decided what shall happen. It will be done."

The two men stared at each other for a moment. The tension in the air could have been bottled. It was obvious who would back down and who would win, but to his credit Avek held out for longer than Dorm thought he would. Or indeed could.

"As my Phirinos decrees," he said quietly bowing his head.

Taslem clapped his hands together suddenly the loud noise starting everyone. He grinned broadly. "Then that is settled. Excellent. Now Avek, show me some of these new observations you have been making."

The Phirinos and Avek walked off towards another part of the temple, the High Priests pace showing clearly that he felt rather lost and dis-empowered by what had just transpired. The others paused for a moment to think. The confrontation had not been completely unexpected, though none of them really knew exactly what would happen.

"Well I should go and prepare," Pianwasal said quietly.

"Perhaps we can accompany you," telly suggested.

"Oh yes let's," Tissie piped up enthusiastically.

"Very well, follow me." She led the ladies off towards a large arched doorway at the end of the sanctum near where they first entered. The men stood around for a few moments, feeling decidedly awkward and out of place, until one of the priests in the room showed them through to another chamber where comfortable seats and low tables allowed them to relax. They were brought refreshing drinks and small fruits to eat, and were actually able to almost pretend that there was no quest and no fate of the world at stake potentially. It was just a group of friends talking and enjoying each others company.

Word reached them a short time later that Pianwasal had prepared for her journey and that they had requested their company. They were escorted back into the Sanctum and into the arched doorway the women had entered earlier. It led to a closed in stairway that wound its way upward to the upper levels of the building.

"What's on this level?" Mac asked as they first started to climb the stairs.

"Cells for the Priests," their guide, a young man with a shaved head replied. "There are chambers for forty priests and priestesses on this level."

They passed by the landing for the next level. The corridor stretched off into the distance, a few priests moved along its length.

"And this level?" Travanos enquired.

"Again more cells," the young man responded. "Again forty."

They continued up another level, and Dorm began to wonder if this staircase ended at all.

"And I suppose this level has more cells?" Ambra commented as they took the last few steps to the next landing.

"No this level has only two peoples quarters. The High Priests' and the Seneschal Priests'. No other rooms are on this level."

They proceeded a short distance down the corridor to a large door, whose lintel was elaborately carved in various traditional Szugabaran motifs. Above the centre of the door stood another symbol of Asen. Their guide politely knocked on the door and waited till it opened. Pianwasal smiled as she saw them. She nodded to the young priest. "Thank you Damas, you have served Asen well today."

"Thank you Seneschal Priest," He bowed and scampered away with a slight spring in his step.

Pianwasal's personal quarters were a vast contrast to the official austerity of the rest of the building, which despite its heavy religious decoration seemed rather impersonal and uninviting. Her floors were covered with deep rugs and several tapestries hung on the walls. The furniture was minimal but comfortable, and there were several vases of flowers around the periphery of the room.

"Welcome gentlemen," she said moving into the chamber. The ladies smiled at them as they entered.

"Well this is certainly different," Zacravia said as he looked about the room.

"These are my personal rooms," Pianwasal explained. "Here I am not just a Priestess, but a person. So I decorate my rooms to reflect me."

"I approve," Ambra stated. "It is nice to find a place that is alive here."

Pianwasal nodded slightly and grimaced. "Yes, the temple can be a bit bland after a while. But it is a place of work and worship."

"So what will happen while you are gone?" Dorm asked her seriously.

"My duties will be shared among the other senior priests. No one will use these quarters until I return."

"And what of other matters?" Travanos politely enquired.

"They shall be taken care of in good time. I am reluctant, but I can see the wisdom of the suggestions that have been made. I will accede to them in this instance."

All knew what they were talking about. But still it seemed somehow criminal to be discussing it. None of them liked Avek after his little display in the Sanctum, but it still made most of them uncomfortable to calmly chat about his possible demise.

Pianwasal continued her packing. She had two large bags and two or three smaller ones out on the large table in the centre of the room. Most seemed to be filled with clothes, and other personal items. She was now sorting through a small pile of objects and selecting some to put in one of the smaller bags.

"What are all these things?" Zacravia asked curiously leaning on the table to inspect them.

"Some are religious icons." She held a lot a strange wooden device that comprised a series of woven wicker circles around a cross like staff. "This for instance is the Akam. It is our ancient symbol for life and rebirth. Given to us by the Gods to represent these concepts and as a sacred symbol. It carries an essence of their power."

Zacravia looked at her trying to see if she was fooling him.

"And this," she said as she held out a tightly bound set of scrolls. "Are some of the ancient prayers and spells that the Gods gave to our first holy men. They are most sacred."

"How is it that you have them then?"

"These are copies," she told him placing them carefully in the bag. "The originals are kept in the Temple of Raked in the capital. But these are copied directly from them by hand. They are blessed in the presence of the originals as well. They may prove most valuable depending upon what we encounter."

"And that is just it," Mac said. "We don't know what we're going to encounter."

There was a polite knocking at the door. Pianwasal went to answer it. The open door reveal a small number of priests, whom the Seneschal Priestess admitted warmly. They noticed the large group of strangers in the room and paused with uncertain looks upon their faces.

"Do not worry," Pianwasal assured them. "These are my companions for my great journey. Friends, this is my First Rank,

Ukavinas. He leads my personal staff."

"A pleasure to make your acquaintance Ukavinas," Dorm said shaking his hand.

"The pleasure is ours, Your Highness," Ukavinas said with an unsure smile. He looked quickly at Pianwasal.

"It is alright," she replied. "They know of our situation, at least generally.

"I do not like this, My Priestess," Ukavinas admitted.

"Neither do I my friend. But it is necessary. You know of what we have planned. It must now simply be delayed for a few weeks, or perhaps months. In the end it will work out for the best." She gave him a knowing look. He watched her for a moment before slowly nodding in agreement.

"I see Mistress," He said slowly. "We will begin adjusting things accordingly. If it is not too impolite to say, My Priestess, we shall be sad for the lack of your company."

"Thank you Ukavinas," Pianwasal told him genuinely. "I shall miss your company also. All of you." She looked at each of them in turn. "You have been my companions, my students, my assistants. But most of all my friends. And for that you will always have my thanks. And my respect."

The group of priests bowed quite low. Several of the younger ones had a glint in their eye. A firm indication of the emotion involved, even if Dorm and his friends didn't fully understand their connection.

"You all know what must be done," Pianwasal said quietly. "I wish you every luck. And I have every confidence that you will succeed."

The meeting with Pianwasal's Priests, as Cal like to call them, was a little strange. No one said very much, and the object of their little conspiracy's name was never mentioned. But all knew what they were discussing. After a time she bade them all good afternoon, and they left. Pianwasal returned to her packing.

"So what time are we leaving?" Lianna asked, changing the subject.

"I think we could afford to spend the night," Dorm considered. "There doesn't seem to be a major rush at the moment. And also if we leave straight away it might make people nervous."

"Sounds like a plan, Oh fearless leader," Telly teased him with a glint in her eye.

"Stop that," Dorm scolded her playfully. "I suggest we all try to get a good nights rest. Tomorrow will probably be a long day."

Chapter 24

The weather remained fine as they again headed east. The sun shone and a light breeze cooled the decks of the *Star of the Sea*, as they sailed along. The departure from the temple had been rather formal and at the same time familiar. Taslem Kanos had taken Dorm aside to ask him to make sure that Pianwasal and Ameks were safe. He also thanked him for opening his eyes to the "larger world". Dorm wasn't quite sure quite what he meant by that, but smiled and took the compliment none the less. There had been little in the way of emotion, except perhaps from Pianwasal, which was understandable; she was leaving her homeland. The Phirinos' ship left first and they watched for a while as its bright red sail slowly shrank into the distance.

They had quickly settled into the shipboard routine, and seemed to have already begun working to bring Pianwasal 'into the fold' as Zacravia liked to call it. Dorm watched as the priestess, Telly, Rhyn and Lianna conversed and laughed nearby on the deck as he stood next to Mac.

"You think she'll blend in?" Mac asked after taking note of Dorms gaze.

"I think so," he replied. "The ladies seem to have that task well in hand."

Mac sighed. "This group is starting to get rather large, isn't it?"

"It is," Dorm agreed. "But it's only going to get bigger. We still have to find the other person in Kiama Mor. And we have at least two more Alliance countries to visit. This little group is going to get quite a bit larger yet."

"I try sometimes, to see what everyone's task will be," Mac said. "I can see the strengths and weakness that everyone has, and can see where you compliment each other. There's still a few gaps I'm not sure about though."

"What's this 'you' business," Dorm asked him noting the mode of his description. "You're here too."

"Me, no," he said with a heavy voice. "I'm just along for the ride. I don't have an amulet remember. I'm just an extra body. I'm not sure that whoever came up with this prophecy even knew I would be here."

"Well whether they knew or not, I'm glad you are," Dorm said putting his arms around him.

"Me too," Mac said. "I don't like the idea of you running all over the world alone. Who knows what trouble you'd get into."

"Probably not as much as what I get up to with you around..." Dorm looked at him intensely. An impish grin slowly spreading across his face.

"Well on that, you may have a point," Mac replied heavily.

The gentle rise and fall of the deck took a bit of getting used to for Pianwasal. There were several times where she looked decidedly "green" as the sailors referred to it as, which after a while Dorm began to see too. She was never sick, but did sometimes close her eyes and inhale deeply of the fresh air. Her attitude seemed to change slightly. Before she had seemed very stern, one could almost say austere. Now there was a certain softening of her. Her look seemed less hard. Her voice had more warmth to it. Dorm wasn't sure if this was because they were away from her normal environment, or because she had seemingly gained the personal confidence of the Phirinos, or for some other reason.

Maybe it was just because she was getting some time off.

Ameks was still very shy. Much as Artur had been in the beginning. It wasn't that he didn't participate in the conversations, it was more that he seemed unsure of himself. Dorm got the feeling that there had been many times in his life where people had put him down, either intentionally or not. And this had rubbed off on him. Whenever he made a good suggestion, or said something positive, Dorm made sure he commented on it. He wanted to build up his confidence. He got the feeling Ameks might be important later on.

Their discussions at night centred mainly on where their journey would take them next. They knew they had to spend more time in Kiama Mor, and as such Ambra had lots of questions to answer. There was only so much he could tell however. The apparent secrecy of the amulets was always leaving them at a certain disadvantage. He suggested that they could travel routinely around with their amulets showing, as they had in the past. That this might prompt someone to talk. He suggested a few people he could contact to try to find out more information, though he admitted it was a long shot.

All in all though, their decisions basically amounted to getting off the ship in Hamij and essentially "following their noses" from there, as Rhyn described it. It was frustrating, but there was little else they could do.

Captain Tamik updated them on what had been happening in Kiama Mor during their absence. He had picked up various pieces of information from other ship captains he knew whilst he had been waiting in Szugabar. Apparently the Sultan had sent many more troops into the area to try to deal with the bands of brigands. No public mention had been made of any possible Peldraksekar connection, but then Dorm guessed that if the authorities did know this fact, they would probably want to keep it to themselves for the time being. Reports had come out of several pitched battles on the desert sands, and the Sultans army was claiming victory against the bandits. Publicly at least. Dorm suspected that not everything had gone the army's way, but if progress was being made then that was a good thing. Perhaps it might even force some of these Peldraksekhr agents to make some mistakes.

The rest of the journey across the Desert Sea was quiet and relaxing. They all knew there was nothing to do until they disembarked so it was a chance to relax. This would all change as soon as they landed of course. The crawling tension of what they were doing would instantly return. There was nothing for that of course; it was something they simply had to endure. At least until they had some more progress.

They sighted Hamij about mid morning and the ship altered course to take them into the harbour. They quickly noticed several thin, but quickly rising columns of black smoke from the far side of the city. The Margrave was instantly on deck scouring the view to determine what had happened to his city. They glided into the wharf and almost before the gangway had been secured to the ship, Hamik was striding down it, demanding to see his staff to find out exactly what had happened.

His wife stood calmly next to the gangway overseeing the organisation of their things. Dorm watched her for a moment curiously.

"My lady, you seem rather unaffected by the sight of your city."

"I am not unaffected, Your Highness. I am very concerned. But I know my husband. He cares very much for this city. Once he gets to working out the problems, the rest of us will only be in the way," she smiled slightly. "Do not worry, our city will be safe. Hamik will see to that."

It turned out that the city had been 'attacked' by several bands of brigands during the hours just before dawn. The city guard, in concert with several companies of the army that happened to be in the city at the time were able to fend them off rather easily. The smoke came from several warehouses and outbuildings outside the city walls, that the brigands had managed to torch before they could be stopped. Overall the damage was light, and the disruption to the city's life was minimal, but it was still a worrying development. If the bandits could amass a force large enough that they thought there might be success against a city as large as Hamij, then they might spell trouble for their passage through the country..

They stayed that night in the Margraves palace. Again they were treated luxuriously, and Hamik provided Dorm with all the reports he had received about conditions throughout the country. He also let Dorm sit in on his meetings with his advisors and the town council. He heard things as Hamik heard them. Dorm was very grateful for this, as he didn't like the idea of walking blind into whatever lay out in the countryside.

They rose and left early the next morning. Their group seemed much larger than it should have with only two extra bodies. Hamik and his wife wished them the very best of luck on their 'great important journey'. It seemed no one wanted to mention the word quest.

They headed through the northern part of the city till they came to the Ferrygate. It was a large imposing defensive structure in the city walls whose only purpose was to protect the ferry landing on the outside. The Kiamans it seemed didn't want to take any chances.

It took a while to get themselves sorted out onto the ferries that would convey them across the mouth of the River Pojdram. The ferries were not designed to accommodate such large groups in one crossing, so they had to take several. On the other side there was another confused melee for a brief moment as they then organised themselves to travel.

For several hours they moved sedately along the shore of the river, following the main road that was crowded with other travellers, mostly merchants, as the day warmed around them. There was a rather pleasant breeze flowing down the slight valley the river ran through that kept away the insects. Again the riverbanks themselves were dotted with fertile areas and small marshes, and several small villages and farmsteads huddled close to them. The travellers on the road with them all carried a sense of tension and a little fear with them as they moved. It was clear that events had rattled people and they were wary.

Their conversations centred on what they would do that day. Dorm wasn't precisely sure what his plan was. He had the idea of just travelling along the river for the day at an easy pace, just to get everyone used to being back in the saddle again, and their new members used to it a little. This part of the country contained many hostels and inns as well, so he had merely intended to travel until it began to grow dark and then stop at the next one.

Everyone accepted that, as there wasn't really that much of a plan to this entire endeavour, when it came right down to it. They stopped for a while around midday at a small village, and ate in a cosy, well-maintained tavern. The size of their group, and the fact that they were clearly not merchants, caused them some curious, almost nervous looks from some of the locals, But they simply smiled and said hello as friendly as possible.

Dorm was worried that as their group got larger, they might have more trouble getting about in these small sort of places. He didn't want to be explaining their presence and purpose to every local constabulary along the way.

Their first day back on the road finally came to an end as the shadows grew long and they saw in the distance another large hostel across the main road from another small village. They made the distance fairly quickly and had taken rooms for the night before it got truly dark. They ate a hearty dinner in the main taproom, before a group of musicians played several songs as entertainment. A tall woman with long dark hair sang an accompaniment to one of the songs. Her voice, like her face was hauntingly beautiful. The song was about lost love and innocence. It almost seemed she was singing from personal experience.

They retired after the last song and settled in for a restful night, before another long day on the road.

It was well dark when he woke. He pushed himself up on one elbow and looked around the darkened room. There was little light, only faintly coming from under the door to the corridor, and the soft moonlight. He had no idea what had woken him. There was nothing that seemed odd. So he lay back down and sighed deeply, trying to remember where abouts in that dream he was up to.

There it was again. He sat up properly this time. Dorm was positive he had heard something. He sat silently for a few moments trying to control his breathing.

There. A faint scraping. It sounded like it was coming from outside. It was probably just a watchman or something, but it did sound very close to the window.

He drew back the bed clothes, being careful not to disturb Mac. He padded on silent feet to the small window, and drew back the rough curtain. At first he could see nothing odd. The sides of the buildings across the courtyard. A tree waving slightly in the breeze. The soft glow of the torches at the main entrance.

He was about to go back to bed, when something caught his eye. A slight movement. Dorm stared for a moment before he realised what he was seeing. Someone had attached some sort of hook to the sill of the window. By the slight movement it was obvious that someone was climbing the rope on the end.

Dorm almost leapt back to the bed to wake Mac. He grumbled a bit at first but was alert enough once Dorm had informed him what he had found. They both grabbed daggers from their packs at the foot of the bed and took up positions on either side of the window to peer out.

After several moments a head appeared. It was covered in black, and was hard to make out in the darkness. The man climbed up until he was able to stand on the ledge outside their window. He paused for a moment, to gather his breath. He reached and took something like a stiletto from some unseen pouch or pocket on his clothing. Dorm looked across at Mac, and both of them retreated to the dark corner of the room. They heard a faint scraping at the window.

On an impulse, Dorm moved back to the bed and quickly arranged the pillows and their overnight bags to look like sleeping bodies. He threw the bedclothes back over it and retreated to the dark just as the window opened. The curtains billowed slightly in the breeze. Two legs descended silently to the floor. The intruder emerged slowly from behind the curtain. He paused for a moment. Probably to see if he had been noticed. He crept slowly towards the bed. He studied the form on the bed for a moment before aiming the stiletto at a point that would have roughly corresponded with Dorms neck had he been lying there.

The ebony clad intruder then gently placed the tip of the stiletto against the bed sheet.

With a sudden burst of strength and speed the man rammed the stiletto into the false body. Dorm suppressed a shudder at the knowledge of how quick this man was. Had he really been there, Dorm would most certainly be dead. There would have been no time to react.

The man withdrew the stiletto and paused for a moment. He looked at the blade. Obviously wondering why it wasn't bloody. He looked at the bed, then flung back the sheets. Only a scattering of pillows greeted him.

He looked around nervously, realising he had obviously made some sort of mistake. He began to retreat towards the window. 'Not this time' Dorm thought.

Brandishing his dagger. He rushed at the man. He intended not to hurt him, but merely capture him. He was worth more to them as an information source. Had he really been trying to kill *him*? Who had asked him to do this? And more importantly, Why?

The man heard his footsteps and dashed towards the window, he tore back the curtain which hit Dorm full in the face. Once he had disentangled himself, he lunged towards the intruded who was by now halfway out the window.

At that moment, Mac crashed into Dorm. Both had rushed towards the intruder but Dorms sudden halt meant Mac couldn't stop in time. Instead of grabbing the escaping assassin, Dorms hand pushed him, before he'd had a chance to grab his escape rope.

With a brief exclamation of fear, he went over the edge. A few short seconds later came a definitive crack from below. Leaning out of the window, they saw the man sprawled on the hard stones of the courtyard. A dark smudge surrounding his head like some sort of negative halo.

"Oops," Mac said contritely.

Understandably there had been a great deal of commotion.

But the hysterical nature of the commotion was now getting a little ridiculous.

After the intruder had fallen to his 'accidental' end, Dorm and Mac had stood stock for a few moments, unsure of what to do. Finally Dorm had made the decision that they couldn't hide the situation. The fact that he was lying on the ground below their window would at least cause questions to be asked. He sent Mac off to wake the others, while Dorm quickly went down to inspect the body; and make sure he had in fact actually departed.

Dorm made it to the body fairly quickly and, finding no pulse and feeling no breath escape from the man's lips, concluded quite positively that he was in fact deceased. He quickly examined the man's pockets and the small satchel that he had looped around his body. Several knives and daggers were in evidence as were several small pots and several small brushes. Dorm had a feeling he knew what these pots contained, but wasn't interested in confirming his suspicions just now.

He found several small scraps of paper in a pocket on the inside of the assassin's clothes. He didn't have much chance to examine them thoroughly as the hostel manager emerged at that moment to see what was going on.

Now of course things had gotten worse.

A small crowd of both guests and servants had gathered around the body, drawn by the hostel managers' boisterous ramblings about his good name and how this incident would surely tarnish it. Dorm and Mac patiently explained what had happened, skimming over the bit where Dorm had suspected something from the beginning, and stated confidently that he had no idea why any one would want to harm a simple traveller such as he. He calmly suggested it might be a good idea for the manager to see who had stayed in that particular room previously, as they might well have been the intended target.

The body was eventually moved to another part of the compound and runners were sent into the town to fetch the local constabulary. The rest of the guests and staff retired to their rooms.

When the officer of the law arrived; still looking like he was asleep, Dorm and Mac reiterated their story. The officer asked them several questions, that Dorm felt he had already answered, but was willing to do so again, given the man was still somnolent. After apparently taking careful note of what they all said, he went off to view the body.

Their group retired to their rooms, everyone asking if the boys were alright. After assuring them that they were, Dorm revealed that he had secreted the pieces of paper. Upon examination of them, they were found to be several descriptive lists of their group. The details were brief but quite specific. Another piece of paper gave the would-be assassin instructions that he was to kill at least one, but if possible two of their group. Preference would be given to Dorm, Mac or Telly, But any of them would have sufficed. There was no signature on the documents, nor was their any other indication of who had written them. There was also nothing to indicate any sort of payment. Zacravia seemed a little puzzled by this.

"It implies that he isn't your normal run of the mill 'knife-for-hire'," he explained. "A man who is hired to kill someone, will want to get something in writing. Even if there is almost no way to trace who wrote it. It's a kind of insurance if you will. Usually the way in which these people are paid requires some sort of instructions. You can't just walk up to him in the street and say "here's the money for killing that person". The fact that there isn't any sort of instruction, says one of two things. One; that he left that 'insurance' wherever he came from tonight so as not to implicate them, or two; that he may believe in the reasons for the killing. And that spells rather large trouble in my book."

"What do you mean?" Telly asked.

"He means that a man who kills for conviction is far more dangerous than one who kills for money," Harmia explained. "The man who kills for money can potentially be bought to tell you who ordered it. The man who kills because he believes the reason, can't be."

"Might I suggest that from now on we keep a watch?" Cal Makor suggested. "I know it sounds a bit extreme, especially in an inn, but it seems we can't be too careful."

"It's drastic but it's a good idea," Travanos agreed.

"Alright," Dorm agreed reluctantly. "I don't like it, but we don't seem to have much choice. I just hope this doesn't turn out to be someone I once beat at dice."

In the end both Cal Makor and Zacravia volunteered to stand watch the rest of the night. Harmia and Travanos agreed to rise a bit earlier than normal to relieve them so they could get some rest before the days riding.

It was shortly after dawn when the gates to the compound had been opened that they left rather hurriedly and headed again on their way.

They rode fairly quickly without much talking for several hours, trying to put some distance between themselves and last nights developments as possible. Around mid-morning though Dorm called a halt. They needed to rest the horses a bit, and it was clear that everyone wanted to discuss what had occurred.

No one was quite sure what to make of the assassin. Dorm as a member of a royal house was an obvious if somewhat innocent target. But there wasn't any real reason for any one to try to kill him. At least nothing political that he could think of. That essentially only left the quest they were on. But who would have known where they were? It was possible that the Peldraksekhr had agents keeping an eye out for them after their trip through Tagradas, but still, there was nothing to directly connect that with their quest. Was there?

Everyone was a little on edge. The fact that the assassins' instructions had said that while Dorm, Mac and Telly were the main targets, the callous, almost offhanded way in which he was instructed that "any of the others will suffice if the main targets prove too inaccessible", chilled everyone.

How could someone like Artur, or Ameks or Tissievilla have provoked that kind of hatred? They couldn't. They were innocent. But now that they had become part of this quest, it seemed that their lives were now very much in danger.

Dorm watched these three in particular. Artur seemed almost to retreat within himself. While he didn't say a great deal at the best of times, he seemed quieter than normal this morning. His face betrayed a sense of fear.

Ameks was similarly quiet though when he spoke he did so with a great deal of bravado. This was obviously a problem that frightened him, but he wasn't going to let *them* see that. Tissie had lost her normal bubbly aspect. Dorm felt a little sorry for her. She had the look of someone who is constantly about to cry for reasons they can't quite put their finger on. Several times she was heard to say quietly to herself, "why us?"

The rest of the day was uneventful. They stopped at their regular times and saw the normal, expected fellow travellers on the highway as they headed eastward. They continued to pass villages and farmsteads as well as small marshes and large piles of rock. It was a strange landscape. Dominated as it was by the river, one would have normally expected much larger areas of arable land. But Ambra told them how the melt waters that fed the river never amounted to as much as some of the rivers in other parts of the world. And there were two rivers that fed off the same source.

The river's course wound its way slowly towards the Desert Sea. It was fairly wide at this point and the current, while not streaming along was calm enough to be pleasant. Several times they noticed small boats and ferries along its length or crossing from one bank to the other. The villagers all seemed fairly friendly, if wary. And occasionally there were small patrols of Kiaman troops. They seemed intent mainly on protecting the highway itself, but were also seen moving around the periphery of villages and farms, and occasionally out into the desert.

They stopped again that night at another large hostel, and again it was decided to have a watch posted. This time Liana and Ameks took the first watch, followed by Artur and Zacravia. Both Dorm and Mac offered to share a watch with someone but both of them were refused.

The night of course produced no events. Exciting or otherwise, and when everyone woke in the morning they almost felt a little let down that nothing had indeed happened. They were of course grateful at the same time.

The next few days proceeded much the same way. There was nothing of any great interest that occurred and they began to suspect that whoever was intending them harm, had either yet to learn of the assassins reversal of fortune, or was taking some time to consider their options.

The river began its ponderous sweeping swing around to the north four days from Hamij, the highway swinging right along with it. They began to notice that the other side of the river appeared slightly less arid than their side did. The next day they also noticed the main junction where the road that lead to Kiama Mor itself branched off from the highway following the opposite bank. They of course continued northward. Dorm had felt inclined to head towards some of the northern towns, and if nothing eventuated possibly head back towards Pardra. Though his inclination to move towards Pardra was now tempered by recent events.

As they headed north the hazy image of the mountains began to rise from the horizon. They appeared an indistinct series of bumps, bluey grey in colour at this distance, but Dorm knew that in a few days they would be able to see much more. They weren't the highest mountains in the world, but they were still high enough to receive snow during the winter months, despite the arid conditions down here on the plain.

Two days after starting the sweeping turn, they stopped for the night at an inn in a village set a distance back from the edge of the river. It was a "quaint little affair", Telly described it as, and it was cheap. The food they were given in the taproom, wasn't the best, but it sufficed for the road weary hungers they had acquired.

It was filled with various travellers from across Kiama Mor and several other Alliance countries. While they ate, the various groups in the room conversed on a variety of topics, including the state of the "actions" against the bandits.

Apparently the attack, if it could be called that, on Hamij wasn't an isolated incident. Several other large towns had also been raided by bands of these brigands. There was a certain tension around this whole part of the country. While this village hadn't seen any action, a few further to the north had. They all seemed worried as to what all this banditry meant. No one seemed completely sure, and all were a little scared by it; even if they would never admit it in front of their peers.

After a relaxing meal, and an hour or two gaining information about the road ahead, they decided to retire.

Their rooms were very small. Almost the same size as the berths they had had on the *Star of the Sea*. The beds were a little lumpy, but comfortable enough for one night.

Again they posted a guard, just in case.

Dorm slept fitfully, mainly because the bed was not as comfortable as he had first thought. He was also worried about what some of the travellers coming out of the north had told them. Several had seen bands of riders off in the distance on occasion, where there didn't seem to be a reason for them. He remembered the names of some of the villages and towns that had been paid visits by them. He tried to place them on the map so he knew how close they would come to them.

He was worried by the apparent increase in their activities. He was beginning to toy with the idea of forgetting about this next Kiaman quester until later. They did after all have to travel back through the country after they had found the questers in Ojliam and Bydanushev. Perhaps it would be safer to just ride northwards and get into Ojliam as soon as possible. Of course there was no guarantee that the bandits wouldn't be operating inside the borders of that kingdom as well.

He was beginning to think it might be a good idea to cut straight across the river and get to the main highway. It would be patrolled so there was less likely to be trouble. Of course that would take several days at least. Days in which they could easily be attacked.

Dorm was starting to regret being the leader of this little expedition.

The next day they continued northward. There were few travellers on the road coming out of the north and those that did seemed intent on keeping to themselves and hurrying on past.

They stopped only very briefly beside the road for a midday meal before heading on. After an hour or two they sighted what appeared to be smoke in the distance. Thick and black it curled skyward, threateningly.

It turned out to be the remains of a large farmstead at the edge of one of the many fertile areas along the river. The main house as well as several of the outbuildings were well alight, and there was evidence that smaller fires were taking hold in some of the others. There was no one around to either indicate who had caused it, or if the residents had managed to escape.

"Perhaps we should head on fairly quickly," Zacravia suggested. "I'm not sure it's such a good idea to linger here."

"Perhaps we should try riding off the road for a while?" Lianna said. "Perhaps if we look like a group of these bandits, the real ones will leave us alone."

"Maybe," Travanos thought. "Or perhaps they'll want to compare notes."

"We should head on," Dorm agreed. "For now we'll stay on the road. It leads eventually to the town of Kamel, so we should be safe if we can get there. But we should be ready for anything."

They left the ruined farm quickly and continued on their way.

The next few hours were spent nervously, as every sound carried on the wind caused them concern. They saw no more travellers on the road, and only a few signs of movement out in the wilderness surrounding them.

And it had become a wilderness to their way of thinking. It was now lawless and dangerous. Anything could be out there, just waiting for them. They pushed their mounts fairly hard in order to try and make it as far as they could.

As dusk was descending they saw in the distance the dust raised from the hooves of many mounts. It rode slowly in their direction, apparently not intent on hurrying. All of them expressed concern as to who these people might be. Weapons were checked and made ready for possible use, and they rearranged themselves into a more defensive formation.

As the group drew closer it was apparent that they did not appear to be bandits, of course that didn't ease their concerns. The riders appeared to be members of one of the nomadic clans that made up a sizable part of the population of Kiama Mor. Several large wagons bumped along behind the main body or riders. After several moments it was clear that these people were most likely not raiders. Women and children sat upon the camels, both unlikely to be part of swiftly moving bands of roving warriors.

A large man in a flowing red robe and with a large elaborately embroidered headdress rode slowly forward, a wary expression on his face. He pulled his mount to a stop a short distance from Dorms and studied them for a moment. His eyes carefully examined each of their faces. Scrutinising and studying. His gaze finally returned to Dorm.

"Where do you travel, friend?" he asked in a thickly accented voice.

"North," Dorm replied after a moment.

"There is a lot that is North," the man replied. "Perhaps you could be more specific."

"Perhaps I could," Dorm told him. "But with everything that's going on in this part of the world at the moment, I'm not sure how sensible that would be."

The man nodded slightly, almost to himself. "True enough, friend," he agreed. "But I have these people's lives to consider." He indicated the large group behind him. "And I would be very remiss if I did not know any dangers they may face."

"You sound like a sensible leader," Dorm told him honestly. "I can respect that. But like you I have these people to consider. And I would be equally remiss if I didn't do everything to protect them."

The man's eyes narrowed slowly. He seemed to consider Dorms

reply. Quite suddenly he burst out laughing. It was a rich, hearty laugh, to which Dorm and his companions couldn't help but smile at least a little.

"Then we appear to be at an impasse my friend. We are too scared to tell you where we are going, and you are too scared to tell us where you are going. And so we will go onward worrying intently about the other." He laughed again. "My name is Kamis. How are you called?"

"I am called Dorm, Kamis."

"Well Dorm. It appears that for the moment we are stuck together on this road. Perhaps we should spend some time to get acquainted and then tell each other of our destinations."

"Do you know of somewhere safe that we could stay for the night?"

"There are no hostels or villages here abouts. But there is a deserted farm not far back the way we have come. We had thought to stay there but decided against it. Come we will lead the way."

He wheeled his mount and headed back towards his people.

"Dorm, are you sure this is entirely wise?" Mac asked.

"Yes, they are after all complete strangers," Telly pointed out.

"How do we know they aren't bandits?" Pianwasal asked his seriously.

"Bandits…" Tissie almost wailed.

"Do you think that these cut throat roving groups of bandits are likely to be travelling around raping and pillaging with their wives and children in tow?" Dorm asked them in response. "And with wagons slowing them down? No these people aren't bandits. And they seem just as wary as we are."

"I'm not sure I like this," Travanos admitted.

"It will only be for one night, and then we can continue on our way. I admit, we should all keep a sharp watch for anything suspicious, but I don't think these people mean us any harm." With that he rode forward after Kamis and his people.

The others exchanged a few looks, before doing likewise.

It took less than half an hour to arrive at the deserted farm complex, which was little more than a collection of shattered walls and fences. It was hard to tell exactly when its desertion might have occurred in the gathering gloom and with the milling of people and camels.

Several fires were lit and preparations were made for an evening meal. Dorm and his companions began to set themselves up at one side of the other group, where they could keep an eye on things, and help protect each other. In case anything went wrong.

Kamis waddled over to their group after they had set up their tents and started a small fire of their own. “My friends,” he began. “I understand your caution, but we are no threat to you. My people are preparing a large meal, there will be plenty for all of you to eat. Please come join us. It will give us a chance to learn of each other.”

A little warily they accepted and took places around the main fire. Several small tables and chairs had been set up in a large circle around it and people were now organising plates and goblets that they filled with wine. The tables stood upon large rugs that were placed directly on the ground. It was clear that these people liked a certain level of comfort, for along with the rugs braziers were set up throughout the camp, and the tents they erected were all thickly canvassed against the wind.

They took various places around the fire interspersed with members of this large group. Both men and women, all dressed in similar flowing attire, but with tight fitting belts and high legged boots began serving the food shortly after. The food came in small portions, that was richly spiced, and quite hot. The portions may have been small, but they kept on coming. Each item was different and seemed to have been spiced quite differently as well. Some of the flavours made ones eyes water, this was usually followed by one that gave you some relief.

“My compliments to your cooks, Kamis,” Zacravia said in a strained and slightly hoarse voice. His face was rather red, even in the firelight.

Kamis merely laughed at that. “So tell me my friend,” he said then turning to Dorm. “Where are you headed?”

“North. We have to get into Ojliam.”

“I see. With all this bandit activity you picked a bad time for travelling.”

“I know,” Dorm agreed looking at his companions. “But we didn’t have much choice. It is a matter of some importance."

"All things are important, in their own way. I would offer to travel with you, but we are headed south. Towards Pardra eventually."

"We had considered going there, but it seemed better to just head north."

"Pardra is a wonderful place, as far as towns go. We of course prefer the countryside. But Pardra presents us with many opportunities."

"I've never met any nomads before," Mac said then. "It must be a very different life."

"It is indeed. We are free to follow our hearts, or our whims. It is not for everyone, but for us…" he swept his arm wide around the circle. "It is who we are. And as you can see, we do not want for the luxuries of the life in towns."

"Well if nothing else, we are glad of the hospitality you have given."

"But of course. I cannot *but* offer it to you. I cannot have you wandering all over Kiama Mor telling how we did not help you. I cannot have the reputation of my clan tarnished by such a thing. The Al Kamash family will always provide hospitality to those in need of it. To do anything else would be unthinkable."

Dorm nodded his headed and smiled in agreement, as Kamis laughed heartily and clapped his hands for some music. Across the circle from him Dorm noticed Ambra sitting at a table with Lianna and several members of the nomads. Ambras' face looked stricken. He seemed almost to be trying to slide down into his chair and not be seen. He wasn't doing a very good job, and if anything was only attracting attention to himself.

And a moment later, this was confirmed.

Chapter 25

"YOU!!!"

It was not something that could be missed.

The voice that spoke the word was loud, determined and full of many different emotions that simply could not be ignored.

Everyone was stunned for a moment into stillness. Dorm turned his head and saw where the voice had come from. A short distance away stood a woman. She was probably around thirty, and was shockingly beautiful. A full head of dark hair falling behind her head, a head held proudly, with confidence, but also at the moment with anger and determination to carry out whatever it was she had planned. Her dark skin, typical of Kiamans, seemed to almost glow in the assorted torch and firelight. Her eyes held a look of steely hatred and as she stood her long fingers seemed almost to flex convulsively.

She took a slow, menacing step forward, her bare feet arching as she did so. Her arm rose slowly to point directly at Ambra, who now sat frozen, directly opposite her. She almost seemed to hiss towards him as she stood there.

Kamis leapt to his feet. "Navista! What is the meaning of this?"

"It is him," she rasped from between clenched teeth.

"Who?"

"Ambra," she said shortly with more venom that Dorm had seen any one use.

Kamis looked towards Ambra. He held his gaze on him for a

moment, then looked back at Navista. "Are you certain?"

"Of course I am certain."

Kamis turned to Dorm. "My friend. This man is called Ambra?"

"Ahh," Dorm began. He didn't exactly know what to make of this situation. He didn't want to lie to these people to save themselves, but at the same time, he didn't want to run the risk of anything happening to Ambra. This Navista was quite obviously murderously angry, and could be capable of anything. He finally decided to stick with the truth, at least for the moment. "Yes, that is his name."

"And how long has he been in your company?"

"A few weeks."

"Do you know him well?"

"Not yet, but we are learning of each other as time goes by."

"Do you trust him?"

Dorm thought for a moment. "I realise that it may sound strange, given I haven't known him for very long, but given the… unique situation we are in… yes I trust him."

Kamis watched Ambra for a few moments obviously trying to decide what to do. His instinct to provide hospitality and comfort to people was weighing heavily on whatever this situation between Ambra and this Navista was. He wanted to act on that, but not in a way that was unfavourable to his cultural needs.

"Stand Ambra," he said finally.

Ambra slowly stood. His hands shook slightly. It was clear he was rather worried.

"You are Ambra, of the clan of Samik?"

"Well," Ambra began haltingly. "You see on that…"

"Yes or no! It is a simple question."

"I was. Though am not any more."

"What do you mean?"

"I am no longer of any family. My clan disowned me."

Kamis thought for a moment, a slightly pained look crossing his face. "I am sorry for that. But that is a matter between you and your clan. If you are Ambra of the clan Samik, then you are indeed him."

"I'm sorry to butt in here like this," Dorm began trying to be as polite as possible. "But what exactly is going on here? What is it you think he has done?"

"He has betrayed the honour of this clan," Kamis said seriously.

"And my personal honour!" Navista shouted angrily across at them. "And he must pay."

"My friend Dorm, we should speak of this in private. I will explain." He motioned to a group of men nearby who moved forward and roughly took Ambra by the arms and walked him off towards one of the tents. Zacravia locked eyes with Dorm, asking if he should do anything. Dorm shook his head imperceptibly to indicate no. Kamis rose and spoke quickly with several of the other high-ranking members of their clan before moving towards his tent. Mac, Telly and Travanos quickly rose and joined Dorm. The others crowded around.

"What the heck is going on?" Mac asked.

"I'm not sure, but I think we are going to find out soon enough."

"Look at her," Telly said nodding her head in the direction of Navista. "Whatever it is she thinks Ambra has done, she wants blood for it. I don't think she'll settle for anything less."

"Then we need to make sure nothing happens to Ambra in the meantime. Rhyn, Harmia, Artur; you go make sure he is okay. And that nothing happens to him. Lianna, Tissie see if you can circulate around and try and find out what is going on. I'm sure we'll get an explanation, but I'd like a bit more than the 'official' one if possible. We'll go see what Kamis has to say. The rest of you return to our places, and start to quietly get us ready for a hasty exit. I hope we wont need it, but in case we do…" he left the possibility hanging.

"I think I will have a look around, if you don't mind," Zacravia said quietly. "See what our options are, if you get my meaning."

"Not a bad idea," Dorm agreed. "Right lets go find out what all the fuss is about."

They all headed off.

They were taken to Kamis' tent. It was rather large, and Dorm wondered where it was stored when they travelled. The floor was covered in thick carpets and braziers stood at various places around the room. Several rather bright lamps provided light. Chairs and cushions were placed around the main area, and along the edges several small tables and cupboards stood, containing only Kamis and his people knew what.

They were invited to sit, and they did so a little hesitantly. Kamis sat in a large chair opposite Dorm. His face was very serious. Whatever this situation was it was one that had to be taken seriously. Dorm knew he had to be careful, not only for the sake of Ambra, but for the rest of them as well.

Navista came in and sat next to Kamis on a low seat, almost like a divan. Her face was drawn, but she seemed to have regained at least some of her composure. The fact that Ambra had come within her influence obviously pleased her greatly. This would be a woman to tread carefully around.

Kamis sighed heavily. "I am sorry this situation has come about Dorm," he said sincerely. "I had only intended to provide you hospitality."

"I believe you Kamis, and I'm sure that if you could you would make it go away," Dorm watched him carefully. "But perhaps you could explain exactly what *is* going on here."

Kamis nodded slowly. "Of course." He stood and began walking abound the room. He indicated to one of his servants, who proceeded to fill several expensive looking goblets with wine and hand them out. "Our clans are nomadic. This you know. We travel all over Kiama Mor, and family is very important to us. Various clans have relationships with various other clans. Different relationships for different clans. Some clans we trade with; others we fight alongside. Others still we have exchanges of people with. Our clan, the Al Kamash, had such a relationship with the Clan Samik. We would have some of our children marry into their family, and some of theirs would marry into ours. It was both profitable and amicable. Our families were great friends. Navista is my daughter. When she was twelve it was decided that she would marry, when she came of age, into the Samik Clan. Her abilities made her very prized."

"Her abilities?" Telly asked. "I don't understand."

"I am a dowser," Navista replied in her accented voice. "We have quite a few, though I am one of the more powerful."

"I have heard of the dowsers," Dorm said. "But I don't know too much about it to be honest."

"We have the ability to be able to find water in the desert," Navista explained. "It is a gift. I can sense with my mind where the waters beneath the sands lie. When I find them we are able to make camps, and survive. Life in the desert is harsh. Finding water is vital."

"I think I can understand the importance of your gift."

"The Samik clan at the time had only a few dowsers," Kamis explained further. "And many of them were getting on in years. Navista was highly prized by them. She would have given them a new lease of life in the desert. She was to have been married to the son of their Chief warrior. He was only a few years older than my daughter. His name was Ambra Osura."

"The man we travel with," Mac concluded.

"The very same. For years everything was fine. Our clans met regularly and the two of them interacted. There was even a great deal of affection between them. As the time of their marriage grew closer we began to prepare. Only a few months before the wedding we met with the Samik clan again. We intended to stay with them for the duration until the wedding could be held. But there was a problem."

"What sort of problem," Telly asked.

"Ambra had apparently fallen in love with a young lady from another associated clan of the Samik. Shortly before we had met up with them he had apparently left in the night, and could not be found. He was tracked and eventually found to be with the girl."

"He betrayed me with that harlot," Navista spat venomously. "He betrayed the honour done to him by my father and our clan."

"Because you are the daughter of a clan leader and a dowser," Travanos concluded.

"Yes," she confirmed. "He should have been greatly honoured to even be seen with me, let alone married to me."

"The betrayal drove a rift between us and the Samik clan," Kamis continued. "The dishonour he did this clan must be addressed. It has festered among us like a wound. We must take action."

"I can certainly understand your anger," Dorm began carefully. "And I can understand your desire for some sort of… recompense. But I must say that Navista is a very attractive woman, and I have no doubt, would be prized by any clan for her abilities, and her position. I'm sure there would be many other clans who would jump at the chance to have her marry into their family."

"You do not understand the way things are here in Kiama Mor, Dorm," Kamis explained. "Unless we can have settlement of this issue, then Navista cannot be married. If it were ever to be known that she had been betrothed and then rejected, we would become social pariahs, outcasts among the clans."

"That changes things a little I guess," Dorm said.

"So what exactly are you going to do about all this?" Mac asked seriously. This was the crucial moment.

"That will be up to my daughter. I can only advise her. Traditionally he would be represented by a member of his family to plead for him, but since none can be found, I may ask you do take on that responsibility Dorm."

'Lucky me,' he thought to himself. Aloud he said "If I was I would want to speak with him first. Find out exactly what is going on from all sides."

"Of course."

"And I would want assurances that he would still be alive at the end of all this."

Navista looked at her father with an angry, yet almost incredulous look. It was clear she had indeed intended harm to him as Telly had suspected.

Kamis held out his hand to still his daughter. "It is the right of the injured in this to chose the form of punishment. The punishment is meant to fit the crime, true, but a clans honour and prosperity are vital things, and must be protected."

Dorm looked at his companions. "Then there are some things that I will need to explain to you as well Kamis. Things that may change your mind about that."

"I do not understand."

"I know, but I think you will after I have spoken to you about them. First though I would like to speak to Ambra. See what he has to say for himself."

"Of course." Kamis clapped his hands together sharply and two of his warrior types entered the tent. "Take our guests to see the accused.

Then bring them back here to me." The two men nodded then stepped back outside holding open the tent flaps. "Dorm, I am trusting you not to do anything… foolish."

"As I am you Kamis," Dorm replied.

They nodded to each other before Dorm and the others followed the men to the other tent.

The tent in which Ambra was being held was across the encampment from Kamis'. They were escorted past the open area where they had been eating, most of the evidence that there had even been a meal taken there was already gone. Apparently no one wanted to be reminded of what had happened.

The guardsmen opened the tent for them and they went inside. Several more of Kamis' men were inside watching Ambra. He was seated on a low bench in the middle of the room. His hands were bound together and it appeared that a chain had been attached from his leg to the leg of the bench.

His face was drawn. He looked almost ashen. He looked up at them as they entered. A faint look of hope and even happiness crossed his face for a moment before settling back to his near melancholy state.

Dorm nodded to Rhyn, Harmia and Artur who stood nearby. They moved over to Dorm and the others as they entered. Before they could speak though, Dorm indicated to remain silent for a moment. He turned to the guards.

"Could we have a little privacy?" he asked. "You can keep watch from outside."

The guards started at him for a moment, obviously not sure what to make of this request.

"I assure you we won't try anything. We are here with Kamis' permission."

They thought about it for a moment, then with a nod, left the tent.

Dorm and the others turned back to Ambra.

"Well I'm glad to see you are still in one piece," Dorm said to the captive.

"Not as glad as I am to be in one," he replied sincerely.

"The guards did some leering and such, but not a lot else," Rhyn reported.

"Yes they seem to be under standing orders not to harm any prisoners until they hear from Kamis," Harmia concluded.

"Well that's good then. Now of course we come to the hard part. Explaining all this."

Ambra looked both sheepish and humiliated at the same time. He bowed his head and rubbed his face with his hands. "I suppose Kamis has told you what happened?"

"He told us a story," Telly reported to him. "But it might be helpful if you told us your version."

"What did he say?"

"That you were once betrothed to Navista, and that you ran away with some other woman you had fallen in love with."

Ambra sighed. "All true."

Dorm groaned. "Ahh Ambra, you aren't making things easy for me."

"I'm sorry Your Highness."

"Did you genuinely love this other woman?"

"Yes. With everything that I was."

"Did you love Navista?"

"Love? No. I did like her a lot. She was a good friend. And I'm sure in time that I would have learnt to love her. But I was already in love with Ujahn."

"So what happened to this Ujahn?" Mac asked.

Ambra stared at him for a moment. "We made our way to Pardra were we had intended to get married. We thought to lay low for a week or two before doing so, in case our families came looking for us." He paused and sighed. Whatever these memories were they were obviously not easy for him to recollect. "But she… she was not honest with me."

"What do you mean?" Telly asked.

"She had never truly loved me. Not in the way she had said. Not in the way I loved her. She had only wanted to escape her family. She didn't want to live the nomadic lifestyle. She wanted to dwell in the cities. And so she used me as a way of getting that." She sighed again. "She left and I have not seen her since. That was nearly fifteen years ago."

They all stared at him for a moment not sure of what to say. They exchanged worried glances at each other, all wanting someone else to be the first to ask the next question. In the end Ambra told them the answer.

"I was stuck in Pardra. I could not go back to my family. As they would have seen it as a betrayal of the arrangement with the Al Kamash clan. I could obviously not go to them, for the same reason. And since there were no other clans I could join up with, without raising suspicion, I was forced to live my life as a city man. I had to relearn how to live. My life has not been the best since then."

"I was an outcast. Alone. With no support and nothing to fall back on. Eventually I gained employment with a herd master and learnt the trade. I eventually worked my way up to taking over part of his business."

"Ambra I'm sorry things have been bad for you," Dorm told him honestly putting a hand on his shoulder. "But right now we are in a bit of a bind. It's fairly obvious that Navista wants your head for what happened. Kamis I think could be talked out of it, but she will take a lot of convincing."

"Once you tell them why we need him..." Artur began.

"That will convince Kamis most likely, yes," Dorm agreed. " But perhaps not Navista."

"Perhaps once she hears what has happened…" Telly suggested.

"You cannot!" Ambra said staring at her with a slightly wild look in his eyes. "She would revel in that kind of humiliation of me. It would give her more pleasure in harming me. I have heard of them over the years. Even sighted them once or twice. Each time I managed to stay hidden from them, But I have seen her face. It is cold. Hard. And I know that it is because of me, and what I did. She will never accept anything other than my death."

"Well let's not get too carried away with ourselves here old boy," Travanos said positively.

"You do not know her."

"Look Ambra," Dorm continued. "You may not want the story to be told, but it may have to be. It might just give us the extra leverage we need to get you out of here alive. I think once I explain our situation

Kamis might be willing to entertain the idea. If I suggest that you have been already punished for all this…"

"Then my humiliation will be complete."

"Well right now I don't care if you're humiliated or not. I just need you alive and well."

"Perhaps we can even make them feel a part of all this?" Artur suggested.

"How do you mean?" Rhyn asked him.

"Well once Dorm tells Kamis what we are doing, he may want to help, if he knows how important it is. Perhaps we could enlist their aid in finding the other Kiaman person who has the amulet."

"The man's a genius," Mac said quietly.

"They would certainly have greater contact with all the nomadic tribes. And they would be able to meet them all without having to explain who they are every time," Travanos agreed.

"Seems you have another reason to stay alive Ambra," Dorm told him. "We should go back and tell him soon, before this drags on for too long."

"What are you going to tell them?" Ambra asked him.

"The truth. All of it. Well as much as I can without worrying him too much." He paused and look at Ambra face. "Don't worry my friend. One way or the other we will find a way out of this for you."

Ambra half -heartedly smiled at him, then lowered his face to his hands again.

Dorm looked at the others. Rhyn, and Harmia indicated they would stay, and Artur simply nodded. Dorm, Telly, Mac and Travanos went to the tent's entrance, Dorm casting one more worried look at his companion as he left.

They went back to Kamis' tent and were again offered wine. It seemed that Kamis wanted them as 'happy' as possible. Navista's face seemed a little more relaxed. Perhaps her father had managed to calm her down somewhat while they had been away. Her brown eyes were still hard though, and her face was set. Her mouth formed a thin, aggressive line across her face, and she held her jaw tightly.

"What did he tell you?" Kamis began.

"Probably lies," Navista said under her breath.

Dorm ignored that. "He confirmed that what you had said was true. He did leave with this other woman, with whom he was in love. It seems however that she lied to him."

"Oh?" Kamis said a curious look crossing his face. Navista also looked up at Dorm.

"Yes. Apparently she had said that she loved him as well, but that was just a ruse to get away from her clan. She wanted to live in the cities, and she used Ambra to get that. Once she had what she wanted, she left him."

A slight smile crept to Navistas' lips, and Dorm knew that what Ambra had said about her was essentially correct.

"Then why did he not return?" Kamis asked sternly.

"To what?" Dorm asked spreading his hands in front of him. "He couldn't go back to his own family, they would have disowned him. He couldn't have come to yours, he would simply have had done to him what you have done this night. There was nowhere he could have gone and been safe. So he stayed."

Kamis stared at Dorm for a few moments. Obviously taking in the truth of his words. There was no escaping the fact that he had had little choice if he had wanted to remain free, and probably healthy. It was clear that he was disappointed, and still a little angry, but it seemed that he was at least leaning towards Dorms side of the argument.

"He has lived the last fifteen years essentially as a homeless man. No family, no heritage. And now you want to punish him again for a leap of faith? For trusting someone who betrayed him as much as you think he has betrayed you?"

Kamis again looked at him sternly. It was clear Dorm's words were getting through. Navista looked at her father and obviously realised the same.

"What he has suffered is immaterial. He has betrayed the honour of our clan and must be punished!"

"Even if his honour was also betrayed?"

She paused for only a second. "Yes."

"There are of course other reasons why we can't let you kill him. If that was your intention."

"And what might they be?"

Dorm looked at the others. He reached into his tunic and withdrew his amulet. Telly, and Travanos did the same. All three stood for a moment and let them be seen.

Kamis stared at them for a moment, as if he didn't see the significance. Gradually though a curious look crept across his face as he realised that all three amulets were essentially identical. He looked across at Navista who also wore an expression of confusion. Her mouth opened and closed several times as she obviously tried to voice her thoughts.

"These amulets are important," Dorm explained. "Each member of our group has one. Except my friend here. They indicate that the bearers are bound together to perform a great task. A task we are still finding out about. It may sound a little ridiculous, but we are on a quest, to find all the bearers of these amulets and bring them together."

"For what purpose?" Kamis breathed.

"Well honestly, that's part of what we are still discovering. But it is important. We have found information that indicates that these amulets were fashioned quite some time ago for some great purpose in protecting the Alliance. It may also have something to do with the Fortress."

"The Fortress?" Kamis briefly glanced first at his daughter then in the general direction of where the Fortress lay. This kind of respect; some might say fear, of the Fortress could only help Dorm and his friends.

"Ambra carries an amulet as well. I cannot let you harm him, and when my group leaves… he must come with us."

"I think I understand," Kamis said slowly. He looked again at Navista, who still wore an expression of worried confusion. "There is something else that you should know then, before you leave us," he continued slowly. He nodded slightly to his daughter.

She returned his nod then slowly reached up to her neck line. They had all seen that she wore several necklaces. In fact most of the women of this tribe, and even a few of the men wore them. Navista wore several. Her father was after all the clan chief it was only natural that she wore some expensive jewellery, and more of it. She took hold of one of the chains with her fingertips and pulled it out. On the end was a large lump of crystal.

Another amulet.

Dorm smiled to himself.

"I don't believe it," Telly said. "We've been led here again haven't we?"

"It will save us some time," Travanos commented. "Also we wont have to worry about asking for their help."

"Why is it on a different chain, to all of ours?" Mac asked noticing the reason why none of them had thought of the possibility before. All the chains upon which their amulets hung were identical, a simple silver link chain. Navista's however hung on a heavier gold chain.

"The chain was damaged some years ago. It had to be replaced," she explained. "We did not know it was so important."

"Oh I'm sure it doesn't matter," Dorm assured her. "It's the crystal that is important I think, not the chain."

"Does this all mean that you will be wanting to take my daughter with you when you leave?" Kamis asked.

"I'm afraid so. We all need to be together. It will take time for us all to figure out what we are doing as a group, and time to get to know one another."

Kamis shook his head slowly. "I had not envisioned any of this when I offered to camp with you this evening."

They all smiled at that.

Navista and Kamis were still both in a certain amount of shock about it all. Dorm, Telly, Travanos and Mac and given them a brief account of what had happened to them so far, and their thoughts on what lay ahead. Kamis finally consented to allow Navista to accompany them, though Dorm got the distinct feeling it was more a case of her agreeing to go with them and letting her father know this.

Kamis agreed to give them an escort back to the main road. Dorm felt it was more in the nature of wanting to keep an eye on his daughter for as long as possible than anything else. But he didn't mind so long as when they parted company it was just them.

They headed back to Ambra to give him the “good” news. They were quite sure he would not be impressed.

Upon entering they informed all present what had transpired in the other tent. Rhyn just smiled with a knowing look, much the same as Telly had. Harmia sighed heavily and chuckled to her self about it. Artur just nodded.

Ambra looked at Dorm for a moment. He too sighed heavily.

“This is the worst news I could have had this night,” he said.

“Why is that?” Mac asked him. “We sorted it all out.”

“And we found the next member of our group,” Telly reminded him. “It means we can be out of here in the morning, with you in one piece.”

“If she comes with us, she will make my life a living nightmare,” he sighed again melodramatically. “She will taunt me the whole way, she will criticise and snipe at me every chance she gets. There will not be a moments peace for me.”

“Some might say that was to be expected,” Harmia observed. “Given the circumstances.”

“No she will be far worse than that,” Ambra told her. “She will be vicious. Vindictive. I fear she may even put her anger at me above the safety of our group.”

Dorm watched him for a moment. He wasn’t quite sure if Ambra was exaggerating or not. His face was certainly serious enough. Perhaps he believed it, but Dorm had trouble believing that once Navista was fully aware of the situation that she would place any sort of revenge upon Ambra over the general well being of everyone else. After all, if the group was harmed in any way, then it was more dangerous for her.

“I think we can take the risk,” he said after a few moments thought. “It’s not like we have a great deal of choice.”

“That is a good point Highness,” Travanos said. “We must all do our bit to contribute to the success of the mission… whatever that might be.”

“Well I’m sure that between the rest of us we can limit her aggression,” Rhyn said confidently.

“What exactly do you mean?”

“There are ways she can be distracted, even diverted from going after Ambra as much. If we do it right she wont even realise that she's being led away from him."

"What makes you think you can do a better job than the rest of us?" Mac asked with a mischievous glint in his eye.

"Girls are better at that sort of thing than boys," Telly agreed with Rhyn. "We're much more subtle than you boys. You tend to go at these things like a brick through a window. Where as we women can do the same thing in a way that the subject wont realise."

"I suppose you have some sort of eloquent metaphor to describe that as well?"

"I do," she admitted. "But I wouldn't want to hurt your feelings too much."

Chapter 26

In the morning the camp was broken and packed away. It all happened so quickly and efficiently that it was clear that these people had performed these tasks quite often. Everything had its place on a wagon somewhere and everything was organised so that it could be gotten out again just as quickly and efficiently.

It was still fairly early in the morning when they left the ruins of the farm, and as they left Dorm again wondered what had happened to the people who had lived here. And what had caused the end of their habitation. The walls that remained didn't really contain any answers to those questions, and so despite his concern he pushed those thoughts from his mind.

Kamis and Navista rode with them. Several of the nomads rode warily alongside them exchanging glances every so often when they thought no one was looking. It was clear that they wanted to know what was going on. All they had been told was that Navista was going with them, and that Ambra was not to be harmed.

The journey back to the main road was filled with small talk about nothing in particular. Navista was obviously preparing herself to say goodbye to her father and the rest of the clan, as Kamis was too, though from the look on their faces it was difficult to tell who was having the harder time of it.

It was times like this that Dorm thought of his own father. He often wondered what he was doing. How he was coping. Dorm had never been separated from his father for as long a time as this would undoubtedly turn out to be. He still occasionally felt the absence of his mother, though that had happened years ago and he had adjusted. Mostly.

At least Mac was close by. With Mac around he didn't quite feel so alone. So isolated. And Telly. He glanced across to her. Her dark hair pulled back from her face. She was a beautiful woman, there was no denying that. He had to admit that his parents had been rather sensible in choosing her as a potential wife for him. A pity. She would have made a wonderful wife. And a wonderful mother.

Alright that's enough of that. I already have a wonderful partner.

They finally arrived at the main road, and there was the obligatory goodbyes. Dorm had expected this. As he expected also Kamis to have a 'quiet word' with him about keeping his daughter safe. Dorm had a sneaking suspicion that he wouldn't have to do much on that front, and that it might just be possible that she would be keeping him safe more often than the other way round.

Finally after what seemed hours they began to head northwards again along the road. The Al Kamash clan slowly receding into the distance through the slowly rising shimmer of heat, as the day began to warm up. Dorm noticed Navista look back several times as they rode. No doubt wondering if she was indeed doing the right thing.

"I think we should stop in a bit," Dorm suggested to Travanos. "And have a bit of time explaining things to our newest member."

The Admiral looked back over his shoulder. He took note of the set of her face. "I think you might be right," he said quietly. "She has the look of someone not completely comfortable with her lot in life."

They rode onwards for another hour or two before Dorm called a short halt to 'water the horses'. They pulled off the rode to a small clump of boulders that sat at the edge of a long slope down to the valley of the river. It was cooler here a slight breeze blowing along the length of the watercourse. Occasional puffs of dust were being blown up below them. The view was quite amazing.

"So Navista," Dorm began. "I guess you would like to know more about what it is that we are doing?"

"I think I deserve that much," she said a little aggressively.

"Well I assure you it is for a good cause. We believe that these amulets have something to do with the Fortress. In fact it's quite possible that they come from there in the first place."

Navista glanced down at her amulet, studying it. Almost as if she thought she could divine its secrets just by looking at it. "What do you think it means? Does it have something to do with magic?" The last word she said almost reverentially. No one liked to talk about magic, that was true, but this was a little different.

"It's possible," he said cautiously. "What specifically did you have in mind?"

"Well," she began haltingly. "When ever I use my abilities… it seems that I can… feel something helping me. Sometimes I have had the overwhelming urge to hold my amulet when I am divining. Almost as if it is helping me."

They looked at each other for a few moments. Was it possible? Could they be carrying around something that was magical? Could they have been exposing themselves to that all this time and not even have known it?

"Well those are questions I think that might be better answered by the Fortress itself. Remind me to ask them."

She looked up sharply at him. "You intend to take me to the Fortress?" Her tone indicated that she hadn't intended that to be a part of her travel plans.

"Well I think that eventually we will all have to go there."

"There are questions that only they can answer," Telly said to her. "We've been getting some indications that perhaps, at some stage, we may have no choice but to go there."

"We survived all our encounters with Rangers so far," Zacravia said sarcastically. "I have every confidence we will make it though the Fortress as well."

"And probably be just as confused," Mac sniped.

"If not more so," Artur suggested pessimistically.

"I assure you Navista," Dorm went on ignoring the others. "That we are not here to harm you in anyway. That would kind of defeat the purpose of finding you."

"Then you are saying that I am important," she lifted her chin defiantly.

"We all are important in this one dearie," Cal said to her. "There's no place for position in this group. I mean just look at 'im," he pointed at Dorm. "You don't see him poncing around his rank do ya?"

Dorm groaned. He'd forgotten that he hadn't mentioned who he really was to either Navista or her father.

"What does he mean?" Navista said with a confused look on her face.

"Oh yeah," Cal said regretfully. "Sorry 'bout that Dorm. I keep forgettin' that you like to keep things low key."

"It's alright Cal. It would have come out eventually anyway. Best to get it over with now before we get ourselves into trouble."

And so they introduced themselves. Properly.

It took a while to get through everyone. It was clear that Navista thought that she came from a more noble group within Kiaman society, and probably did, from what Dorm knew, but her position slid a little once she found out that she was in the company of senior police, and High Priestesses and Princes.

She remained quiet for a time after they had finished, obviously digesting who they all were and trying to figure out how they had all come together. They were admittedly an odd assortment of people.

"Are you alright?" Telly asked her after a moment.

"Yes, I think so. I just wasn't expecting quite this group of people. I was thinking you were adventurers or something."

"We have that effect on people," Zacravia assured her.

"I guess you could say that we are adventurers though," Dorm agreed with her. "We certainly are on an adventure."

"So what are we doing now?" Navista asked him.

"Well for right now, we are heading towards Ojliam. So far we have found two people in each Alliance country. Seems logical to assume that there will be two more in Ojliam and Bydanushev."

"And if we don't get a move on we'll never get there," Travanos reminded them.

"He's full of good ideas isn't he?" Rhyn said.

"I think that's why he's an admiral," Lianna gibed.

"We'll explain some more when we stop for the night," Dorm told her as they all began to get ready around them. "I don't want to overload you too much just yet."

She nodded. Dorm wasn't quite sure that was a good sign.

As they continued on their way north, the land around them slowly changed. It became rockier, and occasionally small stringy looking plants could be seen growing in sheltered places. Over time this vegetation increased, though it was still all rather small and nasty looking. Dorm realised that it was the reverse of what had happened as they had travelled deeper into Kiama Mor several weeks ago. He was glad to be leaving the desert. It was a nice place to visit. It had its beauty, to be certain, but it wasn't somewhere he would want to spend any extended period of time.

On the far side of the river, many miles away, the change seemed much more dramatic. They observed that the land seemed to get much more fertile looking the further north they went. Eventually a large forest appeared and stretched off towards the border.

They stopped each night and over the course of their journey northward, explained in greater detail to Navista everything that had happened to them, and what they thought was going on. She was a little wary about their encounter with the various Rangers and was shocked at the meeting they had had in the Chapterhouse in Lanak Cal. She openly wondered if perhaps they had been infected by magic but simply hadn't noticed. They all assured her that they were in perfect health and that she was in no danger.

Occasionally Pianwasal and Ameks would ask questions to clarify something and Dorm had to remind himself that they were still quite new to the group as well. Tissie also asked a lot of question, but that was for an entirely different reason.

It was a little after midday on the forth day from picking up Navista when things went awry.

The morning had been quite good. They had made fairly good time passing a small village and what appeared to be a mining settlement as the road wound its way through the foothills of the Kebel Mountains. Ambra explained that this was where the River Pojdram originated from and that before too long they would have to cross over it. The land on the other side was much more inviting anyway so no one particularly minded.

They were heading down a long slope when a small group of riders appeared in the distance. At first no one took much notice of them. There was only three or four of them, and they were only moving slowly. After a minute or two the other riders stopped however. There seemed to be a few moments of animated discussion between them.

"What do you suppose that is all about?" Travanos asked curiously, squinting into the distance.

"I'm not sure," Dorm admitted.

"You think it could be something innocent?" Cal asked hopefully. His voice betrayed the fact he thought that unlikely.

"We can hope," Telly said, the forced joviality falling from her voice and face immediately upon completion.

"Well let's just continue on for now shall we," Dorm decided. "We don't want to arouse suspicions."

They continued along the road at a marginally slower pace. They began scouring the sides of the road for possible escape routes. A few small washes and ravines presented themselves, but most would likely lead to them being trapped.

Before they were halfway down the hill, the other group of riders, suddenly wheeled their horses around and galloped off back the way they came.

"Oh I think that could be fairly conclusive proof," Zacravia suggested. "Don't you?"

"We need to get off the road," Rhyn said urgently.

"Back this way," Ambra said. "There was a wash a little way back that went back a fair way. I think it opens into a small ravine."

Navista opened her mouth to protest following any suggestion of Ambra's but Telly cut her off.

"Not now dear," she told her shortly.

They quickly turned their horses and headed back up the road to the point where the wash ended and rode their horses up it. The ground was uneven and a little treacherous for the horses, but they made their way up it without raising much dust. At the top of the wash was a narrow ravine with a few small saplings. Stones and piles of hard dirt also abounded meaning that there wasn't a straight path along the ravine. Going would be slow, but better than the alternative.

They turned their horses along to the north and moved on. Zacravia leapt down from his horse and dashed off with a blanket, presumably to obscure their tracks, like he had done in the desert.

They rode in silence for a few more minutes, before halting to allow Zacravia to catch up with them. When he did he reported that the riders had returned.

"There's probably about twenty of them. I didn't have time to get an accurate count."

"How far away are they?"

"No more than a minute or two," he said catching his breath. "It won't take them long to find where we left the road, but perhaps those few minutes will be enough to put some distance between us. Enough to make them give up and go home at least."

"Then we should keep moving," Dorm agreed. "Keep the horses together and let's not make any more noise than we have to. No sense in making it easy for them."

"That just wouldn't be sporting," Travanos agreed.

They headed further up the ravine. It wasn't too steep, but it was clear that it was heading further up into the foothills, and further away from the course of the road. Dorm hoped this wouldn't be a problem when it came time to go back to it.

There was little talking as they rode. No one was quite sure how far behind them the riders were, or indeed if they even were behind them, but there was a sense that any noise might bring them right down on top of them. After about a quarter of an hour, Dorm called a halt. Everyone strained their ears listening. All that could be head was the breeze blowing through the few trees, and gaps in the rocks; the odd bird calling in the distance, and the occasional noise from their horses.

Dorm was beginning to think that they had evaded them, at least for the time being, when he heard what sounded like a voice off in the distance. He couldn't make out what was said but it sounded as if it had come from further down the ravine.

He signalled silently to the others to move out.

Again they rode on in silence for another while, wondering all the time if the riders were just behind the corner they had only just come round.

It was clear that they would need something more permanent. A cave would have been perfect, but no one was sure of the area. Everyone was studying the land around them, trying to determine if it could reveal the location of some place useful.

Again there was the sound of people behind them and so they moved out again. After another few minutes the ravine began to narrow. They were forced to ride single file, which only made things more difficult, but started giving Dorm and idea. He studied the tops of the ravine. There were a number of small trees, and fairly large rocks even some small boulders. It might be possible to block the ravine off. Or at least block it off enough to halt the riders following them long enough to get away. But they would need somewhere safe to wait.

After a series of twists and turns, the ravine began to open back out a bit, and then ended, looking out into a broad valley. Dorm quickly pulled up and got down. He passed on his thoughts to the others, who quickly agreed.

They began climbing up the ends of the ravines sides. Dorm, Mac, Lianna, Artur and Zacravia went along one side, while Travanos, Ameks, Ambra, Harmia, and Navista went along the other. Rhyn and Telly took care of the horses. Cal stood with his sword drawn at the head of the ravine, just in case this didn't work.

Along the tops of the ravine, each group gathered as much in the way of sticks, logs and rocks as they could and piled them up on either side of one of the narrowest points. Several large boulders nearby would have to levered into position. As the groups began to try and move them to the edges, they began to hear sounds of the riders approach.

Frantically each group tried to get ready, but also to communicate to the other what it was doing, without making any noise.

Finally the riders came into view. They were all dressed in dark clothes, and carried a variety of cruel looking weapons. Their faces betrayed a calm, almost disinterested determination, which Dorm didn't like the look of. These people would never be swayed by mere pleading for mercy.

As the first of them, a large burly looking man with a straggly almost unkempt beard, came into view, Dorm signalled to Travanos to begin. Each group heaved down on the levers they had positioned to push the large boulders down into the ravine below.

There was much sweating, and grunting, and several whispered oaths, before finally the huge stones began to move.

After a few agonising seconds in which it appeared that the stones had suddenly made other plans, the two masses fell with a great clattering roar into the ravine below. As they did, they bounced off the sides bringing down more dirt and loose stones. A great cloud of dust rose up obscuring everything in the ravine. The two groups moved instantly to push more rocks down into the ravine, which sent even more dust and debris into the air.

The shouts of the men on the horse below could be heard easily, as suddenly thick dust filled the air around them, and they were occasionally hit with rocks and pieces of wood. The shout of "Fall back!" was heard before too long and, with a sense of accomplishment everyone headed back to the horses.

But things were not quite as they seemed. As they approached the spot where the others were waiting it was clear that everthing had not gone entirely to plan. The leader of the group, the man with the unkempt beard stood directly in front of Cal, his own sword drawn and pointed at the sergeant. Telly and Rhyn stood shoulder to shoulder a short way behind them, with small daggers drawn trying to protect Tissie and Pianwasal.

The rider was obviously very good at what he did. Cal was after all just a palace guard, but he gave the dark man a steady stare that indicated he wasn't afraid. At least not too much.

Just as they ran up and stopped, Cal looked at them. "Oh good. You're back," he said with a hint of relief in his voice.

"Do you think I am stupid enough to fall for that," the stranger said angrily.

"Well actually you should," Lianna said to him honestly.

The sound of a real voice behind him, caught the man off guard. He half turned to look at them, a look of shocked anger registering on his face for a moment as he realised the size of the group behind him.

It was all the mistake he needed to make.

In a move that was quicker than Dorm would have thought, Cal's sword thrust forward and skewered the would be assassin through the stomach.

The man looked down at the sword for a moment, before giving a groaning sigh, almost as if he was sad about it. He then toppled limply off it to the ground.

Everyone was silent for a moment.

"Well," said Cal quietly. "There you go."

Everyone was quiet for a moment or two, taking in what had happened.

Suddenly Tissie jumped forward and threw her arms around Cal's neck, kissing him on the cheek.

"Oh thank you Sergeant," she said dramatically. "You saved our lives."

"Hang about Miss," He replied attempting to extricate himself from her entanglement, as well as attempting to keep his sword clear so he didn't impale her unintentionally. "I'm just doin' me job. No need for all this fuss."

"But you are a hero Sergeant. You killed that brigand."

"I aint no hero," He said finally getting free of her. His look told Dorm that there was something he wasn't saying. "But your welcome none the less."

Tissie smiled even more sweetly at him.

Zacravia stood over the body and began rummaging around in his clothes.

"What are you doing?" Navista said incredulously. "Have you no decency?"

"You can tell an awful lot about a person from the content of their clothes, and indeed the clothes they wear." He pulled out a small purse with various coins in it, as well as a small pouch tied with string. Upon opening it, were several pieces of parchment. Some containing descriptions of their group, some containing drawn pictures. "What do you make of these Your Highness?"

Dorm looked through the pages. "Seems we still have people after us specifically."

"Good likeness you have to admit," Mac added unhelpfully.

"Yes I can see that," Dorm replied testily. "Which means that someone somewhere has been hired to obtain them. It might be a good idea for us to change our appearance a little."

"What did you have in mind?" Pianwasal asked.

"Well we men can either grow or shave our beards. You women might have to change you hair colours, if we can find someway of doing that. That would be a start."

"If you knew how long this bead took to grow, you may not make that kind of suggestion Dormal," Travanos said quietly.

"Besides dearest," Mac said sarcastically. "You look ridiculous with a moustache."

"Well we don't have much choice."

"Might I suggest that we girls wear our hair differently at least, until we can figure something more permanent out," Rhyn suggested helpfully.

"Good idea." Dorm said. "We probably shouldn't stay here any longer. The rest of those riders will still be after us and if they are even only slightly good, it wont take them long to find another way past that blockage."

They all mounted up quickly and headed off along the edge of the drop into the vast valley. The path they followed gradually lead them downwards, and back in the general direction of the road they had been following. There were more trees here, being higher up in the hills, though as they descended their number thinned out.

It took about an hour of twists and turns and even one brief retracing of steps to finally make it back to the road. Zacravia and Harmia both went forward to have a look, just to make sure that the riders were nowhere about. After about ten minutes they returned to report that the road was clear, and that if they hurried they would be able to get into a small area of trees that would hide them from view for miles around.

They moved forward quickly, but quietly, and emerged on the road not far from where the riders had been when they had first seen them. It only took a few minutes more of concentrated riding to get into the trees. It was cooler and shadier in the trees, and everyone was relieved. They maintained a fast walk, not wanting to be caught unawares if the riders did manage to find their way back to the road.

After consulting his map and both Navista and Ambra, Dorm came to the conclusion that while they would make it to the river crossing by nightfall, they wouldn't get very far on the other side by the time it was completely dark. It was decided to stay for the night in the vicinity of the crossing and get a full days ride in tomorrow. It would be good to rest after the exertion of the last little while.

As the afternoon wore on they rode down towards the river. The land here was actually green, though it looked like some areas could do with a bit more rain. They approached the river as dusk was gathering, and paid to cross on the large ferry. It was a wide beamed, flat bottomed affair, pulled by large ropes from either end. Another such barge could be seen on the opposite shore.

This 'boat' was larger that the one they had used in Tagradas and as such was able to take their entire group. There wasn't a great deal of room left however. The crossing took about fifteen minutes, and after some nervousness from the horses they had disembarked on the other side and ridden into the sizable town here.

It was a little strange to see typical Kiaman buildings and dress in a town that seemed surrounded by the most unKiaman environment. One always associated Kiama Mor with desert. This land was almost anything but. They took lodgings in a large inn near the river, and ate an only slightly burnt meal, before beginning to retire.

Dorm took the opportunity to check on Cal. He knew something was up, but he wasn't sure what. He took him aside on the pretence of checking the horses.

"Is everything alright Cal?" he asked seriously.

"What you mean?" Cal replied feigning ignorance.

Dorm looked at him for a moment. "After you killed that man today, something was bothering you. What was it?"

Cal paused for a moment letting the strap he was holding fall from his fingers. He sighed heavily. "I've never killed no one before," he said quietly. "I didn't really mean to do it even then. It just… he looked at you all, and something inside my head said, that if I didn't get him right then and there, someone would get hurt, maybe even killed. So I just reacted."

Dorm put his hand on the man's shoulder. "Cal you did the right thing. The necessary thing. You're absolutely right. If you hadn't acted someone probably would have gotten hurt. None of us had our weapons with us. You did what had to be done."

"I just feel..." he struggled for a word. "Different somehow."

"Like maybe something inside you is dead as well?"

"Yeah tha's it,"

"That's normal Cal." Dorm hated to admit it but he knew exactly what Cal was talking about. Dorm hadn't killed very many people. Mainly just the ones on this quest. Though there had been a few bands of thieves that had plagued southern Lugemall several years back. He had ridden out with several patrols and had had to deal with this. "If anything, that shows that you're a decent person. If you feel bad about having to kill, then you know that you will only do it when absolutely necessary. And that's a good thing my friend."

"I hope so Your Highness. I really do."

He turned and slowly walked back towards the inn. Dorm watched him go.

~* * * * *~

His footsteps echoed on the polished marble floor as he strode along. The various functionaries and messengers heard him coming long before they saw him. As a consequence, everyone was out of his way before they got in it. That was just as well. He hated having to dodge and weave his way through crowds.

He finally reached the door he wanted. He didn't bother to knock. His rank was sufficient to allow him to ignore such niceties. At least in his opinion. And his position assured him that he wouldn't have to worry about too many platitudes either.

The sergeant behind the desk looked up with an aggravated look on his face and began to protest, until he realised who it was that had so rudely entered the room. He quickly fell silent.

The door to the inner office was closed. No matter. This was important.

He knocked briefly on the door, but didn't wait for an invitation to enter, he simply opened it and stepped through.

The general was seated at his desk as he expected. Opposite him were another general, and a colonel. A major stood nearby holding several large parchments. He recognised the general, but couldn't put a name to the face. The other two men he didn't even bother to look at. They were unimportant.

"Colonel, what is the meaning of barging in here?" the General began.

"Sir, I need to speak to you, it is important," he began. Without giving the General time to answer he pointed at the two other officers. "You two, out. Now!" He held the door open.

The two men looked at each other and then at the generals, not being entirely sure what was going on.

"Gentlemen, would you excuse us for a moment. We will continue this in a few minutes," the General said standing.

The Colonel and the Major nodded warily and then slowly, silently walked from the room. He pushed the door closed behind them, then walked towards the desk.

"Colonel you need to learn some manners…" the General began.

"Sir I am here on instructions of the Emperor himself. I have no time for manners. Besides, they are nothing people, without the seniority to hear what I am going to say."

"This is *my* office Colonel," the General said quietly, with barely restrained rage. "You will treat *me* with the respect *I* deserve. And I would suggest that you treat those below you with a little respect as well. You may find your career cut short if you don't."

He took in the meaning of those words. Assassination wasn't unheard of. Perhaps there was something to what the General was saying.

"Sir," he said pushing those thoughts aside. "We have received the first shipment through the Gate. They are being transported as we speak."

The General nodded and looked at his companion. "Then everything is proceeding well?"

"A few minor difficulties in handling, but we managed to

overcome them."

"And what happens now?"

"We proceed to the beginning of training, Sir. We expect that the basic training will only take several months, but the more in depth training will take longer. We conservatively estimate that we can be ready for full tactical exercises by the end of the year."

The General nodded. "Very well. I will inform the General Staff of your progress."

"I wonder Colonel," the other general said. "How large a force you are expecting to raise?"

"We have an initial consignment of ten units General," he began. That's right. Yabranis was his name. A man you had to be careful around. Very careful. He had a habit of finding "weaknesses" in peoples plans, then "fixing" them so they worked out, and he got the praise. "But we have an agreement to obtain more in groups of ten every three months, from now until the end of the year. At that time, we will need to re-examine our situation."

Yabranis thought on that for a moment. He nodded slightly. Apparently he couldn't find any fault with that… at this stage.

"Very well Colonel, you may continue your efforts. I will inform the Emperor of your progress personally."

"Thank you General Sibrius." He saluted. Showing a little bit of respect didn't hurt.

"I'm sure His Imperial Majesty will be very pleased with your efforts. It will strengthen our forces greatly. *IF* everything goes as planned."

"I'm sure it will, Sir."

"We had better hope that it does Colonel. Because if it doesn't… it could be very bad for everyone involved."

"We will do everything we can to make sure that doesn't happen, Sir."

"Very well, Colonel. You are dismissed."

He saluted again, turned on his heel and left, leaving the door open for the two other men.

As he strode back down the corridor towards the stairs, with much the same effect as his inbound journey, he thought on what was ahead. And a smile slowly came to his lips.

Chapter 27

These northern extremes of Kiama Mor simply did not conform to any one's mental picture of what Kiama Mor should look like.

And that just wasn't fair!

Why couldn't the world do what it was supposed to? Just for once.

The image that one invariably conjured up when thinking of this land, was of deserts, and dusty stone cities. The shimmer of heat over dunes. Great sandstorms that could swallow whole armies, and of a sturdy, friendly, reliable people, who never let the harshness of their environment distract them from having a good time when the situation called for it.

This just wasn't it.

They had ridden north westerly from the town by the river, into a landscape even more fertile than the one they had ridden through to get to the town. This was lush. Trees, a large number of firs and birches dotted the hillsides, and there was long grass growing everywhere. The environment had changed radically on this side of the river, and Dorm was glad that it wouldn't be long till they officially crossed into Ojliam. He had no problem with being in Kiama Mor. He had always found its people to be some of the warmest you could meet, but their strange landscape was weirding him out.

Everyone continually glanced around them at the passing scenery. The Prince wasn't sure if that was for the same reasons he kept glancing around, or if they were just nervous about being attacked again.

The mercenaries were still a possibility. The death of their leader, if they had found him, would probably have rattled them a little, but Dorm was under no illusion that it would make them pack up and go home. No; these men were too hard for that. They would still be out there somewhere. It all just depended on how determined to get them they were. Or would there be other bands ahead of them? Perhaps they only had to patrol a certain area?

Dorm didn't want to think about that. Such thoughts were too depressing to contemplate. It was best to simply take each mile as it came. If more bandits showed up, then they would just have to deal with them.

The border was only twenty or thirty miles ahead. He wasn't sure what sort of affair it would be, but suspected that it would be fairly simple as this wasn't the main highway.

There were very few other travellers on the road, mostly just local farmers and workers, who worked very hard to keep to themselves and avoid eye contact with any one in their group. There was a refreshingly cool breeze blowing down from the hills around them, and they made fairly good time. While the sky grew cloudier as the morning wore on, it didn't rain at all.

Overall the journey was pleasant, but tense.

The forest grew thicker and increasingly darker as they headed north. The trees grew progressively more gnarled and twisted. Zacravia described it as 'gloomy' at one point.

They stopped only briefly for a meal as midday approached, taking only bread and cheese. The road continued to wind its way through the foothills. About an hour after their meal they arrived at the border crossing.

Several small buildings and sheds stood on either side of the road, and soldiers patrolled across the road itself. Nearby another set of similar buildings stood. Above the main buildings of each camp flew two flags. That of Kiama Mor and that of Ojliam.

They rode slowly to the outskirts of the camp. They had to wait for a few minutes for several wagons of a merchant to be fully checked and passed by the customs inspector. The Kiaman soldiers who stood around seemed almost asleep, as the three customs inspectors prodded and poked at the goods in the wagons.

After the merchant had satisfied them that he wasn't stealing the Sultans crown jewels or anything, he was waved through and the customs men turned their attention to Dorm and his friends.

The head inspector, a man of middle years with a thick, close cropped black beard politely introduced himself as Dramos and asked where they were headed.

"North," Dorm replied equally politely. "To Ojliam itself. We have business there."

"May I enquire what business?"

"You may enquire…" Dorm said probably more evasively than he intended.

Dramos watched him for a moment. "And that business would be?"

"Family business. It is a private matter… at least at this stage. I assume you will want to inspect our packs?"

"You assume correctly." He indicated to his two assistants and they began checking everyone's pack. Their inspections were quick and didn't seem that thorough, though Dorm suspected that they actually saw a lot more than it appeared.

"Have you been on the road long?" Dramos asked conversationally.

"Longer than I had thought," Dorm admitted. He realised he was telling the truth. When this had all started he had expected to have only been away for a few weeks before they realised this was all some sort of crazy joke and could go home. Whoops!

"The road south is clear? No blockages or problems? We like to be able to keep travellers up to date with conditions ahead of them."

"No blockages that we encountered," Dorm said choosing his words carefully. He wasn't sure if he should say anything about the bandits.

"We did encounter some trouble though," Telly said.

"Oh?" Dramos asked. "What sort of trouble?"

"Oh some ruffians, who threatened us," she began dramatically, or perhaps melodramatically. "We managed to evade them and one of their number we think met his unfortunate end, but it was terribly frightening."

Dorm began to worry that she was laying it on a bit thick and that he wouldn't believe them.

"We have heard that there are bands of brigands in this region. We have received word that the Sultan is preparing a major push into this region to deal with them."

"Then we wish the Sultan every luck," Travanos said eagerly.

"Indeed, may all the brigands run screaming into the hills and never return," Zacravia concurred.

Dramos smiled. "That is something I would toast to. The Sultan's troops will see an end to them, I have no doubt."

The two inspectors finally reached the end of their inspection and return to Dramos to report that nothing had been found. They headed over to a table piled high with ledgers, into which they began entering various notations.

"There are no major obstructions on the road north," Dramos informed them. "There was some damage near the village of Bevak about thirty miles north of here but it should be mostly repaired by the time you reach it."

"Good news to hear," Dorm replied.

One of the other inspectors came over to Dramos then and handed him a small piece of parchment. He glanced at it then handed it to Dorm. "This is your authorisation to cross the border. You will hand this to the chief inspector on the Ojliaman side once you have crossed."

"Thank you. We appreciate the help."

"Of course." Dramos turned and made a curious twirling gesture with his hand. The soldiers at the crossing took note. One of them walked swiftly to a post that stood at the side of the road, and unhooked something. A chain lowered to the ground. Dorm had not previously seen the chain. It was thin enough that it blended into the background. It was clear that this would be very dangerous to any one trying to force their way across the border.

"Good luck on your journey," Dramos bade them farewell and walked aside.

They nudged their horses forward and headed into Ojliam.

Their group passed the makeshift gate and crossed the short space between it and another similar arrangement on the Ojliam side. Here they were stopped by several Ojliaman guards and made to wait for a moment while the caravan that had passed ahead of them was checked at this end.

Upon completion of this they were allowed to move forward, where they were inspected again. It seemed a little strange to be inspected again, as they had just been so and had no opportunity to pick anything up to conceal, but Dorm wasn't going to argue. He handed the piece of parchment to the head inspector who read it and glanced over their group before nodding and handing it to one of his assistants.

After the inspection had been completed, they were bade welcome to Ojliam and allowed to go on their way.

"Well that wasn't so bad was it?" Rhyn said after they were out of earshot.

"I kept expecting them to declare that they had found something," Zacravia confided.

"That's because you have a suspicious mind, my dear," Lianna told him.

"One of my many charms," he replied.

"We've been held up long enough I think," Dorm concluded. "Lets ride a bit harder for a while. See how much distance we can cover."

They pushed the horses into a canter and covered a far distance in the next few hours, when they took some time to rest. So far they hadn't encountered any villages though they had seen several farmsteads set a ways back from the road. Dorm consulted his map and found that they were probably only a few miles from the first village where they could stop for the night.

They continued on after their stop at a slower pace, discussing what their plan would be in Ojliam. Again they decided to play it by ear, which everyone was beginning to get sick of, but yet agreed was also the best policy with the most likely outcomes.

Dorm briefly considered the idea of visiting the King, one Prinaz X, but his father had never really gotten on with the Ojliaman monarch, finding him "stuffy", and Dorm didn't want to put himself in that position, nor to cause later diplomatic problems for his father.

The road they followed ran northward until it came into the vicinity of the Bozen River. The river flowed southwards from Lake Vikz into the River Pojdram. Once the road got to the area where the river bent towards the lake it swept in a broad curve towards the main highway, near the town of Neftar. Dorm thought this a likely place to properly begin their search, though he fully expected it to take some time.

The forest continued to abound in these hills as they headed northwards. Everyone rode quietly for a while as they took in the surrounding countryside. Occasionally birds would swoop from tree to tree and across the road, and somewhat less often animals could be seen moving around amongst the trees in the distance.

The farms they passed were mainly small. Just a few paddocks or pastures hacked out of the surrounding forest. The houses were small, but well ordered and most had thin streams of smoke rising for their chimneys, reminding everyone of the comforts of home. The road continued to wind its way through the hills following the coarse of least resistance. Only every so often had the builders decided a hill could be cut through. And it avoided big drops in the land like the plague. The few concessions to this were the low wooden bridges that crossed the small streams that flowed towards the river to their left.

The weather had become noticeably cooler as they had entered this part of the world. While it was winter, the fact that there was a huge desert not too far from here, had the effect of keeping temperatures much milder that would otherwise have been the case. They could still occasionally glimpse some snow on the higher peaks, indicative of the fact that winter hadn't totally forgotten this place.

There were still very few people on the road, and both Travanos and Ambra expressed concerns at this, wondering why the road was so deserted. Several of the others picked up on their concerns and began to worry a little as well. Tissie of course, started fretting that the bandits had returned and that they were all in danger of imminent attack, until Lianna told her to keep her thoughts to herself, only a little more forcefully that Dorm thought necessary.

As the afternoon wore on they began to consider their

arrangements for the night. Everyone wanted to stay in an inn, but it was decided to camp that night. They had had a long day and an early start would do them good. Also Dorm secretly didn't want to pamper everyone too much. He had no idea what lay ahead of them, but suspected that a little "roughing it" as one of his uncles often called it, would not be such a bad thing. People might get soft if they had a warm bed to sleep in *every* night.

As the shadows began to lengthen they pulled off the road and followed one of the small streams back into the trees. They found an area where there were fewer trees; not exactly a clearing, but close enough, and pitched their tents. They set a fire and began preparing a meal. Once they had eaten, they sat and talked for a while about what sort of place Ojliam was before all retiring for the night.

During the night it rained. It was only a slight rain; a few drops that fell loudly from the boughs above their tents to strike the canvas with a resounding slpat, but enough to relax Dorm with its rhythmic beat. As he slept he dreamt.

He stood in a forest. Not unlike the one in which he was camped in reality. Though here it was light. A diffuse glow seemed to emanate from all around. A soft mist floated in the air. He cast his gaze around the glade in which he stood taking in the beauty. It was cool, relaxing. Even reassuring. Then he noticed he was not alone.

A man stood several yards in front of him. He wore a dark cloak, similar to that of a Ranger. A small silver circle was embroidered on his breast. He wore the deeply cowled hood up so his face was obscured.

Dorm went to take a step towards the man, but found he could not move. He made to call out to the man but found that like his legs, his voice was immobile.

The man slowly raised his hands and pushed back the hood of his cloak.

His face was kindly, and wise. He had a few lines that suggested some years, but his age was largely indeterminate. His well-groomed hair was silvery grey and hung loosely around his shoulders. He slowly smiled at Dorm, who was overcome with a sense of calm. Of friendship.

He knew, somehow, that this strange man meant him no harm.

The man began to speak, but Dorm could hear no voice. None of the words he spoke could be made out. He talked for some time, but Dorm could hear none of it. He tried to tell the man this, but again, his own voice was denied him.

After several minutes, the old man smiled again, and inclined his head. His face betrayed weariness, then with a brief flicker, he vanished.

Dorm stood for a moment in this transcendental glade, not sure of what had happened, then it began to grow dim.

He awoke with a start.

It was late. Or perhaps early. The drops of water continued to strike the canvas of the tents. Dorm caught his breath, then looked across at Mac, who lay beside him, fast asleep.

He closed his eyes, trying to understand what that had all meant. Nothing was forth coming. He realised that he wasn't scared or worried, like he normally was after he had dreamt. In fact, he almost felt good. Rather more relaxed than he had expected. Calm almost. This particular dream was obviously very different to those he normally had. Something about that man... He got the feeling he would see him again.

He slowly lowered himself back down into his roll. Mac instinctively moved closer, his arm draping across Dorms chest. Dorm took a hold of that arm. It felt good to have it here. He felt grounded. Almost as if he couldn't be taken back to that glade.

He wasn't sure if that was good or bad.

The rain continued for several hours in the morning before finally blowing off. The cloud cover also began to thin and patches of blue appeared. They were all slightly wet, and the breeze served to chill them while it dried them. Everyone was glad when they came to a village around midday and were able to get inside and dry off properly in front of the taprooms' hearth.

They stayed for a little longer than Dorm would have liked, but he had to admit that the room, while plain and uninspiring, was cosy and relaxing.

At least it was dry as they continued on their way. This was something they were all grateful for. As they rode, people began to speculate on who the Ojliaman members of their group might end up being.

There were people from all sorts of backgrounds already in this group, so it was hard to pick a particular type of person. Most agreed that they would probably end up being people from normal backgrounds, with normal jobs. No one particularly expected another Prince of the Realm or High Priestess.

Dorm was glad of that. He had never had much of a chance to really get to know too many normal people. He hated using the word 'common'. These people weren't common. They were anything but. He seemed to only ever have met and interacted with normal people properly, when he had gone off on his "Tours" as his father liked to call them. He had done many of them as he was growing up. Going out into the cities and towns in disguise; that is to say dressed just as a normal person. They had been informative. He had learnt a lot. He believed it made him a better Prince, and his father a better King. Obviously his father hadn't been able to do it for years. It's hard to go unnoticed when your likeness is stamped on every coin.

He had learnt a lot from interacting with these normal people throughout Lugemall, without all the trappings of state, and the pretence that they were talking to someone higher and more important than them. He may have had more responsibilities, to be sure, but he wasn't better than them. That was something he had learnt too. Also it had changed his life when he had met Mac on one of them. He would never have given that up for anything.

On those expeditions he had been taught about the concerns of his people. Not fluffed up with flowery words or 'political speak' but ordinary words, spoken by ordinary people, about ordinary concerns. And that had been the goal. It had been dangerous to be sure. There had been several times when he had been threatened, and one time even slashed in the arm with a knife in a particularly noisy scrap in a tavern. But on the whole he had learnt more than he had risked.

The group considered the values of different sorts of people. Another soldier would be good for protection, something that was on everyone's mind at the moment. A merchant might gain them access to places to hide, or people to interact with to travel in disguise. A labourer would be useful at all the tasks they had to perform everyday, and that were beginning to ware a little thin with everyone. It was suggested that it could be an academic of some sort. It took a while for any one to think of a way an academic could be useful to them, until Lianna suggested that they might know about the history of things.

They all hoped it wasn't a member of the country's parliament or Council of Ministers. It had been hard enough to get the daughter of the High Chamberlain of one kingdom to come along, without the needs of the country in question being put to the test.

Then again, what if it was the King himself?!

That didn't bear thinking about.

In the end the conversation did little more than depress everyone about how little they knew about what was going on, and about the possibilities that this kingdom was going to present to them.

The rain returned the next day and was heavier this time. Very heavy in fact. They began to notice after several hours that many of the small streams were flowing rapidly and were all rather full. Large puddles began to appear on the roadway and the mud seemed to get thicker every minute. After only a few hours of this it was quickly decided that they should pull off the road and try to wait it out; if that was possible.

They began scouting for a relatively protected place, that was preferably a bit higher than the surrounding land. No one particularly wanted to drown in a flooded stream. Eventually Artur spotted something that might be useful and they pushed off the road through the trees, coming to a large outcropping of rocks after a few minutes.

The rocks were typical of the region and not all that big, being only slightly taller than their horses, though they were piled up on top of each other in a sort of horseshoe shape that gave a large enough area to camp in the middle of. It wasn't much but there was a bit of an overhang that they could attach their tent canvases to and create a large enough shelter.

It took a bit longer than originally thought, but eventually they managed to secure the tents well enough to form a workable little camp. They lit a small fire so as not to smoke themselves to death, and did their best to dry off and prepare a small meal.

The rain got heavier and there wasn't much point in trying to talk over the top of it so everyone tried to rest. Travanos and Ambra began checking the horses bridles to make sure none had been damaged at all by the rain; while Lianna, Rhyn and Pianwasal went around and fed them.

Dorm, Mac, Zacravia and Artur stood, or rather sat guard at the small entrance they had left themselves. There wasn't much to watch for. The road was only barely visible through the trees, and the rain just kept falling.

"Well so far I don't think very much of Ojliam," Zacravia said after a long silence. "I mean rain is fine enough. But I think this is a little excessive. Perhaps it might be a good idea if we did stop by the capital after all. Give His Majesty our opinion on the climate of his realm."

"I'm not sure you'd want to do that," Dorm told him with a smile. "King Prinaz has a tendency to think that any criticism is a personal attack on him. He might not take too kindly to it."

"What's the worst he can do?"

"Have you ever spent any time in a dungeon?"

"Actually yes. I found it rather boring to be honest with you. Granted I was only in there for a few hours before I managed to escape but still… I think I would have gone mad if I had had to stay there any longer. They wouldn't have gotten any confessions out of me that's for sure. I would have been too busy drooling and talking about pixies."

"What were you in the dungeon for?" Artur asked.

"Oh a trifling, my friend. A complete misunderstanding."

"A misunderstanding?" Mac asked looking him directly in the eye.

"Oh yes. You see they misunderstood when I said I didn't want to go in there. Silly people."

The rain continued to fall heavily for the next hour or so. It eased slightly then. Around mid-afternoon a rumbling noise was heard off in the distance. At first everyone thought it was another peal of thunder, until it kept going. After a few moments, they realised they were hearing the sound of horses. Everyone fell silent. The noise grew closer until finally, through the trees they saw riders galloping along the road. A large number of them passed by for several minutes. It was hard to see exactly who they were as they were at some distance and all seemed to be wearing travelling cloaks against the rain.

Finally the last of the riders passed their position heading north and the sound of their passage slowly receded into the distance.

They all let out a collectively held breath once the noise had gone.

"Who do you suppose they were?" Lianna asked.

"Not sure. I don't recognise them," Dorm replied.

"You think they might be those bandits again?" Artur asked cautiously.

"Anything is possible I suppose."

"I'm just glad they didn't notice our tracks," Zacravia said. "I didn't bother to try to hide them and with all this rain they should stand out."

"All this rain has probably washed them away," Travanos suggested. "The road surface is probably rather different now."

"So should we leave now?" Telly enquired. "Or should we wait?"

"I think we should wait a little while," Dorm responded carefully. "Let's make sure they don't double back. But lets get ready to move out."

Packs were stowed and the fire extinguished, though they didn't yet take down their shelter. They waited silently for the better part of an hour to see if the riders returned. The slightest little noise made everyone jump.

When no sound of approaching riders was heard they began to strike their shelter. The rain continued but it had lessened. Zacravia took the lead and made his way towards the road to make sure that the riders hadn't just stopped somewhere up the road. He came back after a few minutes to report the all clear. They walked their horses back through the trees to the road, before mounting up and continuing northwards.

The trip was tense and wet. Never a good combination. They moved forward at a measured pace only just above a walk. Everyone quickly decided that giving themselves the most amount of time to deal with the unexpected was the best course of action.

The road continued to slowly wind its way through hills and forest. After about an hour they rounded a bend that crested a small rise.

Mac let out a groan. At the top of the crest was the familiar shape of Rangers.

The three of them stood still in the middle of the road, They stood quite erect and tall, seemingly impervious to the falling rain, or the rushing water at their feet. Everyone exchanged glances, none of their long-term companions really wanting to go through all this again. But since it was equally obvious that they wouldn't have been here, standing in the middle of a road in the middle of Nowheresville, Ojliam, without a very good reason, they proceeded on.

They stopped their horses in front of them and the three dark cloaked people bowed deeply.

"So what is it this time?" Mac sighed heavily.

"Your impatience does not become thee, Quester to be," said the middle figure, which it turned out was a woman. Dorm caught sight of a few wisps of blonde hair, touched by grey. He took note of her face. He couldn't tell the colour of her eyes with the shadow of her hood falling across her face, but there was great wisdom in them. The lines on her face did not make her look older, merely more powerful. Dorm got the distinct feeling he should not underestimate her.

"We have come to warn you of danger ahead," she went on. "The riders you saw earlier."

"How did you know we had seen riders?" Pianwasal asked curiously.

"We know many things, Quester," the young man on her right replied. He seemed barely old enough to be allowed out of the house. But he too stood with an air of confidence. "We would not be here otherwise."

"The riders have been sent to intercept you. But we cannot let that happen," said the other man. He was much older than the first, probably a similar age to that of the woman.

"We will show you to a path that will lead you around them. It will add time to your journey, but it will keep you safe," the woman went on. "Please follow us."

Without another word she turned on her heel and began to walk back along the road. The two men bowed then turned and followed her.

Dorm looked at the others for some advice. No one was quite sure what to make of it. This was by far the most direct the Rangers had ever been involved.

The three Rangers were out ahead of them now, and seemed to be moving quite quickly. This in itself was remarkable. No one had thought them capable of anything resembling speed, given their normal slow, wobbling gait. But the three of them were moving along at a steady pace ahead of their horses.

After a few minutes the three dark clad strangers suddenly turned off the road and proceeded to vanish into what could almost be described as a gap. It certainly wasn't a path of any sort. But with no other choice they led their horses through one by one.

Once they had moved back among the trees a barely discernible path became clear. Probably a game trail, or possibly a woodcutter's track. The ground was covered with short grass and occasionally moss. The dappled light and dripping boughs served only to make the whole situation seem much worse than it probably really was.

The track wound its way back through the trees, heading away from the road for about a mile before it swung lazily around to follow the general course of the road they had been on. Somewhere nearby they could hear the roar of a flowing river, obviously swollen with all this rain.

All the time the Rangers maintained their position just head of their group. It was strange to watch them move so quickly and yet, not seem to be exerting themselves. After about half an hour of following the road, the Rangers stopped for a moment. The three of them stood facing each other, their eyes closed. No one was quite sure what to make of this. The group stood there silently, just long enough for it to start becoming awkward. The woman then turned and faced them again.

"Our apologies. We had to commune with our superiors, and determine if the riders had realised what we had done."

"And have they?" Telly asked.

"Not as yet, Quester,"

"Well that's good then, isn't it?" She asked again.

"As long as it remains the case," said the older of the men.

Again the Rangers turned and lead the way deeper through the forest.

On they pushed through the saturated landscape. A light breeze began to blow from the north-west, rustling the branches of the trees and showering everyone with even more water. The coolness of the air served only to chill them more. Everyone was decidedly unpleasant, and some even started to shiver.

They crested a small rise and found themselves in a clearing. The Rangers stood near the centre, again engrossed in their communing. After a few moments, they turned and smiled at their group.

"The riders are moving on now."

"Away from us I presume your smiles mean?" Rhyn enquired of them.

"Quite correct Quester," said the older man. "We shall wait here for a while until they have passed out of the area, then we will continue on."

"It was a good thing you knew of this trail," Artur said to them.

"Rangers plan for any eventuality," the younger man said.

"Well we are grateful for your help," Dorm said. "I'm not sure what we would have done, if we had encountered them."

"We live but to serve Quester," the woman told him sincerely. "We will take you back to the road. You will be near the village of Tejank. We would suggest that you stay there for the night. If you arrive in smaller groups it will help prevent news of your arrival leaking out."

"That's not a bad idea, Your Highness," Zacravia agreed. "One large group sticks out like an elephant in a cow pasture. But if we go in, in groups of twos and threes…"

"Yes much easier to pretend we are someone else entirely," Dorm finished his thought. "Alright we can try that, but not until we get closer. I don't think it will do any one any good if we start wandering all over this forest."

"Once we get back to civilisation," Ambra began, "Should we not inform the authorities? What I mean is if the Ojliaman army is out looking for them, then they won't be concentrating on us as much."

"That has already been thought of Quester," the female Ranger told him. "Even as we speak this information is on its way to the King himself. It will take a few days but he will muster troops to this area to look for them."

"And what makes you so confident of that?" Travanos asked curiously.

She merely turned and fixed him with a direct look. "As we said earlier, we prepare for all eventualities."

They waited in the clearing for over an hour, as the rain gradually eased. It was still raining very lightly when they headed out. The path once again rose and fell and ducked and wove through the trees and the hills of the countryside. After some time the path straightened out and ran on for several miles before finding the road again. Everyone was quite relieved when they were able to travel on a well defined path.

It turned out indeed to be not far from the village of Tejank. It was quickly decided who would go in what groups to enter the village, and the Rangers informed them of a reputable inn in the northern quarter. The first group of Ambra, Pianwasal, Ameks and Navista headed out, while the next group, which consisted of Cal, Tissie, Rhyn, Telly, Travanos and Artur made ready to leave.

Dorm turned to the Rangers. "Thank you," he said quietly.

"You are welcome Quester," said the woman. She watched him for a moment. Then stepped closer to him. She laid a hand on Dorms hand and fixed him with probably the most intense gaze any one had ever directed at him. "I can see your pain, Your Highness. Do not be afraid of it. It hurts you greatly yes, but it can also be a source of great strength. I hope you will remember that when the time comes."

"What do you mean?" Dorm asked her in a quiet voice.

She paused for a moment. "That I may not tell thee now," she said sorrowfully. "But do try to remember that your pain can help you. Not just harm you."

Dorm had no idea what to say in response. "I will try," was all he could come up with.

"I think it's our turn now," Harmia told him.

"Of course, lets get ready to move," Dorm told her. When he turned back to say goodbye to the Rangers he found they were already some distance away, marching with their familiar gait.

Dorm watched them go.

Chapter 28

The village of Tejank turned out to be rather unimpressive. And more than a little intimidating. It was a medium sized collection of mostly wooden buildings that seemed almost to huddle together and leer at those who passed along its streets. No one felt particularly comfortable as they followed the narrow thoroughfares towards the north of the village.

Some effort had been made in the past to pave the streets but it appeared that not a lot of maintenance work had been carried out in recent years, and the rain had caused all the exposed areas to turn to mud, which subsequently had been tracked all over town.

The villagers scurried about their own business; cloaks and hoods drawn tightly about them against the rain and the chill breeze, and didn't seem to notice, or possibly more precisely, not want to notice their small groups as they moved through towards the inn which was called 'The Travellers Rest'.

Dorm tried to watch these Ojliaman villagers clandestinely. None of them ever met his gaze, and more than a few of them even seemed to go out of their way to avoid looking at him directly. He knew that people in small villages were wary of strangers, that was the same everywhere, but that was a little extreme. Wasn't it?

They stopped only once for directions, from one of the towns' constabulary, who lazed almost nonchalantly at the entrance to the main town square. His directions at first were at best vague, until some hands resting on sword hilts prompted him to be a bit more forthcoming.

After some time they found the inn, which turned out to be one of the few stone buildings in the town and entered the courtyard at the rear. The stable hands took their horses and they headed inside to take some rooms. The inside of the inn was warm and delightfully cosy after the chill of the outside. After depositing their overnight bags in their rooms they all headed down to the large common room to take food and meet up with their other companions.

Ambra, Pianwasal, Navista and Ameks were seated at a table not far from the counter. Their group had been an obvious one. A group of people obviously from either Kiama Mor or Szugabar would not attract much attention. Ambra briefly caught Dorms' eye as they passed and gave him an imperceptible nod.

At the next table, the second group sat talking and smiling and generally having a good time. This also wasn't a bad cover. any one looking for their large group wouldn't be looking for happy people enjoying their time on the road. They'd be looking for serious, concerned, travel worn individuals.

Dorm and his group, which consisted of Mac, Harmia, Zacravia, and Lianna besides himself, took the last table in front of the counter and sat quietly. One of the serving maids came and took their order for food and drink and they sat quietly taking in the warmth.

There were not a lot of other people in the room. Two or three couples, mainly men, who looked like merchants and the like. Two women sat in one corner knitting and gossiping. Though one man did catch Dorms attention. He sat mainly in shadow in one corner of the room. He seemed almost asleep though Dorm could tell he was not.

The man didn't seem to take any particular interest in them, but there was no sense in being too relaxed in this situation.

The food and drink came and was actually quite good. It seemed that the Rangers had indeed directed them to a worthy establishment. The others also seemed to be enjoying their meals well enough.

At the middle table Cal and Rhyn had started a boisterous conversation about some person name Garv, who Dorm presumed was made up, and were telling the others about this Garv's misadventures on the trading routes of the Alliance. It was amazing to see the two of them making up things on the run and reacting to each other as if it were the truth.

After about half an hour or so the 'quiet table' as Harmia had dubbed them, rose and returned upstairs. Dorm felt it would probably be a good idea if they left next, but not too quickly. They all had another drink before returning upstairs. It was now early evening and it was getting rather gloomy outside. The rain continued to fall though it had eased considerably over the afternoon.

There was a little to-ing and fro-ing once they were upstairs, but eventually everyone managed to meet up together in the small room that would be shared by Rhyn, Tissie and Telly.

"So how did you come up with all those stories?" Mac asked Cal once they had settled.

"Oh that," he said simply. "Oh they are real stories. They just didn't all happen to the same person. I sort of put them all together. Tha's all."

"Well I think it was brilliant."

"Well the real credit goes to Rhyn," Cal admitted then. "She went along with everything I said and even added bits to it at just the right moments. Tha's wot made it believable."

"Well I think we should leave this place early in the morning," Pianwasal said. "It does not feel right."

"I agree," Tissie said then. "This whole village makes me feel weird."

"Yes I know what you mean," Dorm admitted. "Alright we'll get out early enough, in our groups and meet up once we are a few miles out of town. We don't want to stay apart for too long."

"That could be an idea though," Travanos mused. "Everyone is still looking for a large group. Three smaller groups would allow us to move more freely, and more importantly, undetected."

"A nice idea, only once we need to find the next people with amulets, I get the feeling we'll need everyone present."

"I agree," Telly said. "Though I think it might be an idea to do this same sort of thing every time we enter a town."

"Not a bad idea at all," Zacravia concurred.

Suddenly there was a knock at the door.

Everyone froze. No one was sure what to do. There was no way they could explain why all these people were in this room at the same time. Especially since they were meant to be from different groups.

Everyone looked at each other.

"Ah, yes?" Telly suddenly answered quite loudly.

"I need to speak with you a moment," a soft male voice said from the other side of the door.

"About?" Telly responded trying to sound curious yet annoyed.

"I have a message for the Prince and the rest of you."

It was obvious this person knew them. But how?

"Prince? Which Prince?" Telly replied trying to maintain the charade.

"I know who you are Quester," said the voice quietly.

Dorm nodded to Mac and Zacravia who stood neat the door. They opened it quickly. It was the man from the common room. The one that had been trying to hide in the shadows.

He quickly stepped inside the room, the door being closed almost before he had passed it.

Harmia stepped in quickly and began patting him all over. No one was quite sure what she was doing. Once she had finished she stood and said to Dorm, "No weapons on him that I can find."

"Who are you?" Dorm asked the man.

"My name is Frandis," he replied quietly. "I have been sent by the Rangers."

"You are a Ranger?" Travanos said a little incredulously.

"I am an Apprentice, yes Admiral."

"And you have a message for us?"

"Yes. The riders you encountered earlier today are now heading back towards this village. They should arrive shortly. You should stay in the inn for the night and leave early tomorrow morning. We will make it so that the riders will not follow you immediately."

" Oh, and how exactly will you do that?" Lianna said slowly.

"We will put something into their ale or wine to… shall we say 'improve their mood'."

"In other words put something in their drink to increase the potency of the alcohol?"

"Yes. They should sleep very well tonight," the young man said almost grinning.

"And hopefully late into the morning," Navista spoke for everyone.

"Isn't that a little immoral?" Pianawasal said then. "Not to mention rather dangerous. What if you are caught?"

The young man stood for a moment with a slightly puzzled look on his face. "But I won't be."

Harmia rolled her eyes.

"I must go now," he said turning towards the door. "Do not take too long before retiring. And from me personally... good luck on your quest." He inclined his head then slipped through the door.

Everyone simply looked at each other for a few moments, unsure of what to say.

"It seems we have our orders," Travanos said finally.

"At least we know they're on our side," Lianna responded. "I think."

They began rising before the sun the next morning. Dorm looked briefly out the window at the steely light of the dawn and saw the clouds still scudding across the sky. It was still rather chilly and the wind could be heard blowing rather forcefully outside, though at least the rain had stopped.

Dorm's group was the first to leave. They headed out into the streets speaking in hushed voices, and rode slowly through the streets. There were few other people about. A few workers cleaning up major pieces of rubbish, and a few labourers on their way to work. The wind was quite chill and they all pulled their cloaks tighter about them as they rode.

The left Tejank and headed north along the main road. They rode slowly until they were out of earshot then galloped for a few miles until they came to a copse of trees near the road. Here they pulled off and waited.

After about a half an hour, Ambra and his group rode up. They noticed their group and rode over to them.

"Good morning," Dorm said.

"Good Morning," Ambra replied. "Fancy meeting you here."

"Yes strange that, isn't it."

"How long do you think we'll have to wait till the others arrive?" Harmia asked the arrivals.

"I'm not sure," Ambra admitted. "We heard some stirrings as we were leaving. But nothing that would indicate they were about to leave."

"I think they are just trying to stay in character," Ameks suggested. "Cal and the others were pretending to be a little 'relaxed' shall we say."

Dorm had to smile at that. "True enough. I just don't want to have to stand here for too long. If any one sees us it would be suspicious and that's the last thing we need."

"You think that someone would tell those riders?" Navista asked in a worried voice.

"Perhaps not intentionally," Dorm explained. "But people do have a tendency to talk…"

"And it would be the kind of thing that would stand out," Lianna added.

In the end they only had to wait about another half an hour. The others had actually been up and ready to leave when their groups had left, but had thought it better to wait and maintain the charade of being 'relaxed'. Once they had all been reunited, they got back on the road and headed northward at a steady canter.

As the day began, they started encountering people on the road. Mainly farmers and labourers. They allowed their group to string out a bit, so that it might not appear at first to be one large group. They passed a few small villages set back from the road. The day remained cool and breezy as they rode. Around midday they stopped and ate a brief meal at a roadside tavern just outside another small village. Dorm quickly looked over his map and after consulting with the others it was decided to head on towards the capital and take things from there.

As they continued on their way there seemed to be a certain uniformity to much of Ojliam. Or at least the buildings. They all seemed to be of an almost standardised construction. Large exposed beams with bright whitewashed walls. Burgeoning thatched roofs and neat gardens. Stonework seemed to be reserved for public buildings and the like.

Minor buildings, such as barns and warehouses seemed to contain a certain amount of wattle and daub in their construction.

It took Dorm some time to realise what he was seeing. This was the after effect of the Second Peldraksekhr Invasion during the Thirty-Ninth Century. Ojliam had all but been destroyed during that cataclysm. It had taken decades to restore all the buildings and much longer to restore the people and their livelihoods. He realised that this uniformity in construction was probably the result of successive governments settling on the speediest and most practical way to build houses and the like in the quickest possible time. It unfortunately had the effect of making every village look the same as every other. Only a few building here and there stood out. They did notice occasionally a part of a building that was different. Most likely due to rebuilding because of domestic accidents; fire and the like, that occurs from time to time. But for the most part there seemed to be a bland sameness about Ojliam so far. It was depressing and even a little foreboding.

The rain returned that afternoon, though it didn't fall as heavily as it had the day before, as they continued to trudge their way northward. They took what little shelter they could in groves of trees when they stopped, and they took the opportunity to escape briefly from the rain at every village they came to.

By evening they came to another village and took rooms, again continuing their subterfuge of being three separate groups, and did their best to stay warm and dry.

The next few days were much the same. The rain fell intermittently and kept everyone feeling soaked and a little miserable. Dorm noticed that the four members of their group from the desert countries seemed to be having the worst time of it. In their native lands rain only really fell during the wet season, which was only a few months of the year. And then usually only at certain times of the day. This was something unnatural to them; something that they muttered to themselves on more than one occasion.

The highlight of their trip toward the capital came around mid-afternoon on their third day out from Tejank when they crested the large hill they were climbing. The trees on their left parted and a magnificent view into the valley below revealed itself. Far below and off in the distance surrounded by mist and rain lay a large lake. It still seemed to shine somewhat despite it's leaden grey appearance. Dorms' map identified it as Lake Vikz. From the northern shore of the lake a long structure could be seen marching towards the north. After some discussion it was decided it must have been the great Lakisklav Aqueduct, the longest in the world. The aqueduct supplied water to the capital. Knowing that this was now within sight gave them all the impetus to go on. The capital was now not that far away. There they would be able to rest properly. After stopping and admiring the view for a few minutes they moved on.

It only took another two days to reach Ojliam. The city itself sat in the middle of a vast rolling plain. The plain had little on it except the odd copse of trees and a village or two. It was just an unending sea of tall grasses blowing before the wind.

The road they followed was now the main highway south, and as such was well defined and well maintained. There were plenty of travellers on it as they neared the national capital. Many merchants, labourers, soldiers and others trundled back and forth along it. As they got closer to the city the waving grass grew shorter and greener. Eventually it stopped and was replaced by an almost manicured lawn. They realised that this was part of something important. Ahead of them they could see large flowering bushes and trees, and here and there stood tall slender spires. The walls of the city still dominated the view, but their eyes were drawn to these pointed edifices.

They stopped near one that was positioned just next to the road. In front of the spire was a formal garden, complete with benches and a small pool of water in a stone foundation. There was a small paved area in front of this that led off the road, allowing them to pull aside and dismount.

They wandered around for a moment of two looking up at the carvings that were inscribed at several intervals up the height of the spire. There was a bronze plaque positioned at the base of the spire. Dorm stood in front of it and read the inscription. It was then that he understood what this was, and indeed what all of the spires were as well as the gardens.

Erected in honour of the men of the
10th Pikeman's Company
Kiaman Army
Who died in valour on this site
Defending the Alliance during the
Second Peldraksekhr Invasion

Long may they be remembered.

One by one his companions came to stand next to him and read for themselves. The inscription was simple, but poignant. Those that were wearing hats removed them and everyone pushed back the hoods of their cloaks. They had probably all heard stories of the great memorials around Ojliam. They had taken decades to build, and nearly bankrupted Ojliam when it had tried to build them all itself. Only when the other Alliance countries had helped had the gardens been finished. Many had wondered why they hadn't been helping from the beginning. But in the end all that mattered was that they were finished. And any one from anywhere in the Alliance, was able to come here and remember what had happened.

The great Battle of Ojliam had cost more lives than any one had though possible. A massive army of Peldraksekhr had marched down through Bydanushev and into Ojliam destroying and capturing all before it. They had laid siege to Ojliam city itself and had brought the capital to the brink of surrender before the Alliance had been able to get its troops properly into position.

The Alliance generals had waited till the Peldraksekhr had committed themselves to the siege. That way the Alliance army wouldn't have to deal with their siege equipment. At least not at first. It meant that the Alliance could destroy a great deal of their support troops, physicians, cooks, armourers and blacksmiths, before the legions proper could respond. Even if they had lost the battle the Alliance would have inflicted a heavy, possibly crippling toll on their enemy.

The battle had raged for a day and a half. And the death toll had been beyond counting. In the end though the Alliance had won. The legions had suffered the worst for the battle, but the Alliance had not had time to celebrate, for a second army was approaching. The second army too was destroyed, but only just. The Second Peldraksekhr Invasion had cost so many lives, these spires were a small but necessary reminder of what had happened. This was a solemn place. One that inspired you to contemplate those battles and that war.

Dorm noticed that both Ambra and Navista seemed quieter than the others. He guessed it was because this was a spire erected in honour of Kiamans. Seeing the graves of ones own countrymen, and thinking of what they had gone through was likely to have that effect on you.

Everyone was very quiet as they moved on back towards the road.

More of these memorial spires reached towards the sky as they approached the city. They stopped at several of them. Each commemorated a different group of the Alliance forces. All from different countries. It started to dawn on you after a while just how many people actually did die during that terrible war. Every one of these spires represented at least several score of men lost. And there had to be hundreds that they could see from the road. And that didn't include what might have been on the other side of the city.

Nor did it count the civilians.

After several stops they found a spire dedicated to a group of Lugemallan troops. Dorm obviously felt a deeper connection with this spire. These were his countrymen. He had served with his country's army for short periods at various times. He knew what they were capable of. He remembered the faces and the voices of those he had served with, and tried to imagine what it would be like if they had been the ones to whom this memorial had been erected.

The Second Peldraksekhr Invasion had wiped out nearly an entire generation of young men, and did untold damage to the women as well. The world had moved on from them, and now increasingly there were women in the various Alliance armies as well.

A hollow thought occurred to him then. This quest they were on. What if it lead to some kind of confrontation? How much damage to this generation would it do? The generation that had lived through the Second Peldraksekhr Invasion had been demoralised. It had taken decades to recover. There were many people who simply were too frightened to have children after it, for fear of bringing them into a world that had spawned such horror.

How would his generation cope?

Mac watched him as he thought. “I wonder the same things,” he said almost as if he had heard Dorms mind.

Dorm could only sigh.

Finally they approached the gates of the city. A small collection of buildings were positioned just in front of the gate. There was an inn or two and a few blacksmiths and liveries and various other odds and ends that one would expect to find beside any major highway. There was also a small guardhouse and a stable where it seemed the Ojliaman army kept a group of riders.

They passed all of this without incident or stopping and clattered across the large wooden decked bridge that crossed the dry moat. Though at the moment it wasn’t exactly dry, what with all the rain of late.

The city gates were huge. Some attempt at decoration had been made when they had been built with several large embossments around the gate itself. After a few moments study Dorm began to suspect that there was a lot less of decoration about them than he had first thought.

They passed underneath the gate and through the walls, which were also massive, being fully sixty feet thick. Dorm wondered where in the world they had gotten the stone for it from. He didn’t recall any giant holes in the world.

After the main wall there was a narrow area that seemed to be closed off to ordinary travellers. Through gaps in the partially ajar gate that lead to it, he could glimpse workshops and possibly stables. It seemed that the kings of Ojliam had decided not to take any chance. This city had been prepared to defend itself if it was ever subjected to another siege. Pity the army that was fool enough to try that.

They passed through another gatehouse in another wall, though this one was only half as thick as the previous one, and entered into the city proper. It, as they had expected was typical of bustling major cities, and for a moment Dorm was reminded of Lugemall city. The shouting of the merchants, though with a different accent, was the same; the hurried almost urgent walking of both traders and bureaucrats followed exactly the same rhythm.

They slowly made their way into the city with the rest of the flowing traffic. Every so often they would come to a square containing a statue or a fountain that simply teemed with people. Every now and again they would see small groups of troops. This was something unheard of in the southern countries in the Alliance, but both Ojliam and Bydanushev and been made a little paranoid after the invasion by the Peldraksekhr. And while that conflict was a very long time ago indeed now, the Empire was still there, and still just as distrusted.

After about a quarter of an hour they asked for directions to an inn and turned off the main avenue onto a smaller street to follow the directions they had been given. When they arrived they found the inn to be a grand multi-storey affair of rather elaborately carved stonework, that made all the ladies eyes light up with the promise of a certain level of luxury.

The interior proved to be just as fancy as the exterior with a great deal of polished wood and paintings and tapestries and soft cushions and curtains. They were informed of the bathhouse and after a brief moment of chittering the women as a group decided it was the first thing they were going off to do. The men all looked at them.

"It might be a good idea for you boys to do the same," Telly said in that voice of hers that challenged you to just try and argue with her.

"What on earth for?" Zacravia asked her.

"Well let's put it this way," she began. "We have been travelling for quite a while without any proper bathing facilities…"

"In other words," Rhyn told them. "You stink!"

"Pong, reek, have become fulsomely odorous, gotten a bit wiffy," Telly detailed to them. "Getting the picture?"

"I think we get the idea, yes," Dorm told her.

"And don't forget to wash behind your ears," Lianna said with a mischievous grin.

"Yes mother," Cal told her.

"Come ladies," Harmia said, and they turned and left.

"What have we gotten ourselves into here?" Travanos posed to the rest of them.

"Nothing good I'm sure," Ambra commented quietly.

"They are right about one thing though," Mac said.

"Oh? What's that?" Artur asked curiously.

"You all do stink."

"Well you're no bed of roses yourself," Dorm told him.

"Me? I always smell wonderful."

"Yeah, right."

After everyone had bathed, and what a luxury that turned out to be, they all dried and dressed and returned to the common room to eat a meal. It was now approaching midday and everyone was getting a bit peckish. The meal was very good and filling. After a brief discussion they decided to venture out for a while to assess the lay of the land, as it were and see if they might not be able to pick up on any gossip.

The city continued to teem with people going about their business. The markets were full, and it seemed that everyone was buying. Dorm had to enquire as to why and discovered that it was the Kings Birthday holiday in two days time. That of course explained it. Leaders birthday holidays were celebrated in every Alliance country. In Lugemall it was a fairly quiet affair. His father would write a short speech that would be sent around the country and there would be a bigger dinner for most people that night. A few minor parades and such, but nothing particularly exciting. Here in Ojliam it seemed that they were going all out. They began to notice bunting being put up at squares and intersections. Nothing like this ever happened in Lugemall. Dorm suspected that his father would be horrified to have this much attention being paid to him.

It seemed that King Prinaz X was better regarded than he had previously believed. Perhaps his earlier assessment of the man was in error?

Ojliam city itself was a mix of different styles of building. One could see the older more solid looking buildings, with little or no decoration, but with an imposing façade that made itself important simply by being plain and unadorned; and the more modern, so-called 'reconstruction' era buildings, again resulting from the damage the great city suffered during the siege. It also seemed that in the intervening centuries some attempts at decoration had been made to liven things up. Squares had more statues and fountains, and some even had trees planted around their peripheries to brighten things up. One large square seemed even to have been ripped up and replaced with a small park complete with flowers and a small duck pond.

Despite all this the city still seemed very stuffy. And almost austere. It was as if the city was perpetually waiting for something cataclysmic to happen. As if they were expecting Imperial legions to come swooping over the hills at any moment.

Dorm felt a little sorry for the people. No one should have to live with that kind of underlying fear. Not a millennium after the event.

They wandered aimlessly for a few hours looking and listening. Nothing jumped out or presented itself as important, and they didn't see any sign of amulets. During their wanderings they had split into different groups to cover more ground and they had finally regrouped in a large market area near several large public buildings. Everyone was tired from all the walking they had done. And no one had anything to report.

"We thought for a moment that perhaps we had found something, but it turned out to be a dead end," Lianna was explaining. "It seems that some people around here aren't as observant as they might like to think."

"We even tried a few jewellery merchants," Artur added. "None of them had ever seen anything like our amulets."

"But they all offered us very good prices should we wish to sell them," Navista observed. "Vultures!" she spat contemptuously.

"Well it was a long shot as best I suppose," Dorm conceded. "No use us getting too depressed over it."

"So I guess now this means we just wander around aimlessly until whatever funny forces keep pushing us in the right direction, do so," Zacravia said dejectedly.

"Can we do that tomorrow though?" Pianwasal asked. "I'm not sure my feet want to try doing that today."

"She is a very intelligent woman," Travanos said. "I can see why they made her a Seneschal Priest."

"Why thank you, Admiral," she replied inclining her head to him.

It was Tissie who noticed them first. She quickly moved close into the group and almost whispered "Soldiers". Across the square a small group of armed men had entered the square they were in. They seemed to be looking for something. The crowd barely took any notice of them as they searched. Obviously soldiers on the streets was a fairly normal occurrence. Which was just as well. It probably meant no one would be suspecting them of being the targets.

"I think it might be a good idea to leave here," Mac suggested.

"See I keep telling you he's not just a pretty face," Telly said to Dorm seriously.

They began to drift apart. Taking a faked, but intense interest in some of the market stalls as they moved. The soldiers continued to search and continued to be ignored by the crowd. Dorm, Mac, Harmia and Rhyn wandered slowly towards a street that would take them back in the general direction of their inn. The others were equally close to other streets that would lead them to safety.

As they made ready to leave the square Dorm suddenly felt something grip his arm.

"Do not be alarmed Your Highness," said a quiet, almost threatening voice in his ear. "No harm will come to you or any of your friends."

"I'm not sure who you think I am," Dorm tried to bluff. "But if I owe you money I'm sure that we can…"

"Do not be silly with me Your Highness. We have been watching you for most of the day. I am not here to harm you. I am simply here to ask you some questions on behalf of His Majesty's government."

Dorm turned slowly to face the man who gripped his arm. He was a fairly nondescript person, the kind of face that would be seen and forgotten moments later. He wore dark clothing and a large floppy looking hat. He thin moustache did little to inspire confidence in him. He was neither rich looking nor poor. He was exactly the sort of ordinary person you would expect to see hundreds, if not thousands of on any given day.

"And what might those questions be about I wonder?" Dorm said slowly.

"Lets say the nature of your mission here in Ojliam," he replied.

"It isn't everyday that the heir to the throne of another country arrives unannounced in our little part of the world. We are understandably curious as to your motives here."

"Well I'm sure we can settle that rather quickly and then be on our way."

"Quite possible, Your Highness," said the man. His voice had taken on an almost oily timbre that Dorm really didn't like.

"My friends…"

"Are very welcome to accompany us," he said catching each of their eyes in turn. "In fact, I'd prefer that. Oh and don't worry about the rest of your friends. We have people talking to them as well. We find it very curious to know why you are travelling with such a… shall we say… diverse group of people."

"I'm sure you would," Mac piped up.

"Shall we?" said the man. He indicated the direction he wanted them to travel in.

"There's no use fighting this," Dorm said quietly to the others. "We seem to have been spotted. I'm sure they'll have people around here watching us. Let's just get this over with."

"Unfortunately I agree with you," Harmia concluded.

They were lead from the square. The crowd still hadn't noticed anything out of the ordinary.

Chapter 29

Dungeons had never really been Dorm's favourite place. He spent as little time as possible in the old dungeons at home. They were used so infrequently, and usually only when it was a matter of great secrecy.

Admittedly this wasn't exactly a dungeon. It was certainly below ground level and had that earthy damp smell that such places always posses, but this room was very well maintained, brightly lit, and was even furnished. Though admittedly that furniture consisted of a rather plain table and several equally plain wooden chairs.

There were no devices of torture or even of intimidation. In fact there was nothing really to suggest that this room was used for anything other than storage. Still the very fact that he and his companions had been snatched off the street and brought here made Dorm nervous.

The journey had been remarkably swift. They had been marched to a small building only a few streets away. There had been little opportunity to talk to any of the others, though they all exchanged worried glances. They were taken down a flight of stone steps at the rear of the building into a cellar. From there they went down another set of steps and found themselves in a long dark tunnel. After following this tunnel for some time they came to a large oak door banded with iron straps. Torches guttered on either side of it and it gave the impression of being the access to something rather important. On the other side were corridors, wider than the tunnel they had been following and better lit. They were taken to a large room, and left alone for barely a minute, before the man with the oily voice returned and had Dorm escorted to the room in which he now resided.

The oily man who had now removed his ridiculous looking hat, sat down in one of the chairs opposite Dorm and smiled at him with that sickly grin he had used all the way here. Dorm was almost at the point where he wanted to punch him in the face just to stop him smiling like that. But evidently he was now 'on duty' as his father always called it. So it was probably best not to do so.

"Thank you for being so co-operative, Your Highness," he said in that sickly pompous voice of his. His accent suggested he had travelled a lot, as it was considerably softer than the common people they had encountered.

"Think practically nothing of it, as my father would say," Dorm retorted with just a hint of cattiness. Well slightly more than a hint.

"Speaking of your father, how is he?"

"He's fine, thank you for asking."

"And what exactly has he sent you here to Ojliam to do for him?"

"Nothing. I am not here for my father."

"Then who are you here for?"

"Is it so unfathomable for you to think that a Prince of another country might simply want to take some time away from official duties to spend some quality time with people he cares about? To see the world and what it has to offer?"

"When he travels without any sort of escort and with such a diverse assortment of people... yes, actually."

"Well if I went around with a full escort, soldiers and trumpets blowing every time I went to step through a door, I never get any time to be with my friends. And I wouldn't see anything real. It would be all banquets and speeches and other assorted official nonsense."

"Then you say your job as heir to the throne of Lugemall is... boring?"

Dorm leaned forward. "You have no idea," he said quietly. "You try standing in a line greeting people you've never heard of who only want you to give them money, for hours on end. Or try having to stand in the bitter cold and remember a speech that everyone in a town square has to hear at an official ceremony in the middle of winter. Or try having no time what so ever to yourself because every three seconds there's someone wanting you to sign something of listen to someone or read some report."

The man smiled. "I'm sure it must be terrible."

"May I ask your name?" Dorm said slowly and with a hint of malice. "I mean, I think I deserve that much. To know who you are and what it is that you do."

The man lent back in his chair. "My name is Cavis. And I work for His Majesty's Intelligence Service."

"In other words you're a spy?"

"Well we don't like that term exactly, but some people call us that. We prefer to think of ourselves as patriots. Working for the greater good of our King, our country and the Alliance."

"Hmmmmm," was all Dorm could think of in reply.

"Your Highness," Cavis continued. "We are merely curious as to why such a prominent person should suddenly turn up in our country unannounced. And with such a strange group of people."

"Well I'm sorry to be unable to satiate your curiosity," Dorm told him. "But it's a private matter that has nothing to do with the security of Ojliam; or Lugemall for that matter."

"Why do I not believe you?"

"I have no idea."

From outside the room there was the sound of a commotion. A voice; male, could be heard arguing with someone, probably one of the guards they had seen upon entering. Cavis seemed slightly annoyed by the intrusion. His eyelid quivered slightly in annoyance, though this smirk remained firmly plastered to his face.

Quite suddenly the door burst open and a man wearing some rather fine looking clothes entered the room. He held himself tall, a bearing that indicated that he was confident of his position here and that those around him had better not try anything. There was almost an air of overconfidence about him. Dorm was beginning to think he wouldn't like this man any better than Cavis. He was vaguely familiar though. There was something about him that he recognised.

"Cavis," the man began. "What is going on here? You were asked to talk with him not arrest and interrogate him?"

Cavis quickly stood upon hearing the voice of the man. It was clear that this new comer was somehow Cavis' superior. "I assure you no harm has come to His Highness. He was never in any danger. And having the conversation here was better than having it in the street somewhere. Wouldn't you agree?"

"Perhaps," the new arrival said after a moment. "But there is a right way and a wrong way to interview a Prince. I'm afraid what you have done is bordering on the wrong way."

"Then I can only apologise, Your Highness," Cavis said bowing slightly.

Now it all made sense to Dorm. He had been right when he recognised the man's face. This was Prince Varain, the eldest son of King Prinaz and heir to Ojliam's throne. Now it all came back to him. He had only met him once or twice, and then only at official occasions, but he had always found the Ojlian Prince to be a little egotistical. And even a little arrogant. He was the heir, and he knew it. He thought that that entitled him to a little more leeway in getting things he wanted. Almost as if he deserved them. Dorm had never really liked him. He'd always thought that his younger brother Prince Kasiv would make a better king. He was quiet and sincere. He had a habit of listening a lot before speaking. Their sister Princess Yalann would also make a pretty good monarch. She wasn't very wise but she was thoughtful, and would probably make decisions that benefited more people than her eldest brother.

But of course the Ojlian succession was none of his business.

"Prince Dormal," Varain began earnestly. "Please accept our most humble apologies. On behalf of both myself and my father we sincerely regret this inconvenience to you and your friends."

"That's alright I suppose," Dorm said rising to stand slowly. "I realise that it was done for a… legitimate reason." He caught Cavis' eye as he said this. "And no harm was done."

"Then please, Your Highness. Let us leave this place and go somewhere where we can partake of wine and you can introduce me to your companions and tell me of your travels."

"Sounds like a great idea," Dorm replied.

He was almost sincere.

Prince Varain led Dorm through the lower levels of the palace and up many different flights of stairs before they finally reached an airy, decorated room, with large windows that looked out over the palace grounds. The floor was deeply carpeted and the room contained various furnishings that had a vaguely feminine touch.

"This is the Private Reception Room," Varain said by way of explanation. "The furnishings were chosen by my mother personally." He led Dorm to a small table and chairs near a set of large glassed doors that led to a small balcony. A soft breeze billowed the curtains and birds could be heard chirping in the distance.

Varain took a small bell from the table and rang it. It's clapping seemed hardly loud enough to be heard across the room, let alone into the next, but none-the-less a butler in an extravagant uniform appeared from a connecting door and waited.

"Would you bring wine and cheese for my self and some guests please," Varain said.

"Of course, Your Highness," replied the butler as he bowed rather deeply. He turned and left the room.

"Thank you," Varain responded as the man left. It sounded as if he almost meant it. "It is so strange to see you again after all these years. You are looking well." He sat down in a rather heavily upholstered chair.

"Thank you, as are you Varain," Dorm said conversationally, also sitting at Varain's invitation, not being quite sure where this was heading.

"Again I apologise for the way you were brought here. Cavis has a tendency to be a little zealous in his duties. Don't get me wrong, he does a wonderful job, but sometimes he forgets that the niceties are called for on occasion."

"It's quite alright. Will my companions be…"

"Oh yes. I sent instructions that they were to be brought here before I went to get you. They should be along very shortly." Varain paused for a moment. "I hope, Dormal, that we might have a chance to talk later on. There is something I might want your opinion on. If you would be willing to listen."

"I'm always willing to listing. I may not always be willing to do, but listening presents no problem."

"I am pleased."

There was a knock at the door. Another ornately dressed butler entered and announced to Varain, "Your Highness, the companions of Prince Dormal, as you requested."

"Ah yes, thank you Rugets," Varain said standing.

Rugets stepped to one side opening the door widely, as Dorm's friends entered. All of them looked relieved to see him and also to be away from where ever it was that they were kept while Dorm was with Cavis.

"My, there are quite a lot of you aren't there," Varain said as they kept on entering. "Such a myriad of companions Dormal. You must introduce me to them."

"Of course. Everyone this is His Royal Highness Prince Varain, heir to the throne of Ojliam." The group responded with mutterings of 'Your Highness', and a few bows and curtsies. Dorm then proceeded to introduce everyone in turn. He made Artur, Ameks, Navista, Zacravia, Ambra and even Cal seem a little more important, by grandiose sounding descriptions of what they did. Varain was not in touch enough with the common man to know the difference.

The wine and cheese arrived soon after, and Varain instructed the butler to return with some more since he hadn't expected quite so many people. They spent the next hour or so chatting about nothing in particular and doing what they could to avoid giving away their real reason for being in Ojliam to the Prince. The use of 'possible future commercial opportunities for the Alliance' seemed to work well enough once Dorm 'explained' that he was doing this for his father and Corm Sanel who were reluctant to have information of it get out in case it wasn't workable. Varain seemed to understand that, at least partially. And he didn't push it any further.

Varain also seemed to be very smitten with the ladies in their group. Tissie seemed most taken with him and even if she didn't know it, was doing a wonderful job of distracting the Prince from their real reason for being here, simply by her presence. She also seemed to be tossing her hair about more than usual. Dorm began to wonder if she was doing it consciously or not.

The afternoon was getting late, and after some insistence they finally managed to leave the Palace. Varain had wanted them to stay in the Palace and meet the rest of the royal family, but they were able to convince him that it wouldn't be fair to the proprietor of the inn, to whom they had already paid money.

Varain did insist on sending several guards with them so that he would know which inn it was and could find them the next day. It seemed he hadn't forgotten about talking to Dorm privately after all.

They returned to the inn through the gradually darkening streets, and took dinner in the inn's common room.

"Can we not see that man again?" Rhyn said as they ate. "I found him insufferable."

"I found him quite charming," Tissie said in the Prince's defence.

"You would," Mac muttered under his breath.

"He wos a bit... forward, with you ladies wosn't he?" Cal concurred.

"He was a little chauvinist, wasn't he," Telly agreed.

"Well I'm afraid we may not have much of a choice," Dorm explained. "Apparently he wants to discuss something with me."

"Any idea what?" Artur asked.

"No," Dorm admitted. "But I get the feeling it's something personal."

"I hate to think what that might be," Harmia said quietly.

"I assure you, I will try to keep most of you out of it, whatever it is."

"Tell him we aren't feeling well," Lianna suggested. "If we have to spend any more time with him, it will have the virtue of being true."

The next morning several of the Palace guard had arrived to escort them back. They were still in the process of getting ready so the guards were forced to wait. Dorm told them that only a few of them would be coming along as the others were either not feeling well, helping those who were not feeling well, or had some of their "mission" to complete. The guards accepted this at face value, though Dorm suspected they had hardly even listened to him.

There was some arguing as to who would go to the Palace. Dorm couldn't blame them for not wanting to go and have to put up with Varain all day, but it would look strange if only he turned up. In the end Dorm was accompanied by Mac, Lianna, Ambra and Pianwasal, who for some reason was actually interested in coming along.

The trip back to the great edifice of political power in Ojliam was swift and uneventful. Dorm suspected this had something to do with both the guards and the Royally crested coach in which they were made to ride.

Varain met them in one of the large echoing vestibules, and escorted them up the large marble steps to his private 'audience chamber'. Dorm felt the Prince having his own audience chamber was nothing short of pretentious. The room pleasantly wasn't that big. Dorm had worried it would be big enough to fit Varains' ego, but it turned out to be a rather simple affair. Varain had a large chair and desk at one end of the room behind which was a large shield emblazoned with the Ojlian coat of arms. A number of plush chairs sat around the outside of the room, presumably for those petitioners, who actually came to see him. There were a number of chairs near smaller desks behind the Prince's own.

Varain indicated for them to all sit where they pleased and he sat at his desk and tried to look relaxed. "I'm glad you could come." He began. "And I hope the others are feeling well soon."

"I'm sure they will be, Your Highness," Mac said before Dorm could respond.

Dorm shot him a glance before continuing. "I'm sure it's just something they ate."

"Good." Varain replied almost sincerely. "Your mission sounds important. I would hate for anything to disrupt it."

"Thank you."

"Dormal, I wish to ask you a personal question if I may."

"Of course."

"I wonder if I might get your opinion on something? Or rather some*one*?" He paused for a moment. "It is a little delicate though."

"I see," Dorm began cautiously. "What does it involve?"

"There is someone I am interested in," the Prince began.

"Someone I could one day see as my Queen." He looked at Dorm seriously for a moment. "But I am having trouble getting together with this woman. For some reason she is always unavailable. I do not understand it."

"Perhaps she isn't interested, Your Highness?" Pianwasal said innocently.

Varain looked at her sharply. "Not interested? In me?!" Varain was quite genuine as he said this. It was obvious that he couldn't fathom of such a thing. "I am the Prince of Ojliam. The future king. I am proposing to make her my Queen in time. What is there not to be interested in?"

"Well, Your Highness…" Pianwasal began to explain.

"What is it that you want me to do Varain?" Dorm cut her off. The last thing they needed was for Varain to get into a shouting match with them. Pianwasal looked at him sharply, but with a hint of confusion on her face.

"I would like perhaps for you to come with me when I go to see her later today. I think I would like the perspective of someone such as yourself. A man of the world. A man with intelligence." A compliment? From Varain?

"Well I'm not sure what to say," Dorm said. He had no real desire or intention of helping Varain catch a woman who clearly wasn't interested in him.

The main door to the room opened and a tall, thin man wearing a formal doublet and hose entered. His boots were expensively tailored and it was clear that he was someone of importance.

"Yes Scanvis, what is it?"

"Something from His Majesty's office that you need to read, Your Highness." Scanvis noticed the others in the room seemingly for the first time.

"His Highness Prince Dormal of Lugemall, and his companions," Varain introduced them. "This is Scanvis the liason between mine and my fathers offices."

"Your Highness," Scanvis bowed towards Dorm. "Ladies, Gentlemen," he nodded to the others.

"Please excuse me for a few moments, everyone," Varain said

standing and moving round his desk. "This shouldn't take too long. Affairs of state you understand."

"Of course," Dorm said with a smile.

Varain and Scanvis left the room.

"I have a headache," Mac said quietly to the room at large.

"Do we really have to put up with this?" Lianna burst out. "He wants us to play matchmaker for him?"

"The things we do for quests," Ambra said under his breath.

"Look I don't like it any more than you do," Dorm admitted. "But the quicker we say yes, the happier he'll be and the quicker we can get it over with. And then the sooner we can leave him for good."

"You seriously want to do this?" Lianna asked him angrily.

"Not in the slightest, but we don't have any choice. Besides, how do we know this won't lead somewhere we want it too?"

Lianna thought about that for a moment. It was a possibility. They had certainly been lead to things before. It would just be nice to know it before these things cropped up. If it wasn't going to lead somewhere, they really didn't have time for it. Lianna looked at Pianwasal who indicated that she was willing to take a gamble on it.

"Ambra? What about you?"

"As much as I hate the idea of traipsing all over the countryside with that man... I guess we have no choice."

"Alright then. We'll go see this woman, and try to convince her to save herself the trouble of marrying Varain. Then we can get on with this."

Once Varain had returned they informed him that while it wasn't what they had intended and they didn't have a great deal of time, they would be willing to help. At least for a short while. The Prince seemed pleased with this and arranged for horses to be made ready for their journey. He showed Dorm a map of the area and indicated the small village not far from the city that they were now going off to. He explained that there were many farms in the area, and the village was were the farmers lived. Dorm was taken a little aback by this. He had expected this woman to be a rich merchants daughter at the least. If not then a low ranking member of the peerage. But a commoner? This seemed too incredible for Varain.

After a short wait they were taken down to the stables and mounted the horses. Dorm was given a large roan mare to ride, who's name was apparently Relann. Relann proved to be a good horse, if a little impatient. Though perhaps that could just have been Dorm and his friends.

They travelled with a small escort of guards lead by one Captain Nikaan. He seemed quite capable, but gave a clear indication when the Prince announced their destination and mission, that this was not the first time he had made this trip. Also it seemed he was as enthused about it all as were Dorm and his friends.

Their journey through the city was again uneventful, though it took longer than before due to the larger volume of traffic they had to negotiate their way through at this later hour. But finally they left the inner walls and passed through the inter-wall zone and then left the city altogether. The weather was cool, there were quite a few clouds in the sky but it seemed likely there would be no rain. They passed again through the memorial gardens. As they had left by a different gate these memorials were ones they had not previously seen. Varain pointed out some of them to his companions as they rode. Commenting about which country they came from and the like.

At one point they came across one that had a group of workmen around it. They seemed to be tending the gardens and washing and polishing the stonework of the spire itself.

"Memorial Keepers," Varain said by way of explanation. "They are employed to tend the gardens and maintain the spires themselves. It is a very important job. In Ojliam we regard it as a sacred duty to maintain these memorials. And as such the Keepers are highly regarded in our country. And I must say they do a magnificent job."

Now this was unexpected. Varain was civil, even nice. And his words about the Memorial Keepers seemed genuinely felt. Perhaps there was more to the Ojlian Prince than Dorm had previously believed.

They paused for a few moments to take some water and watch the men working on the memorial. As they were going to leave, Varain doffed his hat to the memorial, as a mark of respect. He noticed the soldiers guarding them bowed their heads slightly. His companions took note of these acts as well, and so they responded in kind. Perhaps there was much more to this situation than they had first thought.

They moved on.

They rode on through the remainder of the memorial gardens before passing into an area of undeveloped land. Shortly after that they began to notice ploughed fields and short stone walls traversing the undulating landscape. It almost felt like home to Dorm. There was a certain familiar quality to it all.

After about half an hour of this farmland they entered what appeared to be a forest. Dorm didn't recall any forests on his map and asked Varain about it.

"It's a planted forest," he explained. "All the trees here were planted specially to help protect the village. Many of our smaller forests were destroyed during the Second Peldraksekhr Invasion. These replacement ones were planted to break up the landscape. Apparently it has benefits to cropping and grazing to have trees every so often."

Dorm made a mental note to investigate that one day.

The trees did not last long however as they came to a large open space. Clearing was not the right word, as this 'clearing' contained a large village. This was their destination. The village was apparently called Greznick, and had a population of about a hundred or so. Of course they were only here to see one person.

They rode through what could be called the main street of the village, only because it contained the most shops, as well as three taverns. The buildings were all constructed of a drab looking grey wood that gave the whole place a very depressing look. The whole thing should have been accompanied by a rain storm in order to complete the atmosphere. The villagers themselves wore fairly normal peasant clothing for Ojliam, and there were splashes of bright colours here and there. Almost as if they consciously were trying to compensate for the blandness of their surroundings.

Varain and his men lead them across to the other side of town and approached a large building that was surrounded by a spacious verandah. They noticed a few old men sitting quietly on chairs near the door smoking pipes and watching them intently. Dorm felt only slightly conspicuous, rather like he had turned up to a banquet naked, and turned to Varain.

"Now what?" he asked.

"This way," Varain replied turning his horse towards the rear of the building.

At the back there were several other smaller buildings. One was clearly a stable, and the others appeared to be warehouses or stores. They stopped their horse and waited for a moment.

"Well Nikaan?" Varain said after a minute or twos' silence, with a certain impatience in his voice.

"Yes, Your Highness," Nikaan sighed. He got down off his horse, straightened his clothes and walked calmly, and it seemed only slightly hesitantly, towards a door in the back of the main building. He stood for a moment then knocked.

There was no answer.

He knocked again.

After several more seconds, the door was reefed open and a large man with a dark bead appeared. "Yes?" he asked suspiciously.

"I'm sorry to disturb you sir," Nikaan said to him. "But I wonder if the Maiden Kanilma is in residence at the moment."

"In residence?" the man replied.

"Is she here?" Nikaan rephrased.

"Unfortunately for her, yes," he said taking in the group of soldiers that were in attendance. If he recognised the Prince he made no indication so. Though Dorm suspected this was well and truly not the first time this had happened.

"Would it be possible to speak with her?" said Nikaan again. "I bring a message from his Highness Prince Varain."

"Of course you do," the bearded man replied. "Let me go and see if she will deign to speak to you and his highness."

He disappeared back inside all but slamming the door behind him.

There was some muffled yelling for a minute or two before the man again poked his head out of the door.

"She's just coming," he said to Nikaan pleasantly. "Just give her a moment or two more."

Before the captain could respond the door was shut in his face. He looked back to the Princes. "Won't be long, Your Highness," he said unconvincingly.

There was another minute or two of muffled yelling before the door opened and the man returned. With him came two women. One was leading the other. The woman leading had blonde hair was tall and indeterminately aged, but carried herself with an air of someone who has lived a full life and knows what is what.

The other woman was younger. She had dark hair and was quite pleasant looking, despite the smudges of flour and such on her cheeks and brow. Her hair was pulled back from her neck and had a subtle curl to it that reminded Dorm of both Telly and Rhyn's hair.

She stood tall and full, but the look on her face was one of extreme annoyance. That is to say murderous anger. Dorm quickly realised that this woman would be the object of Varain's affection. They could see why. She was certainly pleasing to the eye, and seemed to have a level of confidence far higher than someone her age should have possessed. Varain was kidding himself if he thought that this woman could seriously like a man such as he.

"Miss Kanilma," Nikaan said bowing his head to her. "I give you greetings from His Highness Prince Varain of Ojliam. He seeks and audience with you to discuss certain possibilities for the two of you to get better acquainted."

"Oh does he just," Kanilma replied. Her voice was also very attractive. It was full and rich and had a quality that made her easy to listen to. Dorm got that just from one sentence. "Well you can tell his Royal pain in the Highness, that as usual I am not interested. I have never had an interest in what he has been trying to sell to me, for the past two years, and I am not likely to suddenly want it in the near future."

Varains face went red. It was clear that he was crushed. Dorm almost felt sorry for him. "Mistress Kanilma," he began haltingly from his saddle. "I have come in person this time. I had hoped that we might talk."

Kanilma paused for a moment. It was clear she hadn't expected him to turn up in person. And for a brief second Dorm noticed confusion on her face. Could it be that she was at least flattered that the Prince had taken the time to come here himself?

"Well that's all very well," she began haltingly. "But… but I'm still not interested. I thank you for the offer but it isn't wanted. Now if you'll excuse me I have buns to tend to."

She whirled around and went back inside the door. Dorm watched her go in surprise. He hadn't expected this to be the case. He looked across at Mac and Lianna who both carried a look of happy confusion on their faces. Ambra and Pianwasal also looked at them.

"This is getting too strange," Pianwasal said under her breath.

The other two people who had come out with Kanilma had been apologising to Varain for her outburst. But at no time did they say anything about her not meaning it.

Varain simply sat on his horse stunned. It was clear that he had never been spoken to like that before, except perhaps by his parents, and that he was upset and confused. He probably felt like he had done everything right. Been honest and open with her. Why hadn't it worked?

Dorm sidled his horse over to the Prince's.

"Varain," he said quietly to him. "Perhaps you'd like my help after all?"

"Anything Dormal," Varain replied a little stricken.

"Well if you'd like my friends and I could talk to her. Perhaps some sort of compromise could be reached. Or at least an understanding."

"What do you mean?"

"Well it's clear she doesn't want to marry you. But perhaps we could talk to her and at least get her to sit down and talk with you."

"If you could, there's be a barony in it for you," Varain replied seriously.

"Well I already have a kingdom. I'm not sure what I'd do with a foreign barony."

"Of course. I'm sorry. I don't know what I'm saying. If you can talk to her. Please do."

Dorm looked at the others and nodded. "Show time," he said quietly as he passed them on his way to the door. They dismounted and knocked quietly. After a moment the door was again reefed violently open and the bearded man stood there.

"WHAT!! he yelled at them as the door flew open. "Oh I'm sorry," he said when he realised it was different people.

"That's quite alright. I'm wondering if it might be possible to talk with yourself and Mistress Kanilma, was it?"

"That's her name, yes," the man said cautiously. "What about?"

"Something we'd prefer not to discuss out in the street," Mac said. "Or whatever you call this area out here."

The bearded man thought carefully for a moment scratching at his whiskers.

"I can assure you it's not directly related to what Prince Varain is here about," Dorm explained.

"In fact it will even help her get away from him if we do it right," Lianna put in hopefully.

The man's face brightened considerably at this point. "Why didn't you say so in the first place. Come in please."

He ushered them into the building and closed the door behind them. The room turned out to be a large kitchen. A large stone arched fireplace stood along one wall with several pots heating in the fire. Benches and tables sat around the room, cluttered with various utensils and dishes and even ingredients. The two women stood on the other side of the room glaring at them as a group.

"So what is it you want?" the older of the women said.

"Sorry what was your name?" Dorm asked her.

"Lianka," she replied. This is my husband Gossan. We own the inn."

"And Kanilma is…"

"Our ward," Lianka replied. "She is the daughter of our closest friends, who we opened this inn with nearly twenty years ago."

"I'm sorry your parents are not around Miss Kanilma."

"So what is it that you want to say?" Kanilma said haughtily.

"We have a proposal to put to you. One that may help you."

"What sort of a proposal?" she asked suspiciously.

"A proposal to help you avoid the Prince. At least for a time."

"And it has the benefit of helping us as well," Lianna said quietly.

"How is that?" Gossan asked

"Well that's a long story and we probably shouldn't go into it right now with the Prince outside the door, but suffice it to say, it has to do with that amulet you wear."

Everyone looked at her amulet, then at her.

Dorm and his friends just smiled.

Chapter 30

"What about it?" was the cautious response.

Dorm had to laugh to himself. What about it indeed, he thought as he extricated his own amulet from where it had become hidden during their ride to the village. The others did the same, and very shortly the three people in the room had the beginnings of an inkling of what might have been the issue.

"That's interesting," Gossan said quietly.

"And these aren't the only ones," Mac said.

"Now comes the interesting part. Explaining them. These amulets have something to do with The Fortress. What exactly we don't know but they are important. There is a group of us. The five of us here, plus others who are back in Ojliam. We appear to be on a quest…"

"A quest?" asked Lianaka incredulously. "That's ridiculous."

"Yes of course it is," Dorm agreed. "But it's the truth none the less."

"We all had the same reaction, trust me," Lianna admitted.

"Basically what the amulet tells us is that you are one of the people we are looking for," Dorm explained further. "And we need you to come with us."

"On this… quest?" Kanilma asked slowly.

"That's right," Lianna told her.

"And where are we going?"

"Oh everywhere probably," Mac suggested whimsically.

"Now I know all of this is coming to you as a sudden surprise, but we don't have a lot of time. We are hoping to be gone from the city in a few days at most. And you will have to come with us."

"Just like that?" Lianka said with a hint of steel in her voice. "I'm not sure I like the idea of her going off around the world with you, no matter who you claim to be."

"Madam," Dorm began cautiously. This was the delicate part. "We have no choice. Something very important is happening. Kanilma is a part of that whether she likes it or not. She can no more escape it than the rest of us."

Their faces did not seem entirely convinced.

"She will be quite safe, of that I can assure you. She is too important to let any harm come to her."

"And given the various members of our group, I'm not sure how much harm could come to her," Pianwasal reassured them. "There is great skill in the people we travel with."

"I know this is all very confusing, and strange and weird, and you really have no reason to trust us. But if you come along with us, it's going to get you away from the Prince for months. Maybe even longer. That has to be worth something to you?"

She paused for a moment, twirling one stray strand of hair absently around with her fingers as she thought. Her brow creased slightly as she stood there lost within her mind and its own ministrations. Finally she slowly lifted her gaze to look at them directly.

"I think I want to trust you," she said quietly.

"Kanilma?!" Gossan said moving over to her and taking her by the shoulders. "Are you sure about this?"

"No not at all," she confided to him. "But at the same time, I'm totally sure. I know somehow that I am making the right choice."

Gossan and Lianaka exchanged a look that only parents could swap and both hugged her tightly.

"If you're sure," Lianka said quietly.

Kanilma gave Dorm and the others a look of confidence in her choice.

This was new. Usually people had been very reluctant to join them. Perhaps it had something to do with the situation with Varain?

"So when do we leave?" Kanilma asked them.

"Well that's a good question?" Lianna said. "Do we take her with us now?"

"With Prince Varain outside?" Ambra posed. "I don't think that will go down too well."

"He's right," Mac agreed. "First he'll think we've succeeded in wooing her for him, then we have to come up with some reason why that isn't the case and why she has to leave the country with us."

"Good point," Dorm conceded. "He'll think one of us is stealing her away from him."

"Could we not say," Pianawasal began after a moment. "That we have talked to her and pointed out some positive points to the situation, but that she wanted a few days to think about it all? Then we could return to the city with the Prince, and leave in a day. Come back here and collect her. When the Prince enquires after her, say she has gone off for a few weeks to make up her mind permanently. It could at least give us enough time to get clear of him."

"That's a brilliant idea," Dorm agreed. "Are you two willing to play your parts?" he said then to Lianka and Gossan.

They looked at each other for a moment, and then at Kanilma. "I think we could do that." Lianka concluded.

"It's not every day that one has to lie to one's Prince but… " Gossan sighed. "It is for a good cause I suppose."

"Are you serious when you said it has something to do with The Fortress?" Lianka asked them.

"Yes. I am. I know that sounds bad, but something gives me hope. As if, it wont be what we expect."

They settled their plans to try and collect Kanilma the day after tomorrow from the inn in the early hours of the morning. Hopefully that way there would be less people about to see them and upset their plan. They said their temporary goodbyes and then went back outside to face the Prince.

Varain was waiting patiently, or perhaps impatiently on his horse for their return. The soldiers milled about in a generally bored fashion, waiting to be told what to do.

"Well?" Varain demanded once they had returned to him. "What happened?"

"We talked," Dorm said to him. That was at least true. "She was resistant at first. But we explained a few things to her that she may not have considered previously."

"And then?"

"She seemed more receptive then," Lianna told him earnestly.

"I think perhaps you came on much too strong, Varain," Dorm told the Prince. "She seems a woman who wants to make up her own mind, not be pressured into anything."

"Then my coming to see her would not have helped." This was remarkably insightful for one such as Varain.

"No, not really."

"Then I must go and apologise, and explain to her my reasons." He started forward.

Dorm grabbed his shoulder and halted him. "I wouldn't do that Varain," he said. "She said she was going to take a few days to think about everything. I would stay away for a good week before I tried to talk to her again. You could even wait for her to come to you."

Varain thought on this for a moment. "Perhaps you are right," he said slowly. "I should let her think for a little while."

"Good idea," Dorm agreed. He glanced at the others, who all shared a look of relief.

Varain sat for a few moments staring at the building lost in thought. "I believe our time here has been well spent. Thank you Dormal. I appreciate your help."

"You're welcome," Dorm told him sincerely.

"We should return to the palace now. I have much work to do."

He turned his horse and began to walk away. The soldiers and Captain Nikaan also turned their horses and followed. Dorm and his friends remounted their own horses.

"Well we've given ourselves a window, let's make sure we use it well," Dorm said to them.

"How will we get word to Kanilma of which day it will be?" Ambra asked.

"There should be a courier or something we can find in the city," Dorm suggested.

"We can easily send a simple note. Just in case it gets intercepted keep it to one or two words," Lianna speculated earnestly.

"All this deception," Pianwasal said. "I do not believe it is good for us."

"Oh haven't you always wanted to live a little, Pianwasal?" Mac joked with her.

As they moved off Dorm noticed a small face watching them from the window. He nodded to it as they rode away.

The journey back to the city was again uneventful. Varain told Dorm how he now felt positively about the future and was looking forward to the time when he and Kanilma could sit down and talk about everything. He began sketching in a fairly rough plan to Dorm, of how he wanted to bring her to the palace and have dinner. He thought it would be romantic. Dorm suggested that perhaps he might think of something a little more simpler. Like perhaps going to her inn to have a meal. After he had asked her permission of course.

He seemed to like the idea, and even began to smile a little as he thought about it. Hopefully that will delay things a little longer, Dorm thought to himself.

Once they arrived back in the city the peace and quiet of the countryside was lost and the hustle and bustle returned. It was mid-afternoon now and so there was much to-ing and fro-ing, as people began to prepare for the evening meal, and whatever they were doing that night. Dorm noticed that there were more banners for the King's Birthday celebration flying. He now realised that they would probably have to attend some official function. Dorm really didn't want to have to see King Prinaz but was beginning to suspect that there wouldn't be much choice.

Varain and his men escorted them back to their inn, where they gave the horses back and thanked them for their use. The Ojlian prince seemed quite pleased with the outcome of the day and rode off in the direction of the palace with a smile on his face, chatting pleasantly with Captain Nikaan.

Once back inside the inn they almost flew up the stairs to their rooms to find the others patiently waiting to hear all.

"So how did you do today?" Telly said as they entered.

"Oh we did all right," Mac said suggestively.

"And what exactly does that mean?"

"Well we managed to solve a lovers tiff," Mac went on to explain. "Provided ourselves with a few days of room to leave the city so the Prince wont be following us. We found the next quester… oh and we may have gotten an invite to a party at the palace."

"You found the next quester?" Rhyn said standing quickly.

"Who is it?" Artur asked quickly.

"A young woman who works in an inn at one of the satellite villages to the city. Her name is Kanilma," Dorm told them with a grin on his face.

"Well that's wonderful news," Tissie exclaimed giving a little jump. "Is she here?"

"No, we couldn't bring her with us just yet," Dorm began to explain.

"Yes you see there's a slight problem…"

"Slight?" Ambra said. "I think you mean enormous."

"Well, maybe a bit bigger than slight," Mac responded.

"Would one of you like to explain what that means?" Travanos said patiently.

"It seems that Prince Varain is smitten on her," Dorm told them.

"Oh."

"Yes. He seems to like her very much, only he's been making a mess of things lately. But I think we have managed to smooth things over for the moment. We've told her that we will collect her early on the morning we leave. We just have to figure out when that is."

"Well I don't think it will be any time soon," Harmia said pessimistically. "These King's Birthday celebrations look like they will be fairly intense. It might not be possible to get out when they are on."

"Well that brings us back to the party we may have been invited to," Dorm explained. "Varain is hosting the private party for the King in the palace, and he seems to want us to attend."

"Oh how drab," Telly sighed.

"Drab indeed," Zacravia said then. "But possibly just the thing we need."

"How so? Telly asked him.

"Well presumably there will be a lot of people there. If we make a show of going, and getting roaringly drunk, people will suspect us less. Especially if we all go traipsing back off to our inn. They will all be too hung over the next morning to care less about us. We could use that to get out of the city without any one issuing orders to stop us."

"Good idea," Dorm agreed. "But if we get roaringly drunk…"

"Well we wont *actually* get drunk of course. We all only have to drink enough to make it look like we are. To make our acting believable. We can eat lots and drink plenty of water, that should keep us sober enough. Provided we circulate enough, no *one* person will be able to keep track of what we're not drinking."

They all considered it. "Could work," Dorm concluded.

"It's the only idea we have so it had better," Rhyn said sarcastically.

"Next question," Cal said putting his hand up. "'ow do we let 'er know that we're comin'?"

"I think I can take care of that too," Zacravia said. "I may already have made contact with some, shall we say, less reputable elements here in Ojliam. I'm sure one of them could be persuaded to carry a short message to this village."

"Trust a criminal?" Harmia said shocked. "What kind of fools do you think we are?"

"I assure you my dear, if we find the right people, they can be trusted."

"Well since we can't really go using any official channels, it may have to be what we do. She already knows what she has to do. The message only has to be one or two words. That shouldn't be too hard."

"Wow, that got settled pretty quickly," Mac said.

"I just hope it wasn't too quickly," Ambra wondered out loud.

"You're getting depressing again my friend," Mac told him.

Ambra grinned.

They tried to spend a quiet night in the inn. Everyone wanted to know about their trip to Greznik, and what the new member of their group was like. There were many questions, only some which they could answer, but everyone seemed positive. At least they had managed to locate her. Now they just had to find the man.

They took their meal in the common room again where a group of travelling singers sang various songs from across the alliance on several instruments. They were actually very good. Dorm often found that these sort of travelling minstrels could do with a few days more practise before they gave their performances.

This group, which seemed to consist of a family played rather well, and had fairly good singing voices, which helped considerably. They had a relaxed style that encouraged everyone to join in.

As they sat and sang and laughed, Dorm watched the faces of his companions. It was rare to see them all quite so relaxed. Their journey had a certain stress to it. No one quite sure what was around the next bend, or at the next village. That constant tension was wearing on everyone. He fully realised that. But so far they had crossed almost the entire Alliance and had found all the people they were supposed to. They had that to be proud of that.

After they had retired for the night, Dorm and Mac lay half asleep in the dark. The night was chill and the blankets were pulled up close.

"So where to now do you think?" Mac asked him.

"North I suppose," Dorm responded resignedly. "We know we have to go to Bydanushev eventually. Seems sensible to head in that general direction."

" It still seems like we're being led around by the nose," Mac sighed heavily snuggling in closer against the night chill.

"I know," Dorm replied hugging him closer. "But I don't know that there's much more we can do. These amulets seem to be in control of things."

"Stoopid amulets," Mac said poutily.

Dorm laughed in spite of himself. "They are serving a purpose I suppose. Even if they are leading us on a merry chase."

"So King's Birthday tomorrow huh? Do we have to get Prinaz a present?"

"Oh I think the presence of the Lugemallan heir and his consort should be all the present he'll need."

"You are a bit of a present, that's true."

"Awww thanks you."

"Oh this means we're going to have to go put on a bunch a finery, aren't we?" Mac suddenly said dejectedly.

"I should think so. What's the matter?"

"Oh they always make them out of materials that make my skin itch like mad," Mac complained. "I end up spending the whole night scratching. Then my skin goes all red and blotchy and you won't come anywhere near me. You know what I'm like after a party."

"Yes I have noticed," Dorm replied with an evil chuckle.

Mac opened his eyes and fixed Dorm with a very direct stare. "Why do you think I try to get you to have more parties?" he said huskily with a wicked grin.

Dorm returned the grin.

Things went on from there.

The next day was a good day weatherwise, which was probably just as well given that there would be celebrations going on all over the country. After they had eaten they went out into the street to join with the growing crowd to wait for a parade of some sort. When it arrived, almost an hour later, it turned out to be a large number of Ojlian troops dressed in their full regalia. They were very impressive, and kept perfect time with the large band that followed them.

After the parade they wandered into the nearby square. Here were the usual markets, though Dorm noticed that their prices seemed a little higher than yesterday. No doubt in all the patriotic fervour they hoped people wouldn't notice. There were also several small stages set up around the square upon which different performances were occurring. One had a group of musicians; described by Lianna as 'homely', tootling and strumming their way through songs that were apparently popular in the city at the moment. On another was a rather scaled down performance of "The Trial of the Fairy King" which seemed to always be performed on monarchs day celebrations throughout the Alliance. Dorm watched it for a while but had to leave after the beginning of the famous scene between the fairy king and his daughter. He was beginning to think that it was a good thing that Vebis had died more than fifteen hundred years ago. If he had seen his play being put through this…

After lunch they headed back to their inn, and rested. They knew that come mid-afternoon, there would be messengers sent from the Palace and after that they would be whisked away. Zacravia reported that while they had been out he had managed, after some effort to make contact with someone who could help them deliver their message to Kanilma.

"What do you mean effort?" Artur wanted to know.

"Well there are certain signals that one can give when one wants to contact certain people," Zacravia explained. "But it seems that the people here in Ojliam are a little rusty. It took nearly four hours for any one to contact me. I don't think they appreciated my criticisms either."

"What happened after you finally met someone?" Dorm asked.

"Well after they realised that they were not the person I wanted to speak to," the thief went on. "I was lead, and lead, and lead some more just for good measure, to finally meet the person who could do what we needed. After I explained what it was we wanted, and why we wanted it done this way, he agreed."

"So who was this person?" Harmia said carefully.

Zacravia laughed slyly. "Oh Senior Constable, a very good try. But no prize today I'm afraid. The less said about who they are, the better for all concerned. Trust me on this."

Harmia opened her mouth to say something but thought better of it.

"So the message will be delivered today?" Telly asked him.

"Yes indeed," he confirmed. "In fact it's probably already halfway there. She will receive it soon and know what to do."

"Well then I think that we are all set to go to this rotten party," Dorm sighed.

"Oh I'm sure you'll liven up once you get there," Telly told him. "You always do at parties."

"Well this one will be a little different. There wont be much time for relaxing afterwards. When we leave it will be straight back here, get our things and go. Which reminds me, have we looked at the gate opening times?"

"Yes, Ambra and I took care of that," Travanos said. "The

northern gate will be opening an hour before sunrise promptly. Apparently there are several large shipments that come in at that time."

"Good then we can leave at that time head north till we are out of sight then swing around to the east, pick up Kanilma and go back again."

"Are we all going to go pick her up?"

"No I think just those of us that saw her yesterday should go. Give her a bit more time to adjust to what is happening. If she is even there of course."

"You think she might not come?" Navista asked him seriously.

"It's a possibility," he admitted. "We are asking a lot of her."

"All of us have been asked a lot of. But we are all still here," Rhyn said. "I think she will be there, and that we are worrying over nothing."

"Let's hope so."

Right on schedule a messenger arrived with several troops as escorts to collect their group for the King's party. They arrived at the palace shortly after and were ushered into a small chamber to tidy up and make themselves more presentable. Several ladies in waiting and valets fussed over them, adjusting this and tightening that. And all the while muttering under their breaths that their clothes just weren't suitable for such an occasion.

No one was going to be changing of course. Everyone's clothes were respectable enough. Dorm donned his formal grey doublet and high boots, and made sure that his sword hilt had been given and extra bit of polish. Travanos looked his usual imperial self in his full dress uniform, and Cal had even gone to the trouble of making sure his palace guard uniform was shining. He was after all officially representing his king and country.

The women of course all looked rather radiant in their dresses. Harmia had insisted on wearing her own uniform, which wasn't unexpected, but the ladies in waiting had spruced her up a bit nonetheless, by elaborately doing her hair and make-up. Even Zacravia commented on her appearance.

All this took only about an hour, but seemed like it had been days.

Just as everyone was starting to get restless, and more than a little peeved at the various bodies that were fussing over them, they were ushered into another chamber where various other guests were waiting. Many ladies in finery, and men in uniform milled around talking. Most cast curious glances in their direction, but made no move to talk to them. Dorm made a show of studying the various artworks on the walls of the room. Large paintings of past Ojlian kings and queens. A tapestry or two depicting a famous battle, most probably the Battle of Ojliam, and even the odd bust, of people Dorm didn't recognise, and probably wasn't likely to, even after hearing their names.

At last however Prince Varain entered the chamber and moved slowly through the crowd greeting everyone. Shaking some hands, and kissing others. He was very polite and dignified. Finally he arrived at their group and greeted Dorm loudly and warmly. There were a few shocked looks from people, but that didn't last very long, as Varain swept them all into the main ballroom. Here there were already a large number of guests. Many were dancing to the waltz-like music that was being played by the small orchestra in one corner of the room. On the dais at the other end sat King Prinaz X, sovereign of Ojliam. He was a fairly tall, and wiry man in his late fifties or so with a reddish brown, but greying close cropped beard. His crown perched almost angrily on his head, and despite the festivities being held in his honour, right in front of him, he seemed almost to glower angrily over the room.

Dorm seriously hoped he wouldn't have to talk to the King at all, or at least beyond the necessary niceties for the maintenance of good diplomatic relations.

Queen Hessefah sat nearby in a flowing pale pink dress and light lace. She at least smiled to the people who were talking to her. She seemed a much happier person, and Dorm began to wonder how the two of them had ended up together.

Varain took their group on a whirlwind tour of the room, introducing them to everyone and everything it seemed.

As the night wore on, and they all began their charade of pretending to drink heavily, Dorm received more requests for meetings with just about every Margrave and Archduke in Ojliam. None of which he intended to follow up on. But Varain seemed only too happy to put him in front of yet another member of the Ojlian peerage to go through it all again.

Varain.

He was beginning to be a bit of a problem. No matter what Dorm did to try and get away from him the prince would find him again. If Dorm didn't find a way to separate himself from his unwanted shadow it might make things difficult later on.

About halfway through the evening there were a series of formal speeches, one of which was from Varain. Dorm took the opportunity while he was making his way to the dais to change places. Hopefully Varain might lose him in the crowd.

Varain's speech was full of praise for his fathers' efforts to improve the lives of all of Ojliam's people, and how proud he was to have him as a father. Dorm had the distinct feeling that if he ever pandered to his own father in this way, that Mac Lavin would very likely start an immediate search for a new queen to provide him with another heir as Dorms' replacement.

After Varains speech, Prinaz took the stage and began his own diatribe. He thanked Varain for his 'kind' words, and also thanked his other two children and his wife for their companionship over the years. He then droned on for a while about how much he loved Ojliam, which Dorm gave him, he didn't doubt it for a second, but it was very long-winded and rather repetitive. Finally he thanked the assembled nobility and other guests, as well as the palace staff for the party and he hoped that next year would be even better. In the thunderous applause and cheering that followed Dorm moved further away.

The crowd retuned to moving around the room and Dorm took the opportunity to move quickly away from where he was. He found Telly, Rhyn and Pianwasal standing near the back of the room and joined them quickly.

"Ladies, might I join you?" he asked politely.

"Please do Your Highness," Telly permitted him with a little curtsy.

"We haven't seen much of you so far," Pianwasal noted.

"Yes I seem to have been kidnapped by Varain. He seems intent on introducing me to everybody in Ojliam, tonight! I haven't even seen

Mac for nearly the last hour."

"I think I saw him over with Travanos and Harmia a little while ago. Just before the speeches."

"Can I ask you to help me get away from Varain… please?"

"Well I suppose we should. Since we will need to know where you are when it's time to leave," Telly said a little too haughtily for Dorms' taste.

"Ah, Dormal!" he heard from behind him.

Dorm groaned inwardly, before fixing a grin on his face and turning. "There you are Varain, I thought I had lost you."

"No chance my friend," he said waving his half filled wine goblet about. "Come have a drink with me, there's someone I want you to meet."

Varain grabbed Dorm's arm and began to lead him away. "Excuse us ladies," Dorm called as he was dragged away.

The next few hours became an increasing blur of faces and noise, as Varain swept him from one group of people to the next. He had odd moments of respite, when one or other of his group managed to pry him away from his lecherous companion for a short while, but he always managed to find him again.

Dorm thought he might have had a permanent solution to the problem around midnight, when Varain brought him to a large group of women, whom he 'simply *had* to meet'. Varain seemed very taken with this large group of ladies, many of them young and rather pretty. Apparently they were all Archduchess, and duchess and daughters of duchesses, and probably deputy assistant secretaries to duchesses for all Dorm knew and cared. He let the conversation revolve around Varain for about ten minutes before quietly slipping away. It only lasted about quarter of an hour or so before Varain found him again.

Would the man *never* pass out?

As the morning wore on, bit by bit the number of remaining guests began to dwindle. The orchestra stopped playing and once there was nothing left to dance to many of the ladies began pressuring their male companions to take them home.

Varain continued to try and engage people in slurred and noisey conversation, but after a while there were not enough people to sustain his effort. Dorm signalled to Travanos and Pianwasal who he saw standing near one of the many tables in the room, and they managed to find one of the more senior servants.

After a little persuasion Varain was convinced that it would be better for him to go to bed for a while. It was at least two hours past midnight after all. Dorm played the party of the dutiful guest, saying it was a pity, but that it *was* a good idea. Varain tried to call out after him that they should meet later in the day. Dorm lurched around a bit, pretending he was drunk and therefore didn't hear him, and once in the company of his companions again, made a hasty exit from the ballroom. They met up with the rest of their group who had already left, and were escorted from the palace to waiting coaches. The coaches whisked them back through the chill early morning air to their inn, where they promptly retired.

No one was particularly intoxicated. They had all made sure of that. A few well placed lies about the number of times their goblets had been refilled and a few helpings of rich food; not to mention water at every available opportunity, had helped them all maintain a certain degree of sobriety. Still there would be little sleep to replenish them. And it had been a long night.

Dorm slept only briefly. He was worried about the meeting with Kanilma. And the night's events had indeed put him in the mood for staying up. Damn Varain and his enthusiasm.

He finally dropped off about an hour after they had returned from the palace. He woke briefly a few times during the brief sleep he got. Mac also woke several times, and from the muffled footsteps he heard in the passageway outside their door, so too had some of the others.

Finally he decided that it was time to get up and start this 'day'. It was still dark outside but this was too important to muck up by sleeping in. He had a brief wash, mainly concentrating on his face in an effort to wake himself up, as well as rid his head of some more effects of the wine he had actually drunk.

The others were starting to stir, and it didn't take long for them all to be ready. Zacravia and Harmia carefully checked both the stableyard and the street to make sure there was no sign of being watched, before, after leaving a note and a small gratuity for the innkeeper, they walked their horses out of the yard and a short way up the street.

The rode slowly and quietly through the pre-dawn streets. The air was very cold, and there was even a little frost on the cobblestones. After some time they came to the main northern gate, which was still shut. After quietly conversing with the guard on duty there Zacravia came back and informed them that they had arrived a few minutes early.

Those few minutes crawled by more slowly than any other few minutes in Dorm's life. He expected Varain and his soldiers to come round the corner at any time. Every noise made them jump. But they all turned out to be gates opening and workmen beginning their day.

Finally there was a far off sounding trumpet noise from the direction of the centre of the city. The guards at the gate began issuing orders and with several rather loud sounding at this time of the morning, creaks and clanks the gates were unlocked and began to ponderously swing open. The soldiers held them back till the gates were fully open and had been secured.

They rode their horses through the gate into the interwall zone. There was more noise of work here, which was probably only to be expected given its military nature. Finally they came to the huge outer gate which now stood open. A large caravan could be seen heading towards the gate from the outside.

The guards ushered them through and after just a few moments, in which it seemed everyone held their breath, they were free.

The steely grey light showed little in the way of details as they rode along the highway north of the city. It was chill, everyone was tired and no one really wanted to talk. So they all just pulled their cloaks tightly about them and rode on in silence.

It only took about half an hour to pass over the top of the slight hill to the north of the capital. Once they were safely out of sight they pushed into a gallop and rode until they came to a road that turned off in the general direction of the village, where they called a halt.

"So we part ways here I guess," Travanos said. "At least for the moment.

"Indeed," Dorm agreed. "We all know the plan then?"

"Yes Dorm," Rhyn told him. "We have been over it twice."

"I'm just making sure. This is a little too important to muck up."

"It shouldn't take us too long to get there and back," Lianna said. "We should see you all again by mid-morning at the latest."

"If we haven't seen you by then, we will head north and follow the main highway," Harmia said. "It should be easy for you to find us then."

"Especially if we ride slowly," Artur promised.

"Well then, until later everyone," Dorm concluded turning his horse towards the lane that would lead them in the general direction of the village of Greznick

Chapter 31

The breeze was rather brisk as they pounded along the country lane towards the east. This was actually a good thing, as it helped keep them awake. The sky was still very dark and the stars still shone as they headed past sleeping cattle and silent crops. There was the barest tinge of steely grey to the lower reaches of the sky as they flew along. Dorm worried that the noise of their passage might rouse some farmer or shepard to curiosity, but there was no sign of any one investigating their journey.

The lane meandered across the darkened landscape between hedges and short stone walls that seemed typical of back-country everywhere. The dirt road showed up as a lighter grey streak stretching into the distance. After about half an hour they pulled into a walk to give the horses a rest before pushing on again.

"How long do you think it will take us to reach Greznick?" Pianwasal enquired. She was a little breathless. Dorm had to admit though that she had become a pretty good rider in the time she had been with them.

"Well it took us about an hour to get there before," Dorm considered. "I think it should probably only take about two this time."

"Provided we don't get lost in the dark," Ambra said pessimistically. "You don't suppose there are road signs do you?"

"Oh, I'm sure there'll be something."

"Perhaps we could discuss this on the move," Lianna said, her teeth chattering just slightly. "At least if we are moving quickly I'm moving around and feel a bit warmer."

"I thought you would have been used to this sort of temperature. What with living on a barge all the time," Mac said to her.

"Exactly," she said, almost as if that alone explained it. "I live on a barge. A barge has an inside, not just an outside. It's lovely and warm in there, out of the wind with a few lamps on, maybe the brazier..." she dreamily looked up at the sky. "I miss my barge."

"Well the quicker we get to Greznick, the quicker we can have you back on it."

They pushed the horses back into a canter, and proceeded on their way. After another twenty minutes or so they came to an intersection. The lane they were following ended and another lane crossed over the end of it heading in both directions.

"Now what?" Lianna asked.

"There has to be a sign of some sort surely?" Mac said angrily.

Ambra stared at the embankment at the head of the lane they had been following. A short stone wall had been built to hold back the hill behind it. He got down off his horse and walked over to the wall.

"There is a sign here," he said pointing.

"Oh well spotted," Lianna congratulated him.

"It's too dark here to read it," he said peering at it. "We need a light."

Mac scrounged around in his saddlebag till he found a stub of candle. He then produced a flint, and got down off his horse. As he walked towards Ambra, he grabbed a handful of grass from the edge of the road. He struck the flint several times before igniting the grass. The flames held long enough to light the wick of the candle. He stamped out the embers and held the candle up to the sign.

"Grobel, is apparently the next village this way, and Hazkir is the next that way." Ambra read haltingly.

Dorm pulled out his map and began examining it. Mac and Ambra walked over to him, Mac holding the candle stud up so Dorm could see the map better.

"Lets see," Dorm said under his breath tracing his finger over the surface of the parchment. "There's Ojliam. There's Greznick. And here's Hazkir. So we must be about here." He pointed to a spot on the map.

"So we go towards Hazkir?" Pianwasal concluded.

"Apparently," Dorm said putting the map away as Mac blew out the candle. "Let's just hope they don't hear us as we pass by."

They headed off again in a roughly southerly direction. The land was a little more hilly here, and before long they could make out the trees of the planted forest along the horizon.

They passed through the darkened and very quiet village of Hazkir, without stopping and without seeing any one. A dog barked somewhere at their passing but aside from that there was no reaction.

Not far past the village they entered the forest. Its trees were widely spaced and so there was still a bit of a breeze flowing around them as they rode. The sky had become noticeably brighter now and the odd noise suggested that some of the wildlife was beginning to stir. It didn't take long for them the reach Greznick. The sky was now light enough that they could see the buildings as they approached.

All was dark. All was quiet.

They slowed to a walk, something the horses were grateful for, and as they came to the edge of the trees they stopped. Everything was still quiet. There was no movement either. So there was no way to tell where, or indeed, if Kanilma was waiting for them.

"What do you think?" Mac said.

"I have no idea," Dorm admitted.

"Well that's the inn there," Pianwasal pointed out. "Perhaps we should just go up and knock?"

They all looked at each other. "I've heard stupider ideas," Mac concluded.

"Alright then, lets try it."

They walked slowly towards the building, trying to be as quiet as possible. The grass was wet with dew and their boots became soaked rather quickly. They approached the inn stealthily, feeling rather like criminals doing it, but knowing it was probably the only way.

They arrived at the door.

Dorm raised his hand and rapped quietly.

There was a pause then the door opened. A small dark face looked out.

"I was beginning to think that you had forgotten me."

"Not much chance of that, I can assure you," Dorm said.

The door opened further. Kanilma stood wearing some rather serviceable clothes and a travelling cloak. In each of her hands she carried a bag, which presumably contained her clothes and personal items.

"You really are eager," Mac commented approvingly.

Behind her they noticed Lianka and Gossan standing very close to each other. There had obviously been some tears, but that was past now. At least for the moment.

Mac and Ambra went and put her bags onto the saddle of the spare horse they had brought for her, while Lianna and Pianwasal introduced themselves properly again.

Dorm went to say a few words to her guardians.

"Please look after her," Lianka was saying with a catch in her voice. "She is the daughter we never had."

"I assure you," he replied seriously. "I will do everything in my power to keep her safe. We all will. This is a very special group of people she is joining with. You can trust them with her life. I do with mine."

Lianka nodded.

"We trust you, Your Highness," Gossan said sincerely. "I guess it's just hard to say goodbye."

"Saying it to someone you care about, always is."

There was much hugging and kissing and quiet words, but relatively few tears. The sky was now grey across most of its expanse and they knew that it was time to move off. They made a promise to try and stop by the next time they were passing through, to fill them in on what had happened so far.

It was a sad farewell, but then they always were.

Finally after the last lingering look, the group walked their horses back to the road, before making speed back the way they had come.

Most of the trip back was in silence. Aside from the difficulties inherent in travelling at speed on horseback, no one was quite sure what to say. Everyone wanted to reassure Kanilma that things would be alright, even though right at the moment she didn't feel that. They all knew how she felt. They had all experienced it. Leaving the familiar, the known, to go off on this crazy sounding quest. But somewhere deep inside they knew they had been doing the right thing. This seemed even more pronounced with Kanilma. She at least had been able to put that into words.

The sun continued its stately ascent into the sky as they rode. Once it had cleared the horizon and begun to warm things up a little, they slowed to a walk. There would now be more people about. And it wouldn't do them any good to arouse suspicion by hurrying along quiet country lanes.

They had made pretty good time since leaving Greznick, and they approached the intersection where they had left the others about half an hour after sunrise. Here on the main highway north, there was already a lot more traffic. Several caravans headed towards the capital and others, labourers and some merchants headed in both directions. They merged quietly with the flow and continued on their way north. They did their best to look just like normal travellers, with nothing particularly special about them. No one seemed to take any notice of them, which was just as well.

After about an hour they came to another village, which straddled the highway. It was called Zabczick and contained several inns and taverns, a fair number of houses and various merchants. It was also the sight they were to rendezvous with the others. They made their way past the various inns looking for the horses of their companions. They found them outside the third inn, which was apparently called the Royal Horseman Inn and tied their own horses up out the front. Upon entering they discovered a somewhat smoky interior, ill lit by several oil lamps. It wasn't the best of inns, but then, they wouldn't be there long. The others were sitting at several tables near the doors, trying to look like they belonged there. There was an almost imperceptible acknowledgement between Dorm and Travanos as they entered.

They took tables further towards the bar at the back of the room and ordered some breakfast. They chatted quietly amongst themselves and ate when the food came. It wasn't too bad, but probably not worth the four schillings they asked for it.

When they had finished they rose and left and returned to their horses. As they started out, heading north again, the others began leaving the inn and getting on their own horses.

They all plodded out of Zabczick slowly. It wouldn't do to lose each other now. After a while there was no one within ear shot of them, and they were finally able to merge their groups. There were some very brief introductions, Kanilma seeming to take it all in her stride, before Zacravia suggested they pick up the pace a little, and put some distance between them and the village.

They cantered along for a while as the morning wore on. Around mid-morning they came to a roadside hostel and took a brief meal and rested the horses. While they sat outside in the garden, eating their bread and cheese, and properly introduced Kanilma to the group. As with the other, less affluent members of their group, she was a little intimidated by the high ranking members. Though living as close as she did to the capital she was probably more used to seeing them, and so was relaxed about it sooner.

Everyone took a liking to Kanilma straight away. She was a very likeable person. She was open, and warm, and was possessed of a natural smile, that made you feel she was genuine. It was clear she was going to get on with the girls, Telly and Rhyn were already discussing various female topics with her, and Dorm noted that Tissie and Navista weren't far behind. Harmia, Lianna and Pianwasal seemed a little more hesitant. Dorm wasn't sure if that was because the three of them were slightly older, or had more senior positions in life and so felt a little out of touch with her or not. Though Telly was certainly highly placed and she didn't have a problem.

After they had eaten they got back on the road and continued northwards. The highway wound its way between the rolling hills of central Ojliam. Clumps of trees seemed to top every rise. In the fields cows and sheep and goats could be seen, when they weren't full of crops. Dorm could identify wheat, barely and rye growing, and Artur pointed out several orchards on the horizon.

Their only excitement came just after midday when a small number of soldiers passed them, heading back towards Ojliam. Dorm recognised the man in charge as a Corporal, so it was unlikely that they were anything serious. And indeed the patrol continued on its way after they had passed them.

They decided to camp for the night so as to make an early start the next morning. No one really wanted to, but it was better to try and put as much distance between themselves and Varain as quickly as possible. There was no use in taking any chances.

They found a copse of trees some distance back from the highway and set up their camp fairly quickly. Kanilma it turned out knew nothing about tents, but was a good cook, and quickly took over the meal preparation from Rhyn and Cal who had been doing it most of the time since they had joined. Everyone enjoyed the meal, and it was rather filling despite the small seeming portions. Satisfaction was had all round it seemed.

After they had eaten and washed and packed away their utensils, Navista took out her small oud, and strummed away randomly. The music wasn't any sort of tune, and nothing that could be sung to, but was nice and relaxing, with the crack of the fire. They had gotten used to its soothing sound in the time the Kiaman dowser had been with them.

Kanilma filled them in on more details of herself. Her parents, her guardians, her job at the inn, the run ins with Prince Varain and how she felt about that. Everyone, especially the women sympathised with her situation. Though there was a slight appreciation for Varain's position. Kanilma seemed to have taken it in her stride at first, and even considered it, but after a while it had gotten monotonous, and then annoying, and finally irritating. She had considered leaving Greznick to get away from him, but didn't have anywhere she could go. Their arrival had presented her with an opportunity she couldn't pass up. Amulet or not.

Everyone seemed to be getting on quite well with her, and Dorm noticed that she seemed to have already taken to Rhyn and Telly, and even Artur. He knew that others such as Travanos and Zacravia would work their way into her friendship after a time. They were just that sort of people. Harmia might take a little longer. The constable still seemed to be a little hard around the edges. Dorm and the other members of their group knew better of course, but these things took time to realise.

Finally, with the night fully under way, and midnight approaching, the fire was doused and everyone retired to their tents to sleep.

The sounds of the night filtered through the tent canvas as the hours marched slowly by. The slow creak of the branches above them. The whipping rustle of the leaves as the wind blew. The far off howl of a lone wolf. The occasional flap of the wings of some nocturnal predatory bird in the lonely search for food.

It was cold this night. Winter was still hanging around, though it had been mostly missed. Their constant travel through different climes had meant that they had all but missed the traditional winter that Dorm was used to. They had only seen snow from a distance; none had ever fallen on them. They hadn't gone to any of the festivals that they would normally have gone to. The midwinter festival would be nearly upon them. It was being held a week or two later than normal this year. He vaguely remembered one of his advisors mentioning that the solstice was slightly later this year or some such.

There were now sixteen people in their group. It was starting to get rather large. They had at least one more person to find before they moved on the Bydanushev. How long would that take? He was beginning to think they'd never go home.

Dorm got out of the bedroll and slipped on a tunic. He pulled his cloak around him against the chill and quietly stepped outside. The moon was bright, and the clouds raced across the sky in the wind that blew at that height. It was one of those nights that made you think scary thoughts. You were never quite sure what could happen. A night where there was a sense of barely controlled anticipation in the air.

Dorm walked over to where Zacravia stood guard. The Ambakan seemed to take the watch quite often, and never seemed to be too tired in the morning. Dorm wondered what his secret was.

"Anything?" Dorm whispered to him.

"Nothing yet," Zacravia replied in an almost bored voice. "I thought there was going to be something a little while ago, but it turned out to just be a cow, from one of those fields over that way." He waved his hand vaguely off to the west.

"If it's all the same I think I will take the quiet," Dorm told him honestly. "We might get through all this alive if we do. So what do you think of Kanilma?"

"She seems like a very pleasant young woman," he replied sincerely and turning to look briefly at her tent. "Seems very intelligent and capable. I think she might make a good addition to our little quest."

'I agree. I just hope that everyone gets on. We have a lot of different people here, and a lot of different personalities."

"Dormal, I think you are worrying too much," Zacravia said in an almost fatherly manner. "The last few weeks should have shown you that we are all capable of getting on. I mean just look at Harmia and myself. She hasn't mentioned wanting to kill me for… oh at least a few days now. And I for my part, have to admit that I am coming to respect her more each day. And I suspect that the same is true for everyone. We are becoming a single group. A cohesive unit, instead of individuals. It takes time, but I think we are doing it well."

Dorm looked at the thief for a moment. "You might be right. I don't know what this is all leading to, but I get the feeling we may be called upon to act as some sort of "unit". Perhaps that's a good thing then."

"So where to from here is the big question?"

"Hmmm," Dorm agreed. "Bydanushev certainly. After that? any one's guess. Rikaway seems a likely option though."

"Don't know much about Rikaway, personally. I mean I've heard about it of course."

"I've never been there either. I went to the Council Forts once a few years ago. But we were only there for a few days. We may find out all about them soon enough though."

"Of course we have to get through the night first."

"Aren't you cold out here?"

"Oh slightly chilly perhaps. You forget Dormal, I'm a thief. I am used to hanging around outside in the cold."

Dorm smiled in spite of himself. "I sometimes take your nefarious skills for granted I'm afraid." He admitted.

"Well they will always be at your disposal, Your Highness,"

Zacravia told him sincerely.

Dorm was about to respond when he noticed that the thief's expression had suddenly become very serious. He stared off into the darkness back towards the road.

"What is it?" Dorm asked in a whisper.

"I'm not sure," he admitted. "Wait here a moment."

Dorm watched as he moved off in the direction he had been looking. His feet made no sound as he disappeared into the black.

Dorm waited hugging his cloak about him against the chill of the night air. He stepped from side to side to try to keep warm. He peered off in the direction his friend had gone, trying to make out what had attracted his attention. He couldn't see anything. He just had to hope that it was nothing. Another cow most likely, he told himself.

There was a stirring in one of the tents, and Travanos emerged. "Dormal," he said nodding in his direction. "How goes it?"

"Not sure. Zacravia just went to check something out."

"Indeed. Well in case it is something I had best be quick." The admiral smiled and walked off away from the tents. Dorm returned his gaze to the direction Zacravia had gone. He still couldn't see anything. Perhaps there were just too many trees for him to see what the Ambakan had seen.

Travanos returned a few moments later. "This night is decidedly chilly. I suggest next time we find a barn to spend the night in."

Dorm smiled. "That's a good idea. I will consider it tomorrow night."

Zacravia suddenly emerged from out of the night making both men jump. "Sorry," he apologised.

"Find another cow?" Dorm asked him sarcastically.

"Actually something far more interesting. A group of men. I think it's possible that at least one of them may be Peldraksekhran."

"That isn't very good news Zacravia," Travanos said accusingly.

"I did say interesting, not good, Admiral," Zacravia rebuffed.

"What were they doing?"

"Camping much the same as us, but they aren't very far away. Come morning they will spot us for sure. It might be a good idea if we leave here fairly rapidly."

"And fairly quietly, I should think."

"Indeed."

It was a hard task waking everyone up silently. Trying to get them to take in the seriousness of the situation without making any noise. One by one they managed to get the occupants of the tents awake and dressed. They had all left most of their packs attached to their saddles and so didn't have much to put away. They struck the tents silently, communicating to each other with looks and glances; pointed fingers and nods of the head.

Once the camp was struck and everything put away they prepared the horses as quietly as they could. Once or twice the horses made some noise, but each time they paused to see if there was any reaction from the night. There wasn't, and so they finally were all saddled and ready to leave.

They led the horses for a short distance as the sound of hooves hitting the ground is not particularly quiet. Once they were far enough away they mounted up and walked on towards the road. Now that they were further away they could risk communicating in whispers.

Upon reaching the road they turned to the left, which put them in a generally westerly direction and moved into a trot. The road was bordered by typical short stone walls, so should have kept some of the noise from reaching their pursuers.

After about a quarter of an hour they pushed into a canter to put some distance between them. Everyone was tired and still half asleep. It was probably dangerous to be travelling so fast when so distracted, but it couldn't be helped. If there really was a Peldraksekhran with that group then it was a distinct possibility that they were somehow related to the various other groups they had encountered. And therefore best avoided.

For about half an hour they flew along the country lane ever fearful that they were being pursued. They reigned in and discussed their options.

"We could keep going until sunrise," Ambra suggested. "We could camp somewhere for the day and move off again at dusk. At least till we find a town."

"I think we all still need some sleep," Lianna suggested, looking like she was about to fall out of her saddle with exhaustion. “ We were all awoken in the middle of the night.”

“Is there not somewhere were we could stay for a few hours?” Pianwasal suggested. “If we could at least rest for a while, we can start again when it is light. We’ll be tired for certain, but we can find somewhere secure tomorrow night.”

“We’re in the middle of nowhere,” Mac protested. “In the middle of the night. Where are we going to find somewhere to stay?”

“Could we not stay at a farm?” Ameks suggested. “I have heard often of the hospitality of farmers.”

“I don’t know what farmers you’ve been hearing about, friend,” Artur spoke up. “But not any of the ones I know would be appreciative of a large group of strangers turning up in the middle of the night asking for shelter.”

“I think I see your point,” Ameks said after a moment’s hesitation.

“If we are only planning on staying for a few hours,” began Rhyn. “Could we not just find somewhere and worry about that part of it later? If any one asks we’ll just tell them we got lost. We can always pay them something if they get angry.”

“We’ll still have to find something,” Harmia said. “Mac’s right, we are in the middle of nowhere.”

“Well lets just continue along the road for a while,” Dorm said finally. “Maybe we’ll spot something.”

“Can we find something a bit warmer than the last place,” said Tissie, her lips shivering slightly. “And out of the wind, if possible.”

They continued on at a walk, in deference to the cool night air. After about another half an hour of following the dark winding road, Zacravia spotted something.

“Over there,” he said quietly pointing. “That might be a barn or something.”

“Where, I don’t see anything,” Harmia said angrily.

Just then the moon came out from behind a cloud and spread it's cool light upon the scene. There was indeed a building of some sort out in the middle of an adjacent field. It was tall and dark, but looked big enough to house all of them comfortably.

“It has possibility,” Dorm said. “Let’s check it out.”

He, Zacravia and Travanos walked their horses to a gate several yards further along. After some fiddling with the latch they managed to open it and move through. The field beyond was obviously a pasture. The grass was uneven and the odd stone stuck out of the ground. The unmistakable odour of cow manure wafted occasionally to their nostrils as they rode towards the building.

It was made of wood. What sort and colour it might be they couldn't tell in the poor light. But it was solidly built and had a large door that they could use to gain entry. The three of them opened the door and had a quick look inside. It was mostly empty. A bench held some tools and farm implements, and there was a small wagon in one corner. The floor was covered in straw, that should make Tissie's request easier to fulfil. All in all there was more than enough room for them and their horses. Travanos even discovered a water trough that they might be able to fill if they could find some water.

They decided that it would be decent enough for a few hours. They just hoped that they would be gone before any one noticed them. Zacravia went back outside to send a signal to the others to indicate their success, and a short time later their group of weary travellers approached their nights haven.

Tissie was indeed satisfied with both the structure and the straw, and everyone else seemed to think it was a fine place to stay under the circumstances.

Before long everyone had retrieved their bedrolls and prepared themselves for bed again. Everyone was too tired to argue about privacy or who was sleeping next to whom. Before long the soft sounds of snoring filtered across the barn.

They were awoken to the bloodcurdling screams of Tissie.

Everyone was instantly awake fearing the worst in their half conscious stupors. Everyone groped for weapons expecting to be facing armed men. It took a few seconds for everyone's vision to clear and everyone's brains to comprehend the situation that they saw.

At some stage during the night a cow had entered the barn. It had probably been startled to find a large group of people asleep on the floor. The horses hadn't really taken much notice and had apparently remained silent.

The cow had decided in her curiosity to investigate the nearest object with her tongue. That nearest object was Tissie. As Tissie rolled around, flailing her arms about trying to fend off the rough, wet and rather smelly attack, everyone took in the scene and couldn't help but laugh. Despite their best efforts everyone descended into outrageously long guffaws. Poor Tissie was left to fend for herself for several minutes while everyone tried to compose themselves. Eventually Mac and Lianna got up and led the cow away to the other side of the barn.

Pianwasal and Rhyn attended to Tissie, providing her with some water and a towel to clean her face. She almost genuinely seemed scared of the creature. Dorm could only imagine the thoughts that went through her mind as she woke to the sight of a cows mouth right in front of her face. After some investigation they discovered that there was another smaller door that was unlocked. Apparently the door was intended for the animals of this farm to gain access. Probably to allow them to get out of the weather on cold or wet nights.

The sun had been rising. It had passed through the cold steel of pre-dawn, and the soft yellow of actual dawn was starting to creep over the top of the hills. There was still a lot of shadow across the valley, but there was more than enough light to see. Everyone decided it was time to move on.

They packed and re-saddled the horses. They led them out of the barn and began to head towards the road. Halfway back to the road, Telly piped up, "Umm I think we may have a slight problem."

"Oh why is that?" Mac asked her.

"Because I think we have been discovered." She indicated off towards the west. They all looked. A man on a horse was riding fast towards them. It was obviously the farmer. Most likely out for his morning farming activities. Dorm had no idea what sort of farm this was so had no idea what that might be. It was equally clear that he had seen them leaving the barn and was probably angry.

"I think perhaps it would be best to stop," Travanos suggested.

"Probably a good idea," Dorm agreed.

They halted their progress and awaited the arrival of the farmer.

The man came riding up fast. He stopped his horse a short

distance away, obviously not wanting to get to close to such a large group. If they had been intent on nefariousness, then he wouldn't stand much of a chance.

"Who are you people?" he yelled at them when he had reigned in. "What are you doing on my farm and in my barn? Explain yourself!"

"Our apologies Sir," Dorm said "We had no intention to trespass, but we found ourselves rather lost last night. We saw your barn and thought it would be a good place to stay for the night. We are willing to pay for it, if you'd like."

The man appeared to think about this for a moment. The possibility of some payment was never lost on any one. But their "use" of his barn was obviously something that he couldn't just let go. Dorm understood that. If someone had just decided to make use of his bedroom, he'd be pretty unhappy as well.

"Why are you travelling through this area?" the farmer called out to them.

"We are on our way towards the north. We realised shortly after midnight that we must have taken a wrong turn somewhere. When we saw your barn we thought it a good place to sleep for the night, hoping we could get our bearings in the morning."

"Well this road will take you on towards the general area of Krazclow. It's the main city in that part of the country. You can go north from there… depending on where abouts in the north you are heading for."

"Ah thank you that's good news. You have helped us a lot. And we are still willing to pay something if that will help. "

"We didn't damage anything," Telly said earnestly, hoping to illicit some sympathy.

"In fact I think the only damage done was to our friends pride," Dorm went on. "We got awoken by one of your cows."

"Some of us personally," Cal put in.

The farmer seemed to get at least part of the joke as a faint smile touched the edges of his mouth. He looked around at the barn. It was still standing. This was obviously one point in their favour. He turned back to them.

"Here," Dorm said reaching for his purse. He pulled out several coins. And edged his horse forward. "As a show of good faith." He held out his hand, holding coins for the farmer to inspect. The farmer leaned forward to see what Dorm held out to him.

"I can see that you are trying to be honest about this," he said after a moment.

"I can only apologise. We didn't mean to intrude. It's just that we were well and truly lost."

"I can understand that I guess," he sighed heavily. "I think that the payment would be sufficient under the circumstances."

"Thank you," Dorm told him sincerely. He lent forward and handed the coins to the farmer. "My name is Dormal," he said holding out his hand.

"Poljazak," he replied taking his hand and shaking it.

"Pleased to meet you. I'd introduce you to all my friends but we'd be here all morning," he joked.

"Indeed. There are a lot of you."

"Yes. It makes travelling more interesting.. Perhaps we could get some more directions from you?"

"Of course. It is easy to get lost on all these back lanes, they all look the same."

"Exactly why we ended up here I think."

"Well the first thing you do," Poljazak said smiling. "Is head along this lane in that direction." He pointed off towards the west, they way they had been travelling the night before. As he pointed his jacket shifted. There was a flash of light. The sun had now begun to rise and the rays glinted off something metal. Dorm probably wouldn't have noticed it had it not been flashing right into his eyes. Poljazak went on.

"After about five or six miles you'll come to another lane that heads in a slightly more southerly track. You'll want to take the left hand way. That will lead you to the village of Gozbi. From there…"He stopped noticing that Dorm was watching him. "What is it?"

"I couldn't help but notice that medallion you are wearing…"

"This old amulet?" Poljazak said reaching into his jacket and pulling it out. "It's just an old family heirloom. It's not worth anything. It just has sentimental value to me."

"Oh. I wouldn't say it's valueless." Dorm said pausing and

looking the farmer directly in the eye.

"Why?" Poljazak said cautiously. He obviously wasn't sure if these people were honest after all.

"I guess I had best show you." He revealed his own amulet. He turned and wagged it in the air at the others. They all realised that he wanted them to take them out. Which they did. One by one the morning rays glinted off the metal and the crystal. As each one was revealed Poljazaks eyes watched with nervous fascination.

"Perhaps you could explain this?" he said quietly once everyone's amulets had been revealed.

"I think we could do that for you, friend," Dorm said pleasantly.

"I hope my wife can handle cooking breakfast for such a big group," he said worriedly.

"We can help with that too," Telly said from behind them. "We're used to this sort of thing by now."

Chapter 32

Poljazak's house was a fairly substantial wooden building set in a narrowing of the valley his farm occupied. It had a fairly drab appearance, the wood being mostly grey in colour and the shingles on the roof, merely a darker shade of that forbidding hue. But none the less there was a certain welcoming sense of the place. It's windows were curtained and a large verandah ran the width of the building making it seem more inviting. The thin trail of smoke rising into the air from the chimney spoke of warmth, and food, and family.

The weather seemed to be conspiring to make their arrival more interesting. Wispy mist still hung in the air, but the sun lanced down through breaks in the clouds to dance lightly across the bright green grass.

Several outbuildings stood clustered around the main house. One was clearly a forge, another a hay shed. There was an unwalled shed that held several carriages and wagons, and one or two smaller house like structures that were probably the residences of farm hands.

A number of chickens scratched and pecked at the grass as they approached and scurried away as the horses entered the open area in front of the house. The odd bleating of sheep in the distance announced their presence, and it was clear that this farm had several different types of animals. They realised that this farm was more like a self sufficient community rather than just an isolated farmstead.

Poljazak asked them to wait while he went inside. It probably was a good idea. His wife probably wouldn't be too happy with a large group of people traipsing into her house unannounced. And better for Poljazak himself to explain things.

They heard some raised voices, but couldn't make out what was being said. It went on for a little while. As they stood and waited trying to look like they belonged there, they noticed two small children come out onto the verandah and stand near the steps that lead down to the ground.

"Hello there," Telly said smiling. "How are you this morning?"

"Good," said the boy shyly. "Who are you?"

"My name is Tellsandra. But special people get to call me Telly. Would you like to call me Telly?"

"Okay," said the girl. "Does that mean we are friends?"

"It certainly does. What's your name?"

"Sinka," she told her. "And this is Mikas. He's my brother."

"Well I am very pleased to meet you both." Telly extended her hand. She shook hands with both children in turn.

"Oh they're adorable," Rhyn whispered next to Dorm and Mac. Artur sighed heavily. It was clear that he was missing his own family. Cal also had a slightly sad look in his eyes. It was clear that these two innocent little people had reminded everyone that they had had to leave their family's behind. That was bound to affect people.

Telly continued to chat to the children while the muffled raised voices continued on inside for a bit. There was a period of silence, and they worried what that might mean. Poljazak then emerged from the house, his face unreadable. He tousled the hair of his children as he passed them.

"Sounds like things didn't go as well as you'd hoped," Travanos said carefully.

"Oh I think I just took her by surprise is all," he replied. "She wanted to send for the local authorities until I mentioned the amulet."

"Yes that seems to make people pause for a bit," Dorm agreed.

"Well she agreed with me that we would let you explain all this before we made a decision."

"We are certainly grateful for that," Harmia pronounced.

"Well if you'll follow me," he indicated for them to follow him into the house. They walked up the stairs carefully and followed Poljazak into the hallway. It ran the length of the house and was brightly lit but several oil lamps. There was a rug running the length of the hall and several pictures hung at various intervals.

He led them into a large room which was furnished as a sitting room. A small fire burned on the hearth and several candles gave a cheery light. Chairs and settees sat around the room, and table held several books, which was unusual for a family of farmers in Dorm's experience. The room was warm and smelt faintly of flowers. It was clear that this room was the domain of Poljazak's wife.

Their host did his best to make sure everyone was comfortable. He offered tea, which everyone gratefully accepted when they suddenly remembered that they hadn't eaten anything yet today. There were offers to help prepare it, that were politely refused and he disappeared into the house to comply.

There were several minutes of faint noise coming from somewhere else. Everyone sat quietly and just a little uncomfortably, in this strange room. It was very nice and very homely, but also a little formal. More formal than they had been expecting from the outside.

Poljazak returned with a large tray upon which he carried several ceramic teapots. Behind him came a woman. She was roughly the same height as Poljazak and a full figure, she had a calm, almost welcoming face and her dark brown hair was pulled up into a bun, tied with a ribbon. She wore a rather plain woollen blue dress and currently had an apron tied around her waist. She carried another tray with a number of cups and mugs on it.

They placed the two trays on the table and began to sort out the cups.

"This is my wife, Zaneem," he introduced her.

"Hello, welcome to our home," she said with a catch in her voice. It was clear she wasn't entirely happy with this situation.

"It is a pleasure to meet you madam," Dorm said to her rather formally.

"You have a lovely home," Rhyn said taking a mug from Poljazak. "This room is so cosy."

"Thank you," Zaneem replied a faint smile coming to her lips.

"And your children are just adorable," Telly said beaming. "You must be very proud."

That seemed to help a little. Her eyes softened slightly at the mention of her children. They continued to hand out mugs of tea to everyone. The aroma of the tea was very soothing at this still fairly early time of the day.

"So what were you really doing in our barn?" Zaneem said suddenly.

"A woman who is direct and straight to the point," Zacravia observed. "I think I like her,"

"The truth is we were hiding," Dorm admitted reluctantly. "We discovered that there were some people near where we had camped for the night. If we had stayed there, they would have found us this morning. And that was something we would just as soon avoid."

"Why?" the mistress of the house asked, folding her arms in front of her.

"Because they would probably have tried to kill us," Travanos told them seriously.

"Kill you?" Poljazak said worriedly. "Why?"

"Because we are working against their interests as near as we can work out," Dorm explained. "We are on an important… mission and we think that these people are among those that are trying to stop us."

"And exactly who are you to be going on this *mission*?"

"Here we go again," Cal said quietly from the corner.

The introductions went fairly quickly. The couple didn't interrupt them at all, which helped. Dorm suspected that had more to do with shock than any sense of manners, but he wasn't going to complain. After he had finished they both stood there for a moment. Zaneem then slowly sank into an unoccupied chair and sighed heavily.

"Oh Pol, what have you done now?" she said under her breath.

"This isn't your husbands fault," Telly said. "It's not any one's. It simply is the reality of the situation."

She shook her head slightly trying to clear her thoughts. "So explain what is it about these amulets."

"Lucky you sat down then," Dorm confided in her. "It gets better from here."

That conversation took longer. There were understandable interruptions, explanations and the like. Dorm couldn't fault their inquisitiveness, there was a lot going on and it was a little confusing, unless you had lived through it all from the beginning. The idea that the amulets had something to do with the Fortress worried them, that was also clear. They exchanged glances with each other at the mention of that.

"I don't understand any of this," Zaneem said frustrated and waving her hands in the air. "It makes no sense. What exactly is it that you are trying to do?"

"Well that part we are still trying to figure out," Dorm admitted to them. "We are sort of playing this by ear. We know that we have to find all the people with the amulets. At this stage that is about all we know. Though we suspect that there will be a lot more in the future."

"And what exactly is it that you want my husband to do?"

"Well he needs to come with us," Telly said.

"I can't leave the farm," Poljazak exclaimed. "There's too much to do. I've got several cows that are close to giving birth, and a very sick bull. There is too much to do. I don't have time to go off with you."

"You don't have any choice, Poljazak," Dorm told him quietly. "We have all given up our lives. Artur left his baby son behind at home. Harmia and Zacravia have put aside years of enmity and hatred towards each other to play their part. Tissie had to leave her father behind. Lianna hasn't seen her partner in months. We have all left people behind because we have to be here. And you do too. I know its hard to think about leaving your family, but we have no other choice."

There was silence for a few moments. Poljazak stared at the floor lost in thought. His wife watched him intently.

"I'll think about it," he said after a moment. "I'll give you an answer tomorrow."

"Bugger tomorrow!" his wife exclaimed. "I'll give you an answer right now. He's not going anywhere. I won't have it. I won't be left here to run this farm by myself."

"Zaneem wait…" her husband began.

"I won't wait. Don't tell me to wait!" she raged. "This is ludicrous. These people trespass on our property, showing up out of nowhere and now suddenly you're thinking about just riding off into the sunset with them? I mean seriously Pol, think about it."

He stared at her intently, obviously taking in what she was saying.

The tension in the room was at breaking point. The silence deafening.

Just then it was broken by the bloodcurdling scream of a young female voice. There was suddenly panic in the eyes of the two parents. Both of them were on their feet and flying towards the door before the scream itself had finished, let alone the echo.

Everyone else jumped up and ran after them to find out what was the matter. More than a few hands grabbed the hilts and handles of weapons.

Once outside Dorm saw what had happened. Both parents had clutched the children to them. Sinka was crying and clearly shaken, and clutched at her mothers waist, while Mikas stood close to his father with a worried and confused expression on his face. In the yard in front of the house, standing between their horses and the building stood three familiar robed figures.

"Oh not again," Mac groaned wearily.

Upon sighting them all, the three Rangers bowed deeply. "Noble Questers we greet thee," said the man in the middle. "We must also apologise to the children. Our arrival here startled them."

"I turned around and they were just there," said Sinka through her tears.

"Who are these people?" Poljazak asked.

"They're Rangers," Dorm explained. "Operatives of the Fortress, whose main job seems to be spreading confusing and worry wherever they go."

"Thy cynicism does not become thee, Your Highness." The lead Ranger said again.

"Sometimes it's necessary though," he replied. "Why are you here scaring small children?"

"We are not here to frighten any one," said the female Ranger on his right. "But to make sure that your group is complete upon your departure from this place."

"I think that means you," Cal said looking at Poljazak intently.

"I don't understand."

"Noble Quester," the Ranger began. "Thy hesitancy speaks of your fear. This is a good thing. Fear in this situation will help keep thee safe. But they reluctance to go must be overcome. Thy help is needed.

There is no other choice."

"And to thy wife," began the other Ranger, a younger man by the sound of his voice. "Your husband has no choice in this matter but to accompany these people, for he is a part of the quest. His purpose in it cannot be forsaken."

"What happens if he stays here?" Zaneem asked quietly.

"Then the quest shall fail," said the leader with a finality to his voice that suggested not just failure but something much more permanent. "And all that the Fortress and its Alliance has stood for, for almost five millennia shall crumble and fall into dust."

"Gives you a bit of a new perspective doesn't it," Zacravia said quietly before Harmia elbowed him in the ribs.

"There is no other choice for either your Husband or yourself," said the woman again. "It is what must be."

"Know that one way or another, your husband WILL be with these people when they leave here." The lead Ranger slowly raised his arm and pointed at them. "It wouldst be better for him to go willingly."

Now that was new. Never before had the Rangers done anything that even remotely resembled threatening them. In fact the very idea was almost laughable. The Rangers, despite their confusing interruptions to their journey had been benign, and even occasionally helpful. This was rather different and a little worrying to Dorm. Did this mean that the Rangers were now going to take a more active role in events? And if it did, would that role be necessarily all good?

There was tension in the air as both Poljazak and Zaneem digested the meaning, or at least the possible meanings of those words. They looked at each other for a while trying to decide what to say. In the end it was clear that they indeed didn't have much choice.

"Alright," said Poljazak quietly. "I'll go."

"As it was to be," said the lead Ranger again. "Thy company should prepare thyselves for the journey onward."

"I think I need to sit down," Zaneem said quietly. She then turned and shuffled her children back inside the house. Everyone knew this was the cue to also go back inside. There would obviously be much talking for a while now, explaining everything to the newest member of their group and his wife.

Dorm waited. He wasn't sure about these Rangers. Things had changed. He wanted… no, needed to know why, He slowly began to make his way down the stairs. Mac grabbed his arm as he did so. "Are you sure?" he asked intently. It was obvious that Dorm wasn't the only one to have noticed the change in their behaviour.

"I'll be fine. I just want to ask them some things."

Mac nodded and walked slowly back inside. Dorm continued down the stairs and came to stand in front of the three darkly clad figures.

"I have to say, you've surprised me," he admitted. "I hadn't expected you to be so forward."

"We will act as is necessary, Your Highness."

"But threatening them?" Dorm shook his head. "That seems a little excessive doesn't it?"

"There was no other choice. Poljazak would have remained behind, if not for our intervention. For him to do so would have meant disaster for thy quest."

"You believe that?"

"We KNOW that. There was no other option."

"Does this mean that you and your fellow Rangers are going to be more active in things from now on?"

"We will be as active as is necessary at the times that it is necessary," said the woman.

"Cryptic and confusing as ever I see," Dorm sighed resigned to the fact that he was never likely to understand these people.

"The purpose of our interventions shall be revealed to thee, at the proper time. To tell you sooner would be to disrupt things, and we shall not risk that."

Dorm thought on that. Was that a sideways way of telling him that they wouldn't find out what was truly going on until they got to the Fortress itself? He had always suspected that they would end up there eventually, But would this random wandering continue until then?

"Thy mind is sharp Highness," said the leader again. "You glimpse that which is well hidden. This is most advantageous."

Now that was weird. Had he actually heard what he had been thinking?

"Oh is it just? Well at least I'm doing something right."

"Thy lack of confidence in thy abilities does not become thee, Highness. You are doing what you should be doing, and doing it well."

"Well thank you." He stared at them for a moment. "There's one other thing I don't understand? How did you get to be standing here without the children seeing you walk up?"

A mischievous grin spread slowly across their collective faces. "There are some things, Your Highness," said the leader again. "That you are still not quite ready for… just yet."

Dorm got the intense feeling that the conversation was over. And as if hearing him again they turned and began to walk away. The horses slowly shifted out of their way without so much as a hand to indicate to do so. Dorm watched them for a time before going back inside.

The remainder of the afternoon was spent in explaining everything to Poljazak and Zaneem. Both the prophecy, which they too had a hard time understanding, let alone believing, and their adventures since they had discovered it all. They spent hours telling the new member and his wife all about themselves and their lives, as well as what had happened since they had met.

Their stories about the "attacks" worried both of them greatly. To the point where it seemed at one stage that Poljazak was almost ready to back out. But then they would change topic and recount some funny tale of a cooked dinner gone wrong, or laughing at each others appearance in the rain, and things would change.

This joking and reminiscing was good not only for the new member and his wife but also for those who had been on the journey and experienced the events of which they now joked. It was good to remind each other that there had been good times on their journey, not just difficulties and danger.

"Oh I hope your cooking skills are well developed Poljazak," Telly told him.

"Zaneem does most of the cooking here," he admitted. "She's much better at it than I ever will be. Why?"

"Oh dear," was Tellys response. "We seriously need to find a good cook in one of these questers, Dorm. I'm not sure I can handle the current level of culinary expertise."

"What does that mean?" Zaneem asked curiously.

"Let's just say that none of us are particularly skilled," Rhyn said. "Most of us don't have much chance to cook properly in our normal lives. Other than Kanilma. And it's not fair to make her cook every night."

"Tavanos is not too bad, and Mac and Rhyn can pull together something quite tasty if we have the ingredients. I think Lianna is probably the next best cook among us at the moment," Dorm explained. "But we try not to let Zacravia or Tissie near the fire."

"How rude," Zacravia said with a smirk on his face.

"Yes I used to think that old saying about burning water, was just that, a saying," Dorm explained. "Until Tissie volunteered to cook one night."

Tissie blushed furiously. "My mother tried to teach me. I guess I just don't have the knack for cooking."

"You do make a good cup of tea though," Telly said encouragingly.

She smiled a little at that.

Poljazak seemed to gradually grow more at ease about them as they talked. Zaneem on the other hand still appeared to be a bit reserved. It was clear she wasn't comfortable with this situation, nor happy about her husband having to leave. Dorm made a special point of mentioning the fact that they believed they would have to travel back this way once they had been to Bydanushev. She seemed to brighten a little at that.

The two children didn't quite seem to understand that their father would be going away for a time. It was difficult to explain. No one wanted them to think he wasn't coming back, even though in the backs of their minds they all knew that that might be a possibility.

No one particularly wanted to broach that subject. It wouldn't do any good to worry Zaneem that way, and the children wouldn't understand. They all knew that with his presence the possibilities of them all staying alive were increased, but they had already been attacked several times. There was nothing to indicate that they wouldn't again be in the future. They had been lucky up till now.

It was clear that they wouldn't be able to make a move that day, so it was decided that they would have to stay. Offers were made to assist in the preparation of what would obviously be a much larger dinner than normal for the kitchen, and these were happily accepted. They contributed some of their supplies towards it, and managed to create a very satisfying dinner of beef stew and bread. There was also plenty of cheese to go around.

As night time fell, arrangements were made for everyone to sleep. Dorm offered for them to just sleep in the barn, but Zaneem insisted that they should sleep in the house. There was some rearrangement of furniture in the various rooms of the house to fit everyone in, and it was a tight squeeze for most of them. Zacravia, Harmia and Ambra offered to help by being lookouts and therefore not needing beds. Zaneem got worried at this wondering why a lookout was necessary. They explained carefully, and calmly, that it was just their habit after all that had happened to them, and that the chances of them being tracked to their farm was remote, but it never hurt to be careful. She seemed to be at least partially satisfied by this, though her eyes still betrayed her fears.

Once the sun had finally gone down and darkness had fully descended, everyone settled down to sleep. No one was fully comfortable, being all squished in together, but it was warm and dry, and much safer than what they would have had to make do with on the open road. Dorm and Mac lay close together, listening to the odd snatch of conversation from one of their companions, and in the distance the muffled voices of their hosts as they discussed privately everything that had happened this day.

“Do you think they’ll be okay here?” Mac asked him quietly.

“I hope so,” he replied turning over onto his side to look at him. “Zaneem seems more than capable of running this farm. I don’t think she’ll have any problems on that front.”

“Let’s just hope that the people who keep trying to find us don’t come here. It might be bad if they do.”

“I know. But there’s not a lot we can do about it now. Perhaps they know of someone who can come by and help them. If it looks like a busy farm then we would be less likely to come here, right?”

“Maybe,” Mac conceded. “We just have to hope *they* think like that.”

The next morning was again cool and misty. The sun was out and those “inspirational’ as Tissie called it, lances of sunlight again speared down upon the landscape. They packed quietly and calmly, hoping to be on the road fairly early.

Poljazak chose one of the farms' horses that he thought would be able to make a long journey, and began organising things to take. Saddlebags and packs were arranged and it took only half an hour for him to be ready.

The goodbye took longer.

He spent some time trying to explain to the children why he had to go. From the sounds of things he occasionally had to go to other farms and into the nearby towns and villages for various needs and so they had this reference. He explained that he might be gone for a bit longer this time, and they seemed to understand in their own way.

Zaneem however was different. She *did* understand what was happening. And exactly how long it might take him to get back. And the fact that when he did come back he would probably be leaving almost straight away again.

Everyone gave them the space and time they needed. He made mention of the fact that he would stop by his brothers farm which was further up the valley and get him to check in on things every so often.

Lianna, Zacravia, Harmia and Artur began to walk their horses slowly towards the road as the couple said their goodbyes. Pianwasal and Rhyn followed not too far behind them, and Navista and Cal chatted quietly as they followed behind them.

The rest waited patiently staring out at the landscape. Finally Poljazak came and mounted his horse. He straightened his wide brimmed hat and urged his horse forward to stand next to Dorm’s.

“So I guess this is it?” he said quietly.

“Indeed it is,” Dorm replied. “I know it’s hard to leave. But we are doing all this for a purpose. If we don’t do it. Bad things are going to happen.”

“I get that part of it. It’s just asking a lot to leave ones family behind. It’s hard.”

“Nothing worthwhile isn’t,” Travanos said philosophically.

Poljazak nodded slowly. He understood.

They turned and slowly rode towards the road. Once there they grouped with the others who had waited. There was a last lingering wave, and then they walked off slowly up the valley. The farm buildings slowly fading from view.

After about an hour and a half of fairly easy riding they came to another collection of farm buildings. There was the sound of hammering coming from somewhere, and smoke rose from several chimneys. The smell of baking bread was carried on the air.

"My brothers farm" Poljazak said as explanation. "Wait here while I arrange things."

He rode quickly on down to the farm house and went inside for a few minutes. He came out again and went across to one of the large outbuildings. The hammering stopped and there was happy sounding voices for a while.

They waited patiently in the cool morning air. Eventually Poljazak, and presumably his brother emerged from the building. They stood talking for a few minutes more, before roughly embracing. Poljazak got back on his horse, shook his siblings hand once more and rode back to join them.

"It's all arranged. He'll stop by twice a week to check on things at home," he said. "It's not so bad. We don't have anything pressing going on at the moment. So it should be all fine. The farmhands can handle most things."

"Then if that's all we have to take care of, we should get a move on. There's a lot of this adventure still to come."

Poljazak nodded thoughtfully and then they rode off at a light canter till they came out of the valley and found the main road. Once on it they galloped for a while to get the feel of being on the road. Poljazak was a good horseman, something that they anticipated, him being a farmer. He knew when to rest his horse, and how far he could push her. A little after mid-morning they passed through the village of Gozbi, which Poljazak had mentioned to them the day before.

It was typical of reconstruction villages in Ojliam though did seem to have a few alterations done to some of the buildings to make them a little more individual. They purchased some supplies from several of the merchants in town, who all knew Poljazak and greeted him warmly, and asked after his family.

It seemed that the people here were very warm and friendly, to those they knew. They were never rude to Dorm and his friends, but were rather standoffish. Dorm could understand that. He had heard stories from small towns and villages in Lugemall how it could take decades in some parts to be considered a local. He could only imagine that with their underlying paranoia about being invaded again, that things would be worse here in Ojliam.

They were in Gozbi for about an hour, then headed back onto the road and off towards the northwest and the main highway.

It took four days of fairly steady slog to get to the city of Krazclow. The weather remained fine but quite cold, and the countryside was pleasant enough. As they travelled they slowly began to integrate Poljazak and Kanilma into the group. They were both very pleasant people and Dorm felt that they would make welcome additions to the group.

He watched everyone carefully. The idea that these people would become like a military unit was a little worrying. He didn't want this joviality to disappear and the feeling not of camaraderie but almost of family. He felt that was important. Something that might be beneficial later on. He noticed that everyone did seem to be getting on. Even Navista seemed less antagonistic towards Ambra. She clearly still hated him, but now she didn't snipe at him quite so often. Perhaps she was learning more about him. Dorm thought of how much Harmia's and Zacravia's attitudes had changed towards each other. Perhaps the same thing was happening to them as well.

It was mid afternoon when they arrived at Krazclow. It was a large sprawling walled affair, with a rather grim appearance. At least from the outside. Inside the city was much brighter. Many of the public buildings had been decorated and here and there small flags flew for seemingly no other purpose than to brighten things up a bit.

Like any city it was busy, and noisy, and to a certain extent, dirty. Kanilma mentioned she had heard of a good inn in the city and with

Poljazak's help they were able to find it. They didn't intend to stay in Krazclow very long so they didn't unpack. They ate that night in the common room, and despite some reservations went outside to partake in some festivities that were going on. Some local festival celebrating cabbages or something. Well not seriously. But there did seem to be a lot of them about.

Dorm noticed that many of the private buildings; houses, shops and the like all looked similar. Again another victim of the Great Reconstruction. He vaguely remembered something about several northern towns and cities being simply razed by the Peldraksekhr during their invasion so that they wouldn't have to waste manpower holding and protecting them. Also then the Ojlian partisans wouldn't be able to "liberate" the cities.

Dorm presumed that the various decorations on the public buildings were an attempt to get away from that bland uniformity that the reconstruction had caused. Embellishments could also be seen to a much more limited extent on some of the private buildings.

The festival wound down not long before midnight and they all returned to the inn and retired. They had had a long few days and there were just as many long days to come. If not more.

The next morning was clear but very cold. The sun was out and there were few clouds, but there was no warmth in the air. They left the inn early and headed towards one of the minor gates that lead out of the city to the north. There were a fair number of travellers even at this early hour and they made good time. The day warmed up marginally as they rode and the sky remained clear.

They passed villages and farms as they followed the road in a wavering line to the northwest towards the eventual border.

It took almost a week to reach the last main town before the border, called Cirbah. It was another trading town full of merchants and farmers, here though they could easily make out Bydanushevians. Their accent was slightly heavier than those from Ojliam and their mode of dress was also heavier.

Dorm began to wonder what it would be like to be surrounded by them. He found the accent quite interesting. Some of the women in the group seemed to find it a little more than interesting he began to note.

They passed through Cirbah uneventfully and continued on towards the border. It would take about two and a half days to reach the border and Dorm hoped that one of the villages on the other side would have room in an inn or hostel somewhere.

Around mid-morning on the second day they began passing through the village of Draviak. It was again typical of Reconstruction villages throughout the country, though here the locals had over the years made efforts to change that. Small gardens of flowers and bushes were dotted around the public areas, and many of the houses had been repainted at some stage in different earthy hues. All in all it really only slightly disguised the plainness of the village, but it was still a pleasant change.

They stopped at one of the local merchants to top up on a few supplies. The merchants were friendly enough though they did seem to be actively trying to figure out a way to increase their prices.

After they had completed their purchases they took a few moments to reorganise their packs. Some of the horses had been slowing down a bit and everyone felt that it would be a good idea to distribute the weight a bit more evenly.

After a few moments there was a commotion from up the street. The group exchanged looks that clearly said 'this is nothing to do with us. Just keep your heads down'. Various villagers ran towards the noise from buildings near them. Many women stood back clutching children to them with worried, even fearful expressions on their faces.

Dorm began to get concerned. If this was something that worried mothers, then perhaps there was something going on they should be concerned about.

The commotion continued until suddenly the crowd which had gathered all jumped out of the way. From the melee staggered a young woman. No more then about twenty or so. Her hair was matted, her skin pale, and she had a very haggard look about her. Her plain peasant clothes were dirty and crumpled. Her eyes were haunted; almost as if she couldn't see.

She lurched out into the street and collapsed to her knees, her chest heaving as if she were carrying a great weight. Her fingers flexed and spasmed and she looked as if she were in great pain. Tears streaked her face. Several people ran towards her but didn't touch her.

One of them, a large man wearing an apron, knelt down slowly in front of her. He looked at her with a gravely worried expression. His hands reached out for her but did not touch her.

"This will not go on, Vrandis," shouted a man from the crowd. "She is gone. You must be rid of her."

"She is my daughter!" Shouted back the man apparently named Vrandis. "Have some compassion for once in your life Ravic!"

"She has the magic," replied the one named Ravic. "She cannot stay in this village!"

At the mention of magic the others all began looking at each other. It was clear that this was what the Rangers had previously referred to when they talked about people with magic being victimised in the past. Apparently it wasn't just in the past.

The looks his friends exchanged, told him everyone was of a mind to do something to help this young woman. But what? While they knew they could touch her safely and get her away, it could lead to the villages wanting to harm them as well. And they didn't really have the option of taking her with them. If only there was a chapterhouse here. But a village this small wouldn't have one.

Telly, Dorm and Mac all exchanged a final look. Travanos, Ambra and Zacravia had already adorned some weapons, though they made no moves to brandish them. He knew that Artur and Cal and Harmia would likely be doing the same. He also saw briefly Pianwasal and Navista grabbing blankets, probably to cover the girl.

It was clear they were all of one mind. He nodded to Telly and Mac. They responded in kind, a steely determination on both of their faces.

He marched forward towards the group, now sitting in the middle of the street. He walked up to the girl and her father and knelt down beside them, to the gasps of several people in the crowd.

"Stay back," yelled Ravic. "Lest you be afflicted as well."

"Fool!" retorted Dorm angrily. "You cannot catch magic! It is an illness born within you." He had no idea if that was true or not but it sounded good. He knew he had to maintain the lie the Rangers told, he wasn't going to be responsible for correcting that. "This girl is ill. Have some decency about you man. It is not her fault."

"I don't care! "yelled back Ravic. "She is a blight on our town!"

"She is a human being!" roared back Dorm. "Which right now is more than I can say for you!"

He looked at the girl for a moment. She seemed to have calmed slightly. Though her breath was still laboured and she shook somewhat. "What's her name?"

"Barassa," replied her father quietly. "Thank you for helping me."

"No trouble at all friend." He replied. "Barassa? Can you hear me? My name is Dormal. My friends and I are going to help you."

He wasn't sure if she really had heard him, but her breathing seemed to quieten slightly once he had spoken. Pianwasal and Navista came forward with a blanket and wrapped it around the girl. It was only now that Dorm realised that Mac and Telly were kneeling next to him. Travanos, Zacravia, Cal, and Ambra stood nearby looking menacing.

Dorm reached out and drew a stray strand of hair out of the girls eyes.

"You touch her?" her father said incredulously. "Are you not scared?"

"Lets just say I'm immune. Has any one sent for the Rangers?"

"Yes I sent for them earlier this morning, but I do not know how long it will take them to get here. They have to come from Kevrah."

"I see," Dorm said quietly. "Well we came from Kevrah this morning. We didn't see any rangers on the road." Privately he thought to himself, 'Not that that probably means a great deal'.

"I do not want my daughter to be harmed by them," Vrandis said tearfully. "She is all I have left in the world. If the Rangers do not come, then I shall have to…"

It was clear what he was thinking, and how hard it was for him to think it.

"No," said Dorm. "That isn't going to happen. We will help you. My friends and I have had a little experience with this sort of thing." It was only partially a lie. "We aren't going anywhere till this is sorted out."

"That may be sooner than you think," came the menacing voice of

Ravic. He stood nearby with several large burly men, who seem to populate every village in the world. They brandished a variety of farm and industrial implements. None of them weapons per say, but all of them deadly in the right hands.

This was no longer a village of concerned peasants. It was a massacre waiting to happen.

"Now gentlemen I don't think there's any need for that kind of foolishness, do you?" Telly piped up. "Think of what the women and children will see."

"Better for them to see it, than die from what she will inflict them with."

"Don't be such an idiot," she replied patronisingly.

"I'll show you idiot!" Ravic said from gritted teeth.

He and his friends began to step forward.

Chapter 33

"STOP!"

It wasn't particularly loud. Or forceful, or even angry. But it was commanding.

For some reason you had to stop. There was no other choice. Almost like a compulsion. To stop was… to be.

Ravic and his fellow village barbarians had managed to cross most of the distance from where they had been, and they now stood menacingly close to where Dorm and the others knelt with the stricken Barassa. Ravic and another of the men had even raised their implements; Ravics' a heavy looking smithing hammer, in order to strike at them, before the voice had silenced all movement.

Dorm slowly turned his gaze to where he felt the voice had come from. It was strange. He hadn't actually 'heard' it. It was more as if he had felt it. Looking down the street he saw the familiar figures of three Rangers. Their hoods were up but their faces were clearly visible. The lead Ranger, a man of elder years, carried a stern face. Almost disapproving, as if he were a school master with an unruly class.

For several moments they simply stood and surveyed the scene. None of the villagers moved a muscle. Everyone in the Alliance was taught from an early age to be wary of Rangers. Wary, yet respectful. They did an important job, so everyone believed. They were the only ones capable of keeping everyone safe from Magic.

Or so everyone believed.

The Rangers marched forward purposefully. Their usual swaying gait gone. This was the walk of people on a mission. People who would not be triffled with. Pity the fool who got in their way.

They came to stand next to their group. The lead Ranger fixed Ravic with a look that could almost have been described as contempt, if indeed there had been any emotion in it. He slowly turned and looked at Dorm and his friends. His face softened immeasurably, and that familiar, beneficent Ranger smile crept onto his face. It was clear he recognised them.

"Barassa is under our protection now," he said. "YOU," he almost spat as he turned to face Ravic. "Will be gone from here. Or shall suffer the consequences for disobedience."

Ravic looked as though the Ranger had slapped him across the face. He slowly lowered the hammer and backed away. His face deflating as he realised he had just been put in his place.

The Ranger turned back to the group in the middle of the road. "We came as soon as we received your message, Vrandis."

"Thank you Ranger Navis," he replied sincerely, choking back tears. "Please help my daughter."

"We shall."

He knelt beside the girl and took hold of her jittering arms. He brought her hands together and held them there in front of her for a moment. He fixed her with a penetrating stare. Slowly her shaking subsided. Her short spasms and ticks also gradually ebbed away. She still shivered a little and her breathing was heavy, but she was much calmer.

"You have cured her?" asked Vrandis hopefully.

"I'm afraid not," said Navis sorrowfully.

"We cannot do that here," said the female Ranger with him. "We have only calmed her. Taken away some of her pain."

"Her cure will take much more than we can give her here," said the young man with them. He appeared to be no more than an adolescent, and looked as if he came originally from Kiama Mor. Dorm began to realise that he had never bothered to take note of the previous nationalities of the Rangers they had met along their journey. They had all just been Rangers. That was all they needed to be.

They helped Barassa stand and slowly escorted her over to their groups' horses. Tissie gave her some water to drink, which she accepted gratefully.

"Will you cure her?" asked her father anxiously.

"We will do everything in our power to do so," assured the lead Ranger. He placed a reassuring hand on Vrandis' shoulder. "You do not need to fear for her safety. We will protect her. From herself as well as others."

"What will happen to her?"

"We will first take her to our chapterhouse and help her there. When the time is right she will be taken to the Fortress to be fully cured. Though that will take many years."

"Will I ever see her again?"

Navis glanced quickly at Dorm. Knowingly. "There is always hope Vrandis."

Slowly Vrandis sighed. He clearly was very confused and just wanted his daughter to come home. It was sad that this would probably never happen.

"Thank you for you help friend, Dormal was it?"

"Yes," Dorm replied taking his hand. "I just saw an injustice being done. Your daughter is ill. She doesn't deserve that kind of animosity being directed at her."

"We were just trying to keep it quiet. We had been getting help, but this morning…"

"You have done the right thing Vrandis. You should be proud. Your daughter will always know your love for her." Navis again took his shoulder reassuringly."We will make sure of that."

They walked back to the group. Vrandis going to stand next to his daughter. The Ranger stayed with Dorm and Mac.

"Highness, you took a great risk this morning," he told them.

"As I told her father, I saw an injustice. We couldn't not interfere."

He thought on this for a moment. "You may be right. But you ran the risk of exposing yourself. Or worse getting one of you injured. The quest could be put in great peril at any moment by such an event."

"We had no idea how long you people would be," Mac protested quietly. “We had to do something. She would have been killed if we hadn’t.”

“Indeed she might have,” Navis agreed. “But in the grand scheme of things your protection is more important than hers. As harsh as that sounds.”

“I beg your pardon?” said Telly who was standing nearby. “How do you figure that one?”

“When this situation comes to its climax, she will still only be new. There will be little she can contribute. Do not misunderstand me. We are grateful for that. And any help she can give us will be welcome. But your actions, and the actions of the other Questers, will far outweigh anything she or indeed I can contribute.”

“You’re saying she isn’t important?” Mac asked angrily.

“Far from it. But you are more important than just about any of us right at the moment. This is what you must learn to respect.” He looked back at the group and sighed. “We will take her to our chapterhouse and fully calm her. This should not have happened to her. We had taken precautions.”

“You knew she had magic?” Dorm asked.

“Oh yes. That is what many of us do when we are about. We travel to identify those that have it. We watch them mostly. Try to steer them gradually towards a point where they can be taken. She was still some months away. Something must have happened to upset the balance. We will need to investigate that. But that is no concern of yours Questers. I would suggest that you leave this village as soon as possible. It may not be safe for you for much longer.”

“We were about to leave when all this started anyway,” Telly told him.

“Then you appear to have everything in hand.” He inclined his head towards them. “It has been a great honour to meet you in person.”

He turned and walked back to where Brassa and her father stood with the others.

“Do you think she will be alright?” Telly asked them.

“Something tells me yes,” Dorm told her.

“I still don’t like it,” Mac said. “Saying she isn’t as important like that. Seems rather cruel to me.”

"You forget they know more about all this than we do," Dorm told him.

"Dormal my darling, I think everyone knows more about this whole situation than we do," Telly said. "I just hope they take care of her."

They watched as the three Rangers slowly began to escort her away from the village. They began to slip into their familiar gait as they walked. Their charge walking in their midst. She slowly turned and cast a lingering look at her father, who now openly cried. There was a gentle smile on her face.

They left Draviak soon after.

No one particularly wanted to wait around to see how the villagers would respond to their interference. They cantered out of town along the highway for some distance before slowing down. Traffic on the highway was light, which was just as well. They needed to digest what had happened.

It was clear that they had had no other choice. Everyone was beginning to suspect that magic was going to play some part in this. They had all seen the Rangers doing things that defied normal logic.

There was no denying that there were things going on around them that they didn't fully understand. And probably wouldn't. At least not until they ended up at the Fortress itself, and had it all explained to them. But what exactly that might be was any one's guess.

They probably didn't realise fully how close they had come to injury. Ravic and his goons were obviously serious about hurting them. It was only the intervention by Navis and his other Rangers that had stopped them. Dorm began to think on that depressing and rather worrying thought. Their side would have won in the end, there was no denying that. Travanos and Zacravia alone had more then enough skill to defeat them in a fair fight. And that didn't include Cal, Ambra or even Poljazak. Harmia would easily have given as good as she got and Navista was no stranger to defending herself. But Dorm, Mac and Telly might well have been killed. What would that have done to the prophecy?

More than once concern was expressed for Barassa, and how she would fare in the care of the Rangers. They knew that they would look after her, but would she adapt? Would she thrive? Her father was also of concern to them. It was clear they were a close family. To have them broken apart like that…

They rode in silence a lot of the time. No one being exactly sure what to say about the situation. They all knew that there was no other alternative, but still it hurt that they couldn't have done more. Or that Vrandis hadn't been able to go with her. But they suspected he probably wouldn't have liked watching what was necessary for her long-term health.

There was only one more small village between Draviak and the border. They didn't stop. They didn't want to risk it.

Dorm knew that he would have to find a chapterhouse and talk about this with the Rangers there. Probably everyone did. They had been witness to something special; he knew that, but something a little scary at the same time. He hadn't realised that people could still get so hostile towards people afflicted with magic. There were stories of course, but on one really believed them.

Now he began to.

They approached the border late in the afternoon, and crossed without incident. There was a bit of a line they had to get through and so it was going on dusk when they were finally ushered through. They decided to stay the night at the hostel provided for such eventualities. They were cramped but relatively comfortable, and everyone just wanted to sleep after the events of the morning.

They rose with the sun, and left after a brief meal. Again there was mostly silence. Everyone was still trying to understand it all. Would the same sort of thing happen to them? Would they be forced to 'do things' and have whole villages turn against them? No one knew. But everyone feared it. They were after all mixed up in something quite beyond what any of them were used to. There had already been strange incidents along the way. If more happened, and they weren't able to explain…

The land in this part of southern Bydanushev was much the same as that of northern Ojliam. Picturesque rolling hills, small clumps of trees. The odd stream. There were a few villages set back from the main highway and interspersed between them were farmsteads. All in all it was much as they had suspected. And gave them no clue as to where to go.

According to the maps, this highway lead to the city of Ovgrichenk. No one knew anything about it, and it would take several days to get there.

Dorm had only ever met a few Bydanush in his time. Mostly ambassadors and their families. He had always found them to be likeable people, who loved having a good time. Once, that was, you got past their cold and grim exterior.

He counted on seeing a lot more of that exterior over the coming days.

They tried to stay away from villages for the first few nights, no one wanting to put the group into that situation again just yet. They got better at camping. It was easy to forget that both Kanilma and Poljazak had only been with them for less than a fortnight. It already seemed a lot longer. Perhaps that was just the way recent events made it seem. But the two newest arrivals to their group were integrating well, and everyone was getting on with them. It was clear they were still becoming the group of people they had to be.

The fourth night into Bydanushev they had no choice but to take lodgings. It was late enough that to proceed on would look strange, and be noticed. They were still worried about the possibility of bandits. While they hadn't heard anything to indicate that there were any in Bydanushev, they didn't have anything to suggest there weren't.

The inn they stayed in was small, and not particularly clean, but it was warmer than staying outside. And above all it was cheap. It also removed the possibility of getting attacked during the night. Dorm had had the creeping feeling every night since they had crossed the border that there was something coming. He wasn't sure if that was just because of the events in Draviak or something else.

They left the inn first thing in the morning, Telly, Rhyn and Tissie expressing a desire to find a bathhouse as soon as possible. There were no objections.

It was another two days before they sighted the city of

Ovgrichenk. It wasn't fully walled but did have a series of large fortified towers that would have given any attacker some serious trouble. Most of the buildings appeared to be of yellow looking stone, with slate roofs. The town presented itself grimly as they entered, and they did their best to keep to themselves. There were signs here and there of liveliness, and even some happiness, but it became muted as they passed.

They took shelter for the night in a large hostel and were shown to a small dormitory for their use. This was a new situation. No one was quite sure how everyone sleeping in the same room was going to work, but it was a place to stay. They ate a meal, and discussed searching the town for clues as to the amulets. This was why they were here.

As there were still a few hours left in the day, they decided to risk it and try to see if they could find out anything. They broke into smaller groups so they would hopefully be less intimidating and maybe illicit some more information from the people of Ovgrichenk.

They wandered through various markets and public areas listening and watching, but nothing of any great value turned up. They did hear some rumours of possible bandits in the area, confirming their fears, but also heard how the Bydanushev army had been giving them a severe thrashing in recent weeks. It was good to know some things were going right.

There were no mentions of amulets, and the few people who did seem to notice theirs, seemed to only take a passing interest. It was becoming clear that Ovgrichenk was not somewhere they wanted to remain any longer than necessary.

The next day they sought out the chapterhouse of the Rangers. Again it was hidden on a back street in the industrial part of the town. The ring of smithies and the smell of a nearby tannery confirming that this was the less desirable part of the town.

Again upon passing through the gate, it was like entering another world. Well tended gardens and polished stone gave an elegant almost regal feel to the place. It was much quieter here, and the aroma of flowers and fragrant bushes almost completely blocked the smells of the surrounding area.

This chapterhouse wasn't as large as the one in Kiama Mor that they had gone to, but still had the same feeling of serenity and peacefulness as that building. They were ushered through various corridors and atria to a large waiting room, rather similar to the one on the previous building.

"This feels familiar," Zacravia said quietly to the room as the entered.

After a few moments a woman entered wearing a Ranger cloak. Her blonde hair was curled and hung long down her neck. She stood tall, even though she was shorter than Dorm. She had a presence that seemed to fill the room. This was someone you listened to. She bowed shortly before them. "Noble Questers. Welcome to Ovgrichenk Chapterhouse. I am Ilavis. Master of this Place."

"Thank you for seeing us," Dorm said to her, inclining his head in response.

"You do us great honour by your visit."

"We have some questions…" he began.

"We know. Draviak," Ilavis said cutting him off. "It has been difficult for you all."

"How could you know about that?" Telly asked curiously.

"We have ways of communicating that you do not," was her cryptic response. "You may rest assured that Barassa is doing very well. In fact Navis has suggested that she may be more powerful than he had first thought."

"More powerful?" Lianna said confused. "I don't understand."

"That is another thing that you will have to wait to find out."

"I presume it has something to do with magic," Dorm ventured.

"Indeed," Ilavis said after a moments hesitation.

"Is she still, 'sick'?" Harmia asked curiously. "We wouldn't like to think we went through all that for nothing."

"She is responding well," Ilavis said smiling. "It takes some weeks, but she is well on her way. I assure you no harm will come to her."

"What about that Ravic man and those others that were with him?" Artur asked.

"Yes he is a concern," Ilavis admitted a little reluctantly. "We have not had such animosity directed towards an Awakened for many years. Your presence seemed to both exacerbate and calm the situation."

"Awakened?" Pianwasal asked. "What is that?"

"Our term for those like young Barassa," Ilavis explained. "Who have begun to experience their abilities."

"Magic you mean," Travanos said glumly.

"Indeed Admiral."

"What normally happens then?" Rhyn asked curiously.

"Normally we are able to approach them and help them through the initial transition before anything like what happened to Barassa can occur. It is a gradual process and normally we do our best to keep it private, and away from those around the person involved, other than their immediate family of course. It is a dangerous time for them, as you have seen. More so when people such as this Ravic are around. But he will be dealt with."

"Dealt with?" began Ambra worriedly. "What does that mean exactly?"

"Do not worry. He will not be harmed. We do not do such things unless there is no alternative."

"This is all very well," said Zacravia loudly. "But we have a job to do and all this worrying over Barassa isn't helping us. Is she really alright?"

"I assure you she is well. And he father is also being looked after."

"Sounds good enough for me," Zacravia concluded.

It was good to know that Barassa and her father were both doing well. It was also satisfying to know that Ravic would be dealt with. Dorm was a little ashamed of himself for thinking that way, but in essence the man had tried to kill him and people close to him. When he thought on that, he didn't feel quite so bad about those thoughts. They returned to their inn and left the next morning.

It took them another two and a half weeks to reach Bydanushev itself. Along the way there was little in the way of excitement. A few local events but nothing particularly exciting. And of course no leads. They thought perhaps they may have been on to something once, when on the outskirts of Rusank they heard tell of a woman with a great medallion. After some searching and careful questioning they discovered it was a noblewoman of some sort from Rusank itself, and they headed there with all haste.

After several hours of careful investigation they discovered to their disappointment that the woman in question was the Duchess of Rusank and that the medallion she wore wasn't anything like what they were looking for, being a large round gold weight that hung from a rather long gold chain. It turned out to be embossed with various things including an eagle, and most of the women in the group agreed it was rather gaudy.

There were no sightings of any bandits, and they only saw one group of troops pass them, one day while staying in a village. There were a few rumours, but nothing really very solid. Only vague whisperings of bandits being slaughtered somewhere.

Finally they approached the capital one mid-morning as the weather was starting to turn. Clouds had been building for the last few days so they knew it was coming. Bydanushev city was large. Larger than Lugemall, that Dorm knew. It was a well-fortified place, which had only been enhanced because of the Peldraksekhr invasion. There were plenty of main turrets in the walls, and also a large number of smaller intermediary ones. The gatehouses were even larger than the ones at Ojliam had been, and there were heavy outer barbicans to help protect them. Large ditches had been excavated around the gates, so that any invaders wouldn't be able to attack the gatehouses directly without first taking the barbicans.

All in all Dorm was rather impressed. If Lugemall was ever attacked while he was around, he now knew some things he would do to help defend it.

The city teemed with people, as all capitals did, and the hustle and bustle reminded many of them of home. They wound their way through the streets and avenues towards one of the less crowded districts to take lodgings. The buildings of Bydanushev were tall, and mostly stone. There was a grimness to them, all being rather plain with just a few touches and embellishments here and there. There was a lot more colour than there had been in Ojliam though, which was one thing. And some effort had been made to beautify the main streets with the planting of trees along their edges.

Once they had settled in they went off to begin exploring the city and to get their bearings. They visited several markets in smaller groups and met up with each other at various times to compare notes. A light drizzle began to fall after a few hours, but it hardly seemed to dampen the spirits of the locals. Business went on as usual.

Dorm began to notice that the various public buildings; courts, government offices, public baths, libraries and so on, were decorated beyond what he had expected. It was almost as if the city had been designed to make them stand out, so that they could shout 'I am a public building. I am important!' Statues, engravings, friezes, frescoes, even a few climbing vines on occasion. Copper and lead roofing. Even in some cases multicoloured tiled roofing. And on the extremely important buildings, strangely shaped domes that rose to a short spire.

This city was a clash of expectations and architecture. Dorm began to piece together a theory. Could it be that all the civilian buildings, houses, shops and the like were all similar and plain, in order to create a sense of oneness, of community?

Where as the important buildings, those that defined who and what the Bydanush people were, had been spruced up to the hilt? And in some cases beyond.

They still didn't find any sort of leads, and there was much of the city they couldn't explore in just one afternoon. It got colder as the hours wore on and everyone decided it was best to call it a day and start again fresh tomorrow. Everyone was tired from the journey and it was quite possible they could miss something important. Reluctantly they all returned to their accommodations and relaxed for the rest of the evening.

The next morning, they rose early in order to have a full day of searching. Cal and Harmia intended to try to give the information to the local police, since it had been a good idea in the past. Zacravia intended to try and contact the 'usual element' as he described it. Lianna and Ambra said they knew of a few business people in city and so went off to make contact with them. Ameks elected to contact a local artisans guild he had heard tell of to see if they might know anything.

The rest of them broke up into groups and began wandering the city again. It was never easy, simply going from one market or square to another hoping to find some sort of lead. The streets were full of people, and most of the time, they were too busy watching where they were going, rather than being on the lookout for the amulets.

The weather was still cool, and several brief showers made things interesting. The day proved rather uneventful and also rather unfruitful. While the respective groups had been alerted to their interest, so far nothing had come up.

They spent a rather dejected and quiet evening, talking about nothing in particular, listening to the rain as it fell outside.

Dorm sat next to the window watching the rain splashing into the courtyard outside. He was rather pensive. He could feel that things were moving in the right direction. Somehow he knew that they were here at the right time. But he just didn't know what to do next.

Pianwasal sat down next to him. "What are you thinking of my friend?" she asked him quietly.

"About what to do next," he replied. "I get the feeling there is something we should be doing to help us find the next person."

"We are here now. We listen and watch. And the Gods will provide."

"The Gods?" he scoffed.

"Yes I know you do not believe in such things. But they are important to our people. Ask Ameks some time, why he became a sculptor. His answer may help you to understand." She looked at him thoughtfully for a moment before rising and walking off. He looked across as Ameks. The man was always very quiet. He, like Artur came from some of the lowest rungs on the social ladder. And like Artur felt a little out of place amongst all these important people.

Dorm had tried to engage him in conversation several times, but he had always seemed reluctant. Almost as if he felt that he was taking up Dorms' valuable time or something. He decided to correct that the next day.

No news came the next morning so they decided to break up into groups again and see what happened. Dorm purposely tried to mix up the groups a little. There seemed to be people who always ended up together, and he felt it better to pair people up differently. He asked Mac to go with Kanilma and he took Ameks off so he could try to open him up a bit. They wandered down one of the main avenues in that part of the city, heading towards an area that had a lot of commercial houses. They were all fairly plain but rather larger than the buildings around them. It was clear to see that these merchants had done well for themselves.

After studying one of these buildings for a few moments Ameks gave a scoffing laugh.

"What is it?" Dorm asked him.

"That corner of that house," he said pointing across the street.

"What about it?"

"The foundation was not laid properly. I give it another year or two and that whole lower section of the wall will have to be replaced."

"Why is that?"

"It's started to sink," he said. "You can see it if you look further up the wall. The angle of the stones changes slightly."

Dorm followed Ameks directions and did after a moment notice that the lower parts of the wall were on a tiny angle away from the horizontal. He would never have noticed it if Ameks hadn't pointed it out.

"It's something you notice when you work with stone as much as I do."

"So why did you become a sculptor?" Dorm asked him as they began to move off.

"It will sound silly to you," he said lowering his gaze. "But I was called to."

"Called to? What do you mean?"

"I had always wanted to be a boat worker on the Sacred River. There are so many boats and they are sailing all the time, there is never any shortage of work. I would have had a job for life. But there was this nagging feeling the whole time during my youth, that I was doing the wrong thing. One day I went to a temple to pray on it. It happened to be a temple of Hep."

"And…" Dorm said after a moment, when Ameks didn't continue. "What happened?"

"He told me to become a sculptor. He showed me that one day I would create a great statue in his honour, and one of the Phirinos. Everyday I worked hard to become a sculptor and to try to become the best that I could be." He sighed heavily. "I know I am not the best though."

"You were good enough to win that competition. Without that we would never have found you."

"But what am I contributing High... Dormal?" he corrected himself. "I am just here to make up the numbers."

Dorm stopped. "No my friend you're not. That thing back there with the building. I would never have known that. Never would have seen it if you hadn't pointed it out to me. We don't know what's going to happen once we find everyone. But things like that... they have a habit of coming in handy when you least expect them. I mean you know about buildings and stone. I don't. Telly doesn't. Travanos doesn't have a clue. No one does. Any time we need to get into a place, or maybe get out of one... you're the man we'll be asking for."

Ameks thought on this for a moment. "And how often do you think that will happen?"

"Knowing my luck. Probably more often than we want."

Again that day no one found anything interesting. Zacravia had the feeling that he had been watched at various times during the day, and began to suspect that some members of the "fraternity" as he had begun calling it, were not entirely convinced of his story. He told them he would take extra precautions.

Cal and Harmia had been informed by the local police that one promising lead had turned out to be wrong, but that they were still investigating. All in all it was a rather unproductive day that left everyone feeling rather deflated. Would they ever get anything? It had almost been a given that they would find the first person fairly rapidly. They had commented on this numerous times in the past, about how quickly and apparently easily they had found the various members of their group. So far here in Bydanushev things were going rather slower.

Yet another day dawned and yet another day of wandering around aimlessly beckoned. No one was particularly looking forward to it, but then they didn't really have much choice. Dorm briefly considered going to the palace and enlisting the aid of the Bydanush king, one Nivazlos II in perhaps finding out something. Dorm had only ever met the king once, very briefly when he was in his early teens, when Nivazlos had been on a grand tour of the Alliance. He was a tall, powerfully built man with a thick dark beard and stern eyes. Dorm hadn't really liked him that much, but then hadn't really spent much time with him. The two kings had gone off to discuss whatever kings discussed on those occasions, and Dorm had returned to his tutors.

He eventually dismissed the idea, as he had no knowledge of what sort of man Nivazlos was these days. He might prove very helpful. He might equally prove to be a hindrance. Also it meant they wouldn't get bogged down in any officialness.

The groups broke up again and began their journeys through the city. In the last few days they had actually covered a fair amount of it. There were some areas that they hadn't been to yet. Notably the palace, and some of the more fragrant industrial areas. These areas had a tendency to breed crime, and Dorm was reluctant to let the smaller groups go there. They could wait a few days till they had covered the rest of the city, and therefore take a larger group into those areas.

Dorm, Cal and Navista had found their way to a large market in the northern part of the city. The square contained a large statue to one King Ivab VIII, who had ruled several centuries ago, and was apparently responsible for those trees on the streets they had noted upon arrival.

The market was bustling as was expected. The various groups would all be making their way here over the next little while to meet up, have a meal and compare anything that had happened. They weren't expecting much.

The rain had held off for most of the morning, but now it seemed likely it was going to return soon. There was a definite chill in the air.

The three of them found a spot out the front of a tavern where they could be seen by their friends and sat down to wait. A serving boy took their orders and eventually brought them out. Not long after Kanilma, Lianna, and Travanos arrived, and sat down. They had nothing to report. They had stopped at every jewellery shop and gem merchant they had seen, but none had known anything about their amulets. As was usual, more than a couple had offered to buy them.

A short time later, Dorm saw Zacravia enter the square from a side street not far away. He seemed flustered for some reason. Dorm was momentarily distracted and when he looked back he had lost sight of him. He couldn't see Rhyn or Tissie who had gone with him.

He paid it little heed. It would probably take Zacravia and the girls a bit of time to locate them. Kanilma was commenting on the quality of the meal they had been served, claiming that her and her guardians could make a better meal with their hands tied behind their back. Dorm didn't doubt that for a moment. Kanilma had come into her own once she had realised how little cooking skills there actually were in the group.

Suddenly Zacravia was standing next to them. Dorm had noticed that about their criminal friend. He could sneak up on you quite successfully. He still appeared flustered. And a little confused. His hands twitched convulsively.

"Sit down Zac," Lianna said to him. "Kanilma is telling us what is wrong with this food."

"I didn't say there was anything wrong with it, just that I could do it better."

"Zac, what is it?" Dorm said realising that something was wrong.

"Well I…" he began. "I don't… I mean… I just can't understand…"

This was very unlike Zacravia to be stuck for words. The others noticed it too.

"Wos goin' on Zac," Cal said suspiciously.

"Has something happened?" Navista asked. "You look almost scared."

"Where are the girls?" Travanos asked warily looking around.

"I was just, I mean I had to go and look, but I wasn't gone for…" he continued in his stuttered manner.

"Zacravia," Dorm said sternly. "What has happened? Where are Rhyn and Tissie?"

Zacravia blinked at him for a moment. "I don't understand it." He said confusingly.

"Zacravia tell me what is going on?" Dorm repeated urgently. "Where are the girls?"

"I don't know," he said after a moment. "They're gone. I... I think they've been taken."

Chapter 34

She was hot.

This was the overriding feeling right at the moment. Hot and stuffy.

But then one couldn't really expect anything else with a large hessian bag over ones head.

Rhyn was conscious of the fact that she was helpless, as they half dragged, half carried her to wherever it was that they were taking her. Her hands tied and her feet bound she was utterly useless, and so was at the mercy of those who carried her.

She could hear the odd noise from somewhere nearby that indicated that Tissie was there as well, and that gave her some comfort. At least they were still together. That was something. What exactly, she wasn't sure, but still…

She knew she was underground. It felt cooler, and it was darker. Occasionally they splashed through water, and there were smells. Oh there were smells.

Where they were she had no idea. It had been a very quick change of scenery. They had been walking along a street talking. Zacravia had thought he noticed someone following them, and told them to wait near the entrance to an alleyway, while he went and investigated. He had only been gone a few minutes, when there was a commotion from up the street. The girls had tried to see what it was without going anywhere, but could only make out a large crowd gathering. Before either of them knew what was happening, they had been grabbed from behind and trussed up the way they now were. Tissie had tried to scream, and the way the scream suddenly ended gave Rhyn the impression that she had either been knocked out, or had something put in her mouth to silence her.

Thank goodness for small miracles.

Now they were being taken somewhere. The Fortress only knew where. But wherever it was, was sure to be unpleasant. Rhyn's only hope lay in that Zacravia would be able to find them, or at least get the others to help find them.

Zacravia. He must be going out of his mind right now. He had been moody all day. He had mentioned the previous day how he had thought someone was following and watching them. Obviously his instincts were right. Too right as it turned out. Rhyn knew that he would be blaming himself for this turn of events. It wasn't his fault. They should have been more careful. Made sure they were watching for anything suspicious. She realised now that the commotion on the street was probably intentionally created to distract everyone from what was about to happen to them. But there was nothing that could be done now.

They continued along the twisting and turning route their kidnappers had chosen for them for some time. She began to worry that any one would ever be able to find them. She tried to calm herself, breathing regularly and trying not to worry too much. The smell of the hessian was musty and the coarse fibres seemed to get up her nose and into her mouth no matter what she did to try and stop it.

Finally they were dumped rather unceremoniously on the ground. It was clearly stone, though by the feel of things, there were rushes or straw strewn about as well. She could hear the dripping of water and from somewhere, another rather nasty odour. There were footsteps echoing around them, and she got the impression they were in a large place. Whispered voices could be heard having a hurried exchange. She couldn't make out what they were saying but obviously it was a recount of what had happened.

Rhyn felt some movement next to her. "Tissie?" she whispered.

"Rhyn?" She responded equally quietly, in part due to whatever they had stuffed into her mouth. She hadn't actually said 'Rhyn', it had sounded more like 'Win', but she knew what it had meant. The catch in her voice showed how terrified she was. "Mummf muph muf,"

"Indeed. Just try to stay calm. I don't think these people mean to harm us," She silently hoped that were true. "Just stay focused. We are going to get away from here."

There was another muffled reply.

There was silence for a few moments, and then the bag was taken off her head. She was momentarily blinded. It wasn't particularly bright, there only being a few guttering torches and lamps to light the large space, but after having had her head in the bag for so long her eyes took a moment to adjust. The bag was also taken off of Tissie's head, and after a moments hesitation the rag was removed from her mouth.

The room contained various crates and barrels, lengths of rope and various other industrial looking odds and ends. They were clearly in some sort of cellar. Various men and even a few women stood around the room. All wore common clothing, and had a slightly grubby look to them.

"So what have we here?" said a voice. It came from a man sitting on top of a crate in front of Rhyn and Tissie. He was rather thin, and not particularly attractive. His hair was rather unkempt. He wore clothes that once must have been quite well to do, but had been allowed to go over the years. He needed to shave, and his lips looked rather dry. His skin was pale, and it was clear that whoever he was he didn't venture far into the world during the day. "Why are you here?"

"I could ask you the same question," Rhyn ventured cautiously. "Why have you brought us here?"

"I will ask the questions if you don't mind." The man retorted. "You see we have become very curious about you and your friends."

"Which friends?" Maybe a little misdirection would work.

"The ones you are staying at the Wounded Bull with. The ones you have been venturing out into the city with for the last three days."

Obviously not.

"Oh those friends." Rhyn said non-committally. "What is it you want to know?"

"Why are you here in Bydanushev?"

"We're just passing through. Should be gone in a few days."

"We have heard of this story of yours. Looking for amulets of some sort? We do not believe you."

"That's your prerogative."

"So why don't you tell me the real reason you are here."

"Well since you already know it, and don't believe us, there's not much point in me doing that is there?"

"What do you take us for?"

"Right now?" She looked them over. "Kidnappers. Ruffians. Thieves. No one I would trust."

"Rhyn!" Tissie said worriedly.

"And you would be right," said the man with a smile. "But we look after each other. And this story of yours… It makes us suspicious. I mean such a large group just to find an amulet?"

"Actually it's two…" she began.

"Two?!" the man lent forward. "Interesting. And what do these amulets mean?"

"Oh not a great deal. They have a sentimental value, but not much more."

"Now I know you are lying." The man grinned from ear to ear. He got up and walked towards the girls. He slowly knelt down in front of them. Rhyn would have preferred it if he had bathed first. "People don't gather together such large groups to go find things that are of no value." He said quietly. "Perhaps you should start explaining. Or we wont be able to help you."

"Help us," Tissie said. "How can you help us?"

"Perhaps we know where there is an amulet like the one you seek."

"Perhaps you can help us find it and then we'll tell you?" Rhyn countered.

"Perhaps not. You are in no position to bargain with me little lady. You are tied and cannot escape without getting hopelessly lost. What do you propose to do? Wander around until some city worker finds you? That may take days."

"Perhaps I can make a deal with you. You show us where this amulet is, and my friends don't come and kill you all. How does that sound?"

There was laughter from all around.

"Bravado? I like that." He slowly walked around the room, looking into the face of those around him. "You're friends are that capable?"

"Yes they are."

"We shall see." He paused for a moment. "Watch them."

He stalked from the room, followed by several of the others.

"We'll just wait here then." Rhyn called after him.

It was about half an hour before he returned. A rather long and boring half hour. Rhyn did her best to keep herself occupied, and to look for ways to escape. She watched the people in the room carefully. Noted the way they walked. The way they held their hands, and the way they stood. None of them said very much to them. She knew that any chance to escape would come suddenly and she wouldn't have much time to let Tissie know. She did her best to communicate with her companion, but Tissie may have been too scared to fully comprehend.

She tried to take note of the layout of the room, and where the doors were, like Zacravia had mentioned a captured person should always do. The first duty of the prisoner was to escape he always said. It was hard to get this information without looking at least a little suspicious, but she did learn a thing or two about where they had been brought. Of course that wouldn't help them much once they had gotten out of here. They had both been blinded on their way in. Their captor may have been right. They may just have to wait till some city worker found them.

She did her best to keep Tissie calm, and to her credit she did a good job of it, given the circumstances. Rhyn began to think that perhaps she had underestimated the blonde girl.

The man returned with his cohorts, and took up his previous position on a crate. He stared at them for a few moments before speaking.

"So are you going to tell me the truth now?" he said menacingly. "Now that you've had time to fully consider your situation."

"We have told you the truth," Tissie said to him somewhat haughtily. Rhyn was surprised. It was rather unlike her to be so forceful and upfront.

"Oh is that so?" their captor replied leaning forward and adopting what could almost be considered a concerned expression. "Well in that case I guess I had better let you go."

He paused for a moment. "Of course I don't believe you. We know that you have gone to the police and told them that the amulet you seek… sorry amu*lets* you seek, are a part of a family collection. And that you believe they were stolen."

"Well if you know that, then you also know that we made special mention of the fact that they were stolen a century or two ago, and that any one who possesses one is not a thief," Rhyn replied angrily.

"I have heard that also," he replied quietly. He stood and slowly paced around the room. He seemed to have a need to do so. Perhaps he thought it was intimidating or something. Rhyn just found it annoying.

He stood behind Tissie for a moment. Her expression clearly indicated that she was uncomfortable. Suddenly he grabbed her shoulders and held her. He knelt down behind her and whispered in her ear, "Tell me what the truth of these amulets is and I will let you go."

"We have," she whispered in return, terror clearly evident in her voice. "We have told you the truth."

He released her after a moment. Tissie let out a sob.

He stared at Rhyn for a moment. "Tell me what you intend to do with this person who has the amulet when you find them?"

"Well that is our business."

"Well I'm making it mine, little Miss."

"Little Miss?" Rhyn said with a laugh in her voice. "Who says that?"

A dagger was suddenly at her throat. "I do," said his voice in her ear. "And if you want to stay unharmed I suggest you tell me what I want to know."

She understood that he was serious. She tried to relax a little, which was hard when there is a blade at ones throat. She closed her eyes and breathed in deeply. Something she had seen Pianwasal do on occasion. It seemed to clam her down.

"We will just be talking to them. There is important information that we need to tell them."

"Tell me what that is?"

"Not going to happen," she said defiantly. "It is only for the people with the amulets. Besides it wouldn't mean much to you."

"Oh and why is that? Aren't I smart enough to understand?"

"No, that isn't what I meant. It just won't mean a great deal to any one but the person who has the amulet."

There was a pause. The dagger slowly moved away. She heard it returned to its sheath, and she sighed. Their captor slowly walked back around in front of them, and returned to his perch on the crate. He too sighed.

Something told Rhyn that he was now satisfied. That perhaps he actually believed them. He sat there for a moment or two thinking. He opened his mouth to say something but then closed it again. Then he looked at one of his offsiders who just shrugged.

"Ogn," he called to a young man who stood nearby, his eyes never leaving the girls. "Call the gang together. We need to talk."

Rhyn now had a suspicion.

It was probably another half an hour until they returned. This time their captor and the one he had named as Ogn had several more people with them. Most of them were young. What was this? Rhyn began to think. Some sort of thieves' crèche?

Their captor sat in his usual place and stared at them for a while. It was clear that everyone was waiting for him to say something. They all kept glancing at him.

"I admit that I don't know what to do with you?" he said slowly. "I have taken you for one reason, but now that reason seems to have vanished. But then I can't let you go without risking everything we have here. And I am starting to run out of places I can go."

That was lost on the girls. They had no idea what he meant by that. "Couldn't you just stick those bags on our heads again?" Tissie suggested, quite cleverly. "You could take us back to where you got us from."

"Yeah they wouldn't be able to see anything," said one of the thieves.

"And you have to admit it would be pretty hard for us to identify you without going through every person in this city." Rhyn reminded him. Perhaps escaping from these people wouldn't be as hard as she had first thought.

"We can always create distractions so we won't get caught," suggested another of the thieves.

"And we can always lie low for a few days," the one called Ogn agreed.

"That's not the point," said the leader. He looked at Ogn. "And you know it now."

What did that mean?

"Yes I understand now, Iv," he replied.

Iv. So that was the man's name. Or at least part of it.

"We are willing to make sure our friends don't come looking for you," Rhyn promised. "I think we can convince them that this was all just a big misunderstanding. *If* we are returned to them unharmed… and soon."

Iv, seemed to think about this for a while. It was clear he was torn. His concern for their getting back and telling everyone about them, even describing them, she could understand. It was clear these were criminal elements, and were probably wanted by the police. She could easily understand and to an extent even sympathise with him. He obviously cared for these people and wanted them to be safe.

But there was something else. He was clearly thinking about something else. Some consideration other than that. Rhyn began to suspect that her suspicions were correct. But she didn't want to say anything just yet.

It was clear that he didn't really want to hurt them. That was all just posturing, to try and get them to talk. These people weren't murderers. Thieves maybe, but not killers. Rhyn dearly wished that Zacravia were here. He would know precisely how to handle them.

"The friend you took us from," she ventured. "He is a thief as well." There were some curious looks at that. "Or at least was. He's sort of reformed now."

"Sort of?" enquired Iv curiously.

"Well let's just say we're still working on his edges. And I guess his skills have come in handy on several occasions. Perhaps we don't want to completely reform him."

"That would explain how he knew how to contact us. His techniques are slightly different to what is used here in Bydanushev, so I'm guessing he is from somewhere else…"

"Ambaka yes. Our group is from all over."

Iv stared at them again for a moment.

"This is so confusing," he whispered.

"I think I may be beginning to understand why." Rhyn said. She looked at Tissie and nodded. Somehow that was all she needed. Together the two women removed their amulets from their clothing and let them be seen. There were some that stared. Even a sharp intake of breath or two. A few muttered voices.

Rhyn and Tissie both looked at Iv.

"Well?" Rhyn said. Tissie clearly now understood what Rhyn suspected as she began to smile.

Iv sighed heavily than sat up straight. He reached inside his rather dirty looking linen shirt and pulled out an amulet.

All the thieves stared at it for a moment, before looking at the amulets worn by the girls, then back again.

"They're the same," said Ogn quietly.

Rhyn and Tissie just looked at each other for a moment. Then when they couldn't hold it in any longer descended into peals of laughter. The two of them laughed so hard they both had tears on their cheeks. Rhyn lay down on her back and laughed harder. Tissie was soon as prone as her and just as caught up in the guffaws.

"What, what is it?" Iv demanded to know.

"Can you believe this," Rhyn said to Tissie while they still lay on the floor.

"We should have seen this coming shouldn't we," she replied.

"Probably yes," Rhyn said trying to dry her eyes. "If only the others could see how this turned out."

"They may not quite see the funny side like we do," Tissie admitted.

"Oh dear no." They realised they were being stared at. "Sorry. Just a funny situation."

"I'm sure it is somehow," Iv said to them in a voice that indicated he clearly didn't understand.

"Sorry, We'll have to explain that later," Rhy told him. "But for right now. You have no choice but to take us back to our friends."

"And you have to come with us, so we can tell you what it is that we need to tell you," Tisse said to him.

"I don't really have much of a choice do I?" he asked them.

"No I'm afraid none of us do really."

And so they were free.

At least technically. They still had to negotiate their way out of the maze of tunnels below the city. Their former captors intended to take them to somewhere near their inn, so they could be back with the others as soon as possible. Both Rhyn and Tissie knew that after this amount of time the others would be frantic, and probably fearing the worst. Zacravia would undoubtedly have met up with Dorm and the others and informed them of what had happened. They would all now be engaged, or at least preparing to be engaged in a desperate search across the city for them.

They headed in what Rhyn thought might have been a westerly direction, but could easily have been any direction really. She was so turned around she had no idea. Their hosts asked them questions about the amulets and what was going on, the young people being very curious indeed. The girls tried to not answer their questions with things that sounded like answers, so that they wouldn't be disappointed. But they didn't want to give anything away.

The one called Iv, simply walked in front. He said nothing except to issue directions and occasionally tell people to hurry up or keep the noise down. He seemed a bit withdrawn now. Perhaps he suspected some of what was going to occur. Or he just dreaded the idea of exposing himself to friends of people he'd just kidnapped.

They had been walking for about a quarter of an hour when suddenly he stopped. All the thieves fell silent and listened. Rhyn and Tissie looked at each other curiously not being sure what was happening. After a moment Iv gave the signal to move on, and they did. But not long later he stopped again.

"I heard it too," said the one called Ogn.

"Heard what?" asked Tissie with a hint of worry in her voice.

"I think someone may be following us," Iv replied. He nodded to Ogn who ran ahead and went down a side passage. He returned a moment or two later and nodded. "Let's move on quickly and quietly," Iv said and he lead the way.

They continued on through the gloom and darkness for another little while, the girls getting more nervous by the second. Who was following them? What did they want? Could it be Dorm and the others coming to find them?

"Not far now," one of the young thieves whispered to them reassuringly.

They entered a long straight passage that seemed to have no passages branching off it. Iv and the thieves in the front began jogging along it on nearly silent feet. Rhyn and Tissie were caught up in the pace and went along with it, even though they would have preferred to just walk.

When they were about halfway along there was suddenly shouting from all around them. No one was quite sure what was happening, but figures loomed out of the darkness. Armed figures by the look of things. Looking behind them it was clear that their retreat was also blocked.

Rhyn could see that there weren't that many of them, and they were mostly young, much like their companions, but they were in a difficult position strategically. They would suffer injuries and possibly losses before they enjoyed any victories.

A man stepped from the shadows in front of them and walked slowly towards the front of their group.

"Ivgrachev." He rasped menacingly.

So Iv was short for something.

"Drakiv," Ivgrachev nodded by way of greeting.

"What are you doing in my part of the city?"

"Oh just passing through. Had some people to take back to the surface, and this was the quickest way."

Drakiv looked at Rhyn and Tissie. "They don't seem your usual fare Ivgrachev."

"A long story I'm afraid. Bit of a misunderstanding. Thought it best to send them back before things got bad for any one."

"Not a bad idea. Pity that won't be happening now," replied Drakiv. "I owe you much Ivgrachev, for what you have done."

"A misunderstanding Drakiv. I told you all this already. I already went to T'Zedella like you asked me too."

"Not good enough."

"We had a deal. Will you now dishonour it?"

That seemed to enrage him all the more. "I am not the dishonourable one. You steal what is rightfully mine. Now you betray our deal. You shall pay for that indiscretion."

Without so much as a signal or a word, Drakiv's people sprang forward to attack Ivgrachevs'. It wasn't much of a fight. They weren't trained warriors or soldiers or anything, and even Rhyn could tell that their fighting styles were born out of hard years living on the streets, or in this case below them. But both sides gave as good as they got. Daggers flashed through the air and fists were swung violently.

Tissie grabbed Rhyn and pulled her back against the wall as two scrabbling youths jostled past them.

"Thanks," Rhyn told her.

"You're welcome," Tissie replied almost pleasantly.

After what seemed hours, but was probably no more than a few minutes the fighting was over. Several youths on both sides lay panting and scruffed around the area. There were more than a few cuts that bled. Ogn still had one younger man in a headlock, but was about to let him go, cautioning him not to try anything when he did.

Ivgrachev and Drakiv stood next to each other at the end of the ambush area. They were very still. It almost looked as if they were talking quietly. Rhyn presumed that that wasn't the case. "Ivgrachev?" she called out to him.

Drakiv suddenly slumped to the ground. A dagger protruding from his chest. It was clear that for the two men this had been personal. The fighting of the others had meant nothing to them. Whatever was between them was a personal score that could only be settled by them.

Upon seeing that their leader had fallen, the fight went all out of Drakiv's people. There were sighs and even a sob or two.

Ivgrachev took a staggered step backwards and straightened up.

"Are you alright Iv?" Ogn said moving towards him.

"Yes I'm fine."

They moved towards him. Ogn was the first to reach him. As soon as he did Rhyn realised by his reaction that something was wrong. A sharp intake of breath and a change in expression. When she got to them she saw instantly what it was. During their fight Drakiv had managed to pin Ivgrachev with his dagger as well. While Ivgrachev had gone straight for the kill shot as it were, taking his adversary through the heart, Drakiv had obviously wanted Ivgrachev to suffer, and so had stabbed him in the stomach.

He was already bleeding badly.

It was the sort of wound that would cause you to die very slowly, as you slowly bled to death. So there was a lot of opportunity to be saved. But you would be in agony all the while. Rhyn knew that here in this sewer there would be great chance of infection and disease, if they didn't do something quickly.

"What do we do?" Ogn exclaimed dancing on the spot in confusion and worry.

"How far are we from our inn?"

"About another ten minutes or so," replied the boy.

"Then we have to hurry. If we can get him there, we can get him to a physician."

"But won't your friends…" Ogn began.

"Bugger that for the moment," Rhyn said angrily. "We have to save his life."

Rhyn looked at Tissie. They both knew exactly what Ivgrachevs' death would mean. They didn't even want to entertain the idea, let alone see it happen. If the others had a problem with things, they would soon get over it once they saw the amulet.

Ivgrachev was now starting to pass out from the pain. Tissie was doing her best to try and bandage his wound.

"Ogn," Rhyn said commandingly. "Lead the way."

Chapter 35

Catastrophe.

This was the word that best described the feeling in the group right at the moment.

Other words jumped to mind as well. Fear, desperation, panic, hopelessness. But catastrophe was foremost in their minds, and seemed to sum it all up nicely. The real question now of course was what to do about it?

Dorm and the others had done their best to digest the announcement that Zacravia had made. There was no point in blaming him. Whoever had taken Rhyn and Tissie had obviously planned this well. And to his credit Zacravia had been wary the day before. He had warned them something was happening.

They did their best to hide their fear. There was no point in making a big scene out here in this public place. Everyone was intending to meet them here shortly, so instead of rushing back to the inn or to the authorities, they decided to wait. As each group of their friends arrived they apprised them of the situation. Mac, Telly, Travanos and Artur headed back to the inn to wait, in case the girls managed to escape and make it back there.

The rest headed towards the last place that Zacravia had seen them. It was about the only place they could look. Though when they got there, there was nothing that indicated which way they might have been taken.

They asked a few of the local people, but no one had seen anything. They searched the immediate area, looking in all the doorways and alleys they could find, but there was nothing.

As they searched that slow creeping fear began to sneak up on them. That sick nauseating feeling of dread. They were all feeling it. Zacravia most of all probably. Everyone knew full well what their disappearance could mean. Especially if things went bad. It didn't bear thinking about, but they seemingly had no choice.

In the end there was nothing else for it but to return to the inn.

Once there, the others informed them that there had been no sign of them. No one had seen them return on their own.

Everyone was starting to panic.

What could they do?

There were two obvious options.

One; go to the police. They would have much better knowledge of the city and its inhabitants. And may even have an idea of who might have taken them and where. Option two was to enlist the aid of the Rangers. If any one had an interest in seeing their safe return it had to be them, right?vc

It was decided that they try both. No sense in putting all your eggs in one basket, as the old saying went. Harmia elected to go and contact the police. Travanos and Telly went with her. Dorm, Artur and Poljazak went to see the Rangers. Zacravia wanted to accompany them, but Dorm insisted that he stay behind.

"Why?" demanded the thief. "Is there something wrong with that?"

"No," Dorm told him calmly, sensing how out of hand this could get if not handled properly. "Not at all. But right now you're feeling guilty, and you aren't thinking straight. I need you to think straight, my friend. Stay here and try and rest. You've had a nasty shock. Let us deal with it."

Zacravia paused, then slowly hung his head in shame. "I have failed," he almost whispered.

"Nonsense!" said Lianna. She moved and took him by the hand. She nodded to Dorm. He returned the nod and left with the others.

Harmia, Travanos and Telly found one of the larger constabulary houses in the area, to make their report. The officers there took them seriously, and took note of the details. It was apparent however that they probably didn't intend to do anything about the situation. Harmia therefore had to take matters into her own hands.

"I am here as a special representative of the Ambakan government." She flashed her credentials at the slightly startled officer who was interviewing them. He stood still for a moment.

"One moment ma'am," he said rising and scurrying off to find his superior.

"We appear to be getting somewhere now," Telly congratulated her.

"He just thought we were some common street people. Letting him know that a foreign government is interested in this case may just get something done," Harmia explained.

"I'll have to remember that next time I want my father to buy something from another country," she mused.

"I'll have to remember that the next time my wife does," Travanos mused, though from a different point of view.

The officer returned with his superior and as a group they took descriptions of both Rhyn and Tissie and their last known location. They did their best to gloss over who Zacravia was "just a friend of ours" was their description, though they were truthful when they said how he was quite distraught by their disappearance.

The officers pledged to put every available person on the job and to contact the 'usual suspects'. To their credit there was a hurried meeting not long after that and a scurry of activity following it.

"We seem to be getting somewhere," Harmia said positively.

"I just hope the girls are," Travanos pondered darkly.

Dorm, Artur and Poljazak, had a longer walk to get to the Rangers' Chapterhouse, which was located in another district of the city. They made their way to the main gate, and rang the bell. It tinkled softly in the background, so they knew it had rung.

There was no movement from within.

Dorm pulled the chain again.

Still no response.

Dorm really wasn't in the mood for this kind of thing. He grabbed the chain and yanked it angrily, and continuously. The bell could be heard ringing madly from the other side of the wall. Whoever was in there would have to come and see what was going on eventually.

Finally the slot in the gate opened and the face of a Ranger could be seen. The woman was in her mid thirties and quite attractive. At least physically. Her attitude left something to be desired.

"What do you want?" She demanded angrily.

"Let me in, damn it," yelled Dorm. "I need to see whoever's in charge of this Chapterhouse."

"I do not think so young man," she replied "We are very busy here."

Dorm was taken aback. What was going on here? This wasn't the Rangers he was used to. Most of the time they seemed to fall over themselves to help them with their non-helpful answers, and their riddles and confusion. Now they weren't even allowed in?

"Do you know who I am?" Dorm demanded and pointing at himself. "I am Prince Dormal of Lugemall, and one of the chosen Questers of this stupid quest of yours." He grabbed the amulet at his neck and waved it in front of the woman's' face.

"Well then," she began. "I am honoured to meet you. But it changes nothing. You cannot come in."

"Look you stupid woman," Poljazak said then. "Two of our companions have gone missing. Do you think maybe you might take some sort of interest in that? I mean they are only in danger because of your quest."

The Ranger cocked her head to one side as if she were listening to something. She was silent for a moment. "I'm sorry Your Highness. We cannot help you at this time. But I am told to tell you to stop by here before you leave Bydanushev. We will be able to give you some instructions."

"Well that's nice. I like having instructions for once. But what about our friends?" he demanded to know.

"It shall be as it shall be," was her only response.

She closed the hatch and several footsteps were heard hurrying away. It was clear that the Rangers would be no help to them in this.

They simply stood and stared at the door and at each other for a few minutes, not sure of what to do. They had expected that the Rangers would be eager to help, even desperate to. But not this. This was almost callous. Cold.

In the end the three of them trudged slowly back to the inn, feeling rather dejected and useless. And maybe even a little bit used.

The others couldn't quite believe their experience. It was so out of character for the Rangers to behave in such a way. Granted they had never really been amazingly helpful, and had never quite been going out of their way to assist. But point blank refusing to was something else entirely.

They all felt a little lost and hopeless as they sat. Could this reaction from the Rangers be a sign of how things would be in the future? Dorm sincerely hoped not. Once Harmia, Travanos and Telly had returned they updated them on what had happened, and now knew that the authorities were at least going to try.

Everyone was worried about how Rhyn and Tissie would be faring. Rhyn might be able to look after herself. At least for a while. She had a good head on her shoulders, and could think well on the run if she had to. No one doubted that she would be strong enough to endure a little hardship, but was that all their kidnappers would give them?

Tissie on the other hand was another matter. She wasn't exactly the sharpest knife in the scullery draw, and no one was quite sure how she would go having been kidnapped. She was the daughter of a fairly high profile person in the court of Tagradas though. Perhaps there had been things like this before? No one knew. They had to hope that she exercised the better part of valour and remained silent for most of their ordeal. If she did they guessed she had a fairly good chance of staying safe.

Not knowing who or more importantly, why they had been taken was frustrating. If they had an idea of why that at least might help them answer the who and maybe even the where. Could it be Peldrakhsekr agents? There had certainly been enough of them wandering about the Alliance over the course of their journey. It was possible. But then it could just be some local ruffian trying to make a name for himself. Recognising that she was a foreigner, travelling with a large group of foreigners could be worth something. If that's all it was then there was a good chance they would stay safe.

They waited for a while hoping that they would turn up. It became increasingly more difficult to remain in the inn as time wore on. It felt like it had been days, but it was probably no more than two hours or so. Everyone agreed that they had to get out there and look. They broke up into groups and went in different directions. Dorm insisted that Zacravia stay behind. Despite his obvious skills no one was sure of his state of mind. He clearly blamed himself for this whole situation, even though there was very little he could have done to prevent it. Dorm didn't want to risk him second-guessing himself, or worse still overreacting to something and getting them into more difficulties.

Pianwasal and Lianna offered to stay behind and watch him.

Dorm went with Mac and Navista off towards the north. They found their way eventually back towards the place where they had lost the girls from. Dorm stared at the spot for some minutes hoping he could somehow let them know that they were looking for them.

He didn't want to think about what might happen if they couldn't find them again. The whole prophecy hung on a knife-edge, and he didn't know how to stop it falling. He still wondered at the Rangers reaction. It was so strange.

There was really no point to them even being out here. There were no clues, they had already checked. And there was little if any chance of someone miraculously just walking up to them and saying "I think I might know something."

Slowly they began to return to the inn. They watched for spies, who might be clandestinely watching them. And they kept an eye out for the sort of people who might be involved in criminals. Zacravia had, over the time they had been together, informed them of some subtle things that various criminal gangs did to let each know of their existence. Simple things that would go unnoticed by any one who didn't know what they meant.

They saw a few things that might have been these signs, but nothing that was concrete. Dorm began to suspect that here on the other side of the Alliance, things were done slightly differently, and perhaps the signs were what they were seeing, but they were just that little bit different.

It was mid-afternoon when they arrived back at the inn, and the weather was closing in again. Large dark grey clouds were gathering across the sky and the wind was starting to get a bit chilly. They all hoped that wherever the girls were that they were dry.

A city watch officer came by shortly after to inform them of what resources had been devoted to the search and what had been done so far. It actually seemed like they were indeed taking it seriously, and not just paying them lip service. Everyone was impressed, and congratulated Harmia again on having the forethought to show her credentials.

Shortly after he left it started to rain. A soft drizzle that gradually soaked everything. It reflected the mood of all within their group. Everyone was depressed and pessimistic. No one could see the way ahead.

Everyone sat staring at each other or the walls. Nothing was said as no one had any idea what to say.

Time slowly passed them by as they waited for something. Some news, some inspiration of what to do next.

It didn't come.

Another hour passed with no activity and no word. It was becoming increasingly tense in the room as everyone became lost in their own thoughts. Rhyn and Tissie were family. They were a part of this group. This quest. What would they do if they didn't come back? How would they go on?

Every time they heard footsteps in the hallway they would be filled with a sense of anticipation. Of hope. But tinged with a little dread as well. But no one ever knocked on their door. Every time they opened it they would only find some other patron of the inn, or one of the workers. Never their companions.

After that hour things had sunk from the terrified hope of finding them, to the beginnings of the grim reality that they never would. That their friends had been lost forever, somewhere in the city.

The rain continued to fall. As the afternoon began to turn into dusk it got heavier. Darkness slowly crept into the city and the noise of the world slowly began to fade. Noise filtered up from the taproom downstairs of locals enjoying themselves.

No one in this room was.

Then there were more footsteps.

They had since stopped getting up to look. There was no point. Everyone was beginning to feel it. The start of the loss. It hadn't hit any of them yet, but it was there. Slowly reaching out to them with its icy cold fingers of the grim reality of the situation.

The footsteps in the hallway were soft, almost cautious. No one was really paying that much attention.

There was a knock at the door.

Everyone stopped for a moment. Faces turned to each other. No one was quite sure what to do. Eventually Pianwasal rose and went to the door and slowly opened it. She stood in the doorway for a moment. They all waited.

She stepped back into the room allowing the knocker to pass inside.

They wore a large cloak with a hood. It was fairly ratty looking, with several patches. And it smelt a little too. The person was clearly a woman by the stance, and the slender hands that held the edges of the cloak.

She reached up and pushed back the hood.

Tissie.

Her face was pale, and she had clearly cried at some stage. Her eyes were rimmed in red and her cheeks were flushed as if she had been running. Her hair was a little unkempt, and her whole demeanour suggested she just wanted to curl up and cry herself to sleep.

With a cry of fear and joy several people leapt across the room towards her, to embrace her. There was sobbing and questions, and pained laughter. Tissie took it all rather well. Finally though she had to stop them.

"We don't have time for this," she said earnestly. "We have to hurry. Rhyn is downstairs in the courtyard."

"Why didn't she come up with you?" Telly asked.

"Is she injured?" posed Zacravia, who had hung back from the rest.

"No," Tissie replied. "She's fine. But there is someone who isn't"

"Who?" asked Dorm curiously.

"Someone who we have to help," she responded. "If you get my meaning." She grabbed Pianwasal by the hand and lead her out the door. They followed. It probably looked strange, this large group of people trudging down the stairs like this. But no one cared.

In the courtyard the rain made it difficult to see at first, but in one corner standing under the eaves of the stable was Rhyn. They all ran over to her, anxious to see her safely back with the group.

As they rounded the corner they saw others. Mostly young people by the looks of it. None of them too clean and none of them looking too happy. There was one adult. He was propped up against the wall, with an ashen complexion and a pained look on his face. He held his arms across his stomach and one of the children supported him.

"Rhyn!" Dorm exclaimed as they came up to her. "You're safe."

"Hi everyone," she replied pleasantly. "How has your day been?"

"Not as eventful as yours by the looks of things," Cal told her.

"Probably not, no," She agreed.

"So who is this?" Dorm asked pointing at the man.

"He's the man who kidnapped us, and then saved our lives," she explained.

At the knowledge that he was their kidnapper everyone wanted to take revenge on him then and there. Nothing would have pleased them more. But she had also said saved their lives? How was that possible?

"He took a dagger that probably would have ended up in either Tissie or I eventually," Rhyn explained. "Right now he's badly injured and we need to get him medical attention before he dies."

"Dagger in the stomach," Ambra noted. "Nasty."

"Why should we care if he lives or dies?" Mac asked seriously.

"If he's responsible for kidnapping you two, then I say let him die," Ameks agreed.

"You may want to reconsider that attitude, when you learn he has an amulet," Rhyn concluded the conversation. She looked meaningfully at Dorm.

He returned her gaze for a moment before reaching out and revealing the amulet to everyone.

"Hi there," the man said in a strained voice. It was clear he was in a great deal of pain "Ivgrachev. Nice to meet you. Guess the rest of the introductions can wait for a bit."

"Well I guess we can't kill him then," said Artur softly.

"If we don't hurry we wont have any choice in the matter," Rhyn said. "Cause he'll have died from his injuries."

Dorm looked at Pianwasal and Navista, both of whom had some limited medical training. "Can either of you do anything?" he asked solemnly.

"My training is too limited for this sort of thing," Pianwasal admitted.

"I've only ever mended cuts," confessed Navista. "He needs work on his innards."

"Poljazak?" Dorm asked next.

"I only know cows and horses," he replied. "Maybe sheep. People is something very different."

"Then we have no choice but to take him to a physician," Dorm said reluctantly. "Supposing we can find one."

The man groaned as if he was about to say something, but then slumped into unconsciousness. The girl who was supporting him valiantly tried to keep him upright against the sudden weight of the fully-grown man, until one of the boys and Rhyn helped keep him up.

"Right. Mac go find out where the nearest physician is and hurry," Dorm instructed. "Artur go see if you can find a cart we can use to get him there. We wont be able to put him on a horse. The rest of you get ready to ride as soon as we know where we are going to."

Everyone jumped to their jobs. Pianwasal and Navista began inspecting the wound on the man Ivgrachev, to see how bad it was. Mac darted off into the inn to find out the information they required.

There was a great sense of relief at the return of Rhyn and Tissie. But there was confusion and worry. What had happened to them? How had this Ivgrachev been injured? And why had he kidnapped them in the first place? All of these questions would have to wait. This Ivgrachev was obviously their next quester, or at least knew of someone who was. It was impossible for them to ignore. It was impossible for them to let him die.

Mac returned with information that there was the Bydanushev Royal College of Physicians only several streets away. It was apparently the largest hospital in the country, and was the premier teaching place for physicians. It seemed to fit the bill nicely.

Artur returned a few minutes later with a cart. It was small and rickety but would suffice for the short journey they needed it for. They took several blankets from the horses and laid them out in the back of the cart and placed Ivgrachev on top of them. He exclaimed in pain once, but didn't seem to wake. His bleeding continued unabated, and Dorm wondered how long he had been bleeding for. Could a man lose this much blood and survive?

They covered him over with several blankets to try and keep him warm and then Tissie, Rhyn and Pianwasal climbed in the back, While Dorm and Travanos jumped in the front. The cart was quickly hitched to two of their horses and they began to make their way out of the yard. The rest following closely behind as they mounted up.

It was dark and gloomy in the streets, but there was still a fair amount of traffic out, despite the inclement weather. Lamp lighters were just beginning their rounds, and so one by one small points of light began to illuminate their way.

They made several twists and turns, Mac giving directions from his horse next to the cart, before coming to the right street, which was one of those broad tree lined avenues that seemed to criss-cross the city. They were able to move much quicker here, as the traffic was moving more swiftly. They almost missed the gate to the College as it came up on them. They negotiated their way across the street and went through the high iron arch that surmounted it.

There was some confusion as to where they should go, before Artur spotted a sign that told them where people could be taken in an emergency.

An emergency medical facility. What a brilliant idea, Dorm thought.

They drove the cart round to a portico in the building and all jumped down. Several startled people watched them as they hauled Ivgrachev out of the cart and carried him inside.

The room was brightly lit and very clean. Polished stone seemed to be the main feature of the building. Large balustraded stone steps wound up and down to different levels of the building and corridors led off in various directions. No one had any idea of where to take them.

"May we help you?" said a woman who seemed to appear out of no where, wearing a rather plain gown with a large white apron. One her head she wore a sort of wimple that held back her hair and made her face appear taut.

"Yes, this man has been injured. He needs to be tended by a physician," Dorm explained to the woman. "We were told to bring him here."

"I see," she replied looking at the man. She didn't appear very concerned. "He appears to have been stabbed." She paused for a moment, pursing her lips in thought. "We shall treat him."

"Thank you…?"

"Matron Akera," she replied. She snapped her fingers loudly and several similarly dressed women and men appeared as if from nowhere. "Find a trolley," she instructed them. "And take him to one of the rooms. I shall fetch one of the physicians. Tend to him as best you can in the mean time."

"Yes Matron," they all intoned. There was a flurry of activity and then a strange contraption was brought into view. It looked like a thin bed on wheels. Dorm had never seen the like. Ivgrachev was placed on the bed and the four people began wheeling it rapidly off down one of the corridors.

The group followed them anxiously and found their way into a small room, that was painted white. There were several large tables and large pitchers of water. Piles of bandages and blankets sat on one of the tables and a large covered tray sat on another.

Ivgrachev was taken off the trolley, as the Matron had called it and placed on the table in the middle of the room. The people began working on removing his clothing that had now become quite sticky with blood. They began washing the congealed blood from around his wound and inspected it, being careful not to touch it.

Everyone watched on anxiously. They couldn't let this man die. Not so soon after finding him. He may have taken Rhyn and Tissie but he had apparently saved their lives. That had to count for something.

Very soon the Matron returned with another young woman around Mac's age. She had curly brown hair that was pulled back into a pony tail. She had a kind face, that was now distorted by concern, probably over what she had heard about the condition of Ivgrachev. She wore similar clothes to the Matron, though with a slightly different cut.

She moved purposefully to the table upon which Ivgrachev now lay. She inspected the wound carefully.

"Can you assist in this Physician?" asked the Matron.

"Yes I can," the young woman said shortly. "I will need as much sedative as we have, and any pain relievers you can find." The Matron moved off. "And more bandages and sutures," the physician called out almost as an afterthought.

They all waited expectantly. No one sure what was going on. The young physician began issuing instructions to the four people who had brought Ivgrachev in. No one in their group understood what she was saying to them. They moved around the room swiftly, confidently. Obviously they knew what they meant and had done this before. One of them uncovered the large tray they had noticed. It was covered with a variety of shiny metal objects. All cruel and vicious looking.

The tray was brought closer to where Ivgrachev lay.

"What are you going to do to him?" Zacravia asked in an almost horrified voice.

The woman looked up at them, as if noticing them for the first time. "Are you his friends?" she asked.

"Yes, we are," Rhyn said after a moment. She looked at Dorm, who only nodded.

"My name is Bianeska, I am a physician here in the College," she introduced herself. "I will do what I can to save his life. He is bleeding badly and I must get to work if he is to live." She looked at them seriously for a moment. "He is in a very dangerous place at the moment. I would advise you all to wait outside. It will get rather messy in here. It is not for the faint of heart. The Matron can have someone tend to your needs. We will be some time."

They all slowly agreed and filed outside to the waiting corridor.

There was a grim feeling as they did so. Would this be the last they saw of their newest Quester?

Alive at any rate?

Chapter 36

Dorm paced.

It was all he could think to do.

They had been escorted to a large waiting room nearby. A variety of comfortable chairs and pleasant tapestries and the like tried their best to put them at ease. It wasn't working. For sometime everyone asked Rhyn and Tissie question after question about what had happened to them. How they had been taken? Where? Who this Ivgrachev was? How they discovered about his amulet and how they had escaped. And of course, importantly how he came to be injured.

The girls did their best to answer all of them, Occasionally they had to go over things again, and sometimes the story skipped over parts. But in the end everyone had a rough idea of the events of their day.

Ivgrachev had been injured not too far from where the tunnels they were following allowed access to the surface in the vicinity of their inn, but for the girls and the children that had been accompanying them, it had been a difficult journey. Ivgrachev was weak and had trouble walking, and his condition only got worse as they went on. The most dangerous part had come when they were exiting and had to negotiate a flight of stairs to the surface. Rhyn told how she was very worried at the pained faces and strangled noises Ivgrachev had made as they had climbed them.

The Matron brought them all tea, and that helped relax them a little. But everyone was still desperately worried. If this man died, there would be no answers to their many questions. And Dorm *wanted* those answers.

Both Rhyn and Tissie were kept close to everyone. It was clear that all in the group had felt keenly their apparent disappearance, and started to feel the fear of losing them permanently. No one wanted that feeling to return. It was clear to most of them that they would have to keep a closer eye on each other. They may not be so lucky next time.

The time they spent in this waiting room seemed to stretch around them like days. They had been here so long already as this physician, Bianeska, worked on curing him. And they had no idea how much longer it would take. It could be hours before they heard anything, and presumably he wouldn't be going anywhere for a while.

Dorm noted that both Rhyn and Tissie seemed unharmed by their abduction. In fact both of them almost seemed to be a little more confident. Perhaps this had been somewhat of a growing experience for the two of them. Rhyn's tone towards the blonde girl had certainly softened. Perhaps they had learnt something about each other during the ordeal.

Tissie seemed a little more self-confident. If she was right about something she came out and said it now. She didn't seem to hesitate as much. Perhaps this was a good thing.

Everyone fussed over them somewhat as they sat. They almost couldn't get up to simply stretch their legs without someone offering to get something for them. Dorm understood this. It would fix itself in a few days, once everyone got used to the fact that they weren't going anywhere.

This Ivgrachev still worried Dorm. What sort of a person was he? It was clear that he was some sort of criminal. But then they already had one like that. And Zacravia had proven very useful, and quite resourceful. Another wouldn't be too much of a problem.

But these children? Were they his 'gang'? And if so, what sort of a gang was it? 'I mean really' Dorm thought to himself. 'How useful can children really be in that sort of a venture?' After thinking about it for a while, he began to suspect that perhaps a lot more useful than he first suspected. Perhaps he should sit down with Zac and ask about it?

There were various comings and goings in the corridor as the nurses went about their business. Several times one was seen carrying a bundle of bloodied bandages away, only to return a few minutes later carrying a fresh bundle of clean ones. Several times large pitchers of water were taken towards the room. Everyone worried at what these could mean. No one came to inform them of anything so perhaps that was a good sign? Presumably if he were dead, they would tell them fairly quickly.

At times like these Dorm couldn't help but think of his mother. He had only been about ten or so when she had died. He vaguely remembered following his father to some rooms in the palace where she was whilst she was ill. He had been there a couple of times. She had looked worse each time. Eventually his father forbade him from going there. Mac Lavin rarely ever forbade his son anything, so Dorm had known it was serious.

He hadn't actually been there when she had died. He both regretted this and was grateful to his father for not making him endure that. His mother had been such a towering figure in his life. She had doted on him, and had been his friend, teacher, confidant and more besides. For sometime after her passing he hadn't quite grasped that she wasn't coming back. Every time he made some innocent comment about it, Mac Lavin's eyes would glisten with tears.

It had taken some time but father and son had grown much closer over that period. In order to fill the void left in their lives by the passing of the woman they both loved.

Once he had understood, Dorm had retreated inside himself. His whole world just about had come crashing down around his young ears. And his father, despite his best efforts, had been unable to completely rebuild it for him. For many years people had considered Dorm, aloof, even cold. Until that was, that he met Mac.

Dorm knew that his mother would have been proud of Dorm for finding Mac. He wished the two could have met. They would have gotten on so well together. As it was, Dorm could only live with the memories of his mother. And those his father had of her. Together the two men remembered, and in some ways revered the life and memory of the woman who had loved them both, saved one, and birthed the other.

Dorm noticed that Telly was watching him. Of course. She too would be having similar thoughts to himself. Having been through the same thing. She nodded slightly when she noticed him looking at her. That was all they needed. They both knew what the other was thinking and that they understood. There was nothing in life quite like having someone close who understood what you were going through, because they had been through it too. This was why Dorm appreciated Telly so much. She 'got' him.

Mac of course noticed the two of them exchanging looks and made his presence felt to Dorm. While both of Mac's parents were very much still alive, the fact that they refused to speak to him was a 'death' of sorts. The death of the relationship. His family had ostracised itself from his life. One of his sisters still continued to speak to him on occasion, and Dorm had always found her very pleasant on the few occasions they had met. But in some ways it was worse for his partner. For Dorm and Telly there was no going back. No possibility of rekindling that relationship, that love. For Mac there was, and the fact that every day he had to endure another day where it didn't, Dorm could only imagine would be painful to live through.

Dorm decided to stretch his legs, and walked out into the corridor. It was still brightly lit, despite what he felt the hour was. The building was very quiet. And there was a faint smell of blood in the air. He noticed several small sconces around the corridor emitting wafts of smoke. He lent closer and discovered that it was incense. In a place like this he could imagine how useful that would be.

There were very few people about. Every so often one would walk past. There seemed to be no speaking in this edifice. The faint footfalls they made seemed to echo much louder here.

This was all so confusing. They had found the next member of their quest and yet they didn't know who he was or anything about him. In fact they didn't even know if he was going to live.

And the Rangers? What was going on with them? Perhaps they would explain themselves when they visited them before leaving as they had so politely been instructed to do.

He wandered back to the door into the waiting area. Everyone was quietly talking. He let his gaze wander over the faces of his friends. Even Poljazak and Kanilma felt like friends now. And they had only been with them a few weeks. He couldn't imagine losing any of them. And now they faced the very real possibility of it happening. And they hadn't really even met him yet.

Dorm heard more footsteps echoing down the corridor. He looked and saw the physician Bianeska and one of the nurses approaching from the direction of the surgery. He stepped back inside the room and informed everyone. They all fell silent, dreading what they were about to hear. Everyone fearing the worst, and hoping for the best.

The two entered the room. Everyone was stilled and silenced by their appearance. Their faces were calm but tired. Their clothes however told a different story. A rather harrowing one. Splotches and streaks of blood disfigured the surface of the aprons they wore. Everyone stared at them. It was clearly distressing everyone. Did this mean he was dead? As Dorm had already thought several times this night; can a man lose that much blood and survive?

"We have finished," said Bianeska calmly. "It was difficult, there was a lot of damage we had to repair."

"Is he alive?" Rhyn asked in a quiet voice.

"Yes he is alive," came the longed for response. There was a release of held breath from around the room and a few careful smiles. This was the best news they could have hoped for.

"He is still very weak, and the risk of infection is great, but for now he is stable," Bianeska explained. "He is asleep at the moment. We will keep him sedated for at least the next day. He will need plenty of rest in order to heal."

"How long do you think it will be until he is able to walk again?" Dorm asked her.

"That is hard to say. These sorts of injuries are so individual. But let me say this. You'll be visiting him here for at least the next week."

"A week?" Cal said. "Do we 'ave a week?"

"No idea," Dorm told him. "But it seems we'll have to make room for it."

"I say at least a week," Bianeska went on. "It will most likely be more than that. And even if he is able to walk again in a week, he wont be leaving the College, and he certainly won't be ready for travel on the road, if that's what you're thinking."

"It's just that we are on a journey and we have places to be," Travanos explain patiently. "We don't want to be late for certain things."

"We will do our best to get him healed as soon as possible. But one cannot rush these things too much. The body needs time to heal. If he gets up and moves around to quickly, he risks rupturing his injury and then he will be right back where he began."

"We understand," Telly said. "It's just we were very worried and we have a lot of things to do, and he is a part of that."

"I'm guessing by the look of you all that this is some sort of international thing?" Bianeska asked. "Something to do with the Alliance?"

"You could say that," Mac said looking at the others knowingly.

"Well if you don't mind my saying so, he seems a rather odd person to be helping with that sort of thing," she shook her head slightly.

"We know," Dorm explained. "But he is who we need for parts of it. Sometimes people can surprise you."

"True enough," Bianeska conceded. She turned to the nurse at her side. "Paniz, would you tell Matron that I will be in to see her as soon as I have changed. And lets see if we can keep these people informed about their friend."

"Of course, Physician," replied Paniz. "I'll bring them updates myself if I have to." She turned and went out.

"My staff nurse. Probably the best in the College," Bianeska explained. "Unfortunately she comes from a poorer family and so can't afford to do the courses to become a full physician. I try to teach her what I can without getting into trouble myself. Your friend is in safe hands with people like her working on him."

"We thank you for that," Zacravia said quietly. There was relief in his voice. It was clear he still felt guilty.

"My pleasure," she said to him. "If you will excuse me, I should go change."

"Of course," Dorm said. "And thank you." She realised the sincerity with which he said that.

"You're all welcome," she responded. She half turned to leave. As she did so she seemed to remember something. She opened her mouth to say something but then closed it again, and left before any one could ask her what the matter was.

"Well that's a load of worry off our minds," said Ambra. "He is alive."

"Yes," agreed Pianwasal. "But will he stay that way?"

It felt a lot later than it actually was. Since there was little they could do at the College other than wait, it was decided that they should return to the inn and get some rest. The day had been long. Far longer than any of them had thought it was going to be that morning. The ride of emotions had taken its toll on all of them, and now they felt it. They slowly walked back to the main entrance and took to their horses. The trip back was sombre and quiet, and none too warm, given the weather, which had not improved during their time indoors.

No one said much. Everyone was busy thinking though. Everyone hoped that Ivgrachev would recover swiftly, but of course there was no guarantee of this. It was apparent that everyone secretly feared that he would still die. His injury had been very serious by the sounds of Bianeska. They just had to hope for the best.

They skipped their usual evening chat. No one really felt like sitting and going over the days events. They all knew what had happened now. Everyone did make a point of personally saying goodnight to Rhyn and Tissie, and expressing their relief that they had been able to return to them safely. The girls it seemed took it in their stride. A measure of their character Dorm thought to himself. But he privately wondered if maybe they hadn't been affected by it more deeply than they let on.

He and Mac went to bed quietly. There was little to say even between them. They just lay in each other's arms. It was good to feel that there was someone there. They had had enough fear of losing people for one day. Dorm let the closeness of his partner and the sound of the rain outside carry him off to sleep.

The next morning dawned cold and cloudy, but the rain had stopped. They ate and washed and as a group, went immediately back to the College to check on Ivgrachev's progress. They again met with

Matron Akera and the young nurse, Paniz, who took them to see the patient. Bianeska was apparently still sleeping after having to help another patient after they had left.

They were taken to a quiet room on an upper level, where a large number of cots sat against both walls. There were various other patients in the beds, and one or two other nurses moved about checking on them and talking quietly with them.

Ivgrachev lay covered in several sheets and a blanket. He was still unconscious, or at least asleep, and the Matron said quietly that this was a good thing, as it meant he would move around less.

"He will need plenty of rest over the coming days," she explained. "It will take time for the skin and organs to repair. Any movement could hamper that."

"He will experience some pain for some time still," Paniz told them. "Even after his injuries have appeared to have healed."

Everyone watched him for a time, still trying to figure out who this man was. They still really hadn't met him. All they knew was that there was a very good chance he was another quester.

The Matron and Paniz left them alone for a time and the group crowded around the bed and watched. Of course there was nothing to actually watch, except for a man sleeping, but it seemed somehow good for them.

Dorm noticed a pile of clothes on the small stand next to the head of the bed. From beneath the folds of his linen shirt sat a heavy chain. He took it and brought it forth for the others to see. The crystal caught the light and reflected it onto the ceiling. There was no doubt that this was another amulet. This man could *not* be allowed to die.

"We told you," Rhyn said quietly. "No mistaking it is there?"

"No, it appears not," Dorm said quietly.

"You are sure it is his?" Pianwasal asked seriously. "I mean it isn't something he stole?"

"What a thing to suggest," Tissie said defensively. "He took a dagger for us. He wouldn't have done that if it was stolen."

"It's alright Tissie," Artur said. "We know that, but look at him. It's definitely possible."

"Let's not pretend we haven't all thought about it," Dorm said.

"Because we know we have."

"True enough," said Zacravia looking at the Prince intently. "Until he wakes up, we cannot discount that possibility. He may simply have been trying to find out more about it, and us. I admit it seems likely he is the man we are looking for but…"

"Then let's hope he wakes up soon," Lianna said positively. "At least if we have that answer we can spend some of the time we have now telling him what the story is, or looking for the original owner."

"And looking for the woman," Ameks put in. "We still have no idea where to look for her."

"Oh Ameks," Telly sighed heavily. "And I was just starting to think positively."

"He's right though," Travanos agreed with the sculptor. "We don't know where she might be. We still have a whole country to search."

"And if we have to, we will," Dorm replied quietly. "We aren't giving up just because of this minor setback."

"Minor setback?" Zacravia said. "It seems a little more than minor. A man nearly died."

"But he didn't," Dorm retorted probably a little too quickly. "And now we have a good lead even if we don't have the man himself. I'd say given that, it makes it better than it might otherwise seem."

"I take your point I guess."

"We still have a week at least though," Cal noted. "What are we going to do for a week?"

"Search this city from top to bottom if we have to," Dorm told him.

"That's a lot of top and bottom," Cal responded. "Might take more than a week."

"Which will just give Ivgrachev more time to heal," Rhyn observed positively. "Which means he'll be better able to make up the lost time with us when we do leave."

"See there's always a bright side to things," Telly said beaming.

Ivgarchev struggled back to consciousness the next day. He was still terribly weak, and a little vague and groggy from the medicines he had been given, but he did recognise some of them. He tried to talk to them but got tongue tied and slurred his words terribly. Paniz, who was with them, said this was normal, and that most of the medicines that were causing that should have gone from him by tomorrow.

They didn't stay for too long, as Ivgrachev obviously needed to rest more, and in his vague state there really wasn't much point. Especially when his conversations didn't make much sense most of the time.

On the way out the physician Bianeska was entering the ward. She greeted them warmly and updated them on some of the details of their new friends' condition. She seemed a little on edge. As if there was something worrying her. Dorm couldn't think what that might be. But she didn't seem to be concerned about them in any way, and she seemed to indicate that Ivgrachev was doing well, so it presumably wasn't anything to do with that.

She continued on into the room as they left. Dorm walked slowly behind the others and stole a look back into the ward. Bianeska sat close to Ivgrachevs bed talking to him. Dorm doubted he would make any more sense to her than he had to them. But she seemed eager to talk to him, the way she leaned in close to him.

They returned to the inn. They re-stabled their horses and chatted as they began to return to the building. From behind the stable block came a whistle.

It turned out to have been made by one of Ivgrachevs 'children', who Rhyn identified as Ogn. Now that Dorm saw him in the light of day, he realised that he was probably in his late teen years, which was older than he had first thought. He was pale, and by the look of his eyes, hadn't gotten much sleep lately. His dark hair was a little unkempt and there was a smudge of dirt on one cheek.

He seemed genuinely glad to see Rhyn and Tissie, but appeared to still be wary of the others.

"Is Iv going to be alright?" he asked cautiously. Obviously he was concerned. And no one had told him. For all they knew Ivgrachev could be dead. Dorm felt a little guilty for not having tried to contact them previously.

"He's going to be fine," Rhyn explained. "He just needs to rest for some time to allow his injuries to heal."

The boy seemed to visibly relax. A genuine smile came to his lips and there were almost tears in his eyes. He ran his hands through his floppy dark hair as he composed himself. "That's good news," he said warmly. "Really good news."

"Sorry we couldn't tell you earlier," Tissie apologised.

"That's alright," Ogn assured her. "It's not like you would have had much of a chance."

"I hope all your other friends are okay?" Dorm enquired.

"We're fine," Ogn replied. "We were just worried about Iv. He's like a father to us in many ways."

"I think I understand," said Zacravia quietly.

"But if he's going to be okay, then we'll be okay as well."

"Glad to hear it. If you come back in a few days we'll let you know how he is going," Rhyn offered.

The boy nodded appreciatively. "That would be good, yes."

The next few days went much the same way. Ivgarchev slowly became more coherent as the time went by, but they didn't tell him much about the amulets, informing him that the college ward wasn't really the place for it.

They did introduce him to everyone. At least their names. No ones titles or positions were revealed. It was felt that was safer given the number of strangers in the surrounds. He began eating again, small nibbles at first but gradually building up. He seemed stronger, but still grimaced terribly and even cried out on occasion when he moved.

Paniz continued to administer to him his medicines and game him his food. Once or twice Bianeska came in to check on the progress of his recovery, and to inspect that his injury was actually healing. Everyone gave her plenty of room when she inspected it, and changed the bandages. She seemed rather satisfied with his progress and informed him that he might end up being out of the college a few days earlier than she had first thought.

As the days went by though, Dorm noticed that she became more withdrawn. He couldn't figure out why. It was like there was something worrying at her. Dorm wondered if perhaps Ivgrachev wasn't really doing as well as she was saying. But she did seem genuinely pleased with his recovery.

Once, when they were leaving he hung back a bit from the rest, and noticed her leaning in to talk to him when she thought no one was looking. He couldn't hear what she was saying, nor any response her patient may have given. It was clear that there was something going on. Perhaps she knew him, and there was some personal issue between them?

Dorm knew he had to find out.

He didn't tell the others. Not because he didn't trust them, but he didn't want any one making a fuss, in case it was nothing.

By the time the week was up. Ivgrachev was able to sit up with only a little discomfort. He had tried walking, but the pain had still been too great whenever he was bent over. And he still felt rather weak. He seemed to take an almost perverse delight in showing off his scar to the others. It was still a rather angry puffy red welt along his abdomen. Whenever he did, the nurse on duty would scornfully instruct him to cover it up again.

They knew he wouldn't be able to ride a horse for any great length of time for at least another week, probably more. They had continued their search for the other amulet in the city but hadn't discovered any leads.

It was a week and three days after the misadventure that things came to a head. They had again gone to visit Ivgrachev in the ward. He was getting better, and showing his rather weird sense of humour. He suddenly asked something serious about the amulets. They did their best to explain without being too loud.

Dorm explained how they had been noticing over the last few weeks how some of them seemed almost to fit together into each other, like some sort of giant puzzle. They quietly showed him with several of their own amulets before putting them back around their necks.

"I wonder if mine fits into any of yours?" Ivgrachev asked curiously.

"It probably does somewhere," Mac told him.

"There's an easy way to find out," suggested Navista, who sat on the edge of the bed.

“Good idea,’ said Dorm. “Gives us something to do at least.”

Ivgrachev indicated that his amulet was down with his clothes on the stand. Dorm told him that they had already seen it there.

“Sorry,” he apologised. “I keep forgetting I’ve been out of it for a while.”

Dorm leaned over and grabbed the pile of clothes. “I think before we leave Bydanushev we will have to get you some new clothes,” he observed.

“What’s wrong with these,” Ivgrachev said defensively. “I have had these clothes for years. They are quite comfortable.”

“Yes, that’s the problem,” Telly said quietly.

There was a general chuckle around the bed as Ivgrachev conceded the point himself. He rummaged through the clothes to find his amulet. “Wait,” he said after a moment. “It’s not here.”

“Check in the folds,” Rhyn suggested. “Mine is always getting caught in things.”

He went through the pile of clothes again checking all the folds and creases. There was no amulet. Everyone began to worry a bit. What would happen if they lost an amulet itself? No one had even thought about this. They had an idea of the consequences of losing a quester, but an amulet?

“Where could it have gone?” Ivgrachev said quietly. It was like he had lost the most precious thing in his life. Given it had come from his father, and it was likely his father was no longer around, perhaps it felt that way.

They searched under the stand, under the bed, and under the bed next to Ivgrachevs’ but still there was no sign of the amulet.

Everyone began to feel that weird tingling sensation that always accompanies worry about a lost item. Especially a really important one.

They continued searching for several minutes more, growing ever more restless and desperate all the while. There was a sense of repetition in this. First they thought they had lost Rhyn and Tissie, then maybe Ivgrachev, now his amulet. Dorm would be very glad when they could leave Bydanushev.

There was still no sign of it. Ivgrachev was getting a little frantic. They asked the nurse on duty in the ward if he had seen anything. He replied that he hadn't and hadn't seen any amulet at all. The only person he had seen anywhere near Ivgrachev's bed had been Bianeska earlier in the morning.

Dorm thought about that for a moment. He couldn't imagine it. It wasn't impossible but it also wasn't the first thing that would leap to mind.

They asked the nurse to have Bianeska sent for. He scuttled off to find her as they waited. Telly, Rhyn and Mac, watched Dorm curiously. They recognised that he was thinking something. Of course they weren't sure what.

It took several minutes for Bianeska to arrive from wherever she had been. Her first reaction was predictable and understandable. "Is he alright?" she enquired worriedly as she came into the room. "Has something happened to him?"

"No he's fine actually," Zacravia said. "We just needed to see you is all. Dorm?"

"Something appears to have gone missing from Ivgrachev's things," he explained. "This nurse said that you are the only person who was near his bed today, we thought perhaps you might have seen something?" He didn't want to accuse her of stealing it. At least not right away.

She got a little huffy at his implication. "I didn't see anything. What is it that has gone missing. Perhaps I have seen it and not realised it was his?"

Dorm glanced at the others.

"It is an amulet, not unlike this one," Dorm said bringing his out. He let it hang in front of her gaze for a moment.

A conflict of thoughts and emotions played across her face for a moment. She paused and stared at Dorm full in the face. "I need to speak with you all privately," she said quietly. "All of you. I will have someone bring Ivgrachev."

"This should prove interesting," Cal said sarcastically.

Chapter 37

Bianeska lead them silently to a small office on one of the upper levels. It didn't contain much furniture, just a desk, some chairs and various shelves. The room was cluttered with a plethora of scrolls and parchments and many books. A large diagram was posted on one wall of all the internal workings of the human body, with well drawn but strange looking blobs representing the various organs. Dorm knew the names of most of them, but had no idea they were so unattractive.

It had the same smell as the rest of the College. That faint aroma of blood and the attempts to remove it. Though this room had a vase with flowers in it. While the flowers were starting to get on, there was still the faint smell of them in the air.

The room was small, and it was very crowded once everyone had managed to squeeze in. It was several more minutes of uncomfortable silence broken by the odd little snatch of conversation, before Ivgrachev arrived. He was brought in on a small sedan like chair carried by two nurses. There was some shuffling around to make room for him, before the nurses left.

"So what is it you wanted to discuss with us?" Dorm asked slowly.

She sighed. For a moment she hung her head, almost in shame. But she quickly raised it and looked them full in the eye. Almost as if she had reached a decision and wasn't going to back away from it. "I did see the amulet you mentioned in Ivgrachevs things," she admitted.

"Well that's good," Telly said. "Where was it when you saw it?"

"I first noticed it in among his clothes," she explained. "When he was still on the table. While we were trying to save him, I didn't take much notice of it at that time, as I had more important things to worry about."

"Of course," Rhyn assured her. "We understand that."

"Afterwards though, when I had time to examine it properly, I thought about it a lot." She briefly hung her head collecting her thoughts, or so it seemed. "I couldn't get it out of my mind."

"Why?" Travanos asked her. "What did it mean to you."

She looked at him intensely for a moment before answering. "It was clear to me, from his manner of dress, that Ivgrachev was some sort of thief. It wasn't hard to tell that. I had to be sure before I said anything, so that I knew that what I said was true and accurate. I checked, and found that my first thought had been completely wrong. I felt ashamed. But then I realised that there was something else going on. Something far more important."

"I'm not sure I understand?" Kanilma responded. "What did you think first that you then found you were wrong about?"

Bianeska paused. "That he had stolen the amulet."

"Stolen! From whom?"

"From me," she said revealing her own amulet at her neck.

Several things clicked into place for Dorm. The strange looks she had given them. Obviously she had seen some of the chains and recognised them. She probably hadn't said anything because she couldn't see the amulets themselves, and wasn't sure if they were anything to do with the one she owned. The whispered conversations with Ivgrachev, were probably her attempting to get information from him without shouting down the roof about it. Things began to make sense now. He began to smile, knowingly.

There were several whistles from their group, as well as a few sighs and one or two chuckles. And there were quite a few smiles from the others. No one had quite expected this. It was almost too easy.

"His amulet is not missing," Bianeska went on. "It is here." She reached into the draw of the desk and drew it out, handing it across to be passed back to its owner. "I had to compare it to my own in case I was wrong. I would have returned it this afternoon when on my rounds of the wards. I'm sorry if I worried you."

"Well," began Dorm slowly. "You did. But I think under the circumstances, it's somewhat understandable. Given the story you undoubtedly heard when your mother gave it to you on your sixteenth birthday, you obviously thought it was a one of a kind item. Finding another one would have unsettled you."

"It has all of us," Lianna finished.

"How…?" Bianeska began. The look on both hers and Ivgrachev's face indicated that they were both thinking the same thing. How could they have known these details? "I'm guessing that means there is more to this than what I have known?"

The basic explanation went well. Both of their new members understood it all well enough, and made sense of it. The knowledge that they had to leave however went less well, as it always did. This situation was a little different. Ivgrachev was concerned about his "kids" as he called them. Who would look after them while he was away? How would they protect themselves? Bianeska was worried about the rest of her studies and the people whom she taught at the College. It was of obvious concern to them. No one could fault them for harbouring such considerations, but of course they had all had to leave things behind. Family, friends, homes, lives. Once this was made plain the two newest additions began to slowly acquiesce.

They spent several hours sketching in details as best they understood them. About what the amulets might mean, what they had to do with the quest, and what link they might have had with the Fortress. And of course some of the details of their journey so far. Then of course there were the introductions.

They went as well as might be expected. There were some strangled gulps at the ranks of some, and some relaxed sighs at others. Bianeska was more used to interacting with so called 'high society' and so she accepted it much more readily than Ivgrachev. He seemed to have trouble accepting that they were human too.

He too, he revealed, had learnt about their curiosity about the amulets, and that had been behind his kidnap of Rhyn and Tissie. He apologised to both of them for that, which they readily accepted.

Bianeska was a little confused, and even worried at the mention of kidnapping, but once they had explained things she seemed to understand.

The conversations turned to how they had discovered the amulets and their meaning. And to some of their adventures whilst on this quest. Both were a little amused by the idea of a quest. The use of that word made both Bianeska and Ivgrachev laugh incredulously at first. It seemed to be the theme of things. But once they saw how serious everyone was they began to rethink their initial scepticism. And no one could blame them for that initial reaction. While everyone else, with the possible exception of Kanilma and Poljazak had come to terms with the idea of this being a quest, it still sounded silly.

They discussed how much longer it would be before Ivgrachev would be able to walk properly and to ride a horse for extended periods. Bianeska said to give it another week at least, as she was still concerned about his injury, and didn't want it rupturing. Everyone was annoyed at the delay, but fully understood the reasons. They didn't want to run the risk of losing Ivgrachev a second time. Not after thinking they had lost Rhyn and Tissie so recently. Again Dorm knew how happy he would be to leave this city.

They discussed what they would need to take with them, and organised to buy some new clothes for Ivgrachev. Tissie taking that task upon herself. Dorm secretly wondered at this, hoping she wasn't going to buy him some of the more 'courtly' clothes she wore on occasion at the expense of more sensible clothes. He asked Artur to go with her, supposedly to give her someone to carry things, but really so she could keep an eye on her.

The rest of them began organising to purchase two more horses and the new equipment they would need. Some they already had, but there were some things they realised they would have to get. Like another tent.

Bianeska decided she would have to let the Matron and some of her teachers know she was leaving for a time fairly soon. But she wanted to keep it from the nurses and her students for a while yet. She wasn't sure how she was going to tell them.

Ivgrachev was worried about his 'gang'. He worried about their survival. They were mainly children after all. His concerns hinted that there might be serious threats to them once he had gone.

"Is this more of what that Drakiv was on about?" Rhyn asked him.

"Yes it is," was his response.

"Who's Drakiv?" Mac asked curiously.

"He's the man who stabbed Iv," Rhyn explained slipping into the familiar nomenclature used by his gang. "He seemed to indicate that there was some sort of history between the two of them."

"Indeed there is," Iv conceded sadly. "There are many gangs throughout the city. And we all try to keep out from each others business. We all have areas that are ours, we all have activities that are ours. We try not to intervene in each others lives. It's safer that way. Some months ago some of my boys became entangled in some business that involved some of Drakiv's boys. It wasn't any one's fault. It was just one of those things that happened. Anyway as a penance I was made to leave the city for a time. I went to T'Zedella in the south. I had to run an operation down there for one of Drakiv's men who was performing less than well."

"Sounds complicated," Travanos mused. "I never knew the criminal underworld was so involved."

"Oh yes," Zacravia agreed. "We have similar things in Ambaka. I'm sure there are in all countries. Though I'm guessing that here in Bydanushev it's a little more formalised. I've not ever heard of people having franchises in different cities before."

"Franchises," Ivgrachev mused. "I like that. Anyway, after teaching those kids as much as I could, I came back to Bydanushev to continue my life. But it seems I came back too early. I think Drakiv wanted to take over my gang and the territory that came with it. He was always ambitious. My return stopped his plans to do that. He betrayed the understanding we had, and he got what he deserved."

"Sounds rather cut throat if you ask me," Artur said.

"Well we aren't talking about flower arranging here, my friend," Zacravia told him.

"I guess that explains why he attacked you then," Dorm said. "Which never made much sense to me."

"I suspect that he knew I had Rhyn and Tissie as well," Ivgrachev explain further. “His people watched my people. My people watched his. It was the way of things.”

“He was probably very curious then,” Rhyn went on. “From what you’ve said, kidnapping seems very out of character for you and your kids. He must have wondered what was so valuable about us.”

“Very much so.”

“Well I’m glad you got him,” Tissie said defiantly. “I don’t think I liked the look of him. I think all things considered you treated us quite well. I get the feeling he wouldn’t have been so nice about it.”

“On that you are right,” Iv agreed with her.

Tissie surprised Dorm with her very sensible purchases for Ivgrachev. Artur reported that he hardly had to question anything she looked at at all. Dorm began to think that he had misjudged her a little.

Horses and supplies were bought and essentially they were ready to go. They just had to wait for Ivgrachev’s injuries to heal.

It was a curious time. They were essentially just waiting. They had nothing to do other than wait. Ivgrachevs’ gang did have to be informed, and ‘reorganised’ as he called it. They were a little confused as to what he meant by that, until he explained that since Drakiv had died, Ivgrachev had essentially inherited everything he had controlled. He spent some time making notes on some parchment Bianeska provided him. He didn’t let any one see them, and said that they were only for Ogn. Zacravia informed them that he was most likely working out a chain of command, and trying to fit the best people from both groups into it.

“He’ll want to be careful though,” Zacravia mused. “He’ll want to put some of this Drakiv’s people into high positions so that they see they aren’t being victimised. But not so high that they can’t take over while he’s gone. It’s a very careful balancing act.”

“Sounds a lot like a business amalgamation,” Ambra commented.

“Quite,” Zacravia agreed.

They met with Ogn the next day and passed on Ivgrachev’s instructions as well as the message that he would come and see them before he left. Ogn was shocked at the news that he was leaving. He was clearly worried at how things would pan out in the future without him there to hold it all together. Some gentle reassurances from Dorm and the others placated him, but probably didn't banish his concerns completely.

Every day Ivgrachev got better, and was able to do more. Bianeska commented often that she was pleased with his progress.

As time went on the others became increasingly restless, and Dorm had to admit that he too was growing unsettled. They had everyone now didn't they? There was no further need for them to remain in Bydanushev. Everyone was eager to get out and back on the road. The question of course was where? They had set out from Lugemall so many months ago with the clear idea that they had to travel to all the countries in the Alliance to find the questers. There had been structure to their travels. A purpose. But now that they had reached the end of that plan, the question of where to go next was staring them in the face; without any sort of answer.

He wanted to go home. But he wasn't sure if that was what he was supposed to do.

The Rangers had told him to visit on his way out of Bydanushev. Perhaps they had some information that would lead them in the right direction? He hoped so. He was beginning to feel a little lost.

Wherever they were going to be off to next, Dorm was glad he had these people with him. He couldn't imagine the journey without them.

Bianeska gave Ivgrachev a clean-ish bill of health, saying that he should still take it easy and not exert himself. Since she was to accompany them she could make sure this occurred. He was not to get involved in any heavy lifting for a little while yet.

Before they left he went to see Ogn and the others. They went with him into the sewers again, experiencing all the wondrous sights and smells that that part of the city had to offer. They found the group and there was a long conversation as Ivgrachev explained to them all what was happening. Some of the younger children grew teary, and the various women in the group couldn't help but comfort them.

Ogn expressed his concerns, which seemed to be shared by all the others. Ivgrachev gave them strict instructions as what to do in certain circumstances. He told Ogn how proud he was of him, and that he thought the young man was ready to lead these people on his own. Ogn blushed with pride at this, but still seemed unconvinced. Dorm had seen this reaction in people from time to time. Usually in people he had great confidence in and were found to succeed.

There were many tears and hugs and kisses on cheeks when they had to leave. It was clear that Ivgrachev didn't want to go in his heart of hearts, and none of them could criticise him for that. But in the end as the day grew older, they made their way back to the inn. They would leave the next morning.

The last look they had was of a sad faced Ogn trying to look strong for the others. While inside he was feeling so terribly alone and exposed. Dorm didn't envy him that feeling.

The next morning they rose and went through their usual domestic routine, before beginning their journey. The only places they knew for certain they were going to were the College to collect Bianeska and then the Rangers chapterhouse.

The city was its usual bustling self. It seemed almost uninterested in them. Here they were embarking on an unknown journey, one with no actual destination picked out, and yet the city went about its normal routine as if nothing interesting were happening.

Bianeska was waiting for them when they arrived at the College. Matron Akera and Paniz were the only ones waiting with her, but they got the feeling that there were probably a lot of people watching from windows.

"Right on time I see," Bianeska said as they arrived.

"We endeavour to be punctual," Mac informed her with a grin.

"Besides we probably have a very long journey ahead of us," Telly explained. "The sooner we pick you up the sooner we get to where we're going. And then the sooner we can stop."

"Sounds like a plan to me," Bianeska replied.

She began to organise her things with Poljazak's help. It didn't take long as she only had a few bags. Though she did insist on one medium sized bag being carefully secured.

"What's in it," Poljazak asked her curiously as he tied in onto the rear of her saddle with an extra strap.

“It’s my medicine bag,” she explained. “Something that might come in handy.”

“If the way you helped Ivgrachev is anything to go by, very handy,” the farmer complimented her.

“Why thank you.”

She said her goodbyes to Akera and Paniz, giving her pupil several whispered pieces of advice before leaving. There was much hugging and several tears.

Finally they were ready to leave. Dorm briefly glanced back across the faces of those around him. There was something he wanted to say. But he wasn’t sure what.

He pushed his horse out into the street and began to make his way towards the chapterhouse. The group he led clustered around him as they rode, almost as if they were afraid to get lost in the traffic.

It took only about half an hour to make their way across to the chapterhouse. Again they pulled the bellpull and heard the ringing of the bell. This time however, the gate opened promptly. And beyond, lining the sides of the path were Rangers.

They walked their horses into the courtyard, and saw that this too was surrounded by idyllic gardens. It seemed the Rangers liked their gardens. It was a strange sight. This beautiful garden with Rangers almost standing guard around the edge of it. There was the noise of birds chirping pleasantly over the distant hum of the noise of the city. It was a relaxing place. Calming. Yet there was still a sense of anticipation, and a little trepidation, if Dorm was honest with himself.

On the steps that lead to the main door stood a group of three Rangers. The woman who had met them the last time they came here stood in the centre. She smiled at them, and inclined her head as they approached.

“Noble Questers,” she said. “We welcome you most warmly.”

“Well this is a change,” said Travanos sarcastically.

“We must apologise for our performance last time you visited us,” she went on.

“Performance?” Mac asked her.

“Yes. I’m afraid that’s what it was. We could not let you in for fear that you would not find your next quester."

"You mean you knew that we would find Bianeska through Ivgrachev's injury?"

"Indeed we did," she told them. "If you had entered this chapterhouse whilst looking for Rhynavell and Tissievilla, you would not have found Bianeska. We would have been forced to help you search the city for them, and the opportunity to meet Bianeska would have been lost. And that could not be permitted. We know that our actions hurt and confused you, but there was no other way."

"You could have just told us perhaps," Artur suggested.

"No gentle Artur," she chided him. "If we had you would not have been able to find her. It is the way of things. Do not ask us to explain it."

"Well we did find her," Dorm told her. "In fact we have found everyone, Miss?"

"Raquis is my name," she replied.

"Well Raquis," Dorm went on. "What now? I mean, we have done everything that we knew we had to do when we started this thing. Where do we go now?"

"Oh you have not done everything Your Highness," Raquis informed him. "In fact you have but barely begun. But for now you have achieved much. And you have earnt a period of rest. And so we instruct thee to return to the beginning."

"Return to the beginning?"

"Yes. And spend some time in that rest. For the journey will continue, and be as long or even longer than that which you have now completed, thus far."

Well wasn't that just great. More travelling.

Though Dorm knew exactly how everyone would feel about going back. Presumably the beginning referred to Lugemall. It would be a long journey, but they would be able to see people along the way and give those who had left family behind a chance to catch up. He could only see good coming from that.

"Well despite your strange way of going about it, I suppose you have helped us Raquis," Dorm told her. "So I guess we should say thank you."

"It is our honour to serve you Noble Quester. You owe us no

thanks."

"Still, it is given."

The questers bowed around them.

Dorm turned his horse to face the others.

He looked across their faces, catching the eyes of each one in turn. Telly, the high-born lady who was the closest thing to a best friend he'd ever had; Rhyn, the humble accountant who amazed him everyday with her insights. Travanos, a man of quiet dignity, who had become a confidant; Artur, the quiet, almost shy woodsman who seemed to recall facts at just the right time; Lianna, who was almost like a mother to the group, when she said jump, they asked how high; Harmia, the single minded police officer who had given up her quest for vengeance; Zacravia, the object of that vengeance. A fallen man, who seemed to have somewhat redeemed himself. Cal, the simple guardsman who had already proven he was much more; Tissie, who despite some short comings was starting to prove her worth; Ambra, who was still wary of his former betrothed, but who's quiet strength was comforting to them all; and Navista, who seemed to recently have gotten past her hatred of him, and had maybe even begun to respect him a little. Ameks, the simple stonecutter, who's inner confidence had yet to shine, but could easily be seen. Pianwasal; who's bearing led none to question her. Kanilma, who was still wondering how she had come to be mixed up in all this, but kept them fed so well, they weren't going to lose her in a hurry; Poljazak, the farmer who had given up his young family and somehow instilled confidence in them all. And Ivgrachev and Bianeska, who had only recently joined them but could already be seen to be of great benefit. And finally Mac, the man Dorm shared his life with, and who couldn't be anywhere else.

As he looked over their faces he realised truly that these people were more than companions. They were more than friends even. These people *were* family. As important to him as his father or Mac. He would do anything for these people, and indeed any that were still to come. He didn't know why or how he had come to feel this way, but it was there. And it felt right.

Yes these were the most important people in the world to him right now. And he suspected would be for some time to come.

He thought about them all, the times they had shared. The things they had seen and done. And everything that had happened to them on their journey to this city on the far side of the Alliance. The good, the bad, the raucous and the terrifying. Where would they end up in the future? Where would they go? Who would they meet? Who was still to join them? These questions remained unanswered, but he couldn't imagine facing them or indeed answering them without these people at his side. He laughed in spite of himself.

"What is it Dorm," Telly said to him curiously.

"You people," he said quietly. "You're amazing."

No one was quite sure what to make of that. There were some uneasy coughs and blushed faces.

"I guess we should make a move then," he said.

"Yes," agreed Ambra. "Before you get any mushier on us."

"I think it's nice," Navista said. "And we all know you have no romance in you."

Dorm knew that jibe for what it was. Her eyes betrayed the fact that she didn't really mean it. He noted that change in her, and the changes in the others. All of them had changed over the time he had known them. And he was beginning to recognise those changes. He was beginning to know these people.

"Then let's go," he said simply and started them off.

Chapter 38

And so they were on their way home.

Unfortunately it didn't start very dramatically. They became stuck in the city traffic on the streets of Bydanushev and it took them almost an hour to reach the south gate. They finally managed to make their way through and began their journey home properly. Dorm wasn't sure what route they would take exactly. He wanted it to be more or less directly back to Lugemall. But he knew they would have to make a few stops along the way.

It would be good to let people visit family as they went past them. That was fair. They had missed them. And would continue to do so. It was a little unfair for him to rush home and not let his companions see their families when they happened to be going right past them.

They hurried their way south along the main highway through the city of Rusank again and on to the city of T'Zedella. Ivgrachev showed them a good place to stay in this city, which they found to be rather cosmopolitan, likely due to the fact that it was the first major city that other Alliance travellers would come to.

They stayed overnight and Ivgrachev took Zacravia to meet some of the 'locals'. No one was particularly interested in getting mixed up in anything so they elected to stay at the inn.

The two returned quite late in the evening with nothing hugely interesting to report. Some rumours about Peldraksekhr merchants and 'diplomats' apparently becoming increasingly involved in less than completely reputable deals.

Dorm filed that information away for later.

They continued on their way south and after another few days crossed the border back into Ojliam. After a few more days they found themselves in the city of Tilekzel. It seemed that this city was heavily influenced by the country to the north, as there was a distinct appearance to many of the buildings that was not unlike those in Bydanushev. While the city was another victim of the Great Reconstruction, there seemed to have been a concerted effort over the years to alter things and make the city appear more natural.

They headed south again from Tilekzel but turned off the main highway after two days in order to follow the smaller roads and visit with Poljazaks' family. It took several days of meandering to cross the east-west running highway that lead towards Krazclow, and another day and a half to reach the valley where their friends farm was located. It was mid-morning when they approached the area in front of the farm buildings. They held their horses while Poljazak took in the state of his farm.

It hadn't changed.

A thin trail of smoke rose from the chimney and from somewhere there was the sound of wood being chopped.

Sinka and Mikas were playing some unknown game. They were totally engrossed in their make believe world and didn't notice their father and his companions ride up. Poljazak simply sat on his horse for a minute, watching them. There was a smile on his face, and everyone knew how happy he was to see them.

After a moment the children happened to look up and noticed them.

There were screams of delight as the two little people realised who it was that they were seeing and ran over towards him. Poljazak swung down from his saddle and scooped them up as they crashed into him laughing and squealing in joy, and smothering his face in kisses.

A moment or two later Zaneem came rushing out of the main door to the house. She had a frantic expression on her face. Obviously she had heard the children's cries, but hadn't been able to tell their cause. Fearing the worst she had rushed out to see what the matter was.

Her first reaction upon seeing her children in the arms of a man she didn't at first recognise, with his face covered in small children, and surrounded by a large group of people could not have been good. It was a second or two before she realised who she was seeing.

"Poljazak! She cried, literally leaping down the stairs to the ground to run over to him. She flew into his arms, tears on her cheeks. There was a long rather passionate and intimate kiss between the two, that made everyone just a little embarrassed, but that none could deny them.

For some minutes there was much whispered talk and kisses and hugs and fond touching. It was a wonderful homecoming for him.

Zaneem insisted on making lunch for them, which everyone offered to assist in. The rest of the day was spent in eating and relaxing and filling Zaneem in on their adventures since she had seen them.

She worried at the tale of Rhyn and Tissie's kidnapping and even fussed over them a little. Everyone took it in their stride, knowing that soon they would have to leave again, and also knowing how hard that would be for the couple.

They went to sleep that night knowing that they were safe, but also satisfied at the happiness that the day had brought to Poljazak and Zaneem.

They elected to stay a full day at the farm, so that Poljazak could see what had happened in the time he had been away and issue any instructions he thought necessary. As it turned out, Zaneem and his brother had actually anticipated several decisions he made, and had already taken steps towards them.

"This is why I married this woman," he told the others loudly. "She thinks of everything."

They spent the evening eating a hearty meal and preparing for their departure the next day. They knew it would be bitter-sweet for Zaneem and the children. To have him home for such a short time was not enough, and everyone understood that. But there was a task that they had to perform, and sadly it couldn't be performed here.

They restocked their supplies, and went to sleep knowing that tomorrow would be emotionally draining, but that they would once again be back on the road.

The departure was not as harrowing as Dorm had feared it would be. Zaneem seemed to have accepted that her husband was doing something important. The children didn't quite understand why Poljazak had to go away again so soon, but seemed to accept it when he said that he would return. He had this time hadn't he?

Husband and wife spent some time in quiet conversation before he remounted his horse to join the others. There were many long looks and waves as the group slowly rode away. Dorm realised rather quickly that this was going to be a regular feature of this part of the trip.

They retraced their path as they headed towards their next stop which was to be Kanilma's home. The landscape hadn't changed and the journey was easy. There were no possible Peldraksekhr agents camping that they could see and they made good time.

Having Kanilma with them made the job a little easier as she was able to point out a way to get off the main highway earlier and follow the smaller country roads towards her village. Dorm was very grateful for this. He wanted to avoid the city of Ojliam especially. It wouldn't be a good idea to go through there, with the possibility of running into Prince Varain again. Things would probably be a little uneasy with him if they did. Time was what was needed on that situation. Time for the initial shock and pain to subside.

They arrived back in the village of Greznick early one morning. They paused for a moment as they approached. The village was 'quaint', according to Travanos. No one was quite sure if he meant that kindly or not, but no one said anything. Kanilma sat on her horse taking in the view and smiling at it. It was home after all.

"Are you okay?" Rhyn asked her after a few moments.

"Yes," she replied quietly. "I just wanted to take a moment."

They moved out again and went directly to the inn where Kanilma's guardians worked. They tethered their horses and entered the building as if they were just normal travellers. They didn't want to arouse any suspicion. The taproom was large and fairly dark given the time of day, and there were only the obligatory older generation of men who seemed to always inhabit inns in small villages.

They took seats and did their best to ignore the curious stares of the locals. Kanilma did her best to hide her face from them in a natural sort of way. She didn't want any one to recognise her before she saw Lianka and Gossan saw her.

They ordered a light meal and waited patiently, chatting about the road as if nothing was amiss. Kanilma smiled a lot as she heard the voices of the people in the room, and took in the sights and smells. It was after all a homecoming of sorts. Granted a brief one only, but these things were important and everyone knew it. Besides it was good to remind oneself of what this quest was all about. They had all been discussing over the previous days what the prophecy had said and what it might mean. It had strongly hinted that there might be a war, or at least some sort of conflict that may be important in the survival of the Alliance. This sort of visit was good for that. If one knew what one was fighting for…

Eventually Gossan came forth with a large tray of cooked meat and bread. Lianka came out a few steps behind him with butter, jams and several large pots of tea, and mugs. They put all the food out on the table in front of their large group without really taking in the faces of the people. Dorm remembered that they hadn't met all of them anyway so that was another reason why they didn't say anything.

They bade them to enjoy their meal and began to return to the kitchen to continue their work. Half way back to the door, Gossan stopped. Lianka who was only a step behind him bumped into him cursing him briefly for his clumsiness, until he turned around. The look on his face stopped her.

"What is it Gossan?" she said quietly, fearful of what his answer might be.

He whispered something in response to her query that couldn't be heard at the table. But there were tears in his eyes. And a faint smile on his face. Lianka turned around slowly and followed his gaze. Kanilma, who was the subject of that gaze, slowly pushed back the hood she was wearing and smiled. A tear in her own eyes.

There was no running leaps. There were no exclamations. Just a gentle, sincere, and loving nod of acknowledgement. Both guardians knew that she was back, at least for a time. And both were happy beyond words. They went back into the kitchen and their group ate their meal in relative silence.

"I presume we will be staying here the night?" Artur asked knowingly.

"Of course," Telly agreed. "We have to. Kanilma deserves nothing less"

It was about an hour later, after they had finished and the old men, who Kanilma described as 'bar-flies', had left, that the proper reunion took place. Again there was much hugging and kissing and asking of questions on top of each other with no hope of an answer. But there was joy and warmth in the reunion of what was in reality a family. There was no mistaking the love felt for Kanilma by Lianka and Gossan, nor by her for them.

They closed the inn and spent several hours filling them in on what had happened since they had left and introducing them to everyone. They seemed genuinely pleased that Kanilma had fallen in with such a disparate group of people who were sharing a common experience.

They also informed them of what had happened with Prince Varain in the mean time. It turned out that he had waited a full week and a half before trying to contact Kanilma again. Dorm was impressed. He hadn't expected him to last more than two days.

The information that she had gone away for a time hadn't gone down well, but not nearly as bad as they had thought. He had seemed to accept it and thought that in the end she would be a better person for it and would realise how much she meant to him sooner. Kanilma's response to this was just to sigh.

The inn had to reopen around lunchtime for several hours. They didn't want any suspicion of anything happening to somehow get back to Varain and cause them issues. The last thing they needed was to be chased around by a lovesick prince.

Kanilma took the opportunity to help out in the kitchen and everyone decided to try and do their bit as well. Even if it was only to peel some vegetables or wash some dishes. It made everyone feel almost like they were at home. Which was a strange feeling in this place none of them had been before. Perhaps it was really the company…

The day continued on with sessions of serving and sessions of reminiscing. Both Lianka and Gossan asked some probing questions of the others. No one could blame them for this. They were as a group, after all responsible for the well being of someone who was essentially their daughter. The answers they gave always seemed to satisfy them. Dorm wasn't sure if that was because they liked the answers or they just felt that they had no choice but to like them. But he was almost glad that they did ask the questions. Perhaps this went someway towards setting their minds at ease, and possibly helping them in the future. If these two people were on their side, that was a start.

Day turned into night, as day is want to do, and the conversation continued until well after the crickets had begun their nightly serenade. There was laughter, there were gasps of concern, there was even the odd word of anger. There was confusion and worry at the story of Rhyn and Tissie's adventure, but always it came back to happiness. Happiness that Kanilma was doing something important.

Finally everyone retired for the evening in the various rooms of the inn. They were small, but neat and comfortable, and everyone had a feeling of safety knowing that the rest of the group was all around them.

In the morning they did their best to ease the eventual pain of their departure. They all knew it was coming. They had explained the day before where they were heading. Lianka and Gossan went about their business as if this was just another day with nothing special happening. They all again did their best to help out. And again they did their best to look like normal travellers.

Finally, just after midday the time had come for their leaving. They remained inside in order to keep the emotion away from prying eyes. There was much hugging and kissing, and well wishing, and orders to remain safe. It took them almost an hour, but finally they were mounted up and ready to leave.

The goodbye was still lingering. Understandably. No one likes to say goodbye to people they care about. But it had to be done. Finally they rode off. Promising to return as soon as they were able.

Kanilma was a little quieter than normal as they headed south. It was obvious that this reunion had affected her. She had been reminded of what she had left. That was hard for all of them, but she was, so far at least, the youngest of their group. They had to consider that. Dorm decided to have a talk with Telly at some stage to see what she thought. Perhaps there was something they could do as a group to help her.

They made their way through the back roads till they were well past Ojliam, before turning their way towards the main highway. Once there they headed south at a good speed. There was a steady amount of traffic travelling in both directions, and the weather remained fairly good.

Everyone on the road seemed to be in good spirits, and eventually they were able to pick up snatches of rumours. Apparently King Prinaz's army had managed to defeat a large group of bandits near Zobeka.

Dorm had to admit that he was worried by this. Bandits had been seen active in both Kiama Mor and Ojliam, and there was some evidence that they were operating even further afield than that. It was obviously linked, and probably part of some sort of plan. He suspected he knew who was behind it, but proving it publicly would be difficult. And the reason as to why still escaped him.

They passed through the city of Neftah about a week after leaving Kanilma's home, and they took shelter for the night, and enjoyed themselves. There was nothing quite like pampering oneself after a long time on the road.

Whilst in Neftah they heard rumours of trouble along the border with Kiama Mor. They worked their way to speaking with a group of travellers who had recently passed through there to find out what was going on.

"We made it through just in time," explained the head merchant, whose name was Famix. "They closed the border just after we crossed it."

"Closed it?" Dorm worried.

"Yes," Famix told him. "If you can believe that. They said they'd reopen it again as soon as the situation had calmed down."

"What situation is that?" Travanos asked him curiously.

"All these bandits everywhere," Famix said shaking his head and staring into his tankard. "I tell you, I don't know what the Alliance is coming to, when honest people can't use the roads any more without being in fear of their lives."

“We'd heard a while ago that the Sultan had been getting on top of them,” Telly put in.

“So had I,” the merchant went on. “But apparently they got out from under him again.”

“Well that puts a dent in out plans,” Dorm mused pessimistically. “We have to get to Kiama Mor.”

“You'll have to wait a while, friend,” Famix warned him. “There's Kiaman soldiers all through them hills. They wont be letting any one through till they kill every last one of them bandits.”

“Well we still have a few days before we get to the border,” Lianna said. “Perhaps they'll have taken care of it by then?”

“You can hope,” was Famix's reply.

They again headed south and passed through the various villages and small towns along the highway. They noticed a shortage of accommodation as they went indicative of the number of merchants who had been held up. They began to despair that they wouldn't get out of Ojliam for some time.

Finally they arrived at the small town that had grown up within sight of the border crossing and discovered that the border was indeed still closed. Apparently Ojlian troops had also been active in the area to prevent any bandits from sneaking across into the northern country. They worried for a moment that perhaps this might bring Varain here, but the soldiers were apparently led by one General Tribnest.

They still maintained a low profile. There was no point in making themselves stand out. And no point in getting too vocal about the situation as there was little they could do about it. It was another three days before they heard anything substantial about what was happening. Apparently the Kiamans had eliminated a large group of the bandits at what appeared to be their base. There were no other details they could get, and the border remained closed.

Two days after this news they received word that the border would be reopened, and that both Kiaman and Ojlian troops would patrol the highway to provide protection. While they didn't really want any one to be watching them they were glad of the security.

They moved out and crossed the border into Kiama Mor. The

forest and hills continued to follow them, though this time they knew how long that would last. Dorm spoke to Navista as to where her clan were likely to be at this time. He didn't really fancy the idea of wandering all over the country looking for them. She told him that once they got to a main town she would be able to make some enquiries and pin them down to an area.

It took about two days to reach the first main town on the highway, called Hamishev. Like most Kiaman cities the buildings were fairly low, and plain. There were however a few more 'Ojlian' style building than they had thought. They had pushed fairly hard and so had managed to arrive before many of the other travellers that had crossed the border at the same time as they had, so there was still plenty of room in the inns and hostels.

Navista went off and returned after only an hour or so with the belief that her clan was somewhere in the vicinity of Efgaz. Dorm didn't recall that place and had to look it up. It turned out to be only slightly out of their way and wouldn't really cost them anything to go have a look.

The next morning they headed out of the town by way of the west gate. The road they followed left the hill country behind and entered flat plains, that seemed to stretch forever into the distance. As they continued on their south westerly track the land gradually began to grow more arid, and dryer. The number of farms diminished and the grass grew sparser. Finally it gave way to the desert. It was curious to go through this transition again. Navista informed them that this wasn't proper desert, but that it was close enough. She appeared to be rather uncomfortable at times as they rode. She explained this as being a part of her divination ability.

Dorm was still curious about this. They hadn't had any opportunity to witness it, and he didn't really understand it. He had heard of it of course, but actually seeing it was something else entirely.

It was on the fifth day out from Hamishev that they came to the town of Efgaz. It was an unremarkable little town huddled in a slight depression between two small hills, where the two main roads in the area happened to intersect. They took rooms and did their best to ignore the almost hostile stares of the locals. It was fairly late in the day, but

Navista did some wandering to see if she could learn anything more about her family. She returned empty handed, vowing to try again in the morning.

Navista was more successful the next day, and learnt that her clan had been in the town only a few days prior. She had directions to follow and they set off at an optimistic pace roughly due south of the town. They were probably given some strange looks by the inhabitants, but no one bothered to investigate that.

They rode well throughout the day despite the sandy conditions. They stopped only sparingly, and luckily the weather was rather mild so the horses didn't exert themselves too much. Towards the end of the day they began to encounter the odd trace of the clans passing. Some hoof prints, a short stretch of wheel tracks.

They camped for the night and set out early the next morning following the intermittent signs. Dorm noticed that he now had several people who were good trackers. Zacravia had always been tracking for them. And Navista was obvious, she had lived in this environment for most of her life. She would be well familiar with the signs. But both Ambra and Ivgrachev seemed to be assisting. Ambra had probably learnt the skills in his youth, in much the same way as Navista. Ivgrachev seemed to be only slightly less able than Zacravia. This was a surprise to Dorm. He would have thought that someone who lived their life in a city would not be able to see these sorts of signs out here in the wild.

It was not long after midday when they spotted in the distance a low hanging cloud of haze. There was faint views of movement coming from it and Navista announced cheerfully that their search was over.

“Are you sure that's them?” Harmia said to her shielding her eyes from the glare and squinting into the distance.

“Of course,” replied the clanswoman. “I recognise my family's colours anywhere.”

“Colours?” said Poljazak incredulously. “The only colour I can see is brown.”

“Then there must be something wrong with your eyes.”

“Do not try to explain it to them, Navista,” Ambra told her. “They are all city dwellers. They don't have our eyes.”

She smiled knowingly at him for a moment, almost as if they were friends, before spurring her horse forward. The others hurried to catch up.

As they got closer they saw the 'colours' that Navista had referred to. Flying from the rear of the aftermost wagons, from short poles were small flags of blue and white. There was a series of stripes and chequered squares. From a distance they had been almost impossible to see, and Dorm wondered how Navista had been able to.

As they approached the clan, several riders, who until now had seemed completely unaware of their approach, suddenly wheeled their camels around and drove at an astonishing speed towards their group.

Navista, who was in the lead immediately reigned in, the others following suit. The camels came to a halt quite close and almost before they could blink the riders had bows trained on them.

"Who are you?" yelled the lead man defiantly. "Why do you approach our clan?"

Navista laughed heartily. " Ahh Omsir, you always were funny."

The one called Omsir paused for a moment, taking in her face. He lowered his bow and grinned at her. "Navista! It is good to see you again. Are you back to stay?"

"Alas no my cousin. We are just passing through, but we wanted to see my family before we left the area."

"Then we shall escort you in. I know your father will be very pleased to see you," Omsir instructed one of the other riders to go on ahead and tell Kamis that Navista and her companions had returned. While he went on ahead the other camel riders moved in around them and escorted them onwards. Omsir and Navista chatted happily to each other. Dorm did note that Omsir seemed to ignore the fact that Ambra was present. For his part, Ambra seemed to almost have expected this.

It didn't take long for them to catch up with the rest of the clan, and as they rode through there were shouts of greeting to Navista, and waves, and even a few hurried kisses. Finally they came to where Kamis was erecting his tent. His daughter practically leapt off her horse and flew into her fathers arms. There was much kissing and laughing. Dorm knew they would be in for a good few days.

There was a great celebration for the homecoming, with more

food than Dorm had seen in weeks and music and dancing. They were also treated to a fire-display, where members of the clan did all sorts of wondrous and probably lethal things with fire, like eating it and twirling it about their heads and walking on it. They all had to admit that the displays were very exciting, but also a little worrying. Could people really do this without long term effects? Dorm wasn't about to take up the pastime to find out.

Kamis was grateful to them all for having returned his daughter to them unharmed. He admitted openly that he had been worried that something would happen to her while she was away. Everyone promised him that if anything, things were more likely to go their way with her around. He gave them a knowing, smiling nod at this.

Kamis also seemed to be more relaxed towards Ambra. While he didn't go out of his way to be overly friendly like he did the others, he was at least civil. A difference that Dorm noticed from the reactions of the clan members. Ambra later explained this to him. Kamis, as the head of the clan, was the one who decided when a person who had wronged the clan was welcomed back. No one else would speak to him until it became clear that Kamis was alright with it. His actions during their stay seemed to indicate that he was heading in that direction, but wasn't quite there yet. Ambra hinted that some of the more prominent members of the family might interact with him in a similar way to what Kamis had already, but no more. Dorm found all this very complicated, but Ambra's reaction to it seemed to indicate that he had been pleased with the response so far.

Kamis remained close to his daughter during the evening. A procession of people came and spent some time with her chatting and reminiscing. And it seemed on more than one occasion, gossiping. She went and met all three new babies that had been born during her absence, and chatted to the newly adult members of the clan.

Navista seemed happy to be home. There was a certain joy that seemed to have been rekindled in her eyes as she spoke. It was good to see her feeling this way. Even if it was only for a short while. And Ambra seemed to be a little more comfortable as well. At least he was now surrounded by a culture he understood, and there had been improvements in his relationship.

At one stage, late in the night, Kamis took Dorm to one side and spoke to him. "I commend you friend Dorm. You have taken good care of my daughter. That is no small thing. Will you continue to do so into the future?"

"Of course. How can you even ask me that?"

"Forgive a fathers' need for reassurance," Kamis said. "I understand that you have a long journey ahead of you, and that Navista must go with you. I know I will not see her for some time. Whatever it is that you are doing, I know it is important."

"Yes, very."

Kamis nodded. "Then I entrust her into your care. And know that whatever happens, and if it is ever needed, you have an ally in this clan. We will stand with you if and when the time comes."

Dorm paused for a moment as he took that in. "Thank you Kamis," he said taking the leaders hand firmly. "That means a lot."

They decided to stay the next day with the clan and partake of as much of their hospitality as they politely could. For their part Navista's extended family seemed only too happy to cater to their needs.

A little after midday Navista informed them that she had to go off and help find some water. This presented a unique opportunity to see her use her divination abilities. None of them had had an opportunity to witness it yet and they were all very curious.

Several of them gathered with a small group of clansman headed by Navista's cousin Omsir. They all carried large water skeins and shovels to dig with. They milled around chatting and telling Navista that the other diviner in the clan, whose name was Qu'sam, that she had "felt" things off to the north-west of their encampment, the day before. Dorm wasn't sure what that meant but got the feeling he'd find out.

They rode out soon after and proceeded out into the desert chatting about nothing in particular. The weather was warm, but not overly so, and there was a wind blowing, that stirred the sand a little, which made things less pleasant than they would otherwise have been.

After an hour or so they crested a large dune and looked out over the expanse of the desert, marching away to the horizon. Navista got down off her horse. She looked around for a moment then seemingly having made a decision, took a small mat, that had been curled up on her saddle, and laid it down on the sand. The other clans men got off their camels and stretched their legs, but didn't approach Navista.

She sat down cross legged on her mat sighed heavily, then sat up straight and closed her eyes. She remained motionless for some time. After a while Dorm began to hear a low hum emanating from her throat. It slowly built till it was properly audible, and then just as suddenly stopped. Her eyes slowly opened.

"I am ready," she said.

Her cousin Omsir, helped her to her feet and put away the mat, while she slowly turned around on the spot. After a few seconds she seemed to have picked a direction and began walking.

To Dorm and his friends it seemed almost aimless as she descended the slope of the dune and climbed the next one. Once she had ascended that dune she paused, altered her course slightly and continued on. They trailed along behind her. The other clansmen seemingly used to this strange behaviour.

Navista made slight alterations in her direction as she walked. Dorm noticed that her movements were stiff. Almost as if she had forgotten how to bend her knees and elbows properly. The one time she turned around her face appeared almost blank, as if she couldn't see anything.

Finally after nearly half an hour of this strange wandering, she came to an area that was scattered with rocks and the dry remains of long dead plants. It was clearly an old stream bed, but there couldn't be any more water here surely?

Navista stumbled around the area for a few moments before stopping and pointing frantically at the ground. Her fingers stiff and claw-like. "Here," she instructed them in a slightly hoarse voice. "Dig here, quickly."

The clansmen leapt forward with their digging tools and skeins and began to hack away at the dried earth and sand. The others did their best to help without getting in the way too much. After what seemed an eternity of digging through parched dry sand, it began to become damp, and finally wet.

Eventually they had uncovered a veritable stream of clear water. It tasted very earthy having come straight from the ground, but it was water none the less.

Dorm had to admit he was impressed. He congratulated Navista who merely thanked him, with no sense of pride or achievement. For her, this was normal, something she had always been able to do. There was nothing special in it.

They filled up all the skeins over the next hour and then returned to the clans' camp site.

Despite the hospitality shown them by Navista's family they knew they had to leave. Dorm made this known to Kamis at dinner that evening and he reluctantly agreed that they should leave sooner rather than later.

"We do not want you to become too comfortable here," was his response.

The next day they said their goodbyes. Navista spending time with various people during the morning. The clan gave them food and water to take with them, and even replaced some equipment that had become worn.

Navista and Kamis had a rather sedate farewell, given the circumstances. Dorm had expected much more emotion. There was almost a 'politeness' to it. A hesitancy to go over the top. Dorm hoped this was just because they were confident of meeting up again soon.

The clan rode with them for a time as they headed back in the general direction of Efgaz. It took about two and a half hours to reach the city. Given their less than cordial reception there previously they decided not to stop.

They said their final goodbyes to Kamis and his family before joining the road just past the city and heading off towards the east. For some time Navista was quiet, much as Kanilma had been. Dorm suspected this would be a fairly common feature. Ambra, by contrast, had been quiet during most of their stay with the clan. He almost seemed to liven up a bit now that they had left them. Though he seemed to cast curious looks in Navista's direction, and Dorm wasn't sure what they meant.

They stayed that night in a hostel a few hours to the east of Efgaz.

It wasn't as comfortable as those that could be found on the main highways, and neither was the food as good, but it was cheep and relatively homey. They left first thing in the morning and rode hard for most of the day.

The day after they came to and then passed through the city of El Peradae. They had no desire to stop there, despite its possible promise of better accommodations. The city lay at the junction of the road they were following and the main north-south highway. It was a town devoted to trade and industry, and even though all of them could have done with a decent meal and a wash, everyone agreed this wasn't the place. There was just a bad feeling.

Ambra informed them that he had been here a couple of times, and never had a particularly good time of it. He claimed the merchants here always tried to swindle him.

They decided to camp some miles from the city as evening came, and spent a rather uncomfortable but less nervous night as a result.

Dorm consulted his map before they rode out in the morning and updated its details with the help of Navista and Ambra, who both informed him of several villages that weren't shown on his parchment. As a result they were able to better plan their journey with the least number of stops, but ones that would hopefully be of better 'quality' than what Dorm had originally been planning.

The journey back towards Suaabar would take the better part of a week at least, but would be mostly in a straight line. The only sizable town along the road would be Ebrel, where Ambra informed them there were several good inns that they might use.

They made good time and everyone agreed that they actually felt like they were making progress. Various members of the group had expressed concerns that sometimes they felt like they weren't getting anywhere. Now at least they had the feeling of progress.

They arrived in Suaabar as the weather began to turn again. A sure sign that the world was moving on without them. They took rooms in a different part of town to the last time they passed though, They decided not to stay anywhere they didn't have to for any longer than they had to. Dorm confided in Telly, that he wanted to get to Tagradas as soon as possible. He just had the feeling they would be safer there.

They left Suaabar and headed east again, passing though the border and into Tagradas, they encountered no problems, nor did they hear of any. In fact things seemed to have quietened down significantly since they had passed through this area previously. Several merchants expressed some angst at the fact that the number of Peldraksekhran merchants had fallen off again, and many of their official representatives seemed to have vanished.

Dorm was secretly happy about that and only slightly proud of the damage he and his friends must have done to the plans of the Peldraksekhr who had been here earlier in the year.

They again passed through Lanak Cal, but avoided the Rangers' chapterhouse. They stopped overnight at the town of Malgu and heard rumours that the King had been approached by an ambassador from Peldraksekhr and Szugabar. Dorm would have to have a long conversation with Uncle Sanel when they arrived at the palace.

Several days later they passed through the town of T'Kell again. On a whim, Dorm decided to pay the mayor a visit again. Mayor Yabis hadn't changed at all, but was delighted to see them, once he remembered who they were.

"Well I will admit Your Highness," he explained. "We had some interesting times with various Peldraksekhr over the past few months."

"I can imagine," Dorm agreed with him.

"Yes, at first they didn't want to take the hint, as they say, we had to explain it to them a few times. I even had Habidax, our chief constable, throw one of their underlings in gaol for a night or two over some miscellaneous thing."

"I do hope you made it sound plausible?"

"Oh yes Your highness," Yabis assured him. "We apologised profusely. Habidax spun a brilliant story that he had already arrested two men claiming to be the same man that day. It got them terribly confused."

"Well Mayor Yabis. I, and the Alliance thank you for your efforts. And I will be sure to let the King know as well when I see him."

"You'll be seeing His Majesty then?"

"Yes my companions and I are headed to the capital now. We should arrive in a few days."

"Then please convey my personal greetings to him. I hope he appreciates our efforts on behalf of the country."

"I'm sure he will." As soon as I inform him, Dorm thought to himself.

It indeed only took them two and a half days to reach the capital, and they went immediately to the palace. After a brief argument with one of the guard chiefs, whose name was Jasam, who refused to believe that they were who they said they were, until Cal demanded that he go and find one Captain Wannus, who recognised Cal straight away and personally ushered them through, glowering at Jasam the whole while, they finally made it in to see King Sanel, who was delighted to see them again.

He had arranged a reception as soon as he heard that they had arrived and relatives of their two Tagran members were on hand to greet them.

It was again an emotional homecoming for the two members of their group from Tagradas. Navagahn tried vainly to contain his emotions at seeing his daughter again, but Tissie's overt emotionalism robbed him of that very quickly. He thanked Dorm profusely for keeping his daughter safe and bringing her back home. Now was probably not the best time to tell him about the kidnapping, nor that they would be off again in a few days.

Cal was met by his own family. He rarely mentioned his wife and children. Dorm had never quite understood why. Despite all the conversations he had had with him, the guardsman had rarely ventured into this part of his existence. They knew that his wife's' name was Mafleen, and that he had two sons and a daughter. There had always been a hesitancy from him to talk about them, and Dorm suspected that perhaps all was not well in the family. Though the greeting he was given was warm enough.

Corm Sanel was his usual happy-go-lucky self as he greeted them and seemed to just gloss over the emotional fuss going on around him. His queen Sal Badan also came out to greet them. She rarely made public appearances any more after she had been disfigured some years ago by an illness. While she had recovered, and was these days as healthy as an ox, her face and arms had become horribly scarred. It was a great national sadness that the Queen had so secluded herself, but everyone understood why, and she continued to play her role as consort as best she could. This time she stood next to her husband wearing a rather formal blue dress with a heavy veil that covered her face. One could still see her smile and her eyes through the veil but the details of her face were obscured.

They went inside and were escorted to one of the banquet halls where a large meal was laid out for them. They were all invited to sit and partake of the grandness of the Kings table, And Sanel almost seemed to delight in the unease of those who were not normally used to such finery.

There were many introductions and stories that were told over the next few hours, and slowly everyone seemed to relax. They still glossed over some details, there was no point mentioning the kidnapping, since it would only serve to inflame the situation. Dorm could tell Sanel later and he could decide what to do with the information.

After the meal they were escorted to various rooms that took up a whole level of one wing of the palace, and everyone washed and changed, and in many cases napped. Palace food had a habit of doing that to people.

There was another formal dinner, though this time with less food but more guests, that evening where they were introduced to various dignitaries of the Tagran court. Sanel stopped Dorms' protests by informing him that there had been planned an event for this evening anyway, and he couldn't very well have a foreign prince present without making something of it publicly. Dorm reluctantly conceded the point.

Finally the day was over, and it wasn't as late as they had been fearing. Everyone went to bed rather exhausted by both the road and the festivities.

The next morning Dorm and Mac sought out Sanel to have a long conversation with him.

“Uncle, what are you doing?” Dorm said by way of greeting as he entered the monarchs' study.

“Whatever do you mean young man?”

“Why am I hearing rumours about ambassadors from Szugabar?”

"Oh that," Sanel relaxed into his chair. "Afraid there wasn't much I could do about that. The Szugabar sent a special envoy to us quite out of the blue. Of course I knew about what was happening from your letter and your letter to your father. But I had expected Lugemall to take the lead on this, given your contact."

"Well I guess I can forgive you then. I just don't like secrets I've worked very hard to keep secret, being repeated back to me in taverns."

"Yes I can understand that. It's been a strange couple of months I can tell you. First I have rumours of Peldreaksekhr agents behind every tree in the kingdom; a near riot over it in one town. Then this thing with the Szugabar. Rumours of bandits and all sorts causing mayhem and havoc all over Kiama Mor and Ojliam. Sounds like the whole world is starting to fall apart."

"Perhaps it is Uncle," Dorm said looking at Mac. "We've seen some of this ourselves."

"Had to run from it a few times as well."

"Really?" the king said incredulously. "Perhaps things are more serious than I thought."

"Don't get us wrong," Dorm reassured him. "I think most of it is pretty minor and probably under control now. But we should keep an eye on it."

Sanel grunted his agreement.

"Also you should send a letter or something to the Mayor of T'Kell."

The king thought for a moment. "Isn't that that pompous ass Yabis? What in the Fortress for?"

"For helping us put down possible Imperial espionage," Mac informed him.

"Really? That twit did something constructive?"

"Well he had some urgings on our part."

"But he did quite well," Dorm went on. "

"After some of the things that happened to us in Ziga, and later in Kiama Mor, I'm glad we did it. It seems the Peldraksekhr are definitely up to something."

"Well I'll keep it in mind," Sanel promised.

"I want to send some messages to people quickly if I could

Uncle," Dorm said then.

"Oh, more sneakyness?"

"No more in the way of arranging some reunions without us having to wait too long. If we can have people waiting for us in Lugemall when we get there that will help."

"I think your father will be very glad to see you both, Dorm," Sanel said seriously. "He's written me several letters. I think he's been terribly worried about all this."

"I know, Uncle," Dorm sighed heavily. "But we are on our way home now."

"Have you gotten any closer to learning what this is all about yet?"

Mac started laughing.

Loudly.

"I take it that's a no then?" Sanel said seriously while Mac continued to guffaw.

"You could say that," Dorm replied. "But I think it's going to take a big effort on our part to solve it. I get the feeling there will be war before we're through."

"Great, just what I can't afford this decade."

"I don't think any of us can afford not to, Uncle."

Dorm enlisted the assistance of Sanels' chief aide Thovin to write the letters and have them sent to the Diplomatic Message Service. The Service had been set up centuries ago to maintain speedy communications between the leaders of the various kingdoms of the Alliance. Dorm's letters weren't quite what the Service existed to convey, but they were rather important none the less. Thovin promised not to tell on him.

Dorm was rather satisfied when he saw the first rider leave the palace with his letters. It really made this trip seem like it was coming to an end. Or at least a sort of end. He was under no illusions that this stop in Lugemall would be relatively short. He had no idea where they would end up next, but he knew that his returning home was to be just a brief stop.

He would be glad to see his father and sleep in his own bed for the first time in months. He hated to think what his desk would look like after all this time. While not officially in charge of very much, there were a lot of things that Dorm had, over the years, made sure went via his desk on its way to his fathers. And some things that he had quietly had removed from his fathers desk entirely. Nothing that the Kingdom relied upon, but the sort of things that would take up way too much of his fathers time, away from the important things, had they not been redirected.

They all spent the rest of the day telling their stories and conversing with each other and the families of the local members. Both Tissie and Cal seemed rather chuffed by the attention that was paid them by those around them, including the Queen who seemed genuinely interested in what had happened to them.

This especially impressed Cal, as he mentioned to several people afterwards. He had obviously seen the Queen on numerous occasions, but had rarely spoken to her. The fact that someone so important took a genuine interest in him and his life, seemed to boost his self confidence quite a lot. The Queen also seemed to get on quite well with Cal's wife, Mafleen. She had at first seemed rather aloof, almost cold, but now that they had gotten into the stories of their adventures, and the attention paid to her by the quiet blonde Queen appeared to have brought her out of her shell a little.

Cal even commented on the difference in his wife.

At dinner that evening Dorm watched over the faces of his friends, and their families. This was such a unique group of people. What was it they were being asked to do?

They left around mid-morning the next day. For Dorm it wasn't that big of a deal, though he did have a much more personal connection to the Tagran royal family than he had to any of the previous groups that had had to leave. He watched as Navagahn and Tissie had a lengthy goodbye. There was little the Chamberlain could do now to deny his daughter the rest of the journey. He had seen that she had returned safely, and that indeed she had seemed to grow somewhat as a person. He probably still would have preferred it if she had stayed, but he realised that this was no longer possible.

Cal and Mafleen also had a lengthy goodbye. It still seemed rather stiff, but there was a genuine concern expressed by the wife towards the husband. Perhaps this experience would be good for their relationship? Dorm had to remember to try and find out what the exact nature of the situation between the two of them was. He hated to be a snoop, but this felt important.

Their children were all adolescents. Unlike the situation with Tissie and Navagahn, who were both older and had a much better understanding of the reality of the situation, Cal and Mafleen's children were still mostly at that age where while you knew bad things happened in the world, you couldn't fathom a way that they could happen to you.

They clattered out of the main courtyard of the palace with a full escort, that Sanel insisted they have, despite the efforts of his wife to make him see reason. There was much waving and a few tears, but very quickly they were moving through the city at a fairly steady pace heading towards the eastern gate.

Once they had passed through the gate and travelled far enough away from the city, Dorm thanked the Captain of the escort, one professional soldier by the name of Randik, and told him to take his men to a good tavern somewhere and have a tankard each.

"And exactly how am I meant to pay for that, Your Highness," Randik asked. "I'm not exactly outfitted to pay for a tankard of ale for sixty men."

Dorm rummaged around inside his purse for a moment before producing the last of several High Crowns. His purse was definitely starting to get a little on the light side. "This should help," he said handing the coins to the soldier. "Courtesy of the Lugemallan government."

Randik looked at them for a moment. Then at Dorm. "You keep this up, Your Highness, and you may just end up with a influx of immigrants."

"Lugemall can always do with more good soldiers, Captain," he replied with a grin.

As they left them the Captain was asking for opinions on the nearest decent alehouse.

They crossed the River Lugumo the next day and followed the highway as it wandered eastward. The weather was certainly better than it had been the last time they had travelled this way and they made good time, doing their best to stop in the various towns and villages along the way.

They passed through Lugumoford without incident, though given the size of the town they half expected Sanel to have sent them another escort. Luckily he hadn't and they passed through in anonymity. Several days later they arrived at Junction City, with its many warehouses and merchants shops, and bought what they hoped would be their last purchase of supplies for a while. They purposely didn't buy a great deal as they didn't want to lug anything they didn't have to the small distance remaining to them.

Several hours after leaving Junction City they entered the Great Southern Forest as it was grandiosely called. It was a largely untamed wilderness throughout the hilly region, though there were pockets of 'civilisation' here and there. The forest was a major source of wood for both Tagradas and Lugemall, and despite centuries of logging didn't seem to be getting any smaller.

The forest was like a new world, as most forests seemed to be. Perhaps it was just the change in light or the noises that could be heard, but these large forests seemed like a different place, where anything could happen. And sometimes did.

They did their best to make it to the periodic villages that dotted the forest, but sometimes this wasn't possible as they had sprung up rather randomly along the route of the highway. They were forced to camp several times, made a little more nervous by their past experiences in forests.

After nearly a week they crossed over into Lugemall passing through the rather substantial border posts with little fanfare or fuss. Dorm was glad of this. He kind of liked the idea of sneaking up on his father without notice.

The forest continued unabated and even grew wilder and darker in parts. There were fewer villages in this part of the forest, though the ones that existed were bigger than their Tagran counterparts. After several days they arrived at the town of Temeld, which was a rather large and walled affair.

Temeld was the centre of activity in the forest and as such was given to rather more elaborate buildings than would otherwise have been the case in a town this size and this far out into the countryside. Dorm had only been here twice before and not found it very interesting. Of course both times he had been obliged to stay with the local Baron and attend meetings and other official type functions.

Perhaps the town was more interesting away from all of that?

They only stayed overnight and continued on their way fairly early in the morning following behind a large group of loggers who were heading out. The head logger, one Sabidax, informed them of all the latest gossip from around the kingdom, including that one of Dorm's cousins had recently given birth to a little girl. He hadn't even thought about Olandia since before he had left. He felt a little contemptuous for that. He would have to be sure to send her and her husband a letter congratulating them personally.

A week later they arrived at Lessahn. It hadn't changed much since they had passed through on their way out so long ago. But then Lessahn would probably never change. It was that sort of place. They stayed in one of the better inns near the centre of town and did their best to keep a low profile.

The next morning they moved out and made their way to the punts that carried travellers across the river. There was some negotiation in order to get the ferryman to take them all, but after a few more coins than Dorm considered strictly necessary had changed hands they were on their way. The punt negotiated its way through the river traffic of barges and small ships, as well as fishermen and eelers.

They alighted on the opposite quay and reorganised themselves and calmed down the horses, which hadn't been particularly comfortable ever since they had smelt the river. After a bit of jostling however they were well on their way passing through the buildings on the opposite shore and then leaving Lessahn altogether.

Dorm began to feel that sense of anticipation of arriving back at home. While they were still a couple of days away he knew he was home again. The sights and sounds were all familiar to him. The voices and their accents oddly calming. He finally had a bit of the feeling of what the others must have gone through, being reminded of home.

On the third day from Lessahn they entered Lugemall. This being his actual home, Dorm noticed many more subtle changes. Buildings being completed, trees having grown. All the little things that make a place, a place.

They wound their way through the streets, which were their usual busy self and headed towards the palace. Finally after what had seemed hours they approached the edifice. Dorm noticed a few extra flags flying and wondered at this, hoping his father hadn't been tipped off.

They made their way round to the private entryway near the rear of the palace and dismounted in the same courtyard from where this long journey had begun. Dorm took a moment to look around. It hadn't changed much. The trees were the same. So was the stable block and the guardhouse. The portico into the palace looked like it had been given a scrub recently but that was about all. Somehow he had expected it to be different.

"Are you okay?" Mac asked him quietly as he noticed him looking around.

"Yes," Dorm reassured him. "Just thinking."

Everyone dismounted and took their belongings off and followed Dorm and Mac into the palace. Dorm brushed aside the startled looks from servants and aids he had known all his life, and who hadn't expected him to suddenly come around the corner. He made his way firstly towards the throne room, not really expecting his father to be there given the time of day. It turned out he was right and so off he went towards his fathers office which was several levels above. On the way there, the large group trailing along behind, Dorm almost ran into Ellin, his father chief aide and most trusted advisor.

Ellin nearly yelled in anger at whoever it was who had nearly bowled him over until he realised who it was. His lined face split in a genuine grin of happiness and pleasure. His auburn hair and beard, now more touched by grey than Dorm remembered were a welcome sight for Dorm's travel weary eyes.

"Your Highness," Ellin said with a catch in his voice. "By the Fortress. You have returned my boy." He laughed loudly. "Oh I am so happy to see you."

"And I you, Ellin," Dorm assured him grasping his hand firmly and shaking it.

"And Mac," Ellin went on noticing him. "Oh this is a happy day. Come all of you, I will take you to the King."

"Aren't you on your way with something?" Dorm asked him pointing at the large sheaf of parchment in his hands.

"This?" Ellin said looking at it contemptuously. "Oh bugger that. It's just the budget. It's not important." With that he turned and almost skipped with happiness down the corridor.

They came to Mac Lavin's official study. Which the King rarely used, except when meeting with officials. The real work went on in his private study which was just down the hall. Unfortunately it was rather a bit smaller and would never had held everyone comfortably.

"Wait here. I'll go and get him," Ellin said barely containing his joy.

He left the room through the door that lead through the antechamber to the private study. After a few moments came the familiar voice of the King cursing his luck at having such fussy and pedantic treasurers working for him, and threatening to have a long conversation with his treasury minister.

Until that was, that he entered the room and saw that the people before him were not treasurers.

His eyes skimmed around the room, until they settled on the face of his son.

"Dorm," his voice said meekly. "Oh my boy!" he cried and almost flung himself across the room to Dorm. They embraced roughly but lovingly, ignoring the embarrassment that would normally have accompanied something like this. There was laughter and a few tears as the family was reunited.

Mac Lavin stood back from his son and took his face in his hands. "I am so glad you're home."

"So am I, Father," Dorm assured him.

"Mac," the King exclaimed happily and hugging him too.

"Hello.... Father," he said experimentally.

Mac Lavin looked at him for a moment before glancing at Dorm who stared wide eyed at Mac. The king looked back at his son-in-law .

"Oh my boy I'm proud of you." He embraced Mac again.

There was no shortage of teary grins around the room as they watched this spectacle. But then everyone was genuinely happy for them. Dorm was unofficially the leader of this group and for all of them, they had seen him being quite alone in that. Oh he talked to them all, and major decisions were always a group matter, but still, being in that position was lonely, and they all knew it. They had one by one, all had the opportunity to see their loved ones again. Dorm and Mac, and Rhyn as well had had to wait the longest. And everyone knew that.

There were some introductions, before Ellin sent a messenger off to "bring some other necessary items". Mac Lavin scowled at him for forcing him to do more tedious work when his son had come home, but Ellin just gave a knowing look and vanished. He retuned a short time later with several more people in tow.

First through the door was Lord Kardranos, Telly's father. He hadn't changed much in appearance, but was overjoyed to see his daughter whom he even lifted off the floor while hugging her, despite her height.

Next came Rhyn's father and siblings. She hadn't mentioned her siblings often, but had seemed to have a fairly close relationship with her father. Her father held her tightly for quite some time with happy tears on his cheeks before she was able to greet her siblings. Her family seemed a little bemused by being in the palace but the Kings relaxed bearing seemed to put them somewhat at ease.

Behind them came Travanos' wife, Yamelda. She was a tall woman with slightly greying blonde hair. She was much more striking than Travanos had ever let on. This was a woman of grace, of presence. And Dorm suspected, one not to be gotten on the wrong side of. She at first seemed a little reserved even aloof, though Dorm later suspected that was just because of the overwhelming reaction of seeing her husband again, as she relaxed quite a bit as the time wore on.

Gormall stepped into the room next. His barrel chest was no match for his emotions at seeing Lianna again after such a long time. He lifted her off the ground and spun her around as she kissed him all over his face. Everyone took note of this. Lianna wasn't normally the most flamboyant person. But then this was a special occasion.

Lastly came Lessahna and little Galem. Artur started blubbing almost as soon as he saw them. Lessahna not far behind him. Everyone knew how much Artur loved his wife, and how hard it had been for him to leave her so soon after the birth of their first child. Galem had grown quite a bit since they had been gone and his hair was just starting to come through.

With everyone in the room now reunited with someone, so it seemed, the time came for them to reminisce. This went on for hours and hours, with no end in sight. Food and drink were brought and the conversation went on till after dark. Finally everyone realised that they all needed sleep, and so their guests were taken to various rooms in the guest wing of the palace, while Mac and Dorm walked Mac Lavin back to the royal apartments. Ellin trailed along with them glad to see his oldest friend so happy.

"We have much more to discuss my boys," the king was saying. "There is much work to do and you have many more adventures to tell us all about I'm sure."

"True enough Father," Dorm agreed. "But that can wait till later. We can spare a few days I think before we move on."

"Move on? Ellin said startled. "You only just got back. I thought that was it."

"Not by a long way," Mac said. "We still don't have all the questers."

"Well if you can wait a week or two you can come with us when we go south."

"What's in the south?"

"Apparently the King of Rikaway has requested a personal meeting between the two of us. Could be that major breakthrough we've been hoping for these past few years. The letter arrived a few weeks ago. We've been getting ready for a while now."

"We should probably check with the Rangers but it sounds like it could be a good idea," Dorm mused. "We always thought Rikaway could be a possibility."

"Well that's settled then," Mac Lavin said cheerfully. "It will be good to have you home for a little while."

"It will be good to be home Father." Dorm told him.

They bade the king goodnight and then made their way back to their own rooms. They had that empty smell. While the room had been regularly cleaned during their absence it still retained that unlived in aroma. The fire had been lit and the candles as well, which gave a cheery glow to everything. But the room still felt a little empty.

They relaxed in front of the fire with some wine, glad to be home again and for the first time in what seemed like forever, actually able to rest.

The day had been long and very emotional. It stirred all kinds of feelings in everyone. Dorm took Mac's almost empty goblet and put it on the table. He took his hand and led him across the room, before undressing and climbing into the bed, which was cold.

For a time.

Epilogue

He stood upon the parapet. The clouds boiled above him.

He watched them for a time. Their roiling black ominousness was somehow soothing. Perhaps it had to do with his knowledge of their reality? Perhaps it was just because his mood was blacker than their colour and so he could at least see some light in the world.

The stone was cold, but that was alright. Everything was cold at the moment. The wind wasn't too bad, but even it couldn't blow away his concerns.

He stared out across the landscape. The various towers and turrets rearing into the dark sky. A few lights twinkled back at him. He hated these heights, but somehow they seemed appropriate at this time. And he had to admit that the crenelations were thick.

There was a step behind him. He knew exactly who it would be. And why he was here. He felt sorry for him. Being sent on this errand all the time.

“Councillor?” came his voice.

“Yes I know,” he sighed heavily.

“The Committee is waiting for you in the chamber,”

“Of course they are.”

“Is everything alright with you Councillor?” he said after a moment.

“Oh Ramdek,” he said without turning around. “I don't know any more. I am beginning to wonder that myself.”

"I don't understand," Ramdek replied.

"I wonder if we have done the right thing by them," he said quietly staring out across the landscape. It's desolation, hard to make out properly in the gloom, reflected his thoughts. But then so too did the gloom itself.

"We have done what had to be done, Sir," Ramdek said confidently. "Have we not?"

"Indeed we have Ramdek, and that may indeed be the problem. You know what is going on here. What is being said. And yet we have helped it along. But they are nearly as confused and lost as when they began this."

"If that is what is necessary, Sir, then that should happen."

"I am forced to wonder about the longer term though, my young friend." he turned to face him, smiling in sympathy as he looked at the younger blonde headed man. "I do not mean to dump this all on you."

"It's alright Sir," Ramdek smiled back. "It's a part of my job."

He laughed at that. He remembered his early days when he was the subject of such superior musings. He had just had to grin and bear it like Ramdek now was. But then in those days, the concerns of the Masters were not quite so world shattering. Literally.

"I know we will get through it, but I wonder how they will cope. We are asking so much of them. I only hope they have the strength to carry on and persevere through what is... necessary before they can meet with us."

"I have every confidence in them, Sir," Ramdek said positively. He even squared his shoulders and raised his head slightly as he said it. Ahh the power of youth. "They are people of intelligence, skill, grace, and compassion. I know they will succeed."

He stared at him for a moment. "I hope so too," he whispered. His words snatched away on the wind.

He pulled his hood back up onto his head and folded his hands in front of him. "Well I guess there's no sense in delaying this meeting any longer. I know what the Committee will recommend, but still my arguments against it give them some amusement. No point in denying people their simple pleasures is there."

Ramdek smiled at this, and nodded his agreement, he too then raised his hood. He turned and walked to the door which he opened for his elder.

They went back inside to deal with the Committee, and fate.

Here ends Book One of the *Fortress Saga*. In Book Two, *Alliances*, the Questers shall journey onto strange lands beyond the Alliance, and deepen their understanding of the Prophecy, and what it is really asking of them.

Printed in Great Britain
by Amazon

85773451R00365